She heard a noise behind her

Ramona started to turn, when suddenly a hood was forced over her head. Terrified, she screamed and struggled, kicking backward at her attacker. The man yanked her hands back tightly, and in seconds they were bound with a rope.

"Please just tell me what you want," she begged.

There was no answer. Instead her captor shoved her forward. She went down on her knees, but he wrenched her up to her feet, brusquely pushing her outside and through the brush.

Then, without warning, the man lifted her and placed her on something soft. It didn't make sense. Ramona tried to bolt upright, but he pushed her back hard. Then she heard the soft sigh of metal, like hinges, followed by utter silence and a strange pressure. More frightened than she'd ever been in her life, she tried to get up again. She slammed her head against something solid and fell back. There was a heavy object just inches above her.

Suddenly the linens, which felt plush and satiny against her skin, filled her with revulsion. Utter, choking terror overwhelmed her as she realized exactly where she was.

ABOUT THE AUTHOR

Aimée Thurlo says that *Shadow of the Wolf* was inspired by the strong code of loyalty and respect for family ties she found present in both her Hispanic culture and that of the Tewa people. She wanted to share this quality with her readers. Her love for the Southwest and the ethics that bind the three major cultures there into one are at the heart of the story. Aimée and her husband, David, live and work in New Mexico. When not writing, they enjoy riding, playing with their four dogs and practicing their marksmanship.

Books by Aimée Thurlo

HARLEQUIN INTRIGUE

Don't miss any of our special offers. Write to us at the following address for information on our newest releases.

Harlequin Reader Service
P.O. Box 1397, Buffalo, NY 14240
Canadian address: P.O. Box 603,
Fort Erie, Ont. L2A 5X3

Shadow of the Wolf

Aimée Thurlo

Harlequin Books

TORONTO • NEW YORK • LONDON
AMSTERDAM • PARIS • SYDNEY • HAMBURG
STOCKHOLM • ATHENS • TOKYO • MILAN
MADRID • WARSAW • BUDAPEST • AUCKLAND

To Hilary Sares for helping me wish upon a star.
All my loving children thank you.

The physical setting for Aimée Thurlo's *Shadow of the Wolf* was inspired by the San Ildefonso pueblo in New Mexico, near Aimée's home. To protect the privacy of the individual pueblos, Aimée has created San Esteban, a fictional composite of elements from a number of Tewa pueblos.

Harlequin Intrigue edition published March 1993

ISBN 0-373-22217-3

SHADOW OF THE WOLF

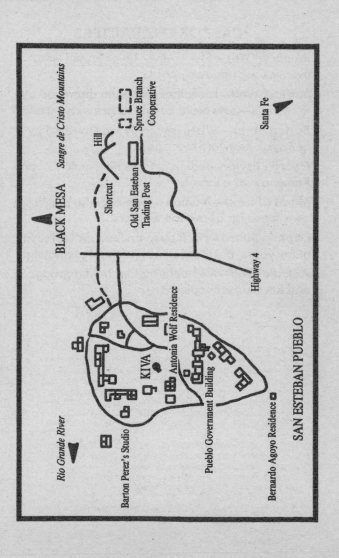

Rio Grande River

Barton Perez's Studio

BLACK MESA

Sangre de Cristo Mountains

Hill

Shortcut

Old San Esteban
Trading Post

Spruce Branch
Cooperative

KIVA

Antonia Wolf Residence

Pueblo Government Building

Highway 4

Bernardo Agoyo Residence

SAN ESTEBAN PUEBLO

Santa Fe

CAST OF CHARACTERS

Ramona Ortiz—She'd never be accepted—not even among her own people.

Michael Wolf—His father had been disgraced by Ramona's—how could he join forces with a traitor?

Barton Perez—When his family was touched by betrayal, he swore revenge.

George Taylor—Indian art was his passion...and Ramona was a threat.

Mario Chacon—A union organizer who put his own needs far above the workers'.

Captain Suazo—He'd been on the tribal force for many years, but the violence just kept escalating.

Antonia Wolf—Michael's mother held a grudge, and Ramona embodied it.

Prologue

May 12, 1975

John Ortiz walked slowly to the front window of his trading post. Dust was thick in the air. It had been weeks since the last thunderstorm and the parched desert earth had little to offer by way of color. Only at sunset did the crimson skies shrouding the Sangre de Cristo Mountains finally overwhelm the grays and browns of the desert. Yet the change was more disturbing than welcome. The bloodred mantle gave the illusion of life spilling away somehow, and enhanced the sun-scorched smell that tainted everything.

Ortiz made sure the Closed sign was in place, then walked toward the worn pine bench beside the main counter. His hickory cane tapped solidly on the wooden floor as he brought his game leg along. He was expecting a visitor and trouble, probably in that order, and he didn't want to be distracted by an unexpected customer.

At least his family was safely out of the way. His wife Loretta was shopping in Santa Fe and his daughter had gone on a field trip with her class. Neither would be home until much later.

Ortiz's gaze drifted slowly around the room. Their place sure wasn't much. The trading post/home adjacent to San Esteban Pueblo dated back to the turn of the century and was always in need of repair. Yet he loved the life he'd

made here. There was an enduring quality and timeless-
ness about the New Mexican desert that suited him. But
now, as he waited for his visitor to arrive, he wondered if
things would ever be the same again.

Whoever was preying on the community had decided to
use him as a convenient scapegoat. Unwilling to take the
blame for someone else's actions, he'd pursued all the
leads he could find. Finally he'd managed to gather some
evidence. Unfortunately, it didn't conclusively prove the
guilt of the person he suspected. Of course, he could have
made public what he'd learned and let others judge for
themselves. But the seed of doubt that remained in his
mind was enough to stop him. He didn't want to destroy
the life and reputation of someone who could turn out to
be innocent.

Finally, unable to think of another way, he'd arranged
for a confrontation here on his own turf, and under his
own terms. He'd planned everything to the last detail. If
there was trouble, he had his ace in the hole. Ortiz glanced
at the spot where his evidence was hidden, second thoughts
gnawing at his confidence. Maybe he should have placed
the stuff in his secret safe. Not even his wife knew it existed. Then again, only a fan of Edgar Allan Poe would
ever find it where it was now.

As footsteps sounded on the porch, John Ortiz hobbled
across the room. "Come in," he said, opening the door
and cocking his head toward the interior.

The man entered and crossed to the far side of the room
as Ortiz shut the door.

"Let's try to make this as quick and as painless as possible," Ortiz said, turning around.

"I couldn't agree more," the man concurred, pulling a
revolver out from beneath his windbreaker. "Get your
hands away from your body," he ordered, his voice distinct and oddly tranquil. "Good. Now we can deal."

Chapter One

December, Seventeen Years Later

Ramona's eyes hazed with memories as she glanced around the small living room. The furnishings were sparse and the few pieces that were left had been ravaged by time. She'd spent her childhood here. Ghostly images of the past flickered at the edges of her mind.

For several minutes she walked around the house restlessly. Finally, she stopped by her father's study. She'd overheard many arguments coming from that room, despite the closed door. But memories often distorted the truth. Had she really been the focus of all her parents' quarrels, or were those just the ones she remembered?

A heaviness of spirit settled over her. Fighting the urge to flee from the house, she went to the window and stared outside. The last glimmers of the short winter day had become a blaze of crimson and lavender hues that bathed neighboring San Esteban Pueblo in their glow. Only a few miles separated her from the pueblo; yet, the real gulf that kept her from her own people was as large and as deep as the Rio Grande Gorge.

Of course, she was certain that someday the tribe would accept her and she'd be able to take her place among them. Her mother had been a Tewa Indian, and by right and custom so was she. But her mother's sudden death meant that she'd have to wage that fight alone. She was already on tenuous ground. It was said that her Anglo father had betrayed the tribe. The wedge that had formed between her family and the people of San Esteban because of the supposed betrayal held firm to this day. But she'd come back to make things right again.

Ramona stepped toward the fireplace, craving its warmth. Then, without warning, the window seemed to explode, sending glass shards flying everywhere. She dived to the floor as one crack was followed by another. Bullets slammed into the walls, showering bits of plaster everywhere.

Terrified, she crawled toward the telephone, staying close to the wall. The shots were being fired from the side of the property that bordered San Esteban Pueblo. That knowledge tore at her heart.

Ramona reached for the telephone cord, pulling the receiver to her without rising any higher into the line of fire. Shaking badly, she managed to dial 9-1-1. "Someone's shooting at me through my window! My name is Ramona Ortiz and I'm at the old San Esteban Trading Post off Highway 4. I need help right now!"

By the time she placed the receiver back on the telephone, the shots had stopped. Silence echoed eerily around her. She remained frozen, afraid the rain of metal would start up again.

Finally, praying the sniper had run out of ammunition, she crawled to a dark corner of the room. Gathering her courage, she peered out the edge of the window. Night was rapidly descending. The desert was shrouded in gray shadows that danced like a gathering of ghostly figures. Unable to stop trembling, she huddled down with her back to the corner, staring at the bullet holes on the far wall. The winter cold that was blowing through the shattered window heightened the chill that filled her soul.

After several long, quiet minutes, Ramona struggled to her feet. Glass crunched underneath her shoes. Careful not to outline herself against the window, she walked around assessing the damage. The family snapshot her mother had treasured and kept over the mantel for years lay on the floor. A bullet had ripped the center, leaving a gaping hole where her parents had been pictured. Now, like her memory of them together, only segmented pieces remained. A whole kaleidoscope of dark emotions knifed through her. Although she'd known her plans to stay would meet with resistance, nothing had prepared her for the violence she'd just witnessed.

Hearing a vehicle coming up the driveway, she jumped and spun around. The flash of red and blue lights announced clearly the arrival of the police. Ramona took a deep breath and pulled herself together. News of the incident would spread, and she had no intention of letting her enemies know how frightened she'd really been. They had enough of an advantage already.

She was by the door waiting when a Tewa officer emerged from the sheriff's vehicle. Her gaze focused on his face, and for a second her heart forgot to beat. Then as if making up for the lapse, it began to pound frantically. She stared at Michael Wolf's familiar features, feeling as if she'd stepped back in time.

He was the same, and different. His incredibly masculine physique was more mature, more . . . solid. His chest had broadened and his shoulders were wider, stronger looking. The textures and hard planes of his face were rougher, too, and belonged to the man he was now, not the boy she remembered. But the impact of him was the same. There was a vibrant maleness about him that made her knees turn wobbly.

She was thirty years old, and in all that time no one had ever affected her the way Michael Wolf could. Through the years, she'd learned to dismiss the feelings as the fading echoes of a bad case of puppy love. Yet seeing him now left her as disconcerted and fuzzy-headed as the thirteen-year-old who'd fallen in love with him. What if he didn't even remember her name?

Ramona walked out to the porch and watched Michael approach. His strides were measured, his movements as graceful as that of a predator on the hunt. His hand rested on the butt of his holstered weapon as he glanced around cautiously.

"I think the sniper's gone," she managed to rasp.

He captured her eyes and held them as he came up the front steps. She felt herself lost in that gaze. His eyes were extraordinary, dark and luminous, so like the volcanic obsidian found in the desert.

"I'm Ramona Ortiz. We used to go to school together," she added, not really wanting to know if Michael had forgotten about her.

"I remember," he answered with a hint of a smile. Quickly he motioned her inside, and out of view. "Now tell me what happened." His voice was quiet, yet reverberated with strength and confidence.

Her mouth felt parched, but she forced herself not to look away. "Someone fired shots into the living room. I'm not sure how many. They seemed endless."

Michael nodded, his expression alive with interest and another emotion she couldn't quite make out. "Any idea who might have done this?"

"No, but there probably isn't any shortage of volunteers. I wouldn't win any popularity contests around here."

"True," Michael agreed, glancing back at her. "People expected you to return for your mother's funeral. But your plans to stay and open a business here has taken everyone who knew your mother and you by surprise." Michael studied the bullet-riddled wall. "Did you hear a vehicle at any time, especially right before or after the sniper opened fire?"

"No. Maybe I should have been more alert, but I never dreamed this would happen."

He nodded thoughtfully. "Who have you been in contact with recently? Anyone you've argued with or who has given you trouble?"

"I haven't had time to meet with anyone. I've been busy settling my mother's affairs."

His eyes fastened on her, his gaze penetrating and bold. "But you had time to place that sign beside the road leading out of the pueblo. Even if it is on your land, you must have known it would incense some people."

Ramona ran a hand through her shoulder-length black hair, pushing it away from her face. "I expected some opposition, but not this," she answered, waving a hand around the room. "The arts and crafts cooperative I plan to open will be a financial boost to the tribe. Eventually the people of San Esteban will realize that and support what I'm trying to do." She sounded more confident than she felt. "It was a portion of the federal funds appropriated to the tribe that paid for my schooling. The tribe deserves a return for their investment."

"There are some who would say that the money was well spent if it kept you away," he said quietly.

His reply stung. She suspected he was among the ones who thought that. The knowledge made her heart shrivel up inside her. "Not everyone believes that. Some of my mother's friends and relatives remained loyal to her throughout the years."

"You're only talking about a handful of people."

"Yes, but it's a start. There's also a new generation at the pueblo now. You and I are part of it."

"Yes, we are," he said slowly, then added, "but as you've seen, old distrusts can be stubborn. They don't just fade away."

Ramona said nothing, unable to argue with the truth.

Michael moved to the edge of the stone fireplace, where bullets had hit and been deflected elsewhere. "When I heard about your plans, I knew it was just a matter of time before all hell broke loose. I wasn't wrong." Michael studied the pattern the bullets had made on the far wall and floorboards.

"Can you tell anything from that?" she asked.

"A bit. For starters, the sniper must have fired from higher ground." He dug out one of the bullets and held the slug up to the light. "It's a rifle caliber .223 round, so to group his shots like he did, he must have been relatively close, inside two hundred yards." He paused thoughtfully. "I'm going outside," Michael said, moving toward the door. "The wind's up and it's supposed to snow. I want to take a look around before it does."

"You're going to try and pinpoint his location tonight? It's as dark as a well out there!"

"I have a hunch. The hill above your house is the perfect place for someone wanting to fire into this room. It would also explain why you never heard a vehicle driving up."

"That's where I put up my sign inviting the tribe to join the cooperative." Anger rose inside her. If the sign had been taken down, she'd replace it. She'd never allowed anyone to deter her from doing what was right, and she wouldn't start now. "I'm going with you," she said, following him outside.

"I can't take you along." He stopped by the door of his squad car. "It's against regulations."

"Then I'll follow you, but I'm going, Michael."

He was relieved to hear her finally say his name. He wore a name tag, but it bore only his surname. Had she known his first name all along, or just remembered a few seconds ago? A lot of years had gone by since the seventh grade, when he'd discovered Mona had written "Michael" all over the cover of her math notebook.

Before he could say anything, she ducked past him. He watched her go to her pickup and jump inside. Her courage impressed him, though it certainly didn't come as a surprise. Her intention to stay was solid proof that she had guts.

A subtle emotion wound its way inside him. Like a spark hidden beneath a stack of kindling, the attraction he'd once felt for her was flickering to life. He'd never run from the truth, but he needed this now as much as a coyote needed fins. It would have been easier if she'd grown ugly, hateful, and lost all her teeth. But fate was determined to taunt him with what he couldn't have.

Mona had matured into a beautiful and appealing woman. He could swear that the gods had expressly designed her to disarm him. Her hair was a true black that fell in heavy masses around her shoulders. Her features were small and delicately shaped. Yet it wasn't her physical attributes that ultimately drew him the most. It was the way she could charm with a smile, or challenge with an iron resolve that was more than a match for his.

His breath eased out in a low, annoyed rumble. Thinking about things like this was a waste of time. Legacies rooted in family history had placed them on a collision course with each other. He had his duties, both to the past and to the present. Nothing could be allowed to interfere.

Michael saw her drive up directly behind his squad car and wait. Easing himself behind the wheel, he grabbed the mike and depressed the transmit button. "This is Unit Three. I'm going to check out the hill behind the trading post. I think that's where the sniper was positioned."

"Stay in touch, Unit Three," a woman's voice came over the air.

"Ten-four, base."

The beams of his headlights sliced through the darkness as he drove up to the high spot by the main highway. She'd placed her sign up here, a smart move in terms of advertising, but not so bright in terms of diplomacy. He'd heard his neighbors at the pueblo talk. Mona's proposed cooperative had stirred up quite a controversy among the tribe.

Ramona Ortiz was said to be an able businesswoman, well trained and competent. She'd earned an M.B.A. at the University of New Mexico and had owned a growing wholesale business before selling it to come home. She'd returned with a well-deserved reputation for success. Some pueblo artisans who didn't want to join her venture were afraid that her company would undermine their business.

Others still viewed Mona's family as enemies of the tribe. Anger at the man who'd harmed so many could be redirected toward his daughter.

Michael arrived at the summit a few minutes later. Staying in the car, he surveyed the area with his spotlight. Mona's sign was nowhere to be found now. He waited, watching and thinking. It was doubtful that the sniper was still around, but caution never hurt. Once he stepped out of the car, he'd be an easy, unprotected target.

Before he'd completed the detailed visual search he'd wanted to do, Mona pulled up and left her truck. Exasperation crept through him. He took a deep breath and, invoking the power of the mountains, struggled not to let annoyance cloud his thinking.

Taking a large flashlight with him, he climbed out of his own vehicle. "Don't come any closer, and don't spotlight yourself. Let me check this out first. I don't want either of us to get shot. Also, if there's any evidence here, it'll have to be carefully preserved."

"What happened to my sign?"

"I don't know yet." He walked ahead, then stopped short. Small stands of tough brush dotted the rocky earth. There'd be no footprints here, the ground would have made a perfect gravel quarry.

As Michael continued to study the ground carefully, he found Mona's sign. He lifted it with the toe of his boot. "I found your sign, but you're going to have to get a new one."

"How come? Will you need it as evidence?"

"Yeah, I'll be taking it in, but it's ruined anyway."

As he crouched down next to it, he saw a small leather pouch. The thought of touching the bag repulsed him, but he had to confirm his suspicions. A closer look told him what he needed to know. He gestured for her to approach.

She stared at the red stain that covered the front of her sign. "Oh, great! Spray paint?"

"It's blood—probably a coyote's." He noticed her look of disgust, then gestured toward the pouch. "Do you know what that is?"

She shrugged. "A leather bag, obviously. Does it give you a clue as to who left it here?"

"It doesn't tell me who, but it does tell me what."

Ramona stared at him, puzzled. "I don't get it."

"You don't remember much about our ways, do you?" Michael put his leather gloves on and carried the items to his vehicle.

"To be honest, I don't. I've been gone for seventeen years." Sensing his reluctance to discuss the matter of the pouch made her more curious than ever. "So tell me about the bag," she prodded.

"It's called a witch's bundle. It's filled with shredded rattlesnakes. Somebody's put a curse on you."

Ramona never thought of herself as superstitious, yet she shuddered just the same. "Someone seems to be going through a lot of trouble on my behalf. And this goody bag really makes me wonder how stable he is."

Michael smiled grimly. "Well put."

"Do you believe this witchcraft has any power?" Her voice shook but she cleared her throat, trying to cover up the lapse.

"I'd like to say no, flatly," he admitted, "but it makes me uneasy. As a cop, I've learned that this kind of thing leads to trouble. It influences people in all the wrong ways."

"Do you think that the sniper is responsible for this?"

"It's possible, but not necessarily. The person who did this probably believes that it has the power to harm. I don't think he or she would resort to more direct ways right away."

"There's another possibility. This might have been left here as part of a campaign to frighten me away."

Michael considered it. "That theory fits the sniper's attack. The room seemed to be more of a target than you were. But in my opinion, the witch's bundle is a separate thing altogether. I can't imagine any Tewa fooling with witchcraft unless they were deadly serious."

"So my list of well-wishers grows," Ramona replied sarcastically.

"Let's go back to your place. I'll collect all the bullets, seal them in evidence pouches, then take them over to the state lab along with the other items."

As they were driving back to the old trading post, Michael's thoughts remained on the evidence he'd collected. A dark sense of foreboding haunted him. The trouble was only beginning. He was certain of it.

When they arrived minutes later, Michael followed her inside. "I'll try not to damage the wall any more than it already is when I take out the slugs," he said, fishing a folding knife from his pocket.

"Don't worry. I plan to tear this building down after the cooperative begins operation. And if things work out, that should be very shortly."

"You're that confident?" Her eyes seemed calm, but he saw a flicker of doubt behind them. Was she afraid?

"I'll succeed because I won't give up," she said simply.

Michael focused on his work, determined not to respond to Ramona. He worked one of the bullets loose, careful not to mark it, then began to dig out a second one. "Are you planning to look into your father's disappearance? Is that the real reason behind the cooperative?"

His bluntness took her off guard. "Well, yes, that's one of them."

"What are the others?"

She took a deep breath then let it out slowly. "My mother was Tewa, Michael. I may be light skinned like my father, but in all the ways that matter I'm Tewa, also. I can't walk away from that part of me. People need their links to the past before they can define their future. I'm no different. I'm back to claim my place among the tribe. But before I can do that, I'll have to find out what happened to my father and clear our name."

Michael wished her well. In fact, the more she learned about the past, the better it would be for him. He still had his own oath to fulfill, and that duty to his family weighed heavily upon him.

Michael shook himself free of memories and forced his thoughts back to the job at hand. He placed one round in a marked pouch, then moved down to the floorboards and began extracting another slug. As he pried at a wood splinter with his pocketknife, trying to force out the bullet without scratching the rifling marks, the board jiggled loose. "It looks like you'll have to replace this section of flooring. The boards are all rotted through." A second later, the board split all the way down. He glanced up and gave her a sheepish look. "Sorry about that, but it really was about to go. It's dry rot, probably."

"That's okay." She pointed to the hole in the floor. "That looks odd. There shouldn't be sand right under there, should there?"

"No. There's usually an air space between the wooden floor beams." He studied it for a long moment, shifting from side to side. "I think something's buried here, see how it's been mounded up?"

"Neither my father nor my mother were much for safety-deposit boxes…" she said, letting the sentence hang as she considered it.

"I can take a look, if you want."

"I think that's a good idea," she said after a moment.

He stood and rolled up his cuffs. "I'll try digging just around the wooden beams first. I don't want to disrupt the other sections of flooring."

"I have a small shovel outside. Let me bring it in." She returned a moment later. "We'll probably end up finding some workman's sandwich wrappers and soda bottles or something."

"Probably," he agreed, taking the shovel from her.

Michael tried to shift the dirt from one end to the other. He was as curious as she was, but wanted to keep damages to a minimum. He dug down several inches, but there didn't seem to be anything down there.

"It looks like we were wrong..." he started. Suddenly he felt something hard strike the tip of the shovel. He lifted the object up to the surface carefully. "What the heck..."

Ramona stared at it in horror, an unhealthy pallor spreading over her face.

Chapter Two

Michael pulled a crooked wooden cane out from the dirt, then brushed the sand away. "It's a walking stick," he said, puzzled.

"My dad had one just like that," she said, unable to keep her voice steady. "He always kept it with him."

Michael's fingers curled hard around the handle of the shovel. "Yeah, I remember. I'm going to keep digging. Stand back."

Ramona's stomach twisted into a tight, painful knot as she watched Michael slowly pull up the floorboards. Unable to stand it any longer, she tore her gaze away and began pacing.

The cane was her father's; she was certain of that. It even had the familiar nick on the handle. Her dad had used that old hickory walking stick for as far back as she could remember. It had helped him compensate for an injury he'd sustained during the war.

Memories, like vignettes from an old movie, flashed in her mind's eye. Her father at her tenth birthday party using it to kick the soccer ball she and her friends were playing with. Then, another afternoon when he'd taught her about fishing. The terrain had been rough going for a man with a handicap, but he'd been determined to take her up the Rio Grande and show her the best fishing holes. Then finally, when he'd disappeared, the police had used the absence of his cane to further the theory that he'd abandoned them.

"I know what's down there," he said at last, interrupting her thoughts. "I'm not digging any farther. You might want to go into the next room. I'm going to call in a crime-scene unit."

"What did you find?" she asked, forcing her voice to remain steady.

"A human body, which was at one time wrapped in plastic."

"Whose body?" she asked in a whisper-thin voice.

"I can't tell. It's been here a long time," he said quietly. "There's not much more than a skeleton in rags."

He saw her step forward to look, and moved to intercept her. "You can't identify it. That's a job for forensic experts."

"I have to at least try, Michael. You'd do the same if you were me."

He hesitated briefly, then finally stepped aside. "Don't touch anything."

She crouched beside the opening he'd scooped out. Floorboards had been lifted away and carefully stacked to one side, revealing a shallow grave of sand. Shreds of black plastic were scattered in the hole. She felt a strange mixture of relief and disappointment as she realized that he'd only uncovered a small portion of the skeleton. But he'd been right. Only forensics could help now. She started to move away when a shiny object in the sand caught her eye.

"What's that?" she asked, calling his attention to it.

He came up beside her and brushed the sand away from that one spot. As he did, a skeletal hand showed. A massive gold-and-turquoise ring encircled one bony finger.

For a moment her head felt light and everything began to spin. Looking away, she took several fast, deep breaths. An excruciating sense of loss grew within her. "That was my dad's ring," she said, finally managing to produce some words.

Michael placed his arm around her shoulders and gently led her into the kitchen. "That's enough for now," he said softly. "I have to radio this in. Wait here."

He returned a few moments later. Her half hearted smile made his gut twist. Ramona was a strong woman. Seeing her so vulnerable touched off a sense of protectiveness in him. "We don't *know* that's your father," he said quietly. "Don't jump to conclusions."

"I do know," she answered. "That cane and ring were both one of a kind. I came back to find out what happened to him. But this . . . it'll take me awhile to accept it. From the looks of it, my mother was right. Dad never hurt anyone. He was someone else's victim."

"Wait until the details are verified." Michael walked to the window and looked outside. "It shouldn't be much longer before the others begin to arrive."

She didn't seem to hear him. "Everyone thought he was guilty of cheating the pueblo artists. Even you stopped coming around to visit that summer before I left for boarding school. I hope this will force the tribe to admit that my dad was as much a victim as everyone else."

He leaned against the door frame separating the kitchen from the front room and gazed at her. "If that does turn out to be your father, Mona, it will answer some questions. But it's also going to raise many others."

"Well, at least it'll be clear that it wasn't his intention to cheat anyone. He didn't run away."

"That's one way of looking at it. But it's also possible that he was killed by someone trying to prevent him from leaving." He hated to hurt her, but it would have been even more cruel to let her pin her hopes on suppositions. "Don't try to mold the facts to fit your beliefs. Your father deliberately withheld information our tribe desperately needed. He'd discovered a deposit of some very special clay. In exchange for telling us, he demanded a year's worth of the best pottery our artisans made. He even insisted that he be paid in advance, as if the tribe couldn't be trusted."

"The agreement made required the consent of both parties."

"The artisans didn't have much choice," he countered gently. "The pieces the craftsmen made with that clay had a very distinctive sheen. The pottery had become popular with outsiders, and we needed the tourist dollars very badly. Some even feared that your father would take the clay to another village and sell it there for a better price, unless we agreed. He had us and he knew it. Then, when the last pieces of pottery were delivered, he refused to accept some of them. He insisted that the potters had rushed the job and were delivering inferior merchandise. More pots had to be made. It became apparent to everyone then that he was reluctant to part with the secret."

"Or he might have been telling the truth, as he saw it."

"Maybe," he conceded. "But when he disappeared, everyone suffered. Fortunately, there was enough food and firewood to share. Still, the potters who'd made the deal on behalf of the others were disgraced. Their families have never recovered from the stigma."

"But if my father died before the deal could be completed, it wasn't their fault. This could exonerate them, as well."

"It doesn't work that way. The ones who made the deal with your father were responsible for the outcome. They owed it to the others to bring back the pottery already delivered or find the location of the clay. Their failure harmed the pueblo and the artisans who'd trusted in them. The matter will never be forgotten until it's resolved."

Ramona nodded slowly. She understood that way of thinking. Until she knew exactly what had happened to her father, she would not be able to put it behind her, either. "So now what?"

He heard the sound of two vehicles coming up the driveway. "That sounds like the crime-scene unit arriving." He started to leave the kitchen, then stopped and turned around. "You'll be asked to stay out of the front room. You may find it difficult to cooperate with strangers in your own home, but it's standard procedure.''

Ramona watched Michael leave. She didn't have the desire or energy to go back into the front room. She knew in her heart that they'd uncovered her father's body. She'd returned home to find him, but doing that had ripped a hole right through her heart.

She filled the teakettle and placed it on the stove. Scarcely aware of what she was doing, she returned to the table and prepared for the long wait ahead.

AROUND MIDNIGHT the body was removed. The detectives and technicians continued to work, searching and photographing the area, but the age of the corpse left little hope of finding clues after so many years.

Ramona went to her mother's sewing room and made herself comfortable on the chair next to the window. Everything her mother had valued was in here and this was where Ramona felt closest to her.

"Mother, I don't know what to do," she whispered to the silence. "You wanted me to make a life for myself away from here. But I can't run from our past. It's part of me. I can't turn my back on who and what I am."

Michael gently placed one hand on her shoulder. Startled, she jumped. "How did you get in here without making any noise?" She shook her head. "Never mind. I remember you have a reputation as an excellent hunter."

"That's probably one of the reasons why I joined the sheriff's department. I would have preferred to be appointed *kwaku tsonin* and work as a tribal cop. They and the *Towa é* are responsible for protecting the tribe."

"I know the *kwaku tsonin* are our officials. But what exactly are the *Towa é*? That sounds familiar."

"Our tribe classifies all existence into six groups, three spiritual and three human. On the human level, the *Towa é* are the protectors, both of our rites and of our people."

"Oh, I remember. We progress through stages. Only the Dry Food People—the lowest, common level of Tewa—are appointed by the chiefs to serve as *kwaku tsonin* and *Towa é*. I think my mother belonged to the Made People, another level."

He nodded. "Made People are the highest mortal category. They're mediators between the spiritual and the human. That's why your mother's marriage to a white man met with such disapproval. Most felt she should have chosen a mate from our tribe."

Ramona smiled. "She fell in love and followed her heart."

"That's why many insist she brought most of her troubles on herself."

Ramona shook her head sadly, suspecting he shared their opinions and didn't understand. "Are the other policemen gone?"

"Yes. I'll be leaving soon, too, but first I thought you'd want to know what we've learned."

"Yes. Please."

"The coroner said that the victim, a male, had been shot in the head twice, execution style. One misshapen bullet lodged in the skull, but the other passed through and wasn't located. They searched the room, but it doesn't look like it's there."

"The trading post was being remodeled at the time my father disappeared. If that is him, and I believe it is, he was probably shot in that room and buried there for convenience. He was a big man."

"Not necessarily. He could have been shot almost anywhere on the property, then brought there because it was one place where the crime would be easily hidden."

"Something just occurred to me. Do you think tonight's sniper had something to do with the murder? It's no secret that I'm planning to have construction work done here. He might have been worried that the body would be found if I went ahead with my plans."

He considered it, then shook his head. "I doubt that the sniper incident is related to any of this. The thought of the body being found after all this time probably wouldn't have worried the killer. He'd realize that whatever evidence we find now would be marginal at best. Look at what we have so far. Also keep in mind that the killer might not be in this area anymore. For that matter, he might not even be alive. Wanting to stop the cooperative seems a much more plausible explanation for what happened."

Ramona shuddered. "I wanted to make things right, not worse...."

"I'm sorry." Michael didn't like to see the tears that welled in her eyes, but the lines separating them were clearly drawn. "We'd like to keep news of the body quiet for now, at least until we have more information. Don't discuss what we've learned with anyone for the time being."

"All right," she answered quietly.

"Is there anything I can do for you before I leave?"

"No, I'll be okay. I'm going to search this room. There are a few things of my mother's I've been trying to locate. Afterward I'm going to bed."

"Can I help you look?"

"No, it's not that important. The items I want aren't valuable to anyone but me. They're small keepsakes I associate with her, and I'd like to have them. They used to be on that shelf, but they aren't there anymore."

He stared at the floor for a moment, saying nothing. Finally he glanced up at her. "The items ... were they religious?"

She nodded. "Yeah, why do you ask?"

"I don't think you'll find them, then. I would expect that the head of the *Kwiyoh,* the woman's society, has already taken them to their rightful place."

"Their rightful place is with me," she answered angrily. "They can't deny me my heritage!"

He shook his head slowly. "You've got much to remember, and much to learn. No one is singling you out
unjustly. Ritual objects owned by a Made Person may not
be used again. They're retired to a lake or mountain shrine
by other members of the society."

The emptiness inside her grew, enveloping her in a soul-
chilling void. His explanation had robbed her of righ-
teous anger. That one emotion could have shielded her
from the pain by giving her something to hold on to. But
now there was nothing. "I spent so many years away. I
know my father's world very well. It's my mother's that I
can't seem to fit into."

"Maybe that's the way it's meant to be."

"No." She squared her shoulders and faced him. "I
won't let it be lost to me forever." Ramona walked Michael back to his car. "Let me know what else the police
find out, okay?"

"Count on it. In the meantime, I'll concentrate on trying to find the gunman who threatened you. I'm also going to go to the pueblo and see if I can find out who left
you the witch's bundle. I still think we're dealing with two
different people."

She stood behind Michael as he opened his car door.
"Tomorrow I'll replace the damaged sign. Then, as soon
as the printer delivers my flyers, I'll take them to the
governor's office and leave them there for whoever is interested. This isn't going to stop me from what I need to
do."

Instead of stepping inside his vehicle, he turned around,
intending to caution her. His abrupt gesture took her off
guard, and for an instant, they stood inches away from
each other. "Be careful, Mona," he said, the meaning he'd
intended altered by the circumstances.

Ramona's eyes were riveted on his. There was something raw, vital and quintessentially male just beneath his
veneer of control. "Are you warning me as a cop," she
asked, "or a friend?"

"Both." The warmth of her breath touched his cheek like a caress. He was suddenly achingly aware of all the years her hazel eyes and full mouth had haunted his dreams. He'd stopped coming to visit after the scandal— he'd had to—but he'd never stopped missing her. For a moment they stared at each other in silence, trapped within themselves, chests heaving, lips moist.

"You're just as I remembered you," Michael finally mumbled.

"Really?" Self-conscious, Ramona glanced at her dirty jeans and blouse, then brushed a strand of hair away from her face. A piece of plaster fell down past her eyes and landed on his boot, leaving a small clump of white powder sitting there. She looked down, then their eyes met.

He gave her a quick, lopsided grin. "Naw. Maybe not. You didn't wear plaster in your hair back then," he said, and heard her laugh. He could feel her tension as well as he felt his own.

Cold, chunky flakes of winter snow began to fall, but the heat inside him could have melted a frozen lake.

"You've got enemies, Mona. Remember that and take care of yourself."

Ramona watched his car disappear into the darkness, then slipped back inside the house through the side door. As she stood in what had once been her parents' home, the reality of her situation hit her full force. Her feelings for Michael were nothing more than a holdover from the past. They meant nothing in the face of the battle that lay ahead of her.

For several seconds, she stood in the kitchen by the doorway to the living room. There was a piece of plywood over the hole they'd made in the flooring. Unable to bear the reminder it posed, Ramona walked to her mother's room and brought out a large folding screen. Carefully positioning it in the front room, she blocked out the area that had served as her father's grave.

Ramona took a deep breath, fighting to break the stranglehold of sadness that engulfed her. She felt naked and isolated, buffeted by a myriad of emotions too raw to contain. Shielded in the silence and loneliness of the house, she finally allowed herself to cry.

IT WAS SHORTLY AFTER eight o'clock the following morning when Ramona set out to replace her sign. She was determined to show whoever had defaced it that she wouldn't be scared away. Yet as she neared that location, a persistent sense of uneasiness crept over her. Memories of what she'd found there the night before were still too vivid in her mind.

Turning the pickup onto the dirt road that crisscrossed her property, she forced herself to continue. To her right, on an adjacent plot of pueblo land, she saw several sheep foraging on the meager grasses. It looked so peaceful here. It was the last place on earth she would have expected to encounter the kind of trouble she'd had.

As she reached the turnoff from the highway, Ramona noticed a sheriff's vehicle parked ahead on the far side of the dirt road. Michael was a few yards from the squad car on the pueblo side of the fence, hunched over the ground.

Ramona left her truck and walked toward him, holding her new sign in one hand. "Have you learned anything yet?"

He joined her at the side of the road. "See where that boulder is? That's the spot the sniper fired from," Michael said, gesturing uphill, where he'd searched earlier. "He had a clear shot into the living quarters of the trading post from there. With your lights on at night, the interior would have stood out clearly, making a perfect target."

"Will those shell casings help you track him down?" she said, glancing at the plastic evidence pouch in his hand.

"Not unless we find the rifle they were fired from. They're from a .223, the same caliber as the bullets I dug

out of your wall. It's a very common weapon. Once we
have a suspect though, these will help build the case against
him." He called her attention toward the place where he'd
found the shells. "I also searched for vehicle tracks, but
too many people use that road on their way in and out of
the pueblo."

"There's a house right down the hill from here. The
owner might have heard or seen something last night."

"I'll go talk to them. I know the families who live over
that way. Someone might be able to help. Can you meet me
at the tribal government building in about an hour? I have
a small office there the county has leased for me from the
tribe. I'm going to need you to sign a statement and fill out
a complaint form."

"Fine. I'll catch up with you there."

Ramona selected another place on high ground for her
sign. From this new location, it would be even easier to see
by anyone who used the highway in or out of the pueblo.
Satisfied, she hammered the post firmly into the ground
with a flat rock, then drove back to the trading post. The
flyers were supposed to be arriving first thing this morning, but she hadn't noticed any delivery truck.

She reached her home shortly afterward, but one glance
at the porch told her the delivery hadn't been made. Disappointed, she went inside. There were many things to do
before the cooperative could get under way. She'd have to
start recruiting members soon. Acting on impulse, she began working on a hand-lettered sign she could leave outside the building where the village council met.

Time slipped by. When she checked her watch, she realized it was nearly time to meet Michael. Grabbing her
coat off the back of the chair, she rushed to the pickup.
She was almost out the driveway when she saw a carton
near the mailbox. From the outside label, she could tell it
was her long-awaited flyers.

She expelled her breath in a tiny hiss. The printer had
promised delivery before eight-thirty, and had agreed to

leave them on her porch if she was out. It was now nine-thirty and here they were, practically on the side of the road where anyone could have taken or vandalized them. Grateful that luck had been with her, she loaded the cardboard box into the pickup.

Ramona drove to the pueblo and parked by the government building. She had one quick stop to make before meeting Michael. She wanted to make sure no one had defaced or removed the poster she'd placed on the bulletin board in there.

She entered the low adobe structure and went down the hall. Seeing a small circle of people ahead, she smiled with satisfaction. At least her ad was still up and attracting attention. When she came close enough to hear the conversation however, her stomach tightened into a painful knot. Barton Perez, a longtime San Esteban resident, was speaking to the others, and their attention was riveted on him.

"How can we trust the daughter of a man who cheated most of our families?" he argued. "We can't form an alliance with her! It would be admitting that we have no hope of righting the wrong done to us."

She watched Barton for a moment, knowing his impassioned plea was swaying the others. Perez had always been a natural leader, and now, in his mid-fifties, he seemed more charismatic than ever. He was also an unusually gifted jewelry maker. His support would have insured the cooperation of many, but it was clear that wasn't going to happen.

She stepped forward, speaking clearly and assertively. "Mr. Perez, the cooperative may not right a wrong of the past," she began, "but it may help today and tomorrow. The pueblo trades mostly with tourists, and the season for that is limited. Winters are lean for the pueblo artists. The Spruce Branch Cooperative will enable the artisans to market their work in stores all over the United States. That would mean paychecks year-round."

"We don't need your help, Miss U.N.M. business school. Your father also made many promises, but in the end, all he did was cause harm. Even after all these years, some of our families are still suffering. Now you come ready to step into your father's shoes, and want us to trust you. This tribe should never again ally with an Anglo, and in your heart that's what you are. You were raised on the outside, in their schools. You think just like them, and we won't be taken in by your words."

"When the tourists aren't buying, everyone in the village suffers. We can make things better if we work together. That's the heart of the Tewa way." She glanced at all the faces, letting her gaze linger on each for a second before going on. "And yes, I was raised in the Anglo world after I left for boarding school, but that can be an asset to the tribe. Those are the people we'll be dealing with. Who better to do that than someone who has lived in both worlds?"

"Your words are nothing more than empty promises," Perez said. "If in your heart you were still a Tewa, you'd be busy searching for the pottery your father stole from us. Or you could try to find the source of the clay, information our families paid for with long hours of labor. That's how you can really help. Not by taking our work and using it to line your own purse."

"Barton's right," an elderly man agreed. "The cooperative may help some, but will end up hurting the artisans who choose to remain independent. You'd be taking tourist dollars away from them."

"How would that be any different than it is now? Tourists have always gone from artisan to artisan, choosing the pieces they like best."

Barton pushed through the crowd and faced her squarely. "Your father wanted to get rich off us. It seems to me that you're the same. Why don't you go back to your big city? You don't belong here."

Anger tore at her restraint. But reason, not emotions, was what was needed to reach them. "I am my *mother's* daughter. She was raised and loved in San Esteban. She never acted against any of you. Yet she was the one hurt most when people turned against her."

"What happened with your parents was before my time," one of the younger men said, "but I remember the stories. Your mother chose to stand with your father."

"She stood by her mate. Who among you wouldn't ask the same of your husband or wife, and value that in them? Before you judge me on the basis of my parents, consider that."

She bent down and started to open the box of flyers. "If any of you want to know about the Spruce Branch Cooperative, then read my flyer. It'll tell you exactly what it's meant to accomplish and how."

She lifted a handful from the box. As she held them out toward the crowd, one of the flyers exploded like a firecracker and burst into flames.

Chapter Three

"What the...!" Ramona gasped, and jumped, dropping the burning papers onto the brick floor. The onlookers all stepped back, but an alert receptionist quickly doused the glowing papers with coffee, extinguishing the flames.

Ramona's heart was beating like a bass drum, and her fingers tingled from the lingering heat.

"She's bewitched," an elderly man said in a hushed tone.

Badly shaken, she fought to regain her composure. She glanced up angrily, ready to defend herself against an accusation that could ruin her. But when she met the man's eyes, she saw no malice there, only fear. His dry, wrinkled skin, with its geography of deep-set lines, made him appear more frail than threatening.

"Someone tampered with the papers," she hastily tried to explain. Her hands were shaking so badly she clasped them together for mutual support.

"Yes, a witch," the elderly man insisted. "Wasn't your father one?"

Ramona was too stunned to reply.

Barton Perez smiled smugly. "Well, witch or not, it just brings home the point I've been making. Your presence brings nothing but trouble." He turned and walked away, followed by many of the villagers.

"You better keep your distance from those papers. Close the box and let me take it to the bomb squad," a familiar voice interjected. As she turned, she saw Michael standing there. He looked like a giant stone sentinel keeping guard. His expression, though thoughtful, was otherwise difficult to read.

Ramona's voice wavered slightly as she folded over the cardboard flaps and handed the box to him. "I'd appreciate it if you'd let me know what you find out."

He nodded. "I thought you were coming to my office," he added, lowering the box carefully into a small metal trash can.

"I wanted to check on the ad I'd posted and hand out the flyers." She explained how the delivery had been delayed and where she'd found the shipment.

"It's obvious someone intercepted it." Michael carefully salvaged several of the burned papers and placed them in the trash can beside the box. Ramona followed as he took them to an adobe storage shed outside and locked up the evidence. "You should have been more alert."

His matter-of-fact tone hurt. "Where do you stand on the issue of the Spruce Branch Cooperative?" she asked pointedly.

"I've heard all about your plans to market what our artisans produce, but I'm not convinced it'll work. With everyone taking a cut along the way, will there be much left for the artists?"

"Their profits should increase because there will be no middleman wholesalers. We'll deal directly with retail outlets. Also, the cooperative will provide the artists with whatever materials they need, so that'll cut their overhead. And they'll get an advance against the sale when they deliver their product. After the item is sold, they'll get the rest, minus the cooperative's fee. As an added bonus, the members will get a percentage of all the profits made, too, so they'll share the net proceeds of a substantially larger merchandise base."

"It sounds good. I'm curious though. How did you come up with the name?" He crossed the grounds leading the way around the side of the building.

"In the Anglo world, spruce is called an evergreen. It bears life despite the season or circumstance. It's also a plant that's used in ceremonies by both the Summer and Winter People, the two groups that make up our tribe."

"Makes sense." Michael smiled in approval. "But even though your plans are sound, they don't alter the facts. The resistance you've encountered already worries me. The tribe only has one very overworked police captain and a sergeant. I lend a hand when they call, but San Esteban isn't used to having trouble." He shrugged. "We haven't had anything serious happen here for at least three years, when John Romero disappeared."

"Yes, I remember. My mother wrote me about that. He was kidnapped, right?"

Michael nodded. "The sergeant who handled most of that investigation is now captain." He stopped in front of the rear door to his office, hearing someone call his name. A beautiful elderly woman stood in the portal of an adobe home and waved.

Ramona smiled. "I'd forgotten that your parents live across the street from the government building."

"Wait here. I'll be right back." He walked to the front steps of his mother's house.

Ramona waved at the elderly woman, but Antonia Wolf didn't wave back. Ramona wondered if Antonia had even noticed her. Antonia's attention seemed completely focused on her son.

Ramona watched the pair as they met. Antonia hadn't changed much through the years. Her hair was now almost completely gray, but she stood straight and as proud as she had during her younger years.

As she stood there waiting, Ramona felt the crushing weight of a past she couldn't escape. She would have liked a chance to visit Antonia Wolf, but from Michael's attitude, she knew she wouldn't be welcome there.

Michael emerged seconds later and rejoined her. "Sorry. Personal business."

"How are your parents?"

"My father died several years ago. My mother hasn't been the same since. I take care of her as much as she'll let me. But she's proud and won't tolerate my interfering too much." He unlocked the door to his office and showed her inside.

"This must be one of the smallest official areas around," she commented with a grin.

"I don't need much. My prisoners go to Santa Fe or Española. The tribe's police captain uses the adjoining offices. The small holding cell in the back is for tribal police use only."

"That's not a lot for them, either."

"It's enough. Remember this is a small pueblo. Our troubles mostly come when we have our ceremonial dances. Outsiders don't always realize that it's part of a religious ceremony."

He went around his desk, pulled several sheets from a file cabinet and placed them before her. "These are part of my crime report. In addition to signing those, you'll also have to make a statement for the tribe's records."

"No problem. I want whoever's after me found and arrested. By the way, did you speak with any of my neighbors?"

"Yes, but they weren't much help. They heard shots, but didn't go outside for a look."

It was an hour later when Ramona finally walked out of his office. Michael accompanied her back to her pickup. "Have you given any thought to what Barton Perez said about trying to find the location of the clay? The information could be among your father's personal effects or his business records."

"If it's there, I'll find it," she said quietly. "I've been looking for it whenever I have some time to spare. I knew that the information rightfully belongs to the tribe. There's nothing I'd like better than to turn it over to them."

As she drove away, Michael started back to his office. He was halfway there when he saw his mother approaching.

"I have to talk to you again, son. There are things that have to be said and clearly understood between us."

"All right. Do you want to come to my office, or would you like to go back home?"

"Let's go home. There's something I'd like you to have."

A few minutes later, they arrived at his mother's house. Michael followed her into the kitchen and sat down across the table from her. For several seconds she said nothing, staring at some indeterminate spot outside the window. Finally, with a long sigh, she glanced back at Michael.

"Your father held a position of honor before his downfall," she said slowly. "As the Hunt Chief, he was the mediator between the Summer and the Winter People. It was that woman's father who caused our problems."

Michael nodded. "I remember when Dad gave back the 'corn mother,' the symbol of the original mother of all. That and the *Pi xen,* the mountain lion fetish that symbolized his office. Without those, and stripped of the job that defined him, he felt like a man without a purpose."

"He believed that he'd failed the tribe and that led to his death, I'm sure of it. He felt he'd disgraced all of us, particularly you." Antonia looked down at her hands.

"I never blamed him for anything. He made that agreement with John Ortiz in good faith. And he lost as much as the others. Dad was one of the potters who delivered his best work to Ortiz for an entire year. All Ortiz supplied was the special clay."

"Yes, but there's more to the story, a part I've never told you." She coughed briefly, then continued in a strong voice. "Your father headed the group who negotiated the deal with Ortiz, you've always known that. But as the head of the Hunt Society, your father felt it was up to him to find the source of the clay or retrieve the pottery. He was also firmly convinced he'd succeed. He believed the gods would show him the way. That's why he went to the tribal meeting and promised everyone he wouldn't fail."

Michael rubbed his hand over his face. "He should have never said that."

"I couldn't stop him," she said quietly. "He assured everyone that they could count on him, and insisted he could do it alone. Then after months went by, he realized he'd never be able to do as he promised. By then, invaluable time had been lost by others who could have also been searching. He knew then that he'd failed the tribe, and that knowledge broke his spirit."

"I remember him spending hours sitting alone in the garden."

"Something inside him died. His body eventually followed. Despite what others may think, I believe that the *Oxua,* our gods, accepted him. His soul now resides with other ancestral souls." She handed him two pouches. "I want you to go to the shrine west of here. Offer these and ask your father to help you. Nothing would please him more. He'll help you find the answers you need."

He looked down at the small leather bags—prayer meal and *pe,* an offering of feathers.

"The meal will nourish the spirits, and the feathers are a gift of clothing and adornment for them. Your message asking for help will then reach your father."

"I'll take care of it. I know that telling me about this was hard for you, but I'm grateful you did. Before he died, I promised Dad I'd find answers. Now the weight of his promise is also part of my own. I'll finish the job he started. Count on it."

"You sound so much like your father. Yet you're distracted. When I saw you with Ramona this morning, I knew what was still in your heart."

He glanced away, then after a pause, looked back at her. "I won't deny that I'm attracted to her, but I know my duty. I won't betray the trust you and others have placed in me."

RAMONA STOOD before the loan officer's desk. The walls of the bank's small office seemed to be closing in on her. Things were starting to fall apart. "I don't understand. You'd said everything was in order. You assured me that I wouldn't have any problem getting the loan. Now you're changing your tune. Why?" She returned to her chair and challenged the woman behind the desk, holding her gaze. "And don't think I can be brushed aside. There's nothing wrong with my credit and my assets are tangible. They more than equal the loan I've asked for."

"Yes, all that's true." The woman leaned back in her chair. "Look, there's been a snag in the paperwork. That's all I can tell you."

"Okay, officially that's all you can tell me, but you and I went to junior high school together, Linda." Ramona softened her tone, deciding on a different approach. "I helped you survive Algebra, remember? Now it's your turn to do something for me. I feel like I'm fighting shadows. Tell me what's wrong. No one will ever know we had this conversation, I promise."

Linda hesitated, looking past Ramona out into the hall. After a long pause, she nodded. "Okay. I don't like having to play these games anyway." She leaned forward and lowered her voice to a conspiratorial whisper. "Our biggest account has put a great deal of pressure on us. He doesn't want you to get this loan."

"I wasn't aware I knew any wealthy people," she joked halfheartedly.

"George Taylor is one of our local businessmen. He has gift shops all over the place and he's also the largest jewelry wholesaler in the state. He feels your business will be in direct competition with his and that this bank would be undermining him by financing you. He's threatened to pull out all his money and investments if we give you the loan."

"So, I'll go to another bank."

"Wouldn't do much good. He's got financial interests all over the state. There isn't anywhere you could go where he couldn't exert some influence. Money talks." She tapped her pen against her desk, lost in thought. "Let me try to push this loan through. I think I can sway the right people. But if he pulls his money out of this bank, I'll have trouble of my own." Her eyes met Ramona's in a level gaze. "You won't exactly be off the hook, either. You'll have an even bigger fight on your hands the minute he learns you have the financing you need."

"A Christian missionary once told me that the best way to destroy an enemy is to turn him into a friend. I thought she was crazy at the time and I still think it's terribly impractical. Yet in this particular case, I think it just might work," Ramona said pensively.

"What do you have in mind?"

"I'll let you know if it turns out right." Ramona smiled, then walked out of the office and the bank. With a plan slowly developing in her head, she stopped long enough to make a phone call, then drove directly to George Taylor's business office.

She was ushered in seconds after she arrived. Taylor's walls were covered with framed collections of military insignias, antique police badges, and old Mathew Brady photographs of the Civil War. Ramona smiled guilelessly at her adversary. "Mr. Taylor, I don't know if you've heard about me, but I plan to start an Indian crafts cooperative on the land my father left me."

"Yes, I've heard of you," Taylor replied icily. "I'm sure you also realize I intend to make things as difficult for you as I can."

"Well, what I did hear was that you were concerned the cooperative would be in direct competition with your shops. I came to offer you an alternative."

"Alternative?" Taylor eyed her suspiciously.

"Yes. Besides selling directly from our location, Spruce Branch Cooperative will have many retail outlets handling our merchandise. If you're interested, we could work out an arrangement with your shops."

"I'd be helping your business far more than I would mine. I already have artisans who provide my shops with a variety of jewelry and crafts."

"By adding what we produce to your inventory, you could offer the public an even greater selection. San Esteban has some fine artists."

He stood by the window, his back to her, staring down San Francisco Street toward the Plaza. "No. I knew your father for many years. Like you, he had ideas that sounded great. The problem was, they never quite worked out to anyone's advantage but his own." Taylor turned and met her gaze. "My business doesn't need help from you."

"I don't intend to justify myself or my father to you. What I'm offering is a simple business proposition."

"It's one I refuse. And for the record, I'm a formidable opponent. I suggest you drop this business venture of yours before you lose every penny."

Ramona rose and faced him. "I'm a tough, well-trained adversary. I won't cave in under pressure. I'll just fight even harder. *Your* business will be the one losing customers."

As she turned to leave, she saw Taylor's secretary staring aghast at her. From her expression, it was easy to tell that few people spoke to Taylor in the tone she'd just used. She stepped around the woman, easing by the gun display case, and strode out the door.

Ramona held her head high as she walked to her pickup. She'd spoken strong words, but inside she didn't feel brave at all. The minute she slipped behind the wheel, self-doubts closed in on her like storm clouds before the sun.

Desperately she tried to recapture her earlier sense of optimism. She'd need to believe in herself if she was going to succeed. If the bank did refuse her loan application, she'd just have to find another way to get financial backing. Maybe she could deal with an individual investor, or someone who'd be willing to take the loan out on her behalf. Either way, she'd get what she needed. No one, particularly George Taylor, was going to stand in her way.

Later, as Ramona approached the trading post, she saw a man near the gates, watching the entrance. Recognizing him, she slowed down. He was one of the pueblo's jewelry makers. Though still young, he was quickly gaining recognition for his work. "Hello, Al. What are you doing sitting out here?"

He looked sheepish and stared at the ground. "I saw the ad you placed in the government building, and I thought I'd come and talk with you."

"You could have waited on the porch. I've got plenty of chairs there. You would have been more comfortable," she prodded, feeling there was something he wasn't saying.

"I was curious to see who else would show up."

"Hop in and don't worry. Others will come soon enough."

"I know. I've heard talk. Some are against this, but many who had hard times last winter are eager for a change. I don't know if you can really help, but I'm interested to hear the details of your plan."

She explained it thoroughly, then continued. "Since the artists will give the cooperative a percentage of each sale, it shouldn't be long before I can recoup my initial investment. Then we'll all be co-owners, working for ourselves within the framework of the cooperative. The more a person puts into it, the greater their individual share, and the more it'll benefit the group.''

He nodded thoughtfully as she parked the vehicle, then followed her inside, where he read a draft copy of her overall proposal. ''It *is* a good plan. I don't see any reason why it shouldn't work. I'll join you.''

''I'm glad to hear that. I'm also glad you haven't let rumors affect your decision.''

''Yes, but then again, I'm the first in my family to work outside of farming. There have been no craftsmen among us for several decades, so there's no bad blood between your people and mine.''

''I see your point.''

''So, when do we get started?''

''I'll need a few more days to get things ready. Once I set up some temporary space, you can move your work over here.'' One way or another, she'd have the financing she needed to boost her existing funds by then. There was no way she'd let them or herself down.

''That'll work fine for me. By the way, there's something you should know. Barton Perez has convinced many of the tribe's most experienced craftsmen to remain independent. Spruce Branch Cooperative won't be able to count on their jewelry or crafts.''

''Hmm. I expected as much.''

Al glanced out the den window, then looked at her. ''But there'll be others who'll come. Here are two now. Juanita Gonzales and Martin Lucero are both good potters. They're not well-known enough to command the highest prices, but they're steady producers and do quality work.''

As the pair came in, they greeted him and spoke for a few moments. As soon as Al left, their attention shifted to her. Gonzales and Lucero were more skeptical than Al had been, but a half hour later, they too agreed to join the cooperative.

Once they were gone, Ramona sank down into the worn cushions of an easy chair. She'd need more than three members to make the cooperative work, but it was a start. With a bit of luck, more artisans would show up this afternoon.

She glanced at the small clock on the mantelshelf. It was nearly noon. Next on her agenda was applying some pressure of her own at the bank. There was no valid reason for them to deny her credit. Perhaps threatening to make their reluctance a bit more public would help. No financial institution needed adverse publicity—not after the savings and loans scandals. She stretched wearily and stood. She'd shower and change, then go pay them a visit.

Ramona went to her old room. As her gaze drifted over the familiar surroundings, memories echoed back at her. When she was young, she'd often sat in the window and kept a curious watch over San Esteban. Her mother had never spoken much about her old life there. The pain from severing most of her old ties had become a permanent shadow of sadness that shimmered just beneath the surface of her eyes.

Ramona had wondered if someday she too would find a love so precious and strong she'd willingly pay any price to hold on to it. As she stared at the pueblo through her window, Michael's face flashed before her memory. Dangerous emotions flickered to life, and she quickly brushed him from her mind.

Even though she'd lost much of her Tewa ways, there was one thing that was too deeply ingrained in her to forget. Dedication to duty was the heart of the Tewa world. It was woven into the fabric of everything they were as a people. She'd honor her own by achieving what she set out to do.

Ramona undressed quickly, but as she stepped into the shower, her heart froze. There, propped on the handles, was a hideous doll made out of animal hide. Prickly pear spines speared it.

With a strangled cry, she staggered back.

Chapter Four

An intruder had been in her house, inside her own room! The realization stunned her. She'd felt safest inside her home, even after the shooting, but now an enemy had defiled her only haven.

Ramona's nakedness accentuated her sense of vulnerability. In a flash, she retrieved her clothing from the floor and reached for the telephone. She dialed the sheriff's office quickly. An expressionless voice informed her that since no emergency existed, she'd have to wait for the next available officer. Response time would take another hour, at least.

Frustration spurred Ramona into action. She searched the house room by room, making sure no other surprises had been left for her. She had no doubt the person who'd done this was long gone. His intent was to build fear. Remaining nameless suited his purposes far better than confronting her face-to-face.

Eventually she discovered how the intruder had gained entry. A window in one of the bedrooms, long ago painted shut, had been forced open with some kind of pry bar or tool. She quickly located a hammer and nails, and sealed the window shut permanently.

When she returned to her room, she walked straight to the bathroom door and slammed it shut. She didn't really believe in witchcraft, but the thought of leaving the doll there until Michael could come repulsed her.

Sitting on the edge of her bed, she tried to organize her thoughts. There was no time to go to the bank now. Other artisans would hopefully be arriving soon.

By the time she reached the den, she heard voices approaching down the driveway. Ramona went to the window and saw six more residents of San Esteban. The small group left ninety minutes later; four had agreed to work with her. The victory lifted her spirits. But as the list of artists committing to the cooperative grew, so did her need to get the financing under way.

Glancing out the window, Ramona estimated she had at least five minutes before anyone else arrived. She strode to the telephone and dialed the bank.

"Has there been any change?" Ramona asked after Linda answered.

"Not so far. The delay is still in the front office. I'm trying my best to get things moving again."

"I appreciate that, but I'd like you to go to your supervisors and convey a message for me. There's no reason for my loan request to be turned down, we all know that. If my application is denied, I'll have to conclude that it's due to my being a single woman, an Indian, or both. My attorney will be happy to discuss it with them—in court. There are federal agencies that would be asking them questions, too, on my behalf. But that would probably take place after the press conference."

"Uh...I'll get back to you. Please don't do anything else yet." Linda cleared her throat, then continued. "You may have found a way to get the ball rolling, but be prepared. They may decide to play tough with you or draw out the process with technicalities."

"I'm taking my best shot. Let them take theirs."

By the time Ramona placed the receiver down, her palms were sweating. It was mostly bluff, of course. She wasn't eager to focus any more negative attention on herself, either. But desperate times called for desperate measures. If it became necessary, she would fight hard and long for her rights.

Hearing someone walking up to the porch, she took a deep breath and prepared to greet them. With a smile firmly in place, she walked over and opened the door. Three more members of the tribe were there, but along with them was a Hispanic man she didn't recognize. He was in his mid-forties and balding. His egg-shaped head looked disproportionately large because of its stark shiny surface. His features were too small for his face, giving him a feral and dangerous look.

She greeted the pueblo artisans warmly, then turned to the man who'd come in with them. "May I help you?"

"My name is Mario Chacon, and I've been hearing about your cooperative. I'm here to ask if you intend to operate a union shop." His voice boomed in the confines of the small den. "I've done some research on your family, Ms. Ortiz. I think the tribe ought to monitor your business very carefully. A union is going to be needed to protect the workers."

"There's no need for you or your rudeness here, Mr. Chacon. There will be no employee-employer relationship in the cooperative. Everyone that signs on, does so as a partner in the venture. We'll set our working conditions by mutual consent."

"You expect these people to believe that? Come on! You put up the money, but you're all equal partners? Yeah, right."

"I'll get my investment back as we share in the profits. The Tewas are part of me, and I'm part of them. By helping the tribe, I'm helping myself."

Chacon turned toward the three men. "You need a contract with representation for yourselves. You can't trust someone with her background to look after your interests. By forming a union, you guarantee protection for everyone."

"We know about her," one of the Tewa artists replied. "We don't know about you. Why would a stranger want to help us?"

"I don't like to see management take advantage of its workers. She talks nicely about partnerships, but who's actually going to do the work?"

"Like I said, we know about her and what she's offering us," the man replied. "What about you? Your services, I assume, don't come free."

"Well, no, the union represents you, and in turn you pay membership dues to cover costs and benefits. But without unity and representation, the individual has no recourse in case of trouble. It sounds terrific to say you'll be equal partners. But if your manager in this so-called equal partnership disappears, you can be left holding nothing but bills."

"That won't happen," Ramona said flatly. "You're forgetting. I'm the one incurring the debts, not them. Without their work, I can't do anything. They have the upper hand—they can stop working for the cooperative at any time. But making the cooperative a success will bring needed employment to the pueblo." She met his gaze with an icy glare. "I care about the tribe because I'm a part of them. You're only interested in them in exchange for the dues they'll be paying. That doesn't put you in a very good light." She held out her hand. "Give me your card, Mr. Chacon, then please leave."

"There are more people coming up the drive. I'm not going anywhere. You're trying to pull a fast one here. Until your initial investment is paid off, you're not all on equal footing. Whether you admit it or not, you'll be management because you'll be in control of the money."

She picked up the receiver. "If you force me to call the sheriff, Mr. Chacon, I'll swear out a complaint and you'll be arrested for trespassing. The choice is yours. Either way, you *will* leave."

Chacon crossed his arms indignantly and glared at her for several seconds. With a shrug, she began to dial.

"Okay, I'm leaving," he said quickly. "But this isn't over. Not by a long shot."

She walked to the door and held it open for Chacon. As soon as he left, she focused her attention on the artisans who'd been waiting. "Please understand that I'd never try to stop you from forming a union, if that's what you want. That decision is up to you. But do remember that this is a cooperative, not a traditional corporation. We're all management, and we're all labor. My funds will finance the start of the cooperative, so I have the most to lose. I'm putting everything I own into this and trusting you. But you also have to trust my business sense. For this to work we have to have confidence in each other."

As a murmur of assent went around the room, Ramona breathed a silent sigh of relief. This was the first sign of progress between the members of the cooperative and her. Her energy and optimism renewed, she waited for the others.

The afternoon went slowly. She recruited several members of the pueblo, but lost others who weren't quite able to let go of past distrusts. It was midafternoon when she accompanied the last artisan down the driveway.

"I'm glad that you decided to join, Saya. You're the best potter in New Mexico. Your traditional black-on-red style is very beautiful."

"It's nothing compared to the work my parents did," the woman commented. "Your father's clay was exceptional. There hasn't been anything like it since. Many said he was a witch." She smiled sheepishly. "Personally I wouldn't have cared. I'd give anything to work with that clay."

"I've been trying to find the source," Ramona admitted, "but so far, I haven't had any luck."

"You have no idea how much that could mean to the tribe. To really understand, you would have had to live through the hard times that came after the clay was gone."

"I know. Sales really dropped."

Saya nodded. "Drastically. It took some families years to recover financially. The tourists only wanted to buy our old style, and we couldn't provide it for them." She paused, her eyes on the sacred mountain to the north. "Of course the Wolf clan never recovered at all."

She looked up, surprised. "Michael Wolf's people?"

She nodded. "His father was the Hunt Chief and responsible for bringing back what was ours. It is said that the *Oxua,* our gods, punished him for his failure. He died shortly after he admitted that he'd lost the trail and he'd have to abandon the search." She paused and, almost as if speaking to herself, added, "A great deal of food had to be buried with him."

"You mean, they forgave him at the end?"

"Not at all," the older woman explained. "An extra pair of moccasins and additional food is provided for anyone who doesn't lead a good life. Although we believe they too will reach the underworld, they'll have a hard journey ahead. Their road will be filled with hazards and it'll take them a long time to find their way." She paused. "Of course the responsibility for finding answers now falls to his son."

As the woman finished speaking, Ramona's thoughts shifted to Michael. Now she wasn't sure that his efforts to help her had been genuine. He'd paid dearly for her father's actions. Even though her heart went out to him in sympathy, the seed of distrust had been firmly planted.

As she reached the end of the driveway, Ramona slowed her steps. "I'm glad we got a chance to talk. I look forward to working with you, Saya," she said sincerely.

Ramona picked up her mail, then started back down the road to the house. Her thoughts raced as she weighed the import of what she'd learned. Michael had deliberately chosen to withhold information from her. The realization filled her with foreboding.

As Ramona stepped inside the house, she heard a noise behind her. She started to turn, when suddenly a hood was forced over her head. Terrified, she screamed and struggled, kicking backward at her attacker. Though she jerked and strained against him, the man yanked her hands back tightly. Then, in seconds, he bound them with a rope.

The air inside the hood was hot and stale. She wondered if she'd suffocate. "Please, just tell me what you want," she begged.

There was no answer. Instead, her captor shoved Ramona forward, hard. She went down to her knees, but he wrenched her up to her feet, brusquely leading her outside. Pushing her along, he forced her to maintain a rapid pace as they walked through the brush.

His silence unnerved her, but she tried to resist the only way she could. The more her attacker prodded her to walk faster, the slower she got, certain that she was going to her death. She struggled continuously against the iron grip that held her prisoner, falling often as she tried to hamper him. Yet her captor remained undaunted, his plan for her seemingly unchanged.

Then, without warning, the man lifted her into his arms and placed her on top of something soft. It didn't make sense. She tried to bolt upright, but he pushed her back hard. Then she heard the soft sigh of metal, like hinges, followed by utter silence and a strange pressure.

More frightened than she'd ever been in her life, she tried to get up again. Ramona slammed her head against something solid and fell back. For several seconds stars seemed to burst in front of her eyes despite the darkness. He must have placed a heavy object just inches above her. What scared her most was that it hadn't even budged when she'd collided against it!

Despair as thick as a January blizzard churned within her. She kicked repeatedly against the obstacle above her, and struggled against the bonds that held her hands. The ropes gnawed into her flesh, but the pain was nothing more than a distant annoyance at the back of her mind. The air, in spite of it being winter, was getting warm and stuffy.

As fear electrified her efforts, she felt the knots begin to loosen. Refusing to give in to panic, she struggled to even her breathing. She would suffocate if she didn't calm down. Dizzy with fear, she gave the ropes one last yank. Miraculously her hands were freed.

Ramona moved carefully in the confined space. After releasing the cord that had been tied around her neck, she pulled the hood away from her face. She blinked furiously, trying to see through the absolute darkness. A horrible feeling of dread gripped her as she blindly felt the sides and the top with her hands, searching for a way out.

Suddenly the linens, which felt plush and almost satiny against her skin, filled her with revulsion. Utter, choking terror overwhelmed her as she realized exactly where she was.

Chapter Five

In the confinement, the sound of her own screaming echoed back in her ears with painful intensity. Quickly Ramona lapsed into a terrified silence. She'd been placed inside a sealed coffin!

Her mind raced forward in time, visualizing her fate as she slowly suffocated. Then a thought passed through her muddled senses, and a glimmer of hope appeared. She wasn't beneath the ground! She remembered the man setting her down, but he hadn't bent over any more than if he'd placed her on an ordinary bed. She was also certain that she would have felt the coffin being lowered, and the sound of earth being shoveled on top of it.

Though her heart was drumming frantically, she forced herself to calm down. She had to find a way to escape before she ran out of air! She pushed with her shoulder, trying to force the lid open. Her position made it impossible to get enough leverage. Reconsidering, Ramona brought her knees up against the lid of the coffin. The best chance was to push with her legs, using every ounce of strength she possessed. If she persisted, maybe she'd spring the latch.

At first, the pressure from her exertions did nothing. She could feel her entire body throbbing, but she struggled not to give in to despair. She worked in spurts, concentrating her bursts of energy on the coffin lid. After what seemed an eternity, she felt it give slightly.

Ramona continued her efforts. Then her legs began to cramp and she knew she couldn't go on much longer. With a yell of rage and frustration, she kicked upward with all her strength. Suddenly she heard a snap and a monstrous bolt of pain shot through her. For a second, she thought she'd broken a bone. Slowly the pain subsided to a tolerable level. Taking a deep breath, she pushed hard with her arms. A heartbeat later, the lid shot open and the last rays of a fading sun burst into her prison.

She scrambled to a sitting position and tried to climb out, but her legs were too wobbly. Ramona fell to the ground hard, but nothing mattered now except that she was out of there. Afraid that her kidnapper was watching and would try to recapture her, she glanced around anxiously. No one was in sight. Breathing a sigh of relief, she looked at the silver gray coffin. It was only yards away from the dirt road. Her captor had taken pains to keep it hidden, however, piling tumbleweeds on both sides. She studied the collapsible cart that rested below it. That's how he'd brought it here. He'd rolled it along, as the tracks leading from the road verified.

Her eyes stayed on the coffin as if magnetized by some unseen force, then shifted to the hinges. The screws had been loosened, that's why she'd been able to kick her way out! Her captor had given her a chance, however slim, of making an escape. If she'd been buried, she would have never been able to get away. Someone was playing a deadly game of chance with her life!

Ramona struggled to her feet, quickly reorienting herself. She was on a dirt road over a hill not far from the trading post. Taking slow, painful steps, she made her way back. Day had given way to a cloudless night by the time she arrived and staggered up the front steps. Suddenly, inches from her front door, she paused, afraid once again.

She'd been gone a long time. Anyone could have come in. Maybe her kidnapper was inside, preparing to terrorize her again. Torn between running away or going inside, she stood frozen. Without warning, the roar of a car sounded from behind, startling her. Ramona whirled around and shrank back against the wall. Had her captor returned?

Her muddled senses slowly registered the flashing red lights. Then in a burst of comprehension, she forced herself to stand upright. A few moments later, Michael emerged from the vehicle. Trembling, she struggled between the need to run into his arms and the suspicion that she'd find no safety there.

As he drew near, the lines on his face sharpened with shock. His gaze, filled with questions, strayed over her. "What happened to you?"

It was only then that she realized what she must look like. One leg of her pants had been shredded from the knee down. Her wrists were bloody and throbbed painfully with each beat of her heart. Her hair hung down her face in strands that were coated with perspiration despite the cold. "I was kidnapped."

He stared for a second, then quickly went to her side. Taking his jacket off, he slipped it over her shoulders and started to lead her inside.

"No," she said, shrinking away. "That's where he was. Anyone could be in there now. That door's been unlocked all afternoon."

"I'll check. Stay here." He pushed the door open with his foot, careful not to touch the knob, and took a look around inside. He returned a minute later. "It's clear. Now come on."

As he supported her, she couldn't help but notice that he was about the same size as the man who'd kidnapped her. Suspicion gnawed at her, though she tried to dismiss it as the aftershocks of fear.

"He ambushed me in my own home," she said, her voice wavering badly despite her efforts. "This man is completely ruthless."

"Who are you talking about?" His voice was cold and extremely professional. "Tell me exactly what happened."

"He slipped a hood over my head before I could turn around, so I can't give you a description," she said hesitantly. "But he was about your size."

Michael's eyes narrowed. "That describes about half the population. I'm going to need some specifics, like did he have an accent? Did you catch the scent of an after-shave? Could you tell what he was wearing?"

"He never said a word, so I don't know if he had an accent. From the feel of the fabric, I think he was wearing a flannel shirt, but I couldn't swear to it. And if he was wearing after-shave, I didn't smell anything. But it all happened so fast!" She described the events in as much detail as she could, her voice dropping to a whisper at times.

"Using lasers, the lab can tell us who touched your doorknob last. If his prints are on record, we'll find him. But I'll have to take the doorknob with me."

She took a screwdriver from a drawer and handed it to him. "Be my guest. I can use the dead bolt for now and replace the rest tomorrow."

He finished moments later and placed the knob inside a large evidence pouch. "Okay. Let's go see that coffin. We should be able to get quite a bit of physical evidence from that. We also might be able to track down where he bought it, and that could lead us straight to him."

"I...do I have to go with you?" Her fear resurfaced, stifling her breath as much as the hood that had been pressed against her face. "I could give you directions." She looked past him out the window, half expecting to find her kidnapper still lurking nearby.

"If you're able to walk, I'd rather you show me your exact route back here, and the sooner the better. There might be clues we can pick up along the way."

"I can walk," she said, forcing her voice to remain calm. It wasn't hard. The effort self-containment took robbed her voice of all expression. "My legs felt as if I'd broken every bone and ligament in them for a while. But right now they're pleasantly numb."

"If this wasn't important, I wouldn't ask." He captured her eyes and gentled his voice. "I know you must have been terrified, but nothing will happen to you now. I'll be there with you every step of the way."

She wanted to trust and believe in Michael, but uncertainty held her back. "Okay, but don't you think you better call this in first? What's going to happen if you need backup?"

"I intend to call in, but I doubt we'll need backup. My guess is that the guy's nowhere near here by now."

"Give me a second. I want to get something." She returned a moment later and unsheathed a long-bladed combat bayonet. The weapon looked as if it could slice though stone, and in her hand it was doubly frightening. "My father carried it during the war. I thought I'd bring it with me. From what's happened, I think someone's declared war on me."

Michael glanced at it, eyebrows raised. "You don't need it, but bring the thing along if it makes you feel better. Just be careful you don't hurt yourself, or me, either."

"By the way, something occurred to me," she said pensively, following him out the door. "There was some play in the ropes right from the start. I got cut up when I tried to break free, not before."

Michael considered it as they moved off the porch. "You think he meant for you to get away?"

"I think he wanted to drive me crazy with fear rather than kill me," she concluded, acknowledging to herself that he'd been very successful. "But if I'd ended up dead in the process, I doubt he would have shed any tears."

She glanced around. "I can only guess the route he took going away from the house," she warned. "I couldn't see.

But I do recall falling into some piñons. The needles really gouged my knees. There's a cluster of those west of here."

"Then let's go that way. I want to have a look before it gets completely dark."

Ramona stopped in midstride. "Would you mind walking beside me? I don't want anyone or anything behind me, and I certainly don't want to lead the way."

He retrieved a flashlight from his police car, then did as she asked. "I know this has rattled you. I can understand that. But why do I get the feeling you think I might be responsible?"

"I'm not accusing you of anything. But I'm not ready to give my complete trust to someone who doesn't play it straight with me," she said evenly. Anger rose as she recalled what she'd been told. Desperate to squelch the fear that rippled through her as she continued on, she held on fast to that emotion. "You've kept things from me that under the circumstances I had a right to know." She challenged him with an icy stare. "I learned what happened to your father. Did you really think you could keep that a secret from me?"

His lips clenched into a thin, white line. "My family's history is not something I normally discuss with anyone. Like you, there are personal things I have to deal with. What my father left undone falls to me. I do want to find the source of the clay, but I'm also a cop and I live by certain rules. Using fear to break someone isn't part of who or what I am."

His words resonated with conviction. For an instant, she felt a rush of sympathy. They were alike in many ways; both shackled by a past they'd played little part in establishing. Then she thought of his omission and everything that had happened to her since. Michael must have grown up hearing what her father had done to his. Could he really disregard a lifetime of carefully nurtured animosity? Caution was the only road to survival now.

"We're almost there," Ramona said, changing the subject. Until she was sure of him, there was nothing left to say.

"He picked his path well," Michael commented. "This ground is filled with rocks. It would be nearly impossible to track anyone here."

She led the way past a dry arroyo and through an area containing stunted piñons. Emerging onto the dirt road moments later, she stopped and looked around in confusion.

"What's wrong?" he asked.

"It was here, Michael, I swear it. The coffin was beside the road not ten feet from where we're standing."

"In this country most places look remarkably similar, especially this late in the day. Are you certain this was where you were?"

"Yes! It was here, I know it!" She hurried forward and studied the ground.

Michael crouched down. "It doesn't look like this area was disturbed by a heavy object." He touched the dried stalk of a small plant. "See how brittle this is?" he asked, snapping it easily. "If anything had rested here, it wouldn't have been upright."

"Do you think I made it up?" She held out her wrists, exposing her bruised flesh. "And what about these? Am I imagining it?"

"Let's walk around a little more. It's possible we're not where you think you are."

She had to work hard not to cry. The incident was making her look like someone who'd engineered a desperate plea for attention. "This is the place. Now help me. There's got to be something that will substantiate my story. He must have brought a pickup or van if he hauled the coffin here and took it back with him." She shuddered involuntarily.

He searched the ground for several minutes, then came to a stop beside a large boulder. Scuff marks had been left on its side by some heavy object. Turning on his flashlight, he stooped down and took a closer look at the streak of gray paint.

Immediately aware that he'd found something, Ramona went to his side. A wide smile spread over her face as she saw his find. "There! That proves I'm telling the truth! He must have bumped the coffin on that boulder either loading or unloading it." She pointed to a spot a few feet away. "And look at all those tumbleweeds. He brought them here to cover up the coffin, just like I said."

"This isn't conclusive proof of anything. It's just marks on a rock, some tumbleweeds, and a bit of paint. If we knew where the coffin was, and we established a match, *that* would be evidence."

Her heart plummeted, but she tried to hold on to her hope. "He's erased the tracks the cart made when he wheeled the coffin here, but maybe you can find tire marks from his vehicle. I've heard of that being done."

"You can identify a make of tire, but not a vehicle. Once you have a suspect, then can you establish a link. But in this case, following up on tire tracks isn't going to do much good. Half a dozen or more vehicles used that road today. It serves as a shortcut to the pueblo for many people in the area. There are just too many tire tracks around to narrow the search to any specific set." He rubbed his jaw pensively. "I'm sorry, Mona, but we don't have enough evidence to confirm your story."

She spun around and faced him. "Don't you see? He's trying to make me look like a liar. But there's more and I do have the evidence to back that up. Earlier today, I discovered that someone had been in my house. They left a disgusting present inside my shower."

He listened to her account as they started walking back. "I'd like to see the figure. You did keep it, didn't you?"

She glared at him. "Of course I did...unless the person who kidnapped me took it! I was going to show it to you."

"I'll tell you one thing. The doll and the witch's bundle we found earlier, that's Tewa. The trick with the coffin is another matter entirely. That seems more in line with Anglo-type thinking." He narrowed his eyes, studying her. "I want you to think carefully. Who around here hates you enough to do that to you?"

"I don't know. No one, that I can think of."

"Someone did."

She thought she detected skepticism in his tone, but couldn't be sure. "I wish I could give you answers, but I can't. You know of the problem between the tribe and my family. As far as the others in the community..." She shrugged. "I can't imagine anyone... well... no, never mind."

"Finish it. What were you going to say?"

She hesitated. "I had some trouble with George Taylor earlier." She didn't want to tell him she'd had a problem with the bank loan that would finance the cooperative. Yet, there was no other way. "Everything was fine until Taylor decided to get into the picture," she said, explaining.

"If they deny you the loan, what will happen to the cooperative?"

"I'll postpone opening it for a month probably, while I find alternate financing."

"Taylor's a very powerful man."

"That's okay. I'm not exactly helpless myself." She smiled grimly. "Now that I think about it, I wonder if he was the one who sent Chacon over." She told him about the union organizer.

"You really *are* making lots of friends, aren't you?" Michael observed ruefully.

"I didn't come home to run for political office. I expected to ruffle a few feathers. But once the cooperative gets going, everyone will see that an Ortiz can do something worthwhile."

"That's the bottom line, isn't it?" he asked quietly. "You want to earn people's respect, both for yourself and for your family."

"Is it so different for you? My guess is that's why you became a cop. You're in the sheriff's department because you couldn't be a tribal cop, not with the problems your family's had. Yet you still wanted to serve the tribe in some way. As a county sheriff, you get to act as liaison between the people of San Esteban and the community. It's a job worthy of respect." As their eyes met, she saw the pain mirrored there. "That's why you, of all people, should understand why I have to follow through on my plans for the cooperative."

"I understand you better than you realize," Michael said softly.

"Then why can't you work with instead of against me?"

"My job is to substantiate the truth with evidence. Without that, I have got nothing."

"But on a gut level, you're not at all certain about me, are you?" Ramona observed as they entered the house.

"No more than you are about me," Michael admitted slowly. "The past comes between us. That's the truth and there's no sense in hiding from it." He stood face-to-face with her for a moment. Unspoken desires and wants that begged to be voiced crowded his throat, but he locked those words inside himself.

"Do you believe I've been telling the truth?"

His gaze was steady as he held her eyes. "I believe something happened to you, and I also know that it frightened you badly. It's your perceptions of what happened that I don't trust."

"Like what?"

"The coffin, for instance."

"It was there."

"But was it a coffin, and not a car trunk or box? It could have been a freezer. Maybe in your fear you've become confused. Witnesses do that all the time." He hid behind professionalism, masking his feelings and becoming brutally frank. "On some level, you may have even been hoping to get some sympathy and find an ally. The suggestion of a coffin is guaranteed to get attention."

Ramona stared at him in stunned silence. Finally she managed to find her voice. "I'm not a weak person. I know what I saw. Yes, I was scared, but hysterics aren't my style." Her heart twisted inside her. How could she be attracted to a man who thought so little of her? She walked across the room, wanting to put some distance between them.

As she stood by the bookcase, she caught a glimpse of him out of the corner of her eye. He was watching her. His gaze was soft and drifted over her gently. It was the look of a man attracted to a woman, not one a hunter gave its prey.

The discovery threw her. The attraction she'd felt was mutual! She'd mistaken his gruff manner for lack of caring, but maybe it was just his way of coping with what was happening. He probably wasn't any more comfortable with it than she was.

"Would you like to see the doll now?" she managed in a husky voice quite unlike her own.

"Yes. The sooner I get that logged in as evidence the better."

Feeling completely self-conscious and awkward, she led the way to her room. Ramona stood by the bathroom door and waved toward the shower. "There."

He went inside. Noting the hide figure was still sitting there, he glanced at it superficially, then took a careful look around. "These ridged handles might look pretty, but it's nearly impossible to lift any prints from them." He studied the shower curtain. "I might be able to get prints from this."

"Don't bother. He would have never touched it. It was open already. I only leave it closed when I'm taking a shower."

"Well, that leaves the doll and the door handle to the bathroom."

"Forget the door handle. The door was open. I was the one who shut it."

He turned his attention back to the hide doll, and spent several seconds looking it over before pushing it into an evidence pouch using his pen. "The person who sent you this wants you dead." He pointed to the prickly pear spines that pierced the middle of the hide figure.

The thought that someone, probably a Tewa, wanted her to die filled her with a sorrow so intense it almost made her ill. "Have you actually seen one of these before?"

"Once, a long time ago," he said in a taut voice. "Someone left one for my dad."

She swallowed. "After he told the others he couldn't find the source of the clay?"

He nodded and continued to stare at the figure.

"And he died shortly after that?" Her voice rose slightly despite her efforts to sound calm.

Michael nodded again. Then, as if realizing what he'd said, he glanced up quickly. "One had nothing to do with the other. You'll be better off holding fast to what you learned in the white world. Our ways can't give you much comfort now."

Ramona could barely breathe over the knot that had formed in her throat. Superstition was a funny concept. Most people shrugged it off, just as she'd done, and claimed they didn't believe any of it. Yet they'd still avoid walking beneath a ladder, or painting the trim around their windows and doors a particular shade of blue to ward off evil spirits. She was no different.

"Did you find out how he got in?" Michael asked, interrupting her thoughts.

"I think so, but I couldn't leave it the way it was until you got a chance to come by. I nailed that window shut."

"I have a fingerprint kit in my car. Let me get it. Maybe I can lift some prints anyway." He returned a few moments later and began the task. It took fifteen minutes before he completed the procedure. "I'll need your fingerprints so I can exclude them right away in a computer search."

"No problem."

He worked quickly and efficiently. Minutes later, Ramona wiped her fingers clean on a paper towel and walked Michael to the front door. "If I can't match the prints I've taken to any on record, I'll go talk to the tribe's police captain. I'll need his permission to interview some of the San Esteban residents about this."

"Do you expect a problem?"

"Not getting the go-ahead. The tough part will be getting Tewas to answer the kind of questions I have to ask."

"No one wants to talk about witches, right?"

He nodded slowly. "Our tribe believes that the *chuge ing*, witches, live by killing. They have no life of their own, so in order to exist, they must rob someone else of their life. To talk about them is to risk drawing their attention, and most people don't want to take that chance."

"But in a small pueblo like San Esteban, people would know who, if anyone, was involved with witchcraft, right?"

"Not necessarily. Anyone practicing that would go to great lengths to keep it secret. Years ago there was talk about an older lady, but nothing was ever proven. Then she died, and that was the last time I ever heard anyone mention the subject."

"If others at the pueblo learn that I'm having this kind of problem, they'll stop coming to see me," Ramona said. "Can you keep this quiet?"

"Once I start my questioning, everyone will know what I'm after and why. After that, it won't take people long to figure out that the threat was against you."

"Then don't ask. The pueblo, strictly speaking, isn't your beat anyway. Take the figure as evidence of the threats against me, but let it drop."

"I can't do that, either. We have to find the person who's doing this. What I can do is couch my questions carefully. I'd do that anyway though, since I don't want to start trouble at the pueblo. This kind of business is likely to cause problems." Michael paused. His voice was reflective when he resumed. "You may not like what I have to do, but our interests do coincide."

"Yes, in a way I guess they do." Ramona watched him return to the squad car. As he drove away, weariness settled over her. If their pasts hadn't been linked by tragedy, they might have been friends. Maybe more...much more. Longing tore at her, leaving her feeling empty inside.

Realizing the turn her thoughts had taken, she strode inside angrily. She didn't need to wish for impossible things. Surely she had enough to worry about already!

Ramona bolted the door securely, then placed a large chair beneath the door handle. After making sure all the windows were latched tightly, she went to her bedroom. She stood at the doorway for several minutes, staring at the familiar surroundings. Knowing that a dangerous enemy had been in there filled her with dread. She wouldn't sleep there again.

Ramona took her clothes and carried them into what had been her parents' bedroom. At least this door locked from the inside. The catch on her own door hadn't worked for as far back as she could remember. There had never been a need to fix it.

She placed fresh linens on her parents' old bed, then crawled between the sheets. Cold gusts of air blew against the windows, whistling through the cracks time had woven around its joints. She closed her eyes, allowing sheer exhaustion to take over. Within seconds, she drifted into a troubled sleep.

It seemed as if she'd just fallen asleep when the shrill ring of the telephone jolted her awake. She jackknifed to a sitting position, turned on the lamp and checked the clock on the nightstand. It was two in the morning! Heart pounding, she picked up the receiver.

"Hello?" For a second, she heard only the sound of someone breathing.

"You cannot stay," a male voice hissed. "Your presence offends. Leave and do not desecrate holy ground."

Her stomach was tied in knots, but she swallowed back her fear. "Who *is* this?" she demanded.

"Your father is *nang opah*. Unless you want your future cut as short as his," the soft hissing voice continued, "leave this place." There was a click, then a dial tone.

Ramona hung up, jerking her hand away from the receiver as if something vile had touched her through the wires. That voice! It had reminded her of a rattlesnake about to strike. Trembling, she wrapped her arms around herself and stared at the telephone. Her body was covered in perspiration. As the cold began to penetrate, she crawled beneath the covers and curled up.

It was one thing to confront an adversary. But dealing with a faceless enemy who stalked in the night filled her with a primitive, savage terror. She tried to soothe her shattered nerves by listening to the voice of reason within her. The worst thing she could do was to let fear take control. That would hamper her thinking and endanger her even more. As the minutes ticked by, Ramona's heart began to beat at a less frantic pace and her breathing evened.

Ramona reached for the lamp on the nightstand and shut it off. The moon filtered through the cracks in the blinds, filling her room with a muted glow. Shadows, like swatches of black cloth, dappled the wall. She was about to close her eyes when the patches of dark melded together, outlining a massive shape right outside her window.

Ramona jumped out of bed and shot toward the door. As she tried to turn the handle, she remembered she'd locked it! Her hands shook frantically as she struggled with the mechanism. In spite of her efforts, the bolt held firm, refusing to open.

Chapter Six

Ramona glanced back, wanting to identify the person outside the window and desperately afraid of the encounter. But the cracked blinds offered her only a limited view. As her gaze darted around the room in search of a weapon, she noticed that the shape on her wall remained frozen. A trick? She studied it for several more seconds, listening and watching.

Only the sound of the wind disturbed the quiet in the house. She was close enough to the telephone now to reach for the receiver, but a thought stopped her. If this was a false alarm, her credibility would disappear completely. Michael already suspected her of embellishing her problems to gain sympathy.

Ramona took a deep breath and inched closer to the window. The shape still hadn't moved. In one quick motion, Ramona drew the blinds up. As she stared into the darkness outside, her knees almost buckled with relief. A cottonwood branch had broken off. It dangled vertically, precariously balanced over another in line with her window. It swayed with each blast of wintry air, straining to free itself from its unstable moorings.

She didn't know whether to laugh or cry. Is this what her enemy had reduced her to? She was a grown woman, running from shadows. Anger fueled her determination. Whoever her tormentor was, he wouldn't win.

She tried to recall exactly what he'd said on the telephone. Something about *nanopah*, or had she heard him right? As his voice echoed in her mind, she shuddered involuntarily. It was a sound straight from nightmares and undoubtedly that was the effect he'd hoped to achieve. Annoyed that she'd been manipulated like that, she leaned over and unplugged the telephone. He wouldn't disturb her sleep any more tonight.

Ramona adjusted her pillow and curled up, listening to the steady ticktock of the alarm clock on the nightstand. Though exhausted, sleep came slowly.

RAMONA AWOKE EARLY the next morning. Her knees were black-and-blue, reminding her of her painful escape from the coffin. After a long, hot shower and breakfast, she plugged in the telephone. As soon as she connected the wire, it rang. She hesitated for a moment, then picked it up.

"Good morning! This is Linda," a familiar voice greeted her.

"I thought bankers didn't get to work before nine," Ramona said, and heard laughter at the other end.

"Not when you're a junior loan officer and want to get ahead. Is it too early?"

"It's eight o'clock. I've been up for a while."

"Well, I've got some good news for you. Your loan application was approved. The file's on my desk, ready to be processed today."

Ramona placed the receiver down moments later, a wide smile on her face. In high spirits, she immediately telephoned the contractor but succeeded only in getting his machine. She left news that the construction work could now begin, then went back to the counter to fix breakfast. Good news was never as wonderful if one couldn't tell someone else about it. She thought of Michael, wishing she could have shared her excitement with him. But only true allies could share each other's victories. Realizing just how alone she really was dampened her enthusiasm.

She had started to toast a slice of bread when she heard a car outside. Ramona peered out the kitchen window and saw Michael's squad car pulling up. Working quickly, she went to the front room and removed the obstacles she'd placed by the front door.

Ramona greeted him as he came up the porch steps. "Hi! Have you found out anything?"

"I got a report back on your flyers. One of the sheets was coated with a tiny amount of an extremely sensitive explosive compound called picric acid. When you picked it up, the flyer touched a small piece of aluminum foil. The contact with the metal triggered the explosion, setting the paper on fire."

"This picric acid...can we trace it? It's got to be licensed or something."

"No, at least not in this case. The chemist thinks it was homemade. According to her, any person who's passed high school chemistry could have made the stuff. Its ingredients are easily obtainable without so much as a second glance. For instance, the phenol used can be bought at any well-stocked pharmacy. It's a well-known disinfectant." He paused. "Consider yourself lucky. Things could have been much worse if the perpetrator had used a larger amount of this stuff."

She shuddered. "Were you able to find out anything from the other evidence you gathered?"

"I'm still waiting to find out about the knob, but there were no fingerprints on the doll. And the only prints on the window were yours."

Her shoulders slumped. "What now?"

"I'm going to approach the investigation from a different angle while I wait for answers from the lab. I'm on my way to the pueblo to meet with Captain Suazo. Since I was early, I figured I'd stop by here and let you know what I'd learned so far." Michael hesitated before continuing. "I also wanted to make sure everything was okay."

"Yeah, I suppose it is," she answered, uncertain of how much to tell him about last night. The call, like the kidnapping, wasn't something she could substantiate. The last thing she needed to do was tell him of another incident when he wasn't even convinced of the first.

"So, something else *has* happened," he observed flatly.

"I've got a question for you," she said, evading his question. "What's *nanopah* mean? Is it a Tewa word?"

"I don't recognize it right off. In what context was it used?"

Ramona hesitated. "Maybe I'm mispronouncing it. Is there anything else that's even close?"

"Say it again."

She tried to pronounce it as she'd heard it. "*Nano-pah.*"

Michael took a deep breath. "That doesn't mean anything, not as far as I know." He puzzled over it. "Could you mean, *nang opah?*"

"I think that might have been it," she said, struggling to remember. "The connection wasn't very good," she added, almost to herself.

"You had a crank call?"

She glanced up at him, realizing that she'd given herself away. "Look, you want facts and there's no way I can prove what happened. If you don't mind, just tell me what it means, and I'll deal with it."

"Tell me how he used the word." Michael listened to her account, and replied, "He said that your father had become 'dust of the earth.' The rest was a death threat aimed at you."

"Yes, I understood the latter part."

"Interesting, though, that he should use that particular Tewa term when referring to your father. It's one a pueblo witch would be familiar with. According to our beliefs, when a witch dies, there's a severe dust storm within four days. That means that the underworld rejected his soul, and the person is doomed to end his existence as nothing more than dust."

"He thought my father was a witch?"

"I remember talk about that many years ago. Some chose to explain his discovery of the clay that way. If this person thinks you also might be a witch, he might be trying to confront you in the way that seems the most appropriate. In other words, he's hoping to scare you with his own powers."

"Or maybe he thinks that by killing me, he'll be helping the pueblo, as well as prolonging his own life."

"Yeah, that's possible, too."

"Well, at least we know that it's someone from the pueblo. Not many outsiders know about things like this."

"That's a logical assumption. Your father, and by extension, you, have many enemies within the tribe."

"He also said I was desecrating holy ground, Michael. Is there a shrine around here? I never knew of one, and I'm sure my mother would have said something."

"Holy ground?" He gave her a surprised look. "I'll check it out, but that's an odd one. Why would someone who thinks he's a witch worry about desecrating holy ground?"

"If it is holy ground, I'll meet with the chief of the Winter People. He's in charge until March. Maybe he can help me. I'll do everything to preserve the shrine, even move the location of the cooperative, but first I have to know where it is. I've got my loan, so I'll be starting construction on the new buildings very soon."

"Whoever's after you will increase the pressure as soon as he learns you're going ahead with your plans."

"I won't be frightened away," she said, hoping her tone would sound more fearless than she felt. She certainly didn't kid herself about her own limitations.

"In that case, I suggest you get some good, strong locks. Even if you plan to tear this building down eventually, some sturdy dead bolts would be money well spent."

"I'd planned to call a locksmith this morning. I'll be needing a new doorknob anyway."

"Something else occurred to me. It isn't a pleasant thought, but it's something you have to be aware of. Yesterday a man attacked you here, and then forced you away from the trading post. That brings up an interesting point. He knew *when* you went outside. He took advantage of the opportunity to sneak in and wait for you. That means he must have been watching all along. And if he could watch the house without your knowing about it, that means he could be out there anytime. You've got to stay on your guard."

She shuddered and looked around warily. "Whose side are you on? Are you trying to unnerve me completely?" she demanded angrily.

"I'm trying to help you," he said.

"By warning me of a danger I can't really protect myself against? That's not much help!"

"You're not completely at his mercy. You can fight him by keeping alert, closing your blinds, and being aware that he could be out there. If you want to stay here, then you have to be willing to face the truth of the situation, no matter how difficult. This might be one of the easiest things you'll have to deal with."

"You think he's got even worse things planned?"

"I don't know, but the more you try to fix the past, the harder it's going to get for you. For one thing, you'll probably learn things about your father that you wish you'd never known," Michael warned softly.

"Someone murdered him, Michael. No matter what he did or didn't do, he shouldn't have had to pay that high a price."

"Many would say he got off easy." Michael saw the sorrow in her eyes and felt a stab of pain twist through him. "Having to live through the aftermath, when the clay and the pottery were gone, was hardest of all."

She glanced away, unable to reply. "Today I'm going to look inside my father's special hiding place. Providing his things are still there, I might be able to find some answers."

"I'd like to be here when you do that."

She hesitated, then shook her head. "If I find anything that will help you, I'll let you know, but my father kept his most cherished possessions in there. This is too personal a duty for me to share with anyone."

"Call me as soon as you can. I've waited so long for answers. The hope that it might be over soon..." He let the sentence trail.

Michael's eyes held a bleakness that wrenched her soul. "If I learn anything of value, I'll call you right away. You have my word."

"Okay. In the meantime, if anything else happens, get to a phone. You're better off risking a false alarm than an encounter with whoever's after you." Without thinking, he grazed her cheek with his fingers. "I'm not the bad guy," he whispered.

Her whole body responded to the light caress, leaving her tingling from head to toe. "I'll try to remember that," Ramona answered unsteadily.

Feeling her tremble in response to his touch made forbidden thoughts rush into his mind. Reluctantly he moved away. "I'll see you soon."

Michael left the trading post, acknowledging that he couldn't have stayed without making things considerably worse. Everything male in him wanted to make the woman his. But having her for one night, even a string of nights, would never be enough. The way things stood, he'd eventually have to let her go. And then, he'd become like a man who'd discovered the sun, only to be sent back to some dark, cold dungeon.

He forced Ramona from his thoughts, remembering the oaths he'd taken at sunrise this morning. He'd left the prayer meal and feathers his mother had given him at a shrine he'd visited often with his father. The ritual had helped him connect with the past and refocus his thinking. Nothing could be allowed to interfere with his hunt for answers. No matter what the cost, he would clear the past. But being around Ramona made it plain that what was in his heart would remain there, undeterred by either logic or duty.

He stepped on the accelerator, eager to get to his office. What he needed now was the discipline of his work. Maybe there'd be news from the lab waiting for him on his desk. He drove to the pueblo government offices and went inside.

There were no telephone messages from the lab, and only a small stack of mail. But the white envelope with no return address immediately caught his attention. His name and address had been typed neatly on the front. Instinct told him he'd want to preserve as much of this one as possible.

He walked to his desk and slit the envelope open with his pocketknife. Holding the letter by the edges, he unfolded it carefully. Though crudely lettered, the message was painfully clear.

Chapter Seven

Ramona crossed to the area of the trading post that had once served as her father's store. It was hard for her to come here. This was her father's place, and it was as if the entire room still held echoes of its former master. She could almost hear the tapping of his hickory cane on the wooden floor.

Ramona walked behind the counter and touched its worn surface. "Your ways were far from perfect, Dad," she said in a half whisper, "but I won't believe that you cheated the tribe. Someone took your life before you were able to finish the deal. It's up to me to prove it."

She went to the walk-in freezer that occupied the far side of the room. It wasn't on, it hadn't been used since her childhood. Grocery stores in the area had made dealing with perishable goods more of a liability than anything else. Ramona unlocked and tried to pull the massive door back. She struggled briefly before the hinges surrendered with a tortured peal.

As she walked inside, she flipped on the light switch. The old freezer had served as an indoor storage shed for years. Now it was almost empty. Her mother had sold or traded most of the things she'd no longer had any use for.

Ramona went to an empty bottom shelf that stood against the wall. To the casual observer it appeared to be just another metal shelf, but as Ramona worked her fingers beneath the lip of the shelf, the catch finally gave and the lid lifted, revealing her father's special hiding place.

Mindful of the stiffness the recent injuries had brought to her knees, she sat cross-legged on the floor. Ramona stared into the interior, disappointment weighing her spirit down. There was nothing in there except a cigar box and a small metal case. Old photographs spilled out as she picked up the cigar box.

Ramona smiled, surprised that he'd actually saved all these snapshots. Her father had always complained when her mother had brought out her camera. She found one photo taken on her third birthday as she blew out the candles. A bittersweet feeling swept over her, making her throat tighten. This was a side of himself that her dad had kept carefully hidden. The gruff exterior had fooled many, but she'd known the real man—the one who'd held her when she'd scraped her knee, and taught her about bicycles.

She sorted through the faded pictures with loving care. Most were of her mother and her, but then toward the bottom she found one that seemed out of place. Along with the collection recording special family events was an old photo of a pueblo man she didn't recognize. It wasn't her maternal grandfather who'd died many years ago, she was certain of that. She studied the face in the photo, searching her memory for a clue, but found none. Setting that photo aside, she lifted the last item. It looked like a fishing-tackle box. Ramona placed it in front of her and unfastened the latch. Inside she found a box of .22-caliber cartridges and a black semiautomatic pistol.

She smiled as memories came flooding back. Her father had taught her to shoot the target pistol on her tenth birthday. He'd been so proud of her marksmanship and she'd tried hard to please him. She'd known even then that he took pleasure in a daughter who was like himself, and dared to try almost anything once. There weren't many things that could actually frighten either of them.

But that was then. Nowadays, she could think of many things that had the power to completely terrify her.

The ringing sound of the telephone in the next room made her jump. For a second, the hissing voice of her anonymous caller echoed clearly in her mind. Taking the tackle box that held the weapon with her, she raced to the living room.

"Yes? Hello?" she said, breathless from running.

"This is Hector Pratt. I got your message on my machine. I'd like to come by today, and have my foreman start familiarizing himself with the site. We should be able to start construction in a day or two since you've okayed the plans."

"That's fine," she answered. "By the way, I'll need you to put up that portable building with the heating unit right away. The members of the cooperative are going to need a work area immediately."

"There's a small problem," he said slowly. "I inspected that shipment when it arrived, and it was fine. But two days ago someone broke into the warehouse."

"A thousand-square-foot building is a rather large item to steal. . . ." she said.

"Well, materials are stolen all the time, but this appears to be more the work of a prankster. Among other small items, he took most of the special fasteners we need to erect the metal building. It'll take a few days to get replacement hardware in." He cleared his throat. "We have security cameras working at our warehouse all the time, so it's possible we might be able to catch the thief, eventually."

She took a deep breath and expelled it slowly. "I'd be willing to bet the prankster is really someone who's trying to obstruct the Spruce Branch Cooperative. Would it be possible for me to see a copy of the photos your cameras took?"

"Sure. I'll bring them over. But don't give this another thought. The construction is my responsibility. I'll see to it that any problems are taken care of right away."

As she placed the receiver down, Ramona stared at the box that held her father's pistol. She'd keep it available just in case. She could hit close enough to scare the pants off anyone with a brain.

The morning went by quickly. She met with the contractor, had the locks changed and also managed to recruit one jewelry maker into the cooperative. It was close to noon when a knock sounded at the door.

"Come in. It's open," she said.

Michael stepped inside. "You shouldn't keep your doors unlocked."

"I'm not being careless. The front is the only one unlocked, and I've been right here all the time. No one could come in without my knowing about it."

"Good," he said with an approving nod. "Did you go through your father's things as you'd planned?"

"Yes, but I didn't find the answers you were hoping for. In fact, his hiding place was almost empty. I expected to find the class ring he'd treasured, and his special-occasions watch, but they weren't there. It's been so long, I don't know why I thought I'd find them."

Michael watched her, wishing he could erase the terrible sadness in her eyes. He could see that the danger and tension were beginning to take a toll. Dark circles rimmed her eyes, and a deep-set weariness marked her movements. He had more bad news, and the thought made his gut twist. She was strong, but everyone had limits. He decided on impulse to postpone his announcement just a little bit longer.

"So, we have no new questions and no new answers," he said softly.

"Well, there is a snapshot that puzzles me." She walked to the bookcase and took it from the top shelf. "This was in among some family photos. It's no one I recognize."

Michael studied the photo. "I don't, either, but this must have been taken thirty or forty years ago. The paper is yellowed and brittle. There's someone at the pueblo I can show it to, if you want. He'd know if anyone would."

"Take it with you, then."

"Sure." He paused, struggling to find the right words and wishing he didn't have to add to the burden she already carried. Later he would tell her about the note he'd received, but there were other things she had to know as soon as possible. "There's something else. I got the call a short time ago. The body we found has been positively identified as your father's."

Her blood turned cold. She'd known it in her heart, but hearing it stated as a fact made her chest constrict. She swallowed hard and glanced up at Michael. His expression wasn't hard to read. "Go on. There's more, isn't there?"

Michael nodded. "I'm going to be working on the investigation as part of my regular duties. Our manpower shortage in the department is so critical that the sheriff is reluctant to assign one of our regular detectives to a crime that took place so long ago."

"They don't believe it's likely we'll find the killer then?"

"I don't look at it that way," he said, avoiding a direct answer. "The trail is cold, sure. But we have a few things in our favor. No news of the body has reached the press, and I have permission to keep this secret for a while. In the meantime, we'll be searching for new information. The killer's bound to have grown complacent by now."

"What about the bullet used to kill my father? Did that give you any leads?"

"No. The one lodged in his skull was badly distorted, so we can't tell much from it."

"You said that there were two bullets, didn't you?"

"Yes, but we have no idea where the second bullet is. Remember it went through him. We searched the room, but nothing turned up."

She gazed at the folding screen that blocked off the section of floor where her father's grave had been. "Then there's still a chance the other bullet is in this house. A complete search will have to be made. It could eventually lead to the killer."

"You're assuming your father was shot here, but we have no proof of that. Also keep in mind that there are hundreds of nails in these walls. It'll be like looking for a needle in a haystack," he said gently. "The department can't afford to fund a wild-goose chase."

"Then forget the department. We'll do it. As long as we work together, we're not likely to miss anything."

He shook his head. "Don't you see? Even if we find the bullet, that won't be enough. We'd need to match it to a gun."

"But it's something to start with. We've got to try, please." She walked to where the partition was but didn't go around it. "My father's final humiliation was to be buried here, with nothing and no one to mark his grave. Even in death, his murderer cheated him of respect and dignity. Yet that killer has walked free all these years, letting my family pay for his crime. I'm not interested in revenge, Michael, but I do want justice."

Her face sharpened and grew taut, torn between anguish and expectation. It was hard for a woman as strong as Mona to ask for help, and the effort was costing her dearly. He couldn't stand to see her like this. "All right. We'll search together."

She smiled. "Thanks, Michael."

The softness of her words touched him like a cool summer breeze. He shook himself free of the spell. "I spoke to Captain Suazo briefly about the witch's bundle and the doll. He referred me to another villager, an elderly man respected by everyone."

"Was the man any help?"

"I haven't visited him yet. I was about to go see him when I got the call about your father."

"Do you think I should be with you when you speak to him?"

"It's probably a good idea, actually, since it directly concerns you."

"Good, then let's go."

RAMONA STARED out the car window as they approached the pueblo. She was curious about the elderly villager they were going to visit. "Who is this man? Maybe I remember him."

"You probably heard his name when you were a kid. Walupi Sanchez is *pu'fona sendo* of the Fire *Pu'fona*."

"The head medicine man?"

"That's the one."

"Yes, I think I recall my mother speaking of him. He's some kind of clairvoyant, isn't he?"

"Basically, yes, that's what a *pu'fona* is."

"But his abilities are supposed to be far above the ordinary, according to my mother."

Michael nodded. "Most of it is probably talk. Rumors about his ability began like tiny piñon seeds. All that was needed to make them grow was a little bit of time. Eventually the legend shaped itself around the truth, obscuring most of it."

Michael parked by Walupi's home at the end of the main pueblo road, and they walked to the front door. A few minutes after Michael knocked, an elderly man answered.

"Michael Wolf," he observed. "Your mother is not sick, and you...well, I can't do anything about what troubles you," he said flatly. Walupi looked solemnly over at Ramona, nodded to her, then returned his eyes to Michael.

Michael stared at Walupi Sanchez. The man's statement unsettled him, but he tried not to show it. "There's nothing wrong with me, Walupi. I'm here—excuse me—*we're* here on a police matter. This is Ramona Ortiz. Her mother was one of our people."

"I know of Ramona's mother *and* father." Walupi offered his hand and she shook it.

"We're hoping you can help us," Michael said.

Walupi smiled. His roughened leatherlike face lightened as if he'd heard a joke he didn't want to share. "Oh, I have no cures for what's bothering you, but I'll answer your police questions."

"That's what I need." Michael glanced at Ramona, hoping she wasn't being particularly perceptive at the moment. He knew Walupi was referring to her.

Walupi laughed. "So proud. But it gets all of us," he said, pointing to his heart.

Michael shifted uneasily, sensing that Ramona was watching his expressions. First his mother, now Walupi. He might as well have been carrying around a sign announcing that Ramona had gotten under his skin.

"I have some very important questions to ask you," Michael said, his tone strictly professional.

Walupi gestured toward a small wooden bench. "Then we must get comfortable. Come and sit by the fire."

Michael knew Walupi couldn't really read minds. The man was just a skilled observer, like any detective. Still he felt like a novice who was at a distinct disadvantage. After they were seated, Michael cleared his throat. "Someone outside the village is having problems linked to Tewa witchcraft. You're the expert on that and I'm hoping you can give me some answers."

"Ms. Ortiz, I don't know how much your mother has taught you about our people, but I'm aware of your troubles. Before you can understand, you need to know something about our beliefs." Walupi's voice grew distant, in cadence with a chant only he heard. "When the Tewa emerged from beneath the lake, those who were of a different breath, the witches, came up with us. They wanted to destroy us, so the supernaturals created the first medicine man. From the beginning, our purpose was to combat the power of the witches." He held her eyes steadily.

"If we had a witch in San Esteban, I would know. I'd feel it here," he said, pointing to his heart.

"So, to your knowledge, we don't have a witch in San Esteban now," Michael concluded.

He nodded once. "The *pu'fona* always tell the truth. There was even a time when we'd tell our patients honestly if they would live or die. But it scared them, so we don't do that anymore." He took a deep breath, then let it out slowly. "If you were my patients, I'd give you bear fetishes to wear for protection."

"You think we're both in danger?" Ramona asked.

Walupi nodded. "It won't come at you head-on. It'll creep up like the snake and surprise you. Guard your hearts and your thoughts, because that's where you'll be most vulnerable."

"Thank you for your help." Michael nodded to Ramona, and they stood up and started toward the door. He could feel the hair at the back of his neck standing on edge. Walupi's prediction was like a daddy longlegs spider creeping over your skin; its feather touch tested the nerves.

After the elderly man waved and shut the door to his home, Michael escorted Ramona to his squad car. Before him, the sun spilled over the Sangre de Cristo Mountains, challenging the blanket of snow that all but covered its peaks. This was his land, and the home of his forefathers. He could understand Mona's need to reconnect to it.

He struggled against the emotions that were coursing through him. His concern should have been solely for the clay, but his feelings were more complicated than that. Somehow, Ramona had turned on a light in a deep, barely acknowledged part of his soul. Places that had been dark and silent now stirred restlessly with newfound life.

Yet without self-discipline and dedication to duty, a Tewa wasn't worthy of the name. With effort, he shifted the focus of his thoughts.

"Michael, is there something else you're not telling me? You seem so distant."

Her voice tempted his mind to stray, but he closed himself off. The case needed his undivided attention. "Someone left a note on my desk today." He paused then continued. "It said, 'Will you betray us like your father did?'"

"Do you know who sent it?"

"No. It came from someone who didn't have the courage to sign his name."

"That's predictable, considering it sounds like a threat."

"That's what Suazo said when I tried to find out how the note got there. He thinks I'm being pressured to work harder." Michael shook his head. "It's only going to make me search to find whoever left the note." He pulled up in front of the trading post.

"It has to be someone who knows you from the village. The note writer was obviously familiar with your family history." She walked with him inside.

"Suazo sent the note to the lab in Santa Fe. It's an outside chance, but there could be fingerprints or something that can lead us to the person responsible."

Ramona's heart twisted. Her father's failings just made him human, but that wasn't something she could make Michael understand. The Wolf clan had paid too dearly for her dad's mistakes. She stood there awkwardly, wondering if there was anything at all she could say that would help.

"I've got to get back on patrol," Michael said at last. He started toward the door, wishing he could have stayed longer. "I'll check out the man in the photo. Hopefully, I'll have an answer for you later this afternoon."

Ramona watched Michael leave. There were times when caring and understanding gentled his dark eyes, bearing silent evidence of emotions that went beyond physical attraction. But then again, maybe she was only seeing what she wanted.

As night enveloped the desert, she closed the curtains and moved away from the windows. She smiled grimly, remembering the story about witches peering in at night and catching victims unawares. Right now it wasn't a witch's power that frightened her. It was knowing that there was someone out there who was determined to harm her.

She crossed to the fireplace and started a fire. It was supposed to be particularly cold tonight. Settling into one of the worn chairs, she stared at the flames. As the relaxing and soothing warmth cocooned around her, she drifted off to sleep.

Suddenly her dreams were shattered by an explosive thump and the crackling of glass. She bolted upright with a strangled cry. Blows were being struck against something metallic. It was a dull, hollow sound, as if someone were hitting a refrigerator with a baseball bat. In a flash of comprehension, she remembered her pickup was parked outside.

Reacting in an instant, she dove for the phone and dialed police emergency. As she placed the receiver down, another sound sent her heart to her throat. Slow, methodical footsteps were coming up her porch steps! She ran to the box that held the pistol, slid the loaded clip into the butt of the gun and ducked behind the doorway leading to the kitchen.

"Don't try to come in here," she said in a loud firm voice. "I'm armed and the police are on their way."

The footsteps stopped, but then she saw the doorknob being turned slowly and noiselessly.

Chapter Eight

Ramona watched the knob turn, then stop abruptly as it reached the end of its axis. It was locked; there was no way he'd get in. She held her breath, hoping he'd give up and go away. Suddenly the door was rattled furiously. The wood groaned, and for a second she thought the hinges were going to give.

Still positioned behind the doorway, she kept her eyes glued on the door. Though her hands were shaking badly, she managed to cock the gun, ready to fire a warning shot. A second later, she heard a siren wailing off in the distance. For a heartbeat, nothing happened, then she heard footsteps hurrying away from her porch. She held her breath and waited, listening and knowing that any hasty decisions could cost her dearly.

A minute passed and she heard the sound of a car engine starting up just outside the front door. She couldn't ignore the chance to try and identify the intruder. She made a frantic dash to the side of the window and peered outside. The vehicle was speeding away in a shower of gravel and dust.

If she could catch the license plate or the make of the car, Michael would have something solid to go on. She unlocked the door just as the vehicle was reaching the end of her driveway. Running as fast as she could, she started up the hillside next to the trading post. She reached the summit, gasping for air. Even though she'd run as fast as she could, all that could be seen were two red taillights disappearing down the highway.

She walked back slowly, disappointed she hadn't been able to expose the identity of the person after her. But at least the incident was over. Now it was time to assess her losses. She hadn't taken a look at her pickup yet, but she had a terrible feeling it had been severely vandalized.

As she neared the trading post, she noticed a police car had arrived and was parked several yards from her pickup. The flashing blue-and-red lights had a mesmerizing strobe effect on everything around her, even the ground.

A moment later, Michael came out of the shadows on the north side of the building. As his eyes fastened on her, he seemed to relax then tense up all over again.

He strode toward her. "What on earth possessed you to leave the trading post? You were safe in there. Out here, you made yourself a target."

"He was nearly gone by the time I came out," she said, and explained. "Anyway, it didn't do me any good." She walked to her pickup. Michael had used the spotlight in his car to illuminate it, and the sight made her cringe. The windows and the windshield were shattered almost completely. Small cubes of safety glass crunched beneath her feet as she surveyed the damage. Her stomach lurched, and for a minute or two she thought she'd be sick.

"If you're insured, and I assume you are, they'll cover this."

"Yeah, but my payments will go up. You can count on it."

"I'm going to take what he left on top of the cab as evidence. I doubt we'll get anything from it, but it's worth a try."

Ramona stood on tiptoe and studied what Michael was referring to. "Shards, from a broken piece of pottery..." she commented. "He smashed it against my truck?"

"Maybe it's symbolic of the pottery your father took from the tribe in payment," he suggested. "That's the only thing I can think of."

She considered the idea. "Maybe."

Michael walked around the area, shining the beam of his flashlight on the ground. "The gravel doesn't leave tire tracks and footprints, so there's not much here to go on."

"So once again, I'm back to ground zero. I can't prove what happened, unless you count my truck as evidence."

"There is that," he conceded. "I also have a little bit of good news for you."

"Please, let's hear it. I can use some good news."

Michael followed her inside the house. "I was able to identify the man in the photo you gave me." He took the photograph out of his shirt pocket and handed it back to her. "Captain Suazo recognized him almost immediately. I figured he'd know everyone in the tribe and I was right."

"Was he a friend of my father's?"

"According to Captain Suazo, he was. I could take you to meet him whenever you want. His name is Bernardo Agoyo. Once the captain identified him for me, I realized who he was. I've met the man's son."

She glanced around, then with a sigh, turned to Michael. "There's nothing else I can do about this tonight. Do you think it's too late to go there now?"

"It's eight o'clock. I think it'll be okay. You want to try?"

She nodded. "I really would, if you don't mind. But I'm going to have to ride with you. My pickup's in no shape for anything except the repair shop."

"It's okay, this is official business. Maybe Bernardo will know something about your father that could shed a light on what's been happening. Either way, I'd like to be there when you talk to him. I might need you to corroborate something."

She picked up her shoulder purse, then went to the door. "Let's get going then."

They arrived at Bernardo Agoyo's home ten minutes later. The small adobe house was at the very edge of the pueblo limits. As they left the squad car, a shaggy mutt began barking from one of the windows.

Bernardo Agoyo came to the door. "Is something wrong?" As his eyes focused on Ramona, he nodded slowly. "I thought you'd be by sooner or later," he said, then glanced over at Michael, perplexed. "Why are you here?"

"Can we come inside?" Michael asked.

"Yes, of course." Agoyo waved them inside. "It's cold out tonight. Would you like something warm to drink?"

After accepting steaming coffee in old white mugs, Michael explained the reason for their visit. "We were hoping you could help us."

"I don't know anything about what's happening now," he said slowly. "I can't help you with that." Bernardo turned to Ramona, his eyes softening. "But I did know your parents well. I know what the others think of your father, but I never believed it. Your father and I were friends. He had his faults. He could be difficult to get along with at times, but in his heart, he was a good man."

The words warmed her much more than the coffee. "Thank you so much for telling me that," Ramona said. "I never thought I'd ever hear anything nice said about him again."

"Your father and mother were very special people. They made enemies, but they never purposely hurt anyone in their lives...except maybe each other."

"I don't understand."

"How much do you know about your parents' marriage?"

"I know they argued constantly, but I really think they loved each other," she affirmed. "You knew them both. What can you tell me about them?"

"You're right about the love between them, but it wasn't a fairy tale, by any means. Your father was constantly worried that Loretta would leave him to go back to the pueblo. He wasn't a wealthy man, and they went through some very tough times. But their biggest problem wasn't money. Your father was very domineering, and your mother was a woman with a fiery spirit. They clashed often. Loretta had her own way of doing things and wouldn't stand for anyone telling her what to do."

Ramona struggled between her desire to know, and fear of what she'd learn. Bracing herself, she asked what was foremost in her mind. "Do you think they were happy? I mean, was it worth it to my mother? Or to my father?"

"For your father, yes. I'm certain of that. He loved Loretta a great deal." He stared at the orange tongues of flame that leaped from piñon logs in the circular kiva-style fireplace. "Loretta was a different story. She was never truly happy. I remember something she told me once. Loretta said she felt trapped by her love, that she would never be free as long as John was alive."

The words, and the implication, cut through her like a sharp blade. She saw Michael straighten in his chair.

Desperately Ramona sought to clarify what she was certain was a misunderstanding. She glanced at Michael, asking wordlessly for his permission to confide in the man, her father's only friend. Michael read the question in her eyes and nodded.

"There's something I think you should know," she said, interrupting Bernardo's thoughts. "My father was murdered."

He stared at her for a moment, not comprehending, then he leaned forward. "I hope you're not thinking your mother had anything to do with his death. She was incapable of violence."

"I know that," Ramona answered, then glanced at Michael. The wariness she saw on his features tore at her, hurting her more deeply than she would have thought possible.

"Until now, I never understood your father's sudden disappearance. It seemed so out of character. He wouldn't have left your mother, or you. Not ever. His biggest fear was that she'd leave and take you with her," Bernardo said.

Ramona smiled. "Thanks for telling me about my parents. I'm glad to know they had a friend like you."

After saying good-night, Michael walked back silently with her to the squad car. Knowing what was occupying his thoughts troubled her. Yet only facts would settle the question of her father's death, and she had none to offer him.

As they drove back, Michael gave her a sidelong glance. "Do you recall anything about the day your father disappeared?"

"My mother didn't do it. *You* knew her. How can you even think that?"

"I don't think anything yet. I'm just exploring the possibilities," he said gently. "I know this is painful for you, but try to remember back to that day."

Ramona stared at the twin cones of brightness the headlights forced through the darkness. A few thin flakes of snow were visible in the glow, swirling uncertainly up and over the windshield as they disappeared. "I'd been on a field trip with my class so I was later than usual coming home. My mother was shopping in Santa Fe, so I didn't expect her to be home when I got there. What surprised me was that Dad wasn't around. I'd never come home to an empty house before. One of them had always been there to meet me. I used my key to go inside, then waited. It was hours before Mom finally got back."

"So the dead bolt was locked, as if he'd left," he commented. "Did you help your mother unload the packages from her car?"

"Actually she didn't have any. I went out to greet her, thinking that maybe Dad had gone with her after all, but she was alone. She said she'd been all over Santa Fe, then drove all the way to Albuquerque looking for material to make some dresses. But she hadn't found anything she liked.''

"Did she normally do that, come home empty-handed?''

"No, but it wasn't that unusual, either. My mother was the kind of shopper who'd make up her mind exactly what she wanted before she ever went to a store. If she didn't find what she was looking for, she often didn't buy a substitute.''

"Was she worried when she found out your father was not there?''

Ramona paused, considering it. "At first she thought he'd gone out to get some materials for repairs. He'd said he might close the store that day so he could fix the flooring and do a few other odd jobs. But she was angry that he hadn't been there to greet me. Then the hours went by, and Dad never appeared. She went all around the trading post looking for a note. She checked everything, and that's when she discovered half the money was missing from the cash register.''

"And is that when she called the police?'' Michael pulled up in front of the trading post, then turned to look at her.

"No, she waited for several more hours. He had never gone drinking or gambling or anything like that, so I think she expected him to eventually come home. She kept going to the window and looking out. I remember that clearly. Finally, she gave up and called the police.''

"What about the floor?''

"I think she assumed the same thing I did. We figured that Dad had finished the work.'' She held his gaze with a challenging one of her own. "She was hurt and confused by the entire thing, Michael. When the police told her that Dad had probably abandoned us and left half the money so we wouldn't be penniless, she couldn't accept that explanation. She always thought that Dad would find his way back to us. She believed that he hadn't left out of choice, but the police couldn't find any evidence to support that. Now, it turns out she was right." Ramona opened the door of the car.

Michael's silence settled over her like a heavy weight as he walked with her to the house. She knew that he'd been looking for an alibi, something that would have removed her mother from the list of suspects. She'd failed to give him one. "You think she might have killed him."

"It happens," he replied softly. "People can take the lives of their loved ones when they're angry, or hurt, or in the midst of a crisis." The pain in her eyes wound its way to his heart and squeezed, but she deserved more than placating lies. "The only way we'll ever know for sure is to find the killer."

"I came back to prove my father's innocence. I never expected that I'd have to risk tainting my mother's memory to do it."

Standing with her back against the closed door of the old trading post and her arms folded across her chest, she looked defenseless and vulnerable. He acted before he was even aware of it, drawing her to him. He needed to hold her and wanted to comfort her, but she pulled away.

"I don't need your pity, Michael."

He started to tell her that what he felt had nothing to do with pity, but then bit back the words. Certain things could not be spoken between them. The best way he could protect Ramona was to shield her from himself.

Michael half turned toward his car. "We *will* find answers, I promise you that," he said, emotion making his voice reverberate with conviction. "But what I can't promise is that you'll like what we learn."

Ramona watched Michael leave, wishing she could have asked him to stay. As she pictured herself nestled in the circle of his arms, a tremor shot through her. But she wanted—no, needed—more than a night filled with the pleasures of love. Without the substance that gave it meaning, the bittersweetness of their union would tear her apart.

She walked to the window and watched the taillights from his car disappear into the darkness. Maybe, just maybe, he'd be thinking of her tonight.

MICHAEL AWOKE the next morning to a country-and-western tune on the clock radio. Hitting the Off switch, he stared at the tiny beams of sunlight that filtered through his curtains and played on the far wall. He hadn't slept much last night. He'd tried not to think of Mona, but his efforts had only entrenched her more firmly in his thoughts.

Nothing seemed the same anymore. There'd been a time when he'd loved his life just the way it was. He'd enjoyed having the freedom to come and go without having to offer explanations to anyone. Now it seemed more like another burden he had to shoulder. He was a solitary man by nature, but a longing sharp as a blade tore through him as his eyes took in the empty room. This place needed a woman's touch. He needed a woman's touch. He needed Mona's touch.

The thought blazed through him, causing an instant reaction. His breathing quickened, his heart raced, and his body became painfully aroused. Then, as if part of the same thought, a rush of guilt ran through him. He was a cop, and he was Tewa. He had a job to do, and lying in bed daydreaming wasn't part of it.

Twenty minutes later, he was on the road. He picked up his mike as he drove, and checked with the department's radio dispatcher. Ramona had left a message for him.

By the time he racked the mike, he was already on his way to her place. Someone had broken into her contractor's warehouse and stolen essential components to her portable building. At her request, the contractor had brought over a photo the security camera had taken of the warehouse thief. It was reaching, of course, but if that incident was related to the other things that were happening at the trading post, he might be about to get his first solid lead. As he sped down the highway, he put in a call to the burglary division. Maybe they'd uncovered something that would be useful to him now.

By the time Michael arrived at Ramona's, he saw the contractor's Chevy Suburban parked outside and a survey crew at work. With a nod to the men, he went inside the trading post.

Ramona glanced up from the set of plans she was studying. "Good morning, Michael," she greeted. "This is my contractor, Hector Pratt," she said with a glance at the tall Anglo man standing beside her. "Have you two met?"

Pratt extended his hand. "No, but it's a pleasure. Ramona said that you'd be interested in looking at the photo our security cameras took."

Michael nodded. He took the photo from Ramona and studied it carefully. "Well, the stocking mask is very effective, but this still gives us some clues."

Ramona came and looked at the picture as he held it. "Like what? I couldn't tell much from it."

"He's standing near that doorway, so we can get a good approximation of his height. I figure he's probably about five foot seven. We also know from the lightning bolt on the side what brand of sneakers he's wearing. Unfortunately, they're fairly common," Michael commented. "But it is something. And a Tewa paintbrush was found on the site."

"You mean the kind that's made with yucca fibers, and used to paint pottery?" Ramona asked.

"Yeah. The burglary team figured that it probably fell out of the thief's pocket," Michael added, handing the photo back to her.

Ramona stared down at the construction plans spread across her dining table, then looked at Hector Pratt. "You'll start preparing the ground this afternoon?"

"That's the plan. I'll call you with the time later. The replacement hardware we need for the metal buildings should be in this afternoon, so there's no reason to delay."

"That's great!" Ramona saw the worried look on Michael's face but decided to ignore it.

Michael waited until Pratt left before saying anything. "I'd like you to call me when the crew gets here, okay?"

"Sure, but why?"

"I want to be around, just in case." He held up a hand, stemming her protests. "It's only a precaution."

Ramona reluctantly agreed. "Okay, but I think that once construction starts, things will ease up. My enemies will be forced to admit that I'm going to see this through."

"If you think that's going to make those who are after you stop, you're wrong. My guess is they're going to fight even harder."

"Thanks so much for cheering me up."

"I won't lie to you, Mona. Not ever. You deserve better than that. I want to protect you, and that's the truth of it," he said, his voice soft.

There was an undercurrent of emotions laced through his words. Ramona was torn between wanting him and accepting the truth of their alliance. "Having you around will even the odds a bit, but I fight my own battles, Michael."

He gave her a sad smile. "Maybe neither one of us knows when to stop fighting." He started back to his squad car. "Call me when the crew arrives."

Ramona watched him leave, then picked up her keys and went to her truck. She spent a busy morning at the wholesale outlets, getting supplies for the artists. By the time she returned to the trading post, it was almost noon. She'd just come in the door when the telephone began to ring. Dropping her coat over the back of a chair, she rushed to answer it.

"This is Hector. I just thought I'd let you know the crew will be there in an hour."

"Terrific!" With a happy smile, she dialed Michael's number. His guarded tone made her uneasy, but she pushed the feeling aside.

When it was almost time for the crew to arrive, Ramona went out to the end of the driveway and stood by the side of the road. Within minutes, a small convoy of vehicles and equipment came down the highway. She met the lead truck, introduced herself and hopped onto the running board.

Excitement pounded through her as she led the small column onto her property. "I'm really glad this is finally getting under way," she shouted to the man at the wheel.

The burly Anglo driver smiled at her. "Hey, so are we. It's usually hard to get a good contract this time of year. Times are lean."

"Turn left as soon as you go past that cottonwood tree." She felt the cold breeze blowing through her hair. A wonderful feeling of freedom and accomplishment left her exhilarated. If only her mother had been alive to see this day!

The man glanced in his rearview mirror. "Oh, great," he muttered. "We've got a sheriff's deputy behind us. I wonder what I did this time."

"No, it's okay. I know him. He said he'd be by for the start of the project."

The driver gave her a sly grin. "Can't say I blame him for finding an excuse to come around."

Ramona chuckled, then shook her head. "No, it's not like that. I think he wanted to see this for himself. He never believed this project would really get under way." She pointed ahead. "That's where you'll be working," she said.

As they drove into the parking area near the trading post, something uphill caught the driver's attention. "You have a crew working up there?"

She followed his line of vision and caught a glimpse of a green truck. Before she could take her next breath, it exploded into flames and began to roll. Her stomach lurched as the vehicle began to build up speed, heading directly toward them.

Chapter Nine

She heard people yelling, then the trucks behind them began to scatter, moving off the road in all directions. Before she could hop off the running board, her driver
stepped on the accelerator. "Hang on!" he shouted.

She was almost swept off as he drove through the thicket
of brush that bordered the road. Her fingers curled hard
around the rearview window bracket and the door handle
as she struggled to ride it out.

"It's a runaway and there's no way to tell where it'll end
up," the driver shouted, trying desperately to maneuver
out of its path. As the flaming truck hit a large rock, it
suddenly veered off its original course, and shifted back
toward them. "We've got to get out of here!"

He increased his speed, heading downhill for an arroyo. Suddenly the truck bounced hard as the right-hand
side tires went over a basketball-sized boulder. Ramona
felt her feet floating in midair, and for a brief second she
managed to hold on by her fingers. Then as the truck slid
to a stop, she lost her precarious grip.

Ramona flew forward, hitting the sand by the edge of
the arroyo. Instinctively ducking her shoulder, she rolled
off the wash and into a thicket of junipers. She landed on
her back about a foot off the ground, suspended by the
branches. Her body felt as if she'd been dragged for miles

by a horse. She tried to sit up, but her vision was blurred. Her eyes were tearing heavily.

Ramona lifted her head slightly as she felt the ground begin to shake. Dazed, she wondered where one ran to in an earthquake. Then she saw the flaming truck looping in a half circle, heading her way again. She tried to scramble to her feet, but her body was sluggish and wouldn't respond.

With her eyes riveted on the pickup, she prepared to face death. Rage all but obliterated fear. *It was so useless! Why did this have to happen now? She'd failed her family and herself.*

She heard men shouting, but the voices seemed too distant to be real. As if trapped in her worst nightmare, she saw the burning vehicle heave itself off the edge of the arroyo. But the front tires suddenly encountered the deep sand, and in a second were buried in the soft mass. Trapped with its wheels half-submerged in the dirt, it abruptly lost speed. Time seemed to shift to slow motion as the truck went end over end twice, landing upside down less than thirty feet away. Then, in an instant, orange flames flared out from its center and licked against the dry brush, igniting it.

The fire spread along the withered sage and dead tumbleweeds that occupied much of the arroyo, working its way toward the mass of junipers she was resting on. She struggled upright, her knees refusing to lock. Her tumble off the truck had aggravated the injuries she'd suffered inside the coffin. As she managed to rise, she realized that it was already too late. There was no place to run, even if she could have managed to move that fast. The tall wall of dirt behind her offered no hope of escape, and she'd never be able to move quickly enough through the fire to avoid getting burned. Slowed to a limp, she moved laterally, searching for a way out. But the smoke and heat drove her back.

"Ramona, no! Don't do anything yet."

She could see Michael, though the heat radiating from the fire made his image waver and float. Men were fighting the fire with extinguishers and shovels of sand, but Michael was busy doing something else. She couldn't make out what was going on until she saw him run forward, his leather jacket covering his head.

He leaped over the fire line as the men eased his passage with three small fire extinguishers. As soon as he got through, the fire erupted again as if nothing had been done to hamper it.

"We're getting out of here." He started to pick her up, but she shook her head.

"No. I'll slow you down. We'll both have to run. Those fire extinguishers are probably about empty!"

"Yes, we have only a few seconds. That's why I'm carrying you," he said flatly. Shoving his left arm beneath her thighs and cradling her shoulders with his right, he picked her up easily. "Don't struggle, or we're both in trouble."

"But..."

"Quiet," he ordered, tumbling her against him. "Pull my jacket over your head. Your hair could catch fire. And hold your breath."

Before she could speak, he shot toward the fire line. She buried her face against his shoulder and closed her eyes. She felt the wave of heat, then suddenly the air was cool again. They were free!

He stopped several yards uphill and met her eyes, his tight hold on her not diminishing. "You scared the hell out of me, Mona," he said in a raw, heartfelt whisper. His expression was hard at first, but then softened. "I don't scare easily," he added.

She wasn't sure who started what, but the next instant his mouth was over hers, hard and demanding. She melted against him, needing everything he offered and more.

She heard the soft groan that seemed to come from the depths of his soul as he deepened the kiss. It was as hot as the fires they'd crossed. His tongue delved into her mouth in a searing primitive dance. A shock wave of pleasure rippled through her, and, with a sigh, she surrendered to his tender assault. She'd faced death, but in his arms, she knew life.

"Well, I guess you two are going to survive," she heard one man say, and others started to laugh.

Michael eased his hold on Ramona and set her gently down. His breathing was uneven and he burned with a need that grew more powerful every time she was near. "Can you walk?"

"Yes, I think so." She took a few steps to make sure. Her legs were wobbly and sore from the fall, but they'd hold her well enough. Staying too near him right now was dangerous. Longings that could never be satisfied ribboned through her, jumbling her thinking.

Michael walked to where several men were shoveling dirt onto the fire. "At least this won't spread. It'll continue across the arroyo and burn itself out when it hits the embankment."

She shuddered, realizing that the area where she'd been standing was now covered with flames and spirals of white smoke.

"We'll keep working on it, just to make sure. There's plenty of sand around," one of the men said with a nervous chuckle.

"I want everyone to stay away from the hilltop. I'll be going up there to take a look around in a minute."

Michael went to his squad car and retrieved his handheld radio. His body still strained with the hunger she'd unleashed in him. She'd yielded so naturally, wanting him and the pleasures he could give her. The memory sent a shudder through him.

With effort, he forced his body under control and concentrated on what he had to do. As he walked around to the back of the smoldering pickup, he noted that the license plate had survived intact. He called in the sequence and, minutes later, had the information he needed. The truck had been stolen from a pueblo family just a few hours earlier. Captain Suazo had started the investigation.

He made a quick visual search of the truck, though it was much too hot to approach closely. The steering wheel had been wired in place and the ignition hadn't been on.

Ramona came up and stood beside him. "So, there was no driver."

"It was carefully set up. This took planning, lady."

"Like I've told you. My enemy is cunning."

He nodded, lost in thought. "I'm going to take a walk uphill."

"I'll help the men put the fire out. I don't think it'll take too many more shovel loads of sand to do it."

Michael returned to his squad car, picked up some evidence pouches and climbed to the top of the hill. From what he could tell, the vehicle had been driven here, and the person responsible had walked off toward the highway on the other side. There was only one slightly faded imprint on the hard ground, but it was enough to establish his direction.

Michael crouched near the spot where the vehicle had been parked. He wanted answers. By attacking Ramona, his one link to the past, they were attacking him. Whoever was behind this had issued a challenge, one he intended to meet both as a cop and as a Tewa.

Something extending out from underneath a tumbleweed caught his eye. Lifting the tumbleweed away with his hand, he studied a length of wire, following it as it extended through another bush and ended, wrapped around a block of wood.

Hearing footsteps behind him, Michael turned around. Ramona approached slowly. "Climbing up here wasn't easy," she said half-jokingly. "So tell me something that'll compensate for my trouble, will you?"

Michael looked at her in admiration. Her inner strength and will never ceased to amaze him. Her courage was in perfect counterpoise to her vulnerability.

He stepped over to the block of wood and turned it with his foot. There were letters on it, crude but distinct.

"Does that mean anything?" she asked, noticing it.

"It says, *'W'itsa Kwiyo.'* It's a name. Do you know who it is?" Seeing her shake her head, he continued. "She's an evil force who's supposed to live north of the pueblo."

"Like I do," she finished for him.

"Yes. Tewas are warned from childhood to avoid it."

She nodded slowly. "That's why it sounded familiar."

He picked the block up by the very edges, using gloves, and slipped it and the attached wire, which he coiled, into the largest evidence pouch. He didn't bother even trying to close it. The wood stuck out the large pouch, making handling difficult.

"I have to ask you a favor," she said.

"You don't want me to tell anyone down there what's on the block," he guessed.

"That's right. It's exactly what this guy expects you to do. I don't know if you noticed, but several members of the crew are from San Esteban. Despite the trouble surrounding me, they showed up for work. That proves they have some measure of faith in what I'm trying to do. Don't let my enemy undermine their confidence even more, please."

He considered it for several long moments. "All right. Nothing would be gained by my telling them. I'm not endangering the crew further since they already know someone wants to stop them from working here."

"Thanks, Michael."

"I'm going to increase my patrols, keeping an eye on the more likely approaches to your land. But I want you to help me by also keeping a watch."

"I'd planned on it. This is my fight, and I don't want anyone else to get hurt."

Michael walked back to the burned-out truck. Now that the metal had cooled, he was able to examine it more thoroughly and verify his earlier assumptions. Before long, the county wrecker he'd requested arrived on the scene. As the men winched the burned-out vehicle onto the bed of a large truck, he signed the forms they'd brought him.

Michael sensed Ramona behind him, though he hadn't looked around. It wasn't her footsteps, or any other audible sound. It was something infinitely more subtle—a feeling—that alerted his senses to her presence. But he couldn't afford to have feelings like that. Other, more pressing matters demanded his attention.

"What happens with the pickup now?"

"It'll be taken to the county impound yard. After the lab boys are finished with it, the owners will be able to claim it." He glanced at the construction crew and saw them watching the proceedings. "Do you want me to assure them that patrols will be increasing?"

"They're not worried about the danger. I spoke to the foreman. He told me the men were more concerned I'd bow to pressure and call off the job." Ramona watched as the crew returned to the task of clearing and leveling the work site. "I told them it would never happen."

He smiled ruefully. "Call me if anything else goes wrong, or even if you suspect something might," he said, walking back to the squad car. "The stakes are getting higher and the danger will increase."

As she started to answer, one of the pueblo men approached and stood a few feet away, waiting. She glanced at him and smiled. "Do you need to speak with me?"

"We have a problem. There's a *kayé*, a shrine, within the area you designated for a parking lot."

"I wasn't aware of that. Let me take a look."

Michael accompanied her, curious about this development. It seemed to tie in with the threat about desecrating holy ground, but no one he'd ever spoken to had mentioned a shrine here at the trading post. As they approached the rocky terrain, Michael hung back, keeping a respectful distance. "It sure looks like a shrine," he conceded. "There's prayer dust right around the edges of the rocks."

"There's also that fetish placed at the base of the rocks," the pueblo man said slowly.

"An offering to the spiritual *Towa é* often includes fetishes, but normally they're not so well crafted," Michael observed slowly. "Of course, that's not a hard-and-fast rule. That bear fetish could be there to guard the shrine."

"We won't disturb anything," Ramona said in a tone that precluded the need for discussion. "We'll rope off this area and move the parking lot back."

"I'll make sure none of the crew strays too close to it," the pueblo man assured her, then left to inform the workers.

Michael crouched by the figure, studying it carefully. "Interesting," he muttered. "It's got Barton Perez's mark. I recognize the slash at the bottom of the figure."

"You think the shrine belongs to him or his family?"

Michael stood up. "I don't know, but I intend to find out." They walked back to his squad car. "I also want to check another possibility. This shrine may not be genuine. It might just be another attempt to divert you. Either way, you've done all anyone would expect you to do for now."

Ramona nodded. "But for some it won't be enough. You and I both know that. Unless I can prove it's not genuine, then I'll be giving some people at the pueblo a reason to fight me."

Michael reached for his radio mike and reported in. A second later he glanced up. He saw her features change subtly, defined by the emotions that flickered just beyond her gaze. He wanted to warn her that courage, though admirable, was a double-edged sword. It could push people into situations they weren't equipped to handle. Yet only one thing could give his words the added strength they'd need to really reach her—allowing her to see what was in his heart. And that was something he couldn't do.

He chose to hide behind his uniform, resorting to police talk, that wonderful barrier that made his job more tolerable at times. "The perpetrators will be caught. So far we haven't been able to lift latent fingerprints, but sooner or later they'll slip up. When they do, we'll make a collar."

As he drove away, he saw Ramona in his rearview mirror, watching him. Feelings that at first had seemed intangible were gaining substance and form. He didn't like it one bit, but, unfortunately, they didn't require his permission to exist.

Michael tried to block her from his thoughts, though instinctively he knew that the victory would only be temporary. Control was valued in a man, and was a quality that before Mona's arrival had come quite easily to him. Once again, Walupi's prediction rang in his mind's ear.

Michael arrived at Barton Perez's studio ten minutes later. Perez was standing by the window and saw him drive up. Business was slow on a winter's day like today. Not many tourists came out when the wind and the cold flowed down off the Sangre de Cristo Mountains.

Barton came to the door as he approached. His gaze was wary, but there was a notable amount of curiosity there, too. He waited for Michael to speak first, blocking his way inside.

"I'm here on official business," Michael explained.

"What's your business got to do with mine?"

Not willing to take his eyes off Perez, he explained in a flat, crisp tone what they'd found by the trading post. "Is it your shrine?"

"No," Perez said.

"How do you account for the fetish then?" Michael asked.

"I can't, at least not definitively," Barton answered, finally stepping aside and gesturing for Michael to enter. "You sure it was my mark?"

"Yes." As they went inside, Michael glanced at the firearms collection kept behind locked cabinets. "I know your workmanship and your style."

Perez nodded, not disputing Michael's judgment. "I'd have to see it before I can tell you anything more."

"That's an impressive collection," Michael said, stepping toward the first cabinet. "I didn't know you were interested in firearms."

"I served a stint in the marines. That's when I first got interested. It's taken me years to buy the pieces I wanted."

"Ever use them?"

Barton's eyes narrowed. "No. They're for show, and as an investment. The gun trade is much more stable than art or jewelry. You never know when you're going to need some cash, and unlike pottery or silver, there's always a good market for these."

Michael started to move along to the next cabinet when Barton blocked his way. Michael challenged him with a lethal stare. After a second Barton moved. Michael looked back down at the collection of early-twentieth-century handguns, mostly revolvers.

"I'm curious about this shrine. I'd like to look at it." Perez moved back over by the door.

"You'd be useful if you can tell me about the fetish," Michael agreed.

"I'll follow you there in my pickup. But let me close up here first."

Michael nodded once, then walked outside. By the time he'd started the patrol car, Barton was ready to go. Michael led the way to the site, hoping that their visit wouldn't disrupt the work going on. He knew people would talk, but there was no way to stop that. Right now, Barton might provide some much needed answers.

When they arrived, Michael stepped out of his vehicle, noting with surprise all the progress the crew had made already.

Barton Perez left his truck and joined him, his gaze studying the area. "Did she bulldoze over the shrine?" Perez asked acerbically.

Ramona came up from around Michael's car. "No. I respect what commands respect," she answered with a directness that made Barton flinch.

Michael tried not to smile. Her fire was unquenchable. For an instant, he pictured her in a much more intimate situation, blazing with fires of a different nature. As he realized the turn his thoughts had taken, he promptly brought them back into line. "The shrine is at the far end, behind that roped-off section."

Perez followed the two of them around the vehicles that were leveling the ground. As Michael himself had done earlier, Barton crouched before the shrine, remaining at a respectful distance. "It's one of my fetishes all right."

"Your shrine then?" Ramona asked.

"No. My family has no shrines off traditional pueblo land."

"What can you tell me about the fetish?" Michael prodded.

"It's one from a group I made months ago for shops in Santa Fe. They sell well there. I have no idea who might have ended up buying it," he said, then with a shrug added, "A tourist, I would imagine."

"So the shrine, if it *is* authentic, is very recent," Michael observed pensively.

"To be honest, I never heard of a shrine so close to the trading post. Of course, it's possible that one of the religious societies established this one. Their rituals are secret and so are their activities." He stood up and gave Ramona a hard look. "This is another sign of the trouble you're going to cause by being here," he said, his voice loud enough to be heard by two pueblo workers nearby.

"Not if I find whoever's behind the trouble," Michael countered smoothly, and escorted Barton back to his truck. "Where were you last Tuesday around 7:00 p.m.?"

Barton straightened his shoulders and glared. "Whatever trouble the woman's been having isn't my doing. You'd do better looking elsewhere."

"I asked you a question."

"I was in my studio, working alone," he spat out defiantly. "Before you ally yourself with that one," he cocked his head toward Ramona, "be sure she's worthy."

"My only alliance is with the truth," Michael shot back, his tone equally curt. "I intend to find it, Perez, and if you're behind what's been happening, I'll take you down."

"Your threats don't impress me. Maybe you've been working for the white man too long. You've forgotten who you are and where you came from," Perez taunted.

"I serve the tribe by serving the law. You'd do well to remember that."

Barton's eyes were stony as he gave Ramona one last glance. "Trouble will follow her. Like her father, she creates it."

Michael watched Perez drive away, then went to his squad car. Ramona was standing there, waiting. "I'm going to talk to Captain Suazo," he said. "He's been working on the theft of the truck. Maybe he'll have some answers."

"I'll be here. We're making good progress. These men need the work, and are just as eager as I am to continue. Like one of the workers put it, once the construction is under way, we'll be building facts."

Or courting death. But that wasn't something he could say to her. He respected her ability to watch out for herself. Yet she wasn't invincible, and he wasn't sure that Ramona would know when to retreat.

"Good luck with Suazo," she said as he closed the door.

Michael drove directly to the pueblo. He knew that investigations took time, but he needed a solid break. He mulled over the possibility that he'd grown too close to the case. So much was at stake that would affect him directly. Then he thought of Ramona. Was he trusting her too quickly and not pressuring her enough?

He had no answers as he drove up to the tribal government offices and went inside. He found Suazo behind his desk, filling out a report.

Suazo glanced up as Michael knocked. "I thought you'd come by. I'm still working on that stolen truck, but I don't have any leads. You know how rare thievery is inside San Esteban. Most of us don't even bother to lock our doors." He slid a copy of a report across the desk. "I interviewed Ramon Archuleta, the owner. He didn't report the truck missing until it had been gone most of the day. He just assumed Juan Cruz, his neighbor, had borrowed it to get some firewood. The keys, it appears, were always kept in the ignition."

Michael nodded. He knew Ramon Archuleta and almost everyone else who lived in the pueblo. There was a kinship that transcended blood relationships here. When one of the tribe suffered, everyone did. "How's he coping with the loss of the truck?"

"The tribal insurance he had was minimal. It was an old pickup. But he'll be okay. His family will see to that. Of course if I find out that one of our people stole that truck, I'll make sure that Ramon is compensated for the loss. The old ways still apply to anyone who wants to continue living here. Restitution will be made." He stared out his window thoughtfully. "What's hardest for him, like it is for all of us, is accepting the changes that have slowly been affecting San Esteban. We're no longer isolated from the whites, nor can we be."

"The whites are not our only source of trouble," Michael observed quietly. "Remember the note I received," he added.

"Yes, about that . . ." Suazo leaned back and stretched his legs out in front of him. "The note writer is probably an artist. Although he tried to hide his skill, the strokes and proportions of his characters indicate considerable ability. I've spoken to several artists I trust, and that seems to be the consensus.''

"Any idea of who's responsible?"

"Not yet, but I'll have one soon."

"The construction crew at the trading post found a shrine there today. Do you know anything about that?"

"I've never heard of one over there. Do you want me to ask around?"

"I'd appreciate it." Michael stood up. "I'm going back on patrol. We're expecting more snow, or so the weatherman said."

"Then it'll probably be a beautiful, sunny day," Suazo replied. "Anglo forecasters don't mean to lie, it just happens."

Michael grinned, then walked out. He didn't share Suazo's disdain for the world outside the pueblo, but he knew where he belonged. He thrived in this world of his, filled with rituals that were incomprehensible to many, but gave meaning to everything he was and did.

The day passed slowly. He'd increased his patrols around Mona's place, and found himself hoping to catch a glimpse of her every time he drove by. He tried to tell himself that he was only doing his job but knew deep down he was kidding himself. Desire was natural, part of the dance of life, but it couldn't be allowed to interfere with what he had to do. Without honor, there was no center, nothing to balance against the troubled winds that often came.

Hours later, ready to complete his shift, he made one last pass by the trading post. The construction people had cleared the work site and were wetting and compacting the earth, preparing for the next step. He saw her standing outside, surveying the work as the others finally began to park their machinery and call it a day.

He pulled up beside her home, then stepped out of his car to join her. "It's going quickly, I see," Michael commented.

"Not fast enough for me," Ramona answered with a sigh. As she turned and looked at him, her pulse quickened and her body tingled in response. Hating herself, she turned away and started back to the house.

"You seem to be in a rush. Am I here at a bad time?"

"Not really. It's just that I have to call a cab. It takes forever to get them to come out here and, unfortunately, I don't have that long. My pickup's been repaired and I've got to go get it."

"Why don't you let me give you a ride?" he said. "It won't take me long to drop off the patrol car and get my own."

"You don't have to," Ramona started to protest, then relented as she glanced at her watch, "but I'd sure appreciate it. It's at Healing Parts, on this side of Santa Fe, and the place is going to close in less than an hour."

"Give me ten minutes," Michael said, and strode back to the squad car.

By the time he returned, she was standing out by her mailbox, waiting. He pulled over, then reached across and opened the door on her side. "We'll make it with time to spare."

As the sun disappeared over the horizon, the desert temperature began to drop. "Sorry," he said as she shivered. "The heater's not working."

"I'm okay," she said quietly, as if her thoughts were miles away.

The idea that she might not find his presence as disturbing as he found hers annoyed him immensely. Enveloped in the darkness of the night with distractions to a minimum, riding alone in the car with her was a test of his willpower. A shudder caressed his spine as her familiar scent and the warmth of her body cocooned sensuously around him. His old pickup made it impossible for her to sit too far away. The springs on the passenger's side forced her to slide over, closer to the center. He'd never fixed it, finding it useful at times. But this wasn't one of them.

As he hit another bump on the road, she bounced even closer. A smile played at the corners of her mouth. "The seat on this side is an effective torture device. Are you trying to flatten parts of my anatomy by hitting every bump?"

He smiled wryly. "The springs are shot."

"And the heater?" She laughed softly.

"It's not on purpose. I bought this truck for a song, but I just haven't had the time to do all the work it needs."

She sucked in her cheeks, trying not to laugh but failing miserably. "You're just trying to get me to move closer to you."

"Well I wouldn't protest," he said slowly. "I'd just figure fate's on my side. None of this was done on purpose, you know."

She smiled. "I remember some talk I heard about you once. The women from the pueblo gossiped about who'd tame the wolf. They said that a tame wolf growls softly for his mate," she teased playfully.

He grinned, remaining silent. There was some truth to that speculation. That reaction came naturally to him at certain times, though he'd never really thought about it much. But he was glad the story had teased her imagination. He wondered what scenes had taken shape in the world of her secret dreams.

"An eligible bachelor from our tribe is always sought after. How come you never married?"

Her words brought him back to reality with a jolt. "I'm not free to do that. Until the past is settled, the future's not my own."

She nodded slowly. "Yes, I understand."

"So many years have gone by," Michael said slowly. "I wonder sometimes if it'll ever be settled." He tried to hold himself superior to normal human needs, but he was just a man. He wanted her, there was no denying that. But he wanted more from her than just her body. And in that lay the biggest danger. There could be no soft words spoken between them. They were locked too tightly into the roles fate had forced on them.

"I have to believe that I'll be able to find the truth. It's what keeps me going. If I lose that hope, I'll have failed my mother, my father, and myself."

He nodded silently, understanding completely.

A moment later, he slowed down and pulled into the repair shop. "There's your pickup. It doesn't look so bad."

She shrugged. "I couldn't afford to get all the dents repaired, just the glass, but it'll have to do. It was practically new," she added bitterly, then shook her head. "Well, someday I'll get everything repaired."

"Take it a step at a time," he cautioned, then followed her inside the shop.

"You don't have to wait for me," Ramona said. "You've done enough by bringing me here."

"I'll follow you back. We're heading in the same direction, and I haven't got any pressing business tonight."

Ten minutes later, he pulled out of the repair shop's parking lot right after Ramona. Regret, frustration and guilt tore at him. He felt like a traitor for wanting to be with her instead of concentrating on the job he had to do. His large hands flexed on the wheel, then regripped it so tightly that his knuckles turned pearly white under the strain. He'd see her safely back to the trading post, then leave. Regret slammed into him.

He glanced ahead at the taillights of her truck, needing the frail connection it gave him. Suddenly his stomach coiled with fear and his heart began to pump like a runaway locomotive. Ramona was weaving into traffic, slowing quickly, then veering dangerously off the road. Something was going on inside her pickup and it was about to get her killed!

Chapter Ten

"No!" Michael shouted helplessly as her truck drifted off the road and the gravel shoulder, disappearing into a field.

Fear twisting through him, he braked his truck hard. His eyes were riveted on the spot where the truck had left the road as he shifted down and drove off the highway, following her path.

In the beam of his headlights, he could see her truck off in the field, stopped. The lights were still on. Relieved that it seemed undamaged, he reached for the rifle he kept behind the seat. Whatever or whoever was attacking Mona was going to have to deal with him.

He slid to an abrupt stop directly behind her, illuminating the truck with his own lights. She was behind the steering wheel, but he didn't see anyone else. Abruptly the door was thrown open, but Ramona didn't jump out. Instead, she climbed up onto the bench seat.

Michael heard Ramona yell, but by then he was already running toward her, levering a shell into his Winchester. As he crossed the few feet that separated them, he saw her tumble out the door.

She fell hard, then crawled backward away from the pickup. He was there the next instant. Jumping in front of her, he pointed the barrel inside her truck.

"Snakes . . . rattlers," she managed. "Three, I think. I didn't notice until I was on the highway and one started rattling. I'd turned on the heater. They were just lying there until things warmed up. Then one started to crawl from beneath the seat toward the accelerator. I was trying to push it away with my foot while keeping it from striking."

"Are you hurt?" He crouched beside her, his eyes on the diamond-backed reptiles that had begun to slither toward the open pickup door.

"No. Only one ever got close enough to strike, and it seemed more interested in getting out of the car than in fighting."

Michael took the rifle back to his pickup, then grabbed a long, thin pine branch. Armed with a flashlight and a gunny sack from beneath his truck seat, he returned to her vehicle. "There're no livestock or houses around here, so I'm going to let them go. The cloud cover is keeping it warm tonight, so they should have a chance to find a hole before they get too cold. If I can avoid it, I'd rather not kill them."

"Bad luck?"

He shrugged. "These aren't *Avanyu,* the water serpents who send water for irrigation. But unless it's necessary for food or defense, killing serves no purpose."

"I agree. As long as they're out of my truck, I'll be satisfied," she managed shakily.

It took twenty minutes before he finally was able to remove the last of the reptiles from the interior. One lodged itself beneath her seat and refused to come out. Only some prodding, a hasty retreat when it coiled, and patience finally persuaded it to leave. He carried the snakes in a gunny sack down to a boulder-strewn hillside, released them, then returned to where she waited.

"Let me take a look and make sure there are no more surprises," he said. He peered underneath the seat where the last rattler had been, then expelled his breath loudly. "Don't go in yet," he said, then walked back to his truck.

"More snakes?" she asked quickly.

"No, this is something else," he said, picking up the
gunny sack again. He didn't have any evidence pouches,
so this would have to do for now. "Let me pull it out, then
I'll know if I'm right." He slipped a pair of gloves on, then
reached underneath. The small leather pouch looked almost like a replica of the one they'd found before by her
sign.

"Here we go again," she sighed wearily.

Michael opened the pouch. "There's animal hair and
cactus thorns inside, and a note," he said, carefully extracting the paper nestled inside with the tip of his pen.
"It's a newspaper article."

As she tried to read the text in the light of Michael's
headlights, she noticed a red smear across it. "And more
blood."

He nodded. "The article is about your cooperative, but
the red over it isn't just smeared blood. It says something."

He laid it flat on the hood of her pickup and directed his
flashlight on it. "'Your presence offends,'" he read aloud.
"'Get off holy land.'"

"I just don't understand," she said, running her hand
through her hair. "*Am* I on holy land? Does this allude to
the shrine? We know it hasn't been there long. Can anyone come around and declare the land holy?"

"No, that's not the way it works. And if a society had
erected that shrine, Captain Suazo would have found out
about it fast and told me. My guess is that this is more of
the campaign meant to frighten you away. The animal hair
may be from a coyote, and cactus thorns are said to be the
food of witches."

Ramona and Michael walked back to her pickup, where
she slipped behind the wheel. "Any hopes of getting the
fingerprints of the person who placed that and the snakes
in my truck?"

"There's a very slim chance. You've had repair people
all over the vehicle. But I'll try to lift some, just in case,

from around the door handles." Michael started back to his pickup. "Let's go. I'll follow you to the trading post."

Ten minutes later, they parked in front of her home. Michael did his best to take latents from the doors, but too much handling and the beginnings of a light drizzle made it impossible to get much of anything except smudges.

She watched him, his expression letting her know the futility of his efforts. "I'm worried about the shrine," she admitted as he began to put his equipment away. "I know so little about it. If what's on my property is genuine, is it enough to just cordon it off? I don't want to be disrespectful, but I'm afraid I might out of ignorance. Who can I talk to?"

Michael wasn't sure who would be willing to speak to her about something like this. Yet he couldn't ignore the need that shone so clearly in her eyes. Rather than send her to someone who would turn her away, he accepted the responsibility. "I get half a day off tomorrow," he muttered. "You won't have workmen here, since it's Saturday. If you want to learn more about us and our shrines, I know of a place."

"Where?"

"It's a northeastern Rio Grande Anasazi site. Two Tewa pueblos, including ours, claim the ruin as an ancestral site. Little remains of the main structures, but the shrines are practically intact. I could take you to see them, and teach you about the significance."

"I'd like that."

He thought of the forty-minute drive, all that time alone with her through an empty stretch of desert. His heart began hammering inside his chest, and he clenched his fists in exasperation. The woman made him crazy and right now that was the last thing either of them needed. He stared at her truck, remembering the snakes. "I'll leave you a map, and I'll meet you there at one-thirty."

"Okay, that'll be fine."

"I'll also be talking to the people at the shop tomorrow morning. Someone had to put the snakes inside your pickup. It's possible someone remembers something that might help." He accompanied her into the trading post.

Michael glanced around the room, then stepped to the doorway leading to the hall. "Do you mind if I take a look around?"

"Not at all. Be my guest."

Michael returned a few minutes later. "Okay. Everything seems clear. If you'll let me have some paper, I'll draw you a map to the ruins. Do you remember visiting there as a kid?" She shook her head. "I just thought your mother might have taken you there sometime."

"I recall her mentioning the site, but that's about it."

He drew a simple but accurate map. "Do you think you can find it from this?"

She studied the drawing, then finally nodded. "Sure. No problem."

Michael went directly home, needing time alone to think. His feelings for her were there, he couldn't deny that, but he could choose not to act on them. Lowering his guard led to deadly mistakes. The least he could do was to see to it that his training and ability gave her some protection.

That night he went to bed early. Every time she crept into his thoughts, he quickly and firmly banished her from his mind. Then, as he drifted to sleep, her face and softness came back. Her arms were open, inviting, and her hazel eyes smoldered with passion. "Lie with me, Michael," he heard her whisper. "Let me make the wolf growl."

RAMONA AWOKE early after a troubled night. She huddled deep into the blankets, trying to ease the heart-wrenching longing that filled her. She'd dreamed of Michael last night, of things that couldn't be. She'd felt his embrace and heard the deep growl that had shattered the night as he'd filled her with his love.

She tossed the covers aside and left the bed, hoping the cold would bring her back to earth. Dreams. That's all they were. As the cold touched her naked body, she shivered and reached for her clothes. What an incredible fool she was! She'd never considered herself a romantic, but here she was acting like a teenager experiencing a powerful rush of hormones. And that of course was all it was. Neither of them would ever be free until the past was settled. And even then, resentments held for decades wouldn't just vanish, no matter how much she might want them to.

Ramona spent the rest of the morning going over the books. They required absolute concentration in order to make them balance. The time soon came for her to drive to the Anasazi site.

She arrived at the isolated location near the Rio Grande tense with expectancy. No matter how she tried to rationalize it, she couldn't deny that her feelings were caused by more than her desire to learn about her tribe. She saw Michael's old truck parked just ahead, and her stomach fluttered as he stepped into her view. Wearing a brown leather jacket and jeans, he looked singularly masculine. She swallowed to aid the sudden dryness in her throat.

"Am I late?" she asked as he came to join her.

"No," he replied.

Ramona saw something flicker in his eyes. Anticipation? Had he also looked forward to seeing her? She ran a hand through her hair, unable to squelch the desire to primp.

"The kiva looks almost intact," she said, forcing herself to look beyond Michael. Only a few low walls remained of the ancient stone-and-adobe village. Most of those were overgrown with sagebrush and wild grasses, stunted now by the coming of winter.

"Do you want to climb down inside the kiva? That's the heart of any pueblo."

"Yeah, I'd like that," she answered, looking into the deep, stone-lined chamber.

Michael led her down an exceptionally long, handmade wooden ladder that had been propped against the inside. "As you can see, kivas extend deep into the earth. Originally it was half above and half below ground."

She followed him down, then glanced around at what remained of the ruin. "Do the ones still in use look like this inside?"

He shrugged. "Yes and no. What's left here is mostly a hole dug into the earth. The others are..." he struggled to find the right words "...more refined."

"How so?"

Michael smiled but shook his head. "Part of what you have to learn is what you may ask and what you may not ask."

Ramona exhaled and nodded. "Right."

She looked toward the center, imagining the scent of burning piñon logs and the sacred ritual chants performed so long ago. She envied Michael, so secure in his heritage, in his customs. She had neither to lean on, just a few fragments woven through the tattered tapestry of memories.

He climbed back up, not interrupting her thoughts, and she followed a few moments later.

"Farther ahead is what remains of the Plaza," he said.

"What are those?" Ramona pointed at the barely discernible paths formed by double rows of rocks. They led in all directions away from the ruin.

"They guide the way to the shrines," he answered, following one at random. "Most are comprised of carefully laid squares or circles of stones. It's been said that when there was a drought, the medicine men and other men of the tribe would spend four days and nights in the center shrine making medicine and offering prayers. On the fifth day, they would walk to those stone tanks," he gestured ahead. "At sunrise, the rain would fall into those tanks, but nowhere else. Then a runner would be sent to the village. People would come with ceremonial cups to drink the water or to gather what was necessary to make medicine. But no one was allowed to touch the water directly. After that, the rain would come, ending the drought."

She heard the echoes of the past singing through him and felt the blood ties that had brought her here. "Is the ceremony still performed?"

"Yes, but there are only a few who know how to do it properly." Michael paused before speaking again. "Our ways are all about survival. They teach us to work with nature, to find her rhythms and harness them to benefit the people. Can you reconcile what you've learned on the outside to that?"

"I know that our ceremonies lend purpose and order, and through them the tribe remains strong. But what you're really asking is whether I believe in the significance behind the rituals." She paused. "I honestly feel there's more to life than what we can see with our eyes. Science answers many questions, but never the ones that are formed by the soul."

Michael nodded slowly. "It's a start." He gestured toward the cliff face that had shielded the small site for so many centuries. "When you're on ground level, it's hard to see what the village must have been like. But from that ledge up there, you can really see the patterns in the ruins and get a feel for life as it was here. Would you like to climb up with me?"

"How? That's quite a cliff."

"We can borrow the kiva ladder. I know it's long enough. I've done this before. There'll be a gap between the last rung and the ledge, but I can climb up and give you a hand."

The prospect frightened her; she'd never been much for heights. She hesitated, unwilling to admit her fear.

"It's safe," he assured. "I wouldn't risk you . . . it otherwise." He cleared his throat and looked away.

"Okay," she said at last.

Together they retrieved the ladder then positioned it carefully against the cliff side. Michael made sure it was steady, then led the way up.

A few minutes later, they reached the shelf high up on the sandy cliff. As she surveyed the ruins below, she caught a flicker of movement from behind a cluster of piñons. Curious, she shifted along the ledge, trying for a better look.

Michael saw her expression change, and his senses sharpened. "What is it?"

She scarcely breathed. "I thought I saw someone...something moving down there, to the left of the shrines."

Michael followed her line of vision and glimpsed the brief outline of a man. But something was wrong. As the figure emerged, he realized what. The person was wearing a coyote mask, like the ones used during rituals.

Michael yanked her down hard and covered her body with his own. A pulse beat later, an arrow came whistling over the place where they'd stood. "Stay as flat as possible. He's got a hunting bow. He could kill a bear with that thing." He pulled a small pistol from his boot. Making sure his body remained between her and their assailant, he moved as close to the edge as possible, ready to respond. "He'll have to come out from behind cover to shoot his arrows. I'll make sure he knows we aren't easy prey."

A second later, as the figure came into view, he fired once. He had to conserve his rounds. He had a total of six, and no way of knowing how many arrows his opponent carried. "At least he's a lousy shot," he added as an arrow plunged into the dirt side of the cliff, then fell, unable to lodge securely in the soft sides. "We'll be okay."

Two more arrows bounded off the cliff face directly below them. As they waited, wondering if another volley would follow, they heard the *thwack* of wood crashing against the ground below.

She tried to rise up. "What the—"

"Don't!" he ordered, yanking her back against the shelf.

"I just wanted to peek over the edge," she protested.

"It's the ladder. He managed to dislodge it."

"That means he's trapped us up here!"

"For now. But he can't get close, either," Michael answered. "It's a standoff." Michael waited, listening, measuring and weighing what to do. "The next move is his. Let's see what he does."

A few seconds later, they heard a car engine starting up. Dust lifted off in the distance, obscuring the vehicle that sped down the dirt road.

Ramona started to move, but he flicked a warning glance at her. "No. Wait a few more minutes. Let's make sure it's not a trick. There could be two of them."

She waited, impatience tearing at her. Finally, when Michael moved, she crawled up to her knees, rubbing a bruised spot on her elbow. "He was one of our tribe wasn't he?" she asked, her voice taut. The possibility sickened her.

"Not necessarily. Outsiders buy masks, though not the real ones, of course."

"I wonder why he picked the coyote mask?" she mused.

"Could be that's the one he saw for sale, or..."

"Go on."

He shrugged dismissively. "It's said that the coyote will be the one who'll eventually bring the news of the end of the world. Symbolically, had he succeeded, it would have been the end of us."

She stood up slowly, glanced down, then shuddered. Silently she assessed their predicament. "He didn't have to kill us. Without that ladder, there's no way down. We certainly can't jump."

"Climbing down will be risky, there's no escaping that. The cliff face is crumbling and getting a firm toehold is going to be a matter of luck." Michael took a deep breath, determination shining in his eyes. "Well, my luck's been good so far. I'll go down, then reposition the ladder."

She shook her head. "No. I'm smaller and the dirt sides of this cliff should hold me without breaking off." She met his gaze. "I'm our best chance and you know it."

"I don't know," he said, and let his breath out in a rush. "Do you think you can handle the climb?"

She heard the tautness in his voice and glanced at him, studying his expression. His face, which normally reflected toughness and responsibility, was tainted with fear. Then she met his eyes and knew he was afraid for her. The emotion seemed more raw and poignant coming from a man who prided himself on self-possession and control. "I'll be fine," she said gently.

"It isn't a solid face, and that will work for and against you. There are enough places to grab hold, but you'll have to make sure of your grip and pick only those openings with enough strength to hold you. There are small apertures all the way down that have been cut by the wind and water. Test each first before you put all your weight on them." He cleared his throat. "Go very slowly. I don't want to see you hurt."

"Don't worry. I'm not really big on pain myself," Ramona countered, and saw him smile. "Okay, here we go."

She took a long, unsteady breath as she turned her back to the drop and pressed her stomach hard against the dirt. She had to take that first step down, but her limbs refused to move.

"I'll go," he started. "I'm more familiar with climbing...."

"I said I'd do it." Ramona bit down the words. Taking a deep breath, she edged over the side. She hung there for a minute, trying not to shake. Desperation and need fueled her courage and she forced her other foot down. Dried mud and clay crumbled away, protesting her efforts to find lodgment.

Fear ate into Ramona, making her light-headed. She worked her way down slowly, leaning into the cliff face, her fingers digging into the earth. Every moment held its own peril. Sometimes there would be something there to grab ahold of, and other times she'd end up with a fistful of dirt and skinned knuckles.

In fifteen minutes she managed to descend about ten or twelve feet down from the ledge. Then she was forced to a halt. The next three feet of cliff was solid, the sand hard packed. She kicked against the side, trying to break off a chunk of earth that would leave a crack big enough to hold her foot. Her balance was precarious, so she didn't dare swing her leg too far back.

"What's wrong?" he yelled down, fear thick in his voice.

"I can see a fissure in the rock face about three feet down, but that's one heck of a long step. There doesn't seem to be anything to hold on to in between." She allowed herself to drop slightly, one foot teetering uncertainly as her fingers dug deeper into a small aperture in the rock. "Wait. I think I can make it anyway. Just a few more inches."

Pain gnarled up her fingers and her stomach did flip-flops as she reached down with one foot. Suddenly her toehold began to crumble away, unable to withstand the shift in pressure. Her fingers clawed into the dirt and rock as her foot abruptly slipped free, leaving her dangling in midair.

Chapter Eleven

Ramona clung desperately to the cliff face, but she wasn't going to last long. She could feel her hands weakening as the weight of her unsupported legs pulled her down. "I can't hold on!" she yelled, although Michael was too far to help.

Fear more powerful than anything he'd ever felt gripped him. "I'm coming down to get you! Just don't let go!"

Frustration and anger knotted Michael's belly. Ramona wouldn't have been in this mess had he been the one who'd gone down. He stripped off his jacket and tied it around his waist, wanting as much freedom of movement as he could get for his arms. The light flannel shirt wasn't much protection against the strong cold wind that had risen from the north, but it scarcely mattered now. Blaming himself, blaming her, and knowing it was the fault of neither, he started down the side, making sure he wasn't directly above Ramona.

As he'd suspected, the ground gave way beneath his weight, sending rocks and clods plummeting. He drew in a steadying breath, gripping the top ledge firmly with his fingers. Feeling with the tips of his boots, he dug into the hard-packed sand until he felt secure, then reached down one hand at a time for more places to hold on. He forced himself not to hurry. If the ground gave, he could loosen a wide chunk of hillside and they'd both be goners.

Larger muscles and body weight were usually an advantage, but this time they worked against him, requiring even larger crevices and handholds to support every move he made. He clung to the jagged protrusions that were carved into one section of the cliff wall, then glanced down. The slight movement made the ground loosen beneath his feet. He shifted quickly, finding another hold.

"I'm going to reach down and grab your arm. Then as I help you, I want you to pull up to where I am. There're footholds at my level that will be firm enough for you."

"No, don't! If you reach for me, you could lose your balance! It won't work."

"We've got to try. Otherwise our muscles will give out and we'll fall anyway. Now let me help you, and don't argue!"

Ramona looked up at Michael. "Untie your jacket if you can, and use it as a rope. I think I can reach it without pulling you off balance."

"Good idea. Hang on just a little longer."

Michael searched for something to grasp with his hand so he could steady himself. He found a jagged rock embedded in layers of packed sand, and gripped it hard. With his free hand, he loosened the jacket. Clenching the sleeve in his fist, he quickly lowered it so she could grab it. "Don't worry, just climb. I won't let go, no matter what." He felt his skin being scraped away as he held the jacket against the cliff.

She wouldn't, couldn't fail him now. She worked her fingers up the jacket and jammed the side of her foot against the earth. Even minor indentations were enough as determination spurred her forward.

After a minute, she reached out to take his hand. "Wrap your jacket back around your waist and let's go up side by side. If either of us gets into a jam, the other can help out."

"Okay. Take it slow." Michael matched her pace, though he had to admit she seemed far more limber than he was. Minutes later, they clambered up onto the ledge and sat with their backs flat against the cliff side.

"I *never* want to do that again!" she whispered, choking back a lump in her throat. "What are we going to do? There's no one around for miles! We're likely to freeze to death tonight."

He glanced over at her, an idea forming in his mind. She was terrified, he didn't doubt that, but she was far from defeated. Good. His idea was going to test her courage to the limits.

"We can't jump down, we can't climb down without falling, so there's only one other option." He unwrapped his jacket from around his waist. "Give me your jacket, then your sweater and the blouse you're wearing."

Ramona's eyebrows arched. "I think the exertion has rattled your brains."

"Listen to me. If we strip..."

"We'll freeze."

"I doubt it." Michael smiled ruefully. "But be that as it may... I propose we make a clothing rope. Then I'll steady it up here while you climb down it. Though it won't take you all the way to the ground, you'll be much closer and your descent will be safer. Afterward, you can get the ladder for me."

Ramona had fantasized countless times about this. She'd stand before Michael, his eyes on her as she bared herself to him. But to do this here, under these circumstances, and not touch him... Her knees turned liquid, and her breath caught in her throat.

"There's no other way, Mona," he whispered, his voice raw. As he started to strip off his shirt, he felt her gaze sear over him. Knowing that she found him as tempting as he did her made him feel powerfully male. Stifling a groan of frustration, he kept his hands busy knotting the sleeve of his shirt to the sleeve of his jacket.

Hearing the rustle of clothing, he glanced up in time to see her slip the sweater over her head. Fire raged inside him as she unbuttoned her blouse. He couldn't think straight. He wanted to touch her and kiss her. Somehow he forced himself to stay still, but he couldn't tear his gaze away. Her skin was smooth and looked as soft as velvet. The dark centers of her breasts were taut. They peeked out from behind the lacy cups of her bra, tempting him past the point of reason.

"Unless you want me to stare at you," she said, her breathing ragged, "don't stare at me."

He looked away, but when he heard the raspy sound of her jeans' zipper, he glanced over again. "Don't ask me not to look, I'm only human." The fire in him grew hotter.

"I seem to be the only one stripping," she said unsteadily.

He unbuckled his belt, feeling her eyes caress him as he slipped out of his jeans. His briefs did nothing to hide his arousal. As her gaze drifted downward, desire clawed at his gut. "Don't tease, woman."

"Look but don't touch," she managed with an uncertain sigh.

He gazed hungrily at her. Her body was all softness and rounded curves that demanded a man's loving attention. Her silk bikini panties provided her with no substantial covering and hid nothing from him. As his eyes drifted over the dark patch of hair at the center of her body, the throbbing inside him grew more powerful and insistent.

All his male instincts were working overtime. He was painfully aware that she hadn't shied from the thoroughness of his gaze. Need pumped through him, making breathing difficult. Ramona was as sensuous as she was bold. She could drive a man wild before he ever took her.

He forced his eyes away. "Let's do this as quickly as possible."

"Is that what you tell all your women?" she joked nervously.

His eyes were smoldering. "If the day ever comes for us, I promise you it'll be long and slow. Time will be the last thing you'll be thinking about."

His voice burned through her, turning her skin to fire. Wild sparks danced in her head as she struggled against the need to step into his arms. His skin was sleek, its coppery sheen tempting her to run her palms over its hard surface. He was lean: ribs overlapped hard, tense muscles. He was so big, so male. There was a breathtaking beauty about him, like a wild animal whose very essence embodied grace and primitive strength.

"Don't, woman," he rasped, his eyes glittering, his features sharp and intense. "Your eyes reveal too much of your thoughts."

Ramona tried to shut out the warm ache that grew deep inside her. "You're seeing only what you want to see."

He looked directly into her eyes. "I know what I see," he replied quietly, then began knotting her clothing to his. "The way this looks, I'd say our makeshift rope will leave you seven or so feet from the ground," he said, shifting his thoughts to the danger at hand.

"That'll definitely help," she said, choking back her fear. She didn't want to go near the edge, let alone down the cliff.

"Okay, I'm ready. This will hold you."

Ramona moved toward the edge. She was light-headed, and dots filled her eyes as she tried to retain her senses. For a moment she couldn't breathe.

"Are you okay?"

"I will *never* again climb anything that doesn't have stairs," she muttered through clenched teeth.

Ramona stepped gingerly off the edge, slipping and sliding over rolling pebbles and crumbling rock. Her fingers were coiled so hard around the clothing rope she couldn't feel her hands. "Don't let go," she whispered.

"Of course not," he said, then shot her a reassuring smile. "Who'd be left to get the ladder?"

She looked up and saw his grin. "You're all heart," she muttered.

Her skin scraped against the rough sides, leaving pieces of her behind as she descended. When she moved too abruptly the clothing rope would shift, swinging her against the dirt and rock face. The rocks were icy cold against her bare skin. She started to shake and had to pause several times, struggling to keep her grip firm.

After what seemed like hours, she suddenly realized she'd gone down the length of the rope. Gripping only with her hands now, she descended as far as she could. She was less than six feet from the ground. It was time to jump. Taking a deep breath, she released her hold on the rope and dropped to the ground, falling into a drift of sand.

"I made it!" she said, sobbing for breath.

"Great! Now get the ladder."

She heard the urgency in his voice and knew he was worried their assailant would return. Though she tried to hurry, it took a few minutes for her to raise the wooden ladder. It was heavy because of its length, and awkward to move. Eventually she had it secure against the cliff. "Okay. It's ready."

He dropped the clothing rope so that it landed by her feet, then scrambled down quickly.

She glanced up, watching Michael descend. In either direction, he was built solidly. He was all muscles and satiny smooth planes. Sensations she could scarcely bear ribboned through her.

As he reached the ground, he turned and captured her gaze. The intensity of his gaze sent a shiver rushing through her. "The temperature's really going down," she said, trying to explain her reaction. "We're going to have to work fast."

He gave her a crooked grin. "First you're worried about too fast, now all you're interested in is speed."

"The prospect of turning into a block of ice does things to my priorities." Ramona started to work on one of the knots in their clothing rope. "Michael, I can't get these loose. I guess my weight really tightened the knots."

As a cold blast of air slammed against them, he saw her skin prickle and her hands begin to shake. The instinct to warm her with his own body sent the sharp sting of sexual hunger shooting through him. "Let me try." He moved her against the rock face, placing his body between her and the wind. "Okay, here are your pants," he said, handing them to her. "Let me see if I can get your jacket loose next."

She slipped her jeans on quickly, then moved to help him. "I can't seem to untie your pants from your jacket!" As she shifted, trying for a better hold, she brushed up against him. Her breasts grazed his arm, sending shock waves all through her.

Michael bit his lip, unable to suppress a groan. He pulsed, throbbing with needs that threatened to take him over the edge of his willpower.

"Michael, I just can't do this! My fingers are so cold, I can't feel them. Nothing's working right."

"Oh, something definitely is," he said, his head sizzling with erotic thoughts. She looked up and he saw her hazel eyes shimmering with needs of their own.

Reason shattered in a violent surge of passion, and he hauled her into his arms. His mouth moved hungrily over hers, his hand cupping her neck and slanting her head so that his kiss could deepen. When he felt her press her nearly naked chest against his own body, a storm of need rocked him, exploding through him in violent shudders.

"It was meant," he said in a raw and sensual whisper.

His mouth devoured her, greedy for all she could give him. Everything existed in two parts, Summer and Winter People, night and day, male and female. To complete the whole, both had to unite. Passions as raw and primitive as the desert drove him. He rubbed her against him, and a sound of need, dark and violent as the emotions that shook him was ripped from his throat.

Ramona heard him moan, it sounded like a growl, and knew the power they shared over each other. The knowledge stirred feelings she didn't dare define or even fully acknowledge. Instead, she gave in to the flames that licked at her body.

A moment later, Michael released her abruptly. He expected to see surprise and hoped for a glimmer of disappointment in her eyes, but all he saw was sadness and comprehension. Guilt enveloped him like a thick, dark, oppressive cloud. "There is no room for this in our lives. Distractions can be lethal. I'll ask the gods to help me focus, so that I can do my work without this confusion."

Ramona's heart twisted. "What we feel is desire. It's neither good nor bad, just natural. Isn't that what our tribe teaches us?"

He stared at her as her response knifed through him. Is that all it was to her? Half of him refused to believe it, but was that pride or reason? He picked up the clothing from the ground and pried the knots open with a force that verged on anger. "Get dressed. There's work to do."

His tone hurt Ramona deeply. Did he see her as someone who brought out his weakness? He was a modern warrior as proud of his strengths as his ancestors had been. "I'll help you look around for something that might help us identify the archer."

Michael nodded, then walked ahead to where he'd seen the figure. Out of the corner of his eye, he saw her moving toward the boulders that stood at the base of the hillside. "There are boot tracks here," she said.

Michael joined Ramona and studied the marks. New soles and metal tips were obvious. He walked to his old truck, retrieved a small 35 mm camera and took several photographs. After a few minutes he walked to the spot where two of the arrows that had missed them had fallen. He handled them carefully, then took them back to his truck. On his way, he stopped by the center shrine. Prayer meal had been sprinkled over it, and several large white stones had been placed there.

"The stones . . . aren't they part of Tewa rituals?"

He nodded thoughtfully. "People ask the stones for what they want. It is said that long ago everything could talk, even stones. Now they're messengers to the Cloud Beings."

"So, he *was* Tewa," she concluded.

"There's a very good chance he was," Michael admitted.

As he accompanied her back to her truck, Michael lapsed into a tense silence. He didn't speak again until she was behind the wheel. "To find the answers we need we're going to have to work together—without diversions. We have to stay focused on what we're trying to accomplish. Indulging physical needs, no matter how tempting, is something neither of us can afford."

Pain wound a constricting knot around her heart as his words sank in. "Don't trivialize our feelings just because they're natural," she replied in a taut voice.

The intensity of emotion behind Ramona's words took him by surprise. The possibility that what she felt for him ran deeper than he'd thought shook him down to the soles of his boots. He studied her expression, but he couldn't be sure.

That doubt was enough to help him pull back into himself. He didn't need to give an edge to feelings that were already too powerful. "Keep your wits about you and watch your back at all times," he said calmly. "When I have something new to tell you, I'll drop by the trading post."

She placed the truck in gear and drove off. In a way, Michael was right. Their futures held nothing but unknown shadows. Giving in to yearnings neither had the right to pursue would only result in heartbreak and failure. The inescapable knowledge left her feeling empty and cold inside.

As the miles stretched out between them, she forced her heart to release Michael and yield to the truth. They would each have to travel alone, trusting in their own confidence and strength to guide them.

MONDAY MORNING Ramona listened to the sounds of workmen arriving in their private vehicles. She was already at her desk, getting the accounting books set up. The activity soothed her, reminding her of a goal about to be met. Suddenly a sharp bang echoed around her and angry shouts filled the air.

Chapter Twelve

Ramona bolted out of her chair and dashed to the door. Hector Pratt was striding toward the house, his face contorted in a scowl.

"We've got a problem," he said, gesturing for her to come with him.

She followed him across the grounds and saw him point to the wheels of the large grader. Two arrows stuck out of flattened tires. "That's not all. Our portable drilling rig is damaged. Someone broke off the control panel with a screwdriver or something. You heard the backfire when we tried to start it up."

She went to the area where the crew had left their equipment and studied the ground. Familiar boot prints were etched clearly in the sand. "Do those belong to any of your men?"

"No, I checked when we found the flats. Only one guy has a boot size that's close, and it doesn't match."

"I better call the sheriff's department." She glanced around at the workers who were waiting, talking among themselves. "Will you have problems keeping your men on the job?"

He laughed. "Are you kidding? These guys are construction workers, not wimps. They're ticked off. Nobody would quit now."

Relief washed over her. "Good. I'm glad to hear that. How long before you can get things going again?"

"Should be another few hours. But I have to warn you. This is going to start costing both of us pretty soon. I have to pay the men when they're out here even if no work gets done. If we can't meet your schedule, it'll hurt the cooperative's income, too."

She swallowed hard. Her budget was tight enough. "I'll see what I can do about security. In the meantime, if you can think of any safeguards, let me know."

She strode back inside the trading post angrily. Her enemies wouldn't win, not after she'd come this far. She called the sheriff's office, then began to go over her figures, trying to see how much extra she could squeeze from the budget.

Michael arrived less than ten minutes later. Hearing his vehicle, she went outside to meet him. After explaining what had happened, she watched him check and record the boot prints and the marks on the vandalized construction equipment.

"I'm going to follow up on these footprints and speak to as many shoe repair shops as I can. These are the same as the ones left at the ruins. It'll take time though, so don't expect quick results. There are a few one-man operations outside Santa Fe and around the reservation that aren't even listed. They rely on word of mouth mostly."

"What about those arrows? They don't look factory made. Those markings are too individual. They must have been made by hand."

"They're identical to the ones we encountered before. I tracked those down to another pueblo farther north. Locals make them to sell to tourists and gift shops." He slipped behind the driver's seat.

"Maybe the culprit isn't Tewa and we're only being led to believe that."

"Possibly, but I still think we're dealing with two or more people."

"Do you suppose Barton Perez hates me enough to be doing some of this? By this afternoon my smaller building will be ready to furnish and house some of the cooperative's workers. He might be hoping to stall that. And he'd certainly know the proper offerings to make at a shrine."

"He has a motive, but then again, so do a lot of other people." Michael started the engine. "I remember the caller that accused you of being on holy ground. That still puzzles me. I spoke to Tomás Naranjo, the *Towa é sehn,* the head *Towa é,* of our tribe. He wants to speak to both of us tonight."

"Why?" she asked quickly. Naranjo wielded a great deal of power. She didn't need any more enemies, nor did she want to risk a confrontation that would turn him into one.

"He said that you should hear what he has to tell me since it affects you and anyone who joins the cooperative."

A shudder traveled through her. "Maybe he's found out it was true, and I am building on holy ground."

"I don't know." Michael shrugged. "It's a possibility. Depending on the kind of shrine it is or who made it, you may be asked to relocate everything. Even with a clear title to the land and a building permit, you would upset a lot of people by going ahead with it."

Ramona glanced back at where the workers were already preparing a section of land to accept the next portable. Maybe her enemies would end up defeating her by attrition.

She shook free of the thought. "I'll just have to find a way to work around it or else compromise with the tribe." She saw the uncertainty in his eyes and knew what he was thinking. She could alienate the people of San Esteban even more if she hedged around sanctions. "Don't worry. It's my problem," she said, moving away from his car.

"Tomás lives at the north edge of the pueblo. He's got the last adobe house before you reach the fields. Why don't you meet me there later today?" Michael's gaze shifted. "I think the foreman wants to talk to you."

She nodded at Hector Pratt, who stood several yards away, waiting. "Is there anything else I can do for you, Michael?"

His eyes flickered with an undefined emotion. "I'll come by at least once before we go see Tomás. In the meantime, be careful."

As Michael drove away, she turned to Pratt. His expression was one of tense expectancy. "You don't look like you've got good news."

Pratt shrugged. "I've got a suggestion. You mentioned hiring security before and there's a man I can recommend. He's alert and reliable, and his fees are reasonable," he said, then quoted her a figure. "That would be for the duration of the project."

She weighed it over in her mind. "All right. Let's do it."

Shortly after lunch, she greeted the members of the cooperative who'd arrived to see the temporary building just erected. "It's just until the permanent building is finished, but I tried to select a model that would give us maximum light. The heater will be hooked up later today."

"I expected it to be cold," Saya said, "but I think it's going to be very comfortable in here. It's getting warm already." She looked up at the translucent skylights that ran along the ceiling.

"You'll have different work areas, of course, and if there's any problem, all you have to do is let me know. We'll work things out."

Hearing a car coming up the driveway, Ramona walked to a window and glanced outside. A brand-new white Cadillac, not a car one saw much in these parts, was parked by the front of the trading post. A tall man dressed in an expensive western-cut suit and hat stepped out.

Saya stood behind her. "George Taylor," the Tewa woman commented. "He's not involved with the cooperative, is he?"

"Not at all. In fact, he's opposed to it. My guess is that he's here to try and talk us into quitting before we go much further." Her own words came as an awakening. Was it possible that Taylor was the one responsible for much of what had happened so far? He'd certainly pulled no punches when he'd gone behind her back at the bank.

She watched him looking around, studying the way he moved. He was here with a specific purpose. Bracing herself, she squared her shoulders and went outside to meet him. "Is there something I can do for you?" she asked.

His eyes were marble cold, but it was undeniable that the man had presence. Something about him challenged without words, and assumed control. "I'm here on business. I have a proposition for you."

Curious, she tried to watch for signs that would reveal what lay behind the hooded eyes. There was a tasteful correctness about him today that automatically kept her at a distance. In the best of circumstances, she would have never described him as approachable, but it was worse now. "I thought you weren't interested in the cooperative."

"Shall we go inside? I hate to conduct business outside in the cold."

Ramona felt as if she were standing before a viper stalking its prey. "Of course." She led the way into the trading post and gestured for Taylor to sit down. "Please, continue."

"I've heard you've had nothing but trouble since you embarked on your plan to open the cooperative," Taylor said, his body erect and formal.

"Anything worth having demands a price."

"But prices can be renegotiated. I've been thinking about the cooperative. The concept of serving the pueblo in this way is worth pursuing."

"So you're interested in the proposal I made you?" she asked. The instant the words left her mouth, Ramona realized she didn't want to do business with a man like Taylor under any circumstances.

"People like Chacon, the union organizer, don't give up. You've already had delays and trouble with your work crews, I hear. Things will get worse, believe me, and you're no match against a big labor union. Don't get me wrong. I admire your courage, but you'd be better off selling out to me now than having the cooperative slide into ruin."

He handed Ramona an unsigned check made out to her. "That figure is more than ample compensation. You'll have enough to clear your debts and make a hefty profit. The members of the cooperative will also benefit since there's enough money to recompense them for whatever time they lose while we get the paperwork settled. If you really want to help the tribe, let someone who can make the cooperative prosper take charge."

She fought the urge to rip up the check in front of his face. Biting back her anger, she gave him a lifeless stare. "Others have already signed up for the cooperative. It's no longer just my decision."

"You do agree it's a generous offer?"

Resentment stirred inside her. "Perhaps, but I'm not convinced you'd be the best person to run the cooperative."

His eyes flashed with a cold fire. "So far, your progress hasn't been spectacular. Surely you *do* see that. And your involvement could place others in danger. Rampant vandalism can lead to nasty accidents. Things of that nature aren't selective in their targets."

For years, the dream of starting the cooperative had kept her centered. She'd cherished the goal, knowing someday it would grow into a reality. Yet, if it was truly something that she was doing for the tribe, and not just a means of exonerating her family, then she had to think of the people of San Esteban first. "The others are here. I'll present your proposal to them and let you know what they decide.'' Ramona stood by the door and waited for him to rise.

"How soon can I expect an answer?"

"I'll go talk to them now. We'll see how they feel about it."

"I'd like to go with you. It's only fair that they should know what they're up against if you continue to try and manage the cooperative. They signed up as artists, not soldiers in the battlefield you've placed them in."

About a dozen artisans stood inside the utilitarian shell of the building when they walked inside. George Taylor made his offer public, reiterating the danger they could be in. As soon as he finished, Ramona turned to look at him. "Okay, you've had your chance to speak. Now, we need a chance to discuss your offer in private." She held the door open for him.

Ramona let Taylor out, then turned to face the artisans. Uncertainty was mirrored in their eyes. Taylor's words had captured their attention. She swallowed back her own fear, knowing that whatever she said could seal her dreams of running the cooperative. "I won't lie to you. There are risks involved. Someone is trying to stop me."

"Taylor is offering a great deal of money. You could turn your back on this and walk away wealthy. No one would lose," Juanita Gonzales said.

Ramona swallowed back the answer on the tip of her tongue. How did one measure the worth of a dream? Her chance of finding a place among them could vanish with the cooperative. But that was something she could never say to them, for at its center was selfishness. She wanted to be a part of them, but not at any cost.

"This danger he spoke of..." Martin Lucero commented. "My brother is in your construction crew, and he's talked about it. I also heard what happened to the flyers."

"You need to think of yourself," Ramona said, assuming he was in favor of accepting Taylor's offer. "I don't blame you," she added softly.

Martin looked at her and shook his head. "No, you misunderstand me. I hate to run from a fight. We're all being pressured to do something we don't want to do. By trying to frighten Ramona," he said, looking at the group, "they mean to control us. I say we stand firm."

"There's also something else we have to consider," Saya said. The elderly woman potter stood up. "Taylor can't be trusted. We've known that for years. He's a coldhearted businessman intent on making a profit at whatever the cost. Many of us have worked for him at one time or another out of necessity. He pays us wholesale for our work, then sells it at a markup of one hundred percent or more. A man like that will never keep the rules of a cooperative. He'll turn this into a company just like the others he runs. We'll be salaried workers making starvation wages for our labor."

Juan Padilla, one of the jewelry makers, joined Saya. He was younger than the others, barely in his mid-twenties. He hardly ever spoke, but his work was known all over northern New Mexico. "Saya is right. I've worked for Taylor. His offer is generous, and on that basis alone, I think we can safely assume he's up to something."

Relief flooded through Mona as she heard the vote going around the room. They wanted her in, despite the risks and Taylor's offer. A lump formed at her throat. "You won't regret the confidence you've placed in me. The cooperative will succeed because it's got the important things it needs to grow. Loyalty, skill and commitment are unbeatable."

"You do your part, and we'll do ours. Working together has kept the pueblo alive since long before the Spanish. The same principle will work now. No one expects it to be a picnic, and you've taken the heaviest load yourself," Saya observed. "But if you're willing, we'll stand with you."

Not trusting her voice, she nodded and left the artisans, who were eager to set up their workshops. As soon as she walked out of the portable building, Taylor came out from the shadows and blocked her way. "You think you've won, but this is far from over."

"I assume you were listening, so you know they don't want you. The decision has been made."

"By the time I'm through with you and your cooperative, the pueblo will rue the day they ever heard of the Ortiz family. You think things have been rough? Just wait until you get a taste of real competition. I'm going to open a wholesale jewelry mart adjacent to a pueblo farther south. That'll place me closer to Albuquerque, New Mexico's biggest market. I'll undercut you and steal your customers before you even have a chance to set out your wares. Lady, I'm going to drive you straight into bankruptcy."

"If you expect me to start quaking with fear because of your threats, think again. The cooperative's pottery and jewelry will be head and shoulders above yours in quality. The people who buy from us wouldn't come near a warehouse operation like you envision. Tamper with our out-of-state customers, and I'll have every regulatory board in the state checking your operation."

He stepped forward, deliberately crowding her, but she refused to give way. "You have no idea what a powerful enemy I can be."

Out of the corner of her eye, Ramona noticed that Michael had appeared from around the corner of the portable building. As her gaze shifted to him, George Taylor twisted around to look.

Michael stood an arm's length behind Taylor. Although he was out of uniform, his bearing projected unyielding authority. "Maybe you'd like to explain exactly what you meant. You'll find me a very interested listener.''

Taylor recovered quickly. His smile was smooth, though a bit too rigid to pass as natural. "It's just a little business rivalry in action—all part of the American way. Nothing for the sheriff's office to concern themselves with." Taylor gave Ramona a benign glance. "But as an able businessperson, I'm sure you realized that."

Ramona watched him go to his car, forcing her face to remain expressionless. There was no way she'd give Taylor the satisfaction of knowing he'd managed to get to her. "He's something else. One minute he's playing the good guy, the next moment the bad. And you know what? I can't stand him in either mode."

"If he's harassing you, file a complaint," Michael suggested.

"No. He's right. This is business. The last thing I want is for him to think he's getting to me."

"All right. I suppose you'll have to go with your instincts on that," Michael answered. "By the way, I'm ready to go see Tomás Naranjo. I wanted to wait until I was off duty so I could be certain I wouldn't be called away unexpectedly. Can you get away now?"

"Sure. Just give me a chance to tell the others I'll be gone." She went back inside the portable building and made sure the artisans had what they needed. Assured Saya would lock up for them, Ramona started toward Michael's truck, then stopped. If she was going to be gone for a while, taking some extra precautions wouldn't hurt.

She turned and hurried to where Hector Pratt was working. "Have you spoken to the night watchman you recommended?"

"Sure did. I was just going to come see you. He's ready to start whenever you want, even this afternoon."

"Could you make sure he's here before your men leave tonight?"

"No problem."

A few minutes later, she was on the way to San Esteban with Michael. The drive to Naranjo's home was short. As they approached the adobe house, she felt her pulse quicken with apprehension. She didn't want any more trouble: she had enough to handle.

She left Michael's truck and walked with him up the dirt path. "It sounds like there's quite a few people inside."

"He's the head *Towa é*. Maybe there's a meeting of some sort going on."

"Should we come back later?"

He shook his head. "It was his idea that we come to-night."

Almost in verification, a short, heavyset man in his late fifties greeted them at the door. An ample belly pooched out from the top of his belt. Sharp eyes assessed them, then with a casual wave he gestured for them to enter. "I'm Tomás Naranjo," he said, his eyes on Ramona.

She introduced herself, feeling oddly uncomfortable by her inability to read him. There was no discernible body language or expression in his eyes to give her the slightest hint of what lay ahead. "Have we come at an inconvenient time?"

"Not at all." He led the way to a small, sparsely decorated room. Thick woolen rugs with intricate Indian designs adorned the floors and the back of the large cloth sofa. "Those you see here are *Towa é*, all except Captain Suazo, who's our sheriff. I felt he should hear what I say also."

She took the seat she was offered, then waited. No one bothered to introduce the others, all men. She recognized some of the faces, like the elderly man who'd accused her of being bewitched, but the rest remained a mystery.

There was an atmosphere of tense expectancy around the room. Michael took a place across the way, watching the faces intently. Naranjo waited, commanding attention by his silence. Then, assured that he had it, he began. "All of us in this house are aware of the trouble you've been having. We know someone is trying to scare you into leaving. Yet it wasn't our place to interfere until now. When we learned of the shrine found on your property, we all grew very concerned.''

"How would you like me to handle this?" she asked, her arms open and palms up in a gesture of acquiescence.

"Any way you wish," Naranjo answered. "It isn't genuine. There are no family or tribal shrines on your property. We've looked into this thoroughly. Someone is trying to use our rituals and our ways to enhance a lie they want you to believe. This is deeply offensive to us. Not all here agree with what you're doing, but we won't stand for anyone subverting our ceremonies for their own ends.''

"She is at the heart of the problem." The old man who had accused her of being bewitched spoke. "What is happening is because of her. Remove her, and the problem disappears.''

"That statement isn't worthy of you, Frank," Michael said quietly. "There isn't a person in this room that wouldn't fight for his right to follow whatever path he chooses for himself.''

"Her father hurt many of us, Wolf, including your own people. How can you defend someone whose presence is already bringing chaos?''

She saw Bernardo Agoyo stand up, and for a moment she was afraid that in order to help her he'd tell the others about her father's murder. "John Ortiz isn't the issue here. He's gone. We have to deal with what's happening now. If Ramona Ortiz stays, despite the pressure, there's hope that someday we might find the clay we already paid for.''

She breathed a sigh of relief, glad to know that her trust in Bernardo hadn't been misplaced. "I won't give up searching for the clay that belongs to our tribe. I promise you that.''

"Word, words!" the elderly Frank Saez answered. "Your father was full of them. Surely experience has taught us to judge people on what they do, not on what they say."

"Yes, judge *her* on that basis, too," Michael interjected. "Not on what others have done or said about her."

Naranjo held up one hand and silence fell around the room. "Enough. Debate isn't the purpose of this meeting." His eyes focused on Ramona, then strayed to Suazo and Michael. "I will rely on you to take care of this matter. We won't tolerate anyone misusing our rites."

Suazo walked out with Michael and Ramona several minutes later. "We better find some answers," Suazo muttered. "Otherwise, they'll start their own investigation."

"I'm working on my end of it. That's the best I can do," Michael replied.

With a curt nod, Suazo walked to his vehicle.

"I want to thank you," she said as Michael started to pull out onto the main road. "I didn't really expect any allies there tonight."

The gentle words touched him like a lover's caress. Just being with her made something harsh give way inside him and start to dissolve. "The truth was your ally much more than I was. I just voiced what needed to be said."

Whether or not he admitted it, what he'd done was the act of a friend. The knowledge warmed her. Ramona glanced outside into the darkness, feeling at peace. White flakes of snow fell and took roost against the windshield, blurring and softening the world around them.

Hearing Michael suddenly mutter an oath, she sat up abruptly and stared straight ahead. Twin headlights were converging down on them. With her heart drumming in her ears, she watched the speeding vehicle hurtle toward them on a collision course.

Chapter Thirteen

Ramona pressed back against the seat, bracing for the impact. "He's going to hit us!"

"Hang on!" Michael yanked the wheel sharply to the right. The old pickup skidded onto the shoulder of the road, then hurtled into the desert brush. "I've got to try and stop. But it's going to be slippery. Grab ahold of something!"

He tried pumping the brakes, but in the scattered snow the truck fishtailed wildly, scarcely slowing. Ramona's teeth rattled as she was thrown against the seat belt. Then, as the headlights cut a path through the darkness, she saw the drop-off ahead. "Look out!"

"I'll have to slide to a stop! It's our only chance."

She closed her eyes and scrunched down into the seat, trying to wedge herself against the cushioned back. Anchored by the seat belt, she was wrenched painfully from side to side, then abruptly the vehicle came to a halt. She opened one eye, then the other. "What happened?"

Michael was reaching down into his boot for his backup pistol. "Keep your head down, and stay in the truck."

"Where . . ." She never got a chance to finish.

Michael crouched low and moved up the hill toward the road.

Ramona caught her breath, then freed herself from the seat belt. Shifting slowly, she tried to figure out where they'd come to a stop. Michael's headlights were still on, shining straight ahead, but she could only see brush and gray shadows there. She suspected they'd stopped dangerously close to the edge, but there was no way to tell for sure from where she was.

She moved to open the passenger's door, intending to leave in a crouch as he'd done, but the pickup shifted and lurched. As she glanced down, wondering if she'd released the brake, she felt the vehicle rock and sink downward slightly again. It didn't make sense. The stick shift was still in gear and the emergency brake was on.

She rolled down her window to look out and realized with horror what was happening. They'd stopped several feet from the edge, but the muddy slope hadn't been prepared for the weight of Michael's truck. The pickup was sliding laterally toward the arroyo as the edge of the cliff began to sag under the weight.

She started to throw open her door, ready to bail out, but then realized that the direction the vehicle was sliding would make that a lethal mistake. The truck would either pin her or force her off the edge.

Quickly she moved over to the driver's side and grabbed the door handle. It refused to give. She yanked at it hard, and a breath later the lever came off in her hand! Stunned, she stared at the metal handle. The door was still firmly closed. Knowing that her time was running out, she hastily rolled down the window. "Michael!" She shouted his name loud enough for the next county to hear.

She saw him an instant later. He was already coming back down the hillside when he heard her voice, paused and looked around. Realizing what was wrong, he shot forward in a run.

Ramona felt the truck jostle under her again and knew she had no other choice. Struggling not to make any abrupt movements, she tried to crawl slowly out the window, but her winter coat made that impossible. Slipping it off, she tried again, deliberately ignoring each halting lurch that rocked the vehicle as it slid toward the edge.

She was halfway out when Michael's strong arms grasped her around the middle. With one mighty pull, he jerked her free. Suddenly off balance, Michael careened backward into the mud, landing with her on top of him.

Before she could gather her wits, the truck creaked, slipped several more inches, then came to a stop less than two feet from the edge. They watched it for several seconds, expecting it to career over the side. But the vehicle remained motionless, as if glued to the mud.

Michael never loosened his hold on Ramona. His arms were wrapped tightly around her waist, pressing her into him. "Are you all right?"

Wild stirrings shook her as she felt his hard, male body beneath her. She moistened her dry lips with the tip of her tongue. The gesture had been unconscious, but his reaction was swift and obvious.

His arousal pressed intimately against her. "Are you all right?" he repeated in a raw, husky voice.

"I should ask you that. I'm the one who landed on you," she said, forcing a shaky smile. As she shifted, she sank into the cradle of his thighs.

He groaned as fire spread through him. "If you have an ounce of compassion you won't move that way."

"I'm sorry," she said, thinking she'd hurt him. "Let me give you some breathing room." She started to jump up, slid, then fell down against him.

He inhaled sharply. "*Don't* do that again."

"Okay. Just tell me what you want to do."

"That's some invitation," he muttered.

"It could be." She'd meant it as a playful retort, but her voice was too tense to have it pass off successfully.

Her breath stirred against his mouth, offering the promise of something even more tantalizing. His heart lurched inside his chest. *Don't, don't.* The words repeated in his mind as he tried to ward off what he knew he'd do next.

Like a starving man reaching for sustenance, he drew her to him harshly, his hand tangling in her hair. He devoured her mouth greedily, taking all the sweetness he'd hungered for. Her tongue moved to meet his, touching, retreating, then returning to twine around his. Her fiery response sent a furnace blast of heat through him. They were well matched, even in passion. The knowledge ripped through him and desire clawed at his gut.

Ramona couldn't think. His kiss was harsh, but his tongue was seductively soft as it enticed and tempted. Everything in her responded, and at that moment, nothing mattered except the exquisite sensations ribboning through her.

The soft squish of mud tugged at his back, and Michael tried to move to one side. He braced himself up on one elbow, but the ooze sank beneath him and he slammed back against the earth with a splat.

Seeing the frustration and sheer misery etched on his face, she laughed. "Our timing is never right, have you noticed that?"

"How could I miss?" He expelled his breath in a soft hiss.

Michael supported her until she moved away from him, then rose to his feet. Together, they approached the truck. It hadn't moved, all four tires had sunk deep into the mud.

"I'm going to have to brace the tires just for safety's sake, then radio Suazo," he said. "We'll have to report this to him since we're still on pueblo land."

She helped him look around for something that would stabilize the truck. "You ran up the hill after the car that ran us off the road. Did you happen to catch the make or license plate number?"

He shook his head. "By the time I reached the top, all I could see were taillights."

Michael picked up a large rock and hauled it over to the pickup. Seeing Ramona move to help him, he shook his head. "No, let me try to position this myself. I don't want our combined weight so close to the edge."

A second later, with the rock in place behind a tire, he reached through the window and lifted out the CB radio mike. He usually kept it on the emergency channel just in case. After relaying a message via a trucker within range, he turned to her. "If the truck driver stops and makes the call I've requested, Suazo should be here within minutes. He'll tow my truck up the hill, and then I'll take you home."

It was freezing. The wet mud that clung to her clothing only added to the chill that enveloped her. He slid out of his jacket and slipped it over her shoulders. She could feel the heat of him still inside it.

"It isn't much, all crusted in mud," he apologized, "but it's something. I'd get your coat, but I can't reach it from the window, and we don't want to disturb the truck any more. It could still go over the edge."

"But you'll freeze." This time when she shivered, it wasn't from the cold.

"This sweater is enough, at least until Suazo gets here."

Ten minutes later, they saw bright headlights of an approaching vehicle cutting through the darkness. The flashing red-and-blue lights made it easy to identify. "That's Suazo," Michael said. "Would you like to come up to the road, or wait down here?"

"I'll wait," she said. "You'll probably want to have a few words in private with him."

"Yeah, I will at that," he acknowledged. "I'll be back in a few minutes."

Ramona saw him at the edge of the road talking to Suazo. Moments later, he stepped into the police carryall with the tribal captain. They made their way slowly down the slippery hillside, then finally stopped twenty yards away from the truck.

Using a powerful winch on Suazo's bumper, it took only five minutes to pull Michael's truck out and retrieve her coat. After the task was completed, Suazo listened to Michael's story, taking notes. "It's going to be almost impossible to track this car down on the basis of what you've given me."

Michael nodded. "I realize that."

Suazo rubbed his chin with one hand. "I do have some news," he added. "I've been searching for the person who sent that note to your office, and I've got it narrowed down to a few possibilities."

Ramona glanced at Michael then Suazo, instantly alert.

"Who do you think sent it?" Michael asked.

Suazo shook his head. "I have no proof against anyone yet, so I'd rather not say. I just wanted you to know I'm making progress." Tipping his hat, he returned to his vehicle and drove back in the direction of the pueblo.

As a cold blast of air whipped against them, Michael zipped up his jacket. "Let's get going."

She eased herself into the passenger's side, wishing she was home where it was warm. As she twisted in her seat to face him, she noticed from his hands that he was shivering. "You're freezing!"

"I'll be okay. My sweater's still a little wet in spots, but it'll dry up fast enough."

"Come inside when we get to the trading post. Maybe I can find something dry for you to wear."

"Don't worry about it. What I would like is some hot coffee in a thermos. I'm going to keep an eye on the trading post tonight from my truck. I want to make sure whoever caused the accident doesn't come back for a visit."

"Do you think he'll do that?" she whispered, her throat deathly tight.

"No, not really, but I don't want to take a chance."

"There's a security guard posted out back, near the construction equipment."

"I'm not worried about your new building and a few backhoes. The guard can take care of that. I'll keep an eye on the house."

They arrived at the trading post a short time later. Ramona unlocked the door and walked inside with Michael close behind. "I'll get that coffee," she said, slipping out of her coat.

She started the electric coffeemaker, then checked the refrigerator. "How about something to eat?"

"No, don't bother," he said. "Coffee is enough."

She glanced outside. The crescent moon had slipped behind a thick layer of clouds, shrouding everything in an oppressive gloom. "Michael, don't you think you can guard me more effectively from inside the house? In the darkness you're not going to see someone who tries to sneak up, especially behind your truck."

He scrubbed a muddy patch off his cheek. She had a point, but in here with her there would also be more to distract him. He hesitated.

Noting it, she continued. "As the night wears on and you get colder, you'll start getting sleepy. Then you'll be vulnerable yourself."

He exhaled softly. "All right. It does make more sense."

She led him to the den and pointed to the fireplace. "Why don't you make a fire? I'm going to take a quick shower and change."

"You may as well go to bed after your shower. You've got a full day of work tomorrow." Michael poured the coffee from the thermos into a cup. "Though I'll still stop by the office, I'm off duty tomorrow. It won't matter if I lose some sleep," he said. Turning off the room light, he took a seat by one side of the window.

"Yeah, I do have to be up early. I think I'll take you up on that," she said, sensing he wanted to be left undisturbed to do his job. "Help yourself to whatever's in the refrigerator or the cupboards."

Ramona said good-night and walked to the back of the house. She showered slowly, enjoying the steamy cascade of water against her skin. As she dried off, she glanced at what had been her favorite sweater. It lay in a heap on the bathroom floor, covered with a reddish clay. If she left it soaking in the washing machine all night, maybe she'd still be able to salvage it.

She picked up her clothes from the floor, then wearing her worn housecoat, peered down the hall. The house was dark, except for the warm flicker of the fire. Michael was obviously still in the den. Quietly she crept down the hall to the utility room off the kitchen. As she stepped inside, her breath caught in her throat.

Michael stood shirtless by the dryer. "I thought you were going to go to bed," he said, his voice unsteady. She looked so warm and pliable and feminine despite that joke of a robe. He could tell that she was wearing nothing beneath it. The folds of the frayed material draped over the curves of her body, tempting him with what lay just beyond sight. Desire forked through him like lightning across a desert sky.

Looking into his eyes was like gazing into his heart's pure fire. Her knees felt wobbly, and butterflies threatened to shake her apart. "I...uh...I thought you'd be in the den," she stammered breathlessly.

"I thought I'd run my sweater through the wash hoping to get the mud off." His voice was a bare, sensual rasp. "It was getting uncomfortable." His gaze drifted over her hungrily. She was barefoot, her toes curled tightly as she responded to the sensual feel in the air.

"Let me take that," he murmured, reaching for the bundle in her hands.

He wanted to do that, if only to see all of her more clearly. As the back of his hand grazed her softness, his body swelled and began to throb. He owed his full loyalty to the duty he'd sworn to do. But he was a man. And she was very much a woman. He placed the bundle aside, his mind racing with dark images. Had they died out on that hillside earlier, their souls would have now been one with the shrines. He would have never known what it was like to share in her sweetness and her fire. Fate had just given them another chance, and everything inside him urged him not to waste it. His jaw clenched tightly as he struggled to control the storm inside him.

Touch me! she screamed silently. Need rippled through her until her skin ached and she was all pulse. She felt violently alone. She wanted to feel the gentleness of his touch, to know him, to ease the emptiness that gnawed at her from the inside.

"We have duties, but stealing this one moment for ourselves, surely that can't be wrong," he whispered. He placed two fingers over her lips, stilling her answer. "But I won't mislead you. There can't be anything more for us than whatever we share in the next few hours. Will that be enough?" Even as he voiced the words, he knew it would never be enough for him. He should walk away, but knew he would not. Reason belonged to the day, the night seemed made for the inner world of passion.

Trembling, she met his gaze. Enough? No, it wouldn't be. But she could accept it. The alternative was to banish her heart into a cold, painful void. The words lodged at her throat and she was afraid to speak. If she said the wrong thing, she knew he'd leave her.

He took her face in his hands, smoothing wispy strands of hair away from her temples. "Give me your answer, love. Do you still want me?"

Ramona turned her head and kissed his palm. Her hands reached out to him and slid gently over his naked torso. "I couldn't walk away even if I wanted to," she whispered.

"I could."

She glanced down the length of him. His jeans were stretched taut. The large, hard bulge beneath his zipper was uncompromisingly male. "What if I said that I want you, very much, and I'd welcome you, but it's not a good idea?''

"I'd kiss you on the forehead and walk back into the den," he answered. His muscles shook slightly as her hands drifted over his bare skin in a feather-light caress.

"Could you really do that?"

"Just barely," he admitted with an unsteady intake of breath. "But not in another few minutes."

"Well, it's too late. I'm not about to let you escape." She met his eyes and smiled, knowing that something very special was about to happen.

Chapter Fourteen

Michael closed the distance between them. "I'm not the type of man who runs away," he murmured in the stillness of the room. "I want to love you tonight, slowly and very thoroughly. I want to hear you cry out my name."

Ramona's blood raced in her veins, and her heart thudded loudly against her side. "Show me, Michael. Show me what you need."

Primitive instincts turned his body to fire, yet somehow he found the strength to slow down. It had to be right for her, too. His hands smoothed over Ramona's shoulders, slipping the robe free of her body. "You're so beautiful," he said with undisguised awe. He would have watched her for a moment longer, but she stepped into his arms.

She rubbed her body against his, an instinctive prelude to the joining that would take place. A sound of anguish, low and primitive, rose from him. It was almost a whisper at first, then grew into a throaty growl of desire.

"Ah," she said with a sigh. "What a wonderful sound. So full of promise."

He lifted her easily, placing his arm under her hot, silky thighs and cradling her with his shoulders. "By the fire. It matches what I feel," he said in a deep voice.

She tumbled against him, enjoying the hardness of his chest and belly and the smoothness of his soft nipples. He whispered in her ear, small cryptic phrases that told her what he'd do. His voice was like a kiss in the darkness. Thoughts came in pieces, jagged and fragmented, interrupted with incendiary sensations that made her quiver.

She nipped his shoulder lightly, then soothed the hurt with her tongue. She felt Michael shudder, and knowing her power over him sent a thrill coursing through her. She buried her face against his neck and was rewarded by the tightening of his arms.

He set her down gently on the Navajo rug that covered the floor near the fireplace, then moved away from her. She whimpered in protest as he disentangled himself from her arms. "Don't be impatient," he murmured. "Before the night is through we'll know each other's secrets. Think of it, Mona."

The rasp of his zipper as he slipped out of his jeans made her shudder. She was exquisitely aware of every sound, every sensation. When he was fully undressed, she gasped, her eyes widening. She ached to feel him inside her.

Expectation sent ripples of heat and desire through her as he lay beside her. Gently he brought her hand down over him. "Touch me, Mona. Know me now as I'll know you." His voice shook.

Her hand closed over him, stroking and loving. He growled softly, his teeth sinking into his lower lip. Eyes heavy with passion, he let her explore him and take pleasure in the knowledge she gained. Beads of perspiration formed on his forehead.

He reached for her breasts, stroking the tightly budded tips, and smiled when she gasped, then moaned softly. "Yes, show me what you feel," he whispered, pushing her back down onto the rug.

She'd had a romantic, girlhood fantasy about him making love to her. In her dreams each invasive stroke was countered and met in an act of perfect mutual surrender. Tenderness and hot sex had been in perfect counterpoise. But as wonderful as it had been in her fantasies, nothing could have prepared her for the emotions and the beauty of the real thing.

It became a journey of discovery that bonded them in a deeper way than a simple physical union ever could. Their souls intertwined, and when he finally prepared himself and moved between her legs, the fire consumed them. Their hearts melted into each other and in a breathless instant they were one heartbeat, one spirit.

He moved away an eternity later. The intensity of emotions that had gripped Michael alarmed him. Even if he couldn't acknowledge it in words, he knew that he'd never be free of the memories they'd forged tonight. The woman was a part of him forever.

"Don't go," she muttered, a peaceful, sleepy smile on her face.

"I'm here, honey," he answered, gathering her to him. "Rest now."

Nestled in the crook of his arm and pillowed by his shoulder, she drifted over the edge into a deep sleep.

He listened to the rhythmic sound of her breathing for a long time. He didn't want to go, but there was no escaping the truth. He'd hoped that once they'd made love, he'd exorcise the needs that drove him. Now he knew just how wrong he'd been. Gently disentangling himself from her, he positioned her head on a pillow from the couch near them.

Michael stood up and silently dressed. Not even the hours until dawn would be fully theirs. He covered Ramona with a blanket and watched her for a moment longer. He couldn't stay. His regret was so intense it manifested itself as a dull ache in his chest and a tightness in his throat. Knowing he could best serve his purpose outside in his truck, he stepped out into the icy wind.

Ramona woke in the middle of the night. Instinctively she reached out for Michael, but only the cold greeted her. He was gone. Gathering her blanket around her, she walked to the window and looked out. Seeing the outline inside Michael's truck, she knew he'd gone back to keep watch.

With a sigh, her gaze traveled around the room. All that empty space, and silence . . . she felt trapped in a yawning void. Nursing the ache in her heart, she walked back to her room.

RAMONA PURPOSELY kept as busy as she could the following day. What they'd shared was over, and it hurt too much to dwell on the memory.

Leaving the cooperative's artists to their work, she made her weekly trip to the bank. She arrived a short time later, parked and started across the pavement to the entrance.

As she passed a large van, three men stepped out, blocking her way. She recognized Chacon immediately. Something about his expression unnerved her, but she forced herself to give him a level gaze. "What do you want?"

"We need to talk," Chacon answered, as the two men with him moved to flank her.

She studied the men with the same contempt she'd have given a cockroach as it emerged from a storm drain. One looked like a portable vault, low to the ground and solid. The other looked like a cartoon strongman, with overinflated biceps and no neck. "And you need Einstein and Socrates here to put the words in your mouth?"

"Don't push it. I'm trying to be a gentleman," he said quietly.

"Really? You do imitations?"

He scowled. "Maybe we ought to go for a little ride."

He nodded to the strongman, who moved a dangerous step closer. Wordlessly he looked down at her.

She was reminded of a vulture over a fresh carcass. "Okay, Chacon. Tell me what you want, then get out of my way."

"I have a deal to make you, and it's one you'll take, if you have any brains."

"Go on."

"I guarantee no labor problems, plus protection from troublemakers, if you sign an agreement and the workers organize a union. You've been making lots of enemies, and right now you could use an ally. Your competitor is as tough as an old cougar, and he's going to eat you alive unless you find a way to balance the fight."

There was no doubt in her mind that he meant George Taylor. Knowing that he was trying to turn her difficulties to his own advantage made her skin crawl. "Why? What's so important about my cooperative? Don't bother denying that greed's behind this somehow."

"You want everything straight? You've got it," he said, squaring his shoulders and challenging her with a glare. "Through you, I'm going to make serious inroads into the Native American community and their growing labor force. If I can get a toehold with your company, the next step will be organizing other tribal industries."

She gave him a thoroughly disgusted look. "You're sleazier than I gave you credit for."

"Don't underestimate me," he countered smoothly. "If you refuse my offer of assistance, you'll be making two very powerful enemies, Taylor and myself. I've got plenty of connections in this county. I could make your life miserable, more so than Taylor ever dreamed of doing."

Ramona took a step closer, standing practically nose to nose with him. "If you think I'm a pushover, try me. You'll find I've got friends, too." She stepped down hard on his instep, then taking advantage of the momentary confusion, slipped past him.

A hand snaked out and yanked her back. Chacon's eyes held a venom that made her shudder. "You need a quick lesson in manners."

Feeling his grip tighten, Ramona began yelling as loudly as she could. Chacon recoiled, jumping back toward the van as people came out of the bank.

"Just what we need," she said, "witnesses!"

"This isn't over, lady, not by a long shot." When the bank's security guard came out, too, Chacon ducked inside the van. The vehicle sped off in a screech of tires, leaving the smell of rubber in the air.

She felt like cheering. Any victory, however small, was something to be treasured.

Ninety minutes later, Ramona started the drive back to the trading post. Although she'd stopped at the county sheriff's office and filed a complaint against Chacon, she wasn't kidding herself. He'd probably have half-a-dozen witnesses swear he'd been someplace else.

By the time she arrived at the trading post, she saw Michael's squad car parked in the front. He'd probably heard what had happened at the bank. As she stepped out of her truck, she watched his expression. Earlier she'd wondered how it would be the next time they met. She hoped for some sign of recognition, a silent acknowledgment of the magic they'd found in each other's arms. Yet as she looked into his eyes, all she saw was a detached curiosity.

"I want you to tell me exactly what happened with Chacon," he said, joining her. "The officer who took the complaint doesn't know your history and might have missed something important."

Her heart aching, she cocked her head toward the house. "Let's go inside. At least it'll be warm in there." Moments later, pacing nervously in her living room, she finished her explanation. "That's about it. Not much more than I told the officer."

Michael mulled things over. "Chacon's playing for high stakes. But if you can tough it out, sooner or later he'll have to crawl back into his hole."

"*Have* to?"

"Snakes need a warm spot and time to shed their skin."

"Okay. I'll cheer myself up with that thought." Ramona smiled slowly. "There's something that still confuses me, though. How did the creep know I'd be going to the bank? I know he didn't follow me there. I'd have noticed that van."

"Do you always do your banking on the same day, at close to the same time?"

Ramona rolled her eyes. "Yeah, I do," she admitted.

"You should avoid patterns like that if possible. You end up making yourself a predictable target."

She walked with him to the door. "Have you come up with any leads so far on those boot prints?"

"Not yet. I'll be checking on some more shoe repair places today, so maybe I'll get lucky." Michael slipped behind the driver's wheel. "You handled Chacon well," he said as he strapped on the seat belt. "But you made him lose face. That might end up costing you. If you see him anywhere again, call me."

As she watched him drive off, a feeling that struggled to make itself understood and acknowledged tore at her heart.

Saya stood in front of the building watching her. The elderly woman's gaze was filled with understanding. "You care about him," she observed slowly. "That won't make things any easier, especially with the burden each of you shoulder."

Ramona thought of denying Saya's words, but knew it wouldn't alter the truth.

"I didn't say that to hurt you," Saya said softly. "But you must remember that the heart isn't always right."

Ramona glanced at the woman, wondering if the statement was also meant as a veiled criticism of the choices her mother had made. "There's one thing I do know. When the heart's involved, pain follows."

"Not always," Saya said gently, "but all too often that's true."

The day passed slowly. With the help of the artisans, fresh supplies were divided according to need. What had been a cold metal shell of a building now rang with creativity and life. Laughter frequently sounded, then died down, only to surface again.

Ramona sat near the window of one of the empty stalls, staring outside at the construction. The easy banter and cheerfulness inside the building had convinced her to bring over her accounting books and set up her office there. Working alongside them, though her job was vastly different, she felt at peace for the first time in months. Progress was now tangible, measurable in facts, not just the development of ideas. When she finished her work, she began glancing through her father's records. Maybe some clue to the location of the clay would appear.

She hated to say goodbye to the others when the evening finally came and she gathered up her ledgers to take home. They had families to go to, but at that moment, she was acutely aware that the cooperative was her life. There was no family to share a meal with at the end of a hard day, or a friendly face waiting to greet her.

Hours later, she sat in the kitchen staring at the enormous meal she'd cooked. The object had been to cheer herself up, but she'd overdone it. The large pot *posole,* a hominy-and-chile concoction, the cheese enchiladas, and the basket of *sopaipillas,* a fried popover sometimes sweetened with honey, were way too much for her. She'd have at least five meals left over.

As she started to set the table, she heard a knock at her kitchen door. Michael stood outside in civilian clothes. "Come in," she said. "Have a seat."

"I won't stay long," he commented. "But I thought you'd like to know. I went to three more shoe repair places and I've drawn a blank. The way I figure it, the man with the boots either went to a cobbler who doesn't advertise, or had his shoes done in Albuquerque or another neighboring town. I'm going to expand the area of my search, but at this point, I'm not too optimistic." As the spicy smell of the food enveloped him, he glanced hungrily at the table. "Expecting company?"

"Not really. I wanted to fix myself a nice meal, only I overdid it. Why don't you stay and eat? Some of this stuff doesn't freeze very well."

"I'd have to eat and run," he warned. "I work a graveyard shift tonight."

"That's fine."

They sat across from each other and began their meal. "Have you ever considered living away from the trading post?" he asked. "I would think you'd be more comfortable after business hours if you stayed at a hotel or rented an apartment."

"First of all, I don't have the budget for that. But more important, I wouldn't think much of myself if I let someone run me out of my home. Think of what you'd do if the situations were reversed."

"It's different."

"Because you're a man?" she challenged, ready to argue.

"No, not at all. Because I'm a cop, and I'm trained to confront problems."

His answer removed the need for any protest. Ramona was almost disappointed. It would have given a safe direction for her thoughts. She remained quiet for several seconds, forcing herself to think of the dangers she'd faced here.

"I wish I were more like my mother. She had courage. I'm a fighter, but that's not really the same thing at all. My mother had a certain calm about her that bred peace. She remained here, sticking by what she believed was right, without ever going on the offensive."

"You have to remember that your mother was a Made Person. That's a very special level of existence. Her peace came from inside, from the knowledge she'd gained from our ways."

Ramona was about to reply when suddenly the lights flickered and went off. Deep inside her something quivered with fear. "I have a flashlight in the drawer. Let me get it."

He stood and walked to the window. "Electricity all over the valley is out. You don't have to worry," he said, his voice oddly toneless. "This happens around here from time to time."

She brought out the flashlight, turned it on and aimed the beam toward the ceiling. The light diffused, illuminating the small room a little. She watched Michael's expression, trying to read his thoughts. His frown was deep, lining his face, and his jaw muscle twitched as he strained to see into the darkness outside.

"The guard is out there someplace," she assured him.

He turned and picked up the flashlight from the table. "Would you mind if I borrowed this for a few minutes? I'd feel a whole lot better if I took a look around."

"You might, but I wouldn't. Trapped in the dark and worried about you isn't what I need now."

"Don't you have another flashlight?"

"Yeah, it's in the nightstand."

"Come on. We'll get that one, then I'll go outside and see if the guard needs anything."

Ramona noticed how Michael had changed his explanation of what he wanted to do, for her benefit. She retrieved a smaller flashlight from the nightstand and then went back with him to the kitchen. As Michael continued toward the door, she saw the determination etched in the rigid cast of his shoulders and the tilt of his head. He was a cop, it was his nature to seek out trouble. She preferred to confront it only when there was no other choice.

Michael started to turn the knob when the window in the adjoining den suddenly lit up in a flash of bright light. Almost simultaneously a blast rocked the house, shattering the window and flinging open the door with a crash. As the concussion slammed against them, Michael was hurled across the room like a doll kicked in the chest.

Gasping for air, Ramona lifted her head off the floor where she'd been tossed. A thin, involuntary cry issued from her throat as she tried to move toward Michael and found her legs wouldn't obey. She crawled, unwilling to give up, and managed to cross a few feet when a second blast tore through the side of the house.

Chapter Fifteen

Ramona tried to stop coughing, but the air was thick with smoke and dust. She forced her eyes to remain open, ignoring the sting, but then realized that wouldn't work. Tears built up in her eyes, hampering her vision even more. "Michael?"

There was silence now, no moaning or other telltale sounds that would reveal where he was and how badly he was hurt. She listened carefully, but the quiet after the blast was so profound she wondered if she'd gone deaf. Ramona brushed aside the pain that corkscrewed through her body. She had to find Michael!

"Michael! Answer me!"

Ramona heard a soft rumbling sound, then silence. Had she imagined it? She gazed ahead blindly. The debris that had clouded the air was beginning to settle. Pieces of stucco dug into her knees as she crawled toward the far side of the kitchen where the table and chairs had been tossed into a heap.

Then she heard the crash of wood and stone. As the air began to clear, she saw Michael ahead, freeing himself from beneath the tabletop and a tangle of chairs.

"Stay where you are," he ordered brusquely. "There's glass all over the floor."

She suddenly realized why her legs and knees hurt like the devil. "Are you okay?"

"I feel like I've been punched by a wrecking ball," he said in a raspy, broken voice.

"I know it was a bomb, two in fact, but how..."

"First let's put out the fire in the den," Michael said, pointing to the adjoining room.

Ramona turned her head and saw the big hole that had been torn through the den's outer wall. Thin white smoke was coming from a splintered piece of wooden frame visible at the margin of the opening. Outside air was fanning the smoldering wood.

She stood up as quickly as possible, the fear of fire supplying her with a burst of energy. Stumbling to the sink, she turned on the tap. Luckily the pipes were intact. Michael appeared at her side and began to fill a big pot he had found thrown to the floor.

Several potfuls later, there was no sign of hot embers, although more than a few gallons of water lay in a pool below the gaping wound in the wall.

Michael stood back, surveying the damage. "Next time, consider waiting until after dessert to bring out the entertainment."

She turned to look up at his weary, dust-stained face and forced a smile. "Ramona's Dynamite Diner. You may never eat anywhere else again."

Michael shook his head slowly. "I've got to check the security guard. See if you can figure out where the source of the explosion was here at the house."

Ramona watched him race out the door, her heart lodged in her throat. What a time to joke! In all the confusion she'd forgotten about the guard posted by the construction site. She'd hired the man in hopes of keeping the equipment safe, but if that had cost him his life... Her heart lurched painfully inside her chest.

She stood near the open doorway, waiting for Michael to appear again. She could see faint puffs of gray smoke off in the distance as the crescent moon illuminated the grounds around the building.

Michael rushed back a few minutes later. "He's fine. He put out a small fire, and is now checking the equipment. When the lights went off, he went to his truck to call in. That's when the first blast went off."

She breathed a sigh of relief. "He's okay, that's the important thing. Equipment can always be replaced."

Michael's face was grim and hard. "I've got to call the bomb squad and get others here fast." He went to the living room, found the telephone still worked, and dialed.

She stared at the ruined den, her heart twisting inside her. There was little left of the room where they'd made love. The rubble and smoke made it look like a scene from hell. So far her feelings for Michael had left little in their wake except sorrow and destruction. Would it ever be different? Even a simple dinner had turned into a battle for life. She shuddered violently.

"The department is sending people over. They'll be here shortly. But there's something you should see." He led her to the front window. People were walking down the driveway, their paths lit by flashlights and headlights from accompanying vehicles.

"Oh, no!" she whispered. What had happened tonight was bound to frighten everyone away permanently. "I might as well go face them."

She saw the Winter Chief approaching and went out to meet him. Her world was slowly coming apart, but she kept her pain hidden from everyone. "We've had some trouble," she managed. Her voice quivered despite her efforts to maintain her composure.

"We heard the explosions," he said quietly. His hair was loose and long. The gray strands stood out and shimmered in the moonlight. His gaze was filled with sorrow. "All this violence..."

"The more I fight, the worse it gets," she admitted with a heavy heart.

"Only because evil fears whatever it can't conquer."

She met his eyes and for a moment saw the grudging respect mirrored there. "The police will be here shortly," she said, surprised and relieved by his reaction. "I appreciate everyone coming to make sure things are under control."

"We came to help you with whatever you need. In the outside world, people often keep away when trouble strikes a neighbor. They sympathize, but from a discreet distance. Our ways demand that we be different. Our strength adds to yours, and in turn, we preserve the best in ourselves."

Ramona opened her mouth, but words wouldn't come.

"Not all approve of what you're doing, but neither do we approve of someone taking away the right of our people to choose."

Emotions too deep for words crowded her throat. "I'm glad you're all here. If you'll come with me, I'll show you what's happened." She led them to the trading post and the area of the blast. "The bomb squad will be here soon. Until they're finished, nothing can be disturbed."

"Then we'll wait. Permanent repairs will take time, but you'll need to seal off that hole right away and keep out the weather."

Saya approached, her expression downcast. "The building, our materials—they're all destroyed."

Ramona stared at her, the words seeping into her consciousness slowly. She'd known about the second explosion, but somehow had assumed it had been directed at the equipment. "Our portable building?" she repeated dully.

Saya nodded. "It's beyond repair."

Ramona's spirit crumbled inside her. For a brief moment, she thought she was going to be sick. Every step of progress seemed to be followed by setbacks. "He must have known that we were working there."

"Maybe we can come up with a new place to work. We were just getting started. We can recover," Saya said.

Saya's courage and support were like a soothing balm that quieted the desperation threatening to engulf her.

Ramona walked toward the building and saw the gaping hole where several side panels had been blasted away. The roof had been torn back like a peeled orange. There had been little fire because the building was of steel, but most of what was inside was damaged or destroyed. "You're right. The building is a complete loss." She bit her bottom lip. "Well, maybe the display area of the trading post will work. It's about this size. If I move the shelving around..."

"Or your construction people could bring you another building," the chief said over the distant wail of sirens that rose in the air.

"I'm not sure. It took us quite awhile to track down one that suited my specifications."

"But the manufacturer should have more than one. And yours was insured, wasn't it?"

Ramona nodded slowly. "Yes, you're right." There *were* alternatives, even though at first she'd been able to see only the destruction.

Saya started to say more, when the sirens grew to an ear-shattering din and flashing red lights appeared down the gravel road. The crowd parted as the emergency vehicles pulled up. "Even our tribal police chief has come," Saya commented. "Things will work out. You'll see."

It took another two hours before the crime-scene unit and the bomb squad had gathered all the bomb fragments and evidence they could. Michael stood with Suazo as the team packed away their gear.

"The people from San Esteban came to help," Ramona said, joining Michael. "Is it all right if we start picking up the rubble and covering the openings? I'm going to have to sleep here tonight."

Michael gave her a surprised look. "You mean you're planning to stay after all this?"

"I have to. If I abandon this place at night that'll give whoever did this free rein to torch or blow up everything else. I can't allow that to happen."

Martin Lucero, one of the cooperative's potters, approached. "I spoke to the others. We won't leave you here alone. We'll all take turns guarding the cooperative until the guilty people are in jail. None of us like being driven off our jobs."

Their loyalty and commitment brought tears to her eyes. Instead of driving her away as her enemy had intended, the evil he'd brought was helping create unity between her and the tribe. "I don't know what to say."

"I do," Suazo said. "None of you are trained for this. What exactly do you expect to accomplish?"

"We're not going to carry guns," Martin said with a shrug. "We'll work in teams, and use CBs. My truck has one, and I'm going to allow anyone on duty here to use it."

Suazo threw his hands up in the air and gave Michael an exasperated look. "This is out of my jurisdiction. It's up to you to keep trouble from escalating."

"I can't stop any of you, nor do I think I should," Michael said to the gathering. "As long as you notify the department if you see an intruder and don't take matters into your own hands, you'll be fine."

Saya stared hard at Suazo. "Are you going to stay and help us board up Ramona's house?"

"Sorry. I've got police business to take care of," Suazo answered, uncomfortable under Saya's direct gaze.

As Suazo walked off, Saya smiled. "No matter. There are enough of us here." Her gaze locked with Michael's.

Michael stared at the sand. "I also have to go. I have to make sure the evidence going to Santa Fe has the paperwork it'll need to be processed. I'm responsible for whatever happens in this district." He turned to Ramona and gave her a level look. "I'll be back tomorrow. You know the emergency numbers to call if you need me."

Ramona watched Michael drive off, then turned her attention to the pueblo residents. They were already hard at work, boarding up the hole the blast had created in her den and picking up debris. Jogging over to them, she picked up a push broom and joined in.

It was close to four in the morning by the time all the outside openings, including windows that had been shattered by the concussion, were sealed up. Her house looked like a set from an old World War II movie, but at least the cold was kept at bay.

Although she knew she'd never be able to get more than two or three hours of sleep before sunrise, she walked slowly to her room. Some rest was better than none. Exhausted, she stripped out of her sooty clothing and crawled between the sheets.

She surrendered easily to sleep, but the peace she'd sought eluded her. Twisted dreamscapes greeted her, offering nothing but terror. She was running, desperately trying to elude a sinister figure stalking her. But she couldn't move fast enough. His face, obscured by the darkness, was nothing more than a skeletal oval with chary holes where the eyes should have been.

By the time she woke up the next morning, she felt more weary than she had been when she'd gone to sleep. Slowly she dragged herself out of bed and went to the kitchen. The door had been patched and the windows covered up, and for that she was grateful. Yet seeing the shambles in the light of the small window that had survived made her cringe.

A knock sounded abruptly at the door, and she jumped and spun around. Ramona took a deep breath, forcing herself to calm down, then went to answer it.

Michael stood outside in civilian clothes, holding a bag from an area fast-food restaurant. "I've got some free time. I thought you could use some more help making repairs and at the same time I could search for anything that might have been overlooked last night."

Thanking him for breakfast, she stepped aside and invited him in. "Have a seat, but first test the chair and make sure it's solid enough to hold you."

"No, let me get to work while you eat." He looked down the hall to the front of the house. "From what I can see, the blast that tore through the den hurled chunks of plaster and wood everywhere."

"It's worse than that. The wall between the den and living room has buckled. I was too tired to care last night, but I'm not sure it's even safe in there."

She ate the pancakes standing up, leaning against the counter. After finishing her breakfast, she went to join Michael. "What do you think? Will the roof cave in on us?"

"No. I've been studying it. The wall between the rooms has been weakened, but the structure hasn't been compromised. That's not a load-bearing wall."

"As long as it's safe, I'm not going to worry about looks. This building will be torn down soon anyway. The cooperative is going to be erected here where the trading post is now. My living quarters will be directly behind it. I'll ask Hector Pratt to fix the windows just so I can look out some of them at least, but I'm going to let the majority go."

"That sounds logical." He glanced around. "Your helpers last night concentrated on the major stuff, but there's plenty left to do. Where do you want to start the cleanup?"

"It doesn't matter to me. Do you have any suggestions?"

"Since the power's still off and there's very little light in here, I think we should start in the living room. The windows facing the front survived, so we'll be able to see what we're doing in there much better."

"Okay. To the front room then." She checked her watch. "The electric company promised to have the power on again by midmorning, so it shouldn't be too much longer."

He went to the living room and stared at the floorboards pensively. "It looks like the blast loosened up everything. There are gaps where the boards have moved apart. Be careful where you step.''

She made her way around carefully. ''I can't just block off this entire side of the house, at least not until I get all of my father's records out of his office.''

''Then we should tack down the boards that are a hazard.''

''Yeah, even though it'll take a while, it beats breaking my ankle by accidentally stepping through a hole.''

They worked side by side, using whatever nails she could find that were long enough. After a few minutes, Michael stopped and looked at Ramona. He had to say it, but he didn't want to make things even worse for her.

She stopped hammering and glanced up as if she'd felt his eyes on her. ''What's wrong?''

''I wanted to remind you that this is the perfect opportunity to search for the missing bullet.'' He hated to see the stricken look on her face, knowing he'd put it there. ''I know that this is a difficult time . . .''

Ramona shook her head and held up a hand. ''If this disaster—'' she waved a hand around the room ''—makes it possible for us to find the killer's trail, then that's a victory for our side.''

Michael nodded. He wanted to offer some comfort, but no words came out of his mouth. Disgusted with himself, he returned to the work. How had things become so muddled between them? Not even words of friendship could be uttered anymore without a rush of guilt.

When the floor was securely in place, they gathered the cardboard boxes that held the debris swept up last night. Ramona worked indefatigably, sifting with gloved hands through the charred rubble of wood, stucco and glass. She studied every particle that she placed in the giant trash bags she'd brought in for that purpose.

Minutes turned into an hour, and she felt a familiar heaviness of spirit settle over her. Using all her willpower, she forced the feelings aside. She would outlive this pain.

Her enemy could only break her if she surrendered, and that was something she'd never do.

"Do you think Chacon was responsible for the bombs?" she asked. "This is just the type of thing I believe he'd do. In his own way, he warned me."

"He's one possibility," Michael said, ripping out several pieces of plaster wallboard that were beyond hope. "Help me look through this. It's been smashed and I want to make sure I don't miss something that falls into the spaces behind the wall studs."

She joined him, methodically inspecting each piece of damaged gypsum board he pried loose. "There's nothing here," she said, unable to hide her disappointment.

"Yeah, well it was worth a try." He gestured to the area at the right of the hole that had been blasted through the outside wall. "We'll clear the debris over there next. You'll also have to get someone to come and check the wiring and make sure it won't cause a fire when the electricity is turned back on."

"I'll take care of that, but do you mind if we patch that spot next to the stovepipe first? The boards they put up last night are great, but there's still a gap, and the breeze shooting through there is freezing."

He nodded. "I feel it. Let's see if we can plug things up without removing what's already there." He studied the small opening the wood hadn't quite covered.

"What are you doing?"

"Trying to see how much of the stucco crumbled behind the pipe. The gap's too wide to stuff with insulation, but maybe we can put a piece of flashing back there. It would be easier than trying to remove the whole stovepipe."

"I'll get you a step stool."

Michael positioned the metal stool as close to the stove as possible. Then he climbed up and pressed his face next to the wall. There was only an inch or so gap between the pipe and the wall, so he had to get at the right angle.

"There's a crumbling spot behind here, and a big nail that wasn't painted over. Whoever painted this house last probably couldn't get a brush behind the stovepipe."

"That was my mother. Don't worry about aesthetics right now. How bad is the damage back there? Can we cover it up easily?"

"I'll poke around the spot with my pocketknife. If it crumbles away, we'll use flashing to cover the entire area." Michael reached over with the tip of his knife, and a piece of plasterboard broke loose, tumbling to the floor. "Check the plasterboard. That wasn't a nail after all."

As Michael climbed down from the stepladder, she retrieved it from the floor. "I think it's a bullet," she said, her voice rising slightly.

Michael dug around the slug that was wedged in a seam between plasterboard panels and freed it with his pocketknife. "I've got it," he said, catching the bullet with his palm. "Maybe it'll give us the clue we need."

She nodded silently. "It'll go to the lab in Santa Fe?"

"I'm going to take it there myself." He carried the bullet to his car and placed it in an evidence pouch, labeling it carefully. "By the way, last night while searching behind the portable building I spotted the same boot tracks we've seen before."

"Michael, we've got to find that guy. If he gets enough chances he's going to end up killing someone, probably me."

Her words cut through him. "We'll find him, and you'll be okay. You've come this far." He slipped behind the driver's seat and switched on the ignition.

She smiled ruefully. "I'll just have to count on my luck holding out."

As he drove down the driveway, he saw her reflected in the rearview mirror. Her vulnerability touched him. She was strong, but even strong women needed someone to lean on sometimes.

He glanced at the evidence pouch on the seat beside him. So much of his future hopes would depend on the answers Ramona found when her father's killer was unmasked. The truth was often cruel. Instead of a new beginning, Ramona could end up finding heartbreak and a pain too intense to endure without creating permanent barriers around her heart.

He brushed the thought from his mind. One step at a time. First, he had a job to do. He'd handle the rest as it came.

IT WAS CLOSE TO NOON when Ramona went outside and watched the men unloading the panels for the new portable building and dismantling the wrecked one. At least Pratt had been able to track down a comparable replacement. Maybe her luck was changing.

Saya stood beside her. "We'll take care of setting ourselves up again. We've brought our own supplies, so we can get started right away. The cooperative can reimburse us later."

"I appreciate that," Ramona said. "I've still got to clear out part of the trading post and seal off the front rooms. The wiring's been damaged."

"Then you take care of that and leave this workshop to us," Saya said confidently. "We'll be fine."

Ramona went back inside, dreading the job ahead. The rooms had been cleaned up, but now she had to gather all her father's records and move them out of his office. She stacked everything into boxes, then stopped, staring thoughtfully at the ledger on the top. She'd searched through these books just the day before and hadn't found any clues. Nothing balanced, but that was to be expected. Her father had never been much of a bookkeeper.

A new idea formed slowly in her mind. Maybe what she should have done was study the books in the way her father might have viewed them, not adding up figures, but looking at the entries themselves.

She carried the boxes to her old bedroom, which was now going to serve as her home office. Even though the possibility of uncovering a clue filled her with energy, the hours passed slowly. Finally she began looking through his last inventory book. The volume contained records of purchases, trades and current stock. Her father had excelled at this type of record keeping. Each entry had been dated, and the amount paid out or received, faithfully recorded by each item.

As she leafed through the pages, something niggled at the back of her mind. Disturbed by a queer feeling that she'd missed something, Ramona started to look through it again. She placed the book on her lap and moved to the chair near the window. She'd only gone through the first few pages when she saw Michael's squad car come up the driveway. Closing the ledger, she went downstairs and met him by the kitchen door.

"Any luck?" She knew it was too soon. Still she couldn't stop hoping that maybe he'd learned something from the bullet.

"I delivered it to the lab personally," he said, and saw the expectant gleam in her eye extinguished. "Give it a few days," he added gently. "What about you? How are things going over here?"

She told him about the ledger. "It's meticulously detailed, but I think I'm missing something. Then again, maybe I just want to find something so badly, I'm imagining things."

"May I take a look?"

She hesitated. The trading post had been her father's passion. He'd loved the small business. Allowing someone who wasn't sure of his innocence to browse through his books didn't quite seem right.

"It can't hurt him now, no matter what I might or might not see there."

She met his gaze, still locked within herself. Finally she nodded. "Okay. Let me go get it. Maybe you can tell me if I *am* imagining things."

He was sitting at the table when she returned. Placing the book in front of him, she pulled up a chair and sat down beside him. "His inventory books are the only ones with legible writing. Well, legible for him."

They went through the first twenty-five pages slowly, comparing each entry against the rest, and looking for a change in the buying-and-selling pattern. Then as they reached the middle of the book, Michael stopped and stared at the page. "These dates are out of sequence, and I think I saw the same one twice."

She studied the page carefully. "The handwriting's wrong, too. Look at the way the capital *G*s are formed. My father used two loops at the top. This one looks more like a large lower case *g*."

"Could it be your mother's writing?"

She shook her head. "My mother's style is radically different. It's smaller and much more precise, like printing that's been joined together."

Michael took the book closer to the center of the room and held it beneath the light. For several seconds he said nothing, leafing the pages back and forth. "These three pages aren't part of the original binding," he said at last. "They've been skillfully glued in place and made to look like they're part of the book. But they don't belong here. They represent dates that appear again elsewhere in the ledger, but with completely different entries."

She took the book from his hands and studied the sheets he'd pointed out. "You're right. Something else is interesting about these, too. The entries were made about a month before my father's death."

"This is a breakthrough, Mona," he said quietly. "If these pages didn't contain something very important to your father, he wouldn't have taken such pains to hide them."

She stared at the ledger, then up at Michael. "The reason he was killed may be staring us right in the face."

Chapter Sixteen

Ramona studied each entry, unable to think of any expla-nation that would clear up the mystery. "I know that my dad never dealt in copper or silver. Why acquisitions like this would be of interest to him is beyond me."

"What we need to find out is whose ledger these came from," he said quietly.

"But how?"

"I'm not sure yet. We can start by compiling the names of people and firms your father did business with. You have the rest of his records, right?"

"Yeah, but a list like that is going to take some time. My father's accounts were a nightmare, believe me."

"Then you might as well get started," he said with a shrug. "As a cop, you develop certain instincts. Right now, my gut feeling is that we've uncovered something that's going to open up all sorts of possibilities. Mind if I use the phone?"

"Go ahead. I'll go get the other books and start listing companies."

Michael waited until she'd left the room, then dialed the lab in Santa Fe. Officially, test results on the bullet they'd found wouldn't be made available to him for days. But Ernie Romero, one of the techs, was from San Esteban Pueblo. Ernie and he had grown up together, their fami-lies longtime neighbors. Ordinarily he would have never asked for a special favor, but there was nothing ordinary about this case.

"Ernie, this is Michael."

"Yo, Mickey," came the cheerful voice at the other end.

Michael cringed. He hated the nickname, and Ernie had used it to tease him ever since grade school. "All right, have you got the test results? I've already agreed to buy you lunch. Now give."

"You're darned right you'll buy me lunch. And dinner. And hey, how about a new car while we're at it? No, better yet. You fix up that dandy truck of yours, and then give it to me as a gift."

Michael groaned. Ernie wouldn't let up now. "Look, I really need this."

"Of course. That's why the price is going up as we speak. It's a *favor*. Quick, Mickey, bribe me fast, or my dreams will get too large for you to handle."

"I promise I won't break your nose next time I see you," Michael said very matter-of-factly.

There was a pause. "Yeah, that seems reasonable. Now how about throwing in a week's worth of dinners, too?"

Michael expelled his breath in a hiss. "Deal. Now tell me what I need, or I'll rescind my offer not to bust you in the nose."

Ernie laughed, revealing how much he thought of the threat. "Okay, Mickey. This is the report you'll be getting in six days after it's typed. Forensics show that John Ortiz was probably killed by a late 1800s Western revolver, a Colt .44. The composition of the bullet fragments found in the victim's skull was identical to the bullet you found. We believe the round you gave to us passed through John Ortiz, then wedged in the wall."

"I wonder if the murder weapon might still be around. Nowadays, you get a terrific price for something like that. Any collector would give his right arm to have it," Michael said thoughtfully.

"Tracking it down is your problem, old buddy. Mine's to ferret out these little gems of information so I can hold you hostage."

"Ernie," Michael said with a chuckle, "give me a break. You're not exactly divulging classified information to the press. Since I requested a rush, I'd get this in less than a week. You're helping me get a faster start, that's all."

"I also have another typed report I'm supposed to drop by your office later today. I *was* going to read the pertinent points to you over the phone, that is, until you pointed out how unappreciated I am."

"Okay, okay. Your prepaid dinners will be at Rosie's Café. How's that? I know you've wanted a date with her for months. If you're there every night for a week, even you should be able to get her attention."

"I'll take it. See? I knew I could get something worthwhile from you after all." Ernie paused and Michael could hear papers rustle. "It's the report on the bullets you retrieved after the sniper incident. It concludes that they were fired from an AR-15 caliber assault rifle."

"I knew that."

"Yes, but now it's official. Also, did you know that George Taylor used to own an extensive antique gun collection? It could have included a Colt .44, though I have no way of knowing for sure."

"That's great information. Did you learn that from your father? He was into gun collecting, wasn't he?"

"Naw, he never had enough money to own any real antiques. He was a gunsmith though, and got the opportunity to work on some nice old pistols. He knew all the collectors in the area, and kept in contact with them just in case he needed parts."

Ernie's father had passed on awhile back, so Ernie's memory would have to serve him now. "Any other collectors who stick in your mind?" Michael asked.

"No, that's about it. If I think of anyone else, I'll let you know." There was a pause. "Hey, how about letting me help you out?"

Michael cringed, knowing how Ernie felt about police work. Had he been able to pass the physical, Ernie would have joined the department instead of becoming a tech. "What do you have in mind?"

"I know guns, I learned a lot from my dad. If I said I was going to reopen the business and was contacting the collectors my dad had dealt with, no one would give it a second thought. Think about it. It would be easy for me to ask Taylor about his collection without tipping your hand."

"I don't know... it's true that he might not be on his guard around you."

"Then you should jump at the offer. I'll even tape the conversation for you. Does that buy me *two* weeks at Rosie's?"

"Okay, you've got it. How soon can you set this up?"

"Is this afternoon soon enough? I'll skip my lunch so I can take off early."

"Sounds fair. You'll probably eat me into the poorhouse these next two weeks anyway."

"Yeah, and it starts tonight. Just think of how hungry I'll be by then."

Michael placed the receiver down, then turned. Ramona was sitting at the kitchen table, accounting books open. "I'll cover one of those weeks," she said. "It's only fair."

Michael smiled. "Since I'm not sure how much you pieced together, let me fill you in." He gave her the details.

"I remember a firearms display case in George Taylor's office, but I couldn't tell you what was in there. I only noticed it in passing."

"Ernie and I are going to go there this afternoon."

"I have a better idea. Let your friend go to Taylor's office. While he keeps Taylor busy, we'll walk around Taylor's store and take a real good look at his merchandise. I know he sells guns and I wouldn't put it past him to sell a weapon he'd used in a crime. Remember that he doesn't know we discovered my father's body."

"Good plan. Let's do it. I'll go meet with Ernie, fill him in, and work out a few details with him."

After Michael left, Ramona continued trying to compile a list of people and businesses her father had dealt with on a regular basis. The chore was tedious and as incomplete as her father's records. When Michael arrived shortly after two o'clock, she was eager to go.

He turned down the offer to take her pickup, insisting they ride in his beat-up truck. "It might create suspicion if Taylor looked out and recognized your truck," Michael explained. "He won't give this old thing a second glance."

"That's true, unless he's into relics."

"I prefer the term *classics*."

As he pulled into the parking area of Taylor's business in Santa Fe he saw Ernie's car parked near the entrance. "One thing you can count on—when it comes to this type of work, Ernie's never late."

Ramona entered the store with Michael, making sure that Taylor was not where he could see them. There weren't any security cameras to worry about, most small New Mexico businesses relied on locked cabinets and big mirrors. The two salespeople behind the center counter were busy helping other customers, so they had the freedom to browse at leisure. "So far, luck's on our side," she whispered.

The guns, kept behind thick glass, were mostly present-day revolvers and pistols. Several rifles were displayed upright on the wall, chained together through their trigger guards.

Ramona glanced at Michael. She knew something about pistols, but very little about rifles and shotguns. Although she was virtually certain that the gun used to kill her father wasn't there, she wasn't so sure about the sniper's weapon.

Michael shook his head slightly, then gestured across the salesroom floor. "There's his Southwestern art collection. Let's go take a look."

Ramona walked over to the large glass display case. The first few shelves held highly crafted squash blossoms, heishi strands, and turquoise-and-silver bracelets. The middle shelves contained a large selection of fetishes, and the bottom section was reserved for expensive polychrome-and-black Indian pottery. But it was the fetishes that held Michael's attention.

Ramona followed his gaze. "None of those look like the one on top of the cairn. I remember it very well."

"But the style and stones used are very similar," he said. "I think these are made by Barton Perez."

A young salesclerk approached. As her eyes fell upon Michael, there was no mistaking the appreciative gleam there. "Can I help you?"

"I was just commenting that this looks like the work of a man I know, Barton Perez."

"It is." She smiled quickly. "He's one of our finest artists. We have quite a few of Perez's recent works featured here."

"Any more fetishes?" Ramona asked.

"No, I'm sorry, that's it."

Probably sensing that neither of them would be buying anything, the saleswoman moved to another customer near the oil paintings.

Ramona and Michael took one last look at everything as they slowly retraced their way to the doors. When they reached the parking lot, Michael noted that Ernie's vehicle was still parked there. "It looks like Ernie's visit might pay off. If he made it past the first few minutes, he's got a chance of getting something for us. We agreed he had until three-thirty before I went looking for him."

They drove out of Santa Fe toward San Esteban and parked off the road near the entrance to the Santa Fe Opera. "He'll meet us here," Michael said, checking his watch. "Did you notice anything unusual about the shelf that had the fetishes?" Michael waited a minute, then continued when she didn't answer. "All the other shelves had a light covering of dust. That was the only one that had been dusted recently."

"I didn't notice." She gave him a sheepish smile. "I guess out here I've grown immune to dust. I don't even see it unless it's so thick that you can write messages on the furniture and save paper."

He laughed. "Yeah, dust is a way of life out here." He gestured down the road. "Here comes Ernie now."

Michael stepped out of the truck and went to greet his friend. Ramona hung back, not wanting to intrude yet wanting to be close enough to overhear. Curiosity was killing her.

Ernie gave her a wide grin as if reading her mind, then came over. "Well, it paid off. I know for a fact that Taylor owns an AR-15 assault rifle. It was inside his display case, and I believe it has been recently cleaned." A thoughtful frown appeared on his face. "But then, all those guns appeared to be well kept."

"What about collector's items. Does he have antique Western pistols, like a Colt .44?"

"I didn't see any antique guns in his case, and when I asked him, he said he'd sold off his collection years ago. He mentioned that some of the guns were disassembled and sold for their parts. I hope you don't end up trying to track down one of those. I have a feeling that would be a nightmare. Gunsmiths will scrounge around for parts to refurbish a weapon, but once it leaves the shop, it can end up almost anywhere." He handed Michael a small cassette tape with the information. "Here it is word for word. About the only other thing I found out that might be useful is that one of our own people is a collector. Barton

Perez is supposed to have a small gun collection. Taylor doesn't think he owns anything that's worth serious money, just some modern-day pieces, but you never know."

"I don't think Barton has the financial resources to buy a piece as expensive as a Colt .44."

"That doesn't mean he doesn't have the old pistol, Michael," Ramona interjected. "If Taylor wanted to get rid of it, he might have sold it dirt cheap."

Michael rubbed his jaw. "We really need to know if a Colt .44 was ever part of Taylor's collection. I bet he has detailed records someplace for insurance purposes, if no other reason. The problem is getting him or his insurance company to hand those over. Neither has to cooperate without a court order, and we don't have enough to take to a judge."

"Well, if you need my help again, call," Ernie said. "I'm off to collect my first dinner at Rosie's. I should tell you I'm going to go right down the menu. I'm just starving." His eyes gleamed mischievously as he glanced at Michael. "I'll make sure Rosie knows you're picking up the tab."

Michael watched his friend drive away. "Ernie's going to enjoy this immensely."

"I hope you're going to let me pick up half the tab. He sounds like he's going to try and rival the national debt."

Michael laughed. "No, Ernie's okay. In the end, he'll be fair. That's just the way he's wired." Michael walked back with her to his truck. "You know, that dusted shelf still bothers me. There's a chance Taylor engineered that phony shrine and left Barton's fetish there, hoping to implicate him."

"Could be. But we now know that Barton Perez and Taylor have business connections. Maybe their ties go beyond that."

"I wish I could get a court order to inspect that AR-15. But without solid evidence to present the judge, I'll get turned down. The problem is that there are two ways of looking at this. You could maintain that Taylor wouldn't actually display a weapon he'd used to shoot up your living room. Then again, you could argue that he was safer leaving it in plain sight."

"Okay, then let's forget that for a while. Maybe we should try to take a look at Barton's gun collection instead."

"Good idea. His studio is on our way. Let's go over there right now."

"Do you think he'll cooperate, particularly since he'll know he doesn't have to?"

"He's got more to gain by cooperating. If he's emphatic about not showing me his collection, then he knows I'm going to wonder why."

"Shall I look around while you keep Barton distracted?"

He cringed. "No, don't. His home is adjacent to his studio and his mother still lives there. Getting thrown out isn't going to help. Just stand by and follow my lead. Opportunities turn up when you least expect them."

They pulled out onto the highway leading north and drove past a van that was sitting off the road farther ahead.

"That van!" Ramona shouted, turning around in the seat. "It's Chacon's, I'm sure."

Michael glanced in the mirror. "You sure?" Seeing her nod, he added. "Can you get the license number?"

Ramona recited the three-letter, three-number sequence, then wrote it down on the back of a receipt she pulled from her purse.

"Now check it against the numbers I've got in the glove compartment inside the little notebook. I've made a list of all the principal suspects," Michael said.

"It's Chacon's, all right. What do you think he's up to?" Ramona looked over at Michael.

"Following us, I suppose." He glanced into the mirror. "At a discreet distance, of course."

Ramona turned around and saw the van far behind them. "Do you think he knows what we're doing, or is involved with Taylor in some way?"

"I'm not sure. I think it's time I did a full background check on him. When we get a chance, I'm going to pull over and use a phone."

A short time later, Michael pulled into a gas station. While the attendant pumped the gas, Michael made a quick call to the department and requested that a search be done through NCIC. The National Crime Information Center was the most comprehensive federal data base around.

Ramona kept watch as they continued their drive, but the van never reappeared. Finally they arrived at Barton's studio. As Michael parked by the side of the building, an elderly woman Michael recognized as Perez's mother came outside. She held her badly scarred hands against her chest protectively.

"Barton's not here," she said, not looking up. "He's away on business. Come back in three days. Okay?" When she drew closer and saw Michael and Ramona, her features hardened.

"What do you want with my son?" Her eyes narrowed as they settled on Ramona. "You've caused enough damage to this family. I don't want you here." Her gaze shot daggers as she turned to Michael. "And why are you with her? You know what her father did to your family." Not giving him a chance to reply, she spun on her heels and went back inside the home.

"What happened to her hands?" Ramona asked in a hushed whisper.

"The family has never spoken of it. All I know is that she used to be a potter. People said it was an accident with a kiln."

"That family has been through a great deal. I don't blame her for lashing out. It makes things more bearable, if you can hold on to anger."

He started the drive back to the trading post. "Is that the way you feel about the person who's trying to run you out?"

"Anger helps, but I have no one I can focus those feelings on. It would be easier if I knew that Chacon was behind everything, or that Barton was guilty of the Tewa-related threats and Chacon for the rest. Or even if Taylor had hired them both, and was the one ultimately responsible. There's a certain peace of mind that comes from knowing who your enemy is. Instead of being afraid, you can afford to bury that under anger."

He parked in front of the trading post and shifted to face her. "I'm going to go back to my office and call the state crime lab. They said I'd get the results of the bomb fragments they found by today. If they're ready, I'll be going to Santa Fe to get the report. That'll save me a good three days."

"It takes that long to mail it to you?"

"No, but it takes that long for them to fill out all the reports that go along with a mailing." He shrugged. "Red tape. What are your plans?"

She considered it for a few moments. "I'm going to track down jewelry outlets that sold copper and silver thirteen years ago. I'll then cross-reference against the names I got from my dad's ledgers. Maybe some will match." She paused. "But I'm not sure how to check on the ones mentioned in the ledgers that aren't in business anymore."

"Try the county courthouse records. But begin with the easier leads first, like cross-referencing against the phone book ads. One lead often takes you to another. By the time you work your way through the list, it's possible you'll know who the ledger pages belonged to. But remember to be very careful."

"I will. You never know what'll crawl out when you overturn a few rocks."

"This afternoon, I'll start a search of gun collectors who might have done business with Taylor, and get the story on Chacon. I'll probably be out of the area the rest of the day, but I'll alert the department. If you have any problems, call in. Someone will respond to your call quickly, I guarantee it."

Ramona walked back inside the trading post. The kitchen door was still difficult to open, though Pratt and his men had done their best to hang it right. The reminder of what had happened sent a cold chill up her spine. She'd tread very carefully this afternoon.

Later Ramona checked the list she'd made against the telephone book's business section. Only one name matched those in her father's records. After letting Saya and the other members of the cooperative know where she'd be just in case of trouble, she set out.

A short time afterward, she arrived inside the shop, a wholesale business. She'd decided to first introduce herself as the cooperative's business representative, then ask the questions. If they saw her as a potential client, not someone who was just taking up their time, she might have better results.

An elderly man came out and beamed her a smile. "You're Ramona Ortiz," he said.

"Do we know each other?"

"My name is Jerry Gage. I had a visit from a man named Chacon," he said with a chuckle. "He told me that you might drop by. You were going to need to find wholesalers." Gage shrugged. "He didn't want me to do business with you. Said the union would appreciate my support, and be very disappointed if I sold you any supplies."

She bit back her anger, knowing it would serve no purpose now. "He's a highly unpleasant person. I'm very sorry that you had to deal with him."

"I didn't deal with him very long. I threw him out. I'm sixty-two years old. At my age, I don't have the time to waste on punks, no matter how well dressed they are."

Ramona smiled. "He picked on the wrong person, didn't he?"

"The guy's a little slow on the uptake, but I think he got the idea." Gage led her to an office in the back and offered her a chair. "Now what can I do for you?"

"I'm trying to track down a silver wholesaler who dealt with the trading post during my father's time," she said, deciding to get to the point. The man had been open with her and deserved the same courtesy.

"I knew your dad, but he didn't deal much with me," Jerry answered. "I wasn't much of a salesman then, I'm afraid. I hope that isn't going to keep you from doing business now. I can give you good prices and I sure would like to make a nonverbal statement to that idiot Chacon."

She chuckled. "Believe me, we'll do business, Jerry."

"Tell me something. Why are you trying to find this wholesaler your father dealt with? Does he owe you money?"

"No. Ledgers show that the trading post had some silver and copper in stock at the time of my dad's disappearance. But my father normally didn't deal with those items. Since I don't have any record of the purchase, it's remained a puzzle to me, and I wanted to clear it up."

"Settling the past is a good thing." The man's eyes gleamed with curiosity. "As long as it doesn't mess up your life in the trying."

"The cooperative is the future, I know that. But the past also needs to be dealt with."

He nodded thoughtfully. "I don't know anything about your father's business, but I can suggest a link between the two metals. Copper is alloyed with silver to make it more durable. But the more copper in the silver, the less valuable the silver is. Jewelers can determine the purity of the silver with certain tests, but the layman probably wouldn't notice the difference unless the copper content started showing up in the color.''

''You've helped me more than you know,'' she said, shaking his hand. ''I'll be back with an order sometime in the near future. You can count on the cooperative's business.''

As she walked to her truck, she felt her heart racing. She'd finally found the reason why the ledger sheets were in her father's records. Her father must have discovered that an unscrupulous silversmith had been duping the others. He'd stolen the pages as proof so he could discredit the silversmith. But that action had probably cost him his life.

Ramona drove to the trading post, thankful that her persistence was starting to pay off. What little there was left of the day went by slowly. Michael was out of town and there was no one to share the news with. Missing him much more than she would have wanted, she settled down to work.

IT WAS NIGHT by the time Michael arrived at the trading post. He climbed out of his car slowly. He shouldn't have been here, he should have telephoned instead. All he was doing was making it more difficult for himself. But he wanted to see Ramona. He'd worried about her today.

When she opened the door, his gaze drifted over her and his mouth went dry. Her cream-colored sweater and snug jeans accentuated the gentle curves and softness he'd loved so thoroughly just a few nights before.

''I came to trade information,'' Michael said, clearing his throat. How long had he stood there just watching her?

Ramona ushered him inside, a tiny smile on her face. ''Take a seat and let's compare notes.'' She filled him in immediately, unable to contain her excitement.

''The more we uncover, the more complex the picture gets. For the moment though, Chacon's behind-the-scenes involvement worries me most. I discovered he was in the marines, and competes regularly in metallic silhouette rifle events. He's a crack shot. It makes me wonder where he was the night all the shooting started."

"He's slippery. It'll be hard to get any evidence against him." She started to say more when the loud, mournful wail of a coyote shattered the night. The sound was so cold it penetrated her bones like an icicle. Ramona shuddered. "I know coyote's supposed to bring us news, but he really should work on his delivery," she joked halfheartedly.

The cry continued like an insidious chant, reverberating inside Michael's head. "There's something wrong with that animal. I've heard coyotes all my life, but that sound...it's not...natural." The sound rose and fell, fluctuating between guttural snarls and a shrill monotone.

Glad he was still in uniform, he thumbed back the safety strap on his revolver. "I'm going out there and take a look around. Whatever's out there is too close to the house."

"It's just an animal. What could it do?"

He saw the worry in her eyes. There was so much he would have liked to have done to remove that look from her eyes. As a slash of heat snaked through him, he squelched the thought.

His hand drifted over to his weapon; the cold touch of the revolver helped him refocus his thinking. Ramona offered him warmth and softness, but the real world held little of either. "I'll be back. Lock the door and stay inside."

Ramona saw the night quickly envelop him as he left the circle of light around the porch. Time passed slowly, and with each second, her fear grew. Her heart was hammering, and her hands were clammy despite the chill of the winter's night. The coyote's wail, like a song of evil, continued without respite as Michael failed to return.

Chapter Seventeen

Unable to stand the uncertainty any longer, Ramona grabbed a flashlight from the drawer, unlocked the door and slipped quietly outside. She moved from under the porch light quickly into the darkness. Then, reaching the shadowed corner of the building, she stopped and waited for her eyes to adjust. The flashlight was only in case of an emergency. If Michael had encountered trouble, she didn't want the beam of light to give away her position.

She listened carefully between the cries of the coyote, hoping to find out where Michael was. Hearing footsteps ahead, she crept toward the sound. Then suddenly the footsteps and coyote cries stopped. Uncertain, she hesitated. She'd heard someone or something moving, and obviously they'd heard her. Deciding to take a chance, she held the flashlight away from her body as far as her arm could reach. Then, with a flick of her thumb, she switched it on and aimed it toward the spot where she'd heard the footsteps.

The light cut through the darkness and she saw the barrel of a gun pointed directly at her. A figure crouched silently in the shadows. As her heart leaped to her throat, she heard Michael swear.

"I told you to stay at the house!" Michael lowered the barrel instantly.

"You were gone so long! I thought you might need my help."

"I could have shot you!" he managed. He stepped forward, though at the moment he wasn't certain if he wanted to haul her into his arms or throttle her.

"Stop! Don't move!" Her voice was sudden and harsh, compelling him to halt. The beam of her flashlight settled on a small cord stretched taut between two small shrubs. "Down there in front of you. There's a string or trip wire."

Michael crouched, aiming his own light at it. "The wire's attached to a cyanide cartridge. It's a trap used for killing coyotes. If I'd caught the cord with my boot, it would have fired the gas right up into my face."

Her stomach fell. Starting to shake violently, she concentrated on trying to hold her flashlight steady. Despite her efforts, the beam continued to jitter. With determination, she grasped it with both hands. "Now what? We can't leave it here. And what about the coyote?"

"The wailing came from a recording on a cheap cassette player. Someone meant to bring me or you out here to investigate so we could get hung up on this."

She shuddered and this time made no attempt to hide it. "Do you know how to deactivate that thing?"

"Yeah." He reached into his shirt pocket and pulled out a ballpoint pen. He unscrewed it quickly, removing the ink cartridge in the middle. "These contraptions have a safety device. If the pin's in there, it can't fire."

"You're going to use the ink cartridge in lieu of the pin?"

"A nail works better, but the ink cartridge will do the job, I think. Stay back just in case, though. Cyanide gas is deadly."

She moved to the side. "Tell me where to aim my flashlight."

He knelt beside the trap that had been hidden in the middle of a young bush. "Keep the light on it while I slip this through and block off the firing pin."

Ramona held her breath as he worked. "Does it fit?"

"Yeah, but I've got to get it just right. Keep the light steady."

She was trying, but her hands were so clammy, perspiration made the plastic cylinder slippery. A terrible quaking seemed to start at her limbs and corkscrew all through her. She took a deep breath and forced her body to grow still.

"Okay." Michael stood up slowly, holding the lethal trap. In the half-light it looked like Fourth-of-July fireworks. "Now I've got to bag both this and the tape recorder for evidence. Why don't you go inside and wait for me there? I'll only be a few minutes, and there's nothing more you can do now."

"No way. I can at least hold the light for you and make myself useful until you're ready to go in."

Michael started to argue, then saw the determined expression on her face. Her efforts to protect him had almost resulted in her death. He wasn't sure she realized how close she'd come to getting shot. And by his own hand. He stared at the trap he'd almost unknowingly triggered. Tonight they could have easily lost each other.

He worked quickly, remaining silent as he tagged the evidence. Too many words, too many feelings crowded his throat to risk speaking.

A few minutes later, he walked with her back to the house. Their brush with death made him acutely aware of everything about her. Her softness tempted him, appealing to every male instinct he possessed. An intense hunger thrummed inside him. Death was oblivion, but passion and love were life at its best.

As they entered the warmth of her kitchen, she turned and faced him. "The cooperative was my dream, but it's nearly cost you your life. I'm the target, but you've been caught up in the danger. Leave, Michael, and get as far from me and the trading post as you can."

The pain mirrored in her eyes almost broke him. Forces as primitive as the desert night compelled him to take her into his arms. "We've shared danger, but through our own choice. We've shared other things, too, through choice, and . . . need."

"Yes," she whispered, answering the unspoken question in his eyes.

Passion ignited his blood. He took Ramona's mouth with his own, demanding, invading, ravaging. Her response was swift and wild. Her undisguised hunger sent wave after wave of heat ripping through him, each one hotter than the one before.

He lifted her into his arms with an easy strength that reminded Ramona how utterly masculine he was. She sighed his name, her mouth pressed against his neck. "Where?" Michael felt the tip of her tongue working lazy circles down to his shoulders as her fingers worked the buttons of his shirt loose.

"Options are narrowing the more you do that," he said, his voice nothing more than a raw murmur in the stillness.

"Down the hall to my old room, if we can make it that far," she said, smiling.

She slipped her hand inside his shirt, loving the flat muscles of his chest and stomach.

As her fingers tickled the flesh just above his belt, he sucked his breath in. "Forget it. Long and slow is out of the question tonight."

Michael laid her gently on the kitchen table, her legs bent at the knees and draped over the edge. As his gaze drifted lovingly over her, her eyes gleamed up at him in slumberous passion. A trail of fire wound itself around him, squeezing tightly. She looked vulnerable, yet so ready for him.

As he worked his belt loose, he watched Ramona slide her jeans and panties downward, letting them slip to the floor. Seeing her naked from the waist down, lying back, legs invitingly open, sent a shock wave spiraling through him. The drive to take her pounded through him in a rhythmic and primitive cadence that turned his blood to liquid flame.

He came forward and rained soft, wet kisses on her stomach, caressing her tenderly until she writhed feverishly. The final, dewy proof of her desire shattered his restraint. Quickly retrieving what he needed to protect her, he lifted her buttocks in his hand and thrust deep.

Wild with a love too long repressed, she absorbed him completely, meeting his movements with an urgency that matched his own.

Her sweet flesh consumed him. She clung to his wrists, lost to the moment. With a soft growl, he bent down and filled her mouth with his tongue, imitating the penetration that joined their lower bodies.

Ramona whimpered, her body ablaze with fires. The warm ache that had started deep inside her exploded into sparks of lightning that showered her senses. Lost in a haze of pleasure, she cried out his name.

Michael thrust hard, his passion beyond control, and filled her with the essence of life. Shudders racked his body as he accepted her final surrender with his own.

Trembling and sated, seconds later, he tenderly gathered her to him. His lips brushed her forehead as he scooped her into his arms. "Now we'll try long and slow," he said, carrying her to her bedroom.

There, in the house where childish fantasies of him had first teased her imagination, she learned of a reality far more precious than dreams.

RAMONA WOKE UP SLOWLY. An emptiness more chilling than the cold desert night greeted her as she discovered she was alone. His absence attested to the barriers the past continued to wedge between them. Her throat constricted as she accepted what could not be changed.

Blinking to clear her vision, she checked her watch. It was a little past six in the morning. Time to get up. Ramona showered quickly and dressed, then went downstairs. As she entered the kitchen, she was surprised to find a pot of freshly brewed coffee. He'd straightened the room, too, picking up her jeans from the floor, folding them and setting them on the chair. As she glanced at the kitchen table, she saw a faded snapshot there. A note, scribbled on a scrap piece of paper, was next to it.

Curious, Ramona picked up the photo, then suddenly smiled. It was of Michael and her, taken years ago at the State Fair. Her mother had driven a group from the pueblo down to Albuquerque for the two-week festival. She remembered that day vividly. She'd left her wallet in the restroom where it had been promptly stolen. Knowing her parent's budget was restricted, she hadn't said anything about it. Instead, she'd begged off the rides, telling everyone she wasn't feeling well. Michael had somehow guessed the truth, and without ever saying that he knew, had shared his money with her the rest of the day. The photo had been taken later that afternoon by one of Michael's friends.

She fingered the worn photo, noting the creases. He'd folded it up and kept it in his wallet all these years. She read the tiny note that had accompanied it. All it said was, "I'd like this back."

A lump the size of a tennis ball formed at the back of her throat. He was telling her, without saying the words, that he cared and always had. Tears fell down her face. Their hearts drew them together, but fate continued to stand in their way. Longing tore through her, but she forced the feeling aside. Wishing for the impossible accomplished nothing.

She placed the photo in her shirt pocket, then poured some coffee into a thermos. It was time to go out to the portable building and set up an office near the artisans.

It was midmorning when Saya came to Ramona's cubbyhole to visit. "We've heard you working in here all morning, and that calculator hasn't stopped. How is the cooperative doing?"

"Everything is within budget." Ramona leaned back in the small office chair she'd bought. "And we have orders to fill. I called and confirmed with buyers I'd contacted awhile back."

"Good. We've had several more potters and two painters join us. I gave them the agreement to sign yesterday and I got them set up. I hope you don't mind."

"Not at all. I'm just sorry that I wasn't here to welcome them. Were you able to get supplies?"

Saya smiled and gestured to an envelope tacked up on the bulletin board. "That's the invoice for what we had to spend to buy more acrylics for the artists. The rest we already had in."

"I've found another wholesaler who I think is going to be a big help. He's eager to do business with us." She offered Saya some coffee from the thermos.

"No, thanks. I need to have a steady hand for my work, and caffeine doesn't help." She gave Ramona a long, thoughtful look. "I know you're still trying to find out about your father's disappearance. Have you made any progress?"

Ramona sighed. "Some, but not enough."

"There's more than that on your mind, isn't there?"

"I suppose."

"Ah, Michael," Saya said in a whisper.

"No, it's nothing," Ramona said quickly, horrified that she'd revealed so much.

"You're human. That's nothing to be ashamed of. You want a companion who'll share in your dreams and build memories with you. Life makes more sense somehow when it's traveled by two who view things in a similar light."

Ramona swallowed. "You see too much, Saya."

"I've been told that before," the woman answered simply.

Ramona turned to stare out the small window at the activity taking place. The construction crew, protected by thick work jackets, continued to prepare a foundation for the permanent building. "We're making progress here, but until the past is settled, the real foundation for the cooperative won't be set."

"Is there any way I can help you?"

Ramona turned around. "Maybe. Do you know which jewelry makers in the area might have used low-grade silver some time in the past?"

Saya considered it for several seconds. "I'm not a jewelry maker, but I know of a man who would know all about that. His name is Alvaro Gutierrez. He lives near the Plaza. But I'm not sure he'll speak with you. He doesn't trust strangers, and he doesn't want to become part of our cooperative."

"Could you take me to see him?"

Saya shook her head. "He and I don't get along too well. His house is behind mine, and his rabbits are always getting into my vegetable garden. Having me along wouldn't help. I'll ask around though. We'll find someone."

Shortly after noon, Michael drove up in his patrol car. Saya invited him inside the portable building, and after showing him around, took him to Ramona's cubbyhole.

Michael said goodbye to Saya then smiled at Ramona. "You've really turned this building into the perfect workplace. There's a good feeling in here. People are comfortable and at ease."

"It's the artisans, not the building. I can't wait for the permanent structure to be finished! That'll have better lighting and large rooms that will be partitioned to their specifications. *That's* really going to be something." She took the photo he'd left that morning from the top of her desk and handed it back to him. "Thanks for showing this to me, Michael," she said. Words sounded so clumsy in comparison to the feelings ribboning through her. But they were all she had to give him.

"I thought you might like to see it," Michael said, putting it carefully back into his wallet. "By the way, I've got some news on the case. That's why I came by," he said, refocusing on business. "The test results on the bombs are back. Both are homemade, like pipe bombs. The ingredients making up the crude black powder, like Glauber's salt and sulfur, are easily obtained locally. They'll be hard to trace."

"So, we have more verification that he's resourceful as well as intelligent."

"That's about it."

"Well, I have something else that might give us a lead." She told him about her conversation with Saya.

Michael chuckled softly. "I know Alvaro. If you wanted to ask him what he did yesterday, he probably wouldn't be able to remember. Yet if you ask him about something that happened twenty years ago, he's as sharp as a fishhook."

"Would he speak to you?"

He took a deep breath. "He might, but he knows I have no jurisdiction inside the pueblo. He'll guess the question has to do with you, and unless you're there, he's going to be suspicious. The best way to deal with him is for both of us to go over. He may not know you personally, but you can bet he knows of you. He certainly knew your mother, they're of the same generation. You wouldn't be a complete stranger, not by any means."

"When would you like to go?" Ramona asked, eager to pursue the lead and hoping he'd have the time.

"How about now? I'm off duty for another forty minutes."

"Fine with me."

She followed him in her truck, and they arrived at Gutierrez's home ten minutes later. Ramona had formed a mental picture of an elderly man, frail but still actively involved with life. Nothing prepared her for the robust Tewa man that met them at the door.

He wasn't more than five foot three or four, but there was no mistaking the sinewy muscles that covered his chest. His checker-patterned flannel shirt was stretched taut around a barrel-shaped torso too big for it to encase. His eyes sparkled with curiosity. "Michael Wolf, what brings you here?"

Gutierrez's gaze shifted to Ramona and he studied her quietly. "You're Loretta's daughter. I remember when you were a child. You've blossomed into a woman, but your face is the same."

She wasn't sure how to answer. It wasn't a compliment really, so she just smiled. "Good afternoon, Mr. Gutierrez."

The man stood aside and gestured for them to enter. Two lop-eared rabbits scampered across the living room and stopped beside a worn easy chair. "They won't bother you, so don't give them a thought."

Ramona saw how gently he handled the smallest one as he placed it on his lap. "Now then. Why have you come?"

Michael cleared his throat. "We hoped you could answer a question for us. We're trying to track down anyone who might have used low-grade silver crafting jewelry about fifteen years ago."

His eyes flickered as memories bubbled to the surface. "Why do you ask that? How much of this is police business?"

"At this point, we're just trying to gather some information," Michael answered, then glanced at Ramona and gave her a nod.

"I believe that this is somehow connected to my father's disappearance. It's possible he made an enemy of someone who was alloying extra copper in with silver. I can't prove it, not yet anyway, but I think I'm on the right track."

Gutierrez rubbed his jaw pensively. "About twenty years ago there was a scandal at San Esteban. White people who'd bought jewelry from our artists started complaining that they'd been sold cheap silver. Appraisals started coming in way too low, and it was claimed that our silversmiths were cheating the tourists." He squinted, frowning, lost in memories. "It was a terrible time for all our jewelry makers, but the one who suffered the most was Barton Perez."

"Barton?" she sat up abruptly. "Why him?"

"His squash blossom necklaces were the best. The tourists just couldn't buy enough of them. That summer he made big money by going over to Albuquerque and Gallup, selling his jewelry. His plan was to start his own store in Santa Fe. He spent every penny he made fixing up a shop near the Plaza, making that store something to be proud of. Then just before he was ready to open for business, things fell apart."

"What happened?" Michael asked. "I don't remember hearing about this."

"You were young, and not everything reaches the ears of children. It was a time of shame." Gutierrez stroked the small rabbit, then set him down on the floor. "Barton's jewelry had been selling for very high prices, but when it was discovered that many of the pieces were made with inferior silver, the district attorney stepped in. Lawyers accused him of fraud. He was forced to buy back all his merchandise or go to jail."

"How did he get the money?" Ramona asked, knowing how anyone starting a business could be extremely cash poor.

"He had to sell off practically everything he owned. His family suffered, too, they were practically bankrupt by the time Barton paid off all his customers. Barton's reputation was gone. No one would buy from him, although he protested he was a victim, too. He went to work for an Anglo in Santa Fe repairing jewelry. It was the only job he could get." Gutierrez exhaled softly. "Barton's mother was a very good potter, and the weight of supporting the family went to her. It was said that she was working around the clock. The kiln overheated and an accident left her hands practically useless. The tragedy broke them. Without the help of their neighbors they wouldn't have had enough to eat."

"Didn't he know who sold him the silver?" Michael asked.

Gutierrez shook his head. "There was talk that he thought it was Ortiz, but he never said that in public. Barton maintained that he'd bought his silver from several sources and used it quickly, so there was no way he could track it down." He lapsed into a long silence, then continued. "That was a hard time for everyone. The pueblo's reputation suffered. When tragedy touches one, it touches all." His gaze settled on Ramona. "The most widely held theory was that your father was to blame for the misfortune."

She shook her head. "My father was hurt as much as the others. The truth will someday come out."

"I hope you both find the answers you need, and that you'll be able to bear the weight of what you've uncovered," he said, standing up.

As Michael followed Ramona out of Gutierrez's home, the man's ominous words rang in his ears. "He had a point, you know. No matter how bad we think things are, they can get worse," Michael said.

Ramona nodded pensively, thinking of her mother. She'd never believed her mom had anything to do with her father's death, but she had a feeling Michael hadn't completely discarded the possibility. "Neither of us can turn away from what we've started. But I firmly believe that the truth will end up benefiting everyone."

Michael remained silent. Or it could drive a permanent wedge between them. "As soon as Barton returns, we'll pay him a visit. Until then, we both better get back to work."

Ramona watched him walk to his squad car. The cold air that whipped through the pueblo wound its way through the folds of her jacket, making her shiver violently. Yet her reaction stemmed from more than just the temperature. It was the sudden, inescapable certainty that truth might turn out to be as cold and cruel as the wind.

Forcing the thought aside, she walked to her truck and drove to the government building. It was time to check on her flyers. If they needed more, she had plenty in the back of the pickup. She parked near the entrance and was about to go inside when she caught a glimpse of Barton Perez. He drove by without seeing her, heading in the direction of his studio.

Ramona glanced around, hoping to catch sight of Michael's squad car, but it was nowhere to be seen. If he was out on patrol, there was no way of knowing when he'd be available again. But waiting for him at this point seemed unnecessary anyway. After hearing what had happened to Barton's family, she no longer saw the man in the same light. At least, he'd refrained from making his suspicions about her father's involvement public. She wanted to speak to him alone and tell him what she'd learned about the silver. Barton deserved that much, and some thanks, if he'd accept that. Eager to meet with him, she turned the truck around and drove to Barton's place.

By the time she arrived, she saw his truck parked near the side. As Ramona walked up the dirt path to his studio, he came to the door. The automatic smile he probably reserved for his potential customers turned into a scowl in the blink of an eye. Then he stepped toward her, narrowing the distance that remained between them. She hesitated for a fraction of a second as she saw the dangerous flicker in his eyes. It suddenly occurred to her that it might have been a serious mistake to come without Michael.

Chapter Eighteen

Swallowing her fear, Ramona strode resolutely toward the door and faced Barton. He didn't step aside. "We can stand out here and freeze, if that's what you want," she said calmly, "but it would be easier if we went inside."

He muttered something under his breath and turned toward the door. "If this is about that fetish, I've told you all I know. Hounding me isn't going to help."

"It isn't about that." As she followed him inside, she saw the gun case near the wall. Her knowledge of weapons was limited but adequate to spot obvious antiques. A quick glance failed to suggest anything but modern firearms.

"What do you want?" he challenged, following her gaze.

"Don't be so quick to judge me, Barton. Our interests coincide, whether or not you believe that. I'm trying to find a connection between the doctored silver the pueblo was once sold and my father's disappearance."

Barton made a sound of derision. "What good would answers do me now? I've always suspected your *father* was the one responsible." It wasn't easy to put a considerable amount of contempt into one word, but he managed admirably. "He was worse than any plague or natural disaster. Ortiz destroyed from the inside out."

She'd hoped to come in friendship, or at least offer a truce, but his attitude made that impossible. "You have no real evidence. You're just selecting him to blame. Help out by telling me who your suppliers were."

Barton's eyes flashed darkly. "You're right. I can't prove it was your father. That's the reason I never accused him publicly. There's honor in my family even if there's none in yours."

"So your suppliers were . . . ?" she asked patiently.

"I only dealt with three. Your father was one of them, and the other two were men with solid reputations."

"Wait a minute. My father couldn't have regularly supplied you with silver. That's not one of the items listed in his purchase records. I'm sure of it."

"He didn't buy silver, that's true, but he often accepted its current value in lieu of cash. Later, he'd sell or trade it. That's why I was fool enough to believe his story."

"What story?" she asked quickly.

"It was just a pack of lies," Barton said, his mouth tightening.

"Then tell me. If it wasn't true, it can't threaten you."

His eyes flickered dangerously. "Threaten me? You're the one who should be concerned. What would happen to your cooperative if it was proved that your father was the one who sold us the bad silver? It wouldn't inspire confidence in his daughter, would it?"

"Why should you worry then?" she persisted. "You have nothing to lose by seeing my family name further dishonored."

Barton smiled mirthlessly. "You've convinced me." He leaned back against the wall and regarded her with suspicion. "After the trouble, we tried for weeks to find out who betrayed us. The possibility of revenge made that time tolerable. I first confronted the owners of The Talisman, and the Silver Eagle, my two largest suppliers. They'd done business with the pueblo for a long time. But after talking to them, I felt certain my trouble hadn't come from either. Then I went to your father. Instead of protesting his innocence, he told me that he was aware of what had happened. He assured me that he had a plan to get the person really responsible.''

''Did he tell you who he suspected?''

''No, of course not. He was *lying*. Don't you understand?''

''But you said you believed him at first.''

''Yeah, I did. It was his attitude—he could be very convincing. He asked me to wait for a few days until he got hard evidence.'' Barton's hands curled into fists. ''Then he took off, disappeared completely.'' Barton's glare was like an icicle plunging through her. ''He treated me like a fool.''

''Don't be so sure.''

''Just leave us. My mother doesn't need to see you or the reminders you bring.'' Silently he escorted her to her truck.

There was nothing else she could say. Ramona stared at the ground for a moment, gathering her thoughts. As she did, her gaze fell on Barton's boots. Casually she glanced behind him, wondering what kind of tracks they left. The ground, however, was too frozen and rocky to be of help. A second later Barton turned his back on her and went inside.

Disappointed, she climbed inside her truck. The hatred emanating from Barton Perez had left her feeling battered. The pain, though not physical, hurt her more deeply than blows ever could have.

Ramona drove away quickly, glad to be leaving Barton's house behind. She'd only gone about a quarter of a mile when she saw Michael's squad car coming up from behind her. He signaled for her to pull over. She did as he asked, knowing with certainty that he'd discovered where she'd been. Wary of a confrontation, she stepped out of the truck and met him halfway.

''Why didn't you wait for me?'' Michael questioned.

''I wanted a few minutes alone with Barton. I thought I could reach him. I was hoping he'd give me the kind of answers he'd never divulge in front of you," she said. "As it was, I was partially right." She filled him in on the details.

Michael nodded in approval. "I had a chance to speak to my mother. She knows of two other jewelers who might be able to help us."

"What do we do next?"

"We need to compile a list connecting all the buyers who were victimized, to sellers. That way we'll be able to establish a common link. Maybe there's another dealer we've yet to discover who could have been responsible for the low-grade silver. I'm not ready to accept Perez's word as fact yet."

"Where to?" Ramona asked, sensing he already had an agenda in mind.

"My mother's home." His eyes met hers directly. "She knows you'll be coming. She doesn't trust you, Mona," he said reluctantly, "but she's willing to give you a chance to prove that you can help our family."

"It's a start."

Ramona's hands were perspiring with nervousness as they drew close to Antonia Wolf's home. Despite the confidence she'd shown in front of Michael, the prospect of entering his home made her uneasy. She'd known from the start how Antonia felt about her. Only now, the woman's opinion of her mattered a great deal. By caring about Michael, she'd become vulnerable. She wasn't sure how she'd cope if she was able to feel nothing except animosity and distrust from Michael's mother.

Ramona took a deep breath as she parked the truck, then followed Michael up the path to the house. Antonia greeted them at the door. She smiled warmly at her son, then her gaze shifted to Ramona. There was wariness there, and a touch of uncertainty. Ramona breathed a sigh of relief. Hesitancy, she could cope with.

Two elderly Tewa men were inside. One she recognized as the grandfather of one of the cooperative's jewelers. His face was like leather that had been left in the desert sun. Lines and wrinkles formed a thick interlacing roadwork that molded his chiseled face, softening it. Bright, piercing black eyes regarded her speculatively.

"You know Victor Fuentes," Antonia commented, "but I don't believe you've met Matias Long."

It was hard to tell ages, but if she had to hazard a guess she would have placed Matias in his eighties. He was tall and slender, but his shoulders were erect as he stood up and offered her his hand. "Pleasure."

Ramona shook his hand and then took the seat Antonia offered. "I've asked them for the names you wanted," Michael's mother said to him. "They were able to come up with a list."

"There were a handful of merchants dealing with the silversmiths at San Esteban during the time you asked about. But only one place besides John Ortiz's dealt with almost everyone we can think of here. It was called the Silver Eagle, but they're no longer in business," Victor said.

"Do you remember who the owner was?"

"I don't think we ever knew," Matias answered. "We only saw the salesman, an Anglo named Ted Hinton. I believe he was killed a few years ago in a car wreck."

"Hinton was never much for conversation. He'd come, do business, then leave. He always drove a hard bargain, but a fair one. No one ever had any complaints. He and the Silver Eagle supplied most of our needs for at least a decade before your father came."

Antonia looked at Ramona, then her son. "Trust existed between the Silver Eagle and the tribe for many years. Pursuing that will lead you nowhere."

"We'll see," Michael said. "It's like you taught me. There are many versions of the truth. But if we search, sooner or later, we find the one that matches the facts."

"And I always thought that my teaching fell on deaf ears," Antonia commented, unable to hide the pride in her voice.

Michael smiled at his mother, then turned to include Ramona in that smile. For one wonderful moment, she felt part of his life, within the circle of those he loved. Then the feeling banished as Matias spoke.

"Are you closer to finding answers?" he asked Michael, his gaze turning for a brief moment to Ramona.

"Closer, yes," Michael replied.

Matias's eyes hardened as they settled on Ramona. "There has been some talk. People say you bring distractions to those who are least able to afford it. If you're as loyal to the tribe as you claim, then remember the disciplines our ways teach. The focus we learn through rituals must be a part of who you are. Otherwise, everything you do will end up in failure."

Michael rose abruptly, but what he began to say was drowned out by a voice coming from his hand-held radio. Summoned on an emergency, he muttered a quick excuse and went out the door.

As soon as Michael was gone, the faces turned back to her. She forced herself to look back at each. "I've done nothing wrong," she said with quiet intensity. "I'll do what I have to, as Michael will. My feelings for him won't interfere with what either of us have to do."

"But they exist," Antonia said fiercely. "And they shouldn't."

"There are times in everyone's life when the heart overrules the mind. And when you think about it, maybe that's a good thing after all." Holding her head high, she said goodbye to them and walked out into the cold.

"Just like her mother," she heard someone whisper as she closed the door behind her.

By the time she reached her truck, her hands were shaking. The words had pleased and frightened her at the same time. Her mother had found love, but with it, her own special kind of hell. Had the pain been worth it? She longed to ask the question, though she suspected that she already knew the answer. Discretion and prudence demanded that she back away from Michael. But in his arms, she'd found a side of herself she hadn't even known existed. In his eyes, so bright with desire, she saw herself mirrored in the kindest light of all.

Ramona drove down the road that led out of the pueblo. Hatred for a past that kept them apart fueled her resolve. It was time to find out once and for all. She couldn't go on not knowing whether her love for Michael would ever have the chance to become more than just wishful fantasies and stolen moments.

Checking to make sure Chacon wasn't following her again, Ramona drove to the state government offices along St. Frances Drive in Santa Fe. Somewhere in the records of the Economic Development Department there had to be a listing that would reveal the officers and owners of the Silver Eagle corporation. For now that was her best lead, and she intended to pursue it.

It took her over three hours searching through microfiche and unwieldy boxes of folders to find the answer. She'd almost given up when one of the folders slipped out of her hands and spilled onto the floor. As she was picking up the three-part forms, George Taylor's name caught her eye. He had filed a form serving notice he was dissolving the Silver Eagle corporation, and applied for a tax number and license as a wholesale jewelry operation.

She stared at the page for several seconds. George Taylor had known her father, and at times done business with him. He'd claimed to be a friend of the tribe, one who considered her father an enemy. Maybe his reasons were far more complex than she'd ever suspected.

The form she was reading had been typed and Taylor's signature had faded. She'd need to get more samples of Taylor's handwriting to check against the sheets hidden in her father's ledger.

She formulated a quick plan. She'd drive across town and sort through the metal Dumpster at the rear of his store after closing time. She was certain to find a sample of Taylor's handwriting there. She glanced at her watch. It was almost five o'clock.

She crossed Santa Fe slowly, stopping for a sandwich at a take-out place along the way. By the time she got there she wanted Taylor and all his staff to be long gone.

She arrived at around six-fifteen, and parked half a block away just to be safe. Night had settled over the desert. Hidden by the darkness, she went to the trash bin and hoisted herself up. Precariously balanced over the side, she peered in and searched through the top layers.

The remnants of someone's pizza, several days old, had seeped onto the papers and boxes that filled the bin to capacity. The stench was so strong she had to breathe through her mouth to avoid gagging.

Refusing to be deterred, she shoved away the gooey mess, stirring up the papers from the bottom. Several old purchase orders came to the surface, and she saw a handwritten note signed by George Taylor. She reached for it carefully, trying to avoid the slippery ooze of tomato sauce that threatened to spill onto it.

As she started to pull it out, bright headlights suddenly illuminated the parking area around her. She looked up quickly and drew in a breath, an involuntary gesture she immediately regretted.

George Taylor's car was turning in the entryway to the lot. Coughing, she dived headfirst into the bin and froze. She lay curled up, rock still, and listened. There was another, heavy-duty truck coming down the road, and unfortunately that was masking the sound of George Taylor's car.

Staying in the deepest shadows, she peered over the edge. George Taylor had parked about ten feet away from the bin and was entering his store through the rear door.

The loud electric whir of machinery made her shift her attention away from Taylor. Turning in the bin and staying low, she saw giant metal prongs descending to grasp the sides of the Dumpster. The enormous trash truck roared ominously as the bin lurched, then started to rise.

Ramona yelled, but the sound was drowned out. Fear gripped her as she realized that she only had seconds left. Unless she acted fast, she'd be crushed under tons of garbage.

Chapter Nineteen

Ramona knew she only had one chance. The driver might see her if she could manage to stand up and get his attention. Jamming the paper with Taylor's writing into her pocket, she grabbed onto the side tightly, struggling to pull herself upright. The trash beneath her feet shifted like quicksand as she used her free hand to wave back and forth.

The trash truck's mechanism groaned as it reached its maximum height and began to slowly tip the bin over. The driver glanced up casually, checking its progress, when suddenly his gaze fastened on her. His eyes looked as if they were almost going to pop out of his head. She saw him mouth words she couldn't hear but understood clearly. She saw him press something forward and the bin slowly descended toward the ground.

The driver's companion jumped out of the cab. ''Jeez, lady, how the heck did you get in there? That's a lousy place to sleep,'' he said, mistaking her for a street person.

Ramona glanced down at herself. Her jeans and sweater were covered with garbage. Something sticky clung to her hair and fell down her face in strings. Though she breathed through her mouth, she was barely able to keep from gagging.

"Thanks for putting me down, guys," she said with a quick glance back at the store. Now, if she could only make her escape before Taylor came out!

She scrambled quickly out of the bin and ran down the block toward the truck. A minute or two later, she was speeding down the street. Now all she had to do was find Michael and let his police contacts verify the handwriting.

Ramona pressed down harder on the accelerator, eager to get home. Suddenly flashing red lights appeared directly behind her. One glance at the speedometer told the story. She pulled over to the side and fished her wallet out of the glove compartment.

As the officer approached her car, she stepped out. She saw the man stop in his tracks and grimace as he caught a whiff of her.

"Believe me, Officer, it's even worse in here. I can hardly stand myself."

"Have you been in an accident of some kind?"

Diplomatically put. He was trying to find out in the nicest way possible if this was her natural odor or the result of a bath in a cafeteria grease trap. "Uh, I had an unexpected problem. I was on my way to find Sheriff's Officer Michael Wolf. Is there any way you can reach him on your radio?"

He narrowed his gaze. "I might, if you tell me what this is about."

"I have some evidence concerning a case he's working on. He'll be interested, believe me."

"Okay, but I'll still have to give you a ticket. You were going ten miles over the speed limit."

"Yeah, I know," she admitted with a sheepish grin. "You'd go fast too, if you smelled like I did and couldn't open a window without freezing."

He nodded slowly. "You do have a point there." He took her license number and started back to his vehicle. "Just stay by your car," he said, rubbing his nose.

The stringy viscous liquid that had coated her hair, had now saturated the shoulders of her sweater, making them cling to her body with the tenacity of paste. She was trying to pry it away from her skin when the officer returned.

He coughed, then spoke. "Officer Wolf's on his way. His ETA is less than fifteen minutes."

She wondered what Michael would say, what he'd think when he saw her, then brushed it from her mind. There wasn't a thing she could do about it now. She considered going back inside her truck, but it was easier to breathe outside even if it was freezing.

Michael made good time. She'd only been waiting ten minutes when he pulled up behind her truck. As he came toward her, she saw the guarded look on his face. It was too guarded, which usually meant he was determined to hide whatever he was thinking. What he couldn't disguise was his cough as he drew near.

"Jeez! You stink!"

"It's my new fragrance. I call it 'Memorable.'"

He coughed again, then stepped back. "Jerry said you had something for me?"

Shivering from the cold, she reached inside her pocket and retrieved the memo. Part of it was damp, but the signature and handwritten note were intact. "Here. You'll want to have one of your people compare it to the writing on the ledger pages."

He took it gingerly by the corners, but the liquid that had accumulated on the bottom made it stick to his palm. He pried it loose. "This gunk has the color of cheese and the tenacity of a barnacle. Maybe you should market it. You could endorse it personally, after such a comprehensive field test."

"Please. I went through a lot for that little slip of paper." Ramona recounted the story as quickly as she could. The temperature was dropping.

Michael stared, shaking his head. "What possessed you to do something like that on your own?"

"It seemed the right thing to do at the time. And I never expected it to turn out this way." Ramona glanced down at the paper. "How soon do you think you'll be able to get an answer for us?"

"I can get an unofficial one tonight. Since you've gone through so much to get this, why don't you come along? But first, you have to take a shower. I'd like Rick to be able to concentrate without an oxygen tank."

SHE WAS IN THE SHOWER for a full fifteen minutes before she managed to get rid of the gelatinous substance that had adhered to her hair and skin. By the time she'd changed her clothes and was ready to go, an hour had passed.

Michael came into the utility room as she started to toss her clothes into the washing machine. His open look of skepticism made her reconsider. Abruptly changing her mind, she bundled the clothes up and stuck them inside a garbage bag. "I might as well forget it. These probably constitute a health hazard of major proportions. I just hope what I went through tonight turns out to be worth it," she said.

"We're going to need the ledger sheets and the memo," Michael said, and waited by the door as she retrieved them.

"Got them!" she said, following him outside.

Michael had taken the squad car home while she'd been in the shower, and now his old truck stood near the door. "Rick doesn't live too far from here. I've already spoken to him and he's waiting."

They arrived fifteen minutes later. Rick, a Hispanic man in his early forties, greeted them at the door as they pulled up. He was huge, nearly as broad as he was tall. His salt-and-pepper hair was cut short, military style. His shirt had been starched into paralysis and was as impeccably clean as his home.

"I'm glad to help you, Mike," he said cautiously, "but unless it's an easy match you might have to wait until morning. Frequently these things take time." He took the papers from Michael's hands and winced when he touched the memo. Quickly he reached for a clear plastic bag and placed the memo inside. "What the heck's on this?"

"We're not sure, but don't inhale too deeply if you take it back out," Michael warned.

He walked to a well-lit drafting table and placed the ledger and memo side by side. He worked back and forth, sometimes sticking portions of the papers underneath a stereo microscope. Finally he glanced up at them. "There's no doubt, in my opinion. The two samples were written by the same person."

"I'll be dropping these off for you at your office tomorrow," Michael said, shaking Rick's hand. "I really appreciate it."

"Don't mention it," he answered, then repeated, emphasizing the words, "*and I mean, don't mention it.*"

As they drove back to the trading post, Ramona remained in pensive silence. "You know, the more we uncover, the more complicated this gets. We now know that George Taylor sold silver that had been excessively alloyed with copper. It's also clear that my dad knew what Taylor was doing. After all, he stole Taylor's ledger pages. But this doesn't prove that Taylor murdered my dad."

"That's true. Barton's motive is still strong, and we still don't know what Chacon's role in this is."

"But if Perez was willing to give my dad time to find the person really responsible..."

"What else could he have told you? That he'd decided to go over there and shoot your father? He had a lot of hatred stored up. First, there was the matter of the clay, then the silver and what had happened to his mother."

She nodded. "I keep remembering the crank caller. He said my father was 'dust of the earth.' Only my father's killer would have known he was dead. And Barton certainly would have known the Tewa expression."

"That doesn't exclude Taylor, though. He's dealt with our tribe long enough. It's very possible he knows the term. At least you don't have to worry anymore that your mother might have been involved in some way," Michael said. "I can't see her taking part in any conspiracy against the tribe."

"I wasn't worried," Ramona said. "I knew in my heart she could never have hurt Dad."

"Well, I hope you understand I didn't want to think she'd done anything, either. But as a cop, I have to consider every possibility."

"We still have no proof that would conclusively point to the killer though."

Michael was about to answer, when his radio came alive. He picked up his mike and depressed the button. Suazo's voice crackled over the air. "I've got some information for you. I think I can identify the note writer. I'm certain from the ink, and the style, that it's Barton Perez. Unfortunately my opinion isn't that of an expert, so I can't bring charges against him yet."

"We might have more in another forty-eight hours. I'll let you know."

"I'll be holding my breath, Wolf."

"Forty-eight hours?" she repeated, after Michael signed off. "What do you plan to do?"

"I spent my afternoon trying to track down the Colt .44 revolver we know was used to kill your father. I spoke to a gunsmith who said he was almost certain that Taylor had supplied him with authentic parts for that type of weapon quite a few years back. My guess is that if Taylor's the killer, he dismantled the weapon, just to make sure it couldn't lead back to him. The gunsmith recommended I talk to the owner of a gun shop on the outskirts of Santa Fe. He's supposed to have the largest stock of antique guns and replacement parts for sale in the area. The guy's going to be a problem though, since he hates cops.''

"Let's both go see him. If we go in as a couple with you out of uniform, he's not as likely to suspect what we're doing."

"If he doesn't pan out, there are two others worth trying. Though their stock is much more limited, they also carry parts." Michael parked in front of the trading post. "It's too late to go now, everything's closed, so I'll pick you up at eight tomorrow morning."

"Would you like to come in for some coffee?"

Michael shook his head. "I don't think that's a good idea."

She nodded. "All right."

He saw the downcast look on her face and felt an enormous tightening in his chest. He struggled against the desire to comfort her, knowing it might lead to events neither would be able to control. "Lock the doors," Michael said, then jamming his hands into his jacket, turned and walked back to his truck.

He waited inside his pickup until she stepped inside. Vivid images of their nights together filled him with a dark, tormenting hunger. Yet no matter how much he wanted her or how deep his feelings went, he knew that soon he might have to let Mona go altogether. If the past didn't give them the answers they needed they'd have nothing to offer each other, and no way of holding on to what they'd found.

With a groan of frustration he slammed his hand against the steering wheel and drove home.

MICHAEL ARRIVED in his old truck early the next morning. He hadn't been able to sleep, nor had he had much of an appetite for breakfast. Ramona filled him with a mixture of thought-crushing passion and heart-wrenching tenderness. Nothing had ever prepared him for the intensity of feelings she evoked.

A moment later she met him at the door, ready to go. She wore tan slacks and a soft peach-colored sweater. The delicate colors enhanced her femininity and made her appear more fragile than he knew her to be.

"You look great," he grumbled, annoyed at his own reaction to her.

"I don't feel great. I didn't sleep too well last night," she admitted.

"Oh?" Somehow, her admission helped soothe his mood.

"I couldn't stop thinking about today. I hate putting off anything."

So her sleeplessness hadn't had anything to do with him. His mood worsened. "This gunsmith we're on our way to see is a bit shady, so watch your step. He stays right on the edge of the law."

"That would explain why he doesn't like cops," she observed. She pointed to the standard police-issue hand-held radio on the floor. "I see you're hedging your bets."

He nodded. "It's got a full charge, so its operable for the next eight hours. You never know when it'll come in handy." He shrugged. "When we get there, just follow my lead. To get his cooperation I'm going to give him the impression that I'm out for a buck and willing to fracture a few laws."

"Okay. Play it any way you want. I'll back up your story."

They arrived in Santa Fe a short time later. Her stomach tightened with apprehension and excitement. They were getting close, she could feel it. They stopped by the door of an old stucco building with iron bars on the windows and rang the bell, like the small sign requested.

After a while, a man in his late fifties came to the door and nodded to them in greeting. He wore green fatigue pants which made him look twice as wide as Ramona suspected he was. Ramona looked at the design on his T-shirt. Below the growling panther were the words Born To Raise

Hell. He looked like a down-on-his-luck mercenary, and an uneasy feeling spread through her.

"Excuse the delay in answering the door. I like to keep security tight and avoid unwanted visitors."

As they entered the well-stocked but dimly lit shop, Ramona tried not to cough. An oily smell, mingled with the scent of gunpowder and solvents, made the air practically unbreathable. The proprietor gave Michael a long, speculative look. "How can I help you?"

"I heard from some friends...well, they said you might be able to help me. I'm trying to assemble an antique gun for a collector. I've got almost everything I need except for the barrel and cylinder. The ones I had were badly pitted, almost rusted out."

"Give me the make and model you want to duplicate. Who knows, I might even have a complete original on hand."

"It would have to be very special. I want one with wear and tear on it that could pass as a gunfighter's weapon. I promised it's a rare find. I'm after a Colt .44-40 revolver," Michael answered, avoiding the man's gaze.

The gun shop owner laughed. "I see where you're coming from. Let me check my stock and see what I can do for you. I'll be back in a few minutes." He stepped through a doorway behind the counter.

Michael glanced at her and shook his head almost imperceptibly. Casually he looked down at a small metal disk on the counter just behind a hardwood duck call.

Ramona followed his gaze. So, they were being monitored. She was virtually certain that was some kind of microphone. She smiled at Michael and gave him a playful wink. "After you finish this job, I don't want any more excuses. You're going to take me someplace special to celebrate."

"I have just the perfect place in mind." He gave her a slow grin, enjoying watching her squirm.

"No. I want to go out for dinner."

"And we'll make love."

"What, over dinner?"

"I was hoping for someplace more comfortable, but if that's what you want, it's okay by me," he countered.

"I suppose I should expect that from someone whose hormones rule his life," she shot back sweetly.

Before Michael could answer, the gunsmith returned. He grinned at her in a way that suggested he'd decided that she'd won the round. "I've got the cylinder you need. What I'm missing is the barrel, but I think I can track it down. Do you have a minute? I could make a phone call for you."

Michael nodded. "Sure. I can't start working until I've got both pieces anyway."

Ramona knew that the barrel was the crucial part needed for identification because of the rifling. She stood by the barred window and stared outside, afraid that the excitement would show on her face.

She heard the man dial, then ask the person on the other end for the Colt .44 barrel.

"Barton Perez? Yeah. I'll tell them," the gunsmith said. "My customer's also from that tribe, unless I'm mistaken," he added, glancing at Michael. "Okay, George, thanks for the help. You're the only person around here I know used to have a .44."

Ramona spun around and stared at Michael. Their plans had gone awry in a way she'd never anticipated. Afraid the gunsmith would sense her reaction, she quickly diverted him. "Um, did your contact say Barton Perez had the barrel?" she asked in a casual tone.

"Yeah. You know him?"

Michael answered for her. "We're both from San Esteban, I can deal with him. But just how reliable is your source? Perez and I don't get along so well, so I'd rather not approach him unless we can actually deal."

"I've known George Taylor for years, before he was a big-time businessman. He's bought from me and sold to me. He's the foremost collector around here." He glanced at Ramona. "Don't worry, ma'am. He's discreet. Most gun collectors are."

Michael thanked him and started to walk out of the store.

"Hey, don't you want the cylinder?"

Michael stopped by the door and turned around. "Let me see if I can get the barrel from Perez first, then you and I will do business."

"If that's a problem, maybe I can get it for you," the gunsmith said, his glance filled with suspicion.

"You may have to," Michael assured him easily. "But let me try to approach him directly first. If he deals with me, I'll get a better price than he'd give you."

They left the shop wordlessly and went to Michael's truck. She remained silent until he'd pulled out onto the highway. "We've got a couple of ways of looking at this," she said slowly. "Barton *could* have the barrel. Or Taylor may have figured out *we're* the ones after the barrel and is hoping to lead us on a wild-goose chase."

"It's possible he's trying to buy time to go get the barrel from the gunsmith who really has it," he answered. "You've got two more names on your list of gun shops, right?"

He nodded. "But unless we move fast and make the right choices, we may never get the barrel at all. Taylor and Barton are friends, or at least business associates. If Barton has the barrel, it's possible Taylor will tip him off. There's no telling what he'll do then, but there's one thing you can count on. The barrel will disappear forever."

Michael pulled the hand-held from beneath his seat. "I'm contacting Captain Suazo and asking him to pay Barton a visit right now. The sooner we move, the better our chances."

Ramona watched him, her mind racing. There was another problem. Even if Barton had owned the piece once, there was no guarantee he still had it now. The barrel could easily have been in the possession of one of the other two gunsmiths. "We're going to have to call the gun shops in case one of them has it. They'll be the key to tracking it to the original owner."

Michael drove down several blocks and pulled over to a phone booth next to a gas station. "Hang tight. The two remaining places on my list are reputable and I shouldn't have any problem getting their cooperation."

He returned several long moments later. "I've got bad news. They've both got a barrel that would fit a Colt .44-40. One's a long-barrel cavalry model and the other is a short barrel, the kind a gunslinger would have used. Either one could be the one we're looking for. They agreed to hang on to them until we get there."

"If the barrel we need is one of those two, the killer has the advantage of knowing where to go get it. We have to split up and make sure he doesn't beat us to it."

"There's no need. I'll call another unit and have them pick one up while we get the other."

After phoning in, he put the radio down. "The units on call are spread pretty thin right now and it's getting close to the end of the shift. There won't be an officer available for a while, and we can't afford to wait until one is able to respond."

"Then we have to go with my plan. Drop me by the trading post. It's on your way to the second gun shop. I'll take my truck and go back to the first address. That's the fastest way."

"Forget it. You're not law enforcement and you could end up in more trouble than you've ever dreamed of. This is the finish line for the killer and he knows it."

"You can't stop me, Michael. I'm going. If we don't split up we'll lose the murder weapon and the answers we both need."

He said nothing for a while. He desperately wanted to protect her, yet what she'd said was true. He remembered the Tewa saying, "Be as a woman, be as a man." The qualities of both made someone strong, but the two halves needed to work as one, both within and without.

He stepped down hard on the accelerator. "I want you to keep the radio with you. Since I'll have to go through the pueblo anyway, I'll switch to my police unit. That way you can use it to contact me if you need to."

"I'll get the barrel then call you. Don't worry."

"No. The only thing you'll do is stake the place out. I'd like to see who shows up to get it. It would cinch the murderer for us. You can use the radio if any of our chief suspects show up. I'll set it on a frequency normally not used, but one I can still monitor from another squad car. You're not to do *anything* except unofficially stake out the shop. Understood?"

"But if one of the suspects does show up . . ."

"I'll be on my way immediately. In another twenty minutes the new shift will report in and I'll be able to call in another unit to assist. *You* don't do a thing. *Is that clear?*"

"All right. I'll just watch the place," she agreed reluctantly.

They were on their separate ways ten minutes later. Finding the gun shop north of Santa Fe was easy. Before long, she'd selected what she thought was the most advantageous spot to park. From there, she could watch the front entrance and the empty parking area in the back. If anyone she knew showed up at either, she'd see them. Best of all, she was well hidden, nestled between the curve of the road and the orange construction barrels that surrounded her. Feeling safe, she forced herself to relax, and settled back in her seat.

Minutes passed slowly and the lack of activity began to take the edge off her mood. Her thoughts drifted to Michael. She felt a mixture of envy and apprehension as she concluded that undoubtedly he'd picked the right gunsmith. There was certainly no action here.

As she accepted the thought and its implications, anxiety crept through her, making her stomach tighten and her hands turn cold. "Take care of yourself, Michael," she whispered.

She forced herself to focus on the gun shop before her, though by now she was convinced it was a waste of time. Traffic went by steadily, and the sameness of the sounds echoed around her, its familiarity soothing. Suddenly a sharp tap on her window startled her. She snapped around and saw the barrel of a small pistol aimed directly at her head.

"Out!" George Taylor shook his head when she started to reach for the radio.

Ramona saw him keep the gun trained on her as he stepped away from the door. She had no choice. There was no way to call for help, and nothing she could do except comply.

Chapter Twenty

Ramona stepped out of the truck slowly. She had to think fast. Even if she did everything he asked, Taylor would still kill her. She knew too much now, and could put him in jail for life. "Murdering me won't help you. Michael Wolf already knows what you've done."

"Knowing and proving are two different things." Taylor cocked his head toward the gun shop. "Come on. We're running out of time. And if you try anything in that store, you'll insure your death and its owner's as well."

"You're going to kill both of us anyway. You can't afford to leave two witnesses behind."

"The shopkeeper doesn't know what I did. Are you going to force me to kill him, too, or do you want to save a life? It's really up to you."

Her heart lodged in her throat. Panic and a horrible sense of helplessness rose in her, all but choking her. "What do you want me to do?"

"We'll go in together. You'll ask for the barrel, pay him for it, then we'll walk out." Taylor stuck his gun hand into his jacket pocket, keeping his grip on the weapon while hiding it from sight.

"But then he'll have seen you."

"It won't matter. You'll disappear, and so will the barrel. Everything else against me will be circumstantial evidence. They can't convict anyone on that."

She'd have until the time they left the shop to think of a way to escape. Hopefully, something would come to her by then. But whatever she did, she wouldn't risk the life of the gunsmith.

Ramona walked inside the shop slowly, stalling for time and hoping that fate would give her a chance to fight back. All she needed was a distraction, anything that would cause Taylor to lower his guard for even an instant.

As they approached the counter, Ramona managed a weak smile at the gunsmith. "We're looking for the barrel of a Colt .44-40. Do you have one in stock?"

"Sure. I'm Harvey, and I held on to it for you two just like you asked," the man replied, peering at her through thick eyeglasses.

Ramona's last hope crumbled. The gunsmith assumed that Taylor was Michael, who'd phoned in a short time ago. Harvey had been told to expect two people, and unfortunately she and Taylor fit the bill. But there was one last hurdle Taylor had to get past. Surely the man would ask for identification!

The shop owner produced the barrel, placing it on the counter. "Here you go, Officer. I've typed up a release form. I need your signature before I turn it over. Otherwise, my insurance agent will kill me."

"I'm just the escort." As Taylor flashed a badge that Ramona knew came straight from the collection in his office, her stomach plummeted. "The lady here is with the district attorney's office. Go ahead and sign, ma'am, we've got a schedule to keep."

Holding the small cardboard box containing the barrel, Ramona remained just a step ahead of Taylor as they walked to the door. She had to act now, or she'd be dead for sure. Thinking fast, she swung the door back hard and ducked out of the way quickly.

ACROSS TOWN, Michael waited as the gunsmith went through his stock. "Here it is," he said, placing the long cavalry barrel on the counter.

Michael signed a receipt. "If this isn't the one I need, it'll be returned as soon as possible."

"No problem, Officer. By the way, Harvey's Place specializes in Western antique guns. Have you tried him?"

"Yeah. Could you call for me and ask if anyone's tried to purchase the one he has since I last spoke to him?" It wouldn't hurt to ask. Stakeouts were tricky and someone might have slipped past Ramona. Michael waited as the man went to the back room and used the phone.

The man returned thirty seconds later. "Nobody answers. Harvey must have his hands full at the moment."

A disturbing thought flew into Michael's mind, and he was out the door in three seconds. As he sped down the highway, Michael tried to raise Ramona on the hand-held radio but got no response. Fear stabbed into him.

Turning on the flashing lights but proceeding on a silent alarm, he picked up the car's mike. "I've got a Signal One suspect," Michael said, letting other officers know by code that they'd be after a suspected killer, "and I need a 10-83 on this." That would mean he'd get backup fast.

He racked the mike and noticed that his hands were sweating. Swallowing hard, he tried to choke back the panic that pumped into him. Mona, the only woman he'd ever loved, could be in mortal danger. There was no way he was going to arrive too late to help her. He gunned the accelerator, pushing the car for all the speed it could give.

"Stay away from that place, baby," Michael muttered. "Give me a chance. I'm on my way."

THE EDGE OF THE DOOR caught Taylor in the chest and knocked him back. "He's no cop!" Ramona yelled the warning as she dove for the front porch, throwing the box as far out into the parking lot as she could.

Taylor reacted in an instant. His hand snaked out and grabbed her by the arm, lifting her off the pavement and trapping her before she could escape. His fingers clenched around her in a viselike grip she couldn't shake loose. Suddenly the squeal of tires and the roar of a car engine rose in the air.

Taylor turned his head toward the parking lot as a squad car screeched to a halt not thirty feet away. The car door swung open and Michael appeared, taking a position behind it. Taylor jerked Ramona around and held her in front of him as a shield.

Another sheriff's unit came speeding down the street. A second later, the officer swung into the parking lot. He came out of the vehicle with a shotgun, but stayed behind the front end, using the engine block as cover.

"It's over, Taylor. Let her go," Michael ordered.

"Think again, Wolf," Taylor roared. "I want *your* car and clearance to the airport. Have your buddy lay down the shotgun and walk away from here. Then set your pistol down and come out into the open, or I'll kill her right in front of you. I haven't got anything to lose at this point."

Ramona's heart leaped to her throat. "Don't! If you do as he says, he'll kill all of us."

"Or maybe no one," Taylor interrupted. "It's up to you, Wolf. If you don't come out and away from the car, I *will* kill the woman. You can count on that." Taylor's hand was shaking, and he cocked the pistol's hammer back with his thumb.

Michael lowered his revolver's barrel. "Okay. I'm coming out."

"Set the pistol down and move away. Don't bother going for that backup gun. I'm not using arrows this time," Taylor snapped.

Michael turned to the assisting officer. "Back off, but keep the shotgun. We're not giving him that, too!"

"Damn you!" Taylor yelled, pointing the pistol back and forth between the men.

"Relax. We're negotiating," Michael said softly, setting his pistol on the ground and moving away from the car.

Horrified, she saw Michael place himself in the line of fire. The other officer backed away, never taking his eye or the shotgun off them. As soon as the deputy reached the sidewalk by the street, Michael began to approach, circling around so Taylor had to turn.

"Michael, don't!"

Taylor snagged her hair around his free hand. "Ramona Ortiz, your interference has cost me everything I've worked for my entire life. It's payback time," he whispered harshly in her ear. "Now watch the man you love die."

"No!" Ramona lunged for his gun hand. A monstrous bolt of pain emanated from her scalp as Taylor jerked her head back. Tears sprang to her eyes, but she managed to bring her free arm down over his in a jarring blow.

Taylor's hand dropped sharply and she took full advantage. Twisting around, she sank her knee into his groin. Taylor gasped, doubled over and dropped the gun. She kicked him again, hard in the chest, and he fell back onto the sidewalk.

Michael was there a second later. Taylor reacted, hurling his foot upward. Michael deflected the blow and grabbed Taylor's foot, twisting it mightily. As the man screamed out in pain, Michael continued the motion, forcing Taylor around onto his stomach. By then, the other officer was there, and they cuffed the cursing man.

Michael jerked Taylor to his feet and pushed him toward the patrol car. Forcing him to lean against the door, he frisked Taylor quickly.

Taylor glanced sideways at Ramona, his hatred pouring out. "I tried everything I could to get you to quit. You were insane not to just walk away."

"You didn't know I'd found my father's body, did you? Nothing could have stopped me after that."

"So that's it. Well, he only got what he deserved. He tried to ruin me. My only regret is that I didn't kill him out on some road and bury him there instead of under the floorboards. But my biggest mistake was in underestimating you."

His lack of remorse and his self-justification stunned her. "You stole my family's future. But now it's your turn to pay."

Michael locked Taylor, handcuffed, in the back seat of the vehicle. "I'm taking him to jail," Michael told her as the second officer drove away. "We'll question him there. Maybe he'll be able to tell us about the pottery or clay."

Michael's words seeped into her consciousness like icy water dripping slowly down her back. They'd found her father's murderer, and now the real story would come out. Her family would be exonerated, but not Michael's. As long as the pottery issue remained unsettled, he wouldn't be free of his duty to his family or the past.

As she drove back to the trading post, aching regret and sorrow hung heavy on her. She felt drained inside, as if there were nothing left within her. She'd been through the trading post many times and searched all her father's things. The clay and the pottery were gone. In another day or so, the trading post would be history, too. Her new beginning would herald the end of the fragile and newborn love she'd discovered with Michael, a love that had never been meant to be.

Ramona went inside the empty trading post. As the walls echoed in gloomy silence, a shudder ran through her. Without Michael, her future seemed to stretch out before her in an endless succession of days without fire, and without heart. "Dad, where did you put the pottery? Help me find it!" she whispered into the darkness.

For several minutes she stood in the hall, looking toward the part of the house that had been sealed off after the bomb. Gathering her courage, she decided to give it one last try. She had nothing to lose and everything to gain.

THE SUN HAD SET by the time Michael drove up. Hearing the vehicle, she peeked out a narrow crack in the wall where the patching boards didn't quite meet. Hoping he'd fared better than she had, Ramona went to the side door to let him in.

Michael's weary stance touched her, but the sadness in his eyes said everything. She knew that he hadn't learned anything about the clay or the pottery. "I've been going through the house one more time. Why don't you help me? It's going to be torn down this week, so I've got to make a list of everything I want to salvage. Maybe while we're doing that we'll think of something we've missed."

He gave her a tired smile. "Like you, I've always been a fighter. But maybe there is something to fate. If that's against you . . ."

"Come on," Ramona encouraged, "at least we can give destiny a good kick in the shins."

"Okay." He gave her a quick lopsided grin that made him look vulnerable yet shining with determination. "We'll do our best. Where do you want to start?"

"How about the store?" she said, leading the way.

Michael gestured toward the safe that stood in one corner. "You might have some use for that," he said, gesturing toward the back of the room.

"Forget it. The locking mechanism has been broken for decades. My dad kept it to misdirect burglars."

"Wait a second," Michael said, an idea forming in his mind. "The safe was unused, and your dad's special hiding place didn't have anything in it except photos and the .22. There might be someplace else where he kept his valuables. Are you certain he didn't have a safety-deposit box?"

"I'm sure. Mother told me more than once that Dad didn't trust banks. He only opened an account after someone broke in here one night and emptied the cash register."

"Maybe your mother taught him a trick some of the elders in our tribe use. Your father might have had two hiding places, one that a thief could find easily, and another known only to him."

Ramona considered it for a few moments. "It makes sense. It would also explain why I didn't find his old watch or class ring. My mother wouldn't have given those away, nor sold them. I'm certain of it."

"Okay, let's go back to your original plan. We'll do our search as you go through everything and decide what you want to salvage."

Ramona ran her hand over the desk that had stood in the corner. "This isn't worth saving. My dad found it at the dump, and refurbished it, but it's long past its day." She placed one hand on it and it rocked slightly.

"Have you checked the legs? I've heard of people hollowing them out."

They unscrewed each of the legs, then dismantled the chair. "Nothing here," she said, "but we've only just started."

They went over the house and its contents inch by inch. Five hours later, they stared at each other from across the kitchen table. "It's not here," she said, her heart breaking. "So what happens to us?"

He shook his head slowly. "There is no 'us,' Mona. You know I'm not free to pursue my own goals. I may never be."

Unable to meet his gaze, she glanced at the scarred wainscoting on the walls, demanding an answer from the silence. "My father must have hidden the pottery someplace. He didn't sell it, we know that from his records."

"I always thought he must have left some note or map that would let your mother know where it was in the event something happened to him. He was a man with enemies and he knew it.''

"But what's left to search?'' She kicked the bottom of the paneling on the wall with the tip of her shoe, then yelped.

Michael smiled as she hopped back on one foot. "You've given me an idea.''

"You want to kick the wall, too?'' she asked, massaging her toe.

"Do you have a candle?''

"You want to hold a séance,'' Ramona countered cynically. She grabbed a tall, thick, scented candle from the kitchen table. "Here. I keep it to get rid of odors. It has a nice scent.''

He lit the wick, then held it beside the kitchen wall.

"What on earth are you doing?''

"I'm looking for drafts. It's possible your dad hollowed out one of these walls. This is the last thing I can think of trying. If there're any crevices behind the paneling, then the air pocket will create a draft of cooler air and the smoke will sink near it. It may not be much of an effect though, so we'll have to watch carefully.''

They worked their way from the back of the house toward the front. "Since the holes that the bomb blasted haven't been completely sealed, will that throw you off?''

"No, as long as we stay close to the walls. There's not enough air leaking through except near the holes themselves.''

He was approaching the old safe when suddenly the candle flickered, almost going out. He blew out the candle and watched the smoke travel toward the wall, then down behind the safe.

"But that safe's useless!''

"What's behind it might not be.'' He started to push it out of the way, but the heavy steel cube barely moved.

Ramona moved to help him. "Okay—on three," she said, then counted it off. Fifteen strenuous seconds later, they crouched by the wall.

Michael tapped a panel and smiled as a distinctly hollow sound issued from the wall. "Get a hammer or crowbar."

She nodded, afraid to trust her voice. The excitement that drummed through her was equaled by the fear that they'd find nothing but dust and cobwebs.

Michael tapped the top of the wainscoting lightly with the hammer and was rewarded when a panel almost jumped into his hands. "This isn't part of the wall, this is attached with spring catches. You press it in just the right spot, and it opens."

As Michael pulled the panel away, the interior framework of the wall became visible. Where framing should have been at the bottom, there was only a dark, cavernous space extending below the floor. "Where's your flashlight?"

"In the kitchen. Just a sec." She ran there and back, her heart at her throat. "Here," she said finally, handing it to him. She waited a ragged infinity for an answer. "What's down there?" she demanded at last, unable to stand his silence.

He lowered his hand deep into the hole, then extracted a small, intricately decorated pot and held it up to the beam of the light. "It's one of the missing pieces, and there are hundreds more down there, probably all of them." He handed it to her.

As she took the pot, she heard something rattle inside. She turned it over and smiled as a watch and class ring dropped into her open palm. "My dad's things." She smiled.

Michael fingered the dirt that had adhered to the bottom of the pot, then rubbed it between his fingers. "Hold the flashlight for me," he whispered excitedly.

"What is it?"

"There's a big hole next to the pots, like someone's been digging down here." He scooped out a handful of the reddish clay. Mica flakes sparkled within it like gold. "The special clay. It's been here all along, right below the house!"

For a moment, Ramona couldn't even breathe. Tears formed in her eyes as long-sustained tensions and fears crumbled away. When Michael's gaze met and captured hers, her tears became a flood. "No more debts to the past. It's finally over," she managed.

"I love you, Mona," Michael whispered, a lifetime of feelings woven into his soft words. Emotions too raw to contain crowded in his throat. "Like this land and our people, we can finally have our own forever." He lifted her off the floor and into his arms. Her gentle smile and the sweet longing in her eyes made him sizzle with a need that cut through his soul.

As darkness embraced the trading post, a sweet hush descended. Fiery words of love breathed through the stillness, joining the primitive song of the desert night.

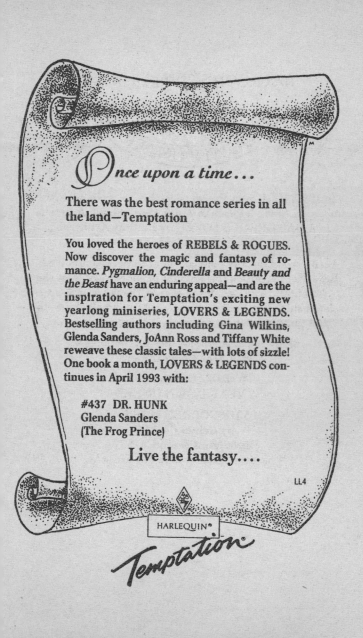

HARLEQUIN ✦ PRESENTS®

A Year
DOWN UNDER

In 1993, Harlequin Presents celebrates the land down under. In April, let us take you to Queensland, Australia, in A DANGEROUS LOVER by Lindsay Armstrong, Harlequin Presents #1546.

Verity Wood usually manages her temperamental boss, Brad Morris, with a fair amount of success. At least she *had* until Brad decides to change the rules of their relationship. But Verity's a widow with a small child—the last thing she needs, or wants, is a dangerous lover!

Share the adventure—and the romance—
of A Year Down Under!

Available this month in
A YEAR DOWN UNDER

THE GOLDEN MASK
by Robyn Donald
Harlequin Presents #1537
Wherever Harlequin books are sold.

 **HARLEQUIN®**

THE TAGGARTS OF TEXAS!

Harlequin's Ruth Jean Dale brings you
THE TAGGARTS OF TEXAS!

Those Taggart men—strong, sexy and hard to resist...

You've met Jesse James Taggart in FIREWORKS!
Harlequin Romance #3205 (July 1992)

And Trey Smith—he's THE RED-BLOODED YANKEE!
Harlequin Temptation #413 (October 1992)

And the unforgettable Daniel Boone Taggart in SHOWDOWN!
Harlequin Romance #3242 (January 1993)

Now meet Boone Smith and the Taggarts who started it all—
in LEGEND!
Harlequin Historical #168 (April 1993)

Read all the Taggart romances!
Meet all the Taggart men!

Available wherever Harlequin Books are sold.

Boyle, T.C.
The relive box and other Stories

Boyle, T. Coraghessan.
$25.99   **3201300381424**

2516			

ACKNOWLEDGMENTS

Grateful acknowledgment is made to the following magazines, in which these stories first appeared: *The Iowa Review*, "The Designee"; *The Kenyon Review*, "The Five-Pound Burrito" and "Surtsey"; *McSweeney's*, "The Argentine Ant"; *Narrative*, "She's the Bomb," "Warrior Jesus" and "You Don't Miss Your Water ('Til the Well Runs Dry)"; *The New Yorker*, "The Relive Box," "Are We Not Men?" and "The Fugitive"; *Playboy*, "Theft and Other Issues."

"Are We Not Men?" also appeared in *The Best American Short Stories 2017*, edited by Meg Wolitzer (Boston: Houghton Mifflin Harcourt, 2017), "The Relive Box" in *The Best American Science Fiction and Fantasy 2015*, edited by Joe Hill (Boston: Houghton Mifflin Harcourt, 2015) and "The Five-Pound Burrito" in *The Pushcart Prize, XLI: Best of the Small Presses*, edited by Bill Henderson (Wainscott, NY: The Pushcart Press, 2017).

THE RELIVE BOX AND OTHER STORIES

THE RELIVE BOX

Katie wanted to relive Katie at nine, before her mother left, and I could appreciate that, but we only had one console at the time and I really didn't want to go there. It was coming up on the holidays, absolutely grim outside, nine-thirty at night—on a school night—and she'd have to be up at six to catch the bus in the dark. She'd already missed too much school, staying home on any pretext and reliving the whole time I was at work, so there really were no limits, and who was being a bad father here? A single father unable to discipline his fifteen-year-old daughter, let alone inculcate a work ethic in her? Me. I was. And I felt bad about it. I wanted to put my foot down and at the same time give her something, make a concession, a peace offering. But even more I wanted the box myself, wanted it so baldly it was showing in my face, I'm sure, and she needed to get ready for school, needed sleep, needed to stop reliving and worry about the now, the now and the future. "Why don't you wait till the weekend," I said.

She was wearing those tights all the girls wear like painted-on skin, standing in the doorway to the living room, perching

on one foot the way she did when she was doing her dance exercises. Her face belonged to her mother, my ex, Christine, who hadn't been there for her for six years and counting. "I want to relive now," she said, diminishing her voice to the shaky hesitant plaint that was calculated to make me melt and give in to whatever she wanted, but it wasn't going to work this time, no way. She was going to bed and I was going back to a rainy February night in 1982, a sold-out show at the Roxy, a band I loved then, and the girl I was mad crazy for before she broke my heart and Christine came along to break it all over again.

"Why don't you go up and text your friends or something," I said.

"I don't want to text my friends. I want to be with my mom."

This was a plaint too and it cut even deeper. She was deprived, that was the theme here, and the whole thing, as any impartial observer could see in a heartbeat, verged on child abuse. "I know, honey, I know. But it's not healthy. You're spending too much time there."

"You're just selfish, that's all," she said, and here was the shift to a new tone, the tone of animus and opposition, the subtext being that I never thought of anybody but myself. "You want to what, relive when you were like my age or something? Let me guess: you're going to go back and relive yourself doing homework, right? As an example for your daughter?"

The room was a mess. The next day was the day the maid came, so I was standing amidst the debris of the past week, a healthy percentage of it—abandoned sweat socks, energy-drink cans, various crumpled foil pouches that had once contained biscotti, popcorn or Salami Bites—generated by the child standing there before me. "I don't like your sarcasm," I said.

Her face was pinched so that her lips were reduced to the smallest little O-ring of disgust. "What *do* you like?"

"A clean house. A little peace and quiet. Some privacy, for Christ's sake—is that too much to ask?"

"I want to be with Mom."

"Go text your friends."

"I don't have any friends."

"Make some."

And this, thrown over her shoulder preparatory to the furious pounding retreat up the stairs and the slamming of her bedroom door: "You're a pig!"

And my response, which had become ritualized ever since I'd sprung for the $5,000 second-generation Halcom X1520 Relive Box with the In-Flesh Retinal Projection Stream and altered forever the dynamic between me and my only child: "I know."

Most people, when they got their first Relive Box, went straight for sex, which was only natural. In fact, it was a selling point in the TV ads, which featured shimmering adolescents walking hand in hand along a generic strip of beach or leaning in for a tender kiss over the ball return at the bowling alley. Who wouldn't want to go back there? Who wouldn't want to relive innocence, the nascent stirrings of love and desire or the first time you removed her clothes and she removed yours? What of girlfriends (or boyfriends, as the case may be), wives, ex-wives, one-night stands, the casual encounter that got you halfway there and flitted out of reach on the wings of an unfulfilled promise? I was no different. The sex part of it obsessed me through those first couple of months and if I drifted into work each morning feeling drained (and not just figuratively), I knew it was a problem and that it was adversely affecting my job performance, and even, if I didn't cut back, threatening my job itself. Still, to relive Christine when we first met, to relive her in bed, in candlelight, cling-

ing fast to me and whispering my name over and over in the throes of her passion, was too great a temptation. Or even just sitting there across from me in the Moroccan restaurant where I took her for our first date, her eyes like portals, like consoles themselves, as she leaned into the table and drank up every word and witticism that came out of my mouth. Or to go further back, before my wife entered the picture, to Rennie Porter, the girl I took to the senior prom and spent two delicious hours rubbing up against in the backseat of my father's Buick Regal, every second of which I'd relived six or seven times now. And to Lisa, Lisa Denardo, the girl I met that night at the Roxy, hoping I was going to score.

I started coming in late to work. Giving everybody, even my boss, the zombie stare. I got my first warning. Then my second. And my boss—Kevin Moos, a decent-enough guy five years younger than me who didn't have an X1520, or not that he was letting on—sat me down in his office and told me, in no uncertain terms, that there wouldn't be a third.

But it was a miserable night and I was depressed. And bored. So bored you could have drilled holes in the back of my head and taken core samples and I wouldn't have known the difference. I'd already denied my daughter, who was thumping around upstairs with the cumulative weight of ten daughters, and the next day was Friday, TGIF, end of the week, the slimmest of workdays when just about everybody alive thinks about slipping out early. I figured even if I did relive for more than the two hours I was going to strictly limit myself to, even if I woke up exhausted, I could always find a way to make it to lunch and just let things coast after that. So I went into the kitchen and fixed myself a gin and tonic because that was what I'd been drinking that night at the Roxy and carried it into the room at the end of the hall that had once been a bedroom and was now (Katie's joke, not mine) the reliving room.

The console sat squarely on the low table that was the only piece of furniture in the room aside from the straight-backed chair I'd set in front of it the day I brought the thing home. It wasn't much bigger than the gaming consoles I'd had to make do with in the old days, a slick black metal cube with a single recessed glass slit running across the face of it from one side to the other. It activated the minute I took my seat. "Hello, Wes," it said in the voice I'd selected, male, with the slightest bump of an accent to make it seem less synthetic. "Welcome back."

I lifted the drink to my lips to steady myself—think of a conductor raising his baton—and cleared my throat. "February 28, 1982," I said, "9:45 p.m. Play."

The box flashed the date and time and then suddenly I was there, the club exploding into life like a comet touching down, light and noise and movement obliterating the now, the house gone, my daughter gone, the world of getting and doing and bosses and work vanished in an instant. I was standing at the bar with my best friend, Zach Ronalds, who turned up his shirt collar and wore his hair in a Joe Strummer pompadour just like me, only his hair was black and mine choirboy blond (I'd dye it within the week), and I was trying to get the bartender's attention so I could order us G&Ts with my fake ID. The band, more New Wave than punk, hadn't started yet, and the only thing to look at onstage was the opening act packing up their equipment while hypervigilant girls in vampire makeup and torn fishnet stockings washed round them in a human tide that ebbed and flowed on the waves of music crashing through the speakers. It was bliss. Bliss because I knew now that this night, alone out of all the long succession of dull nugatory nights building up to it, would be special, that this was the night I'd meet Lisa and take her home with me. To my parents' house in Pasadena, where I had a room of my own above the detached garage and could come and go as I pleased. My room. The place where I greased

up my hair and stared at myself in the mirror and waited for something to happen, something like this, like what was coming in seven and a half real-time minutes.

Zach said what sounded like "Look at that skank," but since he had his face turned away from me and the music was cranked to the sonic level of a rocket launch (give credit to the X1520's parametric speaker/audio beam technology, which is infinitely more refined than the first generation's), I wasn't quite sure, though I must have heard him that night, my ears younger then, less damaged by scenes like this one, because I took hold of his arm and said, "Who? Her?"

What I said now, though, was "Reset, reverse ten seconds," and everything stalled, vanished and started up once more, and here I was trying all over again to get the bartender's attention and listening hard when Zach, leaning casually against the bar on two splayed elbows, opened his mouth to speak. "Look at that skank," he said, undeniably, there it was, coloring everything in the moment because he was snap-judging Lisa, with her coat-hanger shoulders, Kabuki makeup and shining black lips, and I said, "Who? Her?," already attracted because in my eyes she wasn't a skank at all or if she was, she was a skank from some other realm altogether and I couldn't from that moment on think of anything but getting her to talk to me.

Now, the frustrating thing about the current relive technology is that you can't be an actor in the scene, only an observer, like Scrooge reliving his boarding school agonies with the Ghost of Christmas Past at his elbow, so whatever howlers your adolescent self might have uttered are right there, hanging in the air, uned-ited. You can fast-forward, and I suppose most people do—skip the chatter; get to the sex—but personally, after going straight to the carnal moments the first five or six times I relived a scene, I liked to go back and hear what I had to say, what she had to say, however banal it might sound now. What I did that night—

and I'd already relived this moment twice in the past week—was catch hold of the bartender and order not two but three G&Ts, though I only had something like eighteen dollars in my wallet, set one on the bar for Zach and cross the floor to where she was standing just beneath the stage in what would be the mosh pit half an hour later. She saw me coming, saw the drinks—two drinks— and looked away, covering herself because she was sure I was toting that extra drink for somebody else, a girlfriend or best bud lurking in the drift of shadow the stage lights drew up out of the murky walls.

I tapped her shoulder. She turned her face to me.

"Pause," I said.

Everything stopped. I was in a 3-D painting now and so was she and for the longest time I just kept things there, studying her face. She was eighteen years old, a commander of style, beautiful enough underneath the paint and gel and eyeliner and all the rest to make me feel faint even now, and her eyes weren't wary, weren't *used*, but candid, ready, rich with expectation. I held my drink just under my nose, inhaling the smell of juniper berries to tweak the memory, and said, "Play."

"You look thirsty," I said.

The music boomed. Behind me, at the bar, Zach was giving me a look of disbelief, like *What-the?*, because this was a violation of our club-going protocol. We didn't talk to the girls, and especially not the skanks, because we were there for the *music*, at least that was what we told ourselves. (Second time around I did pause this part, just for the expression on his face—Zach, poor Zach, who never did find himself a girlfriend as far as I know and who's probably someplace reliving every club he's ever been in and every date he's ever had just to feel sorry for himself.)

She leveled her eyes on me, gave it a beat, then took the cold glass from my hand. "How did you guess?" she said.

What followed was the usual exchange of information about

bands, books, neighborhood, high school, college, and then I was bragging about the bands I'd seen lately and she was countering with the band members she knew personally, like John Doe and the drummer for the Germs, and letting her eyes reveal just how personal that was, which only managed to inflame me till I wanted nothing more on this earth than to pin her in a corner and kiss the black lipstick right off her. What I said then, unaware that my carefully sculpted pompadour was collapsing across my brow in something very much like a bowl cut (or worse—*anathema*—a Beatles shag), was "You want to dance?"

She gave me a look. Shot her eyes to the stage and back, then around the room. A few people were dancing to the canned music, most of them jerking and gyrating to their own drugged-out beat, and there was no sign—yet—of the band we'd come to hear. "To this?"

"Yeah," I said, and I looked so—what was it?—*needy,* though at the time I must have thought I was chiseled out of a block of pure cool. "Come on," I said, and I reached out a hand to her.

I watched the decision firm in her eyes, deep in this moment that would give rise to all the rest, to the part I was about to fast-forward to because I had to get up in the morning. For work. And no excuses. *But watch, watch what comes next . . .*

She took my hand, the soft friction of her touch alive still somewhere in my cell memory, and then she was leading me out onto the dance floor.

She was leading. And I was following.

Will it surprise you to know that I exceeded my self-imposed two-hour limit? That after the sex I fast-forwarded to our first date, which was really just an agreed-upon meeting at Tower Records (March 2, 1982, 4:30 p.m.), and took us thereafter up to Barney's Beanery for cheeseburgers and beers and shots of peppermint schnapps (!),

which she paid for because her father was a rich executive at War-
ner Brothers? Or that it made me feel so good I couldn't resist skip-
ping ahead three months to when she was as integral to my flesh as
the Black Flag T-shirt that never left my back except in the shower?
Lisa. Lisa Denardo. With her cat's tongue and tight torquing body
that was a girl's and a woman's at the same time and her perfect,
evenly spaced set of glistening white teeth (perfect, that is, but for
the incisor she'd had a dentist in Tijuana remove in the spirit of
punk solidarity). The scene I hit on was early the following summer, summer break of my sophomore year in college, when I gave
up on my parents' garage and Lisa and I moved into an off-campus
apartment on Vermont and decided to paint the walls, ceiling and
floors the color of midnight in the Carlsbad Caverns. June 6,
1982, 2:44 p.m. The glisten of black paint, a too-bright sun caught
in the windows and Lisa saying, "Think we should paint the glass
too?" I was oblivious to anything but her and me and the way I
looked and the way she looked, a streak of paint on her left fore-
arm and another, scimitar-shaped, just over one eyebrow, when
suddenly everything went neutral and I was back in the reliving
room staring into the furious face of my daughter.

But let me explain the technology here a moment, for those
of you who don't already know. This isn't a computer screen or
a TV or a hologram or anything anybody else can see—we're
talking retinal projection, two laser beams fixed on two eyeballs. Anybody coming into the room (daughter, wife, boss) will
simply see you sitting there in a chair with your retinas lit like
furnaces. Step in front of the projector—as my daughter did
now—and the image vanishes.

"Stop," I said, and I wasn't talking to her.

But there she was, her hair brushed out for school and her
jaw clenched, looking hate at me. "I can't believe you," she said.
"Do you have any idea what time it is?"

Bleary, depleted—and guilty, deeply guilty, the narcissist

caught in the act and caring about nothing or nobody but his own reliving self—I just gawked at her, the light she'd flicked on when she came into the room transfixing me in the chair. I shook my head.

"It's 6:45, a.m. In the morning. The *morning*, Dad."

I started to say something but the words were tangled up inside of me because Lisa was saying—had just said—"You're not going to make me stay here and watch the paint dry, are you, because I'm thinking maybe we could drive out to the beach or something, just to cool down," and I said, or was going to say, "There's like maybe half a pint of gas in the car."

"What?" Katie demanded. "Were you with Mom again? Is that it? Like you can be with her and I can't?"

"No," I said, "no, that wasn't it, it wasn't your mom at all—"

A tremor ran through her. "Yeah, right. So what was it, then? Some girlfriend, somebody you were gaga over when you were in college? Or high school? Or what, *junior* high?"

"I must have fallen asleep," I said. "Really. I just zoned out."

She knew I was lying. She'd come looking for me, dutiful child, motherless child, and found me not up and about and bustling around the kitchen preparing to fuss over her and see her off to school the way I used to, but pinned here in this chair like an exhibit in a museum, blind to anything but the past, my past and nobody else's, not hers or her mother's, or the country's or the world's, but just mine.

I heard the door slam. Heard the thump of her angry feet in the hallway, the distant muffled crash of the front door, and then the house was quiet. I looked at the slit in the box. "Play," I said.

By the time I got to work I was an hour and a half late, but on this day—miracle of miracles—Kevin was even later, and when he did show up I was ensconced in my cubicle, dutifully rattling

keys on my keyboard. He didn't say anything, just brushed by me and buried himself in his office, but I could see he was wearing the same vacant pre-now look I was, and it didn't take much of an intuitive leap to guess the reason. In fact, since the new model had come on the market, I'd noticed the same randy faraway gaze in the eyes of half a dozen of my fellow employees, including Linda Blanco, the receptionist, who'd stopped buttoning the top three buttons of her blouse and wore shorter and shorter skirts every day. Instead of breathing "Moos and Associates, how may I help you?" into the receiver, now she just said, "Reset."

Was this a recipe for disaster? Was our whole society on the verge of breaking down? Was the NSA going to step in? Were they going to pass laws? Ban the box? I didn't know. I didn't care. I had a daughter to worry about. Thing was, all I could think of was getting home to relive, straight home, and if the image of a carton of milk or a loaf of bread flitted into my head I batted it away. Takeout. We could always get takeout. I was in a crucial phase with Lisa, heading inexorably for the grimmer scenes, the disagreements—petty at first, then monumental, unbridgeable, like the day I got home from my makeup class in Calculus and found her sitting at the kitchen table with a stoner whose name I never did catch and didn't want to know, not then or now—and I needed to get through it, to analyze it whether it hurt or not, because it was there and I had to relive it. I couldn't help myself. I just kept picking at it like a scab.

Ultimately, this was all about Christine, of course, about when I began to fail instead of succeed, to lose instead of win. I needed Lisa to remind me of a time before that, to help me trace my missteps and assign blame, because as intoxicating as it was to relive the birds-atwitter moments with Christine, there was always something nagging at me in any given scene, some twitch of her face or a comment she threw out that should have raised flags at the time but never did. All right. Fine. I was going to

go there, I was, and relive the minutiae of our relationship, the ecstasy and agony both, the moments of mindless contentment and the swelling tide of antipathy that drove us apart, but first things first, and as I fought my way home on the freeway that afternoon, all I could think about was Lisa.

In the old days, before we got the box, my daughter and I had a Friday-afternoon ritual whereby I would stop in at the Italian place down the street from the house, have a drink and chat up whoever was there, then call Katie and have her come join me for a father-daughter dinner so I could have some face-time with her, read into her and suss out her thoughts and feelings as she grew into a young woman herself, but we didn't do that anymore. There wasn't time. The best I could offer—lately, especially—was take-out or a microwave pizza and a limp salad choked down in the cold confines of the kitchen while we separately calculated how long we had to put up with the pretense before slipping off to relive.

There were no lights on in the house as I pulled into the drive-way and that was odd, because Katie should have been home from school by now—and she hadn't texted me or phoned to say she'd be staying late. I climbed out of the car feeling stiff all over—I needed to get more exercise, I knew that, and I resolved to do it too, as soon as I got my head above water—and as I came up the walk I saw the sad frosted artificial wreath hanging crookedly there in the center panel of the front door. Katie must have dug it out of the box of ornaments in the garage on her own initiative, to do something by way of Christmas, and that gave me pause, that stopped me right there, the thought of it, of my daughter having to make the effort all by herself. That crushed me. It did. And as I put the key in the lock and pushed the door open I knew things were going to have to change. Dinner. I'd take her out to dinner and forget about Lisa. At least for now.

"Katie?" I called. "You home?"

No response. I shrugged out of my coat and went on into the

kitchen, thinking to make myself a drink. There were traces of her here, her backpack flung down on the floor, an open bag of Doritos spilling across the counter, a diet Sprite, half-full, on the breadboard. I called her name again, standing stock-still in the middle of the room and listening for the slightest hint of sound or movement as my voice echoed through the house. I was about to pull out my phone and call her when I thought of the reliving room, and it was a sinking thought, not a selfish one, because if she was in there, reliving—and she was, I knew she was—what did that say about her social life? Didn't teenage girls go out anymore? Didn't they gather in packs at the mall or go to movies or post things on Facebook, or, forgive me, go out on dates? Group dates, even? How else were they going to experience the inchoate beginnings of what the Relive Box people were pushing in the first place?

I shoved into the room, which was dark but for the lights of her eyes, and just stood there watching her for a long moment as I adjusted to the gloom. She sat riveted, her body present but her mind elsewhere, and if I was embarrassed—for her, and for me too, her father, invading her privacy when she was most vulnerable—the embarrassment gave way to a sorrow so oceanic I thought I would drown in it. I studied her face. Watched her smile and grimace and go cold and smile again. What could she possibly be reliving when she'd lived so little? Family vacations? Christmases past? The biannual trips to Hong Kong to be with her mother and step-father? I couldn't fathom it. I didn't like it. It had to stop. I turned on the overhead light and stepped in front of the projector.

She blinked at me and she didn't recognize me, didn't know me at all because I was in the now and she was in the past. "Katie," I said, "that's enough now. come on." I held out my arms to her even as recognition came back into her eyes and she made a vague gesture of irritation, of pushing away.

"Katie," I said, "let's go out to dinner. Just the two of us. Like we used to."

"I'm not hungry," she said. "And it's not fair. You can use it all you want, like day and night, but whenever I want it—" and she broke off, tears starting in her eyes.

"Come on," I said. "It'll be fun."

The look she gave me was unsparing. I was trying to deflect it, trying to think of something to say, when she came up out of the chair so suddenly it startled me, and though I tried to take hold of her arm, to pull her to me whether she fought it or not, she was too quick for me. Before I could react, she was at the door, pausing only to scorch me with another glare. "I don't believe you," she spat, before vanishing down the hall.

I should have followed her, should have tried to make things right—or better anyway—but I didn't. The box was right there. It had shut down when she leapt up from the chair and whatever she'd been reliving was buried back inside it, accessible to no one, though you can bet there are hackers out there right now trying to subvert the retinal-recognition feature. For a long moment I stared at the open door, fighting myself, then I went over and pulled it softly shut. I realized I didn't need a drink or dinner either. I sat down in the chair. "Hello, Wes," the box said. "Welcome back."

We didn't have a Christmas tree that year and neither of us really cared all that much, I think—if we wanted to look at spangle-draped trees we could relive holidays past, happier ones, or in my case, I could go back to my childhood and relive my father's whiskey in a glass and my mother's long-suffering face blossoming over the greedy joy of her golden boy, her only child, tearing open his presents as a weak bleached-out California sun haunted the windows and the turkey crackled in the oven. Katie went off (reluctantly, I thought) on a skiing vacation to Mammoth with the family of her best friend, Allison, who she hardly saw anymore, not outside of school, not in the now, and I went back to

Lisa, because if I was going to get to Christine in any serious way—beyond the sex, that is, beyond the holiday greetings and picture-postcard moments—Lisa was my bridge.

As soon as I'd dropped Katie at Allison's house and exchanged a few previously scripted salutations with Allison's grinning parents and her grinning twin brothers, I stopped at a convenience store for a case of eight-ounce bottles of spring water and the biggest box of power bars I could find and went straight home to the reliving room. The night before I'd been close to the crucial scene with Lisa, one that was as fixed in my memory as the blowup with Christine a quarter century later, but elusive as to the date and time. I'd been up all night—*again*—fast-forwarding, reversing, jumping locales and facial expressions, Lisa's first piercing, the evolution of my haircut, but I hadn't been able to pinpoint the exact moment, not yet. I set the water on the floor on my left side, the power bars on my right. "May 9, 1983," I said, "4:00 a.m."

The numbers flashed and then I was in darkness, zero visibility, confused as to where I was until the illuminated dial of a clock radio began to bleed through and I could make out the dim outline of myself lying in bed in the back room of that apartment with the black walls and black ceiling and black floor. Lisa was there beside me, an irregular hump in the darkness, snoring with a harsh gag and stutter. She was stoned. And drunk. Half an hour earlier she'd been in the bathroom, heaving over the toilet, and I realized I'd come too far. "Reset," I said, "reverse ninety minutes."

Sudden light, blinding after the darkness, and I was alone in the living room of the apartment, studying, or trying to. My hair hung limp, my muscles were barely there, but I was young and reasonably good-looking, even excusing any bias. I saw that my Black Flag T-shirt had faded to gray from too much sun and too many washings, and the book in my lap looked as familiar as something I might have been buried with in a previous life, but then this *was* my previous life. I watched myself turn a page,

crane my neck toward the door, get up to flip over the album that was providing the soundtrack. "Reset," I said, "fast-forward ten minutes," and here it was, what I'd been searching for: a sudden crash, the front door flinging back, Lisa and the stoner whose name I didn't want to know fumbling their way in, both of them as slow as syrup with the cumulative effect of downers and alcohol, and though the box didn't have an olfactory feature, I swear I could smell the tequila on them. They'd gone clubbing, midweek, and I couldn't go because of finals, but Lisa could because she didn't have finals and she didn't have work either. I jumped up out of the chair, spilling the book, and shouted something I couldn't quite make out, so I said, "Reset, reverse five seconds."

"You fucker!" was what I'd shouted, and now I shouted it again prior to slapping something out of the guy's hand, a beer bottle, and all at once I had him in a hammerlock and Lisa was beating at my back with her birdclaw fists and I was wrestling the guy out the door, cursing over the soundtrack ("Should I Stay or Should I Go," one of those flatline ironies that almost makes you believe everything in this life's been programmed). I saw now that he was bigger than I was, probably stronger too, but the drugs had taken the volition out of him and in the next moment he was outside the door and the three bolts were hammered home. By me. Who now turned in a rage to Lisa.

"Stop," I said. "Freeze." Lisa hung there, defiant and guilty at the same time, pretty, breathtakingly pretty, despite the slack mouth and drugged-out eyes. I should have left it there, should have forgotten it and gone on to those first cornucopian weeks and months and even years with Christine, but I couldn't help myself. "Play," I said, and Lisa raised a hand to swat at me, but she was too unsteady and knocked the lamp over instead.

"Did you fuck him?" I demanded.

There was a long pause, so long I almost fast-forwarded, and then she said, "Yeah. Yeah, I fucked him. And I'll tell you

something"—her words glutinous, the syllables coalescing on her tongue—"you're no punk. And he is. He's the real deal. And you? You're, you're—"

I should have stopped it right there.

"—you're *prissy*."

"Prissy?" I couldn't believe it. Not then and not now.

She made a broad stoned gesture, weaving on her feet. "Anal retentive. Like who left the dishes in the sink or who didn't take out the garbage or what about the cockroaches—"

"Stop," I said. "Reset. June 19, 1994, 11:02 p.m."

I was in another bedroom now, one with walls the color of cream, and I was in another bed, this time with Christine, and I'd timed the memory to the very minute, post-coital, in the afterglow, and Christine, with her soft aspirated whisper of a voice, was saying, "I love you, Wes, you know that, don't you?"

"Stop," I said. "Reverse five seconds."

She said it again. And I stopped again. And reversed again. And she said it again. And again.

Time has no meaning when you're reliving. I don't know how long I kept it up, how long I kept surfing through those moments of Christine—not the sexual ones, but the loving ones, the companionable ones, the ordinary day-to-day moments when you could see in her eyes that she loved me more than anybody alive and was never going to stop loving me, never. Dinner at the kitchen table, any dinner, any night. Just to be there. My wife. My daughter. The way the light flooded the windows and poured liquid gold over the hardwood floors of our starter house in Canoga Park. Katie's first birthday. Her first word ("Cake!"). The look on Christine's face as she curled up with Katie in bed and read her *Where the Wild Things Are*. Her voice as she hoarsened it for Max: "I'll eat you up!"

Enough analysis, enough hurt. I was no masochist.

At some point, I had to get up from that chair in the now and evacuate a living bladder, the house silent, spectral, unreal. I didn't live here. I didn't live in the now with its deadening nine-to-five job I was in danger of losing and the daughter I was failing and a wife who'd left me—and her own daughter—for Winston Chen, choreographer of martial arts movies in Hong Kong who was loving and kind and funny and not the control freak I was (*Prissy,* anyone? *Anal retentive?*). The house echoed with my footsteps, a stage set and nothing more. I went to the kitchen and dug the biggest pot I could find out from under the sink, brought it back to the reliving room and set it on the floor between my legs to save me the trouble of getting up next time around.

Time passed. Relived time and lived time too. There were two windows in the room, shades drawn so as not to interfere with the business of the moment, and sometimes a faint glow appeared around the margins of them, an effect I noticed when I was searching for a particular scene and couldn't quite pin it down. Sometimes the glow was gone. Sometimes it wasn't. What happened then, and I might have been two days in or three or five, I couldn't really say, was that things began to cloy. I'd relived an exclusive diet of the transcendent, the joyful, the insouciant, the best of Christine, the best of Lisa and all the key moments of the women who came between and after, and I'd gone back to the Intermediate Algebra test, the very instant, pencil to paper, when I knew I'd scored a perfect one hundred percent, and to the time I'd squirted a ball to right field with two outs, two strikes, ninth inning and my Little League team (the Condors, yellow tees, white lettering) down by three, and watched it rise majestically over the glove of the spastic red-haired kid sucking back allergic snot and roll all the way to the wall. Triumph after triumph, goodness abounding—till it stuck in my throat.

"Reset," I said. "January 2, 2009, 4:30 p.m."

I found myself in the kitchen of our second house, this house, the one we'd moved to because it was outside the L.A. city limits and had schools we felt comfortable with sending Katie to. That was what mattered: the schools. Christine and I both insisted on it, and if it lengthened our commutes, so be it. This house. The one I was reliving in now. Everything gleamed around me, counters polished, the glass of the cabinets as transparent as air because details mattered then, everything in its place whether Christine was there or not—especially if she wasn't there, and where was she? Or where had she been? China. With her boss. On film business. Her bags were just inside the front door, where she'd dropped them forty-five minutes ago after I picked her up at the airport and we'd had our talk in the car, the talk I was going to relive when I got done here, because it was all about pain now, about reality, and this scene was the capper, the coup de grâce. You want wounds? You want to take a razor blade to the meat of your inner thigh just to see if you can still feel? Well, here it was.

Christine entered the scene now, coming down the stairs from Katie's room, her eyes wet, or damp anyway, and her face composed. And there I was, pushing myself up from the table, my beginner's bald spot a glint of exposed flesh under the glare of the overhead light. I spoke first. "You tell her?"

Christine was dressed in her business attire, black stockings, heels, skirt to the knee, tailored jacket. She looked exhausted, and not simply from the fifteen-hour flight but from what she'd had to tell me. And our daughter. (How I'd like to be able to relive *that*, to hear how she'd even broached the subject, let alone how she'd smoke-screened her own selfishness and betrayal with some specious concern for Katie's well-being—let's not rock the boat and you'll be better off here with your father and your school and your teachers and it's not the end but just the beginning, buck up, you'll see.)

Christine's voice was barely audible. "I don't like this any better than you do."

"Then why do it?"

A long pause. Too long. "Stop," I said.

I couldn't do this. My heart was hammering. My eyes felt as if they were being squeezed in a vise. I could barely swallow. I reached down for a bottle of water and a power bar, unscrewed the cap, tore open the wrapper, drank, chewed. She was going to say, "This isn't working," and I was going to say, "*Working?* What the fuck are you talking about? What does work have to do with it? I thought this was about love. I thought it was about commitment." I knew I wasn't going to get violent, though I should have, should have chased her out to the cab that was even then waiting at the curb and slammed my way in and flown all the way to Hong Kong to confront Winston Chen, the martial arts genius who could have crippled me with his bare feet.

"Reset," I said. "August 1975, any day, any time."

There was a hum from the box. "Incomplete command. Please select date and time."

I was twelve years old, the summer we went to Vermont, to a lake there where the mist came up off the water like the fumes of a dream and the deer mice lived under the refrigerator, and I didn't have a date or time fixed in my mind—I just needed to get away from Christine, that was all. I picked the first thing that came into my head.

"August 19," I said, "11:30 a.m. Play."

A blacktop road. Sun like a nuclear blast. A kid, running. I recognized myself—I'd been to this summer before, one I remembered as idyllic, messing around in boats, fishing, swimming, wandering the woods with one of the local kids, Billy Scharf, everything neutral, copacetic, life lived in the moment. But why was I running? And why did I have that look on my face, a look that fused determination and helplessness both? Up

the drive now, up the steps to the house, shouting for my parents, "Mom! Dad!"

I began to get a bad feeling.

I saw my father get up off the wicker sofa on the porch, my vigorous young father who was dressed in a T-shirt and jeans and didn't have even a trace of gray in his hair, my father who always made everything right. But not this time. "What's the matter?" he said. "What is it?"

And my mother coming through the screen door to the porch, a towel in one hand and her hair snarled wet from the lake. And me. I was fighting back tears, my legs and arms like sticks, striped polo shirt, faded shorts. "It's," I said, "it's—"

"Stop," I said. "Reset." It was my dog, Queenie, that was what it was, dead on the road that morning, and who'd left the gate ajar so she could get out in the first place? Even though he'd been warned about it a hundred times?

I was in a dark room. There was a pot between my legs and it was giving off a fierce odor. I needed to go deeper, needed out of this. I spouted random dates, saw myself driving to work, stuck in traffic with ten thousand other fools who could only wish they had a fast-forward app, saw myself in my thirties, post-Lisa, pre-Christine, obsessing over Halo, and I stayed there through all the toppling hours, reliving myself in the game, boxes within boxes, until finally I thought of God, or what passes for God in my life, the mystery beyond words, beyond lasers and silicon chips. I gave a date nine months before I was born, "December 30, 1962, 6:00 a.m.," when I was, what—a zygote?—but the box gave me nothing, neither visual nor audio. And that was wrong, deeply wrong. There should have been a heartbeat. My mother's heartbeat, the first thing we hear—or feel, feel before we even have ears.

"Stop," I said. "Reset." A wave of rising exhilaration swept over me even as the words came to my lips, "September 30, 1963,

2:35 a.m.," and the drumbeat started up, *ba-boom, ba-boom,* but no visual, not yet, the minutes ticking by, *ba-boom, ba-boom,* and then I was there, in the light of this world, and my mother in her stained hospital gown and the man with the monobrow and flashing glasses, the stranger, the doctor, saying what he was going to say by way of congratulations and relief. A boy. It's a boy.

Then it all went dead and there was somebody standing there in front of me, and I didn't recognize her, not at first, how could I? "Dad," she was saying, "Dad, are you there?"

I blinked. Tried to focus.

"No," I said finally, shaking my head in slow emphasis, the word itself, the denial, heavy as a stone in my mouth. "I'm not here. I'm not. I'm not."

SHE'S THE BOMB

Ru ok?

                QQ

Srsly? ur crying?

                I want to kill myself

Dont say that

                I'm saying it

If we had a helicopter, or better yet, a drone, we could hover over Hailey Phegler's shoulder at this juncture and watch her text, but we don't, so we won't. Instead, since fiction allows us to do this, we'll go directly inside her head and attempt to assess the grinding awfulness of this moment, which has stranded her, in cap and gown, among the 332 prospective graduates of the College of Arts and Sciences at Hibernia College in Hibernia, New York, where the trees are just beginning to unfold their leaves after the long winnowing blast of an upstate winter. She is beyond

distraught—she is panicking. Breathing in such short gasps her thumbs actually tremble over the keypad.

When she glances up from her phone in a tic of annoyance, the first person she locks eyes with is Stephanie Joiner, who was in her Introduction to Poetry class last spring and who has zero style and a brain the size of a Snickers bar, but who's here nonetheless, in cap and gown and with her hair combed out and sprayed with shellac, all set to graduate.

"Hi," Stephanie says, coming right up to her so Hailey has to hide her screen, which produces an awkward moment. Somebody, wasted already, shouts "Free at last!" and a low undercurrent of giggly laughter washes through the crowd. "Oh my god," Stephanie chirps, and is she actually going to take her hand, or what, hug her? "I mean, it's been like ice ages, right?" Her contacts have a weird tint, too blue by half, but her eyes are like lasers. "I didn't even know you were still—" she starts, but she doesn't want to go there and cuts herself off. There's a moment of self-congratulatory beaming, the lasers slicing right into her, before Stephanie says, "Congrats, you!" And then, after a quick shuffle of her clunky white platforms that only show off how thick her ankles are, she adds the refrain "We made it! Can you believe it?"

Every word is a nail, and this girl, this nobody with her pasted-on smile, is a human nailgun, and this place, the First Niagara Bank Center quad, with its rearing white tent erected by underpaid illegal immigrants, is the worst place Hailey has ever been in her life. She wants to lash out. Wants to swing her purse like a whatever you call it—a *mace*—and just obliterate the smile from Stephanie Joiner's face, but she hasn't got time for that, so she holds up her phone by way of excuse, turns her back on her and shoots off another text to her best friend, Janelle Esposito, in Annandale-on-Hudson, whose graduation at Bard isn't till the following weekend.

Pls get me out of here!

Wish i could

I'm desprt

Chill it will work out

No, no, no b/c my mothers
here

I thought she wasnt
coming?

I have 2 do something

Like what? like tell her?

I'd rather die

Ur dressed the part ur
walking whos going to
know?

My mom didnt see my
name on the list

So? they make mistakes.

I'm going 2 like off myself

Stop it

Srsly i never thought
i'd wish for a school
shooting . . .

???

Srsly

Her mother, since as long as she could remember, was always harping on her. And what was her main theme? You're a procrastinator, that's what she said. Elementary school, junior high, high school and now college. *You're a procrastinator.* All right, guilty as charged, but then who isn't? The problem wasn't her, really, it was Nathaniel Hawthorne. Back in September, when she couldn't put off her American Lit requirement anymore, she'd signed up for Professor Dugan's course and the first book was *The Scarlet Letter,* which might as well have been written in Mandarin Chinese for all she could make sense of it. *But there is a fatality, a*

feeling so irresistible and inevitable that it has the force of doom, which almost invariably compels human beings to linger around and haunt, ghostlike, the spot where some great and marked event has given the color to their lifetime; and still the more irresistibly, the darker the tinge that saddens it.

No joke, it was just plain boring and so she procrastinated as far as actually reading it went and then, even with the help of Write My Paper Here and Best Term-Paper Service, trying to do the paper on it, and then one thing led to another and she stopped going to Professor Dugan's class because of the embarrassment factor, and once she'd stopped she had to pull the plug on her other courses too, even her poetry workshop, because the classes were all in Fenster Hall and she couldn't risk running across Professor Dugan, who would stink-eye her through his Coke-bottle lenses and wonder why she hadn't been to class and when he could expect her Hawthorne paper, if, like, ever? Plus, it was around then that she met Connor Hayes and fell hard and just wanted to be with him through those warm drifting endless Indian summer afternoons when the sun threw the shadows of the trees across the quad in a thousand rippling variations and the two main student bars—Elsie's and The Study Hall—were offering Happy Hour all day every day until further notice. And there were the other bars in the outlying towns Connor loved to take her to on the back of his turquoise Triumph motorcycle so they could watch their beers sizzle on the bartop and eat peanuts in the shell and snuggle and laugh and feel as if life actually opened out instead of boxing you in with Nathaniel Hawthorne and who, Jonathan Edwards? Jesus. School was bad enough as it was, but Professor Dugan's class just broke her spirit, crushed her, really—it was all so useless, so *stupid*—and then Connor came along and that was that.

What did she tell her mother? Nothing. School was fine, everything was fine, and if she sounded a little down it was just

because she was working so hard. "That's fine, honey," her mother told her over the phone, "just don't put too much pressure on yourself—remember, no matter how dark it may seem now, there's a light at the end of the tunnel. Think of May. May'll be here before you know it."

"Hi, Hail." She's standing there in the crowd of students, frowning at her phone, and there's somebody else squeezing in on her now, somebody calling her name, tall, a guy, and she looks up into the face of Toll Hauser, who used to be Connor's best bud before Connor dumped her and he dumped Connor so he could ask her out without too many complications, and that was okay, because she liked him even if she wasn't all that attracted to him, but really, over the last month she'd been in such a mounting panic she could barely get out of bed, eating nothing but shrimp ramen and sleeping fourteen hours a day, and so she kept putting him off. Six-five, skinny, the gown hanging on him like a shroud, like something Hawthorne would wear in his day, Toll has the mortarboard raked down over one eye, which gives him a kind of comical look that might have cheered her up under any other circumstances, but just leaves her speechless now. "Cool to see you made it," he says, flapping the arms of the gown as if he's going to lift off and soar around the tent. "You must've worked your butt off on those incompletes . . ."

"Yeah," she says, and the word—the single syllable—is like the pit of some sour fruit she's tried to swallow whole.

"You all right?" He's bending over now, his face almost level with hers, his arms dangling and his shoulders tentpoling in back. "I mean, you look . . . you start the party already?"

"I'm okay," she says, each word like a finger locking into place around her throat. "It's just—my mother, you know?"

"Tell me about it." He flashes that smile of his, his best feature,

really, but he isn't Connor and never will be and he's just making her tenser, delaying her, because it's now or never and she really can't see any other way out. Both his parents are here too, he tells her, nattering on, and three of his grandparents, plus his kid sister and his aunt and uncle and like half a dozen cousins, and he's not complaining but all he really wants to do is go down to Elsie's with everybody else and get shit-faced. He says something more, a whole lot more, but she's not listening because she's too keyed up, the words she can't say, the words she's going to say into her phone in the next sixty seconds going off like alarm bells in her head. After a minute, people swarming all around them and some dean or somebody trying to get their attention so they can take their seats before the doors open to the general public, she realizes he's still staring at her and she can't help herself because she just wants this over with and when she snaps *What?* at him he actually steps back a foot.

"I was just saying, will I see you there? At Elsie's? Or have you got some family thing?"

She doesn't answer because she's not there anymore, moving now, the scholarly folds of her robe snatching and billowing, pushing through the crowd of people she mostly recognizes, heading for the exit where they set up the Porta-Pottys so she can have a little privacy, the words she can't say looping over and over like a short-circuit in her brain: *There's a bomb in the Bank Center quad. A bomb, you hear me?*

So i did it

        Did what?

Called in a bomb

        ???

U there?

        Ur joking

OMG my heart is like
  10000 beats a second

What ru saying?

I'm saying i did it

Are you serious? i'm
like, stunned

Real life

Real life? hail, what are
you thinking?

I told you i was desprt

That's when things really accelerate, the dean or whoever he is, the president maybe, going to the microphone on the dais and thumping it with one thick finger so the blast of static makes everybody look up, and then he's saying, "Attention, please— seniors, everyone!" The chatter of the crowd falls off, and at the same time, as if all that noise has somehow been suppressing it, the smell of perfume rises up like some fog that's choking her all of a sudden, Vera Wang, Dolce & Gabbana, Juicy Couture, and her stomach clenches so fast and hard and tight she thinks she's going to be sick right there in the middle of the temporary floor- ing the immigrants magically laid down overnight. "There's a situation here that's just come to our attention," the dean hisses through the speakers, his face a pinched white sack straining at the knot of his bow tie, "and believe me, we're going to get to the bot- tom of this, and I do not find this amusing, people, not at all—"

And what is she feeling? A complete revolution, three hun- dred sixty degrees, suddenly as high as she's ever been in her life, her whole body throbbing with the endorphins rushing through her, and she can already see it, dinner with her mom and Aunt Ceecie, who's come all the way up from North Carolina for the occasion. What a crime somebody had to spoil the day, she'll say over her first margarita, rocks, no salt, some prankster, some idiot, but so they send my degree in the mail, what matters is we're all here together, right? Right, Mom? Right?

"The fact is," the dean says, "somebody called in a bomb threat—" An instant of stunned amazement, and then the tumult breaks out, people gasping, shouting, cursing, as if the whole quad's one big pit filled right to the top with bilge water and everybody's drowning together. The faces around her are worse than ugly, pathetic really, people just chewing at the air, flailing their arms, digging out their cell phones to mindlessly record whatever this is or might be. "So what we're going to have to do," the dean goes on, "and I'm sorry, but we have no choice in the matter, is—"

Cancel the ceremony, she shouts inside the reverberant walls of her own skull, *cancel it and go back to your dorm rooms and your parents and loved ones or whoever—*

"—change the venue to the Threlkeld Arena." The dean has to raise his voice now, because even with the microphone the noise under that tent is too much for him to cope with no matter how much he's fighting to project an aura of calm for the sake of everybody present. "Which means we will convene there in exactly"— she watches in disbelief as he throws back the billowing sleeve of his robe to check his watch—"one hour and fifteen minutes from now. So, everybody"—more shouts, groans, tumult—"the new time will be seven p.m. sharp. Is that clear?"

Ru kidding me?

        Beyond belief

What ru going 2 do now?

        I dont know my moms
         berserk

Tell her?

        U cant be serious!? like
        tell her I lied & then
        what, called in a bomb?

Not the bomb u cant tell
 anybody ever they'll put
 u in jail

Shit dont tell me that,
shit, shit, shit!!!

U have 2 tell your mom
sooner or later so u need
2 tell her now

No way

Way

Sorry got 2 go

There are five thousand people out there waiting to get into the tent, which is something like fifteen friends and relatives for every graduate, and they are definitely not happy about having to traipse all the way across campus to Threlkeld, which, unbeknownst to her, the college always reserves as a backup venue in case of a tornado or lightning storm or any other unforeseen event. Like a bomb threat. Or what, nuclear holocaust. Which, to her mind, would be better than this—anything would be better than this.

She's squeezed in tight with the mass of graduates making for the back exit, the dean and a dozen other functionaries, like Ms. Krentz, the PE teacher who coaches women's soccer and has a face like an over-inflated soccer ball, insisting they all stay together for safety's sake in case the threat is real, which in ninety-nine percent of the cases it isn't, but the college can't take that risk. Obviously. So Hailey's boxed in and sweating—it must be ninety degrees—and her heart is going so hard she thinks she's having a heart attack and here they are out in the sunshine with the trees everywhere and the sweet cool smell of the air and Stephanie Joiner comes out of nowhere like a guided missile to stick her face in hers and crow, "Can you believe it? I mean"—loping along in her big white heels that are like rowboats on the green river of the lawn—"what a shitty thing for somebody to do."

"You don't think it's real, then?"

Stephanie looks almost insulted. "You kidding me? It's just some asshole, some frat rat that thinks he's being cute—"

"What about the terrorists?"

"Terrorists? What are you talking about? In Hibernia? There isn't a Muslim within three hundred miles of here."

"Well, they're not *all* Muslims," she says, matching her stride for stride when all she wants is to get away someplace private because she knows what she has to do, of course she does, and that's make another phone call to public safety because there're bombs all over the place, don't they realize that? In Threlkeld especially. "I mean, what about Columbine? Or what, that elementary school in where was it, Connecticut?"

Stephanie—how did she manage to glom onto her? doesn't she have any friends?—just swings her head round to glare at her without breaking stride, tramp, tramp, tramp. "I'm not going to debate you. It's a prank. Bet you anything."

"Terrorists," she insists, or tries to, but she doesn't sound very convincing, because after all, Stephanie's right, whether she knows it or not. What do they shout, the terrorists? *Allahu Akbar!* Why doesn't some dude in a beard come running across campus shouting *Allahu Akbar* and save her the trouble? Tramp, tramp, tramp. It would be almost funny if she wasn't having a heart attack. Everybody's murmuring and bitching, the whole black-clad crowd of them trudging across the lawn like cattle with Ms. Krentz and a dozen other profs herding them along because the college is running scared now and they all have to stick together, the sun, the trees, the mass of parents somewhere behind them, and all at once she breaks free and makes for the nearest building, Morey Hall, the engineering building she's been in maybe once in her life and she's furious suddenly, because why won't they listen to her?

She needs privacy. She's having a heart attack. She's got her phone in her hand. But here's Ms. Krentz double-timing across the grass to cut her off, calling out to her from fifty feet away, "No, no—you're all to stick together." And then, adding lamely, "Till we get this sorted out. Dean's orders."

It's a moment. Ms. Krentz is right there, pulling up short. "Come on," she says, and she couldn't recognize her, could she? It's been three years since Hailey took PE, and she was hardly a shining light, especially since she couldn't for the life of her figure out how to dismount the parallel bars without crashing on her ass about sixty percent of the time. "I know this is hard, but we need to—"

"I have to use the restroom."

Ms. Krentz—she wears her hair long, unlike any other PE teacher on this planet, and if her face wasn't so puffy she might almost have been attractive, or once maybe—gives her a look of incredulity. "You can't hold it till we get there?"

"It's an emergency?"

Everyone's shuffling past and giving them sidelong looks, as if things aren't unusual enough as it is, and Ms. Krentz just lets it go. "Be careful, okay?" she says, then turns round and starts back across the lawn.

Inside the restroom at the far end of a cool wax-smelling hall with arched ceilings and framed photos of men in lab coats and glasses glinting from the walls, Hailey locks the door and ducks into the farthest stall down and then locks that door too, steadies her phone in one trembling hand and punches in the number. Someone answers on the first ring—a man, the same man she talked to half an hour ago, his voice tense and low. "Hello?"

"I told you," she says. "I warned you. There's bombs all over the place, in Threlkeld too. You need to clear out graduation or things are going to get"—and here she hesitates, all the bad lines

from all the bad movies she's ever seen cartwheeling through her brain—"get ugly," she says finally, and cuts the connection.

Thanksgiving break had been the worst, till now anyway, going home and having to act as if everything was okay and listen to her mother go on about how proud she was of her, the first one in their family to graduate college and could she possibly know how much that meant to her? She actually brought a bunch of books home with her and locked herself in her room with her laptop to keep up the pretense when she wasn't out making the rounds with her girlfriends from high school and some of the guys too, who were all home from their various schools, and she kept up the pretense with them too. Her mother kept asking if she had enough money for books, tuition, housing, and she kept saying she was okay, living off-campus now with these two other girls and telling her how much she appreciated the checks, which were fine, they really were. Did she like lying to her mother's face? No. But she kept meaning to make up the classwork, at least that first semester, but then, after winter break, Connor unceremoniously dumped her to go out with Chrissie Fortgang, a blond stuck-up bitch whose father owned half the building supply stores in upstate New York and Vermont too, and she went into a depression that just kept spiraling down till she hated herself and couldn't get out of bed and for a while there (in February, February was the low point) even stopped going out to Elsie's and The Study Hall. It was like she was in a cell in a prison somewhere, and if she did go out to the bars there was no joy in it because she knew it was inevitable she'd see Connor there, with or without Chrissie Fortgang, and she felt she just couldn't handle that. Spring, which always used to make her feel as if her whole life just got kickstarted and she could do anything there was in the world, slammed down on her like the lid of a coffin, and she didn't go home for spring break because she

couldn't face her mother and she didn't go anywhere else either. Just stayed in her room, hating herself, while her two roommates went to Saint Thomas and soaked up the sun.

She was so miserable that week she even tried Hawthorne again, as if that would help her, as if she could roll that big stone of Professor Dugan's class off her chest and then maybe go to summer school or something, just catch a break, but that didn't happen because Hawthorne was as impenetrable—*boring*—as ever and how he could be some sort of big American writer was beyond her, even in his day when things were so slow and rural and people didn't have as much choice in their lives.

Had I one friend,—or were it my worst enemy!—to whom, when sickened with the praises of all other men, I could daily betake myself, and be known as the vilest of all sinners, methinks my soul might keep itself alive thereby. Even thus much of truth would save me! But now, it is all falsehood!—all emptiness!—all death!

Right. So die already.

U there?

    I'm here but i'm afraid to ask—u ok?

Not

    U really called in again?

What else was i supposed to do?

    Thats crazy

They dont, i mean they're not, like nothings happening & my moms in the stands

    Dont panic

You know what, i wish i did have a bomb

This is the worst moment of her life, maybe of anybody's life, ever, though right there at the dark margins of her imagina-

tion she can picture a whole vast world of refugees and genocide victims and starvation and disease spinning away from her out beyond the towering high ceiling of the basketball arena and the safety and privilege it encloses, but you've got to put it in perspective. None of that matters now, not the kittens in the kill shelters she used to circulate petitions over when she was in high school or the welfare mothers or the Zika babies or anything else—she'd sacrifice them all in a heartbeat, right now, right here and now, if those idiots would only take her seriously. Just for today, that's all she asks, just this once. They're the public safety department, aren't they? What are they, deaf? Don't they care? What if some maniac really did call in a threat? What then?

She is seated now, one of 332 prospective graduates in the crisp white folding chairs that scallop the backs of their black gowns as far as she can see in front of her, and so far nothing is happening. There's a smell of body heat, cologne, that perfume again. Gum maybe. Everyone's chewing gum because the atmosphere's so tense, the crowd in the bleachers buzzing softly, like the yellow jackets that used to hover in the meadow out back of the house on hot, still summer days, the students around her looking vacant and sober, any party atmosphere just squashed dead now. She wants to text. She has to text. It's like breathing. Janelle's the only person in the world that knows what she's feeling right now and she needs her more than anything, but she can't text now, she won't, this is it, the final drop of the final blade, and why aren't they canceling it, why isn't the dean—?

But there he is, rising up out of the first row with a whole troop of dignitaries, older people, white hair and red ears, jewelry, sashes, and that woman, she must be the politician that's supposed to deliver the commencement speech, though nobody's ever heard of her, and—

But again. Always a but, always an interruption.

At first she didn't notice the two men in uniform, not public

safety, but cops, real cops, making their way up the row in the opposite direction of the dignitaries, heightened security, that's what it is, and still she doesn't get it. Not yet. Not until they keep on coming, walking abreast, their heads up and eyes alert, as if they're looking for something, and they finally stop at the aisle where she's sitting, six seats in from the left.

In the days of Connor, the first days and weeks especially, she felt freer than she ever had in her whole life, because she was in love, yes, but not just with him, with the idea of him too. School had been the one constant in her life since the dawn of consciousness, preschool, kindergarten, elementary school, junior high, senior high, college, on and on till she hit the wall in Dugan's class, and Connor—who'd dropped out junior year to sail through the Panama Canal to Puerto Vallarta and back round again and never did bother to reenroll, or at least he was taking his time about it—was contra to all that. He gave her those slow syrupy days, gave her the wind in her face and the smell of the grass and the flowers and the wild rocket ride of a beer and shot for breakfast, though of course he was a bastard and had been all along and she hated him. But back then? There was this one outfit she used to wear—black Topshop jeans, suede ankle boots and a tight tee that read HOME-MADE across her tits—and every time he saw her in it he'd give her a slow smile and say, "Hey, Hail, you're the bomb, you know it?"

If there's irony in that, she's not the one to appreciate it. You can't afford irony when your mother looks at you like she wants to cut you up in small pieces and feed you to the sharks, when you have a lawyer and have to go to court and when the memory of that night at graduation when they traced her calls and came up the aisle and took her away in handcuffs is like a slow drip of acid every minute of every day she has her eyes open.

The good news? She's not getting any jail time, or any more

than the one night she already served before her aunt Ceecie bailed her out because her mother wouldn't. She's currently working as a sales clerk at Nordstrom Rack in Poughquasic Falls to pay down the $10,000 fine the judge imposed on her and she's got two and a half years left of the three years' probation they gave her, with community service thrown in for good measure. Nobody at Hibernia will ever speak to her again, not that that's a bad thing, especially. And Poughquasic Falls, which is fifteen miles south of Hibernia, is just far enough away so she doesn't have to really see any of them. She's down on herself, of course, so far down she sometimes thinks she'll never climb back up, but she's trying, each day that crawls by taking her that much further from that arena and the nightmares that shook her awake every night for the first month. She's got a dirt-cheap efficiency above the thrift store, a neighborhood bar she can almost tolerate, and she's just started seeing this guy who likes to shoot pool there on weekends (he drives a Ford Saturn and if he's ever even heard of a Triumph motorcycle it's only because it's part of the background noise of society).

So there's this one day, maybe ten days before Christmas, the store a madhouse, and she glances up from the cash register and who does she see standing there in back of her current customer but Stephanie Joiner. Stephanie doesn't notice her at first because she's got her head down, mentally adding up the price tags, so Hailey has a moment to prepare herself, fighting down the sick feeling rising in her throat. If anything, Stephanie looks even worse than in college, her hair cut short as if she's the penitent and not Hailey, and she's wearing a white parka that makes her look like the Doughboy. That helps. But still, once the woman in front of her—middle-aged, dandruff like sleet in her hair, taking forever to dig out her credit card and ID—bundles up her packages and steps aside, there's Stephanie, looking as if she's in *Saw II* or something.

"Jingle Bell Rock" rattles out of hidden speakers. The whole

store smells of that Christmasy cinnamon deodorizer the floor manager likes to go around spraying every fifteen minutes and the overhead lights are harsh, blunting everybody's eyes and making death masks of their faces. For a long moment Stephanie just stands there, clinging to her armful of ugly skirts and uglier sweaters, then, without a word, she marches over to the next cash register and gets in the back of the line. And then it's the next customer and the next one after that.

Guess who i saw in the store like ten minutes ago?

Who?

Stephanie joiner

Who's that?

Like really i might as well have a letter A stitched on my sweater

What ru talking about?

Or a B, maybe a B

??? who's stephanie?

I don't know just some girl

So who is she?

Actually?

Yeah

She's nobody

So why mention her?

I dont know maybe b/c i'm nobody too

Dont say that

I'm saying it

ARE WE NOT MEN?

The dog was the color of a maraschino cherry and what it had in its jaws I couldn't quite make out at first, not until it parked itself under the hydrangeas and began throttling the thing. This little episode would have played itself out without my even noticing, except that I'd gone to the stove to put the kettle on for a cup of tea and happened to glance out the window at the front lawn. The lawn, a deep lush blue-green that managed to hint at both the turquoise of the sea and the viridian of a Kentucky meadow, was something I took special pride in, and any wandering dog, no matter its chromatics, was an irritation to me. The seed had been pricey—a blend of chewings fescue, bahia and zoysia incorporating a gene from a species of algae that allowed it to glow under the porchlight at night—and while it was both disease- and drought-resistant it didn't take well to foot traffic, especially four-footed traffic.

I stepped out on the porch and clapped my hands, thinking to shoo the dog away, but it didn't move. Actually, it did, but only to flex its shoulders and tighten its jaws around its prey, which I now saw was my neighbor Allison's pet micropig. The pig

itself—doe-eyed and no bigger than a Pekingese—didn't seem to be struggling, or not any longer, and even as I came down off the porch looking to grab the first thing I could find to brandish at the dog, I felt my heart thundering. Allison was one of those pet owners who tend to anthropomorphize their animals and that pig was the center of her unmarried and unboyfriended life—she would be shattered, absolutely, and who was going to break the news to her? I felt a surge of anger. How had the stupid thing got out of the house anyway, and for that matter, whose dog was this? I didn't own a garden rake and there were no sticks on the lawn (the street trees were an edited variety that didn't drop anything, not twigs, seeds or leaves, no matter the season) so I stormed across the grass empty-handed, shouting the first thing that came to mind, which was "Bad! Bad dog!"

I wasn't thinking. And the effect wasn't what I would have hoped for even if I had been: the dog dropped the pig, all right, which was clearly beyond revivification at this point, but in the same motion it lurched up and clamped its jaws on my left fore-arm, growling continuously, as if my forearm were a stick it had fetched in a friendly game between us. Curiously, there was no pain—and no blood either—just a firm insistent pressure, the saliva hot and wet on my skin as I pulled in one direction and the dog, all the while regarding me out of a pair of dull uniform eyes, pulled in the other. "Let go!" I demanded, but the dog didn't let go. "Bad dog!" I repeated. I tugged. The dog tugged back.

There was no one on the street, no one in the next yard over, no one in the house behind me to come to my aid. I was dressed in the T-shirt, shorts and slippers I'd pulled on not ten minutes earlier when I'd got out of bed, and here I was caught up in this maddening interspecies pas de deux at eight in the morning of an otherwise ordinary day, already exhausted. The dog, this cherry-red hairless freak with the armored skull and bulging muscula-ture of a pit bull, showed no sign of giving in: it had got my arm

and it meant to keep it. After a minute of this, I went down on one knee to ease the tension in my back, a gesture that only seemed to excite the animal all the more, its nails tearing up divots as it fought for purchase, trying, it occurred to me now, to bring me down to its level. Before I knew what I was doing I balled up my free hand and punched the thing in the head three times in quick succession.

The effect was instantaneous: the dog dropped my arm and let out a yelp, backing off to hover at the edge of the lawn and eye me warily, as if now, all at once, the rules of the game had changed. In the next moment, just as I realized I was, in fact, bleeding, a voice cried out behind me, "Hey, I saw that!"

A girl was striding across the lawn toward me, a preternaturally tall girl I at first took to be a teenager but was actually a child of eleven or twelve. As soon as she appeared, the dog fell in step with her and everything became clear. She marched directly up to me, glaring, and said, "You hit my dog."

I was in no mood. "I'm bleeding," I said, holding out my arm in evidence. "You see this? Your dog bit me. You ought to keep him chained up."

"That's not true—Ruby would never bite anybody. She was just . . . playing, is all."

I wasn't about to debate her. This was my property, my arm, and that lump of flesh lying there bleeding into the grass was Allison's dead pet. I pointed to it.

"Oh," she said, her voice dropping, "I'm *so* sorry, I didn't . . . is it yours?"

"My neighbor's." I gestured to the house just visible over the hedge. "She's going to be devastated. This pig"—I wanted to call it by name, personalize it, but couldn't summon its name for the life of me—"is all she has. And it wasn't cheap either." I glanced at the dog, its pinkish gaze and incarnadine flanks. "As I'm sure you can appreciate."

The girl, who stood three or four inches taller than me and whose own eyes were an almost iridescent shade of violet that didn't exist in nature, or at least hadn't until recently, gave me an unflinching look. "Maybe she doesn't have to know."

"What do you mean she doesn't have to know? The thing's dead—look at it."

"Maybe it was run over by a car."

"I don't believe it—you want me to lie to her?"

The girl shrugged. The dog, panting, settled down on its haunches. "I already said I'm sorry. Ruby got out the front gate when my mother went to work—and I came right after her, you saw me—"

"What about this?" I demanded, holding up my arm, which wasn't so much punctured as abraded, since most of the new breeds had had their canines and carnassials genetically modified to prevent any real damage in situations like this. "It has its shots, right?"

"She's a *Cherry Pit*," the girl said, giving me a look of disgust. "Germline immunity comes with the package. I mean, everybody knows that."

It was a Tuesday and I was working from home, as I did every Tuesday and Thursday. I worked in IT, like practically everybody else on the planet, and I found I actually got more done at home than when I went into the office. My coworkers were a trial, what with their moods, opinions, facial tics and all the rest—not that I didn't like them, it was just that they always seemed to manage to get in the way at crunch time. Or maybe I didn't like them, maybe that was it. At any rate, after the little contretemps with the girl and her dog, I went back in the house, smeared an antibiotic ointment on my forearm, took my tea and a handful of protein wafers to my desk and sat down at the computer. If I gave the dead pig

a thought, it was only in relation to Allison, who'd want to see the corpse, I supposed, which brought up the question of what to do with it—let it lie where it was or stuff it in a trash bag and refrigerate it till she got home from the office? I thought of calling my wife—Connie was regional manager of Bank USA, by necessity a master of interpersonal relations, and she would know what to do—but then it was hardly worth bothering her at work over something so trivial. I could have buried the corpse, I suppose, or tossed it in the trash and played dumb, but in the end I wound up doing nothing.

It was past three by the time I thought to take a lunch break and because it was such a fine day I brought my sandwich and a glass of iced tea out onto the front porch. By this juncture I'd forgotten all about the pig, the dog and the grief that was brewing for Allison, but as soon as I stepped out the door it all came back to me: the trees were alive with crowparrots variously screeching, cawing and chattering amongst themselves, and they were there for a very specific reason. (I don't know if you have crowparrots in your neighborhood yet, incidentally, but believe me, they're coming. They were the inspiration of one of the molecular embryologists at the university here who felt that inserting genes of the common crow into the invasive parrot population would put an end to the parrots' raids on our orchards and vineyards, giving them a taste for garbage and carrion instead of fruit on the vine and having the added benefit of displacing the native crows, which had pretty well eliminated songbirds from our backyards. The only problem was the noise factor—something in the mix seemed to have redoubled not only the volume but the complexity of the birds' calls so half the time you needed earplugs if you wanted to enjoy pretty much any outdoor activity.)

Which was the case now. The birds were everywhere, cursing fluidly (*Bad bird! Fuck, fuck, fuck!*) and flapping their spangled wings in one another's faces. Alarmed, I came down off the porch

and for the second time that day scrambled across the lawn to the flowerbed, where a scrum of birds had settled on the remains of Allison's pet. I flailed my arms and they lifted off reluctantly into the sky, screeching *Turdbird!* and the fractured call that awakened me practically every morning: *Cock-k-k-k-sucker!* As for the pig (which I should have dragged into the garage, I realized that now), its eyes were gone and its faintly bluish hide was striped with bright red gashes. Truthfully? I didn't want to touch the thing—it was filthy. The birds were filthy. Who knew what zoonoses they were carrying? So I was just standing there, in a quandary, when Allison's car pulled into the driveway next door, scattering light.

Allison was in her early thirties, with a top-heavy figure and a barely tamed kink of ginger hair she kept wrapped up in various scarves, which gave her an exotic look, as if she were displaced here in the suburbs. She was sad-faced and sweet, the victim of one catastrophic relationship after another, and I couldn't help feeling protective toward her, a single woman alone in that big house her mother had left her when she died. So when she came across the lawn, already tearing up, I felt I'd somehow let her down, and before I knew what I was doing I'd stripped off my shirt and draped it over the corpse.

"Is that her?" she asked, looking down at the hastily covered bundle at my feet. "No," she said, "don't tell me," and then her eyes jumped to mine and she was repeating my name, "Roy, Roy, Roy," as if wringing it in her throat. *Fuck you!* the crowparrots cried from the trees. *Fuck, fuck, fuck!* In the next moment she flung herself into my arms, clutching me to her so desperately I could hardly breathe.

"I don't want to see," she said in a small voice, each syllable a hot puff of breath on the bare skin of my chest. I could smell her hair, the shampoo she used, the taint of sweat under her arms.

"The poor thing," she murmured and lifted her face so I could see the tears blurring her eyes. "I loved her, Roy, I really *loved* her."

This called up a scene from the past, a dinner party at Allison's, Connie and me, another couple and Allison and her last inamorata, a big-headed boor who worked for Animal Control, incinerating strays and transgenic misfits. Allison had kept the pig in her lap throughout the meal, feeding it from her plate, and afterward, while we sat around the living room cradling brandies and Benedictine, she propped the thing up at the piano, where it picked out "Twinkle, Twinkle, Little Star" with its modified hooves.

"No," I said, agreeing with her, "you don't want to look."

"It was a dog, right? That's what"—and here she had to break off a moment to gather herself. "That's what Terry Wolfson said when she called me at work—"

I was going to offer up some platitude about how the animal hadn't suffered, though for all I knew the dog had gummed it relentlessly, the way it had gummed my arm, when a voice called "Hello?" from the street behind us and we broke awkwardly apart. Coming up the walk was the tall girl, tottering on a pair of platform heels, and she had the dog with her, this time on a leash. I felt a stab of annoyance—hadn't she caused enough trouble already?—and embarrassment, that too. It wasn't like me to go shirtless in public—or to be caught in a full-body embrace with my unmarried next door neighbor either, for that matter.

If she could read my face, the girl gave no indication of it. She came right up to us, the dog trotting along docilely at her side. Her violet gaze swept from me to the lump on the ground beneath the bloodied T-shirt and finally to Allison. "*Je suis désolée, madame,*" she said. "*Pardonne-moi. Mon chien ne savait pas ce qu'il faisait—il est un bon chien, vraiment.*"

This girl, this child, loomed over us, her features animated.

She was wearing eyeliner, lipstick and blusher, as if she were ten years older and on her way to a nightclub, and her hair—blond, with a natural curl—spread like a tent over her shoulders and dangled all the way down to the small of her back. "What are you saying?" I demanded. "And why are you speaking French?"

"Because I can. *Puedo hablar en español también und Ich kann auch in Deutsch sprechen.* My IQ is 162 and I can run the hundred meters in 9.58 seconds."

"Wonderful," I said, exchanging a look with Allison. "Terrific. Really. But what are you doing here, what do you want?"

Your mother! the birds cried. *Up yours!*

The girl shifted from one foot to the other, looking awkward, like the child she was. "I just wanted to please, *please* beg you not to report Ruby to Animal Control, because my father says they'll come and put her down. She's a good dog, she really is, and she never did anything like this before, and we never, never, ever let her run loose. It was just a—"

"Freak occurrence?" I said.

"Right," she said. "An anomaly. An accident."

Allison's jaw tightened. The dog looked tranquilly up at us out of its pink eyes as if all this were none of its concern. A bugless breeze rustled the trees along the street. "And what am I supposed to say?" Allison put in. "How am I supposed to feel? What do you want, forgiveness? Well, I'm sorry, but I just can't do it, not now." She gave the girl a fierce look. "You love your dog?"

The girl nodded.

"Well, I love—*loved*—Shushawna too." She choked up. "More than anything in the world."

We all took a minute to gaze down on the carcass, then the girl lifted her eyes. "My father says we'll pay all damages. Here," she said, digging into her purse and producing a pair of business cards, one of which she handed to me and the other to Allison. "Any medical treatment you may need, we'll take care of, one

hundred percent," she assured me, eyeing my arm doubtfully before turning to Allison. "And replace your pet too, if you want, *madame*. It was a micropig, right, from Recombicorp? Or if you want—my father authorized me to say this—we could get you a Cherry Pit, like Ruby, or even a dogcat, if that sounds like a good idea at all—"

It was a painful moment. I could feel for Allison and the girl too, though Connie and I didn't have any pets, not even one of the new hypoallergenic breeds, and we didn't have children either, though we'd discussed it often enough. There was a larger sadness at play here, the sadness of attachment and loss and the way the world wreaks its changes whether we're ready for them or not. We would have gotten through the moment, I think, coming to some sort of understanding—Allison wasn't vindictive and I wasn't about to raise a fuss—but that same breeze swept across the lawn to flip back the edge of the T-shirt and expose the eyeless head of the pig and that was all it took. Allison let out a gasp, and the dog—that crimson freak—jerked the leash out of the girl's hand and went right for it.

When Connie came home, I was in the kitchen mixing a drink. The front door slammed (Connie was always in a hurry, no wasted motion, and though I'd asked her a hundred times not to slam the door, she was constitutionally incapable of taking the extra two seconds to ease it shut). An instant later her briefcase slapped down on the hallway table with the force of a thunderclap, her heels drilled the parquet floor—*tat-tat-tat-tat*—and then she was there, in the kitchen, saying, "Make me one too, would you, honey? Or no: wine. Do we have any wine?"

I didn't ask her how her day had gone—all her days were the same, pedal-to-the-metal, one *situation* after another, all of which she dealt with like a five-star general driving the enemy

into the sea. I didn't give her a hug or blow her a kiss either. We weren't that sort of couple—to her mind (and mine too, to be honest) it would have been just more wasted motion. Wordlessly, I turned to the cabinet, took a glass down from the cupboard, poured her a glass of the Sancerre she liked and handed it to her. Though I had the window open to catch the breeze, there was no sound of the birds, which must have flown off to haunt somebody else's yard.

"Allison's pet pig was killed today," I said, "right out on our front lawn. By one of those transgenic pit bulls, one of the crimson ones they're always pushing on TV?"

Her eyebrows lifted. She swirled the wine in her glass, took a sip.

"And I got bit," I added, holding up my arm, where a deep purplish bruise had wrapped itself around the skin just below the elbow.

What she said next didn't follow, but then we often talked in non sequitur, she conducting a certain kind of call-and-response conversation in her head and I in mine, the responses never quite matching up. She didn't comment on my injury or the dog or Allison or the turmoil I'd gone through. She just set her glass down on the counter, patted her lips where the wine had moistened them and said, "I want a baby."

I suppose I should back up here a moment to give you an idea of where this was coming from. We'd been married twelve years now and we'd both agreed that at some point we'd like to start a family, but we kept putting it off for one reason or another— our careers, finances, fear of the way a child would impact our lifestyle, the usual kind of thing. But with a twist. What sort of child, that was the question. Previous generations had only to fret over whether the expectant mother would bear a boy or girl or if the child would inherit Aunt Bethany's nose or Uncle Yuri's monobrow, but that wasn't the case anymore, not since CRISPR

gene-editing technology hit the ground running twenty years back. Now, not only could you choose the sex of the child at conception, you could choose its other features too, as if having a child were like going to the car dealership and picking the options to add onto the basic model. The sole function of sex these days had become recreational; babies were conceived in the laboratory. That was the way it was and that was the way it would be, until, as a species, we evolved into something else. The result was a nation—a world—of children like the tall girl with the bright red dog.

To my way of thinking, this was intrusive and unnatural, but to Connie's it was a no-brainer. "Are you out of your mind?" she'd say. "You really want your kid—*our* kid—to be the bonehead of the class? Or what, take career training, cosmetology, *auto mechanics*, for Christ's sake?"

Now, tipping back her glass and downing the wine in a single belligerent gulp, she announced, "I'm thirty-eight years old and I'm putting my foot down. I've made an appointment at GenLab for ten a.m. Thursday, and I'm sacrificing a day of work for it too. Either you come with me"—she was glaring at me now—"or I swear I'm going to go out and get a sperm donor."

Nobody likes an ultimatum. Especially when you're talking about a major life-changing event, the kind of thing *both* people involved have to enter into in absolute harmony. It didn't go well. She thought she could bully me as if I were one of her underlings at work; I thought she couldn't. She thought she'd had the final word on the subject; I thought different. I said some things I wound up regretting later, snatched up my drink and slammed through the kitchen door and out into the backyard, where for once no birds were cursing from the trees and even the bees seemed muted as they went about their business. What

came next was dependent on that silence, because otherwise I never would have heard the soft heartsick keening of Allison working through the stations of her grief. The sound was low and intermittent, a stunted release of air followed by a sodden gargling that might have been the wheeze and rattle of the sprinklers starting up, and it took me a minute to realize what it was and that it was coming from the adjoining yard. In the instant, I forgot all about what had just transpired in my own kitchen and thought of Allison, struck all over again by the intensity of her emotion.

We'd managed to get the dog off the carcass, all three of us shouting at once while the girl grabbed for the leash and I delivered two or three sharp kicks to the animal's hindquarters, but Allison's dead pig was none the better for it. The girl, red-faced and embarrassed despite her IQ and whatever other attributes she might have possessed, slouched across the lawn and down the street, the dog mincing beside her, and we both watched till she was gone, at which point I offered to do the only sensible thing and bury what was left of the remains. I dug a hole out back of Allison's potting shed, Allison read a passage I vaguely remembered from school ("The stars are not wanted now: put out every one; / Pack up the moon and dismantle the sun"), I held her in my arms for the second time that day, then filled the hole and went home to make my drink and have Connie slam the front door and lay her demands on me.

Now, as if I were being tugged on invisible wires, I moved toward the low hedge that separated our properties and stepped across it. The first thing I saw was Allison, hunched over the picnic table on her patio. She was still dressed in the taupe blouse and black skirt she'd worn to work, and she had her head down, her scarf bunched under one cheek. When I got closer I saw she was crying, and that got to me in a way I can't explain, so that

before I knew what I was doing I'd fallen down a long dark tunnel and found myself consoling her in a way that seemed—how can I put this?—so very *natural* at the time.

It was dark when I got home. Connie was sitting on the couch in the living room, watching TV with the sound muted. "Hi," I said, feeling sheepish, feeling guilty (I'd never strayed before and didn't know why I'd done it now, except that I'd been so furious with my wife and so strangely moved by Allison in her grief, as if that's an excuse, and I know it isn't), but trying, like all amateurs, to act as if nothing were out of the ordinary. Connie looked up. I couldn't read her face, but I thought, at least by the flickering light of the TV, that she looked softer, contrite even, as if she'd reconsidered her position, or at least the way she'd laid it on me. She didn't ask where I'd been. Instead, she said, "Where's the glass?"

"What glass?"

"Your cocktail? The one you mixed before you stormed out the back door?"

"I don't know—outside, I guess." I shrugged, though most likely I'd left it next door, at Allison's, the MacGuffin that would give me away and bring our marriage crashing to the ground. "I'm sorry," I said, "but I was upset, okay? I just went for a walk. To clear my head."

She had nothing to say to this.

"You eat yet?" I asked, to change the subject.

She shook her head.

"Me either," I said, feeling the weight lift, as if ritual could get us through this. "You want to go out?"

"No, I don't want to go out," she said. "I want a baby."

And what did I say, from the shallow grave of my guilt that

was no deeper than the layer of earth I'd flung over the shrunken and lacerated corpse of Allison's pet? I said, "Okay, we'll talk about it."

"Talk about it? The appointment is Thursday, ten a.m. That's non-negotiable."

She was right—it *was* time to start a family—and she was right too about cosmetology and auto mechanics. What responsible parent wouldn't want the best for his child, whether that meant a stable home, top-flight nutrition and the best private-school education money could buy—or tweaking the chromosomes in a test tube in a lab somewhere? Understand me: I was under duress. I could smell Allison on me still. I could smell my own fear. I didn't want to lose my wife—I loved her. I was used to her. She was the only woman I'd known these past twelve years and more, a known quantity, my *familiar*. And there she was, poised on the edge of the couch, watching me, her will like some miasma seeping in under the door and through the cracks around the windows until the room was choked with it. It was like the moment in a wrestling match where the whistle blows and the grip gives way and nobody gets pinned to the mat. "Okay," I said.

Which is not to say I gave in without a fight. The next day—Wednesday—I had to go into the office and endure the usual banalities of my coworkers till I wanted to beat the walls of my cubicle in frustration, but on the way home I stopped at a pet store and picked up an eight-week-old dogcat. (By the way, people still aren't quite sure what to call the young, even now, fifteen years after they were first created. They're not kittens and they're not puppies, but something in between, as the name of the new species implies. Kitpups? Pupkits?) The sign in the window read simply *Baby Dogcats On Special,* and so I picked out a squirming little furball with a doggish face and tabby stripes and brought it

home as a surprise for Connie, hoping it would distract her long enough to reevaluate the decision she was committing us to.

I'd tucked the thing inside my shirt for the drive home, since from the minute the girl behind the counter had put it in its cardboard carrying container it had begun alternately mewing and yipping in a tragic way, and it nestled there against my chest, warm and content, until I'd parked the car and gone up the steps and into the house. Connie was already home, moving briskly about the kitchen. There were flowers on the table next to an ice bucket with the neck of a bottle of Veuve Clicquot protruding from it and the room was redolent with the scent of my favorite meal—pipérade, Basque-style, topped with poached eggs— which, I realized, she must have made a special stop for at Maison Claude on her way home. This was a celebration and no two ways about it. In the morning, we would procreate—or take our first steps in that direction, which on my part would involve producing a sperm sample under duress (unlike, I couldn't help thinking, the way it had been with Allison).

We didn't hug. We didn't kiss. I just said, "Hey," and she said "Hey" back. "Smells great," I said, trying to gauge her expression as we both hovered over the table.

"Perfect timing," she said, leaning in to adjust the napkin beside her plate, though it was already precisely aligned. "I got there the minute they took it out of the oven. Claude himself brought it out to me—along with a fresh loaf of that crusty sourdough you like. Just baked this morning."

I was grinning at her. "Great," I said. "Really great."

Into the silence that followed—neither of us was ready yet to address the issue hanging over us—I said, "I've got a surprise for you."

"How sweet. What is it?"

With a magician's flourish, I whipped the new pet from the folds of my shirt and held it out triumphantly for her. Unfortu-

nately, I seemed to have startled the thing in the process, and it reacted by digging its claws into my wrist, letting out a string of rapid-fire barks and dropping a glistening turd on the tiles of the kitchen floor. "For you," I said.

Her face fell. "You've got to be kidding me. You really think I'm that easy to buy off—or what, distract?" She made no effort to take the thing from me—in fact, she clenched her hands behind her. "Take it back where you got it."

The pupkit had softened now, retracting its claws and settling into the crook of my arm as if it recognized me, as if in the process of selecting it and secreting it in my shirt I'd imparted something essential to it—love, that is—and it was content to exist in a new world on a new basis altogether. "It's purring," I said.

"What do you want me to say—hallelujah? The thing's a freak, you're always saying so yourself every time one of those stupid commercials comes on—"

Suddenly the jingle was playing in my head, a snatch of the last lulling measures of Pachelbel's Canon, over which the announcer croons, *Dog person? Cat person? It's all moot now.* "No more a freak than that girl with the dog," I said.

"What girl? What are you talking about?"

"The one with the dog that bit me. She must have been six-four. She had an IQ of 162. And still she let the dog out and still it bit me."

"What are you saying? You're not trying to back out on me, are you? We had a *deal*, Roy, and you know how I feel about people that renege on a deal—"

"Okay, okay, calm down. All I'm saying is maybe we ought to have a kind of trial or something before we—I mean, we've never even had a *pet*."

"A pet is not a child, Roy."

"No," I said, "that's not what I meant. It was just, I'm just—" The crowparrots started up then with one of their raucous din-

nertime chants, squawking so piercingly you could hear them even with the windows shut—*Big Mac, Big Mac,* they crowed, *Fries!*—and I lost my train of thought.

"Are we going to eat?" Connie said in a fragile voice, and we both looked first to the microwave and then to the animal excreta on the kitchen floor. "Because I went out of my way," she said, tearing up. "Because I wanted this night to be special, okay?"

So now we did hug, though the pupkit got between us, and, coward that I am, I told her everything was going to be all right. Later, after she'd gone to bed, I took the pupkit in my arms, went next door and rang the bell. Allison answered in her nightgown, a smile creeping across her lips. "Here," I said, handing her the animal, "I got this for you."

Fast-forward seven and a half months. I am living in a house with a pregnant woman next door to a house in which there is another pregnant woman. Connie seems to find this amusing, never suspecting the truth of the matter. We'll glance up from the porch and see Allison emerging heavily from her car with an armload of groceries and Connie will say things like "I don't envy her," and "I hope she doesn't have to pee every five minutes the way I do" and "She won't say who the father is—I just hope it's not that A-hole from Animal Control, what was his name?"

This is problematic on a number of levels. I play dumb, of course—what else can I do? "Maybe she went to GenLab," I say.

"Her? You're kidding me, right? I mean, look at that string of jerks she keeps dating. If you want to know the truth, she's lower class, Roy, and I'm sorry to have to say it—"

"I don't see her dating anybody."

"You know what I mean."

I'm not about to argue the point. The fact is, I tried everything I could to talk Allison out of going through with this—

finally, to my shame, falling back on the same argument about
the whole Übermensch/Untermensch dynamic Connie used on
me, trade school, cosmetology, self-denigration, back-of-the-
classroom, the works, but Allison merely gave me a bitter smile
and said, "I trust your genes, Roy. You don't have to be involved.
I just want to do this, that's all. For myself. And for nature. You
believe in nature, don't you?"

You don't have to be involved. But I *was* involved, though we'd
had sex only the one time (or two, actually, counting the night I
brought her the pupkit), and if she had a boy and he looked like
me and grew up right next door playing with our daughter, how
involved would that be?

So there comes a day, sometime during that eighth month, a
Tuesday when I'm working at home and Connie's at the office,
and I'm so focused on the problem at hand I keep putting off my
bathroom break until the morning's nearly gone. It's the way it
always is when I'm deeply engaged with a problem, a kind of
mind-body separation, but finally the body's needs prevail and
I push myself up from my desk to go down the hall to the bathroom. I'm standing there, in mid-flow, when I become aware of
the sound of a dog barking on the front lawn, and I shift my torso
ever so slightly so that I can glance out the window and see what
the ruckus is all about. It's the red dog, the Cherry Pit that set all
this in motion, and he's tearing around on my hybrid lawn, chasing something. My first reaction is anger—anger at the tall girl
and her fixer father and all the other idiots of the world—but by
the time I get down the stairs and out the front door and into the
sunlight, it dissipates, because I see that the dog isn't there to kill
anything but to play. And that what it's chasing is being chased
willingly (Allison's dogcat, now a rangy adolescent and perhaps
a third the size of the dog).

For all my fretting over the lawn, I have to say that in that
moment, with the light making a cathedral of the street trees and

the neighborhood suspended in the grip of a lazy warm autumn afternoon, I find something wonderfully liberating in the play of those two animals, the dogcat especially. Allison named him Tiger in respect to his coloration—dark feral stripes against a kind of Pomeranian orange—and he lives up to his name, absolutely fearless and with an athleticism and elasticity that combines the best of both the species that went into making him. He runs rings around the pit bull, actually, feinting one way, dodging the next, racing up the trunk of a tree and out onto a branch before leaping to the next tree and springing back down to charge, dog-like, across the yard. "Go, Tiger!" I call out. "Good boy. Go get him!"

That's when I become aware of Allison, in a pair of maternity shorts and an enormous top, crossing from her front lawn to ours. She's put on a lot of weight (but not as much as Connie, because we opted for a big baby, in the eleven-pound range, wanting it— her—to have that advantage right from the start). I haven't spoken with Allison much these past months, once it became clear that whatever we once felt for each other was over—or to put it more bluntly, whatever business we'd conducted—but I still have feelings for her, of course, beyond resentment, that is. So I lift a hand and wave and she waves back and I watch her come barefooted through the glowing grass while the sun sits in the trees and the animals frolic around her.

I'm down off the porch now and I can't help but smile at the sight of her. She comes up to me, moving with a kind of clumsy grace, if that makes any sense, and I want to take her in my arms but can't really do that, not under these conditions, so I take both her hands and pull her to me to peck a neighborly kiss to her cheek. For a minute, neither of us says anything, then, shading her eyes with the flat of one hand to better see the animals at play, she says, "Pretty cute, huh?"

I nod.

"You see how Tiger's grown?"

"Yes, of course, I've been watching him all along . . . Is that as big as he's going to get?"

The sun catches her eyes, which are a shade of plain everyday brown. "Nobody's sure, but the vet thinks he won't get much bigger. Maybe a pound or two."

"And you?" I venture. "How are you feeling?"

"Never better. You're going to be seeing more of me—don't look scared, that's not what I mean, just I'm taking my maternity leave though I'm not due for, like, six weeks." Both her hands, pretty hands, shapely, come to rest on the bulge beneath her oversized blouse. "They're really being nice about it at work."

Connie's not planning on taking off till the minute her water breaks because that's the way Connie is and I want to tell her that by way of contrast, just to say something, but I notice that she's looking over my shoulder and I turn my head to see the tall girl coming up the walk, leash in hand. "Sorry," the girl calls out, "—she got loose again. Sorry, sorry."

I don't know what it is, but I'm feeling generous, expansive. "No problem," I call out. "She's just having a little fun."

That's when Connie's car slashes into the driveway, going too fast, and all I can think is she's going to hit one of the animals, but she brakes at the last minute and they flow like water round the tires to chase back across the lawn again. It's hard to gauge the look on my wife's face as she swings open the car door, pushes herself laboriously from behind the wheel and sets first one foot, then the other, on the pavement (I really should go help her, but it's as if I'm frozen in place), then starts up the walk as if she hasn't seen us. Just as she reaches the front steps, Connie swivels round. I can see she's considering whether it's worth the effort to come greet our neighbor and get a closer look at the tall girl who hovers behind us like the avatar she is, but she decides against it. She just stops a moment, staring, and though she's thirty feet away I can

see a kind of recognition settle into her features, and it has to do with the way Allison is standing there beside me as if for a portrait or an illustration in a book on family planning, male and female, the *xy* chromosome and the *xx*. It's just a moment, and I can't say for certain, but her face goes rigid and she turns her back on us, mounts the steps and slams the door behind her.

When the CRISPR technology first came to light, governments and scientists everywhere assured the public that it would only be employed selectively, to fight disease and rectify congenital deformities, editing out the mutated BRCA1 gene that predisposes women to breast cancer, for instance, or eliminating the ability of the *Anopheles* mosquito to carry the parasite that transmits malaria. Who could argue with that? Genome editing kits (Knock Out Any Gene!) were sold to home hobbyists, who could create their own anomalous forms of yeast and bacteria in their kitchens, and it was revolutionary—and beyond that, fun. Fun to tinker. Fun to create. The pet and meat industries gave us rainbow-colored aquarium fish, sea horses that incorporated gold dust in their cells, rabbits that glowed green under a black light, the beefed-up supercow, the micropig, the dogcat and all the rest. The Chinese were the first to renounce any sort of regulatory control and upgrade the human genome, and as if they weren't brilliant enough already, they became still more brilliant as the first edited children began to appear, and, of course, we had to keep up . . .

In a room at GenLab, Connie and I were presented with an exhaustive menu of just how our chromosomes could be made to match up. We chose to have a daughter. We selected emerald eyes for her—not iridescent, not freakishly bright, but enhanced for color so that she could grow up wearing mint, olive, Kelly green, and let her eyes talk for her. We chose height too, as just about everybody did. And musical ability—we both loved music. Intellect, of course. And finer features too, like a subtly cleft chin

and breasts that would be optimal, not too big but not as small as Connie's either. It *was* a menu, and we placed an order.

The tall girl is right there with us now, smiling like the heroine of a Norse saga, her eyes sweeping over us like searchlights. She looks to Allison, takes in her condition. "Boy or girl?" she asks.

The softest smile plays over Allison's lips. She ducks her head, shrugs.

The girl—the genius—looks confused for a moment. "But, but," she stammers, "how can that be? You don't mean you—?"

But before Allison can answer, a crowparrot sweeps out of the nearest tree, winging low to screech *Fuck You!* in our faces, and the smallest miracle occurs. Tiger, as casual in his own skin as anything there is or ever was, erupts from the ground in a rocketing whirl of fur to catch the thing in his jaws. As quick as that, it's over, and the feathers, the prettiest feathers you'll ever see, lift and dance and float away on the breeze.

THE FIVE-POUND BURRITO

He lived in a world of grease, and no matter how often he bathed, which was once a day, rigorously—and no shower but a drawn bath—he smelled of *carnitas, machaca* and the chopped white onion and soapy cilantro he folded each morning into his *pico de gallo*. The grease itself was worked up under his nails and into the folds of his skin, folds that hung looser and penetrated deeper now that he was no longer young. This was a condition of his life and his livelihood, and if it had its drawbacks—he was sixty-two and never married because what woman would want a man who smelled so inveterately of fried pork?—it had its rewards too. For one thing, he was his own boss, the little hole-in-the-wall café he'd opened back in the sixties still doing business when so many showier places had come and gone. For another, he was content, his world restricted to what he knew, the sink, the dishwasher, the griddle and the grill, and he saw his customers, the regulars and one-timers alike, as a kind of flock that had to be fed like the chickens his mother had kept when he was a boy. What did he do with himself? He scraped his griddle, took his aprons, shirts

and underwear to the Chinese laundry that had been in operation nearly as long as he had and went home each evening to put his feet up and sit in front of the TV.

His only employee was a sour woman named Sepideh, an Iranian (or, as she preferred it, Persian) immigrant who had escaped her native country after the regime change and was between forty-five and sixty, depending on what time of day you asked her. In the mornings she was unconquerably old, but by closing time her age had dropped, though she dragged her feet, her shoulders slumped and her makeup grew increasingly tragic. She was dark-skinned and dark-eyed and she dyed her once-black hair black all over again. People took her for a Mexican, which was really a matter of indifference to him—he didn't care whether his waitress was from Chapultepec or Hokkaido, as long as she did her job and took some of the pressure off him. And she did. And had for some twenty years now and counting.

On this particular day, mid-week, dreary, the downtown skyline obliterated by fog or smog or whatever they wanted to call it, Sepideh was late because the bus she took from the section of town known as Little Persia, where she lived with her mother and an equally sour-faced brother he'd met once or twice, had broken down. As luck would have it, there was a line outside the door when at eleven o'clock on the dot he shuffled across the floor and flipped the sign from *Closed* to *Open*. In came the customers, most of them wearing familiar faces, and as they crowded in at the counter and unfolded their newspapers and propped up their tablets and laptops on the six tables arranged in a narrow line along the far wall that featured the framed black-and-white photo of a dead president, he began taking orders.

First in line was Scott, a student from the university who had the same thing five days a week, black coffee and the chorizo and scrambled egg burrito he lathered with jalapeños, *Just to wake up,* as he put it on the mornings when he was capable of speech.

Next to him were Humberto and Baltasar, two baggy-pants old men from the neighborhood who would slurp heavily sugared coffee for the next three hours and try to talk him to death as he hustled from grill to griddle to the refrigerator and back, and here were two others easing onto the stools beside them, new faces, more students—but big, all head and neck, shoulder and belly, footballers, no doubt, who would devour everything in a two-foot radius, complain that the portions were too small and the burritos like prisoners' rations, and try to suck the glaze off the plates in the process. Of course, he should be happy because the students had discovered him yet again—and how many generations had made the same discovery only to fade away in the lean months when he could have used their business?

He dealt out a stack of plastic menus as if he were flipping cards like the dealer at the blackjack table at Caesars, where he liked to spend his two weeks off every February, bathed in the little spotlight that illuminated the table, a gratis rum and coke sizzling at his elbow. Then he leaned over the counter and announced in the voice that was dying in his throat a little more each day as he groped toward old age and infirmity, "No table service today. You people back there got to come up to the counter if you want to get fed." That was it. He didn't need to give an explanation—if they wanted Michelin stars, let them line up over in Beverly Hills or Pacific Palisades—but he couldn't help adding, "She's late today, Sepideh."

And so it began: breakfast, then the lunch rush, furious work in a hot cramped kitchen, and all he could see was people's mouths opening and closing and the great wads of beans and rice and marinated pork, chicken and beef swelling their throats. It was past noon before he could catch his breath—he didn't even have time for a cigarette, and that put him in a foul mood, the lack of nicotine—and when he saw the face in the tortilla that provided the foundation for the burrito he was just then constructing, he ig-

nored it. It was nobody's face, eyes, nose, cheekbones, brow, and it meant nothing except that he was exhausted, already exhausted, and he still had six and a half hours to go. And sure, he'd seen faces before—Mohammed, the Buddha, Sandy Koufax once, but Jesus? Never. The woman over on Broadway had seen Jesus, exactly as He was in the Shroud of Turin, only the shroud in this case was made of unleavened flour, lard and water. He could have used Jesus himself, because that woman got rich and the lines for her place went around a whole city block. If he only had Jesus, he could hire somebody more competent—and dependable—than Sepideh and sit back and take a load off. That was what he was thinking as he smeared *refritos* over the face of the tortilla and piled up rice and meat and guacamole and *crema,* cheese, shredded lettuce, *pico de gallo,* the works—and why not?—for yet another pair of footballers who were sitting there at the back table like statues come to life. Call it whimsy, or maybe revenge, but he mounded the ingredients up till the burrito was as big as a stuffed pillowcase. Let them complain about this one.

That was when he had his moment of inspiration, divine or otherwise. He would weigh it. Actually weigh it, and that would be his ammunition and his pride too, the biggest burrito in town. If he didn't have Jesus, at least he would have that.

We each live through our time on earth in an accumulation of milliseconds, seconds, minutes, hours, days, months and years, and life is a path we must follow, invariably, until the end. Is there change—or the hope of it? Yes, but change is wearing and bad for the nerves and almost always for the worse. So it was with Sal, the American-born son of Mexican immigrants who'd opened Salvador's Café with a loan from his uncle James when he was still in his twenties, and now, nearly forty years later, saw his business take off like a rocket on the fuel of the five-pound burrito. Sud-

denly his homely café was a destination not only for his regulars and the famished and greedy of the neighborhood, but for the educated classes from the West Side who pulled up out front in their shining new German automobiles and stepped through the door as if they expected the floor to fall away beneath the soles of their running shoes and suck them down to some deeper, darker place.

This was change, positive change, at least at first. He hired a man to help with the dishes and the sweeping up and a second waitress, a young girl studying for her nursing degree who gave everybody in the place something to look at. And on the counter, raised at eye level on a cloth-covered pedestal, was the big butcher's scale on which he ceremoniously weighed each dripping pork, chicken or beef burrito before Sepideh—or the new girl, Marta—made a show of hefting the supersized plate and setting it down laboriously in front of the customer who had ordered it. A man from the newspaper came. And then another. The line went around the block, and never mind Jesus.

Sal was there one early morning—typically he arose at five and was in the kitchen by six, preparing things ahead of time, and, of course, with success came the need for yet more preparation— when he felt a numinous shift in the atmosphere, as if those timid first-timers from the West Side had been right after all. The floor didn't open up beneath him, of course, but as he cut meat from the bone and shucked avocados for guacamole, he felt the atmosphere permeated by a new presence, and no ordinary presence but the kind that makes a dog's hackles rise when it sniffs at the shadows. For a moment he felt dizzy and wondered if he was having some sort of attack, the inevitable myocardial infarction or stroke that would bring him down for good, but the dizziness passed and he found himself in the kitchen still, the knife clenched in his hand and the cubes of pork gently oozing on the chopping block before him. He shook his head to clear it. Something was different, but he couldn't say what.

The morning wore on in a fugue of chopping, dicing and tearing up over the emanations of habaneros and jalapeños, his back aching and his hands dripping with the juice of the hundred-millionth tomato of his resuscitated life, and he forgot all about it till the knock came at the alley door. This was the knock of Stanford Wong, who delivered produce to the restaurants of the neighborhood and was as punctual as the great clock in Greenwich, England, that kept time for the world. Sal wiped his hands on his apron and hurried to the door because Stanford, understandably, didn't like to be delayed. There might have been a noise outside the door, a furtive scratching as of some animal trying to get in, but it didn't register until he pulled back the door and saw that it wasn't Stanford stationed there at all but an erect five-and-a-half-foot rooster dressed in Stanford Wong's khaki shorts and khaki shirt with the black plastic nameplate—*Stanford*—fixed over the breast.

Was he taken aback? Was he seeing things? He'd had his breakfast, hadn't he? Yes, yes, of course: eggs. Chicken embryos. Fried in butter, topped with a sprinkle of Cotija cheese and served up on toast. He just stood there, blinking, but the bird, which somehow seemed to have hands as well as wings, was impatient and brushed by him with a crate of lettuce and half a dozen clear plastic bags of tomatillos, peppers and the like balanced against his—its?—chest, setting the load down on the counter and swinging round abruptly with Stanford's receipt book in hand. But there were words now, the bird saying something out of a beak that snapped and glistened to show off a pink wedge of tongue, and yet the words made no sense unless you were to interpret them in the usual way, as in, *Same order tomorrow?* and *You take care now*.

The door swung shut. The crate sat astride the counter, just as it had yesterday and the day before and the day before that. It took him a moment—and maybe he'd better have another cup

of coffee—before he went to the crate and began shoving heads of lettuce into the refrigerator, all the while thinking that there were two possibilities here. The first and most obvious was that he was hallucinating. The second and more disturbing was that Stanford Wong had been transformed into a giant rooster. Either way, the prospects could hardly be called favorable, and if he was losing his mind in the uproar over the five-pound burrito, who could blame him?

Next it was Sepideh, dressed in black skirt and white blouse, but with her head covered in feathers and her nose replaced by a dull puce beak and no shoes on her feet because her legs, her scaly yellow legs, supported not phalanges and painted toenails but the splayed naked claws of an antediluvian hen. She was never talkative, especially in the morning, but whatever she had to say to him came in a series of irritable clucks and gabbles, and he just— well, he just blew her off. Then came Marta and she was a hen too and by the time Oscar Martí, the cleanup man, showed his face, it was no surprise at all that he should be a rooster just like Stanford Wong—and, for that matter, once the door opened for business, that all the male customers should be crowing and flapping their wings, while their female counterparts clucked and brooded and held their own counsel over pocketbooks stuffed with eyeliner, compacts and lipstick that had no discernible purpose. Something was wrong here, desperately wrong, but work was work and whether he could understand what anybody was saying, customers or staff, really didn't seem to matter, as everything by this juncture had been reduced to routine: spread the tortilla, crown it with toppings, fold it, dip the ladle in the salsa verde and serve it up on the big white scale.

That was Monday. Mondays were always a trial, what with forcing yourself back into the routine after the day of rest, the Lord's day, when people went to church to wet their fingers with holy water and count their blessings. Sal locked up after work that

night and if he noticed that everyone, every living man, woman and child on the streets and sealed behind the windows of their cars, was a member of a different species—poultry, that is—he didn't let it affect him. Even so, the minute he came in the door of his apartment he went straight to the mirror in the bathroom and was relieved to see his own human face staring back at him out of drooping eyes. He poured himself a drink that night, a practice he found himself engaging in less and less as he got older, heated up a burrito (regular size) in the microwave, and watched reality TV till he couldn't hold his eyes open anymore. It would be one thing to say that his dreams were populated with hens, roosters and bobbing chicks, but the fact was that he dreamed of nothing—or nothing he could remember on wakening. He was a blank canvas, tabula rasa. Mechanically, he shaved. Mechanically, he broke two eggs in a pan and laid three strips of bacon beside them, and he drove mechanically to work. In the dark.

When Stanford Wong's knock came precisely at eight, Sal moved briskly to the door, his mood soaring on his second cup of coffee—with a shot of espresso to top it off—and the prospect of yet another record-setting day. If things kept up like this, he'd soon be sitting in a chair all day long watching the world come and go while the new grillman he'd hire and train himself did the dirty work. And it was all due to the inspiration of that day six months back when he'd brought out the scale and piled up the burrito and made his statement to the world. The five-pound burrito. It was a concept, an innovation unmatched by anybody in the city, whether they had a sit-down place or a lunch cart or even one of those eateries with the white tablecloths and the waiters who looked at you as if you belonged on the plate instead of sitting upright in a chair and putting in an order. People just couldn't understand what it took to consume a burrito of that caliber—no individual, not even the greediest, most swollen footballer, could

ever hope to get it all down in a single sitting. Though people placed bets and Sal had agreed to advertise that if you could manage to eat the whole thing, it was on the house. Very few could. In fact, only one man—skinny, Asian, the size of a child—was able to accomplish the feat incontrovertibly, and it turned out later that he was world famous as a competitive eater who'd won the Nathan's hot dog–eating contest three years running.

But here was Stanford Wong's knock, and as he opened the door, he didn't know what to expect, least of all what he saw standing there before him on its hind legs—*his* hind legs. This wasn't Stanford Wong and it wasn't a chicken either—no, this was a hog, with pinched little hog's eyes and a bristling inflamed snout, but it was dressed in Stanford Wong's khaki shorts and khaki shirt with the black plastic nameplate fixed over the breast. It—he—trotted brusquely into the kitchen and set the crate of lettuce and plastic bags of vegetables on the counter, then swung round with Stanford Wong's accounts ledger clutched under one arm and grunted and snuffled out a sentence or two that could only have meant, *How they hangin'?* and *See you tomorrow, same order, right?*

Right. So he chopped peppers and grilled pork and made a pot of *albondigas* soup, shredded lettuce and stirred up yesterday's steam trays of rice and *refritos* and thought nothing of it when Sepideh appeared as a grunting old sow in her black skirt and white blouse and then Marta, resplendent in red shorts and a clinging top, in her guise as a smooth pink young shoat who nonetheless stood five feet seven inches tall on her cloven hoofs and managed to wield her tray and heft the big burritos as if she'd been born to it. As on the previous day, work consumed him, and if his customers vocalized in a cascade of snorts and aspirated grunts, it was all the same to him. Back at home that night he passed on the burrito left over from work, though he

hated waste, and instead slipped a package of frozen meatless lasagna into the oven and poured himself not one but two drinks before he let the TV lull him into a dreamless sleep.

He found himself on edge the next morning and drank a cup of tea instead of coffee and had toast only instead of his usual fried eggs with bacon, ham or chorizo. It was dark as he drove to work and if his headlights happened to catch a figure walking along a shadowy street or spot a face behind an oncoming windshield, he made himself look away. What next? That was all he could think. Cattle, no doubt. Huge stinking lowing steers speaking their own arcane language and demanding big burritos, the biggest in town. When Stanford Wong's knock came this time, he was prepared, or thought he was, but oh, how mistaken he turned out to be. This wasn't Stanford Wong and it wasn't a rooster or a hog or a steer either—it was an alien, and not one of the *indocumentados* of which his late sainted parents were representatives, but one of the true aliens, with their lizard skin, razor teeth and eyeballs like ashtrays. Of course, this one was wearing Stanford Wong's clothing and was carrying his crate of lettuce, but its claws were wicked and long and scraped mercilessly at the linoleum, and when it spoke—*How's business?* and *That five-pounder's going to make you rich*—it could only hiss.

All day, as the aliens crowded the café and his own aliens, Sepideh and Marta, served them their big dripping chile verde–drenched burritos, he kept wondering about their spaceship and if it was like the ones in the movies, all silver and gleaming and silent, and, more to the point, where they'd parked it. No matter. The aliens lashed at their food with a snap of their gleaming teeth and a quick release of their forked tongues and the cash register rang and the line went round the block.

It was around then, on that day, the third day, almost at closing time, that Sal saw a new face in the tortilla he laid on the grill for the burrito he was preparing for a big square-shouldered

footballer alien. This face—the brow, the blind eyes and moving lips that swelled against the pressure of his tongs—was one that leapt out at him in its familiarity. And who was it? Not Jesus, no, but someone . . . someone more important even, if only to him. It was his father, the man who'd held him in his arms and pushed him on the swing and showed him how to grip a baseball and fig-ure his equations in algebra—his father, dead these thirty years and more. The lips moved—and here Sal felt himself lifted into the arena of the fantastic—moved and spoke.

"You're over-reaching, Salvador. Pushing your luck. Flirting with excess and exception, when the truth is you're not excep-tional at all but just a mule like me, made to work and live an honest proportionate life. Go back to two pounds, Salvador. Two maximum. And please, for the love of God and His angels too, dump some aromatic salts in that bathtub . . ." And then the lips stopped moving in that impress of dough and the voice faded out.

But there it was, revelation from the mouth of a flour torti-lla, and the next day, despite the complaints of his customers—human beings, just like him—he went back to the standard-sized burrito. Trade fell off. He had to let Marta go and then Oscar too. The chickens went back to their henhouses and the hogs to their pens and the aliens trooped out across the lot to wherever they'd parked their spaceship and whirred off into the sky in a blaze of light, still traveling as day turned to night and the stars came out to welcome them home.

THE ARGENTINE ANT

(PACE CALVINO)

The baby had been ill, we'd exhausted our savings and our patience too, equally weary of the specialists who seemed to specialize only in uncertainty and of the cramped noisy conditions of our apartment in student housing, so when the chance came to rent the place in Il Nido we jumped at it. We'd never been that far south, but my uncle Augusto had lived in this particular village during the happiest period of his life and had never stopped rhapsodizing it—and since the rent was a fraction of what we were paying for our apartment and my fellowship would provide us with a small but steady income for the coming year, there was nothing to stop us. Provided that the baby stayed healthy, that is. At sixteen months, he was a fine, sturdy-looking child, whose problem—a super-sensitivity to touch, which might have been dermatological in origin or perhaps neurological, depending on which specialist you talked to—seemed to be improving as he grew into the squat stance of his chubby legs. Would there be

specialists in this flyspeck of a fishing village on the tip of the southern peninsula? Pediatricians? Neurologists? Dermatologists? Not likely. But in a way, that would be a relief, since his condition was hardly life-threatening and the various diagnoses and explanations for it were more worrisome than the condition itself. No, what our son needed was to get out from under the impress of our dreary northern clime, with its incessantly dripping gutters, and into the sunshine where he could bask and thrive—and, no small consideration, so could we.

A Signora Mauro was the landlady, and our connection with her was through my uncle, who'd rented the house from her twenty years back when he was between marriages and working on a novel that was never published. I don't remember anything of the novel, portions of which he'd read aloud to me and my sister when I was a boy and he was occupying the guest room over the garage, but I recall vividly his portrait of the village and the tranquillity he'd found there, though, in retrospect—in light of what fell out, that is—I suppose this was fiction too.

My wife and I questioned nothing. This was an adventure, pure and simple. Or more than an adventure: an escape. We took the train and then a succession of buses, the last of which deposited us in front of Signora Mauro's rambling house in the village, and all the time the baby was well-behaved and my wife, Anina, and I stared out the jolting windows and dreamed of a long period of respite in our lives, she no longer trapped in a minimum-wage job as a temporary secretary and I free to work on solving the projective algebraic problem known as the Hodge Conjecture and thereby winning the one-million-dollar Millennium Prize, a sum that would set us up handily for some time to come. Did I have unrealistic expectations? Perhaps. But I was twenty-eight years old and terminally exhausted with the classroom and academic life, and it is a truism that mathematicians, like poets, do their best work

before thirty. So we packed our things, boarded the express and found ourselves on Signora Mauro's doorstep in the sun-kissed embrace of Il Nido.

The house we were to rent was on a bluff overlooking the sea and it was crowded between two others—both, like ours, modest single-story structures of two or three rooms. Signora Mauro, exhibiting traces of a former beauty that was now for the most part extinct but for the low-level radiation of her eyes, found two men to help carry our things up the parabolic hill to the house on the bluff and spent the next quarter hour showing us the essentials—how to light the gas stove and regulate the temperature of the refrigerator and such—before nudging me to hand over a few crumpled bills to each of the workmen and then vanishing down the hill, looking satisfied with herself.

It took no more than half an hour to put away our things— clothes, books, baby paraphernalia, a box of kitchen items Anina had insisted on bringing along though the house had come furnished and the essentials were all in place—and get a quick impression of the living space. There were three rooms—kitchen, bedroom, sitting room—as well as an indoor bathroom featuring a grand old claw-foot tub big enough to bathe armies, and the casement windows in back gave onto a narrow elongated garden (or former garden: it was dried up and skeletal now) that ended in a low hedge and another fifty feet or so of scrub that fell away to the ocean below. "Look, Anina," I called, pushing through the back door and out into the yard, "there's space for a garden! We can grow tomatoes, squash, cucumbers. Beans, beans too."

My wife, so reticent in public, so proper (humorless, was how my mother put it), was anything but in private. She took a critical view and always seemed to see things for what they were while I tended to romanticize and hope for the best. I watched her come out the door to me, after having set the baby down

in his carrier at the foot of our new bed, where he'd promptly fallen asleep. She was grace incarnate, the wafting streamers of her hair caught up in the breeze she generated, her hips rotating in the earthy way that defined her and her lips parted as if in passion, but what she said wasn't at all graceful or passionate. "You call this a garden? It's nothing but stones and leached-out soil."

"The house has been sitting empty—what do you expect? Some seeds, a little water, manure—"

"Where's the water? I don't see any water."

I snatched a look round me. There was a birdbath—or former birdbath—set beside the central path that bisected the yard, the blistered remnants of a wheelless bicycle that looked as if it had been there since Uncle Augusto's time and a rusted watering can snarled in a tangle of yellowed vines, evidence that the garden had once been provided with water. "But there"—I just now looked behind me to the whitewashed wall of the house to discover the faucet and a length of ancient hose coiled beneath it. I pointed. "What do you call that?"

She didn't say a word but just walked back up the path to the house, bending to the hose bib as if to twist open the valve and prove me wrong, when she pulled up short and let out a low exclamation. "My god," she said, the voice dwindling in her throat. "What is *that*?"

What it was—and I hurried across the yard to see for myself—was a black sinuous ribbon of ants emerging from the ground beneath the hose bib to flow up the wall of the house and vanish into a crevice where the stucco met the overhang of the roof. I didn't react at first, rooted in fascination over this glistening display of coordination and purpose, a living banner composed of thousands, hundreds of thousands of individuals in permutations unfathomable (though already I was thinking in terms of algorithms). "Ants," I heard my wife declare. "I hate ants."

Without going into detail about her unhappy undergraduate

romance with a biologist at the university who happened to be ten years her senior, married and a myrmecologist to boot, I'll just say that when she snatched up the hose and leveled it on that column of ants she saw nothing fascinating about the creatures— quite the opposite. The hose flared, a stream of water jetted out and the ants fell away, only to mass at the base of the wall, realign themselves and start climbing again, this time in two separate ribbons that converged just above the locus of the spray.

"That won't help," I said. "It's only temporary."

My wife abruptly shut off the faucet. "You'll have to go into the village for poison then. Some sort of powder, what is it? My father used to use it. You sprinkle it along the base of the walls—"

"We can't use poison here, are you crazy?" I said, thinking of the baby, and in that very moment a high sputtering scream echoed from the depths of the house. We stared at each other in horror, then my wife dropped the hose and we both bolted for the bedroom only to discover that the floor had been transformed into a sea of ants—dislocated ants, angry ants, ants that had fled the wet and come to the dry—and that the baby, all considerations of skin tone aside, was black with them.

The irony wasn't lost on me. Here was a child whose condition one specialist likened to the feeling of having phantom ants crawling all over him, and now the sensation was real and the ants no phantoms. He threw back his head in his extremity, screeching till we thought his lungs would burst while I lifted him out of the cradle and my wife tore off his terrycloth pajamas, balled them up and employed them in frantic quick jerks to swipe the ants from his torso and limbs. They were everywhere, these ants, foaming in miniature waves over our sandals to work their way between our toes even as they scurried up our fingers and arms where we came into contact with our son. When finally

we'd succeeded in brushing him clean, I went for the broom and attacked that roiling black horde with a pestilential fervor until many thousands of them, crushed and exuding their peculiar acidic odor, were swept out the door and into the courtyard. The baby, whimpering still, was in my wife's arms as she rocked with him, cooing little nonsense syllables to soothe him, and the remaining ants retreated into one of the crevices where the tile of the floor joined the wall. "This is intolerable," my wife spat, spinning and rocking, but with her eyes fixed on me like a pair of tongs. "We can't live here. *I* can't live here—not like this."

I told her, in a quiet voice, though I was seething too, that we really had no choice in the matter, as we'd already put down a deposit and first and last months' rent and that I had my desk to set up and my work on the prize to do if we ever hoped to rise to the next level.

"The prize?" She threw it back at me. "Don't make me laugh. You're going to become a millionaire by solving an all but impossible problem that every other mathematician in the world is probably working on right this minute—without ants? In real houses, in university offices, with air-conditioning, polished floors and *no insects* at all!"

This stung. Of course it did. Here we hadn't been in our new home—in our new life—for more than an hour and already she was questioning the whole proposition, and worse, my abilities, my intellect, my faith in the exceptionalism that set me apart from all the others. I'd been close to a solution—it had floated there, just out of reach, for months now, a matter of discovering and applying the right topology—and I knew that if I could just have these months of tranquillity here by the sea to focus my mind, I could do it. I dropped my voice still lower. "I'm going to try."

A long moment transpired, I standing there in the doorway to the bedroom, she bouncing the baby, before she turned to me again, conceding the point but obstinate still, upset, her nerves

frayed by the move and the baby's fragility and everything given figurative expression in these swarming insects that didn't even belong here, migrants from across the sea in South America. "All right," she said, biting her lower lip and swinging round on me with the baby as if she'd taken him hostage, "but you'd better find a solution to *this* problem, to these, these *pests,* before you even think about sitting down at that desk."

We hadn't eaten, either of us, and as it was now late in the afternoon, I thought I'd walk down to the village to pick up a few things for a quick meal—bread, cheese, salami, a fiasco of wine, milk for the baby—and take the opportunity to inquire about whatever non-toxic powders and sprays might be available for application, anything to discourage the ants—especially after dark. I had a grim vision of tossing all night in a strange bed as the ants boiled up from a crack in the floor and made a playing field of the expanse of my flesh. And my wife's. I could already foresee hanging the baby's cradle from a hook in the ceiling like a potted plant—ants couldn't fly, could they? Or not this species, anyway. In any case, I'd just started down the flagstone path for the front gate when I heard music (jazz violin, sensuous and heartrending over the rhythmic rasp of the bow) drifting across the yard from the house next door and a low murmur of voices punctuated by laughter. On an impulse—and out of a feeling of neighborliness, that too—I changed direction and made my way to the low hedge that separated our property from that of the house next door and peered over.

I was immediately embarrassed. Here were my neighbors, a man and woman in their forties and dressed in swimsuits—he in trunks and she in a two-piece that left little to speculation—staring up at me in surprise. They were seated at a glass-topped table, sipping Campari and soda, and they both had their bare feet propped up on the two unused chairs in the set of four. She was dark, he

was fair, and they both looked harmless enough—in fact, once over their initial surprise they both broke out in broad smiles and the woman, whose name, I was soon to learn, was Sylvana, cried out, "Hello, there! You must be the new neighbor." And the husband: "Come join us. You must. I insist." And then the wife: "No need for formality—just hop over the hedge. Here, come on."

I was dressed in khaki trousers and a rayon shirt with sleeves I'd rolled up to the elbows, nothing formal, certainly, but here they were all but naked, so I put away my scruples and vaulted the hedge, and if I came away with a handful of ants where I braced myself atop the vegetation to swing my legs and hips over, it was nothing to eliminate them with a covert clap of my hands. Neither husband nor wife rose, though the wife shifted her (very shapely) legs to prop her feet on the same chair as her husband's, making room for me. I sat and we made our introductions—he was Signor Reginaudo ("Call me Ugo")—and soon I was enjoying a cool Campari with ice and a slice of lemon.

How long was it before I began itching? Minutes? Perhaps even seconds? Both the Reginaudos let out a little laugh. "Here," Sylvana said, a flirtatious lilt to her voice, "put your feet up beside mine—"

It was then that I noticed that the legs of the chairs—and the table as well—were anchored in old pomodoro cans filled with what I presumed to be water, and it was my turn to laugh. "The ants," I said, and suddenly we were all laughing, a long riotous laugh shot through with strains of relief, frustration and commonality, a laugh of friendship and maybe desperation too. Nodding his head and giggling till he had to steady himself with a deep draught of his Campari and a hyperactive pounding of his breastbone, Ugo repeated the noun, the plural noun, as if it were the most hilarious term in the language.

This was succeeded by an awkward pause, during which I

became aware of the violin again and we simultaneously sipped our drinks, trying not to look too closely at the stems, leaves, fronds and petals that surrounded us as if in some miniature Eden for fear of spoiling the illusion. Every blade of grass, every stone, every object in that yard was animated by a dark roiling presence as if the earth itself had come to life. Sylvana gave me a look caught midway between mortification and merriment and I heard myself say, "We have ants next door too," and then the three of us were howling with laughter all over again.

"This is a fact of life here in Il Nido," Ugo began, once he'd recovered himself (again, with a gulp from his glass and a rapid thrust of one fist to his breastbone), "but we've devised ways of dealing with it."

I lifted my eyebrows even as Sylvana shifted her feet so that her sun-warmed toes came into contact with mine and rested languidly there.

"Hydramethylnon," he pronounced, giving me a tight grin. "That's the ticket."

A frown of irritation settled between his wife's eyebrows. "Nonsense. Sulfluramid's the only way to go."

Ugo shrugged, as if to concede the point. "Azadirachtin, pyrethrum, spinosad, methoprene, take your pick. They're all effective—"

"At first," Sylvana corrected.

Another shrug. He held out his palms in a gesture of helplessness. "They adapt," he said.

"But we stay one step ahead of them," Sylvana said. "Isn't that right, darling?" Her tone was bitter, accusatory. "One step ahead?"

Ugo pushed himself impatiently up out of the chair, his fair skin showing a pink effusion of sunburn across the shoulders and into the meat of his arms. "What is this, a debating society?" he demanded. "Come, friend, follow me out to the shed and I'll give

you a good healthy sample of them all—and you can decide for yourself which is best."

I was on my feet now too, gazing down on the gap between Sylvana's breasts and the long naked flow of her abdomen, which, I have to admit, stirred me in spite of myself.

"Come," Ugo repeated. "I'll show you what I've got."

"But what about the baby?" I gazed from him to Sylvana and back again even as I felt the itch start up in my feet and ankles. "He gets into everything. Worse: everything goes in his mouth."

"That's a baby for you," Ugo said. "But this stuff's harmless, really. Even if he—is it a he or she?"

"He."

"Even if he somehow gets into it, it won't do him any harm—"

"Ha!" the wife exclaimed, stretching her legs so that I could see the muscles of her inner thighs flex all the way up to the tiny patch of cloth that covered the mound where they intersected. "And it won't harm the ants either. Least of all the ants."

Though I felt a bit tipsy from the effects of the alcohol on an empty stomach, I had no problem vaulting the hedge with two large shopping bags full of various cans of insect powder Ugo had insisted I take, including one labeled "Ant-Away" and another called "Anti-Ant." When I entered the house to tell my wife what I'd discovered, I saw that both she and the baby were asleep, Anina stretched out diagonally across the bed and the baby tucked in beside her, and perhaps because I wasn't exercising the soberest of judgment, I spread a healthy dose of Anti-Ant along the base of the outside walls, and, for good measure, dumped a can of Ant-Away (active ingredient malathion, whatever that was) atop it. I didn't see any ants in the house and I suppose I didn't really look all that hard for fear of what I'd uncover, but instead made my way back down the hill to the grocery.

This was an old-fashioned grocery, dimly lit, kept cool by the thickness of its ancient walls and smelling strongly of the meats and cheeses in the refrigerated cases—provolone, with its potent smoky aroma, above all else. It was a pleasant smell, and as I carried my basket through the deserted aisles and made my selections, I began to feel at home, as if everything were going to work out as planned and the solution to all our problems was at hand. I selected the wine, found milk and butter in the cooler and a dry salami hanging from its string in the front window, added bread, cheese, olives, artichoke hearts. Once I'd concluded my business, I carried my basket up to the checkout counter, behind which waited a solitary woman in a stained white apron. We exchanged greetings, and as the woman rang up my purchases I couldn't help inquiring if she knew of a reliable product for ant control. At first I thought she hadn't heard me, but then she lifted her eyes to mine before dropping them again. "Signore," she said, her voice no more than a whisper, "here we don't talk of such things."

"Don't talk of such things?" I repeated incredulously. "What do you mean? I see that you carry several ant powders, including Anti-Ant, and I just wanted to ask if you find it effective. If it's the best product, that is. And safe. Is it safe?"

She just shook her head, refusing to look up from the counter as she wrapped my things, then shifted her eyes furtively to my left and I saw that we were not alone. A man stood there beside me, not young, not old, wearing some sort of official uniform—matching trousers and shirt, which bore an insignia patch on one shoulder. He wore his hair long and slicked it back beneath an undersized cap in the same hue as his clothing and he was giving me a quizzical smile. "And you are—?" he asked, his voice a kind of rumble that rose on the interrogative.

I introduced myself and we shook hands.

"Ah, of course," he said. "I should have known—you're the new tenant of the Mauro place, am I correct?"

"Yes," I said, "we just moved in—today, in fact. And I was just, well"—I shrugged by way of adducing the age-old relation between the sexes—"my wife sent me down here to the grocery to pick up a few things. For our first meal in the new house." I shrugged again, as if to say, *You know how it is*.

"I'll be there first thing in the morning," he said. "Would six be too early?"

I gave him a look of bewilderment. "I'm sorry," I said. "And who are you, exactly?"

He straightened up then and perhaps I was imagining it but his heels seemed to click as if ready for action. "Forgive me," he said, digging a card out of his shirt pocket and handing it to me. "Aldo Baudino," he said with a bow. "Of the Argentine Ant Control Corporation."

I wanted to question him further—*Ant Control? Six a.m.?*—but the woman behind the counter was shaking her head and jerking her eyes toward the door, trying to warn me off, trying to tell me something, but what? I thanked her, paid, bade them both farewell and went out the door sans further comment.

Arriving at home, just as I swung open the gate and started up the path, I was startled by a shriek that all but stopped my heart. I dropped my packages and broke into a run. At that moment the door flung back and Anina came down the steps with the baby clutched to her and I saw in an instant what had happened: the baby was dusted all over with the ant powder and there was a greenish crust of it round his mouth where he must have crawled across the floor to ingest it. "The doctor!" Anina cried. "We have to get him to the doctor!"

My heart was pounding and I felt nothing but guilt and horror: How could I have been so stupid? What were ants, a plague of ants, every ant in the world, compared to this? But where was the

doctor and how would we find him? We didn't have a phone—or we did, but it hadn't been connected yet—and the only thing I could think of was the Reginaudos. They would know. Without a word—and here Anina must have thought I'd lost my mind—I veered right and sprang over the hedge into their yard, expecting to find them still seated at the table with their feet up, sipping Campari. They weren't there. Ants boiled up around my feet and I saw then that a whole swift roiling river of them was heading for our house, as if the powder had attracted rather than repelled them. Anina shrieked again. And then I was pounding on the Reginaudos' door, peering through the glass and shouting for help.

A moment later, Ugo appeared, looking annoyed—or perplexed, perhaps that's a better word. "Yes?" he said, pulling back the upper half of the Dutch door to his kitchen. "What is it, what's all the commotion?"

"The baby!" I could barely get the words out—and now, even as I noticed that Ugo was wearing a pair of rubber galoshes and that the concrete floor of the kitchen seemed to be glazed with half an inch or more of water, Anina was there beside me, jabbering excitedly and holding the baby out in evidence.

That was the tableau we presented, the four of us—and the ants, of course. The baby, for his part, seemed calm enough, grinning a broad greenish grin and clinging to his agitated mother as if nothing were amiss, as if ant poison were no more a concern than lime Jell-O and every bit as irresistible. Ugo waved a dismissive hand. "I see he's been into the Ant-Away," he said. "But not to worry, it's nothing. No more harmful than sugar and water."

My wife just stared at him, her eyes—her beautiful olive eyes—so swollen they looked as if they would burst. "What do you mean, it's nothing? Can't you see? He's eaten ant poison!"

And here came Sylvana, still in her skimpy two-piece, sloshing barefoot across the floor. "I told you," she called out, "—it's harmless."

But my wife wouldn't be assuaged—and nor would I, though I was trying to make sense of this. Why would anyone market an ant powder that was harmless, unless it was harmless only to humans and fatal to the insects? But if that was the case, then why were there so many of them?

Finally, leaning over the frame of the door even as a single column of ants worked its way down along the wall to join the phalanx heading for our house, Sylvana said she'd call the doctor if we really insisted. "But he'll do nothing, believe me. He's seen it before, a hundred times. You want my advice? Give the kid a tablespoon or two of olive oil and let him bring it up."

"No," my wife said, shaking her head emphatically, and I realized, absurdly, that she hadn't even been introduced yet. "The doctor."

Both the Reginaudos exchanged a look and shrugged, and then Ugo sloshed across the kitchen to where the phone hung from the wall. I turned to my wife, ignoring the boots and the soaked floor and what they implied. "Anina," I said, "this is our neighbor, Sylvana. Sylvana, my wife, Anina."

The baby grinned and stuck a green finger in his mouth.

"Pleased to meet you," Sylvana said, extending her hand.

The doctor came on foot, toting his bag up from the village below. He was a jaunty, bowlegged man of indeterminate age, though I figured him to be twice as old as I, if not more. "Ah, you must be the new people," he exclaimed, pushing through the front gate as I came up the path to meet him, followed by an anxious Anina clutching the baby in her arms. "And this," he said, slipping a pair of reading glasses over the bridge of his nose and bending to the baby, "must be the patient." He held out his arms and Anina handed the baby over. The doctor hefted him,

then clucked his tongue in the way of doctors everywhere—even specialists—and stated the obvious: "I see he's been into the Ant-Away, eh?"

This was the signal for Anina to pour out her concerns to him, beginning with the story of awakening to find that the baby had crawled down from the bed and somehow managed to push open the screen door that someone had carelessly left ajar (and here she shot me a look), then segueing into the medical issues we'd had with the child over the past six months and ending with a long unnecessary coda about our trip down from the north and our surprise—shock, really—over finding the house infested with ants.

The doctor wasn't really listening. He was shuffling his feet and whirling about with the baby thrust high in his arms, cooing baby talk, as our son, giddy with the attention, peeled back his lips in a wide green smile and cried out his joy. It was then that I realized that all three of us were unconsciously shuffling about—motion the only thing to discourage the ants underfoot—and I found myself giving in to impatience. "But the baby," I said, trying to get the doctor's attention as he cooed and spun, "—is he all right?"

"Oh, he's fine," the doctor assured me, handing the baby back to Anina. "A little malathion never hurt anybody." The birds were settling into the trees by this time and the sun sat low in the sky. My stomach rumbled. It had been a long day and still we hadn't eaten. "And you, little mother," the doctor said, focusing on Anina now, "feed him nothing but pastina for a day or two and examine his diaper carefully. If the result is in any way greenish, you must bring him to my offices; if not, forget the whole business and feel blessed because there isn't a thing in the world wrong with this little fellow." And here he leaned in to mug for the baby. "Isn't that right, Tiger?"

"But aren't you going to examine him?" My wife, usually so reserved with strangers, was in a state, I could see that. She'd practically attacked the Reginaudos and now here she was making demands of the doctor—and this was only our first day in town.

Shifting from foot to foot in a kind of autonomous tarantella, the doctor just grinned. "No need," he assured her, "no need at all," and already he was swinging round to go. "Just remember," he called over his shoulder, "pastina and a close scrutiny of the diapers."

Furious and muttering to herself—I distinctly heard her spit out the term *quack*—Anina spun round and stamped back up the path and into the house, murdering ants all the way, while I followed the doctor to the gate to see him out. "What about your fee?" I asked, pulling open the gate for him.

He seemed to shiver all over and he brusquely swiped one pantleg against the other. "No need to worry about it now," he said, grinning and twitching as the sinking sun made a lantern of his deeply fissured face, "I'll send a bill tomorrow." He held out his hand and I took it. "*Specialists*," he pronounced, and for an instant I thought he was going to spit in the dirt, but he merely squeezed my hand, swung his bony shoulders round, and headed back down the track to the village below.

It was then, just as I plucked the paper bags of groceries up off the ground, almost idly brushing the ants from them and thinking of dinner and a glass of wine—some surcease to all the turmoil of the day—that I heard a "Pssst-pssst" from the hedgerow that divided our southerly neighbor's property from ours and turned to see a man beckoning to me from the shadows there. He was squat, big-bellied, with an enormous head and eyes that seemed to absorb all the remaining light till they glowed like headlamps.

He was known only as "the Captain," he was a foreigner, from Mexico, and he'd formerly been enforcer for one of the narcotics gangs until he was shot three times in the abdomen and his

wife, who'd been sitting beside him in their convertible where they were stopped at a red light, was killed by yet another bullet meant for him. Now he was retired and—according to the Reginaudos, who'd filled me in on the details and warned me against him (they called him an extremist)—he didn't get out much. Which, I suppose, was only understandable.

I crossed to the hedge and offered him a "*Buona sera,*" but he didn't return the greeting or bother with introductions. He merely said, "The Reginaudos? Don't trust them. She's a slut—and come to think of it, so is he. All they do is throw down their powders and lie around screwing all day."

I lifted my eyebrows, though I wasn't sure if he could read my expression in the fading light. I wasn't especially happy—I didn't want to hear criticism of my neighbors or get caught up in pitting one against the other, and the ants, naturally, had begun to discover me standing there with the bags of groceries in hand—but I was polite, polite to a fault. Or so Anina claimed.

"You want to know how to deal with this scourge? Huh? I mean, *really* deal with it, the final solution and none of this pussyfooting? Here, step over the hedge and I'll show you."

The Captain didn't use powders or sprays. He used traps of his own devising. Baited wires suspended over coffee cans filled with gasoline, into which the ants, in their frenzy, would drop singly and sometimes by the dozen, as well as electrical connections timed to give a fierce jolt to a rotting fish head or scrap of stinking meat every thirty seconds. For the next half hour, though I wanted only to go home, sit down to dinner and devise some sort of plan to keep my own ants out of the bedroom for the course of a single night, this night when I was so exhausted I could barely make sense of what the Captain was saying in his vertiginous accent, I patiently followed him around and forced myself to make little noises of approbation over one device or another.

"This is the Argentine ant," he said at one point, "and I

don't know if you quite comprehend what that means. They are invaders"—and here he paused to give me a sharkish grin—"like me. But they're from the true south, in the Americas, in the jungle where you have to fight without quarter every minute of every day even to have a prayer of staying alive. They've out-competed the native ants everywhere they wash up, destroyed them, devoured them. You know what these ants are like?"

I shook my head.

"Like the cells of your body, each ant a single cell and all work-ing in concert, one thing, one living organism, and the queen is the brain. My plan is to starve her by taking her workers away from her in the way you cut up a corpse, piece by piece." There was a silence broken only by the snap of electricity and the faint hiss of ants dropping into cans of gasoline. "Here," he said, and he gestured toward one of his suspension traps, "take as many of these as you like—it's your only hope."

In the morning, at first light, after having spent an all-but-sleepless night at war with the ants (resorting finally to encircling the bed with a frangible wall of green powder, despite any fears for the baby), I was awakened by a noise in the garden. I arose, pulled on my slippers and went to investigate, crushing ants underfoot all the way across the bedroom, through the kitchen and out the back door. I saw a figure there, bent to the wall of the house, and though my mind wasn't as clear as I would have liked, it took only a moment to identify him—the undersized cap, the slicked-back hair, the shoulder patch—as the Ant Man, come as promised. Or threatened, if you prefer. "Good morning," I said, irritated and relieved at the same time—here was intrusion, here was hope.

He didn't look up. "You have a problem," he said. His voice rumbled like a tremor in the earth.

"A problem?" I said, throwing it back at him. "Isn't that stat-

ing the obvious? Don't we all, as you say, *have a problem?* My question is, what are you going to do about it?"

Down on one knee now, working the dirt with a trowel, he glanced over his shoulder and gave me a sardonic smile, as if to concede the point. "My intention," he said, speaking slowly, his voice a rolling fervent peal, "is to eliminate that problem. Come. Look here."

I bent closer.

"You see this?" I saw now that he had set a clay saucer in the depression he'd made in the soil where it came into contact with the wall of the house. There was something in the depths of the saucer, a thick amber substance that glistened in the early-morning light as if it were a precious gift. "This is my special formula— honey, yes, but laced with an insecticide so fast-acting and fatal that you'll be ant-free here within the week. I guarantee it."

"But what of the baby?" I said. "Won't the baby—?"

He made a small noise in the back of his throat. "This is for ants, not babies," he said. "If you're so anxious, why not keep the infant inside—you can do that, can't you? Don't you think it's worth the effort, considering the alternative? Wake up. This is the planet Earth we live on—and it has its terms and conditions like anything else."

"Yes, but—"

"Yes, *nothing.* Just do as I say. And these traps the Captain has given you"—he made a rude gesture toward the traps I'd set up in the garden the night before—"don't you think gasoline is fatal to babies too? Eh? Or don't you think at all?" And now he rose, giving me a hostile look. "Amateurs," he said, jerking his chin first toward the Captain's house, then the Reginaudos'. "Do you really suppose that eliminating a few thousand workers will have any effect at all? No, you have to get the queen, you have to entice the workers to bring her this incomparable bait, to feed it to her and worry over her as she withers and desiccates and the

whole stinking horde goes caput. You're a mathematician, aren't you? Or so I've heard—"

I nodded.

He held me with his acerbic eyes, then nodded back, as if we were in agreement. "Do the math," he said, and then he bent to set the next saucer in the ground.

A week went by. Several times during that week, and at the oddest hours—dawn, midnight—Signor Baudino appeared to refill his saucers, a secretive figure who became almost as much of an annoyance as the ants themselves, which, despite his promise, seemed even more abundant than ever. We slept little, though I finally resorted to setting the four posts of the bed in their own pomodoro cans of water, and that gave us a measure of relief, though Anina and I tossed and turned, dreaming inevitably that the swarms had overtaken us and gnawed us right down to our meatless bones. For the baby, even his waking hours were a kind of nightmare, the ants attacking him the moment we released him from his cradle, and when I look back on that period I have a vision of him itching himself, his former condition complicated now by a melding of the imaginary and the actual so that he could never be sure what he was feeling, just that it was a perpetual harrying of the flesh, and I felt powerless to console him. I see Anina too, growing more sullen and combative by the day and blaming me for all our problems, as if I had any control over this plague in our midst. The Reginaudos stopped by to offer advice and yet more powders and sprays, and the Captain, unbidden, twice slipped into the yard to set up his gasoline traps. For my part, I felt as harried as my wife and infant, trying gamely to pursue my work at a desk set in cans of water and scratching my equations across a page only to see them devolve into streams of ants that were as insubstantial as the ones crawling through my dreams.

On the seventh day, a Monday, Anina came to me at my desk, the baby clasped in her arms. "This is fraud," she informed me, her voice rigidly controlled but right at the breaking point.

I glanced up, noticing a thoroughfare of ants descending the wall before me—or no, they were ascending. Or no, descending. Descending and ascending both. I'd been lost in concentration, in another world altogether, and now I was back in the world of existence. "What is?"

"The contract. The old lady." And here she spat out Signora Mauro's name as if it were a ball of phlegm. "She never once mentioned the ants—and the ants negate that contract, which was made under false pretenses, fraudulent pretenses. This isn't paradise, it's hell, and you know it!"

I was being berated and I hardly deserved it or needed it either. I was going to throw it back at her, going to say *Can't you see I'm working?* but in that moment the truth of it hit me. She was right. We'd come to the end of pretense. "Get your handbag," I said.

She just glared at me. The baby twisted his mouth and began to cry.

"We're going down to the village to see Signora Mauro. And demand an explanation."

The landlady's house, which we'd scarcely noticed the day we stepped off the bus, was a long low meandering structure with an intricate web of iron grillwork out front that must have dated from the Renaissance. It was situated in the better part of town, surrounded by imposing villas, the vegetation lush, the air so fresh it might have been newly created. My wife threw back the gate and marched up the walk to the front door, where she jabbed at the bell with a vengeful thrust of her finger. A moment passed, the two of us framed there beneath a trellis shaped like an ascending angel, the baby for once quiet in my wife's arms. Anina

drew in an angry breath, then depressed the doorbell again, this time leaving her finger in place so that the bell buzzed continuously. Finally, the heavy oaken door eased open just a crack and a maid the size of a schoolgirl stood just behind it, gaping up at us. "We've come to see the signora," I said.

The maid's face was like a wedge cut from a wheel of fontina. Her eyes were two fermented holes. "The signora is not at home to visitors today," she said.

"Oh, but she *is*," my wife countered, forcing the door open and striding into the foyer as I followed in her wake.

We found ourselves in a dark echoing space, the only light a series of faint rectangles that represented the margins of the drawn shades. Furniture loomed in the darkness. There was a smell of dust and disuse. To this point, I'd been swept up in my wife's fervor, but now, standing there in the gloom of a stranger's house—a house we'd forced ourselves into, uninvited—I began to have second thoughts. But not Anina. She raised her voice and called out, "Signora! Signora Mauro! We've come to see you—we *demand* to see you. Right this moment!"

There was a stirring at the far corner of the room, as if the shadows were reconstituting themselves, and then a match flared, a candle was lit, and Signora Mauro, in a widow's colorless dress, was standing before us. "Who are you?" she demanded, squinting through the glare of the candle.

"We've come about the lease," I said.

"It's a fraud," Anina added, her voice rising. "The conditions," she began, and couldn't go on.

"Vermin," I said. "It's infested with vermin and you never said a word about it."

Signora Mauro's voice was the voice of a liar and it came to us in a frequency that wasn't much more than a liar's rasp: "I know nothing about it."

"Ants," my wife put in. "The ants." At the mention of his

nemesis, though he could hardly have been expected to know the term, the baby began to squirm and gargle.

"You've got to keep things clean," Signora Mauro said. "What do you expect, with your filthy ways? I've got a mind to double your rent for abusing my property. And don't think I haven't had reports—" Even as she spoke I could see that she was twitching in some way, furtively scratching, rubbing one leg against the other, flicking a hand across her hips and abdomen.

I threw it back at her. "What about you? What makes you impervious?"

"Me? I don't have pests here. I keep a clean house. Scrupulously clean." Again she twitched, though she tried to suppress it.

"But you do," I said. "I know you do."

"I don't."

"We want out of this contract," Anina said. "We demand it."

The signora was silent a moment. I could hear her drawing and releasing her harsh ragged breath. "Demand all you like, but I'll take you to court—and you'll never see a penny of your deposit, I guarantee it."

"No, we'll take *you* to court," I said, surprising myself by taking a step forward—what was I going to do, attack her? Even as I said it, I knew I was bluffing. She had the power, she had the position, she had our first and last months' rent and absent the house on the bluff we wouldn't even have a roof over our heads.

"Go ahead," she said, her voice jumping an octave as she squirmed in her clothes and stamped her feet on the carpet that must suddenly have come alive there in the dark. "I'd like to see that. I really would."

In the next moment, Anina, my sweet Anina, transformed now in her rage and grief beyond all recognition, shoved me roughly aside, stormed out the door and slammed the iron gate behind

her so furiously the entire house seemed to shake. I was left there in the gloom to make an awkward bow and bid the old woman a good afternoon before awkwardly hurrying after my wife. When I reached the street, I jerked my head right and left, in a panic over what she might do next—I'd never seen her like this, violence erupting from her like a lava flow, and I was afraid for her and the baby too. The street was busy enough, pedestrians and vehicles alike making their way from one end to the other, and at first I couldn't find her in that shifting chaotic scene, but finally I made out the unmistakable rotating motion of her hips as she veered left down a side street at the end of the block. I ran to catch up.

By the time I turned into that block, she was already at the next, swinging right now, descending toward the section of town where the fishermen lived in their ancient stone houses amidst a petrol station and a few tumbledown canneries that once processed the sardines that had become rarer and rarer over the course of the years. "Anina, what are you doing?" I called, but she ignored me, her shoulders dipping over the burden of the baby in her arms, her legs in their faded blue jeans beating double-time along the walk. Then I was beside her, pleading with her—"Let's go home and talk this over, there's got to be a solution, calm yourself, please, if not for me, then for the baby"—but she just kept on going, her mouth a tight unyielding slash in a jaw clenched with rage.

We went down another street, then another, until finally I saw where she was headed—a warehouse just a block from the sea, a place of concrete block and corrugated iron that had seen better days. As I followed her up the walk to the front door, still pleading, I spotted the hand-lettered sign over the lintel—*The Argentine Ant Control Corporation*—and at the same time became aware of the smell. And the ants. The smell was of rot, of the spoiled fish heads and lumps of offal the Captain might have used for bait, and the ants were swarming over the walls in such le-

gions they must have been six inches deep. Anina tried the front door—locked—and then began pounding on the metal panels, dislodging ants in great peeling strips like skin. "Come out of there, you son of a bitch!" she shouted. "I know you're in there!"

I snatched at her arm, shook her, and now the baby had gotten into the act, bellowing till he was red in the face. "What are you doing?" I demanded.

There were tears in her eyes. The baby howled. "It's true what they say, don't you see? He claims to be doing a governmental service, this Ant Man, but in fact he's breeding them. Don't you get it?"

"No," I said, "frankly, I don't. Why would he do a thing like that?"

She gave me a look of contempt and pity, a look for the fool blind to the realities of life. "If the ants are eliminated, so is his job. It's as clear as day. He's not baiting the insects, he's *feeding* them!"

Of course, that couldn't be. I saw that distinctly. And I saw that through no fault of our own we'd been distracted from our path in life, that we'd become disoriented and at odds with each other. And all for what? For *ants*? I still held on to her, my grip firm at her elbow, and even as the idea came into my head I swung her around, the baby still mewling, and began guiding her down the street to where the sea crashed rhythmically against the shore. We made our way amongst the rocks to the pale bleached sand of the beach and I just held her for a long moment, the baby calming around the deceleration of his miniature heartbeat, the sun a blessing on our upturned faces.

In that moment, the solution to Hodge's conjecture came to me, or the hint of a solution that would require pencil and paper, of course, but the intuition was there, a sudden flashing spark in my brain that made everything come clear. It was an abstraction, yes, but math was the purest thing I knew, a matter of logic, of

progression, of control. The ants were nothing in the face of this. We could learn to live with them. We *would*. I took a deep breath and looked out to sea, Anina and the baby pressed to me as the surf broke and receded and broke again. Here was a gathering force that predated everything that moved on this earth, the waves beating at the shore until even the solidest stone was reduced to grains, each a fraction of the size of an ant and each lying there inert on the seabed, stretching on, clean and austere, to infinity.

SURTSEY

All he could think about was bailing, one bucket after the other, as if the house he'd lived in all his life was a boat out on the open sea. The front door was sandbagged, inside and out, but the waves kept rolling across the yard, already as high as the seat on the swingset he used to play on as a kid, and there was no stopping them. The ridiculous thing was, where was he supposed to put the water? He just opened the window and flung it out, but since the whole yard was the lagoon now it would have taken the sorcerer's apprentice—or no, the sorcerer himself—to put an end to it. Every bucket he tossed was one more bucket leaking in around the doorframe. His father had the mop, really going crazy with it, and his sister, Corinne, was bailing too, but they had the same problem he did, just dumping the water out the window as if the window was on top of a mountain somewhere, and the wind blowing half of it back in again anyway. As for his mother, she did what she did anytime they had a crisis, like when the stovepipe overheated and burned a hole in the roof so for two weeks it was as cold inside as it was outdoors or when his father had an accident

on his ATV and broke his collarbone in two places: she just got in bed with one of her books and started reading.

That was where she was when the storm surge hit, and though the house was four feet up off the ground on pilings, that wasn't really going to help all that much because this was a storm surge riding in on a supertide, the sun and moon in alignment on the autumn equinox and the bad luck of a major storm on top of it. A.J. didn't like seeing her there in the bed with the water already rippling across the floorboards in little wavelets and the bedposts dark with wet, but that was her way—what was going to happen was going to happen and there wasn't anything anybody could do about it. Try arguing with her. Try telling her they needed to bail and mop and save what they could, stack the best things on top of the not-so-good things and the not-so-good things on top of the throwaway things, make do until they had no choice but to go over to the school, which sat on the highest ground of the island—all of eight feet above sea level, but that was better than where they were—and she would just say, We'll go when we go, and, What do I look like, Noah?

He tried hard, he did. Everybody knew what was coming because this wasn't the first time and the science teacher at school, Mr. Adams, took them through the global warming thing like it was the Bible or something, nobody arguing about it now, the shore ice that used to protect the island forming later in the season and melting earlier, ocean levels rising all around the world, carbon dioxide building up in the atmosphere, the loss of the albedo effect with the loss of the ice and all the rest. When they'd seen the eclipse the night before, that was the giveaway, the sun and moon on the same line and pulling together, tug of war against the earth, and he put his best clothes in a knapsack along with his video games and his basketball trophy and got ready to evacuate to the school. His father—he was a genius, he really was—got the idea of anchoring hooks in the ceiling beams so they could

pulley his and Corinne's beds up off the floor by a couple of feet and so they did that, but their parents' bed was too heavy so they just put cement blocks under the bedposts and hoped for the best. And yes, he was hopeful, of course he was, sixteen years old and full of his own strength, thinking if they just kept at it everything would be all right—they could live with an inch or two in the house, no problem, and the storm would stop and the water recede, like always—but this was different, this was the supertide, and there was his mother, wrapped up in bed, her eyes tracking across the page while the edge of the one blanket, the one that was slipping off the end and she didn't even seem to notice, was turning dark where it was soaking up water like a sponge, and he didn't know what to do except keep on bailing.

By the time they finally gave up and made for the school, most people were already there, and the only way they could get to it at that point was in the boat, which wouldn't start, so his father had to row and his mother sat in back, in the stern, but she was so heavy it was like a seesaw up front, where he and Corinne were trying to balance out the weight. His mother was the heaviest woman on the island, fat actually, obese, though he didn't like to think of her like that or use that term either. She always said she was big-boned, that was all, and laughed when she said it. Still, no matter what you wanted to call her—and the kids at school never stopped ragging him about it, as if any of them were any better or their mothers either—just getting her into the boat was a trick, the water at the level of the front porch now and bubbling up through the floorboards and the waves beating at the windows and sending jets of foam right up to the roof, but Corinne helped her put on her boots and her rain slicker and the two of them got her down the hallway to the porch while his father held the boat as steady as he could. Himself, he could

have walked, the water up to his waist and the wind screaming and flapping the hood of his parka, no problem, the school
only five blocks away at the end of town, but his father needed
him there in the boat to help balance out the weight. They didn't
bring much with them because they didn't think they'd be gone
more than maybe overnight, just a couple black garbage bags of
emergency things, flashlights, sleeping bags, cereal, underwear
and socks, his mother's nightgowns that were like army tents in
the movies and an armload of her books too. The house, if it
didn't get wrecked, would stink till summer with that rot smell,
and the thought of that depressed him—he really didn't want to
go anywhere, least of all back to school, but when they finally did
make it up the flooded steps and through the front door, everybody was there and it felt like a holiday.

The first thing, the first order of business, as Mr. Adams would
say after he got done checking the roll each morning, was to get
his mother out of her wet clothes and into something warm, blankets, spare blankets, and did anybody have any spare blankets?
The problem was, just when they'd got the boat there on the beach
that just yesterday afternoon was the playground, and his mother,
with him on one side and Corinne on the other, stepped out of
the boat, a wave came shooting in and the thing surged forward
and took her legs out from under her and she went down hard.
It wasn't that cold, low forties maybe, but the water was always
freezing and even if you were used to it (and she wasn't) you didn't
want to be sitting in it up to your neck. In a storm. With sixty mph
gusts riding in across the Chukchi probably all the way from Si-
beria. That wasn't fun for anybody, and he was shivering himself,
pretty much wet to the crotch, and so once they got inside he'd
had to go around to everybody and see if they could borrow a
couple of blankets because theirs were wet, or damp anyway, and
the sleeping bags wouldn't fit her. And no, he wasn't one of these
kids who's ashamed of his parents, he was bigger than that, but still

people were making jokes and that would have got to him except the whole situation was so weird, like Christmas and a basketball game and the community monthly movie all rolled in one.

Corinne took their mother into the girls' room to help her out of the wet clothes and he and his father went down to the gymnasium, where people had already staked out the best spots and had their sleeping bags laid out and all their stuff scattered around them as if it had crashed through the ceiling, radios tuned to a whisper, a rustle of potato chip bags, crackers, whatever, and the men were all squatting in little groups, talking in low voices and drinking coffee out of stained mugs. And smoking. Everybody was smoking so it was like they were drying sheefish inside except the smell was totally different, not appetizing, not at all.

He didn't feel hungry, or not yet, though he must've burned through ten thousand calories with all that bailing and the rest of the frantic activity around the house, so he just made the rounds, not only in the gymnasium but the classrooms too, looking for his friends and wondering where Cherry was, if her family had even come here or if they were waiting it out at home—they had a two-story house, which meant they could all just go upstairs. Her father, Mr. Pollard, was one of the four white teachers at school, along with Mrs. Cato, Mr. Nordstrom and Miss Rumery, who taught the elementary school classes, and if he was pretty clueless about hunting and even fishing he was all science and math and maybe the single smartest person on the island, which meant that he was ahead of everybody else when it came to emergency preparation because everybody else was like his mother with all those generations of wait-and-see in their blood. So maybe Cherry wasn't there, that was what he was thinking, and he was depressed all over again. But then a wave came up and slapped the window of Mrs. Koonook's classroom, which was impossible, and the wind raised its voice till it was the only thing he could hear, and he knew she had to be there somewhere.

When he found her—Jimmy Norton said he thought he'd seen her go into the library, and that was where she was, way in back, though he'd already looked twice—she was sitting with his cousin Charlotte Swan and the other A.J., the one that made his stomach turn. The other A.J., first of all, didn't have a name that stood for anything—it was just initials (he himself was Arthur James, after his father). The second thing was that this A.J., who'd only been at McQueen for six months, was black, African American, whatever you wanted to call it, and not only did that make him special right off as the only one in the whole Northwest Arctic Borough School District, but it gave him instant basketball cred even though he couldn't hit a three-pointer to save his life and his father was a crazy man who'd come to the island to go native and kill beluga and bowfin and caribou and live off the fat of the land, none of which he did at all—he just lived off his army pension and drank alcohol in his shack all day even though alcohol was banned in the village. The third thing, the worst thing, was that this A.J. had a crush on Cherry, or he was coming on to her anyway, and Cherry was *his* girl. Period. And nobody was going to tell him different.

So he came up to them and made as if it was no big thing, them sitting there together like that, and said Hi at just the very instant the lights began to flicker. The other A.J. rolled his eyes and waved a hand at the lights and said, All we need, and Cherry said Hi and scooted over one chair and then, in a lower voice, We saved a place for you.

Pretty crazy, huh? he said. I mean, last year was bad—but you weren't here, were you? he said, looking the other A.J. dead in the eye. Remember? They thought those HESCOs were going to hold and they wound up all smashed and scattered in like the first hour?

This is worse, Cherry said.

Yeah, Charlotte put in, and was she wearing eye makeup? She never wore eye makeup because her mother wouldn't let her,

and here she was wearing eye makeup on a night they might all have to evacuate the island? They say it's a supertide, she said.

What's a hesco? the other A.J. asked, but everybody just ignored him.

They were a stupid idea in the first place, HESCOs, these wire mesh things like supersized crab traps with a white fabric lining and filled with dirt, as if that was going to withstand a sea as angry as this. Now, at a cost, his father said, of over a million dollars, they had a rock revetment built by the Army Corps of Engineers, which the other A.J.'s father used to be a part of.

The lights went out then, a sudden switch from seeing to not seeing, from three dimensions to none, and all they could hear was the wind and the barking of the dogs, all the island's dogs, out there cold and wet and mean-tempered, going at one another in the black void beneath the building. He didn't say anything more, though Charlotte let out a little scream and the other A.J. said, Motherfucker, and then repeated himself, All we need, shit! No, he just took Cherry's hand there in the dark, her hand he knew as well as his own—better—from holding it through all the never-ending days of sun and on into the dark tunnel of the winter that was coming on day by darkening day, and then he pulled her to him and put his lips to hers and felt her tongue in his mouth and just stayed there like that, hard as a rock, till somebody started up the generator and the lights came back on and he saw that Charlotte and the other A.J. were doing it too.

Food was not going to be a problem, even if they had to stay longer than just the one night, and with a storm like this—a blizzacane, Mr. Adams was calling it now, the rain predicted to turn to sleet by midnight and then snow after that—it could be two or three days, maybe even more. By the time people began to realize it was too late to evacuate because the airstrip was un-

derwater and there was no way to get a boat across the mouth of
the lagoon with waves cresting at twenty feet, the most amazing
smell began seeping through the whole building from the direction of the cafeteria. The lights had come back on and Cherry
had just pushed him away—you didn't make out with people
watching, and especially not in school—when the smell hit him
and he realized he was ravenous.

Smell that? He looked at Cherry and the other A.J. looked at
him. You know what that is?

Stew? Cherry guessed, and she guessed right, because what
else would it be?

My uncle Melvin, he said.

What, the other A.J. said, your uncle smells like stew now?
Should be sweat. That's what he smells like to me.

Charlotte said, Hey, that's my dad you're talking about, but
she said it with a laugh and he couldn't help wondering if she was
going to start going around with the other A.J. now, the black
A.J., and how his aunt was going to feel about that. Or Melvin.
Though Melvin, as one of the village's best hunters, was out on
the ice or away inland most of the time, getting meat, which he
shared in the way of the old times and which was how he got the
things he needed in return. Mr. Adams talked about that a lot,
how the people were balanced on a razor's edge between the old
ways and the consumer society of all the vast country strung out
below them, the place where there were palm trees and Holly-
wood and New York City and alligators, which they only knew
from satellite TV and the books and magazines in the library.

My uncle got a caribou yesterday morning—before the storm
hit? There was a rumbling beneath the building, as if the whole
thing was shifting under their feet. Nobody said anything for a
long moment, the four of them just listening. Then he reached
over and gave Charlotte a nudge. Isn't that right, Charlotte?

Charlotte nodded.

Okay, he said. Okay, right? That means caribou stew, and I don't know about you, but I'm going to go down there and get me some of it, like right now?

So they pushed themselves up from the library table with its scatter of books and the computer screens that were like poked-out eyes and went out the door, down the hall past the gymnasium and on into the cafeteria, where the bubbled-up smell of caribou stew was a hundred times stronger and made him feel almost dizzy with hunger. Everybody was there already, lined up outside the kitchen with bowls in their hands, and a couple of the women stood at the stove by the big shining pots of stew, ladling it out one person at a time. He picked up a tray and bowl and utensils and tried to ignore the screech of the wind and the way the waves shook the building—and the dogs, the dogs that were howling now, just howling, and he wondered whether they were all going to drown or get washed out to sea because the school barely had room for the people, and the dogs were going to have to fend for themselves.

What about your dogs? he said to Cherry, and they were like anybody else's dogs, sled dogs, though she only had three and nobody's dogs pulled sleds anymore, not when they all had snow machines and ATVs. Which were all going to be ruined if the water got any higher.

My mom put them in the house, like, upstairs in the hall?

Cherry's mother was blond, like her daughter, and she had a face like a three-quarters moon shining out over the ice, but she was all right really, and she fit in as well as anybody, even people who'd lived here their whole lives (which was about ninety-eight percent of everybody he knew).

The smell of the food was overpowering. He said, I hate this. You know what I'm going to do, like, when this is over?

Hate what?

I don't know, like, this, this storm. It used to be we would just stay inside till it blew itself out, but now we have to worry if

the island's even going to be here when it's over. Plus the house stinks. Everybody's house stinks.

So what're you going to do about it? You heard Mr. Adams— this whole place'll be underwater in ten years. Cherry was wearing the white sweater her mother had knitted her, the one that clung to her across the chest and showed the outline of her bra straps in back. He could still taste her on his tongue.

I'm going to go to California, he said, and, I don't know, go surfing, pick coconuts all day.

Right, she said. And I'm going to Washington. I'm going to be president, didn't I tell you?

No, he said, really. I am. I am so out of here. This was a theme he'd been developing lately, trying it on for size, though they both knew he wasn't going anywhere. Her father had met her mother at college and they expected Cherry to go to college too and the whole idea of that—of her going away—just froze his heart like the ninth circle of hell Mr. Nordstrom told them about in English class, no devil breathing fire but a big frozen-over place just like this would be if the skies never grew light again and the ducks never came back and the winter went on forever.

He was going to say more, puff himself up, show her how cool he was, how dedicated to her, how worthy and true and not really desperate, not desperate at all, when Corinne came up to him, took hold of his arm and hissed, Mom needs you. Like, right *now*?

His father had found a place for them in the gym, but not up against the wall where you could at least have a little privacy— all those spots were gone—but out in the middle of the room, right where the key of one of the baskets was painted on the floor. The *Go, Qavviks!* banner from last weekend's three-day tournament with Kotzebue, in which they'd got killed and his

legs had felt so heavy he might as well have been playing under-water, was peeling away from the wall behind the backboard, one long fold of brown construction paper drooping to the floor like the tongue in the dead head of a whale. Everybody who wasn't in the cafeteria was here except for some of the kids who were out there in the halls doing whatever, and whether they'd eaten yet or not he didn't know, not that it mattered—the stew would last for days, just like the loaves and fishes in the Bible story, plenty for everybody even if the storm went on for a week.

The thing that surprised him was seeing his mother lying there on her back in a pile of blankets and black garbage bags of clothes instead of sitting up cross-legged, which was her usual pose. Was she going to bed already? It was only eight-fifteen. And she was a book addict who'd stay up all night sometimes when she really loved a story, so this wasn't what he'd expected. That was when he saw the look on her face, all the color gone out of her till she was as white as Cherry's mother, and that brought him right to attention. What? he said. What is it, Ma—you sick?

She forgot her medicine, Corinne said, and she didn't look scared the way she had the last time their mother'd had an attack and went all pale like this—just pissed. Or exasperated, that was a better word.

Where's Dad? He found himself staring into the face of Joe Sage's mother, who was perched on her bear rug not three feet away, but then Mrs. Sage, who never missed a thing, turned her face away and pretended to watch somebody else.

He says he's not going back out there. Nobody is.

You mean for her medicine?

He says she's just going to have to tough it out.

That was when his mother's eyes opened up like two breath-ing holes in the ice and she whispered his name and he went down on one knee and bent close to her. You all right, Ma? he asked.

Nothing. All he could hear was the soft murmur of the hun-

dred conversations sifting round him—that and the wind. And the howling of the dogs down there beneath the floor that was just like the wind, only angrier.

Ma?

Her voice was weak and fluttery, caught deep in her throat. I need my medicine. The heart medicine?

What about your insulin? You have your insulin?

She shook her head against the bag she was using as a pillow. The black plastic rippled and glittered dully under the overhead lights. Go get it for me. You know where it is.

Corinne was hanging over his shoulder now with her big face and crooked teeth and her breath that smelled like seal oil. She said, You heard Dad. He says it's too dangerous.

He wants me to die, I guess. Is that what that means? And you—you want me to die too?

His sister said, No, no, Ma, it's not that, but he was already on his feet and picking his way across the gymnasium floor, dodging little kids and stepping over people's things. He didn't care what his father said or anybody else either—he was going out there and he was going to get in that boat or do anything, swim, whatever, because he wasn't going to let his mother suffer like that, not for one minute more.

The dogs were right there, right at the door, a whole pack of them fighting for purchase on the two wooden staircases that sloped down into the rising water. He pushed his way through the door and the wind snatched the breath out of his lungs. The rain was a presence, all-enveloping, and it wasn't rain anymore but ice, windborne pellets rattling against the side of the building like bird shot. Get down! he shouted at the dogs. Get! And they all nosed up to him, whirling and fighting and scratching at the door, and when he kicked them they snarled at him and that just

set him off so he kicked harder until he was down the stairs and into the icy water that was up to his knees and rolling in with that crashing surf—the whole island, as far as he could see, just rolling and rolling. That scared him. If it was up to his knees here, what was it like at the house?

The school loomed above him, a big dark box with the waves disappearing under it. He saw right away the boat was no use. It was straining at its tether, pushed deep under the building along with everybody else's boats, and it was a miracle the rope hadn't snapped. He tried to pull it to him but it felt like it weighed a hundred tons and he realized the boat was tangled up with the other boats and maybe wrapped around one of the pilings, and even if he could get it out there would have been no way to row into this wind anyhow. What he did, and he was already wet through and shivering, was double-tie the knot, to make sure it was secure, then he hunched into the wind and started wading.

The buildings across the street helped because they broke the wind and the surge of the water and it came to him that the best thing to do was pull himself along the side of the near building and then the next one and the one after that. By the time he got to the Native Store, which was only halfway, the water was up to his chest, running at his face, and basically he was swimming now, but that wasn't any good because his parka was dragging him down and he took a lungful of water and before long he was just hanging there, clinging to the rail out front and coughing till he thought he was going to black out. And the cold—he was numb with it. Outsiders, like the other A.J., were always saying how his people didn't even seem to notice the cold because they were born to it, they were used to it, it was in their blood (*You got ice in your veins, man, but me, I'm African and I tell you I can't take this shit*), but that was only partly true. You get wet, you die, like Ray Kinik, who'd fallen through rotten ice last spring and never came back again.

So what was this? Hypothermia, that was what it was. And

if the water was rolling in here and the wind whipping it up, his own house must have been flooded right up to the top of the door frames and all their clothes and all their things and his mother's medicine flooded along with it. He was sixteen years old. He had a thing for Cherry—he loved Cherry, *loved* her—and Cherry was going away to college and he wasn't because he couldn't fool himself and he knew damn well he was going to end up working the Red Dog Mine digging zinc out of the ground like everybody else, and what was the sense of that? The cold gripped him. It lulled him. That was the way you died on the ice when a floe took you out to sea: you went to sleep. He was sixteen years old. He had a thing for Cherry. And he loved his mother and his father and Corinne too, and he wasn't going to be able to get back to the house and he wasn't going to die here on the washed-out steps of the Native Store either—he was going to turn around and go back to the school and get warm and drink black coffee and eat caribou stew, bowl after bowl of it, steaming hot, hot as the shower at the Washeteria when you turn it up full and don't use any cold, so what was he waiting for?

He pulled himself along, everything black-dark and the wind slapping his face the way women slap men in the old movies when the men get out of line and try to kiss them, and why he was thinking of movies when all the blood was going to his core and he couldn't feel his feet or his hands either he couldn't say. Maybe he was hallucinating like that time when Lucy Kiliguk had a marijuana blunt and shared it with him. He concentrated on keeping the water out of his mouth—and his legs, his legs that had to keep going, just like in the basketball tournament, only he was drowsy now and he was freezing and he couldn't have held on to a basketball if it was made out of solid gold. Then he came around the corner of Leonard Killbear's house and saw the lights of the school and the water let him go. All at once he was wading again, the wind shoving him forward like a pair of hands pressed to his shoulder

blades, and when he reached the stairs and the dogs clawed at him and snarled and barked he just hoisted himself up by the railing and jerked open the door and went inside, back inside, and if one of the dogs bit the hell out of his numb right hand—a cross-eyed bitch that belonged to the Adamses—he didn't hardly even notice.

Long night, long, long night. Everybody made a fuss over him, people called him crazy for going out there, but they knew he had heart and they knew he'd done it for his mother, to try and help, to save her. His father chafed his limbs and helped him into dry clothes and he sat right by the furnace for the longest time and Mrs. Nashookluk, the school nurse, bandaged his hand. His mother was asleep on her back on the floor of the gymnasium, snoring the way she did, and when he looked down on her he had to smile because under any other conditions he would have been embarrassed for her, but not now. She's going to be okay, his father said. Just let her sleep. And his father chewed him out in front of everybody, but you could see it was just for show. Cherry came and sat with him for a while, but then it was one o'clock in the morning and her mother came to get her because it was time for everybody to settle down to bed and listen to the wind scream and the dogs howl and the waves crash against the windows of Mrs. Koonook's classroom until the next day broke and they could see if there was anything left out there except water.

He closed his eyes for a while, trying to sink down into sleep, but it was too strange with the whole village sprawled all around him and everybody snoring in their own key till it was like one of the atonal compositions Mrs. Cato made them listen to in Music Appreciation. It was hot, too hot, and if there was irony in that, he was way beyond it. His father was asleep beside his mother, spooning into her, their faces gone slack, and Corinne lay just beyond them, her cheek pressed to her pillow and her mouth

squeezed like a fish's, softly snoring to her own rhythm. In the morning, first thing, no matter what, he was going to go get his mother her medicine because she would need it then more than ever and he was thinking about the times when she overslept and her blood sugar plummeted and she was like a crazy woman, fighting everybody with her eyes dilated and the veins standing up in her neck till they got some juice in her and she balanced out. The wind blew—kept on blowing. Somebody moaned in their sleep.

The gymnasium was the biggest room in the school, and most people had set up in here, but they were scattered around in the classrooms, the library and the cafeteria too. Cherry's family was camped in the library with maybe six or seven other families, including—and this got him—the other A.J. and his father. That was nothing intentional, just luck of the draw, but it rankled him anyway and that was another reason he couldn't sleep. Not that he was worried. The last thing she'd said to him, just as her mother came picking her way across the room to come fetch her, was, Two o'clock, okay? If you can stay awake that long. Think you can? For me?

He'd kissed her then, a public kiss, just a quick brushing of the lips, but he had an instant hard-on and he lifted his head to watch her all the way across the floor and out the door before he bent to set the alarm on his watch, because here was the deal: she was going to get up to go to the bathroom at two and so was he. Except they weren't going to go to the bathroom at all but cruise right past the doors marked "Girls" and "Boys" and on down to the end of the hall, where the janitor's closet was. If nobody was looking—and why would they be at two o'clock in the morning?—they were going to go in there and be together for as long as they could. The promise of that, of what she might let him do, kept everything else at a distance, because the house was wrecked, he knew that in his heart, and the island was doomed and Cherry was going away, but not now, not tonight, not when

they had the janitor's closet all to themselves and nobody the wiser.

In his dream, the whole school and everybody in it was lifted off the pilings and swept up into the sky on the tractor beam of an alien spacecraft that hovered over him like a bird beating against the sun, and whether the aliens were going to put them down in Hawaii or Tahiti or even California, he never knew because his alarm was going with a soft *ping, ping, ping,* and his eyes flashed open on the darkened room and the shadows humped there like seals pulled out on the ice in the twilight. Cherry, he thought, and he was already pushing himself stealthily up, thinking of the last time—at her house—when they had half an hour before her mother came home from her card game and how they'd both got naked and she'd let him touch her everywhere.

The only illumination was from the emergency lights glowing red at both ends of the room, but it was enough to see by so he could avoid stepping on anybody, though that was a trick in itself because people slept in all sorts of bizarre positions and they moved in their sleep too. He was almost at the door when he lost his balance and came down square on somebody's stretched-out arm—one of the men, he couldn't see who it was—and there was a curse in the dark and he froze and whispered Sorry, and was going to add, Just going to the bathroom, but then there came a quick sharp snort of air that was like a gunshot and who-ever it was was asleep again.

The hallway was as strange at this hour as if he was still in his dream, time frozen, nobody there, no kids, no teachers, no shouts and taunts and girls giggling and lockers slamming, but then the door to the boys' room opened and out came Jimmy Norton rubbing his eyes. A.J. murmured Hi, but Jimmy didn't say anything, dead on his feet. He waited till Jimmy brushed by him before he pulled open the door to the bathroom, but that was just for show, and he stood there, his heart beating fast, watch-

ing Jimmy out of sight, then eased the door shut and tiptoed the
length of the hall to the janitor's closet.

She was already there. He opened the door and the faint light
of the hall seeped in and there she was, in her white flannel nightgown that was like the ones his mother wore, only smaller, a
whole lot smaller, and she said, Shhhhh. Come on. Come in.
Shut the door.

He was confused—electrified, yes, so excited he was trembling, but there was no light in the closet and he'd forgotten to
bring a flashlight or even matches. Or no, he hadn't forgotten—
he'd never even thought of it.

But there's no light in there.

Shhhhh! Just shut the door!

Her eyes were red flecks that gave back the glow of the emergency light at the end of the hall. He couldn't see her face or
her hair or anything else but her voice was right there front and
center, impatient now—exasperated—and he realized she was
as excited as he was. Which excited him all the more.

He did as he was told, the door pulling shut behind him with
an audible click that was like a thunderclap, and then he had hold
of her and they were kissing and he could feel her breasts flat-
tening against his chest. Usually, when they were kissing, he had
his eyes closed and it was like when he sang along with a song
he liked, just feeling it, but now his eyes were open wide and he
couldn't see a thing and it made him feel strange, as if he wasn't
anyplace at all.

I want to see you, he said.

No.

Come on, just let me open the door a crack, I mean, an inch,
just an inch, and he reached back for the knob but she took hold
of his wrist and her grip was like iron because she was strong and
beautiful and like nobody else on the island and he loved her, he

really loved her more than anything. He could have thought of all the things they'd done together, a whole DVD of their life, of wrestling on the shore when they were kids, hiking to the end of the island and back, playing board games, video games, racing their ATVs on the airstrip, of their first kiss and the first time he told her he loved her, could have reminded her, but all he could say, there in the blackness, were two words he thought he'd never utter: I'm scared.

Scared? Of what—the dark?

No, he said, and faintly, beneath the floorboards, he could feel the slap and slash of the waves. Not the dark. Just, I don't know, *scared*.

Of me? She let out a laugh and now it was his turn to shush her. You didn't seem so scared at my house the other day.

He could feel her breath on his face. Don't be scared, she said, liking the word, liking the notion of it, and she moved into him and they kissed again, the deepest kiss, the warmth of her all there was in the world, but he broke away and said, Please? Just a crack?

In answer, she pulled the nightgown over her head—he could hear the soft whisper of the material letting go of her skin—and pressed herself to him. Feel me, she said, feel me here.

There was a smell of the janitor's things—bleach, floor wax—and when they went to lie down, using her nightgown and his shirt as protection against the cold of the floor, their limbs kept banging into things in the dark—brooms, he guessed. Mops, buckets. She had never let him go all the way with her and she wasn't going to do it this time, he knew it, and he didn't have a condom anyway, but her skin was on fire and so was his and he kissed her all over. He kept closing his eyes and opening them again, the whole universe spinning there in the dark with him, the flecks of light Mr. Adams called floaters strung out like constellations in a depthless black void. He came twice, both times

on her belly, and she squeezed him so hard it was like he was back out there again in the crush of the water gasping for air.

He lay there awake after she fell asleep with her head pressed to his chest and her nightgown wrapped around them like a sheet. It took him the longest while to make out the faint sliver of light at the bottom of the door, which must have been there all along because it couldn't be morning yet, could it? Soon he would have to wake her so they could both sneak back before they were missed. But not yet. For now he just lay there, letting the night spin round him, his mother drifting there in his consciousness and the dogs too, the dogs that were quiet now so that the only sound was the keening of the wind and the hiss of the water running on and on, unstoppable, in the darkness beneath them.

He felt her breathe, in and out, rhythmically, and tried to time his own breathing to hers and that made him feel strong again, in control, no matter how dark it was or what came next. His mother was going to die and his house and the village and the school were all going to die too and Cherry was going away. The whole thing was too depressing and it would have brought him back down again, except that just then the image of Surtsey came into his head, Surtsey, the island that had risen up out of the sea fifty years ago off the coast of Iceland, in the other ocean, the Atlantic. He had to smile at the thought. Mr. Adams had done an entire lesson on it, on how the underwater volcano erupted and made this new place high above the waves, and how things had blown across the water—seed pods, insects, pollen—to make it alive, a whole new island, a whole new world. That was something, Surtsey, and maybe he would go there one day, he thought, maybe he would.

He shifted his arm ever so slightly and Cherry snuggled in closer. He listened to the wind, listened to the waves, and then he was asleep.

THEFT AND OTHER ISSUES

THE DOG

The dog was old, arthritic and fat, and she belonged to my live-in girlfriend, Leah, who'd had her for eight years before we met. The dog's name was Bidderbells (don't ask) and you couldn't really leave her at home for long stretches because of her tendency to chew up the cushions on the couch, or at least gum them, and then take a dump on the kitchen floor. So I had her with me the day I brought my laptop to the library to work in peace (they're renovating the building across the street from the apartment and the noise is multidimensional) and, of course, I couldn't park on the street because the sun would make a furnace of the car. I got lucky at the parking garage. Just as I took my ticket and the gate lifted I spotted an SUV backing out of a prime space on the left-hand side and I eased right in, feeling good about myself and the little unexpected rewards of life. I

cracked the windows, gave the dog a rawhide bone to gum and walked down the ramp and out into the sunshine.

The library is one of my favorite buildings in town, a sandstone monument to culture and learning built in a time when people cared about such things. Of course, it's principally a repository of bums these days, men mostly, who crowd the armchairs and big oak tables with their oozing bags of possessions and idle away the hours bringing up porn sites on the computers, scribbling in their journals or snoozing with their heads thrown back and their mouths hanging open. Not that I'm complaining. They've got a right to live too and we've got a lot of bleeding hearts in this town (read: bum advocates) and though I'm not really one of them I guess you'd have to say I'm tolerant, at least.

At any rate, I worked for maybe an hour and a half, then packed up and headed back out into the sun for the stroll across the street to the parking structure. Was I thinking I was about to be violated? No. I was thinking nothing—or just, I suppose, that it was a nice day, it was time for lunch and the world was an equable place.

THE ABSENCE

The car wasn't there. I walked directly to the spot where I'd left it and found a motorcycle parked there instead. The motorcycle was a handsome thing, a chopper actually, with high handlebars and a dragon decal on the fuel tank, but it wasn't my car and I was at least ninety-nine percent sure that this was where I'd parked. Now I began to exercise my neck, looking up and down the row of parked vehicles, wondering if I was somehow mistaken, if my internal compass had confused this trip to the library with the last and that it was on the last visit I'd parked here and today elsewhere. Like up there at the top of the ramp. I started walking up the gradual incline, scanning

the vehicles on both sides, and when I got to the point where the ramp gave on to the second floor of the garage, I went back down again, rechecking every spot. Still no car. So back up the ramp I went, turning the corner to Level 2, and I checked every space there as well before continuing on to ascend all the levels, including the sixth and top floor, which was outside in the glare of the sun and no possibility at all because I was certain I would never have parked there with the dog in the car, not on this day or any other.

I didn't really know how much time dribbled away in this wasted effort, this idiotic obsessive-compulsive tramping through the entire parking structure checking and rechecking the same cars over and over as if one of them would magically morph into mine. Half an hour? More? And wasn't this the definition of true idiocy, repeating the same behavior and expecting a different result? It was at this point that I realized the car must have been towed—and yet why I couldn't imagine, since this wasn't metered parking and the gate wouldn't have admitted me in the first place if I hadn't taken a ticket. Suddenly I was in a hurry, thinking of what this was going to cost me—and of the dog, of course, who at the very least would have been confused if not disturbed or even frightened by the clanking of the tow truck and the unnatural elevation of the car—and I was practically jogging as I descended through the levels and made my way back down to the exit. Here was a sharp curve and a narrow lane that led from the mouth of the parking structure to a kiosk and gate, and I found myself squeezed between the unforgiving concrete pillars on the one side and the autos backed up at the ticket kiosk, feeling awkward and vulnerable on foot in the domain of big-grid tires and steel.

The ticket taker was a high school kid in a hoodie who looked startled when I popped my head in the door. In his idle moments he'd been underlining passages in a creased paperback of *Crime*

and Punishment, which lay on the scratched aluminum counter before him. I was beginning, deep in that place of flap and panic in the center of my chest, to see a theme revealed here. "Did you guys tow any cars today?" I asked him, hopefully, and I must have looked confused or disoriented, like one of the bums he no doubt had to negotiate at regular intervals.

There was the screech of tires somewhere above and behind us. A sweetish smell of exhaust hung in the air. He gave me a wary look. "We don't tow cars out of here," he said. "Unless they're like left for a week or something . . ."

"No, no," I said. "I just parked two hours ago"—I flipped my wrist to consult my watch—"at ten past ten or so."

He was shaking his head so that the flaps of the hoodie generated their own little breeze. "I've been on since eight and I definitely haven't seen any tow trucks."

That gave me pause. I looked off across the street to the courthouse and saw the way the sun drew radiant lines across the sandstone blocks a previous generation had stacked up there in defiance of time, temblors and the depredations of weather. Then I brought my gaze back to the kiosk, to which a shining white Lexus was just pulling up. The driver of the Lexus, a faux blonde with a reconstructed face, gave me a look, then handed the ticket to the kid in the hoodie, and I stood there observing the gate rise and listening to their parting remarks ("Have a nice day now"; "You too"), feeling helpless and embarrassed.

"That's a camera there, right?" I said, after the Lexus had wheeled off down the street.

The kid looked to where I was pointing, just to his right and above his head. "Yeah, I guess," he said.

"So if anybody"—and here the word caught in my throat for just a moment—"*stole* my car, you'd have it on film, right?"

UNRAVELING THE MYSTERY

The kid called his supervisor, a lean, gum-chewing athlete in his forties with a little pencil mustache and a name tag affixed to his sportcoat that read GREG. Greg shook my hand and asked, "What seems to be the problem?"

"I think somebody stole my car."

"You parked it here?"

I said yes.

"You're sure? Absolutely sure?" Greg had been through this before, you could see that. And you could see that in ninety percent of the cases it turned out that people had parked on the street or in another lot or had simply walked right by their own vehicle without recognizing it because people got confused, especially if they'd been in the library focused on a page or computer screen and not on the real and actual.

I nodded. A slow pounding had started up in my chest and quickly migrated to my head, where it began to beat like a big bass drum. "And my dog was in the car," I said. "My girlfriend's dog, I mean." Here a vision of Leah rose before me, Leah when she was perplexed by the spill of coffee grounds leading across the kitchen floor from the counter to the trash or upset over something she'd heard on the radio, her brow contorted and her eyes coiled, ready to strike. How was I going to break the news to *her?*

"Make and year?" Greg's gaze never left my face. He was trying to get a read on me and I didn't blame him for that. I could only imagine the sort of nut cases he had to deal with on a daily basis.

"Crown Victoria, 2003. Blue. Dark blue, that is. Almost looks black, depending on the light?" The car had belonged to my mother and it had come my way when she passed on last

year. It was a bit of a gas hog, but it was in prime condition because she'd hardly ever driven it and it had less than thirty thousand miles on it. When we went on trips—up to Oregon to visit Leah's sister or to Vegas for R&R—we took Leah's Honda to save on gas.

Greg gave me a smile that stretched his mustache to the breaking point. "Let's go have a look," he said.

So I spent the next half hour tramping back through the parking structure, this time with Greg at my side. "I'll be your point man," he said, and we started off up the ramp on the first level, Greg keeping up a stream of chatter the whole time though the drum was beating ever louder in my brain. I heard him as if at a great distance, the ramp swaying under us as cars labored on by. He filled me in on the problems of running a public parking structure, the fistfights over spots when there was a big event going on, the graffiti, the vomit, the sex in the stairwells and the bums making their nests in cars people had foolishly left unlocked. Anytime we came to a car of any make that happened to be blue or black, he pulled up short and asked, "This it?"

But of course it never was.

"All right," he said finally, "let's have a look at that tape and see if we can find out what happened to your vehicle."

THE PERPETRATOR'S SLEEVE

I don't have any tattoos, though Leah has a blue and gold butterfly just under the crease of her right buttock so that it seems to flutter when she's walking ahead of you on the beach in her bikini. I mention it because the perpetrator—the thief—was a tattoo junkie and it was his sleeve that gave him away.

Greg and I went back to his office, which turned out to be a room not much bigger than the ticket kiosk located on the lower level of the parking structure, and waited for his "tech person"

to come across town from one of the other garages to extract the feed from the camera and play it for us. "Fifteen minutes," Greg said. "Twenty at most." Then he looked into his computer and I pulled out my laptop, though I couldn't concentrate and wound up staring at the wall above Greg's desk for the hour and a quarter it took the tech person, another high-schooler, to arrive (and that was frustrating because the thief had obviously stolen the car in a narrow window of time and the sooner we got the cops on it the sooner the situation would be resolved, the car restored and Bidderbells returned to me. And Leah. Who was at work and as yet didn't know a thing about it.).

The high-schooler, who actually turned out to be a university student, played the feed for us on Greg's monitor, all three of us leaning in to watch the kid in the hoodie jump and dance and sit and spring up again as we fast-forwarded through the morning's transactions till finally I shouted out, "There! There it is!"

My car had entered the scene, a grainy presence, sleek and substantial, and here was the window rolling down and the shadow of the dog in the backseat, pressing her nose to the glass there. The kid in the hoodie extended his hand and the thief handed him my ticket, his arm casually resting there on the window frame until the amount showed on the kiosk's display—$1.50, first seventy-five minutes free, $1.50 for each hour after that. Which meant that the car had been broken into, hot-wired and driven to the exit just minutes before I emerged from the library, *minutes*! What was I feeling? Anger and regret in equal parts. If only I'd been there I could have stopped him before he'd even got started, the son of a bitch, but the problem was he was a son of a bitch without a face—or at least we couldn't see his face given the perspective of the camera and the shadows inside the car resulting from the angle of the sun at that hour. All we could see was his sleeve—the tattoos he wore on his left arm, dark solid blocks of color like a grid of railroad ties running from his

wrist to his bicep. Then the money was exchanged, the gate rose and my car was gone.

OFFICER MORTENSON

Two hours later Officer Mortenson pulled up in front of the parking structure in a Crown Victoria very much like the one that had been stolen from me, with the exception that hers—a newer model—carried a roof rack of flashing lights and bore the San Roque city logo on both front doors, with POLICE emblazoned beneath it in block letters. I was sitting on the low concrete wall outside the library in the company of half a dozen bums and watched her pull up opposite the kiosk and park along the curb in the No Parking Anytime zone, at which point I rose and hurried across the pavement to where she was just emerging from the car. "Hi," I said, tense still but feeling just the smallest relief of the pressure that had been building in me over the course of the past two hours. Here she was, the servant of the law, ready to put things to rights.

Unfortunately, I seemed to have taken her by surprise, approaching the car too eagerly, I suppose, so that as the greeting emerged from my mouth she was in the act of squaring her shoulders and adjusting her duty belt, her fingers running familiarly over the service revolver, the nightstick, mace and handcuffs, and she swung round on me so precipitously you would have thought I was the perpetrator. Or *a* perpetrator. A perpetrator in potentia.

So there we were. The sun beat at the back of my head. I tried for a smile but couldn't quite manage it—I was that wrought up. Nor did it help that I towered over her, my six-three to her five-five or -six. Add to that that she looked too young to be a cop and maybe a bit heavier than the ideal, which made me think of the junk food she must have been forced to bolt down during her busy rounds taking statements from agitated citizens whose

safe, secure little worlds had just been cracked open like so many walnuts.

She surprised me then by coming up with the smile I couldn't manage and a soft sympathetic gaze out of eyes the color of the caramel chews Leah likes in lieu of dessert every once in a while. "You're the one whose car's missing?" she asked.

"Yes," I said, and in the next moment it was all pouring out of me in a rush of verbiage, every detail I could think of, from the car's description and license plate number to where I'd parked and how I'd spent my morning and the salient—and most corrosive—fact that Bidderbells was in the backseat and for all I knew being held hostage.

She heard me out, but she wasn't writing anything on her pad beyond the make, model and plate number. When I'd run out of breath, she said, "Let's back up a minute here. Name?" she asked. "And I'm going to need an address and a number where you can be reached."

Once she'd recorded the information, she straightened up and swept a look round the area, scanning the faces of the bums, to whom this was all in a morning's entertainment, and then she turned back to me. "Well," she said, "let's have a look at that video feed, shall we?"

We were in stride now, heading into the shadow of the parking structure, when another thought came to me. "It's not just the car. And the dog. I just remembered my golf clubs are in the trunk. And my fishing equipment. Which includes my fly rod? That my grandfather gave me? I mean, it's handmade split bamboo and pretty much irreplaceable."

She gave me a sidelong glance and I shortened my stride to stay even with her. "You say he has tattoos?"

In the agitation of the moment I thought she was talking about my grandfather, but then I saw my mistake and nodded.

"Don't you worry," she said, "we'll get your car back and

your dog and your golf clubs too. My bet? He's got a rap sheet, which means those tats are going to give him away."

I wanted to thank her, wanted to thank her extravagantly and tell her I was feeling much better and that I appreciated her help in resolving this matter as expeditiously as possible, but all I could think of was Leah and the dog and what would happen if Officer Mortenson was wrong. Or maybe overconfident. Maybe that was a better word.

THE BLAME GAME

One thing I like to do in the late afternoon once I'm done with work (I consult for a couple of the big wine-growing operations on the Central Coast) is pour a glass of wine, put on some music and wait for Leah to get home so we can decide what to do about dinner. Half the time we wind up going out. We're not foodies per se, but there are a whole lot of fine restaurants in this little tourist enclave by the sea, and our choices are virtually limitless. Plus, our two favorite places are an easy walk from the apartment. On this particular afternoon, the afternoon of the theft of the car and abduction of the dog (whether planned or incidental), I got back late, having declined an offer of a lift from Officer Mortenson only to wind up walking the twenty blocks home. Every step of the way I'd been thinking about Leah—her look of shattered disbelief when she found out, the tragic extenuation in the way she would freeze her lips and pinball her eyes, her uncanny ability to hurtle from shock to sorrow to accusation and play the blame game—and if I'd already put away half a bottle of an ambrosial Santa Rita Hills pinot by the time she came in the door, who could blame me? It had been a day. And it was far from over.

About Leah: she's thirty-seven, a year older than I, and she works for a sometimes intemperate older woman named Mar-

jorie Biletnikoff, who has her own interior design business here in town. Most days are placid, meeting with clients, choosing fabrics, carpets, antiques, that sort of thing, but every once in a while—once a week, it seems—things can get inordinately stressful because Marjorie Biletnikoff goes off the wagon in a major way (if she ever even bothered to climb up on it in the first place) and tends to take her frustrations in life out on Leah. Maybe I'm imagining things, but from the moment I heard Leah's key turn in the lock I thought I could detect the sort of forward thrust and abrupt wrist action that would indicate that today was one of those days.

The door yawned open, slammed shut, and here came Leah down the entrance hall and straight into the kitchen, where I was standing at the counter, cradling my wineglass. She didn't say hi and I didn't either and there was no pecking of kisses or embraces or anything usual because as soon as she came through the door I said, "Something happened," and she said, "You're drunk," and I was on the defensive.

Finally, when I got the news out that the car had been stolen from the parking structure at the library, she softened and murmured, "Oh, James, that's awful," even as she went to the cabinet to reach down a wineglass for herself. "You must feel terrible."

"Yeah," I said, shifting my gaze, "but that's not all."

She'd swung round, glass in hand, and had lifted the bottle by its neck before she paused, her eyes boring into me.

"They got Bidderbells," I said. "I mean, she was in the car. They probably didn't even know. And the police, I went to the police, and they said they—"

"What are you telling me? You took my dog? To the library? Left her in the *car*? And you, you—you lost her?" Implicit in this, which rode in on an accusatory tone I didn't particularly need or like, was her history with Bidderbells, a rescue dog she'd

got after her divorce, the dog who had *literally saved her life* when she was so depressed all she could think about was killing herself every minute of every day and nothing on this earth seemed worth living for. Until she went to the shelter and saw that sweet thing with the big-eyed gaze and her furry front paws scrabbling there on the wire mesh till it was like to break her heart, etc.

"It's not my fault. How was I to know? And I'm just as upset as you are."

Very slowly, she set the bottle back on the counter and put the empty glass beside it. I watched her face, the interplay of emotions there, as if something caught under her skin was trying to fight its way out.

I gave her a pleading look. "You know we can't leave her alone in the apartment."

"But why? Why did you even go out? I thought you were supposed to be *working*—?"

I pinched my lips together and pointed out the window to the construction site. "The noise," I said. "I couldn't concentrate."

I thought she was going to say something more then, something with a barb in it, overgenerous with blame, as if I was the criminal and not the loser with the tats who'd started all this in the first place, but she just looked past me and murmured a soft exclamation. "Jesus," she said, and then she did fill her glass.

THE PHONE CALL IN THE NIGHT

Dinner was sandwiches washed down with wine and tap water, Leah far too agitated even to think about going out. We tried to watch an old movie on TV, one of those screwball comedies that feature people running in and out of rooms while mistaking each other for somebody else and hiding Jean Arthur in one closet or another, but neither of us could really get into it. For one thing, Leah kept pacing and fretting, the wineglass held out before her

like a mood sensor. For another, without even realizing it, we both drank more than was good for us—three bottles, in all. She kept saying, over and over, "The cop did say he'd call, right, if they heard anything?" and I kept correcting her with regard to the pronoun. "*She*," I said. "I told you, it was a woman cop. Officer Mortenson."

"Not *Julie* Mortenson?"

I was on the couch. Jean Arthur flickered by on the screen. "I don't know. She didn't give me a first name. Officer Mortenson, that was all."

"Christ," she said, flinging back the dregs of her wine. "That's all I need. Of all people, *Julie Mortenson*—"

"What, you know her?"

Furious now, every twitch of her brain focused in her eyes, which were focused on me: "Know her? She's a backstabber and a slut, is all. She bullied me on the volleyball team in high school till I had to quit and then turned around and stole my boyfriend senior year, who I'd been going with, like, from my sophomore year, Richie, Richie Lopez? If it's the same Julie Mortenson, and how many could there be in a town this size?"

That was when the phone rang.

I won't say it was like a bomb going off, because that's a cliché, but it did stop the conversation dead in its tracks. I got up and answered it.

"Mr. Mackey?"

"Yes?"

"This is Officer Mortenson. We haven't yet located your vehicle but we did find your dog."

I said something like "Wow, great," while mouthing the information to Leah, whose face froze in expectation.

"Apparently the suspect let her out on the off-ramp at Glen Annie Road and a witness saw what was happening and stopped for the dog, otherwise things could have been a lot worse."

I was trying to process this information, picturing the dog mangled on the freeway but for the intercession of some dog-loving Good Samaritan, when Officer Mortenson added, "The dog—Bidderbells, is that right, a basset mix?—she's at the animal shelter on Turnpike and all you have to do is present ID to reclaim her."

"But I can't—I mean, I've had maybe a glass of wine with dinner? And I wouldn't want to, you know, get behind the wheel—"

Officer Mortenson—she had a voice like honey heated on low in the microwave—just laughed. "I meant, in the *morning*. They close at five weekdays. Open at eight, I think—you can check it out online."

I would have felt relief, but for the fact that Leah was glaring at me, all the tension and blame-assigning of the past few hours livid in her face. I looked down at the rug. Cupped the phone to my mouth. "Okay," I said. "Thank you so much. This is huge." The conversation should have ended there, but the wine sat thick on my tongue and thicker in my brain. "Could I ask you something?" I said, lulled by the patient rhythm of her respiration on the other end of the line. "Is your first name Julie, by any chance?"

There was a pause that allowed me to feel just how far I'd stepped over the line here, attempting to personalize what was a purely formal, bureaucratic transaction, but then her voice came back to me, soft and almost sugared. "It's Sarah," she said, and broke the connection.

THE THIEF REVEALED

Leah was still furious with me in the morning. She'd hardly slept at all, she claimed, thinking of Bidderbells locked up in that cell with strays and pit bulls and she didn't know what else. Did I

realize that since Bidderbells had come into her life, they'd never spent a night apart. Never?

I hadn't realized it and I was sad to know it now. I kept my counsel, leery of provoking her, though my own sorrow was a new and festering thing that the loss of a car to a car thief couldn't even begin to contain. Breakfast was a cold and hurried meal. We were out of the apartment by seven-thirty because I had to drive Leah to work so I could use her car to go rescue the dog. Which I did. Promptly at eight. Here came the dog scrabbling down the linoleum hall on a leash gripped by a humorless woman who made me sign a form and pay a fine because Bidderbells' license had lapsed, and then I was in the Honda and heading home to sit at my desk and work as best I could through the noise of the construction across the street. The dog ate lustily and looked no worse for wear, though one account had the thief flinging her out the door while the car was still moving.

The next call from Officer Mortenson came at half-past two, when I was deep into my work—a proposal for expanding the acreage of the Escalera Vineyards on the south slope of the foothill property they were thinking of acquiring from the rancher next door—and didn't at first hear the phone ringing. There was a distant sound, and it finally woke me from my trance on what might have been the fifth or sixth ring for all I knew. No matter. There was Sarah Mortenson's soft, soft voice on the other end of the line, betraying not the least hint of impatience.

"Mr. Mackey, good news. We've located your golf clubs, or what we think are your clubs, which you'll have to come down and identify, and we have the suspect in custody."

I was still in the vineyards. I murmured something incoherent.

"Actually, he was already in custody, arrested early this morning on a drunk and disorderly, and the tats we ran yesterday came up bingo."

I felt my mood elevate. "So you have my car?"

There was a pause. "Unfortunately, no. The suspect—he's known to us, minor perp, long rap sheet—admits taking the car but claims he doesn't remember what he did with it. The golf clubs he sold to two other suspects, who tried to fence them at Herlihy's, out by the public course?"

I tend to get wrapped up in things, I admit it. Someone else might have taken this little violation, this theft of his late mother's and grandfather's property, in stride, but in that moment I couldn't let it go. I wanted my car back. My fly rod. And I wanted to see some punishment meted out too. "What's his name?" I asked. "The car thief? Mr. Tattoo?"

"We don't disclose that information. Not at this stage of the investigation."

"Come on," I said. "Sarah. Look, I'm the victim here."

Another pause, longer this time. I listened to her breathe, pictured her caramel eyes and the eyeliner she wore on duty to emphasize the depth of them. "Reginald Peter Skloot," she said. "A.k.a. the Reg-Dog."

COUNTY

"County" was the diminutive people intimate with the San Roque County Jail used in a familiar way, be they inmates, gang members, jailers or attorneys, and it was the temporary residence of the man who'd stolen my car and my girlfriend's dog and was the only link to the whereabouts of the car and the things contained in its trunk. I'd been to County once previously, in the bad old drinking days before I met Leah, to bail out a buddy who'd spent the night there on a DUI after he'd dropped me off at the apartment because I'd had my own DUI in the past and wouldn't get behind the wheel if I'd had more than three or four drinks. And I had. And did.

At any rate, Officer Mortenson—Sarah—had warned me to stay away from the suspect, the Reg-Dog, because my talking to him would only complicate things, might endanger me in the future and would serve no good purpose. So, naturally, and without even thinking twice about it, I dropped Leah off at work two days later and drove out to County for visiting hours, thinking maybe the Reg-Dog would take pity on me and tell me what he'd done with the car, especially since I'd discovered through a lawyer friend that the Reg-Dog had some money in the bank from his insurance settlement (motorcycle, gravel) and once he was convicted—and he would be, no question there—I could put a claim in and take that money away from him. Tit for tat. Of course, there was a second reason for my driving out there—to get a look at him, at this dirtbag who'd unthinkingly reached out and inflicted damage on a total stranger, me, who'd been put through the wringer and whose live-in girlfriend had stopped speaking to him. Period. Because she couldn't trust him anymore. And why not? Because he had bad judgment. Fatally bad. As it was, she was reconsidering their whole relationship vis-à-vis what she was giving and what she was getting back and he—I—could only thank his lucky stars that Bidderbells hadn't been physically abused, though she saw signs, painful signs, of what the mental toll had been. The dog was eating compulsively, she was skittish, peed secretly in the closet and had gummed Leah's best pair of Liz Claiborne pumps till they were fit for nothing but the garbage.

That was what the Reg-Dog had inflicted on me and I wanted some of my own back—or if not that, just to look at him, to see the sleaze of him and the shame in his eyes.

I wasn't nervous, or not particularly, but as I showed my ID at the desk and stepped through the metal detector, I was afraid that maybe someone had bailed him out or that he wouldn't bother with seeing me, because what was in it for him, but my

fears were misplaced. A guard showed me to a chair set before a window in a whole line of them, and there he was, the Reg-Dog, the thief, sitting right in front of me. He was about my age or maybe a couple years younger, with the kind of electric-blue eyes that can be so arresting on people with dark hair. He was in an orange prison jumpsuit, which covered up his tattoos and somehow even managed to seem elegant on him, and he wore his hair short but with long pointed sideburns like daggers.

It took him a minute, assessing me with those jumped-up eyes, then he leaned into the speaking grate in the window that separated us and said, "Don't tell me *you're* my lawyer?"

"No," I said, and I tried to hold steady, but had to look down finally. "I'm the victim."

"Victim? What are you talking about? Victim of what?"

I raised my eyes, fastened on that magnetic blue gaze that must have let him get away with a whole lifetime of petty and not-so-petty crime, and said, "Of you." I gave it a beat to let that sink in. "That was my car you stole. With my girlfriend's dog in it?"

He just blinked at me, no apology, no shame, no recognition even. I was wound up, and I couldn't help delivering a little lecture about what he'd cost me, emotionally and financially too, and if I went into detail about Leah and Bidderbells and my grandfather's fly rod, I'm sorry, but in a society like ours where everything is instant gratification and nobody even knows their neighbors, somebody's got to take responsibility for their own actions. I didn't like what he'd done to me and I let him know it.

And here was where he surprised me. He heard me out, even nodding in agreement at one point. I'd expected he'd throw it right back at me, maybe threaten me, but he didn't. He just bowed his head and murmured, "I'm sorry, man. I wasn't thinking, you know?"

THE CONFESSION

"Look, since my accident? It's like I'm just not right in the head. And tell me that doesn't sound lame because I know it does, but it's the truth. You want to know something? I wasn't even stoned or boozed up or anything when I saw your car there— and I swear I didn't know the dog was in the backseat, or not at first anyway. My father, before he killed himself, used to have a car like that, or maybe not exactly, but you know what I mean. Boom, goes my brain. Time for a *ride*. And you're right, man, I wasn't thinking about you or whoever or what kind of damage I was doing because I just kind of *went off*—"

"So where's the car?"

"Truthfully? I can't remember."

"What if I told you I have a lawyer friend who says I can take your bank account for damages—would that help you remember?"

"Oh, man, don't do that to me. I got my own troubles. As you can imagine. But hey, I'm straight up with you here—I just don't have any recollection because, well, you know, *forgive me*, but that change and dollar bills and all you had in the glove box? I started boozing it, I'm sorry. And then somebody had some oxy—"

"So you're really not going to tell me?"

"Uh-uh. But I'll tell you something else—that lady cop's really got it for you."

MISSING LEAH

I do miss Leah, with that empty bottomless-pit kind of feeling that hits you first thing in the morning, the minute you open your eyes, and I miss Bidderbells too, because you'd have to be one

cold individual to live with a dog for a whole year and not feel affection for her, even if she was the kind of animal who would gum the pillows and make her deposits on the kitchen floor so that you were all but compelled to take her to the library with you. In your car. Which just sits there in the shade waiting for somebody like Reginald Peter Skloot to come along and covet it with his burning blue-eyed gaze. But then, if it weren't for that particular chain of events—and their aftermath—I might not have discovered just how intolerant, unfair and vindictive my live-in girlfriend really was. This is what's called experience.

Did I ever get the car back? No. Will I ever see restitution from the Reg-Dog? That's a question of time. Geologic time. I picture the glaciers rolling in again and my friend the lawyer (I'll name him, Len Humphries) pulling a check out of the inner pocket of his zipped-up parka and the three of us, Len, the Reg-Dog and I, retiring to the nearest pub to tip back a celebratory glass.

The car I have now is a newer model, harder to steal, and pretty much unremarkable, the kind of thing nobody would really notice even if it did have its windows cracked and a dog in the backseat. I'd just parked it the other night in front of the apartment after a trip into the Santa Ynez Valley to meet with the Escalera people when a police cruiser pulled up at the curb behind me and Officer Mortenson swung open the door and stepped out onto the sidewalk, adjusting her duty belt as if she were wriggling into a girdle. I saw that her eyes were done up and that she'd changed her hair and maybe even lost a bit of weight, I couldn't say. She said hi and then told me she was sorry to say there was nothing new to report about my car. "My guess?" she said. "They took it straight down to Tijuana. Or somebody chopped it."

"Chopped it?"

"You know, for parts? Like auto body shops. It's a scam. And a shame too, a real shame."

"I see you've still got *your* vehicle," I said, nodding at the cruiser where it sat sleek at the curb. "Crown Victoria, isn't it?"

She gave a laugh. "Yup. All mine. Except I have to share it with about six other officers."

There was a silence, during which the little sounds of the street came percolating up, the buzz of a distant radio, a window slamming shut, snatches of conversation drifting by like aural smoke.

"You know, did I ever tell you what I do for a living?" I asked, following her gaze down the block to where a small cadre of bums was just settling down for the night in the alcove out front of the auto parts store. I waited till she came back to me and shook her head no.

It was a golden evening, the sun just cresting the line of buildings above us to illuminate the windows up and down the far side of the street. There was a faint breeze wafting up from the sea. Birds flared in the palms like copper ingots. "Here," I said, digging a card out of my wallet and handing it to her. "That's me. I'm in the wine business. And you know, I wouldn't call myself a connoisseur, or maybe I would, but I was just thinking—"

I watched her turn the card over in her hand as if it were a piece of evidence, then smile up at me.

"What I mean is, I was just wondering, do you like wine?"

SUBTRACT ONE DEATH

Riley didn't like dogs, or not particularly. They were like children (of which he had none, thankfully), bringing dirt, confusion and unlooked-for expense into your life. But here was a dog, a darting elaborately whiskered thing in the seventy- to eighty-pound range with a walleye and one collapsed ear, barking inquisitively at him from the terminus of its chain. Behind him, in the drive, Caroline stuck her head out the car window, her face leached of color. "Don't tell me *this* is the place?"

"Wait'll you see inside," he called over his shoulder, the dog's explosive barks underscoring the dreariness of the day, which was gray and coldish for mid-May.

He'd rented the house for a week because the few local hotels had been booked for graduation across the river at West Point and he most emphatically did not want to go down into the city, which was what Caroline most emphatically did want but wasn't going to get. He hated cities. Hated the seethe of people, the noise, the crush of everybody wanting everything at the same time. What he liked was this, simplicity, nature, the river spread

out at his feet and his gaze carrying all the way across to the wooded mountains on the other side, which, apart from the rail line—and what was that, an oil tank?—couldn't have looked all that much different when Henry Hudson first laid eyes on them. He felt his heart lift. All was right with the world. Except for the dog. And Caroline.

But Caroline liked dogs, and she was out of the car now, striding across the wet lawn in her heels, calling to the dog in a clucking high childish voice. "Oh, that's a good boy, he's a good boy, isn't he? What a good *boy*," she called until she was right there and the dog was fawning at her feet, rolling over on its back so she could apply her two-hundred-dollar manicure to its underbelly. After a minute of this—and Riley was just standing there watching, not with the proprietary pride he'd felt after their marriage four years ago but with a vague kind of quotidian interest, the same interest, dulled and flattened, that just barely got him out of bed in the mornings—she turned round to him and said girlishly, sweetly, "This must be Meg and Brian's new dog. I wonder why they didn't say anything? I mean, I remember the old one, when they came to visit that time? The one that died—I'm picturing German shepherd, right? Wasn't it a German shepherd?"

He just shrugged. One dog was the same as another as far as he was concerned. Meg had said she'd be home from work by four to give him the keys to the rental, which belonged to her next-door neighbors, an older couple who were away in Tuscany for the month on some sort of culinary tour. But it was already half-past four, there were no cars in Meg's driveway, and her house—a modest one-story place shingled in gray that had had its basement flooded twice in the past year after storms upriver—looked abandoned. Except for the dog, that is, which was clearly Meg's, since its chain was affixed to a stake on her side of the rolling expanse of lawn the two properties shared. If Meg was home—or Brian—the dog would have been in the house.

"Give her a call, why don't you?" he said, and watched Caroline straighten up and dig in her purse for her phone. He didn't carry a cell phone himself—one, because he despised technology and the grip it had on the jugular of America, and two, because he didn't want the federal stooges mapping his every move. Might as well have them attach one of those tracking devices. Like with wolves—or parolees. Or better yet, just tattoo your social security number across your forehead.

Caroline, slim still, with gym-toned legs tapering down to those glistening black patent-leather heels, had turned her back to him, as if for privacy, the phone pressed to her ear. It was a picture, her standing there framed against the river like that, and he would have snapped a photo too—if he had a cell phone. But then what was the use of pictures anyway? Nobody would ever see them. It wasn't like the old days, when he was a kid and Polaroid was king. Then you could snap a picture, hold it in your hand, put it in a photo album. Today? All the photos were in the Cloud, ready for the NSA to download at their leisure. And pleasure.

Leisure and pleasure. He liked the sound of that and made a little chant of it while he waited for Caroline to turn round and tell him Meg wasn't answering, or Brian either.

It began to drizzle. This had the effect of intensifying the otherworldly greenness of the place, and he liked that, liked the weather, liked the *scene,* but the shoulders of his new sportcoat seemed strangely sponge-like and his coiffure—the modified pompadour he still affected—was threatening to collapse across his forehead. He let out a curse. "What now?" he said. "Jesus. She *did* say four, didn't she?"

There was something in his tone that got the dog barking again, which drove a fresh stake through his mood. He was about to swing round, get back in the car and go look for a bar somewhere when Meg's generic little silver car swished into the

drive next door and he moved toward her, foolishly, because that put him in range of the dog, which reared up on its hind legs to rapturously smear mud all over his white linen pants and attempt to trip him in the process. "Shit," he cursed, shoving the dog down and trying vainly to wipe away the mud, a good portion of which transferred itself to his hands. But was it mud—or the very element he'd just named?

No matter. So what if his jacket was soaked, his pants ruined and dirt of whatever denomination worked up under his fingernails? He wasn't here to show off his fashion sense or dine out with celebrities or sit for press interviews. No, Lester was dead. And he was here for the funeral.

One thing, among many, that Caroline didn't know was that he'd been involved with Meg all those years ago, long before he met her—or either of his first two wives, for that matter—but if she did he suspected she wouldn't have cared much one way or the other, except to drop the knowledge like a fragmentation device into the middle of one of their increasingly bitter squabbles, squabbles over nothing. Like whose turn it was to empty the litter box and why they needed a litter box in the first place when the cats could just shit outside, but no, she insisted, that was the kind of thinking that was driving birds to extinction and how could he be so short-sighted, and he, in his shortsightedness, countering with *What birds? There's nothing but crows out there. Crows and more crows.* And she: *My point exactly.* Or who'd conveniently forgotten to fill up the car or buy cheese at the market, and not blue cheese, which tasted like hand soap, but a nice Gruyère or Emmentaler? Or how you pronounced her brother Cary's name, which he rendered as "Carry" and she as "Kierie" in her Buffalese.

And what was that all about? Boredom, he supposed, the two of them locked away in their restored eighteenth-century farm-

house in the midst of a peace so unshakable it was like living in a tomb. Which was all right with him—he was a novelist, "high midlist," as he liked to say, bitterly, and he'd chosen to isolate himself for the sake of his writing—but after the remodel was done and she'd selected the antiques and the rugs and the fire irons and dug her flowerbeds and landscaped the front portion of their six-point-five acres, what was left for her? You choose rural, you choose isolation. And Caroline didn't especially like isolation.

But none of that mattered now because Lester was dead and Meg was crossing the lawn to him, her eyes already full. Before he could think he was wrapping her in a full-body embrace that rocked them in each other's orbit far too long while Caroline stood there watching and the mud staining his trousers imperceptibly worked itself into Meg's jeans. He was feeling sorrow, a sorrow so fluent it swept him in over his head, Lester gone and Meg pressed tight to him, and it really hadn't come home to him till now because now he was here, now it was real. He'd always suppressed his emotions in the service of cool, of being cool and detached and untouchable, but suddenly there were tears in his eyes. He might have stood there forever, clutching Meg to him, so far gone he couldn't think beyond the three questions he and Lester used to put to each other when they were stoned (*Who are we? Where are we? Why are we?*), but for the fact that Brian's car had somehow appeared in the drive, right behind Meg's. If Caroline didn't know how he'd once felt about Meg, Brian certainly did, and the knowledge of that—and of some of the extracurricular things Brian had said to him at a party a few years ago—made him come back to himself.

He became aware of the rain, which was more persistent now. Lester's face rose up suddenly in his consciousness, then melted away, as if he'd taken a match to a photograph. He let go of Meg, dropped his arms to his sides, took a step back. "Hi, Brian," he called, lifting one hand in a crippled, fluttering wave though Brian

couldn't have heard him since the window was rolled up and the motor running. Still, he couldn't help adding, "Great to see you!"

The house was one of twelve set on a slim strip of land between the river and the train tracks, a smallish 1940s bungalow that had been recast as a two-story contemporary, with fireplace, boat mooring and panoptic views of the river. It was nothing like the farmhouse, of course, but once you stepped inside it gave a good first impression: rustic furniture, framed photos of Hudson scenes on the walls, a brass telescope for stargazing or catching the eye-gleam of the tugboat captains who pushed barges up and down the river all day long. The second impression was maybe a hair less favorable (cramped kitchen, a smell of what, bilge?) but he was gratified—and relieved—to see that Caroline was going to be all right with it. "I love the view," she said, striding across the parquet floor to pull the curtains open wide. "It's"— she searched for the word, turning to him and holding out her hands. If he thought she was going to say "inspiring" or "sub-lime" or even "awesome," he was disappointed. "It's nice," she said, and then clarified—"I mean, it works, right?"

They were just mixing their inaugural cocktail—vodka gim-let, Lester's touchstone—when the first train entered the scene. On a theoretical level, Riley had understood that the proximity of the tracks might give rise to a certain degree of noise now and again, but this was something else altogether. There was a sudden shattering blast, as of a jet fighter obliterating the sound barrier, then the roar of the wheels, the insult of the horn and the chattered-teeth rattle of every glass, cup, dish and saucer in the cupboard. The whole thing, beginning to end, couldn't have lasted more than ten seconds, but it managed to spike his blood pressure and induce him to slosh Rose's lime juice all over the

granite countertop the older couple had installed to fortify their barely adequate kitchen. "Jesus," he said, "what was that?"

Caroline, deadpan: "The train."

"How're we supposed to sleep? I mean, what's the schedule? Are there night trains—or no, there wouldn't be, right?"

"Ask Meg and Brian."

"You get used to it, is that what you're saying?"

She shrugged. Implicit in that shrug and the tight smile that accompanied it was the reminder that they wouldn't have been having this discussion if they were on the twelfth floor of the Algonquin or even the Royalton or Sofitel and that any train they might have run across would have been a conveyance, only that, a means of getting them from the city to this benighted place and back again.

"Jesus," he repeated, looking round for the paper towels, and he was just sopping up the mess—sticky, redolent, probably ninety percent sugar—when there was a tap at the sliding door and Meg was there, framed in the glass panel as in a Renaissance painting, *Our Lady of the River*. She'd changed out of her jeans and into a skirt and she'd done something with her hair. He waved, enjoying the moment, till Brian's head and shoulders entered the frame, and then, at hip level, the dog. She tapped again, grinning, and held up a handle of vodka.

They had a round of gimlets in memory of Lester, then another, after which they switched to wine, a Bordeaux from the case Riley had brought down from Buffalo to help ease Lester's passage, or at least his own immersion in it. He'd written about death to the point of obsession, but he'd been spared the experience of it, if you except the death of his parents, which had happened so long ago he couldn't even remember what they looked like, and he was finding the process of mourning in someone else's living room increasingly disorienting. He tried to make small talk, but small

talk wasn't going to work, not with Lester hanging over them like some great-winged bird. The shadows deepened. The river went the color of steel. Everything he said seemed to begin with "You remember when?" And here were Meg's eyes, inviting him right in, the most patient, salvatory eyes he'd ever seen. He was drunk, of course, that was it, and if Caroline and Brian were forced to hover on the fringes of the conversation, that was something they'd just have to get used to because they hadn't been there with Lester right from the beginning and he had. And Meg had too.

"You're slurring your words," Caroline said at one point, and he looked up, wondering how it had gotten dark so quickly—and without his noticing.

"Maybe we should eat something?" he heard himself say, even as the lights of a barge drifted by on the dark shoulders of the river and the dog, agitated by something beyond the range of human senses, began to whine.

Brian pushed himself up from the easy chair in the corner, an empty wineglass in one hand. He was big-headed, white-haired, and, Riley noted with a certain degree of satisfaction, he'd begun to develop a pot belly. He looked old, tired, bored. "I'm ready for bed."

"Pizza?" Meg made a question of it. "They'll deliver."

"Count me out," Brian said, and gave a little laugh that was meant to be self-deprecating but to Riley's ears sounded just this side of rude. He was a killjoy, Brian. A nonentity. And Meg was wasted on him. "But if you three want"—Brian waved at the air—"I mean, go ahead."

"I don't eat pizza," Caroline put in, her voice light and incisive, no slurring for her though she'd had as much to drink as anybody. She let out a laugh. "It's not Paleo."

"You're telling me they didn't have pizza delivery in the Stone Age?" Riley had used the joke before, somewhere, sometime, and nobody responded to it now. He was sunk deep in the easy

chair beside Brian's, feeling as if he'd never summon the volition to move again. Somehow he found the dog's head in his lap, and he began idly stroking its collapsed ear.

"We could go out," Meg offered, but Caroline just shook her head and he sank deeper into the chair, wondering how he was even going to get up the stairs to bed, let alone negotiate the car and deal with lights, people, waiters, menus.

Just then there was a tap at the glass, which sent the dog into a frenzy, its head rocketing up out of Riley's lap, paws scrabbling on the floor, the barking rising in pitch till it was nearly a scream, and Riley looked up to see a ghostly face illuminated there at the door, a woman's face, nobody he knew, but it made his heart seize all the same.

As it turned out, she was Meg's neighbor from the next house up and she had some bad news to impart, some very bad news, in fact. Meg slid the door back and the funk of the river rushed in to overwhelm him. "Turn on the TV!" the woman shouted, thumping into the room and going directly to the television—a wall-mounted thing Riley hadn't to this point even noticed—and clicked it on. "I can't believe it," she sang out as images of wreckage, flames, emergency flares and stunned onlookers played across the screen in a way that had become the nightly reality and every bit as believable as anything else out there in the world. The feed at the foot of the screen read *Florence, Italy,* and gave the time there, *5:30 a.m.* "They got Ted," she said.

Meg gave her a look of disbelief. "What are you talking about? *Who?*"

"The *terrorists.* I just had a call from Nadine." And here her voice broke. "It was, I don't know, wrong place, wrong time." She was fiftyish, this woman, bottom heavy, her hair cut short but for a spray of pink-dyed strands sprouting like feathers at the back of her neck. "She's going to be okay, but Ted—he didn't make it."

Loudly, in a rising wail, Meg denied it.

"Who's Ted?" he asked, puzzled, even as the tension began to sink its claws in his stomach, deep down, where he was most vulnerable.

"Ted Marchant," Meg said without turning her head. "I can't believe it," she echoed, her eyes jumping from the screen to the woman who'd come to destroy their evening. Or night. It was night now. Definitely. "When?" she demanded. "Are you sure?"

"Who's Ted Marchant?"

Brian loomed over him with his big white head, the empty glass arrested in mid-air. "The guy," he said flatly, "whose chair you're sitting in."

So there were two deaths. First Lester, and now this. Ted Marchant. Whose name Riley must have written across the face of a check, though he had no recollection of it, who'd sat in this very chair and trained his telescope on the stars or maybe a girl going topless in a speedboat on the far side of the river, who, as it would turn out, had been unlucky enough to be sitting at a corner table in a Florentine café, sipping his espresso, at the very moment the black-clad gunmen had rumbled up on their stolen Ducatis and begun shooting. He'd never met Ted Marchant or his wife of forty-five years either—Nadine—but here he was in possession of the dead man's home and all the dead man's things, drinking out of the dead man's wineglasses. It made him queasy to know it.

The television talked to them and they leaned forward in their chairs and watched the images play across the dead man's screen, listened to the voices of the reporters, the same old thing, the tiredest thing, except that one of the seventeen dead had plodded across these floors and breathed this same dank river air that smelled of a whole array of deaths, from fish to worms to clams and the algae that bloomed on a bounty of phosphates and died back to nothing again. It was staggering. He almost wanted to

protest—this wasn't about Ted Marchant, whom he didn't even know, it was about Lester—but instead, into the void, he said, "Maybe we should leave?"

Meg turned away from the screen, her features saturated with the garish light, and looked him full in the face. "No," she said, fierce suddenly, as if the killers were in the room with them, "no way. You're going to stay."

He glanced at Caroline for support, but Caroline's eyes never left the screen. "But won't the wife—? She'll be coming back now, she'll have to, the widow, I mean—"

"Are you serious? Something like this—it could be weeks, months, who knows." Meg's voice caught in her throat. "Poor Nadine—can you imagine?"

"The weirdest thing"—and here the woman who'd brought the news gave him a long look—"is that you're here . . . for a funeral, right?" A glance for Meg. "Or that's what Meg said. And that makes this whole thing so, I don't know, *spooky*, I guess you'd have to say—"

He didn't deny it. In fact, he was spooked right down to the superstitious God-denying soles of his feet. It was like that time in Alaska when the surviving pilot of a two-man air service told him his partner had crashed while delivering a family of Inuit to the next village for the funeral of a family of Inuit killed in an air crash the previous day. Was that how the fates were aligned? Did death come in pairs, like twins? Lester had died of melanoma, a cruel, preposterous thing that had begun as a blister on the little toe of his right foot and spread to his brain and killed him so fast Riley hadn't even known he was sick, let alone dying. It wasn't cool to die, wasn't hip, that was how Lester felt—he had an image to maintain—and so he'd done it alone. That was what hurt. He hadn't called, e-mailed, written, hadn't breathed a word. He'd just crawled off to some hospice in California and spared them the pain.

Later, after Caroline had gone up to bed and Brian took the

dog back across the lawn to his own house and shut out the lights one by one till the fading image of it vanished into the night, there were just the three of them left there in the dead man's living room. Everything was quiet, the lights muted, the TV screen gone blank now. He was the one who'd finally got up and shut it off, Meg whispering "Thank you" and the other woman (her name was Anna or Anne or maybe Joanne, he never quite caught it, not that it mattered—she was the Messenger of Death and that was all he needed to know) seconded her. "These media hyenas," she said, waving her hand in dismissal. "Really, it's just disgusting." For a long while no one said anything, the only sounds the tap of bottle on glass and the consolatory splash of the wine, but then the house began to quail and rattle and here came the blast again, that violent rending of the air, and a train hurtled past with a last fading shriek.

"Oh, my god, I didn't realize it was so late," the woman said, rising from her chair and setting her glass down on the nearest horizontal surface—an inlaid end table, already blemished with a dozen fading circular scars, not that Ted Marchant was going to care. In the next moment she was embracing Meg, the two of them tearful, exuberant in their grief, and then the woman was gone and he was alone with Meg. She looked at him and shook her head. "It's terrible, isn't it?"

He didn't know what to say. It was. Of course it was. Everything was terrible—and getting worse.

He watched her as she bent for her glass, stood up and drained it, one hand on her hip. She looked dazed, uncertain on her feet, and she set the glass down carefully beside the one her neighbor had left, then sank heavily into the couch. "Here," she said, giving him a tired smile, "sit here beside me. Take a load off. It's been a day."

So he sat beside her and felt the warmth of her there in the house that had taken on a chill with the lateness of the hour, and then he put his arm around her and pulled her to him and they

kissed and though he felt the tug of her like some elemental force of reconciliation and surcease, he didn't give in to it. What he did do, with the smallest adjustment, was stretch out his legs and lay his head in her lap so that the warmth became a heat and his eyes fell shut, and the death, the two deaths, faded into oblivion.

The next morning, Caroline, declaring the situation "too weird for words," took a train into the city to lunch with her roommate from college and engage in a little resuscitative shopping, and by the time he extracted himself from the bed he'd somehow managed to find his way to at some unfathomable hour of the night, he was just in time to see Meg pulling out of the driveway on her way to work. Brian's car was gone too, as was his own— Caroline had taken it up to the Garrison station and left it there because he was too enfeebled by the night's reversals to get up and drop her off. So he was alone there in the dead man's house (the *murdered* man's house) poking through the cupboards with the idea of coffee in mind—and maybe something to ease his stomach, like dry toast. Or . . . the zwieback he somehow found in his hand, the pastel rendering of a baby grinning up at him from the front of the cardboard box. But why would the old couple stock baby crackers? Grandchildren? Dental issues? He put a zwieback in his mouth, experimentally, then spat it back out in the palm of his hand. Milk. Maybe milk would settle his stomach. He poured out a clean white glass of it, set it on the counter, and stared at it a long moment before trying, with mixed success, to pour it back into the carton. In his distraction, it must have taken him five entire minutes before he remembered that Lester was dead. And that the funeral, at which he'd be expected to get himself together long enough to deliver a eulogy, was tomorrow.

He looked up at a sudden noise—a thump—and there was the dog, pressing its nose to the glass of the sliding door, a rup-

tured length of chain trailing away from its throat like essential jewelry. The day was bright, he noticed now, yesterday's clouds and drizzle driven back over the hills and the sun dividing the lawn like a chessboard into patches of shadow and light, and the irritation he would normally have felt at the intrusion gave way to something lighter, more tenable, something almost like acceptance. He was glad Caroline had gone into the city and Meg to work, glad to be alone here so he could slow things down, take a walk, sit by the river, commune with Lester on his own terms, and never mind Ted Marchant—Ted Marchant was another issue altogether and he wasn't going to go there.

The thump came again. The dog was pawing the glass as if it wanted something, as if it had a message to convey, some extrasensory glimpse into the process that had claimed Lester and Ted Marchant and would repurpose itself, in good time, to claim the survivors too. Or maybe it was just hungry, maybe that was it. Or, more likely, it wanted in so it could go take a crap on the carpet—wasn't that what dogs were famous for? But then it occurred to him that the dog shouldn't be there at all, that it had, in fact, broken free of its chain, which meant that it was in danger, or potential danger—hadn't Meg complained about how vigilant you had to be or it would bolt out the door and make straight for the train tracks? He got up from where he was sitting at the kitchen table, thinking to let the dog in—to trap it in the house—and then see if he could do something about reinforcing the chain.

But what was the thing's name? Something with a *T*—Tuffy? Terry? Or no, Taffy, that was it, because of its coloration, as Meg had explained shortly after it had annihilated his pants. Anyway, he got up from the kitchen table, went to the door and slid it open, which, far from having the desired effect, caused the dog to back away from him so precipitately it fell from the porch in an awkward scramble of limbs. For the briefest moment it lay there on its back, its legs kicking in the air, and then it sprang up and bolted

headlong away from him, straight in the direction of the tracks. "Taffy!" he called, feeling ridiculous, but nonetheless coming down off the porch and hustling across the lawn after him (or her; he wasn't even sure what sex the thing was). "Taffy! No!"

It was at that moment the train appeared, the 9:50 or 10:10 or whatever it was, the air shrieking, the wheels thundering, a great onrushing force that eclipsed the animal as if it had never been there at all. Running now, his heart slamming at his ribs, Riley reached the tracks just as the last car—*the caboose*, a term that came to him out of a buried past, childhood, Lionel, mittens pressed to ears, *Take Daddy's hand now*—raged on by and the tracks stood vacant, shining malevolently in the hard gleam of the sun. What he expected was death, another death, the dog's remains dribbled like ragout up and down the line—and what was he going to tell Meg?—but that wasn't what he found. The dog was there, intact, remnant chain and all, sitting on its rump on the far side of the tracks and staring at him stupidly across the void.

"Taffy," he called, trying to control his voice, the edge of hysteria there, of fury. "Come!"

But Taffy didn't come. Taffy never budged, except to contort himself (he was a male, Riley saw now, the sheath of the organ, the tight dark balls like damson plums) so he could reach up and scratch his chin with one back paw. Riley looked up and down the tracks, a long tapering *V* to the vanishing point in either direction, then called again, again without response. *Maybe if I turn my back on him*, he thought. Or maybe—and here he felt embarrassed with himself, because what was he now, a dog whisperer?—maybe he should just say fuck the whole business. Let the dog take his chances. Right. Fine. He swung abruptly round and made his way through the damp grass to mount the porch of the dead man's house and see if he could find the means to make himself a cup of coffee.

He wasn't really tracking the time, but it must have been

around noon or so, the sun high overhead and the dog frisking back and forth across the lawn, chain in tow, when he looked up from his coffee and toast and his eyes came to rest on the canoe where it lay overturned on the dock. He'd been reading a very dull book, trying not to think beyond the next dull paragraph, wondering how he was going to get through the rest of the day, and there it was, this vision: the canoe. It was just the thing he needed—to get out on the river, clear his head, let nature be his guide. What could be better? The sun-spanked waves, the breeze fresh out of the north, a little exercise—he could always use the exercise, and really, how often did he have the opportunity to get out here on the Hudson, the river of his boyhood, of his connections, of his past, of *Lester*? All right. A plan. A definite plan.

It took him a while to find the paddles, secreted as they were in the back of the garage behind a six-foot-tall rusting metal cabinet that contained the other boating things: blue flotation cushion, orange life vest, various fishing rods, crab traps, gigs and landing nets. He took the cushion, a spinning rod and a tackle box stocked with Ted Marchant's lures—why not?—balanced a paddle over one shoulder and crossed the lawn to the dock. If he didn't bother with the life vest it was because he never bothered with life vests—he knew what he was doing, and even at his age (he would be fifty-six in December, though officially he admitted only to fifty) he was a strong swimmer, had always been, and for a moment he saw himself in his twenties, racing Lester out to the raft on Kitchawank Lake over and over again, one sprint after the other, the loser having to swig a shot of the tequila their girlfriends, leaning over the edge of the raft, held out for them even as they laughed and cheered and kicked up a froth with their pretty, tanned feet.

The canoe—aluminum, indestructible—was surprisingly heavy, but he managed to flip it over, stow his gear and slide it into the water before lowering himself into it and equalizing his

weight. In the next moment he was stroking hard against the tug of the current, the first strokes the best, always the best, all the power gone to your shoulders and upper arms in a flush of resurgent joy. It was sensational. Transformative. Dip, rise, dip again. He must have been a hundred feet from shore when he realized he'd forgotten a hat, which would have been nice to have to keep the sun out of his face, and his water bottle too, but that wasn't a problem because he wasn't going to stay out that long. Cruise up the river and back again, forty-five minutes, an hour. Max. Though, admittedly, he did feel a bit dehydrated and maybe hungover into the bargain, and the thought flickered in and out of his mind that he might paddle up the river to Garrison, to the bar there, and then drift back down when the tide reversed, but that was too ambitious . . . no, better to keep it simple.

Ahead of him on the right, just past the promontory where the last of the twelve houses sat, was a low trestle that gave onto the marsh on the far side, and he paddled for the entrance, thinking he'd do a little exploring. Meg had taken him back there the last time he'd visited and he remembered it as a magical place, alive with birds of every description, turtles stacked up like dinner plates on the butts of half-submerged trees—and better yet, the sense of enclosure and privacy it held, as if you were miles away from anyone. The point, he realized, as he dug the paddle in and flew across the gray froth of the river, was that Lester was dead and he wasn't. He was alive, never more alive. The burden of grief was a burden we all carried—*Lester! Lester!*—but there was this too, this living in the moment, the sunstruck chop, the breeze, the scent of the wildflowers clustered round the mouth of the trestle till it could have been a bower in a Rossetti poem. He flew for it. But then, drawing closer, he saw that the tide was up higher than he'd realized—the space seemed barely adequate for the canoe itself to pass under, no more than three feet of vertical clearance, if that.

Riley, for better or worse—worse, actually—never backed

down from a challenge, and once he'd made up his mind to shoot the entrance, he just kept going. At the last moment, he slid down supine on the floor of the canoe and let the inrushing current carry him, which wouldn't have been a problem if he'd arrived fifteen minutes earlier, when he would have had another two or three inches between him and the concrete belly of the trestle. As it was, he could have glided right through if he'd been in a kayak or riding a surfboard, but unfortunately the twin high points of the canoe, at bow and stern, struck the ceiling with a sound like grinding molars, the current dragging the canoe forward till finally, a dozen feet from the far side, it stuck fast.

He saw his predicament and experienced a moment of regret, but regret wasn't going to get him out of this, was it? The water was streaming in and soon it would engulf the entire space, right to the ceiling, or at least that had to be a possibility, didn't it? All right. No need to panic. He raised his arms and pushed hard against the concrete above him and the boat edged forward, scraping in protest. What he hadn't counted on—but he hadn't counted on anything, just acted, and acted stupidly, suicidally, really—was the unevenness of the structure, which, as it turned out, had subsided ever so imperceptibly on the far side, not that it was any of his business, but what, exactly, was wrong with the maintenance people on the New York Central Line? Didn't they inspect these things?

Whether they did or not, the fact remained that he was stuck. On his back. In a space that was like a coffin, with the tide rushing in and no more than a few spare inches of clearance between him and the cold gray lid above him that might or might not have been home to various spiders and biting insects and water snakes too, an example of which had just whipped past him in a display of muscular urgency. What else? The cold. The smell of mud, muck, the decay the river fostered and throve on, and all at once he was

remembering the story his father had told him of the drowned woman in Annsville Creek whose corpse had floated to the surface in a twitching scrum of blue-claw crabs. This was serious. He was in trouble. He was going to drown, that was what was going to happen, and he could already see the headlines—*Author Drowns in Boating Accident*—and the pre-packaged rudiments of his obituary: his books, his wives, the early promise, the bloated middle years, the prizes, the checks, survived by his loving wife. Minutes, that was all he had till the water started pouring in over the gunwales, but in that moment he could picture the newspaper account as clearly as if he were sitting at the big oak table in the kitchen at the farmhouse, the overhead lamp bright and his reading glasses clamped over the bridge of his nose.

He'd often wondered how he'd respond in a crisis, at the same time praying he'd never be obligated to find out (and how was it for Ted Marchant, protecting Nadine with the shield of his own body in the millisecond before the AK rounds split him open?). To this point, the closest he'd come was some thirty years ago in the company of Lester, both of them drunk on cheap scotch and saturated with the triumph of their selves and their wise ways and the hipness that cloaked and absolved them, when the lip of the dune they'd been sitting on gave way beneath them so that they were rudely plunged into the ice bath of San Francisco Bay, but—and here was the charm—wound up none the worse for it. So all right. The water was rising but he wasn't panicking—he was too humiliated for panic. He was just—concerned, that was all. And amused. Struck between the eyes with the force of his own stupidity—of all the millions of deaths that come raining down each and every day of our lives, how many involve aging novelists trapped under train trestles in canoes?

We fear death because all we know is life, and once you're alive the safest bet is to stay that way. He knew that, subscribed

to it as a principle, and it provided his motivation now. What if—experimentally—he were to tip the canoe ever so slightly, purposely letting the water in so he could gain another six inches to free himself and take his chances in the water before the air gave out? He could do that, but then his wallet would be soaked and his clothes ruined, yet what were wallets and clothes when he was so close to joining Lester and Ted Marchant in the Land of the Dead? Nothing, nothing at all. Still, he did take the time to wriggle out of his jacket, shirt, jeans and hiking boots and ball the whole business up in one hand as he pushed hard off the ceiling, found the surge of the water and squeezed into it . . . yes, and Jesus, it was freezing!

A lesser writer than Riley might have said something like "Time stood still," but that wasn't it at all, not even close: time accelerated. One instant had him in the canoe, passively awaiting his death by drowning, and the next saw him flailing his way through cattails and muck, his shirt, shoes and jacket gone but his jeans—and wallet—still clutched sopping in one hand till he reached the high stony embankment some previous generation had erected here in the backwater to carry the locomotive freight. It wasn't easy, his feet battered, the stones slippery, a dense growth of briars and poison ivy impeding his way, but finally, too cold and wet and residually shaken even to curse, he was able to pull himself up by stages and emerge on the tracks, and so what if he was in his Joe Boxers and his shoes were missing? He was alive, alive all over again.

He didn't say a word to anyone, not the old man bobbing in his boat or the two women sitting in lawn chairs at the house across the way. He just limped up the tracks in his bare feet and wet underwear, and here was the dog to greet him, dashing by with its length of chain rapping at the rails, and of course it was inevitable that in the interval yet another train would come hur-

tling by to rake him with its tailwind, faces pressed to windows, a young girl waving—waving, for god's sake—and he, nothing else for it, waving back.

After the funeral, once everyone had exhausted their praise for the emotional intensity of his eulogy and the tears had dried and the drinks circulated, he bowed out early, pleading a headache. He and Caroline drove back to the rented house on the river, where the dog, its chain reinforced, twisted round and round the steel post Brian had pounded angrily into the ground just that morning, and they spent all of ten minutes throwing their things together and bringing the suitcases down to the car. Then Riley locked up, gave the dog a wide berth and hurried across the lawn to leave the key under the mat at Meg and Brian's before they could get back from the reception or wake or whatever you wanted to call it. The tear-fest. The slog. The canoe had un-wedged itself on the turn of the tide, but Riley hadn't been there to recover it. He didn't leave a note. If Nadine noticed it missing he'd send her a check, no problem, glad to do it, in fact, glad to help out, but no sense in worrying about that now.

Traffic was light and they made good time. Caroline was silent most of the way down, but her face was composed and she looked good—better than good—in the black velvet dress and single strand of pearls she'd worn for the funeral. They checked into the Algonquin, the only hotel where he really felt appreciated, a homey place, a *writer's* place, and while Caroline went down to see about theater tickets he settled in a chair by the window, high above the crush and grab of West 44th Street. For a long while he gazed out into the grayness, then he picked up the dull book he'd been working his way through, found where he'd left off and started reading.

YOU DON'T MISS YOUR WATER ('TIL THE WELL RUNS DRY)

A light rain fell at the end of the second year of the drought, a female rain, soft and indecisive, a kind of whisper in the trees that barely settled the dust around the clumps of dead grass. We took it for what it was, and if we were disappointed, if we yearned for a hard soaking rain, a macho rain crashing down in all its drain-rattling potency, we just shrugged and went about our business. What were we going to do, hire a rainmaker? Sacrifice goats? There were vagaries to the weather, seasonal variations spurred by the El Niño Southern Oscillation and the Pacific Decadal Oscillation and the Northern Hemisphere Hadley Cell, and certainly the dry years would be followed by the wet in a cycle that had spun out over the centuries, the eons. Daily life was challenging enough—people had to go to the dentist, sit in traffic, pay taxes, cook dinner, work and eat and sleep. It would rain when it rained. No sense worrying over it. Nobody gave it much thought beyond the scaremongers in the newspaper and

the talking heads on the television screen, until the third year went by in a succession of cloudless days and no rain came, not male, female or androgynous.

It was that third year that broke our backs. We began to obsess over water, where it came from, where it was going, why there wasn't enough of it. It got to the point where everything that wasn't water-related, whether it was the presidential election, the latest bombing or the imminent extinction of the polar bear, receded into irrelevance. The third year was when it got personal.

For our part, my wife, Micki, and I had long since cut back our usage, so that when the restrictions came we were already at the bare minimum, the lawn a relic, the flowerbeds, once so lush, nothing more than brittle yellow sticks, the trees gaunt, the shrubs barely hanging on. If before we'd resented the spendthrifts with their emerald lawns and English ivy climbing up the walls of their houses, it was all the more intense now. When those people were forced to cut usage by thirty percent, they were dropping to the level at which we'd already arrived, and so our thirty percent cut amounted to a double penalty on us, the ones who'd been foolish enough to institute voluntary cuts when the governor first made his appeal. Not only was it insupportable—it was deeply unfair, the sort of thing that made a mockery of the notion of shared sacrifice. I began shaving dry, with only the spray foam to moisten my beard, and Micki stopped using makeup because she couldn't abide the waste of having to wash it off. When our son came home for spring break (from Princeton, where it rained every other day) Micki taped a hand-lettered notice to the bathroom door: *If it's yellow, let it mellow; if it's brown, flush it down.* Next morning, when he turned on the shower—the very instant—I was there at the door, pounding on the panels, shouting, "Two minutes max!"

He was a good kid, Everett, forthright and equitable, and

if he had a failing, here it was revealed: *He'd actually turned the shower on*. I couldn't believe it. And neither could Micki. She and I bathed once a week—in the tub, together—then used the bathwater to wash the clothes and bedsheets until finally we scooped up the remainder in plastic buckets and hauled it out to moisten the roots of our citrus trees, which were my pride and joy and the very last thing that would go in the vegetative triage that had seen the lawn sacrificed and then the flowerbeds and finally even the houseplants. At dinner that night (a hurried affair, Everett eager to go out prowling the local watering holes—bars, that is—with his cohort of friends who were likewise home on spring break), I tried to smooth things over and deliver a hydrological lesson at the same time. "Sorry if I overreacted this morning," I said, "but you've got to realize it's the whole southwest. I mean, there just isn't any water. At any cost. Anywhere."

The sun was caught in the kitchen window, hanging there like an afterthought. It was warm, but not uncomfortably so. Not yet anyway—all that still lay ahead.

Everett looked up, his fork suspended in mid-air over a generous portion of green curry shrimp and sticky rice takeout. He shrugged, as if to say he was fine with it. "I should have known better," he said, dipping his head to address his food.

"I hear they're recommissioning the desalination plant," Micki put in, hopeful, always hopeful. She had her hair up in a do-rag and was wearing a white blouse that could have been whiter.

"Two years *minimum*," I said, and I didn't mean it to sound like a rebuke, though I'm afraid it did. I was wrought up, all the little things of life magnified now, the things you take for granted during the good times. That was how tense the situation had become. "And something like nine million dollars, not that the money has anything to do with it—at this stage people'll pay anything, double, triple, they don't care—"

"But you can't bleed a stone," my son said, glancing up slyly.

"Or squeeze water out of it either," I added, and we were all three of us grinning, crisis or no.

So we had a sense of humor about it, at least there was that. Or at least at first anyway. Still, as much as I loved my wife and enjoyed seeing her au naturel, two in a tub was a crowd, and I'm sure she must have felt the same though she never said as much. She was a good sport, Micki, and if my knees were in the way and the water felt faintly greasy, she made the most of it, but for me the weekly bath began to feel like a burden. "Remember the old days?" I'd say, soaping her back or kneading shampoo into the long dark ropes of her hair. "You know, when you could just get up with the alarm and step into the shower before work?" And she would nod wistfully, the water sloshing at her armpits and the tender gaps behind her knees, before heaving herself out of the tub to snatch up her thrice-used towel. I'd give her a moment, my eyes averted, then ease carefully out of the water to drip-dry and wield the bucket. Was this good for our sex life? Or was it too much of the usual, her body shorn of mystery so that when we did finally slip between our graying sheets at night, all I could think of was the tub and the soapy slosh of wasted water? I don't know. Maybe. Maybe that was part of the problem, but I found myself reaching out for her less and less, I'm afraid.

Of course, we weren't alone in this. You didn't see couples hugging or holding hands much anymore and at restaurants they sat across the table from each other and as close to the windows as possible. People began to smell a bit off. You especially noticed it on public transportation, which we tried to avoid as much as possible and damn the consequences, because this was all about water, not gasoline, and if we were contributing greenhouse gases to the atmosphere and exacerbating the global warming that was

the biggest factor in the drought, then so be it. There was a run on deodorant and various body lavage products for a while there, but eventually people gave up and just lived with their own natural scent. In fact, it became a kind of badge of honor to stink, just as it was to display a lawn as brown as the Gobi Desert.

We were all of us, the whole community, learning to adjust, even the spendthrifts, who were threatened with governors on their intake valves if they exceeded their ration, and I have to admit I took a certain degree of satisfaction in watching their lawns wither and their ivy fade to brown. This was the new normal, and as the days went by I began to feel all right with it, and so did Micki. Then one morning, as I strolled through our modest grove of citrus trees, selecting oranges for fresh-squeezed juice, I noticed something odd. Here were my black plastic drip lines snaking round the root systems of our eight Valencia orange trees, with subsidiary connections for our three lemon, two grapefruit and half a dozen fledgling avocado, but now there seemed to be another line altogether—one that branched off the main line and disappeared under the hard compacted earth of the yard. Which, as I saw now, wasn't so compacted, after all, but seemed to have been disturbed recently. We didn't have a gardener, not anymore—what was the point?—so it wasn't anything he might have done, unless he'd slipped into the yard while sleepwalking. I certainly hadn't put in a new line—again, what was the point?—and unless Micki had been working in the garden, which I doubted, since she'd never shown much interest in anything outdoors aside from maybe the parking lot at the galleria, then this was simply a mystery.

I bent to tug at the hose, but it was held in place by means of a series of metal fasteners, and this just compounded the mystery. What I did then was fetch a hoe from the shed at the back of the house and very carefully scrape the dirt away from the length of the hose, which was clearly newer than the old line, the plastic glistening blackly under the sun. Puzzled, I kept at it, fol-

lowing the direction of it all the way across the yard to the fence
that separated our acre and a half from the acre and a half of our
neighbors, the Veniers. Where, even more puzzlingly, it seemed
to vanish under the fence.

Now, in this community of pricey homes and expansive lots,
we kept our distance for the most part, our adjoining properties
walled off with six-foot fences of stone, stucco or redwood, and we
knew our neighbors in the vaguely familiar way we knew the
birds that formerly gathered on the former lawn to peck about for
worms and grubs and such. So it was with the Veniers. His name
was Bill—or maybe Will—and the wife, a shoulderless blonde in
her forties, must have had a name too, but on the few occasions I
did encounter her out on the sidewalk, she never once glanced up
from her cell phone, and I don't think it ever registered with me.
Maybe Micki would know, I was thinking, even as I gripped the
top rail of the fence and peered over into their yard.

At first, I couldn't quite comprehend what I was seeing: the
Veniers had a virtual oasis back there, shrubs, flowerbeds, trees
heavy with fruit crowning a sod lawn as green as creation and
stretching all the way across the property to the far wall, on the
other side of which lived the Chinese couple (or maybe they
were Korean—I never could get that straight). For a long while
I just stood there, straining on tiptoe and trying to make sense of
the situation. What it looked like to me was that my neighbors—
the Veniers, who I'd assumed were decent-enough people with
an income level commensurate to buy into the neighborhood—
were stealing our water. My next thought was that it couldn't be.
Couldn't possibly. Not in this neighborhood. Maybe they had a
well or a secret spring or something and they'd run the hose into
my yard in a gesture of pure altruism, as a way of sharing the
bounty. *Yeah, right,* I told myself, angry suddenly, as angry as
I'd ever been, and then I was up and over the fence, my slippers
making a telltale indentation in the dense green sod beneath.

Did they have a dog? Not that I knew of—I couldn't recall having heard any whining or barking nor seen either of them out on the street with an animal on a leash. Still, I tensed for a moment, half-expecting the black slash of a Rottweiler or Doberman to come hurtling out of the shadows and make a grab for me. All was still. It was seven-thirty of a Saturday morning. Were they awake, the Veniers? Sitting in their breakfast nook reading the *Times* on their tablets and gazing idly out the window to see an intruder in shorts and bedroom slippers planted in the far corner of their secret lawn? Or sleeping in, their faces slack with the moist compress of their dreams? No matter. The length of hose plunged into the ground and ran beneath the sod to where a dense stand of water-hungry carnations and azaleas crowded the foundation of the house. I could see the faint raised outline of it in the sod and was about to follow it, to rip it up if need be and demand an explanation of Bill—or Will—Venier, but then there was the soft whoosh of a sound I hadn't heard in years and a whole series of sprinklers popped up round the perimeter of the lawn and within moments my slippers were wet.

Fifteen minutes later, after having cut the hose and railed at Micki while her face hardened over this grim evidence of perfidy in our midst, I was standing on the Veniers' front doorstep depressing the buzzer. They apparently didn't have chimes (unlike us), but just a hissing mechanical buzz that reverberated through the house like the sound of an oversized electric shaver. It took a moment, during which I mentally rehearsed various speeches and settled finally on a tone of outraged disbelief, and then the wife was standing there before me, blinking against the light. She was dressed in shorts and halter top, and if she was shoulderless I saw that she was breastless too, and her skin was so pale and leached out she might have been dipped in milk from her toes to her transparent eyelashes and fluff of vanilla hair. "Oh," she said, "hi. You're from next door, right? Jim? Or is it Joe?"

"Actually," I said, "the name's Scooter. But what I wanted to know, I mean, what I'm here for, is this." I brandished a length of the hose, its black plastic aperture gaping raggedly where I'd hacked it off with the garden shears.

She was a liar of the first stripe, this woman (whose name, I was later to learn, was Alta, married to Will, not Bill). She never flinched. Just narrowed her eyes in a look that suggested puzzlement shading into umbrage and maybe even annoyance. "What is that?" she asked, all innocence. "A hose? You want to borrow a hose?"

"I found this attached to the drip line in my yard."

She lifted her eyebrows.

"*Attached*," I said, giving it some emphasis, "and running under the fence to your, your *oasis* back there. How do you explain that, I'd like to know. I really would."

An elaborate shrug. From behind her, in the depths of the house, came the lilt of Debussy's *Images*. Cut flowers decorated a vase on a table just inside the door. I could sense the presence of someone else there, the husband, lingering in the shadows and unwilling to show his face. "It must be some mistake," she said, her hand—beringed, lithe, youthful—already easing the door shut.

"You bet it's a mistake," I shouted, a threat about my attorney—my attorney and the town water board—rattling around in my head, but then the door closed firmly and I was left alone with my complaint.

Summer came early that year and lingered late into fall, the afternoons burned clear and the temperatures toppling records day after day. Everett had planned to come home for summer vacation and take up his former job as lifeguard at the community pool, but the pool had been drained and Micki and I encouraged him to stay back east. "Go to summer school," we said. "Get an internship. Work at

McDonald's." Forgive me if we were both thinking of those showers of his and the extra burden of washing his clothes and dirty
dishes and even of the glass of water he kept on his nightstand. We
missed him. Of course we did. But we told ourselves we'd see him
at the end of the year, at Christmas, when the rains were sure to
come and all this privation would be no more than a memory. As
for the Veniers, I never heard a word from them, either of apology
or denial. I did report them to the water board (if that makes me
a snitch, so be it, because everybody was snitching on everybody
else all across town and god forbid if anybody should actually be
caught wielding a hose) and I made a practice of peeping over the
fence now and again to watch their lawn lose its sheen and their
azaleas wither. I soaped Micki's back. She soaped mine. Our knees
got in the way. And our sex life dwindled down to nothing.

The next development—inevitable, I suppose—was the appearance of the water trucks. They looked like gasoline trucks—
tankers—but with the difference that their insignia, if they
carried any at all, bore images of waterfalls or huge trembling
blue raindrops. Twice a day, in mid-morning and again after dinner, they began a slow seductive sashay through the neighborhood, dispensing water—with a thousand-gallon minimum—at
prices that redefined gouging. We weren't exactly poor, Micki
and I, but we did have Everett's tuition hanging over our heads
and Micki had recently lost her job, while my hours had been
reduced, and there was no way we could afford what they were
asking. The problem was we both worked in the tourist industry
and the tourists just weren't showing up anymore—they wanted
showers, swimming pools, ice in their drinks—and they began
to discover that the beaches of Washington and British Columbia really weren't so bad after all, not if you factored in rising
sea temperatures and considered that that was actual water flow-
ing without stint from the taps and showerheads of their motel
rooms overlooking Puget Sound and the Strait of Juan de Fuca.

By this point, sad to say, Micki and I had begun to get on each other's nerves. She was home twenty-four/seven now and I was only going in to work sporadically, so we both had too much time on our hands. We bickered endlessly about the pettiest things—who'd used the last clean towel or let the dishwater seep down the drain—and when Micki shaved her head I knew it was only to spite me, though she claimed it was to save her the trouble of washing her hair. She looked ridiculous. Her ears, shorn of their camouflage, stuck out as if they were somebody else's ears altogether, random flaps of cartilage grafted to her head, and I wondered how I'd never noticed just how extreme—and unattractive—they were till now. I made the mistake of commenting on it and we wound up not speaking for a week.

Then one morning she came to me at my desk in the makeshift office I'd set up in the guestroom and finally broke the silence. "You see what's going on next door?" she said, her voice a conspiratorial whisper. The guestroom was on the second floor and from where I was sitting I could just see down into the Veniers' front yard, albeit at a sheared-off angle. Alta Venier was there in the driveway, which was lined on both sides with French lavender in full bloom, and one of the water trucks was just easing in through the gate as she directed it with hand gestures. She was wearing a two-piece swimsuit in the European style that left her all but naked and I could see that her face, even at this distance, was a mask of greed and seduction. Sure enough, as Micki and I watched, she climbed up on the step of the truck and leaned into the window to give the driver—a guy in his thirties with a baseball cap reversed on his head—a lingering kiss, then took his arm as he stepped out of the truck and led him into the house. My wife and I looked at each other and all our animus seemed to dissolve in that instant: we were in league together, in league once again. How long was that

driver in the house? Forty-five minutes. I timed it. We both did. He wasn't adjusting his belt or anything like that when he finally emerged, but what had gone on—what sort of bargain had been struck—was clear. He looked round him, and maybe he was smirking, I couldn't say, then paid out his hose, stretched it to the water tank the Veniers had installed at the far side of the house, and began pumping.

Everett did come home for Christmas, but there was no water to greet him. It hadn't rained. Temperatures were above normal, the sun oppressive. There was no snowpack in the mountains, and the Colorado River, from which we'd formerly derived thirty percent of our water via various engineering marvels and pumping stations, was, according to the latest reports, nothing but a muddy trickle. Worse yet, our son, who'd been away so long now, seemed like a stranger to us. In fact, when he walked through the gate at the airport, I didn't recognize him—he seemed taller, heavier, and he'd grown a beard that swelled his face till he looked more like a professor than a student. When Micki rushed forward to embrace him, he seemed to stiffen and even took a step back. "Mom?" he said.

I could see the consternation on his face even as Micki wrapped her arms around him, the slick smooth dome of her scalp flashing an SOS under the glare of the overhead lights. People stopped to stare. One woman, clearly arriving from some wetter place, stood stock-still on the gleaming tiles, working her fingers through her own hair as if to reassure herself. "It's not cancer," I blurted. "Just the drought."

Everett was holding his mother at arm's length now, as if she was somebody else's mother and he'd been wrapped in a counterfeit embrace. Who could blame him if he was confused?

Micki gave him a thick smile, broke away from him, spun out a little pirouette. "It's my new look. You like it?"

Christmas Day came sere and bright, the hot high sun spoiling the pretense of the season, no wreath on the door and the tree from the lot gone yellow with thirst. I tried spraying it with the lawn paint but half the needles fell off and the whole business wound up being more trouble than it was worth. And, of course, season of good cheer or no, the question of water and what to do about Everett's usage soured the mood. I'd sprung for a membership at the local health club, just so I could use the shower, but management was wise to that strategy and installed sixty-second regulators on the showerheads and hired an inflated teenage kid in a pair of board shorts to sit on a stool in the shower room and make sure nobody cheated. I took Everett as my guest, but he did cheat, moving from one showerhead to the next, and the inflated kid reported him and they canceled my membership, so it was back to the tub with Micki for me and a frigid salty dip in the Pacific for Everett. And then Everett returned to school and January came, sans rain, followed by a dry February and drier March, and the fourth consecutive rainless rainy season ended not with a bang but a whimper and we braced ourselves for the long dry year to come.

It was around then—at the beginning of the fifth year—that the Veniers showed up on our doorstep late one afternoon. The winds had been especially bad that day and the yard was all but buried in blowing sand, tumbleweed and the flapping tendrils of wind-whipped plastic bags. I don't know where Micki was—shopping, I suppose, or maybe brooding in the basement. She seemed to do a lot of brooding lately, and whether that was healthy or not I couldn't say, though I did begin to wonder if she might not want to think about seeking professional help. Just for the short term. Till things eased up a bit, I mean.

At any rate, the carillon chimed and I pulled back the door to see my neighbors, the Veniers, standing there hunched against the wind, and a third figure beside them whom I at first took to be a child. Alta was wearing a chador, but she still had her hair, the ends of which whipped around her face in a blond frenzy. Will (at least I presumed this was Will, though I didn't really know him well enough to say one way or the other) was in a hoodie, his face haunted and his eyes as inflamed as a seer's. I saw that he wasn't as tall as I, and it felt good to look down on him, especially considering what he and his wife had done to us—which I hadn't forgotten, not by a long shot. The third figure—I saw now that she was a woman, no more than waist high and with a face so rippled and desiccated it might have been hide—stood there between them with her head bowed and her hands clasped before her as if in prayer. Alta was the first to speak. "Can we come in?" she asked.

I stepped aside, too surprised to respond, the word "effrontery" making a quick tour of my brain as the three shuffled in and I slammed the door against the wind-borne refuse that chased at their heels. We stood there awkwardly in the foyer a moment, the Veniers' eyes scouring me while their companion—she wore ropes of beads over a faded denim shirt and what looked to be a polyester housecoat in a shade of pink so blanched it was almost white—stared down at the floor, until I heard myself say, "Here, let's go into the living room where we can be comfortable."

Custom, manners, the way we respond to and treat one another—these are the first things to go in times of duress, and I have to admit I wasn't very gracious. I didn't offer them anything to drink. I didn't make small talk. I just gestured to the sofa and settled myself wordlessly in the armchair.

Alta stripped back the hood of the chador and shook out her hair. "This may seem like an odd request," she began, "but Will and I are going around the neighborhood taking up a collection, pooling our money collectively, that is"—she paused, snatching a

quick glance at the woman, who'd seated herself between her and Will. "For Yoki, I mean. For her fee."

Will spoke up now, his face expressionless, his lips barely moving: "It's a shared responsibility. For all of us. The whole community."

"Fee?" I echoed. "For what?"

Another pause. "She's a—what would you call her, Will?—a rain-bringer. A shaman."

The woman lifted her eyes for the first time and said something then, her voice a dry rasp that rattled in her throat.

"What was that?" I asked.

"She says she can help us." Alta shrugged. "She has powers."

At this point I just let out a laugh. "Good luck with that," I said, rising from the chair and making my way back across the room to the foyer, where I stood waiting with my hand on the doorknob while they exchanged glances and finally, reluctantly, got up and followed me. I held the door for them. The sun blazed on the doorstep. The wind blew. "Just out of curiosity," I said, "how much is she asking?"

They were already out the door. Will hunched his shoulders, swung his head back round. "She doesn't want money."

"What does she want, then?"

Alta turned now too, as did the dwarf woman. "She wants a Mercedes," Alta said.

"450 SEL," the woman put in, her voice as dry as the wind itself. "Verde Brook Metallic. Amaretto interior. And twenty-inch wheels—only the twenty, not the nineteen."

Absurd, right? Effrontery to the *n*th power? When I told Micki about it she gave me a look of disgust. "How did people like that even get into the neighborhood?" she demanded, as if it had been up to me in the first place.

I shrugged and pointed out to her, as gently as I could, that

it was a matter of income. "The people on the west side, in the condos? I'm sure they're even worse."

We were in the kitchen. It was hot. Her scalp glistened with sweat. "Tell me about it," she said, crossing to the sink for a glass of water, then thinking better of it when she saw the yellow tape I'd wrapped around the faucet as a reminder. "And I'll bet they flush their toilets too, don't they?"

Yes, yes they did. And they showered and let the water run while they were brushing their teeth and god knew what else. This was what it had come to, a universal resentment of anyone who used water for any purpose, when it was meant for us— for us and us alone. Here was the lesson of the village green, writ large, but then the village green wouldn't have been there to abuse in the first place if it hadn't rained, would it?

A few days later, when I was out in the yard assessing the condition of the orange trees (there'd been no fruit for two years now and no blossoms either), I heard the thin keening of a voice struggling against the wind and realized, after a moment, that it was coming from the far side of the fence, in the Veniers' yard. Puzzled, I crossed to the fence, went up on tiptoe and peered over. There was the dwarf woman, the shaman, dressed in Indian regalia—feathers, deerskin, a bone breastplate—and doing a slow-motion dance around the faded remnant of lawn the Veniers had been able to keep alive through their illicit means. She was chanting, her voice rising and falling on the wind, and she held a rusted Chock full o'Nuts can in one hand, from time to time dipping her fingers into the mouth of it to extract droplets of the liquid it contained and fling them over her shoulder. The liquid—it was a bright arterial red—stained her fingertips and shone greasily under the assault of the sun. I understood then that it wasn't paint she was releasing into the air and in the same instant felt something open up inside me, a kind of awe I hadn't experienced since childhood. Absurd, yes, but there it was. "Hi, hi, hi-hi," she

chanted. "Heya-heya-heya." The sky stood motionless. Nothing moved, not even a bird. I stood there and watched her till the muscles in my calves felt as if they'd been soldered in place.

I'd like to report that it rained the next day, but that didn't happen. Things just got worse. A man whose water had been cut off after he'd exceeded his ration three months in a row attacked the director of the water board as he bent over a bowl of *pasta e fagiole* at a three-star restaurant downtown. Water vigilantes began to patrol the streets. Car washes closed. There was legislation on the table to criminalize golf. On a more personal level, Everett called to say he was getting married and Micki sobbed over the phone for half an hour because there wasn't even the faintest hope we could attend, our credit cards maxed out and our frequent-flier miles long since depleted. Through it all the dwarf woman never stopped chanting. A week went by, then two, then a month, and still she kept at it, her voice a thin plaint that conspired with the trills and whistles of the birds till it passed beyond recognition. The Veniers' lawn grew browner, greasier, the blades of grass gone heavy with coagulated blood. "Hi, hi, hi-hi," the woman chanted. Nights fell. Days broke. Nothing changed.

And then one morning I woke to a presence I couldn't have named, a lightness, a release, as if a band had been stretched beyond capacity till it snapped. Micki was there in bed beside me, snoring softly. The air was fecund, crouching over us like a living thing, daylight just beginning to show at the windows. That was when the sound started in, a sound so alien I didn't recognize it at first. It began as a patter on the roof, and then it quickened, and then the drains *were* rattling, macho, macho as all hell. I snatched my wife's hand and pulled her from the bed and in the next moment we were out in the yard, our faces lifted to the sky as the rain beat down around us and beat and beat again till we were soaked through and fell to our knees laughing

in the mud, the glorious mud that clung to us and saturated us and promised everything.

Science, meteorological science specifically, tells us of weather patterns, of hemispheric changes, of cycles of drought and plenitude, but science is cold and disinterested. It models, describes, predicts. All that is small comfort to a community under constraint and a grove of citrus trees stressed to the tipping point. I'm not saying that the Indian woman in the Veniers' backyard knew something the scientists didn't or that superstition is anything but just that, and yet she did get her Mercedes (we even kicked in what we could, though it wasn't as much as we would have liked) and when the rains had gone on for a month and people began to worry about flooding and mudslides and the like there was a movement afoot to bring her back and make it all stop. The water board even did a cost-benefit analysis—what would she have wanted, we wondered, a Jaguar? Two Mercedeses? Her own dealership?—but eventually, in the way of these things, the rains did finally come to an end.

The reservoirs are full now and Micki's growing her hair back. We shower separately, though old habits die hard and we both keep to a two-minute limit, and when I see her wrapped in her terrycloth robe, toweling her hair dry, I just want to reach out and pull her to me, thinking how very, very lucky we are to be alive in this moment on this planet that provides us with such abundance and such everlasting grace.

THE DESIGNEE

THE BOREDOM

What he couldn't have imagined, even in his bleakest assessments of the future, was the boredom. He'd sat there in the hospital while Jan lay dying, holding her hand after each of the increasingly desperate procedures that had left her bald and emaciated and looking like no one he'd ever known, thinking only of the bagel with cream cheese he'd have for dinner and the identical one he'd have for breakfast in the morning. If he allowed himself to think beyond that, it was only of the empty space in the bed beside him and of the practical concerns that kept everything else at bay: the estate, the funeral, the cemetery, the first shovel of dirt ringing on the lid of the coffin, closure. There was his daughter, but she had no more experience of this kind of free fall than he, and she had her own life and her own problems all the way across the country in New York, which was

where she retreated after the funeral. A grief counsellor came to the house and murmured in his direction for an hour or two, people sent him cards, books and newspaper clippings in a great rolling wave that broke over him and as quickly receded, but nobody addressed the boredom.

He got up at first light, as he always had. The house was silent. He dressed, ate, washed up. Then he sat down with a book or the newspaper, but his powers of concentration weren't what they once were, and he wound up staring at the walls. The walls just stood there. No dog barked, there was no sound of cars from the street—even the leaky faucet in the downstairs bathroom seemed to have fixed itself. He could have taken up golf, he supposed, but he hated golf. He could have played cards or gone down to the senior center, but he hated cards and he hated seniors, especially the old ladies, who came at you in a gabbling flock and couldn't begin to replace Jan anyway, not if there were ten thousand of them. The only time he was truly happy was when he was asleep, and even that was denied him half the time.

The walls just stood there. No dog barked. The water didn't even drip.

THE LETTER

The letter came out of nowhere, a thin sheet of paper in a standard envelope that bore a foreign stamp (England: Queen Elizabeth in brownish silhouette). It was buried in the usual avalanche of flyers, free offers and coupons, and he very nearly tossed it in the recycling bin along with all the rest, but it was his luck that at the last minute it slipped free and drifted in a graceful fluttering arc to the pavement at his feet. He bent for it, noticing that it was addressed to him, using his full name—Mason Kenneth Alimonti—and that the return address was of a bank in London. Curious, he wedged the sheaf of ads under one arm and pried

open the envelope right there in the driveway while the sun beat at the back of his neck and people drifted by like ghosts out on the street.

Dear Mr. Alimonti, the letter began, *kindly accept my sincere apologies for contacting you out of the blue like this but something very urgent and important has come to our notice and we seek your consent for the mutual interest of all.*

His first thought was that this had something to do with the estate, with Jan's death, more paperwork, more *hassle,* as if they couldn't leave well enough alone, and he glanced up a moment, distracted. Suddenly—and this was odd, maybe even a portent of some sort—the morning seemed to buzz to life, each sound coming to him separately and yet blending in a whole, from the chittering of a squirrel in the branches overhead to a snatch of a child's laughter and the squall of a radio dopplering through the open window of a passing car. And more: every blade of grass, every leaf shone as if the color green had been created anew.

The letter was in his hand still, the junk mail still tucked under one arm. When Jan was alive, he'd bring the mail in to her where she'd be sitting at the kitchen table with her coffee and a book of crosswords, and now he was standing there motionless in his own driveway, hearing things, seeing things—and smelling things too, the grass, jasmine, a whiff of gasoline from the mower that suddenly started up next door. *I am Graham Shovelin,* the letter went on, *Operations & IT Director, Yorkshire Bank PLC, and personal funds manager to the late Mr. Jing J. Kim, an American citizen. He died recently, along with his wife and only son while holidaying in Kuala Lumpur, and was flown back to England for burial. In our last auditing, we discovered a dormant account of his with £38,886,000 in his name.*

This is a story, he was thinking, a made-up story, and what did it have to do with him? Still, and though he didn't have his glasses with him so that the letters seemed to bloat and fade on

the page before him, he read on as if he couldn't help himself: *During our investigations, we discovered that he nominated his son as his next of kin. All efforts to trace his other relations have proved impossible. The account has been dormant for some time since his death. Therefore, we decided to contact you as an American citizen, to seek your consent to enable us to nominate you as the next of kin to the deceased and transfer the funds to you as the designated heir to the deceased.*

There was more—a proposed split of the proceeds, sixty percent for him, thirty-eight percent for the bank, two percent to be set aside *for expenses both parties might incur (if any) during the transaction.* At the bottom of the page was a phone number and a request to contact the bank if the above-mentioned transaction should be of interest, with a final admonition: *Please also contact me if you object to this proposal.* Object? Who could object? He did a quick calculation in his head, still good with numbers though he'd been retired from the college for fifteen years now: sixty percent of 38,886,000 was 23 million and something. Pounds, that is. And what was the conversion rate, one-point-two or -three to the dollar?

It was a lot of money. Which he didn't need, or not desperately anyway, not the way most people needed it. While it was a sad fact that the bulk of what he'd set aside for retirement had been swallowed up in treatments for Jan the insurers had labeled "experimental" and thus non-reimbursable, he still had enough left, what with social security and his 401(k), to live at least modestly for as long as he lasted. This offer, this letter that had him standing stock still in his own driveway as if he'd lost his bearings like half the other old men in the world, was too good to be true, he knew that. Or he felt it anyway.

But still. Thirty million dollars, give or take. Certainly there were places he'd like to visit—Iceland, for one, the Galápagos, for another—and it would be nice to leave his daughter and his

grandson something more than a mortgaged house, funeral expenses and a stack of bills. There were stranger things in this world—people won the lottery, got grants, prizes, estates went unclaimed all over the place, and it wasn't as if he was desperate. A voice warned him against it, but what did he have to lose? The cost of a phone call?

THE PHONE CALL

The phone picked up on the third ring and the first thing he heard was music, a soft trickle of music that was neither classical nor pop, but something in between, and for a moment he thought he was being put on hold before the music cut off abruptly and a deep crisp voice—so deep it surprised him—swelled inside the receiver. "Yorkshire Bank PLC, Graham Shovelin speaking. How may I help you?"

He'd rehearsed a little speech in his head, along the lines of establishing his authority as the person solicited rather than soliciting, but it deserted him now. "Um, I," he stuttered, "I, uh, received your letter?"

There was the faintest tick of hesitation, and then the voice came back at him, so deep he couldn't help thinking of Paul Robeson singing "Ol' Man River" on one of the old 78s his grandmother used to play for him when he was a boy. "Oh, yes, of course—delighted to hear from you. We have your number here on the computer screen, and it matches our records . . . still, one can never be too careful. Would you be so kind as to identify yourself, please?"

"Mason Alimonti?"

"Mason *Kenneth* Alimonti?"

"Yes."

"Ah, well, wonderful. We'll need verification of your identity before we can proceed, of course, but for the moment, since

we're just beginning to get acquainted, I am satisfied. Now, what do you think of our proposal?"

He was in the living room, sitting in the armchair under the reading lamp, using the old landline phone his daughter told him he ought to give up since the cell was all anybody needed these days and she really didn't know anyone, not a single soul, who still paid for a landline. But for something like this—an overseas call—he somehow felt better relying on the instrument he'd been using for thirty years and more. "I don't know," he said. "It sounds too good to be true—"

The man on the other end of the line let out a booming laugh, a laugh that scraped bottom and then sailed all the way up into the high register, a good-natured laugh, delighted, a laugh of assurance and joy that proclaimed all was right with the world. "Well, of course, it *is*," the man boomed, and here came the laugh again. "But sometimes we just have to accept the fact that luck has come our way—and be grateful, Mr. Alimonti, kick up our heels and embrace what life brings us, don't you think?"

For a moment, he was confused. He felt as if he'd gone out of his body, everything before him—the love seat, the houseplants, the blank TV screen—shifting on him so that it all seemed to be floating in air. The phone was in his hand. He was having a conversation. Somebody—the man on the other end of the line—wanted something from him.

"Mr. Alimonti—you there?"

"Yes," he heard himself say. There was something odd about the man's accent—it was British, proper British, *Masterpiece Theatre* British, but the syntax was off somehow. Or the rhythm, maybe it was the rhythm. "Why me?" he asked suddenly.

Another laugh, not quite so deep or pleased with itself as the last. "Because you've lived an unimpeachable life, because you pay your debts and you're as solid an American citizen as anyone

could ever hope to find. Oh, rest assured we've vetted you thoroughly—as we have each of the nine other final candidates."

Nine other candidates? The receiver went heavy in his hand—molded plastic, but it might as well have been cast of iron.

"Am I hearing surprise on your end of the line, Mr. Alimonti? Of course, you understand, we must protect ourselves, in the event that our first choice doesn't wish to accept our offer for any reason—and I can't really imagine that happening, can you?—but as you *are* the first on our list, the single most qualified individual we've examined to date, we have to say—*I* have to say—that we are delighted you've contacted us ahead of any of the others."

He felt a wave of relief sweep over him. The phone was just a phone again. He said, "What next?"

"Next?" the voice echoed. "Well, obviously we have to make certain that you're the man for us—and that we're the men for you too. Do you have any question about the figures I presented in my letter to you? You agree that a sixty/thirty-eight percent split is equable? You're content with that?"

He said nothing. He was back in himself, back in the moment, but he didn't know what to say—did the man want him to negotiate, to quibble over the way the money would be split?

"Again, let me anticipate you, Mr. Alimonti. You are wondering, no doubt, what's in it for us?" The laugh again, but truncated now, all business. "Self-interest, pure and simple. If this account has not been claimed within a five-year period, the whole of it goes to the government and we receive nothing, though we've been the guardians of the late Mr. Kim's fortune for a quarter century now. We *need* you, Mr. Alimonti, and that is the bottom line. We need an American citizen in good standing, with an unblemished record and absolute probity, to be the designee for your fellow American, Mr. Kim." A pause. "Otherwise, none of us receives a shilling."

"What do I have to do?"

"Oh, nothing really, not for the moment. We'll need banking information, of course, in order to transfer the funds, and our solicitors will have to draw up a contract so as to be sure there are no misunderstandings, but all that can come in time—the only question now is, are you with us? Can we count on you? Can I hang up this phone and check the other nine names off my list?"

His heart was pounding in his chest, the way it did when he overexerted himself. His mouth was dry. The world seemed to be tipping under his feet, sliding away from him. *Thirty million dollars.* "Can I have some time to think it over?"

"Sadly, we have but two weeks before the government accounting office swoops in to confiscate this account—and you know how they are, the government, no different, I suppose, than in your country, eh? A belly that's never full. Of course you can think it over, but for your sake—and mine—think quickly, Mr. Alimonti, think quickly."

A NIGHT TO THINK IT OVER

The rest of the day, he really couldn't do much more than sit—first in the armchair and then out on the deck in one of the twin recliners there—his mind working at double speed. He couldn't stop thinking about England, a country he'd visited only once, when he was in his twenties, along with Jan, in the year between grad school and the start of his first job, his daughter not yet even a speck on the horizon. They'd gone to Scotland too, to Edinburgh and where was it? Glasgow. He remembered he took to calling Jan "Lassie," just for the fun of it, and how one day, leaving a fish and chips shop, she'd got ahead of him on the street and he cried out, "Wait up, Lassie," and every woman's head turned. That was England. Or Scotland anyway. Same difference. And they had banks there, of course they did, London the banking

capital of Europe, though he couldn't remember actually having gone into one. He closed his eyes. Saw some sort of proud
antique building, old, very old, with pillars and marble floors,
brass fixtures, an elaborate worked-iron grate between customers and tellers, but here again, he realized, he was bringing up
an image from one BBC drama or another, and what was that
one called where they showed the lives not only of the lords and
ladies, but the servants too? That had been Jan's favorite. She'd
watch the episodes over and over, and sometimes, at breakfast,
she'd address him as "My Lord" and put on a fake accent. For
the fun of it.

Yes, sure. And where was the fun in life now?

At some point, when the shadows began to thicken in the
trees, he went into the house and clicked on the TV—sports,
a blur of action, a ball sailing high against a sky crippled with
the onset of night—but he couldn't concentrate on it, and really, what did it matter who won? Somebody had won before
and somebody had lost and it would happen again. And again.
Unless there was a tie—were there ties in baseball? He couldn't
remember. He thought so. In fact, he distinctly remembered a
tie once, but maybe that was only an exhibition game . . . Or an
all-star game, wasn't that it?

It was past eight by the time he remembered he ought to eat
something, and he went to the refrigerator, extracted the stained
pot there and ladled out half a bowl of the vegetable-beef stew
he'd made last week—or maybe it was the week before. No matter: he'd been rigorous about keeping it refrigerated and in any
case the microwave would kill anything, bacterial or otherwise,
that might have tried to gain a foothold in the depths of the pot.
The important thing was not to waste anything in a world of
waste. He poured himself a glass of milk, scraped two suspicious
spots from a slice of sourdough bread and put it in the toaster,
then sat down to eat.

The walls just stood there. But the silence gave way to a sound from the other room, where the TV was, a long drawn-out cheer and the voice of an announcer unleashing his enthusiasm on the drama of the moment, and that was something at least. What was the time difference between here and England? Eight hours? Nine? Whatever it was, it was too early there to call yet. He was thinking he might like to endow a fellowship in Jan's name at the college—maybe in the Art Department; she'd always liked art—and if he gave enough they'd install a plaque, maybe even name a building after her. Or a wing. A wing at least. Maybe that was more practical, really. He saw her face then, not as it was in those last months, but her real face, her true face, fleshed out and beautiful even into her seventies, and he pushed himself up from the table, scraped his bowl over the trash can and set it on the rack in the dishwasher, decided now, his mind clear, really clear, for the first time all day.

In the morning, after breakfast (no rush—he wouldn't want to come across as over-eager), he would settle himself in the armchair, pick up the phone and make the call.

THE SECOND PHONE CALL

Of all days, this was the one he wound up oversleeping, so that it was past eight by the time he sat down with his morning coffee and punched in the bank's number with a forefinger that didn't seem to want to steady itself, as if this wasn't his finger at all but some stranger's that had been grafted on in the middle of the night. This time, there was no music and the phone picked up on the first ring. He was all set to tell Mr. Shovelin—*Graham, can I call you Graham?*—that he'd found his man, that they'd grow rich together, though, of course, as a bank employee, he didn't imagine that Mr. Shovelin would actually get any of the money,

but a bonus maybe, there had to be that possibility, didn't there? Imagine his surprise then, when it wasn't Shovelin, with his rich booming basso, who answered the phone, but a woman. "Yorkshire Bank PLC, Chevette Afunu-Jones speaking," she said in a thin weary voice. "How may I help you?"

Again, he drew a blank. This whole business made him nervous. The phone made him nervous. *London* made him nervous. "I was," he began, "I mean, I wanted to—is Mr. Shovelin there?"

A pause, the sound of a keyboard softly clicking. "Oh, Mr. Alimonti, forgive me," she said, her voice warming till you could have spread it on toast. "Mr. Shovelin, who I am sorry to say is away from his desk at the moment, instructed me to anticipate your call. And let me say, from all the good things he's had to say about you, it is a real pleasure to hear your voice."

He didn't quite know how to respond to this so he simply murmured, "Thank you," and left it at that. There was another pause, as if she was waiting for him to go on. "When do you expect him back?" he asked. "Because—well, it's urgent, you know? I have some news for him?"

"Well, I can only hope it's the good news all of us on Mr. Shovelin's staff have been waiting to hear," she said, her voice deepening, opening out to him in invitation. "Rest assured that Mr. Shovelin has given me full details and, in my capacity as his executive secretary, the authority to act on his behalf, though he's—well, he's indisposed today, poor man, and you can't begin to imagine what he's had to go through." Here she dropped her voice to a whisper: "Cancer."

This hit him like a blow out of nowhere. Jan's face was right there, hovering over him. "I'm sorry," he murmured.

"Believe me, the man is a lion, and he will fight this thing the way he has fought all his life—and when he returns from his treatment this afternoon, I know he will be lifted up by your

good news, buoyed, that is . . ." Her voice had grown tearful. "I can't tell you how much he respects you," she whispered.

What he heard, though he wasn't really listening on an intuitive level, was an odd similarity to the accent or emphasis or whatever it was he'd detected in Shovelin's speech, and he wondered if somehow the two were related, not that it mattered, really, so long as they stayed the course and checked those other nine names off the list. He said, "Please tell him from me that I hope he's feeling better and, well, that I've decided to take him up on his offer—"

She clapped her hands together, one quick celebratory clap that reverberated through the phone like the cymbal that strikes up the band, before her voice was in his ear again: "Oh, I can't tell you how much this will mean to him, how much it means to us all here at the Yorkshire Bank PLC . . . Mr. Alimonti, you are a savior, you really are."

He was trying to picture her, this British woman all the way across the country and the sea too, a young woman by the sound of her voice, youngish anyway, and he saw her in business dress, with stockings and heels and legs as finely shaped as an athlete's. She was a runner, not simply a jogger, but a runner, and he saw her pumping her arms and dashing through what, Hyde Park?, in the dewy mornings before coming to work with her high heels tucked in her purse. He felt warm. He felt good. He felt as if things were changing for the better.

"Now, Mr. Alimonti," she said, her voice low, almost a purr, "what we need you to do is this, just to get the ball rolling— officially, you understand?"

"Yes?"

"We will need your banking information so that we can begin transferring the funds—or at least cutting you a preliminary check—before the Royal Fiduciary Bureau for Unclaimed Accounts moves on this."

"But, but," he stammered, "what about the contract we were supposed to—?"

"Oh, don't you worry, darling—may I call you darling? Because you are, you really *are* darling—"

He gave a kind of shrug of assent, but nothing came out of his mouth.

"Don't you worry," she repeated. "Mr. Shovelin will take care of that."

THE FIRST DISBURSEMENT

Once the banking details were in place (within three working days, and he had to hand it to Shovelin for pulling strings and expediting things), he received his first disbursement check from the dormant account. It was in the amount of $20,000 and it came special delivery with a note from Shovelin, who called it "earnest money" and asked him to hold off for two weeks before depositing it in the new account, "because of red tape on this end, which is regrettable, but a simple fact of doing business in a banking arena as complex as this." The check was drawn on the Yorkshire Bank PLC, it bore the signature of Graham Shovelin, Operations & IT Director, and it was printed on the sort of fine, high-grade paper you associated with stock certificates. When it came, when the doorbell rang and the mailman handed him the envelope, Mason accepted it with trembling hands, and for the longest time he just sat there in his armchair, admiring it. He was sitting down, yes, but inside he was doing cartwheels. This was the real deal. He was rich. The first thing he was going to do— and the idea came to him right then and there—was help out his daughter. Angelica, divorced two years now, with a son in high school and barely scraping by, was the pastry chef at a tony restaurant in Rye, New York; her dream was to open her own place on her own terms, with her own cuisine, and now he was going

to be able to make it happen for her. Maybe she'd even name it after him. Mason's. That had a certain ring to it, didn't it?

That evening, just as he was ladling out his nightly bowl of stew, the phone rang. It was Shovelin, sounding none the worse for wear. "Mason?" he boomed. "May I call you Mason, that is, considering that we are now business partners?"

"Yes, yes, of course." He found that he was smiling. Alone there in his deserted house where the silence reigned supreme, he was smiling.

"Good, good, and please call me Graham . . . Now, the reason I'm calling is I want to know if you've received the disbursement?"

"I have, yes, and thank you very much for that, but how *are* you? Your health, I mean? Because I know how hard it can be—I went through the same thing with Jan, with my wife—?"

The voice on the other end seemed to deflate. "My health?"

"I'm sorry, I really don't want to stick my nose in, but your secretary told me you were, well, undergoing treatment?"

"Oh, that, yes. Very unfortunate. And I do wish she hadn't confided in you—but I assure you it won't affect our business relationship, not a whit, so don't you worry." There was a long pause. "Kidney," Shovelin said, his voice a murmur now. "Metastatic. They're giving me six months—"

"Six months?"

"Unless—well, unless I can qualify for an experimental treatment the insurance won't even begin to cover, which my physician tells me is almost a miracle, with something like a ninety percent remission rate . . . but really, forgive me, Mason—I didn't call you all the way from England to talk about my health problems. I'm a banker—and we have a transaction to discuss."

He didn't respond, but he was thinking of Jan, of course he was, because how can anybody—insurers, doctors, hospitals—put a price on the life of a human being?

"What I need you to do, Mason—Mason, are you there?"

"Yes, I'm here."

"Good. I need you to deposit twenty thousand dollars American in the account we've opened up at your bank, so as to cover the funds I've transferred to you until they clear. You see, I will need access to those funds in order to grease certain palms in the Royal Fiduciary Bureau—you have this expression, do you not? *Greasing* palms?"

"I don't—I mean, I'll have to make a withdrawal from my retirement, which might take a few days—"

"A few days?" Shovelin threw back at him in a tone of disbelief. "Don't you appreciate that time is of the essence here? Everyone in this world, sadly enough, is not as upright as you and I. I'm talking about graft, Mason, graft at the highest levels of government bureaucracy. We must grease the palms—or the wheels, isn't that how you say it?—to make certain that there are no hitches with the full disbursement of the funds."

There was a silence. He could hear the uncertain wash of the connection, as of the sea probing the shore. England was a long way off. "Okay," he heard himself say into the void.

But it wasn't a void: Shovelin was there still. "There are too few men of honor in this world," he said ruefully. "Do you know what they say of me in the banking industry? 'Shovelin's word is his honor and his honor is his word.'" He let out a sigh. "I only wish it were true for the unscrupulous bureaucrats we're dealing with here. The palm greasers." He let out a chuckle, deep and rolling and self-amused. "Or, to be more precise, the *greasees*."

A PROBLEM WITH THE CHECK

Two weeks later, he was on the phone again, and if he was upset, he couldn't help himself.

"Yes, yes," Shovelin said dismissively. "I understand your concern, but let me assure you, Mason, we are on top of this matter."

"But the people at my bank? The Bank of America? They say there's a problem with the check—"

"A small matter. All I can say is that it's a good thing we used this as a test case, because think of the mess we'd be in if we'd deposited the whole sum of $30,558,780, which, by the way, is what our accountants have determined your share to be, exclusive of fees. If any."

He was seeing the scene at the bank all over again, the cold look of the teller, who seemed to think he was some sort of flim-flam man—or worse, senile, useless, *old*. They'd sat him down at the desk of the bank manager, a full-figured young woman with plump butterfly lips and a pair of black eyes that bored right into you, and she'd explained that the check had been drawn on insufficient funds and was, in effect, worthless. Embarrassed— worse, humiliated—he'd shuffled out into the sunlight blinking as if he'd been locked up in a cave all this time.

"But what am I supposed to do?"

"Just what you—and I, and Miss Afunu-Jones—*have* been doing: exerting a little control, a little *patience*, Mason. The fact is, I am going to have to ask you to make another deposit. There is one man at the RFB standing in our way, a scoundrel, really— and I'll name him, why not? Richard Hyde-Jeffers. One of those men born with the gold spoon in his mouth but who is always greedy for more, as if that were the only subject they tutored him in at Oxford: greed."

"He wants a bribe?"

"Exactly."

"How much?'

"He wants twenty thousand more. Outrageous, I know. But you've—*we've*—already invested twenty thousand in him,

the greedy pig, and we wouldn't want to see that go down the drain—do you use that expression, 'down the drain'?—or watch the deal of a lifetime wither on the vine right in front of our eyes."

Shovelin was silent a moment, allowing him to process all this. Which, he had to admit, was difficult, increasingly difficult. Nothing was as it seemed. The house slipped away from him again, everything in motion, as if an earthquake had struck. Spots drifted before his eyes. The phone was cast of iron.

"I promise you," Shovelin said, his voice gone deeper yet in a sort of croon, "as I live and breathe, *this* will be the end of it."

THE FLIGHT TO HEATHROW

He'd never been comfortable in the air, never liked the feeling of helplessness and mortal peril that came over him as the great metallic cage lifted off the tarmac and hurtled into the atmosphere, and over the years he'd made a point of flying as little as possible. His most memorable—and relaxing—vacations had been motor trips he and Jan had taken, usually to one national park or the other or just exploring little out-of-the-way towns in Washington, Oregon, British Columbia. The last flight he'd been on—to Hawaii, with Jan, to celebrate their golden anniversary, or was it the silver?—had been nightmarishly bumpy, so much so he'd thought at one point the plane was going down and he'd wound up, embarrassingly, having to use the air-sickness bag. He couldn't help thinking about that as he found his way down the crowded aisle to his seat in economy, both his knees throbbing from his descent down the Jetbridge and his lower back burning from the effort of lugging his oversized suitcase, which he'd randomly stuffed with far too many clothes and even an extra pair of shoes, though he was only staying two nights in London. At the expense—and insistence—of Yorkshire Bank PLC.

In the four months that had dragged by since he'd first received the letter, his expenses had mounted to the point at which he'd begun to question the whole business. That little voice again. It nagged him, told him he was a fool, being taken, and yet every time he protested, Graham—or sometimes Chevette—telephoned to mollify him. Yes, there was graft, and yes, part of the problem was Graham's health, which had kept him out of the office at crucial junctures in the negotiations with Mr. Hyde-Jeffers of the Royal Fiduciary Bureau, but he needed to have faith, not simply in the Yorkshire Bank PLC, but in Graham Shovelin's word, which was his honor, as his honor was his word. Still, Mason had posted funds for fees, bribes, something Chevette called "vigorish," and beyond that to help defray Graham's medical expenses and even, once, to underwrite a graduation party for Chevette's niece, Evangeline, whose father had been run over by a bus and tragically killed the very week of his daughter's graduation (Mason had been presented with an itemized bill for the gown, corsage, limousine and dinner at a Moroccan restaurant that had cost a staggering $1,500). All to be reimbursed, of course, once the funds were released.

It was Graham who'd suggested he come to London to see for himself "how the land lies," as he put it. "After all this time, to tell me that you don't have absolute faith in me, my friend—my friend and partner—is to wound me deeply," Graham had said, pouring himself into the phone one late night in a conversation that must have gone on for an hour or more. "You hurt my reputation," he said in a wounded voice, "and worse than that, Mason, worse than that, you hurt my *pride*. And really, for a man in my condition, facing an uncertain future and the final accounting up above, what else is there for me to hold on to? Beyond love. Love and friendship, Mason." He'd let out a deep sigh. "I am sending you an airline ticket by overnight mail," he said. "You want your eyes opened? I will open them for you."

TWO DAYS IN LONDON

If the walls just stood there back at home, he didn't know it. His life, the life of the widower, of the griever, of the terminally bored, had changed, and changed radically. Graham Shovelin himself took time off from work—and his chemo—to pick him up at the airport in a shining maroon Mercedes and bring him to his hotel, all expenses paid. Of course, there was a little contretemps at the airport, Mason, exhausted from a cramped and sleepless night and at eighty no steadier on his feet than he'd been at seventy-nine or expected to be at eighty-one, had mistaken this heavyset fortyish man with the shaved head and hands the size of baseball mitts for a porter and not the Operations & IT Director of the Yorkshire Bank PLC. But then he hadn't expected him to be black. Not that he had any prejudices whatsoever—over the years he'd seen and worked with all types of students at the college and made a point of giving as much of himself as he could to each of them, no matter where they came from or what they looked like—but he just hadn't pictured Graham Shovelin this way. And that was his failing, of course. And maybe, he thought, that had to do with *Masterpiece Theatre* too, with the lords and ladies and the proper English butler and under-butler and all the rest. So Graham was black, that was all. Nothing wrong with that.

The hotel Graham took him to wasn't more than a twenty-minute drive from the airport, and it wasn't really a hotel, as far as Mason could see, but more one of these bed-and-breakfast sort of places, and the staff there was black too—and so were most of the people on the streets. But he was tired. Exhausted. Defeated before he even began. He found his bed in a back room and slept a full twelve hours, longer than he could ever remember having slept since he was a boy at home with his parents. In fact, when he finally did wake, he couldn't believe it was still dark outside and he had to tap the crystal of his watch to make sure it hadn't stopped.

He lay there for a long while after waking, in a big bed in a small room all the way on the other side of the world, feeling pleased with himself, proud of himself, having an *adventure*. He pushed himself up, fished through his suitcase for a pair of clean underwear and socks. Just then, an ambrosial smell, something exotic, spicy, began seeping in under the door and seemed to take possession of the room, and he realized he was hungry, ravenous actually. Vaguely wondering if he was too late for breakfast—or too early—he eased open the door and found himself in a dim hallway that gave onto a brightly lit room from which the odor of food was emanating, a room he took to be the kitchen.

He heard a murmur of voices. His knees hurt. He could barely seem to lift his feet. But he made his way down the hall and paused at the door, not knowing what the protocol was in a bed-and-breakfast (he and Jan had always stayed in hotels or motor courts). He gave a light knock on the doorframe in the same instant that the room jumped to life: a gas stove, spotless, with a big aluminum pot set atop it; a table and chairs, oilcloth top, half a dozen beer bottles; and someone sitting at the table, a big man, black, in a white sleeveless T-shirt: Graham. It was Graham Shovelin himself, a newspaper spread before him and a beer clutched in one big hand.

THE EXPLANATION

"Really, Mason, you must forgive me for any misunderstanding or inconvenience regarding the accommodations, but I am only acting in your best interest—*our* best interest—in putting you here, in this quite reasonable bed-and-breakfast hotel rather than one of those drafty anonymous five-star places in the heart of the city, which is where Mr. Oliphant, President of the Yorkshire Bank PLC, had urged me to put you up. And why? To save our partnership any further out-of-pocket expense—*unnecessary*

expense—until we are able to have the funds released in full. Tell me, have I done right?"

Mason was seated now at the table across from Shovelin, a bowl of stew that wasn't all that much different from what he ate at home steaming at his elbow while a woman who'd appeared out of nowhere provided bread and butter and poured him a glass of beer. She was black too, thin as a long-distance runner and dressed in a colorful wraparound garment of some sort. Her hair was piled atop her head in a massive bouffant and her feet were bare. She was very pretty and for a moment Mason was so distracted by her he wasn't able to respond.

"Just tell me, Mason," Shovelin repeated. "If I've done wrong, let me know and I'll get in the car this minute and take you to the Savoy—or perhaps you prefer the Hilton?"

He wasn't tired, that wasn't it at all—just the opposite, he was excited. A new place, new people, new walls! And yet he couldn't quite focus on what Shovelin was saying, so he just shrugged.

"I take that to be accord, then?" Shovelin boomed. "Happily, happily!" he cried. "Let's toast to it!" and he raised his glass, tapped it against Mason's, and downed the contents in a gulp. His eyes reddened and he touched one massive fist to his breastbone, as if fighting down indigestion, then turned back to Mason. "Now," he said, so abruptly it almost sounded like the sudden startled bark of a dog, "let's get down to business. This lovely lady here, in the event you haven't already divined her identity, is none other than my executive secretary, Miss Afunu-Jones, who is taking time out of her hectic schedule to devote herself to your comfort during your brief stay. She has my full confidence, and anything you feel you must say to me you can say to her and she can handle any and all inquiries . . ." His voice trailed off. "In the event . . . well, in the event I am, how shall I put it?, *indisposed.*"

Mason felt his heart clench. He could see the pain etched in the younger man's face and he felt the sadness there, felt the

shadow of the mortality that had claimed Jan and would one day claim everyone alive, his daughter, his grandson, this man who'd reached out across the ocean to him and become not only his friend but his confidant.

Shovelin produced a handkerchief, wiped his eyes and blew his nose. "Forgive me for injecting an element of what, *pathos*, into this little party meant to welcome you to our land, and I know it's not professional"—here he employed the handkerchief again—"but I am only human." He looked up at the woman, who hovered behind them. "Chevette, perhaps you will take over for me, and give Mr. Alimonti—Mason—the explanation he's come for—"

Chevette, her eyes full too, pulled up a chair and sat beside Mason, so close their elbows were touching. She took her time, buttering a slice of bread and handing it to him before taking a sip of beer herself and looking him right in the eye. "We will see this business through to the end, believe me, Mason," she said, her voice soft and hesitant. "We will not desert you. You have my word on that."

"About tomorrow," Shovelin prompted.

Her eyes jumped to his and then back to Mason's. "Yes," she said, "tomorrow. Tomorrow we will take you to the central office, where you will meet with our president, Mr. Oliphant, and iron out the final details to your satisfaction." She paused, touched a finger to her lips. "I don't know that all this is necessary, but as you seem to have lost faith in us—"

"Oh, no, no," he said, fastening on her eyes, beautiful eyes, really, eyes the color of the birch beer he used to relish as a boy on family jaunts to Vermont.

"But the explanation is simple, it truly is. What I mean is, just look at us. We are not wealthy, we are not even accepted by many in white society, and I'm sorry to have to repeat it like a mantra, but we are diligent, Mr. Alimonti, diligent and faithful. The fact

is, as my—as Mr. Shovelin—has told you, we are dealing with corruption, with thieves, and all the unconscionable holdup in this matter is to be laid at their feet, not ours, Mason, not ours." And here, whether conscious of it or not, she dropped a hand to his thigh and gave him the faintest squeeze of reassurance.

UNFORTUNATE CIRCUMSTANCES

The next day, his last day, and not even a full day at that, as his plane was scheduled to depart at 6:45 in the evening, he was awakened from a dreamless sleep by Chevette, who stood at the foot of his bed, softly calling his name. She was dressed in the sort of business attire he'd envisioned when he'd first heard her voice over the phone, she was wearing lipstick and eye shadow and her hair had been brushed out over her shoulders. "Mr. Alimonti," she said, "Mason, wake up. I have some bad news."

He pushed himself up on his elbows, blinking at her. His knee throbbed. He seemed to have a headache. For a minute he didn't know where he was.

"Unfortunate circumstances have arisen," she was saying. "Graham has had a seizure and they've taken him to hospital—"

He fumbled to find the words. "Hospital? Is he—will he?—"

She made a wide sweeping gesture with one hand. "That is not for me to say. That"—her eyes hardened—"is in the hands of the insurers, who keep denying him the lifesaving treatment he so desperately needs. And we, we are but humble bank employees and we are by no means rich, Mason, by no means. We've exhausted our savings . . . yes, *we*, because now I must confess to you what you must already have suspected—Graham is my husband. We didn't want to have to tell you for fear you might think us unprofessional, but the cat is out of the bag now." She caught her breath. Her eyes filled. "And I love him, I love him more than I could ever put into words—"

He was in his pajamas in a strange bed in a strange place, a strange woman was standing over him and his heart was breaking.

"Please help us," she whispered. "Please?"

THE FLIGHT BACK

He'd given her all he had on him—some eight hundred dollars in cash he'd brought along for emergencies—and written her a check he'd be hard-pressed to cover when he got home. As the expenses had mounted, he'd taken out a second mortgage and depleted his retirement account so that things were going to get very difficult financially if the funds didn't come through soon. But they would, he was sure they would, every minute of every day pushing him closer to his goal. Chevette had tearfully assured him that Mr. Oliphant would see things through, whether her husband survived his emergency operation or not. "Truly," she told him, "he lies between this life and the next."

It wasn't until he'd buckled himself in and the plane was in the air that it occurred to him that he never had gotten to meet Mr. Oliphant, see what an English bank looked like from the inside or even sign the agreement Graham had kept forgetting to produce, and now—he felt his heart seize again—might never be able to. He had two drinks on the plane, watched bits of three or four jumpy color-smeared movies, and fell off into a sleep that was a kind of waking and waking again, endlessly, till the wheels touched down and he was home at last.

ANGELICA STEPS IN

Three months later, after having missed four consecutive mortgage payments and receiving increasingly threatening let-

ters from the bank, letters so depressing he could barely bring himself to open them, he telephoned his daughter to ask if she might be able to help him out with a small loan. He didn't mention Graham Shovelin, the Yorkshire Bank PLC or the windfall he was expecting, because he didn't want to upset her, and, more than that, he didn't want her interfering. And, truthfully, he wasn't so sure of himself anymore, the little voice back in his head now and telling him he was a fool, that he'd been defrauded, that Graham Shovelin, whom he hadn't heard from in all this time, wasn't what he appeared to be. He had hope still, of course he did—he had to have hope—and he made up excuses to explain the silence, excuses for Graham, who for all he knew might be lying there in a coma. Or worse. He could be dead. But why then didn't anyone pick up the phone at the Yorkshire Bank PLC? Chevette, though she may have been grief-stricken, would certainly have had to be there, working, no matter what had befallen her husband, and then there was Mr. Oliphant and whatever secretaries and assistants he might have had.

At one point, despairing, after he'd called twenty times without response, he went online and found a homepage for the Yorkshire Bank PLC, which didn't seem to list the names of the bank officers at any of their branches. He did find a general purpose number and after having been put on hold for ten minutes spoke to a woman who claimed she'd never heard of a Mr. Oliphant, and, of course, he was unable to supply any specifics, not with regard to which branch Oliphant was affiliated with or even what his given name might be. He felt baffled, frustrated, hopeless. He called his daughter.

"Dad? Is that you? How are you? We've been worried about you—"

"Worried, why?"

"I've called and called, but you never seem to be home—what

are you doing, spending all your time at dance clubs or what, the racetrack?" She let out a laugh. "Robbie's starting college in a month, did you know that? He got into his first-choice college, SUNY Potsdam, for music? The Crane School?"

He didn't respond. After a minute, when she paused for breath, he said flatly, "I need a loan."

"A loan? What on earth for? Don't you have everything you need?"

"For the mortgage. I—well, I got a little behind in my payments . . ."

It took a while, another five minutes of wrangling, but finally she got it out of him. When he'd told her the whole story, everything, the thirty million dollars, the disbursement, the bribe money, Graham's treatments, even the two-day debacle in London, she was speechless. For a long moment he could hear her breathing over the phone and he could picture the expression she was wearing, her features compressed and her lips bunched in anger and disbelief, no different from the way Jan had looked when she was after him for one thing and another.

"I can't believe you," she said finally. "How could you be so stupid? You, of all people, a former professor, Dad, a math whiz, good with figures?"

He said nothing. He felt as if she'd stabbed him, as if she was twisting the knife inside him.

"It's a scam, Dad, it's all over the papers, the internet, everywhere—the AARP newsletter Mom used to get. Don't you ever read it? Or listen to the news? The crooks even have a name for it, 419, after the Nigerian anti-fraud statute, as if it's all a big joke."

"It's not like that," he said.

"How much did you lose?"

"I don't know," he said.

"Jesus! You don't even know?" There was a clatter of pans or

silverware. He could picture her stalking round her kitchen, her face clamped tight. "All right," she said. "Jesus! How much do you need?"

"I don't know: ten?"

"Ten what—thousand? Don't tell me ten thousand."

He was staring out the window on the back lawn and the burgundy leaves of the flowering plum he and Jan had planted when their daughter was born. It seemed far away. Miles. It was there, but it was shrinking before his eyes.

"I'm coming out there," she said.

"No," he said, "no, don't do that."

"You're eighty years old, Dad! Eighty!"

"No," he said, and he no longer knew what he was objecting to, whether it was his age or the money or his daughter coming here to discipline him and humble him and rearrange his life.

ONE MORE PHONE CALL

The house belonged to the bank now, all of it, everything, and his daughter and Robbie were there helping him pack up. He was leaving California whether he liked it or not and he was going to be living, at least temporarily, in Robbie's soon-to-be-vacated bedroom in Rye, New York. Everything was chaos. Everything was black. He was sitting in his armchair, waiting for the moving van to take what hadn't been sold off in a succession of what Angelica called "estate sales" and haul it across the country to rot in her garage. In Rye, New York. For the moment, all was quiet, the walls just stood there, no dog barked, no auto passed by on the street. He was thinking nothing. He couldn't even remember what Jan looked like anymore. He got to his feet because he had an urgent need to go fetch a particular thing before the movers got hold of it, but in the interval of rising, he'd already forgotten just what that particular thing was.

So he was standing there in the ruins of his former life, a high desperate sun poking through the blinds to ricochet off the barren floorboards, when the phone rang. Once, twice, and then he picked it up.

"Mason?"

"Yes?"

"Graham Shovelin here. How are you?"

Before he could answer, the deep voice rolled on, unstoppable, Old Man River itself: "I have good news, the best, capital news, in fact! The funds will be released tomorrow."

"You're"—he couldn't find the words—"you're okay? The, the treatment—?"

"Yes, yes, thanks to you, my friend, and don't think I'll ever forget it. I'm weak still, of course, which is why you haven't heard from me in some time now, and I do hope you'll understand . . . but listen, we're going to need one more *infusion* here, just to assure there are no glitches tomorrow when we all gather in Mr. Oliphant's office to sign the final release form—"

"How much?"

"Oh, not much, Mason, not much at all."

WARRIOR JESUS

In the first panel of the very first issue you see Him striding across the desert with maybe nothing around Him but sand and the ruins of a shattered village in the distance. He's not wearing a robe and sandals but bike shorts and black lace-up combat boots and a tight black tee and He's not the skinny hippie all the paintings make Him out to be, but buff, as if He's been doing weight training, but of course, like Wolverine or the Hulk, He doesn't really have to sweat anything to be built like that. He just is. And His hair—it isn't that long, actually, just long enough to give Him a topknot like a samurai, and His beard isn't shaggy like some biker's beard, but trimmed close to His rock-hard jawline. His eyes—at first—are calm, and they're not blue like in the paintings either, but green like Asia's (she's my girlfriend). What you see, right off, is that this isn't the sort of hero who'll turn the other cheek or out of some misguided notion of fairness or love or whatever won't use His powers to the very fullest degree. No, just the opposite. Warrior Jesus is the scourge and the whip—the Cleanser—and He's come to wipe up all the slime of

the world, the Al Qaedas and Boko Harams, ISIS, the Mexican Mafia and all the rapists and slavers and drug dealers out there, dog abusers, wife beaters, anybody evil who seeks to inflict pain on the weak—they're going to be dust. All of them. Just like what He's walking over in that first panel, the sand grains symbolic of what He's going to reduce them to. No hell, no trial, no punishment: just dust. Or sand. Or whatever.

Saturday night, the place mobbed, and I've got my head down pretty much the whole shift, just trying to keep up with the orders. Stressed isn't really the word for it, just busy, so busy I'm startled when one of the customers—an older woman who comes in on a regular basis—asks me how my drawing's going and the best I can do is rotate the upper half of my body away from the grill, show her some teeth and say, "Great, just great." There must be twenty steaks up and I'm working my tongs like a master conductor waving his baton, only the stage here is a ten-by-three-foot space between the grill and the salad bar and the audience is a snaking line of semi-drunk people with big oval salad-bar plates in their hands, but I'm the main attraction, make no mistake about it. And the meat, of course, sizzling there over the tiny yellow fingers of flame and sending up that authentic mesquite-seared aroma that has them all choking back saliva as they lean over the sneeze guard and fish out cherry tomatoes or avocado slices with the salad tongs. The truth is, on this particular night, I all but blanked on the public-relations aspect of the job until the woman brought me out of my reverie, and that isn't good, because my boss, Mike Twombley, always makes a huge deal of it. *You are representing Brennan's every minute you're standing there at the grill, never forget it. People like to see their steaks go up and they like to see somebody cool, somebody friendly, flipping them, right?* Well, yeah, I get that. But they also like rare rare

and medium-rare medium-rare, and if the grillman's busy bending over backwards for everybody—especially on a night like this—then there are going to be fuckups, and what would you rather have, dinners sent back or a grillman who's focused on the task at hand?

Toward the end of my shift, after I've already dumped the grease and taken the wire brush to the grill, Mercy, the cutest waitress, who just happens to drive all the old men at the bar gaga because she's older (thirty-two, divorced, one kid), brings me a late order, party of two, a New York well for the guy, prawn-and-scallop kebab for the girl. Normally the kitchen closes at nine-thirty, after which it's burgers only, flipped in a pan in the kitchen and served at the bar, and it's nine-forty now, but I'm in a good place, really riding high on Warrior Jesus and seeing the panels unfolding in my head as if I've already drawn them, and it's nothing to throw one more dinner on the grill, which will have to be scraped again, but it's not as if it hasn't happened before. The restaurant is in the business of making money and I'm a good employee, a model employee, really, as I try to remind Mike every chance I get, and if it costs me an extra twenty minutes, so what? I'm only going to sit at the bar anyway. Asia's out with her girlfriends—a movie, she said, then barhopping—and there's nothing for me at home except staring at the walls, unless I want to play video games (I don't) or watch TV (I doubly don't).

"I can't see them," I say, "where are they?" My eyesight isn't the best and I don't like to wear my glasses at the grill because they tend to steam up, which means everything out there in the dining room is just a blur.

"Around the corner? Table thirteen?"

"Okay," I say, "okay, great," and why do I always feel so stupid—or awkward, I guess—around Mercy when I've got my own girlfriend and Mercy's too old for me anyway? It's the eternal urge, the mating urge, common to us all, though not War-

rior Jesus. He's beyond all that—He doesn't have the time, for one thing. And this isn't Greek mythology, with gods pulling the wires behind the scenes or bickering with each other or coming down to have sex with mortals—this is the One God, the Only God, and He's here for vengeance. "Just tell them we're about to take the salad bar down any minute, so they need to get to it ASAP, okay?"

"I just want to get out of here," she says, giving me a tired grin, and I watch her glide off in her black miniskirt and the low-cut top that adds an extra five dollars to her tip when it's a male paying the bill, which is about ninety percent of the time.

So here they come, the late diners I've gone out of my way to stay open for, a guy and a girl, and the guy's wearing some sort of headgear that flashes white all the way across the restaurant so even I can see it in my semi-blind state. And what is it? A turban? The term *raghead* shoots in and out of my mind, a term I don't think I've ever used because it's not p.c. and Asia's always on me if I make any kind of ethnic reference to anybody, whether in my comics or in person, and then he's there at the salad bar and the girl right beside him (she's mid-twenties, cute, dyed-red hair with black roots showing and a sleeve of tattoos running up her left arm). I can tell they've been dating for a while because he goes ahead of her, flipping a plate off the pile as if he's going to start juggling with it and bending low to dig into the bowl of romaine and pick out the crispest pieces—and he has to bend low, I realize, because he's tall, as tall as me at least, and that doesn't seem right somehow, as if people like him, from wherever he's from, should be shorter than that. He's got a beard, of course, a full beard that just about touches the cracked ice cooling the stainless-steel serving trays, and his skin's not much darker than mine used to get in the summers when I was a lifeguard at the lake. And what is he, a Paki or a Hindu or something? I don't know much about it, one way or the other, though the guy that delivers produce in

the mornings is some sort of Arab and there's a Hindu, definitely a Hindu, running the Conoco station. Plus, what do I care? He's just another customer and I probably wouldn't have noticed him at all if he'd come in during the rush.

It's just then that he glances up and gives a little start as if he didn't expect to see anybody there, though even first-time customers seem to get the drill—suck down your cocktail, put in your order, troop up to the salad bar and let the grillman provide the entertainment till you've heaped up your plate and trooped back to your table again. As I say, he was bent at the waist, picking out his toppings, and now suddenly he straightens up and gives me a look. "Oh, hi," he says. "I guess you're our chef, huh?"

"Right," I say, and I'm looking at her too, wondering if I know her from someplace—high school? Pratt?—and what she's doing with him. "You're the New York well."

He lets out a laugh then, which is meant to be all urbane and above it all, and says, "Well, I hope I'm more than that"—and here he gives the girl a sly look—"though for our purposes, that designation suits me just fine." He's got a trace of an accent, which I'm just now picking up—British or something, or maybe Indian. From India.

"It's a crime," I say and watch his grin waver, which gives me just the faintest little tick of satisfaction. He thinks a lot of himself, this guy, this *dude,* and maybe I don't, maybe I take an instant dislike to him.

"What do you mean? What's a crime?"

I glance at the girl and back at him, then turn away to toss his steak on the grill, where it lands with a hiss and sends up a puff of smoke. "Oh," I say, turning back to him now and letting my eyes run first to her, then to him, "the steak. I mean, well-done is kind of like sacrilege. The other grillman—Bobby Reyes?— I've seen him refuse to do well-done." (And once, when he had a buzz on, actually go into the dining room and stand over a

party of four, pleading with this woman to at least let him do hers medium.)

The guy in the turban bends down to dig into the artichoke hearts, but when he comes up he's grinning again. "Don't I know it," he says and puts his free arm around the girl. "Jenny's telling me the same thing all the time, right, babe?"

That's when I let my mouth get ahead of me, and I have to attribute it to just being tired at this juncture, that and dehydrated because the heat of the grill really does wring the sweat out of you, no different than if you were sitting in a sauna all day. "I thought Hindus didn't eat meat."

I watch the smile fade and then come up strong again, and he takes his time with me, dipping the ladle for the Roquefort dressing and pouring a half ton of it over everything on his plate. "I'm not Hindu," he says, and then he and the girl are turning their backs on me and heading back to their table.

That's all. That's all there is. Just that little exchange. And I am not prejudiced, or not any more than anybody else, and if you want to know the truth I hardly knew my cousin Bruce— Bruce Tuttle? That ring a bell?—because his family moved out to California when we were still kids and if I saw him more than two or three times over the years that was it. And yes, I did know he was some sort of minor journalist for CBS News—could my mother ever let me forget it?—and I knew he was covering the Middle East and all of that, but I don't know if I felt personally violated when they took him prisoner and then, without even negotiating, went out and beheaded him six days later, and I only watched the video once, on YouTube, but I felt something, let me tell you. I felt sick, sad, shocked, confused, angry, of course I did—who wouldn't? It didn't matter who they were doing this to—that video is the purest expression of evil that's ever come into my life. But that doesn't excuse what happens next, once the guy in the turban and his girlfriend disappear round the corner,

and I don't feel good about it, but you have to understand how I was feeling that night, not only because of Asia, who might or might not have been lying to me about who she was going out with, but because I was tired and maybe a little fed up and I'd been listening to my mother go on about Bruce over and over for the last six months till I was either going to have to build a shrine to him in the backyard or go out and shoot myself in the head.

I flip the steak. Press down hard with the tongs till the juices sizzle and the flames jump up, then I put the girlfriend's kebab on, and all the while I'm working this ball of phlegm in my throat—I've got the cold to end all colds and the Dristan I took at four is wearing off. So he gets his steak, cooked through till it could have come right from the tannery, and if it has a nice translucent glaze on it, I just feel it's the least I can do for him.

The second panel shows Him coming into this burned-out village, which is still maybe a hundred yards off, and you can see figures there now, shadowy, wreathed in smoke, and in the third panel He's there and the people—civilians, victims, little kids, old women in head scarves—are all looking flabbergasted at Him as if they're wondering what next, expecting the worst, only the worst. That's when your eye jumps to panel four and you see the bad guys, all dressed in black with black ski masks and AKs and grenade launchers slung over their shoulders. One of them has a knife, and not one of these seven-inch Ka-Bar things like they used in the video, but a huge blade, curved like a scimitar—do they still use scimitars?—and it shines against his all-black clothes, or maybe it's a robe he's wearing, a black robe, till it definitely focuses your eye. Panel five is the knife, foregrounded, and just beyond it are the victims, a skinny kid and his father, kneeling in the sand with hoods over their heads. You wonder, What have they done to deserve this?, and the answer is nothing, they

just had the bad luck to live in a godforsaken place where the bad guys have sway over everything, stealing their cars, their houses, their food, their wives and daughters and mothers. Maybe the father's the village mechanic, maybe he owned the burned-out service station you can see in the distance, maybe he tried to stop them when they dragged his twelve-year-old daughter into the back room and shut the door. No matter. The knife's already in the air, already coming down, and we cut away to just the head, the father's head, in the sand.

That's when Warrior Jesus comes on the scene, just striding ahead, taking His time. The guards see Him coming and they give Him a curious/hostile look, but He's got nothing in His hands and His shorts and tee are so tight He couldn't be concealing anything like a suicide vest or a gun or even a box cutter, so though they level their AKs on Him, they're hardly worried. At worst—or best, depending on how you look at it—He'll be the next victim, once they get done with the boy. Warrior Jesus doesn't say a word. And this is something that separates Him from the other superheroes out there—He doesn't need to talk, only act. Plus, another thing about this character is His power is absolute. He doesn't have a nemesis, no Lex Luthor or Professor Zoom or Red Skull, and He doesn't rocket around like Neo or Superman or the Flash. He doesn't need any of that: He just is. He has immanence. And no one can threaten Him.

The executioner is raising the blade over the boy's head when Warrior Jesus lifts His finger, just one finger—His index finger—and points it. In that instant the scimitar clatters to the ground because there's no one holding on to it, no one there, in fact: the executioner is gone, converted, as you see in closeup, into a knee-high pyramid of dust. The others, the henchmen, that is, open up with their rifles and the bullets are depicted hanging there in the air (think *The Matrix*) but they never reach their destination because they dissolve like vapor and the weap-

ons themselves vanish too, along with the henchmen, who form their own piles of dust, even as Warrior Jesus frees the boy and restores the father's head, perfectly, just as it was before (which is tricky, but if the old Jesus could raise the dead, why not?). No sutures, no scars, no operating room, just a dip into the immediate past, a time warp that fixes everything. Except for the executioner and the henchmen, that is. They are dust forever.

One more thing, because this is just the introductory episode and the readers won't really know what they're getting into yet, what the rules are, I mean—the village springs back up around the astonished onlookers as if it's a stage set, every building, every storefront, even the burned-out service station instantly recreated, only better than before, with trees, lawns, a glittering fresh-water stream emerging from the place where the father's blood saturated the sand, maybe a KFC franchise—or no, Subway, which is way healthier. The people look around them—and they're all wearing new clothes and their wounds are healed, even their dogs are back—and they're wondering who this savior is. Or where He is. Because the next panel shows the village from afar over the squared-up shoulders of Warrior Jesus, who, we see, is already on to His next adventure. Or not adventure, that's not the right word, though there's plenty of adventure in the book—call it correction, His next correction. What's changed? Word is out now and all the psychopaths and murderers and dictators are in for a rude surprise.

And cheats, cheats too.

The next day's my day off and I wind up sleeping in, which means I blow off my date with Asia for a late breakfast at the brioche place before she goes into work at noon (irony of ironies, she's the hostess at Cedric's, our rival steak house on the other side of town, a place that's pricier than ours and a whole lot less

fun, the waiters strictly in jacket and tie—no waitresses—and a bar scene that's pretty well dead no matter the hour; plus, if you want a salad, the waiter's going to go into the kitchen and bring it out to you). The minute my eyes open I reach for my phone and text her, but she doesn't text back and I figure I'll try again later, when she's at work and so bored she's going to be checking her messages every ten seconds. Her job, like any hostess's, is to look great, open up her megawatt smile and lead diners to their tables, which doesn't leave much room for creativity or job satisfaction, but like me she's two years out of college (with a degree in art history) and trying to make ends meet any way she can.

There's not a whole lot in the refrigerator beyond a couple of bagels as hard as horseshoes and a take-out box of mistakes from the night before (you might think it sounds cool having all the filets, New Yorks and lamb chops you want, but that gets old fast), and so I just pour myself a glass of orange juice and sit at the window awhile, looking out on a bleak February day with a crust of grimy snow on the lawn and a cold drizzle fuzzing the windows. The place I'm renting is a spare room, with full bath and private entrance, in a tract house like the one I grew up in, but it's my own to do anything I want with and it has a big picture window with a southern exposure, which gives me the kind of afternoon light I like for my work. Am I hungry? Not really. I'm still dogged by the cold, stuffed up when I get out of bed and then sniffling to the point where I'm going to have to go out and buy more toilet paper at some point, and maybe that has something to do with why I overslept and why I'm not hungry, or at least not hungry enough to get in the car and go out and pick something up. At any rate, before I can think about it, I'm at my desk (a Martin drawing table, actually, which my mother got for me two birthdays ago) and I'm deep into Warrior Jesus, inking the first couple of panels and letting the story come to me,

no speech bubbles yet, but a couple captions running through my head just to set things up so people aren't confused (Is this Syria, or what? He can replace a severed head? Really? What about donor heads? What about all the heads already lopped off in all the other villages?). It doesn't take much. The way I see it, if the drawings don't tell the story, or ninety-nine percent of it anyway, you're dead in the water.

It's two-thirty on the dot when she calls, off work now till they reopen for dinner at five, and finally remembering she has a boyfriend, me, that is, who got shut out the night before and must have called her a dozen times and even, at one a.m., tried her at her parents', though admittedly he—I—hung up after the third ring because the last thing I wanted was for her mother to see the caller ID and answer in that spooky accusatory voice she has.

"Hey," I say.

"Hey."

"Sorry I missed you this morning. I guess I overslept. This cold's a real bitch, you know?"

She doesn't say anything, or if she does—my ears seem to be stuffed up too—it's "Yeah," which isn't much more than a space filler (Yeah, she knows? or Yeah, it's too bad? or Yeah, I'm at the dentist having my teeth drilled?).

"How was the movie?"

"What?"

"You know, the movie you guys saw—Stephanie and who-all? What was it again?"

"Oh, that," she says, her voice dropped low and clogged up, as if she's the one with the cold. "We wound up not going. It was Steph's birthday, did I tell you?"

"No, you didn't mention it. And you didn't answer your phone or your messages either. I even tried your parents' at like one—"

"What can I say, Devon—girls' night out, okay? I guess I just didn't feel like checking my phone—I mean, it's not like we're Siamese twins."

I let that hang a minute, then I'm irate, and I'm sorry, because this isn't the first time and I know something's going on, *I know it*. "Shit, you don't have to jump down my throat—I'm not the one that didn't call. I'm the one that had to sit at the bar and get shit-faced till Tonio shut out the lights and locked the door, and *still* you wouldn't answer."

"I'm not going to argue," she says.

"No," I say, "me neither. If you want to know the truth I'm working, really working for the first time in like months, and you—this call?—you're interrupting me, you're *distracting* me, okay?"

Another pause. And then, her voice dwindled down to practically nothing, she says, "What is it—Warrior Jesus?"

For some reason, this sets me off even more, and yes, I've told her all about the concept, talked it up for weeks, but right now, in the mood I'm in, I can't abide the idea of her horning in on it, of getting between me and my character, which is a kind of intimacy I never asked for. I don't know what comes over me, but I shout into the phone as if I'm shouting across the street at her. "Fucking A!" I yell. And then repeat myself, even louder: "Fucking A!"

The next scene He enters isn't all that much different from the first, though it's a matter of degree. We're in a city now, not a village, a big city like Ramadi, which is where they think Bruce was killed, though the backdrop of the video was so generic—dirt, rocks, rubble—nobody could really be sure. I've downloaded a ton of pictures to give me an idea of what it's supposed to look like, which is no different, really, than what you see in photos of

WWII or Vietnam and, it goes without saying, in all the apocalyptic comics and graphic novels, as if it's a genre, *Shell Cities*. I do try to make it my own, give it a little originality, but you don't want to go overboard—it's a bombed-out city, that's all you need to know. Anyway, there's a whole lot more of it than what you got of the village, so in the splash you see Warrior Jesus' head in profile and the city, with all the rubble and one-sided storefronts rolling out to the gutter on all four sides. Where is He? You see that in the next panel, when He walks up to a towering mosque-like edifice decorated with all these wedding-cake curlicues around a pair of big reinforced double doors, which can only mean He's heading up the stairs of the palace where the big guy, the caliph himself—al-Baghdadi—is holding court. Or hiding. Or whatever.

There are guards, of course, hundreds of them, ranged up and down the street and perched on the roofs of the buildings that are still standing, but Warrior Jesus never even bothers to give them a glance—He's after bigger game. Up the steps He goes, completely ignoring the shitstorm of bullets and rockets and grenades blasting all around Him, which even if they're direct hits, just fall harmlessly to the ground. He doesn't have to open the doors: they swing open automatically and in He steps, which is when we cut away to the deepest hold in the deepest subbasement of the place, where all the drone strikes in the world couldn't even begin to penetrate, and here's the big guy, looking scared—he's heard the rumors—and his minions are strapping suicide vests on two little girls, retarded girls (all right, *Asia*: mentally challenged), which are his last line of defense. Then back to Warrior Jesus, inside this big glittering palace-like place with maybe a few shell holes in the roof and the far wall, and here come the girls, hurrying up the steps to take Him out, whether they know what they're doing or not.

But that doesn't happen. That's the point: it *can't* happen.

There's no kryptonite in this universe, no Mist or Magneto or Dr. Polaris: Warrior Jesus is all-powerful. And, as we see now, merciful too. He doesn't lift His finger to annihilate the girls, but just winks one eye and the suicide vests are gone—and better, the girls are instantly cured, which you can see in their smiles and the way their eyes radiate intelligence. Then it's al-Baghdadi's turn. He's cowering in the subbasement with its bomb-proof walls and three-foot-thick tungsten-steel doors and all the rest, but it's not going to do him any good. Warrior Jesus just steps right through the steel door as if it's made of paper like in manga or the old samurai movies. And then He lifts His finger, and the big guy is dust.

I wind up working all day, just on fire, really, and the funny thing is I keep seeing Bruce in flashes, as if there's something in this that's for him, as if I'm doing this for him, when really, as I say, he was nothing to me. To my mother, maybe—he was her sister's only child, taken from her in this incredibly senseless barbaric way, and how could people be like that, et cetera—but I wouldn't even know what he looked like if my mother hadn't taped him every time he did a story from one dusty outpost or another. To me, he was like any other reporter or TV personality, completely disembodied, as unreal as the image itself flickering there in a haze of pixels, and if I felt any emotion at all it was disgust, especially with the bland smugness of his face as he mouthed the words nobody was listening to and nobody cared about, palm trees waving in the background and him going through the whole battery of facial tics they taught him in broadcast journalism school. But still, as the day wears on and the light goes bad and I'm working under my lamps, I keep seeing him, scenes from ancient times shuffling in a loop over and over in my brain. An example, a thing I hadn't thought of in years, is the time his mother, my aunt Marie, took him and me to

the Central Park Zoo when I must have been five or six, I guess, and we both broke away from her and ran up to the leopard's cage. It was summer. Or no, spring. I remember I had a jacket on, and the colors, I remember the colors, everything concrete-gray and the black bars of the cage cutting the backdrop in neat rectilinear sections and then this cat, this huge muscle-rippling cat, that stood out as if he'd been dipped in Day-Glo. Bruce was older than me, faster and taller, and he got there first so I arrived at the moment the leopard let loose with a sudden soul-stripping roar that scared the living shit out of us because this thing wasn't a stuffed toy and we both knew it could hurt us beyond repair, that it *wanted* to hurt us. One of us cried, I remember that too.

Anyway, though I never did get hold of Asia, which really irritates me (did that earlier conversation qualify as a fight, in her mind anyway?), I nonetheless get in the car come nine and go to pick her up at work, which is what I usually do on my day off. She's got her own car, but over the past couple of months, it's become a ritual for us to meet at the bar at Cedric's, which might be a mortuary, but it's convenient and they pour a killer drink. We have maybe two, on her employee discount, and then go out to get something to eat or hit a late movie or just go back to my place, where the most essential thing is—the bed—because with her living at home it's pointless to go to her place. Unless her parents take off on a cruise, which they did last month and we had the whole house to ourselves, with the bed the size of a life raft, the Jacuzzi and the Samsung forty-inch TV and a freezer full of frozen entrées like Stouffer's lasagna and Bistro sesame-ginger salmon bowl.

The bar is separate from the dining room at Cedric's, unlike at Brennan's, where you can sit at the bar while you're waiting for your table and see people eating, which, in theory, gets you to drink more. At Cedric's, you come into a vestibule where you can stomp the snow off your boots and hang up your coat. The swing-

ing doors straight ahead lead into the dining room and the ones to your right open directly on the bar. On this night—it's starting to freeze up outside, the drizzle whitening under the headlights until it's suspended there like in a Japanese print—I don't bother with my coat and just push through the doors and step into the bar, which isn't as dead as usual, three or four older couples getting raucous at the bar and a scatter of people at the tables, and I don't at first see Asia, which isn't unusual, because sometimes she's in the kitchen or still out in the dining room, depending on the dinner crowd. But then—and this is the strangest thing, like something out of the Believe It Or Not! strip—I spot the white turban floating there in the candle gloom like a seagull, and it's the non-Hindu from last night and his girlfriend right beside him and I'm thinking he's either a restaurant critic or he must really like steak. I hear Asia before I see her, this distinctive machine-gun laugh she's got—*ack, ack, ack*—and now I'm really confused because she's sitting right next to the guy in the turban and laughing at something he obviously just said.

There's no room at the bar—some guy I've never seen before has his stool pushed right up against hers and he's laughing too, all of them part of some joke or routine and all of them, I realize, smashed. So what *is* going on here? I don't have a clue. But I push my way in and slip my arm around Asia's waist, which causes the guy next to her (weasel face, long black hair) to practically jump out of his seat, and I say, "What's up?" and Asia turns around and gives me a look like she doesn't even recognize me.

"Oh, hi," she says, after a minute, and the turban guy turns his head too, like this has anything to do with him. She pauses, everybody does, as if in freeze-frame, then says, "I didn't think you were coming. I mean, after—"

"After what?"

"When I called? And you yelled at me?"

The new guy—he's so close I can smell the old-fashioned

limey aftershave he's got on—is just looking at her now, studying her, as if she's some kind of experiment he's been working on, and then the turban guy, in his fruity tones, says, "Hey, don't I know you?" And all of a sudden he slaps his head and comes on with a big lemon-sucking grin. "From last night, right—you're the chef." The grin goes wider. "So what's this, a busman's holiday?"

I am full of Warrior Jesus, the whole dividing line between how intense work was and this moment here as confusing as if I'm just now waking up from a dream, and I don't know what to say—don't, in fact, want to say anything. These people are nothing to me. And they're drunk, way ahead of me, and even if I started throwing down shots I'd never catch up to them. What I say, and I don't even glance at anybody but Asia, is "Time to go." And because that might sound maybe too abrupt or harsh, I add lamely, "I've got a cold? And I'm really wiped from working all day."

Asia gives me a steady look. "I'm not ready," she says. There's half a drink in front of her and a full one backing it up, which somebody obviously bought her—a mai tai, which she only drinks when she's in interplanetary space, which is where she is now.

"Yeah," I say, and both guys are watching me, one from the left, one from the right, and the tattooed girlfriend too, "but maybe you didn't hear me. I said, *it's time to go.*"

Asia doesn't like to be told what to do, nobody does, really, but I have certain rights here—she's my girlfriend, not theirs—and when she says, for the second time, "I'm not ready," something just goes loose in me and I say, "The fuck you're not," and the Turban starts in with, "Hey, hey, now, no need for that," but there is a need, every need in the world, my need, and before I know what I'm doing, I'm stalking out the door and into the cold, cold night.

Which is where I see the Mercedes parked at the curb, two

cars down. It's an older model, a classic, I guess, the sort of thing your parents might hand down to you once you get your license and they go for an upgrade. It's a mustard yellow, more gold where the streetlight hits it, and everything else bordered in the black of the night so it stands out as if it's the only car on the street. And didn't I see this very car in the lot at Brennan's just last night? One of the last cars there and the Turban and his girl-friend lingering at their table over after-dinner drinks? Maybe. Maybe so. It doesn't really matter at this point—and it only takes me a minute to extract what I need from the trunk of my car, and yes, I do occasionally tag around town, very distinctive, eyeless faces usually, with my own DD insignia underneath, and I will not apologize for it because it's public art, at least the way I do it. Nothing so exacting as that tonight, though. Tonight it's just one word, in black, dripping right down the driver's side door. Can you guess what it is? I'll give you a hint: seven letters, starting with *R*.

The scene changes for Warrior Jesus, no more desert, no more ISIS and Al Qaeda. He's in the tropics now, palm fronds stirred by a gentle breeze, butterflies hanging like mobiles in the air, and the place He's approaching is in a block of storefronts, a glitter of windowpanes, white stucco, red-tile roofs gone dark with night. Out front a sign that says *Cantina*. Who's in there? The narcos and their minions, some of them out-of-uniform *federales* even, everybody bought and sold and every business on the street—in the whole city—paying the extortion tax. We see them partying in a tier running down the right side of the page, tequila bottles, cocaine, video games, and their whores hanging all over them, women they've forced into prostitution because it's either that or die, and some of the girls as young as thirteen, though obviously I can't show all of that without getting into some serious back-

story. Just let the drawings give you the picture and you can fill in the rest from general knowledge. The point is, these are bad guys, very bad guys, and at the center of the action, just like in Ramadi, is their kingpin, a kind of El Chapo figure, only bigger, the way El Chapo would be if he was younger and pumped iron. They look menacing, armed to the teeth, and yet for all that they don't stand a chance—we've already seen Warrior Jesus in action and they are half a beat from being reduced to dust. Or at least that's what you think.

But—and I had to backtrack here, trying to dredge something up from all those years I went to church with my mother as a little kid—a new element enters the picture, and it's so obvious I have to slap myself for not having thought of it earlier. Of course there's a nemesis—what was I thinking? It's Lucifer, the Devil himself, Satan, the original nemesis, the one that ruined Adam and Eve and tempted the old Jesus in the desert. All this evil, what they did to Bruce, the mass killings, all of it—it's got to be coming from someplace, and here it is, evil incarnate. Anyway, he's lounging in back, just behind the kingpin, and he doesn't have horns or a pointed tail or anything like that, but you can see from the way he's built and from his eyes—slit yellow eyes, like a goat's—just who he is and what he thinks of himself.

That's when Warrior Jesus comes through the door and the whole room freezes. We see Him run His eyes over the narcos and corrupt cops and the whores and then the kingpin before coming to rest on Satan, who you see in closeup in the next panel is sporting a mercury tattoo that reads EL ÁNGEL CAÍDO, just in case you're not getting it. Right. And though this part isn't really worked out yet, you see Warrior Jesus raise His finger and point it right at Satan and nothing happens. The whole room is one big smirk, the joke's on Him. What comes next is the fight scene, the two antagonists, with all their powers, locked together in a Manichean struggle as if the forces of good

and evil neutralize each other all the way down the line. You see fire, radiation, suns exploding, and they wrestle over the oceans and the continents and all the way out into deep space, way beyond the glittering satellites and even the spacecraft of aliens we haven't even dreamed of to this point, and then the panel goes black, as if we're in a black hole and all the energy's been sucked out of the universe.

The next day I'm at work, the lunch crowd heavier than usual, and more demanding too—one clown even wants me to Pitts a steak for him (cover a filet in fat, prop it three inches above the grill on kebab skewers and incinerate the outside while leaving the middle all but raw). The meat goes on the grill. The exhaust fans suck back the smoke. I'm sweating, dehydrated, I still have a cold. And I'm upset about the night before, my second night in a row back at home with nothing to do but draw, and she hasn't texted or called so I have no idea what the resolution of that little gathering at the bar turned out to be, whether she's fucking one of them or both of them or if she's going to start wearing a turban now or what. So I put my head down and lose myself in work, and when I look up it's two-thirty and time for my break, at which point I make myself a burger and a salad, sit down at one of the tables in back and dial her number.

I count four rings, five, and just when I think she's not going to pick up, she's there saying, "What do *you* want?"

"What do you mean, what do I want? I want to talk to you."

"Well, I don't want to talk to you."

"Don't give me that shit, because I want to talk to *you*, hear me?"

She doesn't answer.

"All right, fine—I don't want to talk to you either," I say, but

still she doesn't say anything and it takes me a minute to realize the phone's gone dead.

A spread now. You see Him way in the distance with all the turmoil and quasars and all the rest diminishing behind Him till He's back in the scene out front of the cantina and stepping through the doors all over again, and for a minute you think nothing's changed, the panel almost identical to the one two pages back, until you realize Satan, with his goat's eyes and mercury tattoo, is gone. And then you realize that the rest of them, everybody in the room, though they draw their weapons and start blazing away, are doomed, just like bad guys everywhere. Warrior Jesus points His finger, the narcos vanish and their weapons clatter to the floor. There's nobody left in the room now but a bartender, a couple waitresses and the whores, maybe fifteen or twenty of them. These are innocents, the whores, that's what we're thinking—forced into the trade, sold into it—and He will free them from their chains and restore them to what they once were, sisters, daughters, mothers, just like He took the burden of retardation off the two Syrian girls.

We're wrong, though. The whores are beyond redemption, we can see that in their faces, cheaters, sinners, betrayers, riddled with every kind of STD known to man, and we linger on them in a panel that takes in the whole scene. The one in the middle, the prettiest one, I give her Asia's face, and I don't need a photograph to work from, just the implant in my memory, and I give her Asia's green eyes too, though I shade them more toward olive so as to take nothing away from His eyes. It's a moment of tension. He lifts His finger, but the whores don't turn to dust—no, that would be too easy. What happens is they begin to melt, like wax, and we see the one in the middle screaming out her pain with every waxy drop of her flesh that sizzles on the floor beneath her. Then a full-page spread: Warrior Jesus' face

in closeup, so huge it bleeds off the edges of both pages, and for the first time since He's come on the scene, He's smiling. It's not a happy smile, that wouldn't work, not at all—He's still got a job to do—but more rueful, as if He's just about to shake His head in a go-figure kind of way. And then the final image, and I'm still not sure about this, though it could work as a branding icon and I could see it on a line of tees, easily, you get a closeup of His finger, just His finger, pointed right at you.

So what do you think? Is it a go?

THE FUGITIVE

They told him he had to wear a mask in public. Which was ridiculous. It made him feel like he had a target painted on his back—or his face, actually, right in the middle of his face. But if he wanted to walk out the door of the clinic he was going to walk out with that mask on—either that or go to jail. Outside it was raining, which made everything all that much harder, because what were you going to do with a wet mask? How could you even breathe? Here, inside the office, with the doctor and his caseworker from health services, there was no sound of the rain, or if there was, he couldn't hear it—all he could hear was the rasp and wheeze of his own compromised breathing as he sucked air through the fibers of the mask.

The doctor was saying something to him now and Marciano watched him frame the words with his hands before they both looked to the caseworker, a short slim woman with a big bust and liquid eyes he would have liked to fuck if he wasn't so sick. She was named Rosa Hinojosa, and he kept saying her name in his

head because of the way it rhymed, which somehow made him feel better.

"You understand what the doctor is telling you?" she asked in her clipped north-of-the-border Spanish he could have listened to all day under other circumstances. But these were the circumstances and until he got better he would have to play their game, Dr. Rosen's game and Rosa Hinojosa's too.

He nodded.

"No more lapses, you understand that? You will report here each morning when the clinic opens at eight for your intravenous medication, and"—she held up two plastic pill containers—"you will take your oral medication, *without fail,* every night at dinner. And you must wear your mask at all times."

"Even when I'm alone?"

She looked to the doctor, said something to him in English, nodded, then turned back to Marciano, her breasts straining at the fabric of her blouse, a pink blouse that made her look even younger than she was, which, he guessed, was maybe twenty-four or -five. "You have your own room in this house"—she glanced down at the clipboard in her lap—"at 519 West Haley Street? Is that right?"

"Yes."

"There are other roomers there?"

"Yes."

"All right. When you're alone in your room, you can remove the mask, but only then and never if you're in the common area, in the kitchen or the living room or even the bathroom, except to brush your teeth and wash your face. You're highly contagious and if you were to cough without the mask on, the bacteria could get into the air and infect your roommates, and you wouldn't want that, would you?"

No, he agreed, he wouldn't, but now the doctor was saying something more, his tone harsh and hectoring, and though Mar-

ciano didn't register what he was saying, or not exactly, he got the gist of it: this was his warning, his final warning, and now there could be no appeal. He watched the doctor's eyes that looked at him as if he were less than human, something to step on in the street and crush, angry eyes, hateful, and what had he done to deserve this? He'd gotten sick, that was all—and couldn't anybody get sick?

Rosa Hinojosa (her lips were fascinating—plump and adhesive—and he wanted desperately in that moment to get well if for no other reason than to kiss them or even for the promise of kissing them) told him what he already knew, that because he'd stopped taking his medication a year ago, his case of tuberculosis had mutated into the multi-drug-resistant form and his life was at risk because after this there were no more drugs. That was it. They didn't exist. But more, and worse: if he did not comply fully—no lapses—Dr. Rosen would get a court order and incarcerate him to be sure he got the full round of treatment. And why? Not out of charity, entertain no illusions about that, but to protect society, and at a cost—did he even have any idea of the cost?—of as much as two hundred thousand dollars for him alone. She paused. Compressed her lips. Looked to the doctor. Then, as if she were tracking the drift of the very microbes hanging invisibly in the air, she brought her eyes back to him. "You agree?" she demanded.

He wanted to say yes, of course he did—he wanted to be cured, but he was already feeling better, much better, and this whole business was so cold, so hard, he honestly didn't know if he could go through with it, and wasn't that the problem last time? He'd taken the medicine, which was no easy thing because it made him sick to his stomach and itch as if there were something under his skin clawing its way out. They said he'd have to stay on the regimen anywhere from six to thirty months, but within three months he'd felt fine, his cough nearly gone and his

arms and chest filling out again, so he started selling the pills because he didn't need them anymore and then he stopped coming
to the clinic altogether and that would have been fine until the
disease returned to shake him like a rat in a cage and he spat up
blood and came back here to their contempt and their antiseptic
smells and their masks and dictates and ultimatums. He wanted
to say yes, and he tried to, but at that moment the cough came up
on him, the long dredging cough that was like the sea drawing
back over the stones at low tide, and the inside of the mask was
suddenly crimson and he couldn't seem to stop coughing.

When finally he looked up, both the doctor and Rosa Hinojosa were wearing masks of their own and Rosa Hinojosa
was pushing a box of disposable surgical masks across the desk
to him. He couldn't see her lips now, only her eyes, and her
eyes—as rich and brown as two chocolates in the dark wrappers
of her lashes—didn't have an ounce of sympathy left in them.

Before he got sick the second time, he'd been working as part
of a crew that did landscaping and gardening for the big estates
strung out along the beach and carved out of the hills, a good
job, steady, and with a *patrón* who didn't try to cheat you. One
of his jobs was to trap and dispose of the animals that infested
these places, rats, gophers, possums, raccoons and whatever else
tore up the lawns or raided the orchards. His *patrón* wouldn't
allow the use of poison of any kind—the owners didn't like it
and it worked its way up the food chain and killed everything
out there, which to Marciano's mind didn't seem like such a bad
proposition, but it wasn't his job to think. His job was to do as
he was told. The gophers weren't a problem—they died under-
ground, transfixed on the spikes of the Macabee traps he set in
the dark cool dirt of their runs—but the possums and raccoons

and even the rats had to be captured alive in Havahart traps of varying sizes depending on the species. Which raised the question of what to do with them once you'd caught them.

The first time he did actually catch something—a raccoon—it was on a big thirty-acre estate with its own avocado grove and a fish pond stocked with Japanese koi that cost a thousand dollars each. It was early, misty yet, and when he went to check the cage he'd baited with a dab of peanut butter and half a sardine it was a shock to see the dark shadow compressed inside it, the robber itself with its black mask and tense fingers grasping the mesh as if it were a monkey and not a *mapache* at all. In the next moment he was running down the slope to where the *patrón* was assembling the sprinkler system for a new flowerbed, crying out, "I got one, I got one!"

The *patrón*, big-bellied but tough, a man who must have been as old as Marciano's father yet could work alongside the men on the hottest day without even breathing hard, glanced up from what he was doing. "One what?"

"A raccoon."

"Okay, good. Get rid of it and reset the trap. Is it a female?"

A female? What was he talking about? It was a raccoon, that was all, and what did he expect him to do? Flip it over and inspect its equipment?

"Because if it's a female, there'll be more."

Breathless, excited, the microbes working in him though he didn't yet know it, he just stood there, puzzled. "Get rid of it how?"

"I thought you were a trapper?"

"I am, it's just I want to be sure to do things the way you want them, that's all."

A steady look. A sigh. "Okay, listen, because I'm only going to tell you once. Take one of those plastic trash cans lined up

there behind the garage and fill it with water, right to the top, you understand? Then just drop the cage in and it'll be over in three minutes."

"You mean drown it, just like that?"

"What are you going to do, take it home and train it to walk on a leash?" The *patrón* was grinning now, pleased with his own joke, but there was work to do and already he was turning back to it. "And do me a favor," he added, glancing over his shoulder. "Bury it out in the weeds where Mrs. Lewis won't have to see it."

Why he was thinking of that, he couldn't say, except that he missed the job—and the money—and as he walked to the bus in the rain, the box of face masks tucked under one arm, he wanted to be back there again, under the sun, working, just that, working. They'd scared him at the clinic, they always scared him, and he was feeling light-headed on top of it. The blood was bad, he knew that, he could see it in their eyes. Thirty months. He was twenty-three years old and thirty months was like a lifetime sentence, and even then, there were no guarantees—Rosa Hinojosa had made that clear. He was sick from the intravenous. His arm was sore. His throat ached. Even his feet didn't seem to want to cooperate, zigging and zagging so he was walking like a drunk, and what was that all about?

The sidewalk before him was strewn with the worms that were coming up out of the earth because if they stayed down there they'd drown, whereas up here, in the rain, they'd have a chance at life before somebody stepped on them or the birds got to them. He liked worms, nature's recyclers, and he was playing a little game with himself, trying to avoid them and hold in the next cough at the same time, watching his feet and the pattern the worms made on the pavement, loops and triangles of pale bleached-out flesh, and when he looked up he was right

in front of the bar—Herlihy's—he'd seen from the bus stop but had never been inside of. It was just past ten in the morning and he wasn't working today—his new job, strictly gardening, was with an old white-haired *campesino* who booked the clients and sat in his beater truck and read spy novels while Marciano did all the work—and his ESL class at the community college wasn't till five, so there really wasn't anything to do with himself but sit in front of the television in his room. That had something to do with it. That and the fact that his new boss—Rudy—had just paid him the day before.

He didn't go directly in, but walked by the place as if he was on an errand elsewhere, then stripped off the mask and stuffed it in his pocket, doubled back and pushed open the door. Inside were all the usual things, neon signs for Budweiser and Coors, a jukebox that might once have worked, the honey-colored bottles lined up behind the bar and the head of a deer—or no, an elk—jammed into one wall as if this was Alaska and somebody had just shot it. There were three customers, all white, strung together on three adjoining barstools, and the bartender, also white, but fat, with big buttery arms in a short-sleeve shirt. They all turned to look at him as he came in and that made him nervous so he chose a stool at the far end of the bar, rehearsing in his head the phrase he was going to give the bartender, "Please, a beer," which made use of his favorite word in English and the word wasn't "please."

The bartender heaved himself up off his own stool and came down the bar to him, put two thick white hands on the counter and asked him something, which must have been "What do you want?" and Marciano uttered his phrase. There was a moment of ambiguity, the man poised there still instead of bending to the cooler, and then there was a further question, which he didn't grasp until the man began rattling off the names of the beers he stocked, pointing as he did so to a line of bottles on the top

row, ten or twelve different brands. "Corona," Marciano said, unfolding a five-dollar bill on the bar, and all at once he was coughing and he put his hand up to cover his mouth, but he couldn't seem to stop until he had the bottle to his lips, draining it in three swallows as if he were a nomad who'd just come in off the desert.

One of the men at the end of the bar said something then and the other two looked at Marciano and broke out laughing, and whether it was good-natured or not, a little joke at his expense, it made him feel tight in his chest and the cough came up again, so severe this time he thought he was going to pass out. But here was the bartender, saying something more, and what it was he couldn't imagine, because it wasn't illegal to cough, was it? But no, that wasn't it. The bartender was pointing at the empty bottle and so Marciano repeated his phrase, "Please, a beer," and the heavy man bent to the cooler, extracted a fresh Corona, snapped off the cap and set it before him.

He sipped the second beer and watched the rain spatter the dirty windows and run off in streaks. At some point he saw his bus pull up at the stop across the street, a vivid panel of color that made him think of what was waiting for him at home—nothing, zero, exactly zero—and he watched it pull away again as he tried to fight down the scratch in his throat. He was scared. He was angry. And he sat there, staring out into the gloom, drinking one beer after another, and when he coughed, really coughed, they all looked at him and at the wet cardboard box of face masks, then looked away again. Nobody said another word to him, which was all right with him—he just focused on the television behind the bar, some news channel, and tried to interpret the words the people were saying there while the backdrop shifted from warplanes and explosions to some sort of pageant with models on a runway looking raccoon-eyed and haughty and not half as good as Rosa Hinojosa. The bloody mask remained in his pocket, and

the box of masks, the new ones, stayed right where it was on the stool beside him.

All that week he went into the clinic at eight as instructed and all that week he felt nauseous and skipped breakfast and went to work with Rudy anyway, and the only good thing there was that Rudy didn't like to start early—and he didn't ask questions either. Still, Marciano was lagging and he knew it and knew it was only a matter of time before Rudy said something. Which he did, that Friday, TGIF, end of the week, the first week of his new life with the new cocktail of antibiotics running through his veins and making him nauseous, one week down and how many more to go? He did a quick calculation in his head: fifty-two weeks in a year, double that and then add twenty-six more. It was like climbing a mountain backwards—no matter how many steps you took you never got to see the peak.

They were on their third or fourth house of the day, everything gray and wet with the fog off the ocean and the sun nowhere in sight. His chest felt sore. He was hungry, but the idea of food—a taco or burger or anything—made his stomach turn. "Jesus," Rudy said, startling him out of a daydream, "you're like one of the walking dead. I mean, at that last place I couldn't tell whether you were pushing the mower or the mower was pushing you." The best Marciano could do was give him a tired grin. "What," Rudy said, staring now, "late night last night?"

Rudy was helping him lift the mower down from the back of the truck, so he couldn't avoid his eyes. He just nodded.

"Youth," Rudy said, shaking his head as they set the mower down in the driveway of a little mustard-colored house with a patch of lawn in front and back and a towering hedge all the way round that had to be clipped every other week, and this was that week, which meant hauling out the ladder too. "I used to be like

that, burn the candle at both ends, drink till they closed the bars and get up for work three hours later." Rudy sighed, paused to give him a look. "But no more. Now I'm in bed before the ten o'clock news on the TV—and Norma's already snoring."

He'd heard all this before, twenty times already, and he didn't say anything, just leaned into the mower to push it up the drive-way, but the mower didn't seem to want to budge because he felt weak all of a sudden, weak and sick, and here came the cough, right on cue. He really hacked this time, hacked till he doubled over and tears came to his eyes. When he straightened up, Rudy was watching him and his smile was gone.

"That doesn't sound too good," he said. "You ever go to the clinic like I told you?"

"Yes," he said. "Or no, not really—"

"What do you mean, *not really*? You sound like your lungs are shot."

He paused to catch his breath, because he couldn't really cough and talk at the same time, could he? Not even Rudy would have expected that of him. He lifted one hand and let it drop. "It's just a cold," he said, then turned and pushed the mower up the drive.

They were waiting for him when he got home, a cop in uniform and Rosa Hinojosa, who looked so fierce and grim she might have been wearing somebody else's face. He'd run into her at the clinic the day before and she'd asked him if he was sticking to the regimen and he told her he was and she flashed a smile so luminous it made him feel unmoored. *Good*, she said, *good. Do it for me, okay?* But now, here she was, and at first he didn't under-stand what was happening, and he saw her before he saw the cop, the crisp line her skirt cut just above her knees, her pretty legs,

the heels she wore to work, and for the briefest flash of a second he wondered what she was doing there and then he saw the cop and he knew. Rudy had just dropped him off, already pulling away from the curb, and Marciano wanted desperately to climb back into the pickup and go wherever Rudy would take him, but everything was in slow motion now like in the outer space movies where the astronauts are just floating there on their tethers and the ship slides away from them in a long smear of light and shadow.

Before he decided to run, he pulled a mask from his pocket—a dirty one, to show it had been used—looped it over his ears and snapped it in place, as if that would make him look better in Rosa Hinojosa's eyes, but her face showed only disappointment and something else too, anger. He'd let her down. He'd had his warning, his final warning, and he'd been caught out, but how had she known? Had somebody informed on him? Some sneak? Some enemy he didn't even know he had?

The cop, he could see at a glance, wasn't a real cop, more some sort of health services mule, and he was old and slow and his head was like a big *calabaza* propped up on his shoulders, and Rosa Hinojosa, for all her youth, was no runner, not in those shoes. So he ran. Not like in the track meets at school when he was a boy, because his lungs were like wet clay and he was weak, but still he put one foot in front of the other, hustling down the alley between his house and the one next door, to where the fence out back opened onto the dry streambed and the path through the weeds he sometimes used as a shortcut to the corner store. He got as far as the fence before he gave out, and, he had to admit, both Rosa Hinojosa and the *calabaza*-head were quicker than he would have thought. He was just lying there, pathetic, humiliated in front of this woman he wanted to prove himself to, and he watched them pause to snap on their

own masks before the cop bent to him and encircled his wrists with the handcuffs.

The next sight he saw was the hospital, a big clean white stucco box of a building that had secondary boxes attached to it, a succession of them lined up like children's blocks all the way out into the parking lot in back. He'd been here once before, to the emergency room, when he'd nearly severed the little finger of his left hand with the blade of the hedge trimmer, and they'd spoken Spanish to him, sewed and bandaged the wound and sent him on his way. That wasn't how it was this time. This time he was wearing a mask and so was Rosa Hinojosa and so was the mule, who kept guiding him down the corridors with a stiff forefinger till they went through a door and briefly out into the sunlight before entering an outbuilding that looked like one of the temporary classrooms you saw when you went by the high school. What was funny about it, or maybe not so funny, was the way people made room for them in the corridors, shrinking into the walls as they passed by in their masks.

When they'd arrived, when he'd had a chance to take in the barred windows and the heavy steel door that pulled shut behind them with a whoosh of compression, Rosa Hinojosa, cold as a fish, explained to him that he was being remanded to custody as a threat to public safety under the provisions of the statutory code of the state of California, and that he would be confined here temporarily before he could be moved to the Men's Colony in the next county, which was equipped with a special ward for prisoners with medical conditions. He felt sick, sicker than ever, and what made it worse was that there was no smell to that room, which might as well have been on the moon for all it seemed to be attached to this earth. He saw a sterile white counter and a man in thick-framed glasses and some sort of hospital scrubs

stationed behind it. Rosa Hinojosa was doing all the talking. She had a sheaf of papers in one hand and she turned away from him to lay them on the counter. There was a flag of the U.S. in the corner. A drinking fountain. Black-and-white tiles on the floor. "I didn't do anything," Marciano protested.

Rosa Hinojosa, who was conferring with the man behind the counter, gave him a sharp glance. "You were warned."

"What do you mean? I took my medicine. You saw me—"

"Don't even give me that. We have you on the feed from the security camera at the 7-Eleven making a purchase without your mask on—and there was testimony from the bartender at Herlihy's that you were in there without a mask, *drinking,* and on the very day you gave me your promise, so don't tell me. And don't tell me you weren't warned."

"I'm an American citizen."

She shrugged.

"Look it up." This was true. He'd been born in San Diego, two years old when his parents were deported, and so he'd never had a chance to learn English or go to school here or anything else, but he had his rights, he knew that—they couldn't just lock him up. That was against the constitution.

Rosa Hinojosa had turned back to the counter, riffling through the stack of forms, but now she swung angrily round on him, a crease of irritation between her eyes. She wasn't pretty anymore, not even remotely, and all he felt for her was hate because no matter what she said, when it came down to it she was part of the system and the system was against him. "I don't care if you're the president," she snapped, "because you're irresponsible, because we bent over backwards and now you've left us no choice. Don't you understand? The order's been signed."

"I want a lawyer."

He saw that she had a little dollop of flesh under her chin—fat, she was already going to fat—and he realized she was nothing to

him, and worse, that he was nothing to her but one more charity case, and what he did next was born of the sadness of that realization. He wasn't a violent person, just the opposite—he was shy and he went out of his way to avoid confrontation. But they were the ones confronting him—Rosa Hinojosa and the whole Health Services Department, the big stupid-looking mule who'd clamped the handcuffs on him and had made the mistake of removing them after they stepped through the door, and the man behind the desk too. Marciano took as deep a breath as he could manage and felt the mucus rattling in his throat, the bad stuff he kept dredging up all day and spitting into a handkerchief until the handkerchief went stiff with it. What he was about to do was wrong, he knew that, and he regretted it the instant he saw it before him, but he wasn't going to any prison, no way. That just wasn't in the cards.

So he was running again, only this time they weren't chasing him, or not yet, because mask or no mask they were all three of them frantically trying to wipe his living death off their faces— and good, good, see how they like it, see how they like being condemned and ostracized and locked up without a trial or lawyer or anything—and he didn't stop spitting till he had the door open and was back out in the sunlight, dodging round the cars in the lot and heading for the street and the cover of the trees there. His heart was pounding and his lungs felt as if they'd been turned inside out, but he kept going, slowing to a stiff-kneed walk now, down one street, then another, the windshields of the parked cars pooling in the light like puddles after a storm, birds chattering in the trees, the smell of the earth and the grass so intense it was intoxicating. He patted down his pockets: wallet, house key, the little vial of pills. And where was he going? What was he doing? He didn't have any money—no more than maybe ten or fifteen

dollars in his wallet—and there was nobody he could turn to, not really. There was Sergio, the only one of the other roomers he was close to, and Sergio would loan him money, he was sure of it, but Sergio probably didn't have much more than he did. The only thing that was for certain was that he couldn't stay around here anymore.

He hadn't seen his mother in two years, hadn't really given her a thought, but he thought of her now, saw her face as vividly as if she were that woman right there slipping into the front seat of her car—she'd nursed him through the measles, whooping cough and the flu and whatever else had come along to disrupt his childhood, and why couldn't she nurse him through this too? She could, if he was careful and took his pills and wore the mask every single minute of every day because he wouldn't want to infect her—that would be the worst thing a son could do. No matter what the doctors said, his mother would save him, protect him, do anything for him. But how was he going to get to her? They'd be watching for him at the bus station and at the train depot and the airport too, even if he could scrape up enough for a ticket, which he couldn't . . . But what about Rudy? Maybe he could get Rudy to drive him as far as Tijuana—or no, he'd tell Rudy he needed to borrow the truck to help one of his room- mates move a refrigerator, or something big anyway, a couch, and then he'd do the driving himself and get somebody to bring the truck back, pay somebody, make promises, whatever it took. That was a plan, wasn't it? He had to have a plan. Without a plan he was lost.

He kept moving, breathing hard now, the sidewalk like a treadmill rolling under him, but he had to fight it, had to be quick because they'd have the cops after him in their patrol cars, all- points bulletin like on TV, and they weren't going to be gentle with him either. Up ahead, at the end of the street, was a park he'd gone to once or twice with Sergio to drink beer and throw

horseshoes, and there were bushes there, weren't there, along the streambed?

Pushing through the park gate—kids, mothers, swings, a couple of bums laid out on the grass as if they'd been installed there along with the green wooden benches—he tried to look casual, even as the sirens began to scream in the distance and he told himself it was only just ambulances bringing people to the emergency room. He went straight across the lawn, looking at nobody, and if he had to pause twice to let the cough have its way with him, there was nothing he could do about that, but then he was in the bushes and out of sight and he dropped to the ground and just lay there till his heart stopped hammering and the burning in his lungs began to subside. It would be dark soon and then he could make his way back to the house, borrow somebody's phone, call Rudy, pack a few things and be gone before anybody could do anything about it.

Paranoia was when you felt everybody was after you even if they weren't, but what would you call this? Common sense? Vigilance? Wariness? They'd come to his house and handcuffed him and put him in that white room and he hadn't done anything. Now they'd charge him with escaping or resisting arrest or whatever they wanted to call it—and assault too, assault with the deadly weapon that was his own spit. It didn't matter—the result would be the same, thirty months in a sterile room with the fans sucking in and the warders wearing masks and gloves and pushing a tray of what passed for food through a slot in the door and coming in twice a day to stick the intravenous in him. He'd rather be dead. Rather be in Mexico. Rather take his chances with his mother and the clinic in Ensenada where at least they spoke his language and wouldn't look at him like he was a cockroach.

He was thirsty, crazy thirsty, but he forced himself to stay

where he was till it was dark, then slipped back into the park
to get a drink at the faucet in the restroom. Only problem was,
the door was locked. He stood there a long moment, rattling the
doorknob, feeling disoriented. There was the steady hiss of cars
from the freeway that was somewhere behind him in the intermediate distance. The trees were shrouds. The sky was black
overhead and painted with stars and it had never seemed so close.
Or so heavy. He could almost feel the weight of it, all the weight
of the sky that went on and on to infinity, outer space, the plan-
ets, the stars, all of it pressing down on him till he could barely
breathe. Desperate, he went down on his knees in the grass and
felt around till he located one of the sprinkler heads. At first it
wouldn't budge, but he kept at it till the seal gave and he was
able to unscrew it and put his mouth to the warm gurgling flow
there, and that made him feel better and pushed the vagueness
into another corner of his mind. After a while he got to his feet,
eased himself down into the streambed and began working his
way back in the direction of the house.

It wasn't easy. What would have taken him ten minutes out
on the street took an hour at least, his feet unsteady in a slurry
of mud and trash, stiff dead reeds knifing at him, dogs barking,
the drift of people's voices freezing him in place—and what if
somebody sipping a beer on their back porch decided to shine
a flashlight down into the streambed? What would they think?
That he was a fugitive, a thief, a drunk, and before he could even
open his mouth they'd be dialing the police. He was breathing
hard. Sweating. His shirt was torn at the right elbow where he'd
snagged it on something in the strange half-light of the gulley,
and he was shivering too, sweating and shivering at the same time.

He didn't really know how far he'd gone or where he was
when he emerged, scrambling up a steep incline and into the
yard of a house that was mercifully dark, not a light showing
anywhere. There were lights on in the houses on both sides of it,

though, and the black humped shape of an automobile parked in the driveway. He moved toward the car and then past it and if he was startled by a voice calling out behind him, a single syllable he would have recognized in any language—*Hey!*—he never hesitated or turned round or even looked over his shoulder, but just kept going, down the driveway and straight across the street to the sidewalk on the far side where he was just another pedestrian out for a stroll on a cool night in a quiet city.

When he got to his own street he made himself slow down and scan the cars parked on both sides of the road, looking for anything suspicious, the police or the health services, Rosa Hinojosa, though that *was* being paranoid—Rosa Hinojosa would be at home with her parents at this hour, or maybe her husband, if she had one, absorbed in her own life, not his. He took his time, though he was feeling worse by the minute, shivering so hard he had to wrap his arms around himself, his shirt sweated through and too thin against the night and the temperature that must have dropped into the mid-fifties by now. And then, steeling himself, he slipped across the street and into the dark yard of the rooming house where they'd come for him once and would come for him again.

He ducked in the back door, tentative, all the blood in his brain now, screaming at him, but there was nobody in the hall and in the next moment he was in his room, the familiar scent of his things—unwashed laundry, soap, shampoo, the foil-wrapped burrito he'd set aside to microwave for dinner—rising to his nostrils in the ordinary way, as if nothing had happened. The cough was right there waiting to erupt, but he fought it down, afraid even to make the slightest sound, and though he was tempted to turn the light on, he knew better—if anyone was out there, this was what they'd be watching for. He found his jacket thrown over the back of the chair where he'd left it that morning and wrapped himself in it, then went to the window and opened the

blinds so that six thin stripes of illumination fell across the bed. That was when he remembered his pills—he had to take his pills no matter where he was or what happened, that was the truth of his life, whether he ever saw Rosa Hinojosa again or not.

He went to the sink for a glass of water, shook out two of the little white pills and swallowed them. Then—and he couldn't help himself—he lay down on the bed and closed his eyes, just for a minute.

The knock startled him out of a dreamless sleep, the knock at the front door that thundered through the house as if the wrecking ball had come to reduce it all to splinters. But who would knock? Everybody who lived here had a key so there was no need for knocking, not unless you were immigration or the police. Or health services. For one fluttering instant he pictured Rosa Hinojosa in police blues with a cap cocked over her eye, a nightstick in one hand and a can of mace in the other, and then he was pulling the door softly shut and fastening the latch, as if that would save him—and what was he going to do, hide under the bed? Coughing now—he couldn't help himself, really dredging it up, the weakness squeezing him like a fist, then letting go and squeezing again—he slammed round the darkened room in a panic, thinking only to get away, far away where they'd never find him, where there was sunshine and he could stretch out in the hot sand and bake the microbes out of him. He didn't know much, but he knew they'd be at the back door too, just like in the movies when they nailed the gangsters and the pimps and the drug lords and the whole audience stood up and cheered . . .

No time for his backpack, no time for clothes, his toothbrush, for the change he kept in a pickle jar in the top drawer, no time for anything but to jerk up the window in its creaking frame while the knocking at the front door rose to a relentless

pounding and the voices started up there, Sergio's and some-body else's and a dog barking, and then he was down in the grass and scrambling hunched-over for the next yard and then the next one after that. It took everything he had. Twice he tripped in the dark, going down hard on somebody's patio, all the little sounds of the neighborhood amplified now, every TV turned up full-blast, motorcycles blaring like gunfire out on the street, even the crickets shrieking at him, and that dog, the ratcheting bark of that dog back at the house, a police dog, the kind of dog that never gave up, that could sniff you out even if you sprouted wings and flew up into the sky.

Where was he? Some dark place. Some citizen's backyard with its jade plants and flowerbed and patch of lawn. A cold hand went down inside him, yanking at his lungs, squeezing and bunching and pulling the meat there up into his throat so he couldn't breathe. He went down on his hands and knees, shiv-ering again, sweating again, and there was no plan now but to find the darkest corner of the yard, the place where nobody had bothered to cut the grass or trim the shrubs, where the earth was real and present and he could let the blood come up and forget about the pills and Rosa Hinojosa and his mother and Rudy and everybody else.

Time leapt ahead. He was stretched out in the dirt. What was on his shirt was hot and secret and wet. He closed his eyes. And when he opened them again, all he could see was the glint of a metal trap, bubbles rising in the clear cold water and the hands of the animal fighting to get out.

T.C. BOYLE is an American novelist and short story writer. Since the mid-1970s, he has published sixteen novels and more than 150 short stories. He won the PEN/Faulkner Award in 1988 for his third novel, *World's End,* and the Prix Médicis étranger (France) for *The Tortilla Curtain* in 1995, as well as the PEN/ Malamud Award for Excellence in Short Fiction in 1999. *The Harder They Come* was a *New York Times* bestseller. In 2014 he won the Rea Award for the Short Story, and he was the editor of *The Best American Short Stories* (2015).

CONTENTS

I love not Man the less, but Nature more.

−George Gordon Byron, *Childe Harold's Pilgrimage*

Man hands on misery to man.
  It deepens like a coastal shelf.
Get out as early as you can,
  And don't have any kids yourself.

−Philip Larkin, "This Be the Verse"

For Milo, Alexis and Olivia

THE RELIVE BOX AND OTHER STORIES. Copyright © 2017 by T. Coraghessan Boyle. All rights reserved. Printed in the United States of America. No part of this book may be used or reproduced in any manner whatsoever without written permission except in the case of brief quotations embodied in critical articles and reviews. For information address HarperCollins Publishers, 195 Broadway, New York, NY 10007.

HarperCollins books may be purchased for educational, business, or sales promotional use. For information please e-mail the Special Markets Department at SPsales@harpercollins.com.

FIRST EDITION

Designed by Michelle Crowe

Library of Congress Cataloging-in-Publication Data has been applied for.

ISBN 978-0-06-267339-8

17 18 19 20 21   LSC   10 9 8 7 6 5 4 3 2 1

THE
RELIVE
BOX

AND OTHER STORIES

T. CORAGHESSAN BOYLE

ecco
An Imprint of HarperCollins*Publishers*

ALSO BY T. CORAGHESSAN BOYLE

NOVELS

Water Music (1981)

Budding Prospects (1984)

World's End (1987)

East Is East (1990)

The Road to Wellville (1993)

The Tortilla Curtain (1995)

Riven Rock (1998)

A Friend of the Earth (2000)

Drop City (2003)

The Inner Circle (2004)

Talk Talk (2006)

The Women (2009)

When the Killing's Done (2011)

San Miguel (2012)

The Harder They Come (2015)

The Terranauts (2016)

SHORT STORIES

Descent of Man (1979)

Greasy Lake & Other Stories (1985)

If the River Was Whiskey (1989)

Without a Hero (1994)

T.C. Boyle Stories (1998)

After the Plague (2001)

Tooth and Claw (2005)

The Human Fly (2005)

Wild Child & Other Stories (2010)

T.C. Boyle Stories II (2013)

ANTHOLOGIES

DoubleTakes (2004) co-edited with K. Kvashay-Boyle

may not be done in the way you want it, in the time you want, but it will be done. This is what you must understand. Once you give this problem or these children or these people to God, you must leave them to God in full trust.

Striking the Rock Ourselves

❖

Numbers 20:5–11

The Israelites say to Moses, "WHY DID YOU LEAD US OUT OF EGYPT, ONLY TO BRING US TO THIS WRETCHED PLACE? IT IS A PLACE UNFIT FOR SOWING, IT HAS NO FIGS, NO VINES, NO POMEGRANATES, AND THERE IS NOT EVEN WATER TO DRINK!" (20:5). These people were constantly aggravating poor Moses, and no matter what great wonders the Lord performed for them, they were always looking back on what they had lost. We all have a tendency to look back and to focus on our past lives or on the things that happened before. The past seems to be so much better than what's happening now. We edit out all of the bad stuff and only recall the happiness of the past—then we compare that to the misery of the present moment. Pretty soon we're recalling "the good old days." You look back in your life and you say, "Oh, when my husband and I were courting it was so beautiful." The first year you were married you looked forward to his coming home with great anticipation. Now you look up at the clock and when that little hand hits the six you think: "Here comes the monster. Well, he'll be gone by eight o'clock tomorrow. He's not the man I married." This is just something in our human nature, I think. The evil one perhaps puts these things in our minds in order to make us dissatisfied with God's will in the present moment. The important thing to remember is that you have the Lord who is eternally young, eternal happiness, eternal joy, eternal strength. And you have Him. Don't be grousing like the Israelites.

Leaving the assembly, Moses and Aaron went to the door of the Tent of Meeting. They threw themselves face downward on the ground (20:6). Did you ever pray that way? It's a very efficacious way to pray. And Yahweh spoke to Moses and said (20:7), "take the branch and call the community together, you and your brother Aaron. Then, in full view of them, order this rock to give water. You will make water flow for them out of the rock, and provide drink for the community and their cattle" (20:8). Now, you know, it would be very easy to draw water out of the ground, but to draw water out of a rock is something totally different. Sometimes the Lord does that in your life. He lets you wait until you get down to the bare rock of your soul—until you feel nothing. There is no place to go, there is nothing to do, everything is dark and bare and absolutely hopeless. Then suddenly out of nowhere comes water: relief, hope, a new life. Sometimes the Lord permits everything we desire to turn into its opposite; the things we wanted turn to ashes. Why does He permit this? So that when I am relieved, when I am comforted, I will recognize that it is from God alone.

Moses took up the branch from before Yahweh, as he had directed him (20:9). Then Moses and Aaron called the assembly together in front of the rock and addressed them, "Listen now, you rebels" (20:10). Moses is finally getting impatient. "Shall we make water gush from this rock for you?" (20:10). Question mark. And Moses raised his hand and struck the rock twice with the branch;

WATER GUSHED IN ABUNDANCE, AND THE COMMUNITY DRANK AND THEIR CATTLE TOO (20:11).

First of all he said, "YOU REBELS." Do you remember how meek and gentle he's been up till now? He's always interceding for these people, always praying for them. Now he's had it up to here. He says, "Shall we get water out of this rock, you rebels?" and he hits it twice. Ah, what's happened to Moses? He has looked at the difficulty—and that's all he saw. He has looked at the impossible situation, getting water out of a rock. He has looked at the meanness, the ingratitude, the impatience, the unkindness of this people and he's let it get to him. He's so angry that he doubts God. He thinks: "Shall we do this? I wonder if the water will come after all this. Maybe God's mercy has reached its limit." Moses's patience has reached its limit and he has judged God by himself. We are constantly doing the same. We are constantly judging God by ourselves. "I will not forgive, so God will not forgive. . . . I will love you if you do this, but if you do that, brother, that's it. That's it!"

So Moses reached a limit in his life; he got angry with these people. He didn't see a people wandering in the desert needing God; he saw only a stiff-necked, rebellious, selfish, ungrateful people. He let that situation come within, and once it got within, he doubted the mercy of God toward them. You see he *insulted* God, and we do this all the time. I say, "Lord, I believe in your providence but I worry about tomorrow." I say, "Lord, I believe your infinite wisdom has planned everything for me, but I still don't understand why things happen or their timing." I say, "God, I believe You have created all things." Then I wonder, "Did He create me, and if He did, why? I believe God that You have a plan for everything, and yet I doubt I exist for any reason."

Are we doing the same as Moses? I say, "Lord, I believe in Your healing powers." Yet I refuse to believe that the pain I have could be the healing for a sickness more serious than physical—the physical illness could well cure a more lethal spiritual malady that I am riddled with. We look at God and claim to believe in Him, but our actions and our thoughts don't correspond to our beliefs. Here's the difference between belief and faith: Belief is to know. Faith is to see.

God Uses the Weak
❖
Judges 6:10–16; 7:2–7

Look at Gideon in chapter six of the book of Judges. God again uses a very weak man (and a few others) to confound a strong army.

You might have heard the story of Teresa of Ávila who was riding in a carriage one day on her way to build a foundation. The carriage got stuck in the mud and the Lord appeared to her. She asked Him, "Why did You do this? You know I am in a hurry." And the Lord said, "This is how I treat my friends." Teresa replied, "No wonder You have so few of them." Gideon is saying the same thing here.

God says, "I AM YAHWEH YOUR GOD" (6:10). Then Gideon says, "FORGIVE ME, MY LORD, BUT IF YAHWEH IS WITH US, THEN WHY IS IT THAT ALL THIS IS HAPPENING TO US NOW?" (6:13). Finally Yahweh says, "GO IN THE STRENGTH NOW UPHOLDING YOU, AND YOU WILL RESCUE ISRAEL FROM THE POWER OF MIDIAN" (6:14). GIDEON ANSWERED HIM, "FORGIVE ME, MY LORD, BUT HOW CAN I DELIVER ISRAEL? MY CLAN, YOU MUST KNOW, IS THE weakest in Manasseh and I am the least important in my family" (6:15). He had the same idea we have today. You have to have a name to do anything, you have to be somebody, or you have to belong to a particular class of people. You need a degree with a couple of letters behind your name. Gideon had the same idea. Yahweh answered him, "I will be with you and you shall crush Midian as though it were a single man" (6:16).

We know that Gideon got an army together. The Scripture tells us that Yahweh said to Gideon, "There are too many people with you for me to put Midian into their power; Israel might claim the credit for themselves at my expense: they might say, 'My own hand has rescued me' (7:2). Therefore, make this proclamation now to the people: 'Let anyone who is frightened or fearful, go home!'" . . . Twenty-two thousand men went home, and ten thousand were left (7:3). They looked at Gideon and said, "This man is going to deliver us?!"

Today we have forgotten that for all the technology and intelligence in the world, it is still God Who does everything. God went so far as to have Gideon take all his remaining men to the waterside and observe how they drank. If they drank like a dog, lapping with their tongue, the Lord put them aside. These were the three hundred imbeciles God chose to save Israel. Gideon ended up with three hundred stupid idiots (Jgs 7:4–7). And as Gideon began to see his army dwindle from ten thousand to three hundred he got a little scared, and he thought, "Maybe I am not hearing God. What's the whole purpose behind this?"

Today we are fighting tremendous invisible armies. Armies who are more intelligent than we are—evil spirits. We are weak, we are oppressed on every side by the flesh, the world, and the devil: the three great tempters. Gideon was strong with the strength of God. God wants to tell the whole world: I am going to do it. The weaker we are, the more confidence we should have. God uses the weak things of this world to confound the strong. Whether you are a child, an old person, or a sick person, if you love Jesus, you can be a terror to the invisible foe.

God Wins the Battle

❖

Judges 7:12–22

When Gideon's enemies, the Midianites, descended on their camels THE VALLEY [WAS] AS THICK AS LOCUSTS (7:12). That's how many men there were. THEIR CAMELS WERE INNUMERABLE LIKE THE SAND ON THE SEASHORE (7:12). I want you to visualize in your imagination this throng of people and poor Gideon standing there with only three hundred uncouth, uncultured men. GIDEON CAME UP JUST AS A MAN WAS TELLING HIS COMRADE A DREAM [HE HAD HAD] (7:13). The Lord was trying so hard to encourage Gideon. The Midianite said: "I HAD A DREAM: A CAKE MADE OF BARLEY BREAD CAME ROLLING THROUGH THE CAMP OF MIDIAN; IT REACHED THE TENT, STRUCK AGAINST IT AND TURNED IT UPSIDE DOWN" (7:13). HIS COMRADE ANSWERED, "THIS CAN BE NOTHING ELSE THAN THE SWORD OF GIDEON. . . . GOD HAS PUT MIDIAN AND ALL THE CAMP INTO HIS POWER" (7:14).

What happened? Psychological warfare. The Lord had allowed the Midianites to have such a fear of Gideon. The poor guy hadn't even done anything yet, not one thing. Now, you're talking about a throng of people so large that they couldn't even be counted. Probably 300,000 people.

When Gideon heard the dream ... he fell to his knees; then he returned to the camp of Israel and said, "On your feet, for Yahweh has put the camp of Midian into your power!" (7:15). There, now he's brave. Oh, boy, is he brave. Gideon then divided his three hundred men into three companies (7:16). This is one of the most unbelievable battles. To each man he gave what? An arrow? A bow? A sword? Nope. He gave each of them an empty pitcher with a torch inside, and a horn. He lights the torch, hides it under a pitcher, and holds onto the horn.

Gideon says, "Watch me, and do as I do. When I reach the edge of the camp, whatever I do, you do too" (7:17). Now you know those three hundred men had to have a certain level of stupidity. Absolute stupidity, because they've already seen the Midianites in the valley, like locusts, and here they are like people going to a New Year's Eve party. Just imagine these men walking in the dark, hiding a torch, and a horn. A horn!

Scripture says, Gideon and his hundred companions reached the edge of the camp at the beginning of the middle watch, when the new sentries had just been posted; they sounded their horns and smashed the pitchers in their hands (7:19). Toot-do-la-loooo. Smash! The three companies sounded their horns and smashed their pitchers; with their left hands they grasped the torches, with their right hands the horns ready to blow (7:20). What a way to win a battle. And they shouted, "For Yahweh and (for) Gideon!" (7:20). And they stood still. . . . Then

THE WHOLE CAMP WOKE UP AND THE MIDIANITES FLED, SHOUT-
ING (7:21). WHILE THE THREE HUNDRED KEPT SOUNDING THEIR
HORNS, YAHWEH MADE EVERY MAN IN THE CAMP TURN HIS
SWORD AGAINST HIS COMRADE (7:22). That was it. See, they
thought they were fighting Gideon! It was dark and they saw
these three hundred torches, which must have looked like
thousands of people coming down into the valley, and they all
fled. Gideon's army never moved a step.

Lord, we pray that we can be your Gideons today. Where
they stood on a mountain with a horn and a covered torch, we
stand before the Blessed Sacrament with the horn of confidence and the torch of our love, and we stand still. We stand
still. We don't turn to the right or to the left—shaky knees and
all—we stand still. That is our own method of fighting a massive battle. God has to win every battle for us.

So today in our interior lives let's be like Gideon. God calls
us to great holiness. God calls us to help save His people and
return them to their Father's house. We must be willing in all
our weakness, in all our infidelities, in our lack of virtue, to let
the Lord use us as He did Gideon. We have only to stand still
with our torches, with our love, and pray. That's it. God Himself will destroy the locusts of this age; those who are eating up
the fruits of the Lord, those who have forgotten that it is God
Almighty who is victorious, no one else.

Ruth and Obedience

❖

Ruth 1:1–22

At an investment ceremony for one of her nuns, Sister Ruth Marie, Mother Angelica offered this off-the-cuff meditation on the Old Testament heroine Ruth.

As you know from reading the Scriptures, the name of Ruth is very important. She left the land when the Moabites were getting after the Israelites. She was a Moabite. She could have gone home. Moabites were not very loved by the Israelites—they were kind of pagan. Her mother-in-law, Naomi (who had one other daughter-in-law) said to Ruth, "You go back to your people now." Ruth said, "No, no. I'm not leaving you. Your people will be my people. Your God, my God." The essence of Ruth is a willingness to follow in darkness.

She didn't know anything about the real, true God. But she had what it took to believe in the One True God! She's kind of the grandma of Jesus. Ruth was a strong woman. Ready for anything, and God rewarded her for her obedience and her love.

If there's one thing people who want to follow the Lord need today, it is to have no fear, no excuses, and no concern for human respect. Loyalty was Ruth's great gift from God. She remained with her mother-in-law—and it was the love for her mother-in-law that sustained her. She was loyal, and because she was loyal, she was obedient. That's something we never think about. Disobedience is a crime against loyalty. Ruth was the epitome of obedience in the Old Testament. In a new land, among new people, she was always obedient.

Some of us think we have to like what we're doing to be obedient. You're not being obedient until you do what you don't like to do. If you don't believe me, ask Ruth.

Saul and the Will of God

❖

1 Samuel 15:17–21

Like Saul we often think that what we want to give God is better than what God asks of us. That's why Saul was punished. The whole kingdom was taken away from him. He exercised a lot of self-will, which came from his pride. Saul forgot to give God credit, and only obeyed God halfway.

In his mind Saul thought: "Well, I'll take the best livestock and I'll sacrifice those." But that isn't what the Lord asked! The Lord said, "Do away with everything, and don't save anybody." But Saul saved the king. That's called disobedience, and the Lord was angry. There's nothing that angers the Lord like disobedience. Nothing. It's one of the traps Saul fell into (we all do from time to time). He felt his idea was better than the Lord's. His idea was "I'll give the animals I spare to the Lord." And the Lord said, "[O]BEDIENCE IS BETTER THAN SACRIFICE" (15:22).

See, you can't use your own human reason when you're talking about God's will. You can't add to His will or detract from it. Just do what He is asking of you. Saul used his head and lost the kingdom, lost the inspiration of God—and when that happens everything else rushes in: concupiscence and jealousy and all the rest.

Now, we with our modern minds think, well, gee, it doesn't look too bad. He did sacrifice to God what he kept (and then he kept the king). But that was total disobedience. You may want to do something novel and it may seem better to you, but is it better in the eyes of God? Saul thought he was enhancing the Lord's will. But it wasn't pleasing to God, and if you do that in your daily life, you can knock yourself right out of the box because that's the way God is.

He cares about obedience to His will. We see it most dramatically in the nakedness of death. When you die, you don't take anything with you. What would you use it for anyway? Are you going to give Saint Peter a $10 tip for getting you in the gate? At that point it is all about how obedient you were to the will of God. Are you using reasoning to be disobedient? It doesn't work. It didn't work for Saul. And it is not going to work for you.

Saul's reasoning was "Look, I have all these nice fat calves. God would like these." Then he tries to get clever. He even said, "I did what the Lord told me to do. I killed all the men, all the children. I took the animals for sacrifice, which I gave to the Lord." Now, that looks very reasonable. He kept the king, which he didn't mention. But he did not do God's will and the Lord just knocked him out. Saul did a typical human thing: He reasoned himself out of obedience. Do not follow his error.

David and the Love of God

❖

1 Samuel 17:22–51

The battle between Goliath and David is instructional. It's reasonable that a rock, be it ever so small, thrust at the right speed, could embed itself into your head, especially if it was guided by God Himself. What amazes me about that incident is that everybody, including King Saul, was so petrified that they allowed this kid to face Goliath. They probably thought they had lost the battle. They weren't even embarrassed to send this young man over there. It shows how scared they were and apparently paralyzed—all the generals, the soldiers, everyone was paralyzed.

This Goliath could have very well been eight, nine feet tall, and nobody was going to take him on. It shows how our souls become paralyzed by the appearance of an obstacle—and that's when we make wrong decisions. See, King Saul already knew he was not blessed by God—that God was very displeased with him, and the way he executed his office. His mission had been taken away from him. But let's not get so spiritually paralyzed by our own faults, the faults of others, by circumstances, by work, by our health, by the events in the world, that we lose sight of the most important thing: the call of God.

The thing to remember about David is he was really a sinner and yet Our Lord loved him so much that He's known as the Son of David. David did some pretty bad things: he shed a lot of blood, he was cruel in battle, he had that thing going with Bathsheba and then he murdered her husband. David should be an encouragement to any of you who might get discouraged over your little peccadilloes. Once the Lord loves you, I tell you, it's unbelievable. His love is forever.

Elijah and the Still, Small Voice

❖

1 Kings 19:5–14

It's so easy to be holy. So easy to give our total self to the Lord, in total abandonment to His Love and to His will. What a wonderful goal. What a mission. We're often sent into the wilderness *of ourselves* to seek the true light. That's where we're all sent: into the wilderness of ourselves. . . . We're sent by God on that journey of the soul, sent into the interior wilderness to find the One Who sent us there. That's why I like the prophet Elijah so much.

I'm so glad he's going to come back. I hope I'm around when he does. I've always pictured him as a small, scrawny little guy with a long beard and a squeaky voice, aggravating everybody all the time. Getting real discouraged and saying, "Lord take me, I'm no better than my fathers." An angel wakes Elijah up at one point. He looks at the angel, and he's not impressed. The angel gives him a cake, he eats it, and falls back to sleep: that is depression. Depression! The angel wakes him up again, "Eat. You've got to go to Mount Horeb." Hmm. He gets up, eats, and he walks for forty days and forty nights. Can you imagine walking without ceasing for forty days and forty nights—no sleep, no food, just walking?

He gets all the way to the top of Mount Horeb and here comes an earthquake. He watched and looked for God, but

God was not in the earthquake. Then there was a fire on the mountain—big fire—and God was not in the fire. Then there was such thunder and lightning that the whole mountain shook, and there was no voice of God at all. Elijah is standing there wondering, "Why am I here? I'm soaking wet, it's cold. I've gone through an earthquake, a fire, and a storm." Then comes the most beautiful passage: [T]HERE CAME THE SOUND OF A GENTLE BREEZE (19:12). And he took his mantle and hid his face with it. You know what I think the fire and the storm and the earthquake were? His soul. His soul, his wilderness was like an earthquake, fiery and storm-tossed. God had to manifest to Elijah exteriorly what he was interiorly.

Remember Elijah had killed all of Baal's prophets. Jezebel was after him and she said, "May I be cursed if by tomorrow morning you're not as one of these prophets"—the ones Elijah chopped up. So he runs. What else can he do? He's discouraged, he's disgruntled, he's unhappy, and I think that was a reflection of the inside of Elijah. Only when he came to a deep awareness that "there's something wrong with me," only then did he hear that gentle voice, that still, small voice of God. And he covered his face and he said . . . nothing. He was absolutely silent. The next sentence is so perfect that only God could have come up with it. He said, "Elijah, what are you doing here?" and Elijah said, "I have fled. There's not anybody left but me, and I know better than the rest of them. Jezebel is after me because I killed all the prophets. And I'm tired of this being a prophet. I'm tired of the whole thing. I want out." The Lord said, "Elijah, go back where you were." Another forty days and forty nights' walk. Only there was no little angelic biscuit this time. . . . God tells him, "There are others who have also been faithful. Now go back and do your duty as a prophet of the Lord." Just imagine what that poor guy's soul had to go through before he could hear the whisper of God.

Like Elijah, we will only hear God's voice when we allow our wilderness to be calm and quiet. As long as your wilderness is consumed by storms, earthquakes, or fires, you can't hear His voice. You can't hear His voice—and you need to.

God Is Watching

❖

Psalm 139

If you are ever in a kind of tragic situation and you don't know what to do, and your mind just goes blank, I would go to the Psalms. Look at a Psalm that I like very much. It's Psalm 139 and it praises the omnipotence of God. It starts like this: YAHWEH, YOU EXAMINE ME AND KNOW ME, YOU KNOW IF I AM STANDING OR SITTING, YOU READ MY THOUGHTS FROM FAR AWAY (1–2). Now, can you imagine that? You don't pay attention to anybody whether they're standing or sitting, you're just happy if they're quiet. But He knows your every move. "You examine me, and know me." Some of you don't think God knows you. Sweetheart, you're no surprise to God. He decided you would be before time began.

I love that line: YOU READ MY THOUGHTS FROM FAR AWAY. You know the Lord did just that. When Jesus called Nathaniel to be one of the apostles, He said to the others, "Here's a man without guile." And Nathaniel heard Him and said, "How do You know me?" Jesus looked at him and said, "When you were under the fig tree, I saw you." Just think about that. When you walked in and picked up this book, and sat down on your sofa or laid in your bed, God knew you did it, and He saw you do it. I mean, that's the kind of attention you get from God. All the sin that you commit in the dark—you are not hiding it from anybody, especially from God. You can rob a bank in the dead of night, but it's bright as the noonday sun to Him.

It says here: [W]HETHER I WALK OR LIE DOWN, YOU ARE WATCHING, YOU KNOW EVERY DETAIL OF MY CONDUCT (3). There are no secrets hidden from God. You know, sometimes you come home from work and you're tired and you think, "Well, I'll just lie down on the sofa for a few minutes and rest." He sees you, He knows you, and He loves you. We don't have that kind of love, do we? We don't have the kind of love that envelops everything a person does whether it be good or bad or sorrowful—but God loves us at every moment.

It says here: THE WORD IS NOT EVEN ON MY TONGUE, YAH-WEH, BEFORE YOU KNOW ALL ABOUT IT; CLOSE BEHIND AND CLOSE IN FRONT YOU FENCE ME ROUND, SHIELDING ME WITH YOUR HAND (4–5). If we knew this one little truth about God, we'd never be lonely again. Many times God shields you with His hand and you don't even know it. We need to thank God for those times. We need to thank God for all the things He does for us without our knowledge!

I remember one time after my spinal operation many years ago, I was driving with this woman to receive some follow-up treatments, and she was talking and talking. She was about to turn in to the hospital and all of a sudden in front of me, on the passenger side, was the approaching radiator of a big bus. I could feel the heat because this woman didn't look to her side as she started to turn. Had that bus driver not turned onto the sidewalk, I would have been killed. We probably would have both been killed. But you see, God shielded us with His hand there. This happens to all of you at various points in your lives.

The Psalmist continues: SUCH KNOWLEDGE IS BEYOND MY UNDERSTANDING, A HEIGHT TO WHICH MY MIND CANNOT ATTAIN (6). I love this Psalm. WHERE COULD I GO TO ESCAPE YOUR SPIRIT? WHERE COULD I FLEE FROM YOUR PRESENCE? (7). You know, often in our spiritual lives we act as if God is not present. So many of you feel abandoned, alone—you think God is not there. When you feel dry, you think God is not there. When you can't pray, you think God is not there. How easily we forget about this one sentence: WHERE COULD I FLEE FROM YOUR PRESENCE? (7). IF I CLIMB THE HEAVENS, YOU ARE THERE, THERE TOO, IF I LIE IN SHEOL (8). IF I FLEW TO THE POINT OF SUNRISE, OR WESTWARD ACROSS THE SEA (9), YOUR HAND WOULD STILL BE GUIDING ME, YOUR RIGHT HAND HOLDING ME (10). There's just no way and nowhere you can go without God going with you. You can be devastated in weakness, and yet His strength is there. His presence is there. It is an awesome reality.

Isn't it wonderful to have somebody who loves you that much, always. And He's not going on vacation! He's not going to leave you! He's never going to let you down! He's always there. You know, when I was a young Sister, I was kind of ornery. Well, I still am, I guess. Reverend Mother was teaching us how to meditate, and she said, "You place yourself in the presence of God." I would think to myself, "Well, that's not so hard. I can't get out of His presence. He's everywhere." (The smart novice suddenly enters the order and knows everything.) I was stupid. . . . But it's true! Where can you go to escape His presence? Even though you may be alone and even though people abandon you and your children don't pay attention to you, you have God. You have God! And He has always been there.

A little further down the Psalm reads: YOU KNOW ME THROUGH AND THROUGH (14), FROM HAVING WATCHED MY BONES TAKE SHAPE WHEN I WAS BEING FORMED IN SECRET, KNITTED TOGETHER IN THE LIMBO OF THE WOMB (15). Isn't that awesome? God is there at your first moment. Without God nothing living would exist. If God were to stop thinking of me at this moment, you would see a great big grease spot and a habit on this chair.

Let's go to the end of Psalm 139; it's a prayer really. Pray this whenever you can: GOD, EXAMINE ME AND KNOW MY HEART, PROBE ME AND KNOW MY THOUGHTS (23); MAKE SURE I DO NOT FOLLOW PERNICIOUS WAYS, AND GUIDE ME IN THE WAY THAT IS EVERLASTING (24). Amen. Seek His presence and listen for His call. He is there.

DON'T BE A WHAT'S-NEXTER

There's always a grave temptation, very subtle at times, to say: "I've heard it all. What's next?" Well, if you say that, it means you don't know a thing.

Saint Francis used to spend a whole night, a whole night, in prayer and he'd say nothing but "My Lord and my God." That's all he said all night long, and then he'd think about it. Now, in our brilliant minds we'd say, "Yeah, okay. My Lord and my God. I know that. What's next?"

You see, when you become a what's-nexter, then pride— and that's what it is—pride will destroy you because you close your mind to grace, to the grace and the power of the Spirit to give you more light on the same line of Scripture. Nobody can plumb the depths of one passage of Scripture—not if you spent your whole life. How many times have you heard the Scripture? I've been in religious life forty-three years this year and so I've heard every part of Scripture—heard the Gospel preached more than forty times, not counting my earlier life. Assuming that you've heard it before and you already know it, what in the world would you ever learn from this Book? Why read it every day when you've already read it? It isn't going to change. It isn't like you get a revised edition every year with new information and new revelations.

Well, you can't treat the inner self and this Book as if you're cramming for finals, because if we don't meditate on what we already know, we don't grow. If we don't let the Spirit open up new vistas and new light and new grace, what a great gift we are missing. You wouldn't have to learn a darn thing more if you were to meditate on God's Word and just allow it to come into your soul. We're talking about grace; we're not talking about knowledge. If you want knowledge, go get a degree. You can learn a lot. You can learn Scripture, but you may never *know it!*

We don't open ourselves to the light and grace of the Spirit because pride shuts the door. Pride says, "I've already heard that," and shuts out His Word in the Present Moment—in this new reality. I'm here to *experience* God. I'm here to have the kind of faith that brings Him into my life every day, every moment. I'm here to know God. I'm here to love God. You've got to get your mind out of the knowledge stage and into the experience stage.

God's Constancy

❖

Jeremiah 31:3; Isaiah 46:4

In Jeremiah it says "I HAVE LOVED YOU WITH AN EVERLASTING LOVE, SO I AM CONSTANT IN MY AFFECTION FOR YOU" (31:3). The Lord does not appeal to our animal nature. He appeals to our spiritual nature. He's trying to make us live now as we will in heaven.

He loved you from your mother's womb, before you were created (Psalm 139:13,15). God's eternal memory fascinates me. He wants to assure us that it doesn't change, that His affection is constant. He says in Isaiah 46:4: "IN YOUR OLD AGE I SHALL BE STILL THE SAME, WHEN YOUR HAIR IS GREY I SHALL STILL SUPPORT YOU. I HAVE ALREADY DONE SO, I HAVE CARRIED YOU, I SHALL STILL SUPPORT AND DELIVER YOU."

Our love varies and our affection is not constant, so we automatically attribute our puniness to God. But it just isn't so. I heard the mother of a pretty ornery kid say: "I look at him sometimes and I just can't imagine that he's still the same little, sweet, cute baby I used to hug. To think that this monster is the same child!" Our Lord is saying that He began with us and He will end with us. That's what it means to be constant. What a grace we have in God's constancy.

The New Testament

The Birth of Christ
(A Meditation)
❖
Luke 2:4–14

*In the 1970s Mother conducted a Bible study in the parlor of
her monastery for an ecumenical group of women for nearly
five years. She called the teachings "Journeys into Scripture."
Many of these were recorded for distribution and for broadcast on
a local radio station in Birmingham. The following meditation,
and subsequent ones, are excerpted from Mother's "Journeys."*

On our spiritual journey we are going to Bethlehem and
we see Joseph and Mary looking for a room. Joseph is quite
confident that he will find a place for the night. So he goes
to the best inn in Bethlehem, and they say, "There is no room
here. Can't you see we're overcrowded?" So he goes to another
inn and there is no vacancy there. They go to the house of relatives and there is no room there either. He goes to Mary and
she smiles, she understands.

They make their way toward the gate of the city. Joseph
spies a cave there and he looks at Mary. She nods. He lays
his cloak out and puts some fresh hay in the corner and he
asks Mary to sit down. Then he goes to the mouth of the cave
and lights a fire and sits down. As I look at the scene I think,
How strange this is. So many people waited for centuries for
this night and when it comes, there is no one here. Suddenly
the whole cave is filled with the most brilliant light: beautiful
and soft. At the end of the cave is Mary. She is kneeling and

she has the most lovely Infant in her arms. My heart begins to pound with joy and I go over and kneel, and I say to her, "May I touch him?" She says, "Yes. Don't be afraid. This is why He came so that you would see your God in the flesh and never be afraid again." I go to grasp His hand and instead He clasps my little finger and holds it so tight. I realize how much God loves me—that He would come in such a tiny form to such a cold, simple place. That He would consent to be so dependent on His creatures: Mary and Joseph to give Him food and drink and to care for Him. This God who created the whole universe is dependent upon two creatures, all out of love for me.

When I go out of the cave it is so dark. There is no one in sight. I see a great light in the sky and hear angels' voices. Perhaps now people will come? But only a few shepherds appear: the simple, the lowly, the humble; those whose hearts were made ready for His coming by poverty and suffering. They heard the angels. We go in together and we kneel down before the Child and He looks at us and smiles—a smile of such love as if to say, "I came for you." I say: "Oh God, give me the humility to give love for love—that as You came for me, so I may live for Thee. In my heart may You always find shelter and a warm inn where You may dwell, as in a temple, in splendor and glory. At every moment I wish to say I love Thee my God, I love Thee." Mary and Joseph look at me happily. They determined long ago that God would always find a place in their hearts.

Following the Star

❖

Matthew 2:9–11

L et's take up the second chapter, ninth verse of Saint Mat-
thew's Gospel, where he speaks of the wise men. HAVING
LISTENED TO WHAT THE KING HAD TO SAY, THEY SET OUT. AND
THERE IN FRONT OF THEM WAS THE STAR THEY HAD SEEN RISING;
IT WENT FORWARD AND HALTED OVER THE PLACE WHERE THE
CHILD WAS (2:9). THE SIGHT OF THE STAR FILLED THEM WITH
DELIGHT (2:10). It is amazing that no one else seemed to see
the star. Which is a kind of lesson for us, because obviously
that star was very big, very bright, and moving—so much so
that they could follow it. Isn't it strange that they were the only
ones who saw it? You would think that a phenomenon of that
proportion would be seen by everybody.

It makes you wonder if maybe there are stars in our lives
that we don't see for whatever reason. If there aren't great graces
that God has in store, moving in front of us, but because we're
so caught up in things—people, events, work, health, whatever—we don't see them. We don't see the stars; we don't see
the opportunities. Every opportunity for virtue is a moving star.
The very fact that it passes so quickly indicates that it moves.
These are stars in your crown, a gift from heaven created by
God just for you. So I think we need to be careful that we're
not like the people of the city of Bethlehem or Jerusalem.

I think we need to just ponder this. You know, that's one of
the things Our Lady did, at least twice, according to Scripture.
When the shepherds told her what the angels said about her

Son, she "pondered" it in her heart (Lk 2:19). At the finding of the Child Jesus, she STORED UP (all she had seen) "IN HER HEART" (Lk 2:51). You've got to ponder what this means. What does God really want you to do? There are times when the star is moving and you have no time to ponder.

The will of God is manifested in the present moment; it's a moving star, and sometimes you've only got a few seconds to follow it. And if you follow it, it will always be a bit ahead of you. Then there are times it disappears, totally. It comes and it goes. The Lord has something definite in mind, just as He had something definite in mind for the wise men.

The Gift of the Magi
(A Meditation)

❖

Matthew 2:1–12

We see a caravan outside of Jerusalem after the birth of Christ. There are three kings called wise men. You can see they are very wealthy. Yet each of them has a beautiful humility. They ask some of the citizens of the town: "Can you tell us where the infant King is?" The people are puzzled. "We have no king but Herod," they say. Have the wise men been mistaken? Was the star a figment of their imaginations? No, they are certain that this is the time for the birth of the great King. So they go to the king of the Jews, the great Herod. They ask him to lead them to the infant King. When you look at Herod, you see only hatred and jealousy. There will be no rival—no king but Herod. He calls the chief priests and the scribes and he demands to know what this is all about. They say, "This is the time when God was to send the Messiah, and He is to be born in Bethlehem."

We see Herod stroke his beard. He has a plan. He returns to the wise men and tells them to go on to Bethlehem and when they find Him, they are to report back to Herod so that he might also worship the Child. The wise men leave and they are once again led by this miraculous light that takes them to a house where they find Jesus, Mary, and Joseph. They kneel down and worship the infant King.

How odd it is: When He was born, Joseph and Mary saw only poor illiterate shepherds, now there are wise, wealthy, gentile kings. God is for all men, for all people, even as an infant, He came to save us all, and He would have homage and worship from all who are humble of heart. For those who seek Him no matter the obstacles, for those who are not ashamed to ask, "Where is the King?" for those who believe when they discover Him, He always reveals Himself.

What faith it takes to kneel down before this Infant and adore God so small. But these were truly wise men, who forgot their greatness before the majesty of God's Son: so humble, so tiny. Mary and Joseph are humbled that these great men would come to their home. I see in all of this not only love, but a great lesson. It is possible to be great and do great things and still be humble. It is possible to be poor and have nothing and to still be humble. It is possible to find our greatest treasure in God by being willing to give up the greatest things in the world. It is necessary to give up everything in me that is not Christlike and childlike. Oh Father, make me like Thine Son: small in the estimation of the world, but great in Thine eyes.

The Holy Innocents
(A Meditation)
❖
Matthew 2:13–18

The Scripture says: HEROD WAS FURIOUS WHEN HE REALISED THAT HE HAD BEEN OUTWITTED BY THE WISE MEN (2:16). We are at the palace of Herod in Jerusalem. Suddenly the chief priest comes in and says, "We have heard news that a king has been born in Bethlehem. Some say angels appeared and foretold this." Herod calls the palace guards and orders them to kill any male child two years or younger. Oh the evil of this man. Imagine this: He thinks he can destroy God's Son. Can it be that pride has reached its height?

What of God's Son? We go to Bethlehem and we see Jesus and Mary and Joseph and the wise men. They are all asleep. An angel of the Lord appears to the wise men in their sleep and he says, "Make haste, Herod wants to kill the Child. Do not go back to him. Return home another way." And the angel says to Joseph, "GET UP, TAKE THE CHILD AND HIS MOTHER WITH YOU, AND ESCAPE INTO EGYPT" (2:13). They rise and prepare the best they can, and each leaves by a different route.

Then I hear the soldiers coming. They are stomping through the streets and knocking on the doors. Any child two years and younger, they kill. Weeping and lamenting are heard all around, and I think, Why do these innocent children suffer for the greed and the ambition and the evil and the hatred of one man? For Herod? Why does God permit these children to die? Could He not have destroyed Herod? I look at the scene and I face a mystery, the mystery of life itself: evil, heartache, poverty, sickness. Why? And I realize that these children have had the privilege of dying for their God before their God died for them. God sent His Son to die for us. These children were given the privilege of being Christianity's first martyrs. Their mothers must have wondered and lamented. But as we look back we can see the good that came from this evil.

The glory of these children in heaven is incomprehensible because they were martyred for God's Son. So God permitted evil to bring about a greater good. Because they died, He lived. Because He died, WE live. It is a mystery that unless the seed falls to the ground and unless it dies, it remains alone. I realize that there are many things in me that must die before He can live: my pride, my ambition, my impatience, my anger. The difficulty I find in loving my neighbor, or listening to the problems of another. There is much that I must die to. But unless I die, unless these things are conquered, He cannot live in me. He cannot. For God must reign supreme in my soul. He must have all of me. He must know that I prefer Him to everyone and everything. I remember something He said on another day: I must take up my cross and follow Him—then like these Holy Innocents, I will have glory forever.

The Flight to Egypt

❖

Matthew 2:13–15

Aᴼ FTER THEY HAD LEFT, THE ANGEL OF THE Lᴼʀᴅ APPEARED TO JᴼSEPH IN A DREAM AND SAID, "Gᴇᴛ ᴜᴘ, TAKE THE CHILD AND HIS MOTHER WITH YOU, AND ESCAPE INTO Eɢʏᴘᴛ, AND STAY THERE UNTIL I TELL YOU, BECAUSE Hᴇʀᴏᴅ INTENDS TO SEARCH FOR THE CHILD AND DO AWAY WITH HIM" (2:13). Sᴏ Jᴏsᴇᴘʜ GOT UP AND, TAKING THE CHILD AND HIS MOTHER WITH HIM, LEFT THAT NIGHT FOR Eɢʏᴘᴛ (2:14), WHERE HE STAYED UNTIL Hᴇʀᴏᴅ WAS DEAD. Tʜɪs WAS TO FULFILL WHAT THE Lᴏʀᴅ HAD SPOKEN THROUGH THE PROPHET: I CALLED MY SON OUT OF Eɢʏᴘᴛ (2:15).

God does things so differently from the way we would. That's why we miss the boat many times—because we don't think like God. You can't imagine the virtue of Saint Joseph, because here he is, faced with a dream and off he goes.

It's strange that Herod wanted every child murdered two years old and under. Now we don't know how much time elapsed between the birth of Jesus and Herod's decree. What we do know is that Joseph had all the responsibility of protecting the Lord and Mary. Can you imagine that? We have to feel the weight of the responsibility God has given to each of us for our own souls and for the souls around us. You could say, "Well, I don't know what my mission is." No one wrote Joseph a detailed description of his mission either. He knew only one thing at a time. He knew he had to take care of Mary and Jesus, and that's all he knew.

Now, he's sent to a foreign country, full of idols. What

does he do? He had umpteen opportunities to practice faith. Having Mary and Jesus there didn't make it any easier on him. He didn't say, "Wait a minute, angel, you're telling me to go into Egypt tonight. Where?" He didn't ask the angel: "Where will we live?" or "How long will we stay?"

You see, we don't understand Joseph. We don't want uncertainty in our lives. You talk about uncertainty . . . the temptation certainly would have been for Joseph to say, "Look, I'm told this is the Son of God. This is the Messiah. Why should we be running to Egypt?" Our Lady had to give him faith and courage. But, you see, they didn't question God. When they heard "go," they went. Joseph could only do that if he was a great man of faith. And he was.

The Trust of the Holy Family (A Meditation)

❖

Matthew 2:13–15, 19–23

During our "Journey into Scripture" we are going to Bethlehem to a small house. The wise men have gone. Jesus, Mary, and Joseph are preparing for a journey. Their few belongings are placed on the back of a donkey and they go.

They begin their long trek into Egypt. The night is cold, and Joseph removes his cloak and places it around Mary and the Child. I can see Joseph looking a little anxious, worried perhaps. They stop beside a big palm tree. Mary and the Child rest beneath the branches of this beautiful tree, and Joseph sits beside them and looks out into the cold desert. As they sleep he wonders, Will they accept him, a stranger, a Jew in Egypt? Will he find work? Will there be a synagogue where they can worship the Child's father? Will they make friends? How long will they stay, and how will he know when to return?

I realize that he had the same problems that I have had many times: doubts and fears about the future, the hesitancy and the distrust of the present. The "whys" in my life are a mystery that I can only look at with trust—I must trust the Father, trust His love, and trust His will. As I look at the scene, I know what comes after. I can see God's will in this, but Joseph and Mary cannot. So I must learn a beautiful and very necessary lesson: During the times in my life when everything seems so dark and uncertain, I too must trust. I must believe that this is happening to me out of love: God's love, that somewhere in it there is good, my good. We see the Holy Family rise in the morning and begin their journey, and they go into Egypt. It is difficult, difficult to find work and to make friends, but in time they do.

Then another night comes, and during sleep, once more, Joseph is told he must return. He is told that the one who wanted to kill the Child is dead. What a mystery it is that God's Son waited until the danger was over, just as I must wait for many dangers to pass. Like Jesus and Joseph and Mary, I too must wait for God's will to unfold in my life. I too must pray and wait and love and hope—and never lose faith in the providence and love of my Father. So we see the Holy Family and we are not sure how old the Child was, perhaps He was five or six or eight. You can see them going back to Nazareth. On the way back Joseph wonders, Will he find his home in tatters? And what will his friends say when he returns?

They go back to Nazareth to begin a new life. I realize as I look at this scene that they needed deep faith and hope and love, and that I too, no matter what happens, must have faith and hope and love and great joy to do whatever my Father asks of me, because He loves me, and you.

The Disappearance of Jesus

❖

Luke 2:41–51

Let's look at that moment in Scripture when Jesus left the Holy Family. EVERY YEAR HIS PARENTS USED TO GO TO JE-RUSALEM FOR THE FEAST OF THE PASSOVER (2:41). WHEN HE WAS TWELVE YEARS OLD, THEY WENT UP FOR THE FEAST AS USUAL (2:42). WHEN THEY WERE ON THEIR WAY HOME AFTER THE FEAST, THE BOY JESUS STAYED BEHIND IN JERUSALEM WITHOUT HIS PAR-ENTS KNOWING IT (2:43). THEY ASSUMED HE WAS WITH THE CAR-AVAN, AND IT WAS ONLY AFTER A DAY'S JOURNEY THAT THEY WENT TO LOOK FOR HIM AMONG THEIR RELATIONS AND ACQUAINTANCES (2:44). WHEN THEY FAILED TO FIND HIM THEY WENT BACK TO JERUSALEM LOOKING FOR HIM EVERYWHERE (2:45). THREE DAYS LATER, THEY FOUND HIM IN THE TEMPLE, SITTING AMONG THE DOCTORS, LISTENING TO THEM, AND ASKING THEM QUESTIONS (2:46); AND ALL THOSE WHO HEARD HIM WERE ASTOUNDED AT HIS INTELLIGENCE AND HIS REPLIES (2:47). THEY WERE OVERCOME WHEN THEY SAW HIM, AND HIS MOTHER SAID TO HIM, "MY CHILD, WHY HAVE YOU DONE THIS TO US? SEE HOW WORRIED YOUR FA-THER AND I HAVE BEEN, LOOKING FOR YOU" (2:48). "WHY WERE YOU LOOKING FOR ME?" HE REPLIED[.] "DID YOU NOT KNOW THAT I MUST BE BUSY WITH MY FATHER'S AFFAIRS?" (2:49). BUT THEY DID NOT UNDERSTAND WHAT HE MEANT (2:50).

Our Lady thought Jesus was with Joseph, and Joseph

thought He was with her. All of a sudden they came together at a stopping point, and you can imagine Our Lady saying to Joseph, "Where's Jesus?"

He says, "I thought He was with you."

She says, "No, I thought He was with you."

"Well, He has to be around here somewhere, so let's look." So they're looking around and nobody saw Him.

Imagine going to the supermarket and there's a husband and wife. The wife thinks the little kid is with him, and he thinks the child is with her. What would they begin to feel? Guilty. They would feel responsible that they hadn't checked to see if their child was with one or the other. So Our Lady's first thought was probably that they had been negligent . . . or that the Pharisees had kidnapped Him, or that He had fallen somewhere and was injured perhaps.

It is likely that Our Dear Lord didn't tell her where He went so that she could experience the sense of loss. She was sinless but she wasn't Mrs. Omnipotent. All of that was part of her cross. She had to suffer everything any human being suffers in his or her interior life. Otherwise she would never understand. In fact, that's why Jesus came. He came to show us how to suffer, how to accept the uncertainties in our life, and that it's okay not to understand what He does or why. Otherwise you and I would never know that the darkness of faith is just as pleasing to God as the consolations of faith. In fact, the darkness of faith is what prunes you, detaches you, and makes you love God with a pure love. Consolations don't do that.

When you or I experience a sense of losing Jesus, we feel it terribly. And what do you ask yourself? "What did I do wrong? Did I sin in some way?" Or we treat God as if He has done us an injustice the moment we feel a lack of His presence, a lack of consolation, or a lack of knowledge.

Our Lady asks simply, "MY CHILD, WHY HAVE YOU DONE THIS TO US? SEE HOW WORRIED YOUR FATHER AND I HAVE BEEN, LOOKING FOR YOU" (2:48). In other words, "What did we do to displease you?" She placed the blame on herself. She would never have thought, "Look here now, I took care of You. I have believed in You. I said 'fiat' to the Father. I have fed You. Joseph taught You how to walk, and in spite of all that, why would You do this?" Now, a fallen, human mother would do that. But the Blessed Mother wanted to know if either she or Joseph had done some wrong in their hearts. Did they not love Him enough? Did they do something that made Him disappear for three solid days? What did they do? She would want to know so she would never do it again.

Parents don't feel that way when their kids disappear; they want to wallop them—"By God, when I get done with you, you'll never do that again." That wasn't Our Lady's attitude at all. Why did you *do this to us*? And He answered correctly, "DID YOU NOT KNOW THAT I MUST BE BUSY WITH MY FATHER'S AFFAIRS?" (2:49).

What did that response tell Mary? It told her that she hadn't done anything wrong—neither had Joseph. "You didn't disappoint Me," the Lord is telling her (I'm improvising here a little). "I was not displeased with you, but I had to give the teachers in the Temple a hint. I had to enlighten them in the Scriptures so that they would know I'm here, I'm coming." And they were astounded, it says, that He knew so much. You see, the first thing God would do is enlighten the doctors and the Church.

That incident did many wonderful things. It gave the Blessed Mother a real understanding of the sense of loss of God in her life. Our Lady, to be Queen of martyrs, Queen of confessors, Queen of virgins, Queen of everybody, had to go through every single kind of spiritual pain, physical pain, mental pain—she had to experience it along with her Son, Jesus.

Then it says He went down and was subject to them (Lk 2:51). He didn't do any more disappearing acts. But He was obliged, as God, to tell the Jews and the doctors, the Pharisees, the Sadducees, and the scribes first. Some of them must have wondered, "Well, there's His father, what's He talking about?" God speaks to us today as He spoke to those teachers, and to Our Lady, and to Saint Joseph: in mystery.

UNION WITH JESUS

Immersion in Scripture is a critical part of knowing Jesus. My whole religious life is bound up in the one reality of Jesus. The thrust of my entire life must be a profound union with Jesus— a union of my heart: to love like Him; a union of my memory: to remember the Father as He did; a union of my intellect: to be humble of heart, to see the world as He does in the Scriptures; and a union of my will: to see the Spirit moving and to follow wherever He leads. . . .

My union with God is uppermost and has to be the criteria by which I judge everything, because that's how I'll be judged at death. I shall only be judged by love. That's why I keep telling you to keep your eyes on the top of the mountain, to keep your eyes on the essence of Jesus and His wondrous, immense, fiery, burning love for you.

The Boldness of John the Baptist

❖

Matthew 14:3–4; John 1:19–23

John the Baptist was such a strong man. If you have a concept of humility as somehow being weak, or requiring you to become a doormat, you ought to look at John the Baptist. He was so bold. You know, he yelled at Herod (who was sleeping around with his brother's wife): "IT IS AGAINST THE LAW FOR YOU TO HAVE HER" (Mt 14:4). This is the king he's yelling at. Nobody, not the Pharisees, not the Sadducees, not the doctors, not the high priest, no one would tell Herod that he was wrong. When this group asked, "WHO ARE YOU?" (Jn 1:19) he could have, right then and there, said, "I'm a prophet." They asked, "ARE YOU THE PROPHET?" (1:21)—meaning the Messiah—and John answered, "No." "WHO ARE YOU?" they asked (1:22). He answered, "I AM, AS ISAIAH PROPHESIED: A VOICE THAT CRIES IN THE WILDERNESS: MAKE A STRAIGHT WAY FOR THE LORD" (1:23). What great strength.

Humble people are not patsies. When the time comes, and if the opportunity comes to give honor and glory to God, they are strong people. They are not going to back down either. So some of our overly pious concepts of humility are just ridiculous.

John knew Jesus and he was single-minded. Single-minded. That's what the saints are: single-minded. They have one thing in mind: the Lord. We stray. We go back and forth. Sometimes we are like a reed shaking in the wind. We alternate; we change our course every so often. Other things, other people, other events crowd in upon us, and they prevent us from keeping our mind on Jesus. But we've gotta keep pulling ourselves in, because of our poor human nature. We've gotta keep pulling ourselves in and pushing our egos aside.

That's why we need to pray to the Spirit—pray that we don't lose sight of why we're here, that we don't become loners or become distracted or fragmented—that we don't become a people who slowly push God to the periphery. We've got to be single-minded, like John.

People should never keep you from God, and neither should events. Nothing on this earth should keep you from the love of God. You have to strive to see the Lord in the present moment. You have a job to do; do it well and do it with love. If you have to deal with people, then see Jesus in those people, love them with the same love with which you love the Lord.

If you look at yourself you will find that 99 percent of the problems you have stem from your own will. We want things this way, we want this person this way, and we want this event this way. Well, life is not here to give you everything you want. Follow the Lord and be bold like John the Baptist—be bold with the world and with yourself and watch where He takes you.

The Baptism of Jesus

❖

Matthew 3:13–17; John 10:40–42

THEN JESUS APPEARED: HE CAME FROM GALILEE TO THE JOR-
DAN TO BE BAPTISED BY JOHN (Mt 3:13). JOHN TRIED TO DIS-
SUADE HIM. "IT IS I WHO NEED BAPTISM FROM YOU[,]" HE SAID[,]
"AND YET YOU COME TO ME!" (3:14).

BUT JESUS REPLIED, "LEAVE IT LIKE THIS FOR THE TIME BE-
ING; IT IS FITTING THAT WE SHOULD, IN THIS WAY, DO ALL THAT
RIGHTEOUSNESS DEMANDS." AT THIS, JOHN GAVE IN TO HIM
(3:15).

Our Lord had to be baptized in order to sanctify the water for all of us. He allowed Himself, the Sinless One, to be
baptized. He instituted the sacrament of Baptism, by being
baptized Himself. He instituted all of the seven sacraments;
that's why you can't change them and you can't add or subtract
anything from them. That's why women cannot be priests.
Whatever Jesus did, we must do. The only sacraments we can
have are those sacraments that He instituted. The Church has
no authority whatever to institute a sacrament. It cannot create one.

Anyway, as Adam and Eve closed heaven to the world, the
sacrament of Baptism opened heaven to the world. That's why
He said, "Unless you are baptized by water and the Spirit, you
shall not enter the kingdom of heaven." And baptism is an awesome, awesome gift. John had the baptism of repentance. His
baptism did not open the gates of heaven to anyone. He only
prepared the people by calling them to repentance. As SOON

AS JESUS WAS BAPTISED HE CAME UP FROM THE WATER, AND SUDDENLY THE HEAVENS OPENED AND HE SAW THE SPIRIT OF GOD DESCENDING LIKE A DOVE AND COMING DOWN ON HIM (3:16).

AND A VOICE SPOKE FROM HEAVEN, "THIS IS MY SON, THE BELOVED; MY FAVOUR RESTS ON HIM" (3:17). At that point, heaven opened. The Father spoke and the Holy Spirit was there (in the appearance of the dove)—you could say it was the first "public appearance" of the Trinity. The Trinity, Who was so angered by the sin of Adam and Eve, were pleased with the coming of Jesus.

And before we move beyond John the Baptist, look at this passage in the book of John: JESUS WENT BACK AGAIN TO THE FAR SIDE OF THE JORDAN TO STAY IN THE DISTRICT WHERE JOHN HAD ONCE BEEN BAPTISING (Jn 10:40). MANY PEOPLE WHO CAME TO HIM THERE SAID, "JOHN GAVE NO SIGNS"—see here it is—"BUT ALL HE SAID ABOUT THIS MAN WAS TRUE" (10:41); AND MANY OF THEM BELIEVED IN HIM (10:42). So you can be a prophet and not give signs. You can be holy and not give that kind of miraculous sign. That was certainly the way of John the Baptist—and yet of all the men born of women, Jesus said, no one is as great as John the Baptist (Mt 11:11). So John the Baptist was greater than Moses, Abraham, Jeremiah, everybody. I've always felt sorry for these humble prophets. Here's little John, skinny and scrawny—I mean how much weight can you gain on locusts and honey? He wore these smelly camel skins. He looked and smelled like a prophet should look and smell. You know what I mean? He was the greatest of all the prophets yet there's not one sign from John. So that ought to encourage all of us peons, you know. It's not necessary to have ecstatic prayer, or to have visions or locutions; it's not necessary to go into ecstasy every three minutes or to levitate. It's not necessary to heal and to deliver and to do all of those things—have all those charisms.

a little portion of this miracle that we easily overlook: it was cooked fish the Lord multiplied.

The Scripture tells us in John: "THERE IS A SMALL BOY . . . WITH FIVE BARLEY LOAVES AND TWO FISH" (6:9). The boy couldn't carry raw fish around for three days. It would have been stinking. He had dried fish. So what the Lord multiplied was dried fish, not fresh fish. It must have been like baccalà. The Italians used to hang fish up and it would dry until it was like a board. Then you dropped it in water and it would fluff up and get thick. Just beautiful. The bread the Lord broke must have been stale, but I'm sure what He distributed was fresh. Look at me focusing on the menu. . . .

Anyway, there were a lot of people there, lots of children. You can imagine how they were eating. This was not a brunch at the Ritz. They're sloppy. They're caressing their food, it's all over their hands, it's all over their clothes—it's everywhere. It's a mess. It's important for us to understand the utter chaos and mess it must have been.

And what does the Lord say to do? What does He say? "PICK UP THE PIECES LEFT OVER, SO THAT NOTHING GETS WASTED" (6:12). SO THEY PICKED THEM UP, AND FILLED TWELVE HAMPERS WITH SCRAPS LEFT OVER FROM THE MEAL (6:13). *Pick up the pieces.* Pick up everything that's left. He was so interested in picking this stuff up. What do you think happened to this slop? I'll bet the apostles ate it for days and days, like that Thanksgiving turkey you eat until New Year's. Symbolically this is a foreshadowing of the Eucharist: not one particle of it is to be left behind. Every fragment must be consumed.

There is a lesson in those fragments lying there in the grass. In our lives we take something God gives us that is good and we turn it into garbage. We fragment it. We pull it apart.

We scatter it all over the place. Sin kind of squashes it, or just destroys it, or makes it ugly. God is saying to us, "Don't throw it away. I'm going to make it nourishing for you, even in this state."

Your life and my life are full of scraps that we would like to hide in the tall grass. But we can't. Look, I have a tendency to temper, I have a tendency to jealousy, I have a tendency to impatience, I have a tendency to be overly sensitive. Now we think, "I know I have these failings, so I'm going to pray and they're going to go away." That's not necessarily true. We won't know until we die and face God how even the failures of our lives have been used by Him, and transformed by His power for our good. Isn't that great? God can grow roses on your garbage heap. He can actually use your scraps. Don't toss them away. Give them to the Lord.

A Different Vision of Heaven

❖

Matthew 22:23–32

THAT DAY SOME SADDUCEES—WHO DENY THAT THERE IS A RESURRECTION—APPROACHED HIM AND THEY PUT THIS QUESTION TO HIM (22:23), "MASTER, MOSES SAID THAT IF A MAN DIES CHILDLESS, HIS BROTHER IS TO MARRY THE WIDOW, HIS SIS-TER-IN-LAW, TO RAISE CHILDREN FOR HIS BROTHER" (22:24)— they're always trying to trick the Lord—"NOW WE HAD A CASE INVOLVING SEVEN BROTHERS; THE FIRST MARRIED AND THEN DIED WITHOUT CHILDREN, LEAVING HIS WIFE TO HIS BROTHER" (22:25). It goes on and on like that, and eventually all seven brothers marry this poor woman. "NOW AT THE RESURRECTION TO WHICH OF THOSE SEVEN WILL SHE BE WIFE?" (22:28). Isn't that a clever question? Jesus says: "YOU ARE WRONG, BECAUSE YOU UNDERSTAND NEITHER THE SCRIPTURES NOR THE POWER OF GOD (22:29). FOR AT THE RESURRECTION MEN AND WOMEN DO NOT MARRY; NO, THEY ARE LIKE THE ANGELS IN HEAVEN" (22:30).

This is a very good place to stop and meditate, because Jesus is saying that heaven is vastly different from what we imagine. You're not going to need all the people you need here to make you happy. We will love everyone there and we will be loved by everyone there, but we definitely will not be the same as we are here. Because no matter what state of life you're in now, it's the place where you're tested, proven, purified for the kingdom, and your entire glory forever and ever depends on what you do in this place.

And He said, "AT THE RESURRECTION MEN AND WOMEN DO NOT MARRY; NO, THEY ARE LIKE THE ANGELS IN HEAVEN (22:30). AND AS FOR THE RESURRECTION OF THE DEAD, HAVE YOU NEVER READ WHAT GOD HIMSELF SAID TO YOU (22:31): I AM THE GOD OF ABRAHAM, THE GOD OF ISAAC, AND THE GOD OF JACOB? GOD IS GOD, NOT OF THE DEAD, BUT OF THE LIVING" (22:32).

So He taught them two lessons. First, the reason we cling to earth is because we're so attached to people, to things, to our opinions, to ourselves, and we cannot imagine life without any of this. And second, the purpose of life is to get you to a place where you love everybody, accept everything in order to purify yourself, so that you may arrive at that place in the kingdom God has destined for you.

The Woman at the Well

❖

John 4:5–29

Please understand that I have my own personal rendition of
Scripture, but it helps me and I hope it helps you. You've
got to put fire and life into your reading of the Scripture—use
your imagination and live it. Don't just sit there and read it like
a newspaper. It is Someone, not something.

It says here, ON THE WAY HE CAME TO THE SAMARITAN
TOWN CALLED SYCHAR, NEAR THE LAND THAT JACOB GAVE TO HIS
SON JOSEPH (4:5). JACOB'S WELL IS THERE AND JESUS, TIRED BY
THE JOURNEY, SAT STRAIGHT DOWN BY THE WELL. IT WAS ABOUT
THE SIXTH HOUR (4:6).

Can you imagine God being tired? Can you imagine anyone loving you so much that He wants to feel what you feel?
Before redemption we might have said to God, "Have you ever
been persecuted and hated and treated unjustly, when You

didn't know where to go or where to turn?" But now we have a glorious God Who knows. He knows what it is to be lonely, to be rejected, to be tired. I appreciate that because I rise and go to bed tired. When I am most tired I think of Him, and unite my fatigue with His, and somehow there is enough strength for another hour, another day.

So here it is the sixth hour and the Samaritan woman came to draw water. Now, no decent woman drew water at noontime. She was ostracized by the women of the village, so she came when there was no one around. Imagine her tiredness. Jesus said to her, "Give me a drink" (4:7). Oh that was a no-no. No Jew asked a Samaritan for anything, but Jesus was free and he said, "Give me a drink." The woman did exactly what we do to God: She questioned Him. We have the impression that if God knew us He would not love us. That's sick. Let me burst your bubble. Not only does He know what you've done, He knows what you might have done—and He still loves you.

The Samaritan woman said to him, "What? You are a Jew and you ask me, a Samaritan, for a drink?"—Jews, in fact, do not associate with Samaritans (4:9). Jesus replied: "If you only knew what God is offering and who it is that is saying to you: Give me a drink, you would have been the one to ask, and he would have given you living water" (4:10). And what does she do? Just what you and I would do. "You have no bucket, sir," she answered (4:11).

"You don't have a bucket." God just gave her the words of eternal life, and she says, "You don't have a bucket." And you do the same thing. You say to God, "Look at what I did twenty years ago. You couldn't love me." She then tries to educate God. She says, "The well is deep: how could you get this living water? (4:11). Are you a greater man than our father Jacob who gave us this well and drank from it him-

SELF WITH HIS SONS AND HIS CATTLE?" (4:12). See, she's trying to talk God out of his love. JESUS REPLIED: "WHOEVER DRINKS THIS WATER WILL GET THIRSTY AGAIN (4:13); BUT ANYONE WHO DRINKS THE WATER THAT I SHALL GIVE WILL NEVER BE THIRSTY AGAIN: THE WATER THAT I SHALL GIVE WILL TURN INTO A SPRING INSIDE HIM, WELLING UP TO ETERNAL LIFE" (4:14). You know what she says? "Lay it on me Lord." She says, "SIR, . . . GIVE ME SOME OF THAT WATER, SO THAT I MAY NEVER GET THIRSTY AND NEVER HAVE TO COME HERE AGAIN TO DRAW WATER" (4:15). She was probably thinking about all those gossipy women staring at her from their tents every time she went to the well. That's what we tell God: "If You love me, then You will give me all these good things." But the good things in life are those that are sometimes the most painful, because they mold and shape and transform us.

The Lord says, "GO AND CALL YOUR HUSBAND . . . AND COME BACK HERE" (4:16). Ah, here comes the truth. THE WOMAN ANSWERED, "I HAVE NO HUSBAND." HE SAID TO HER, "YOU ARE RIGHT TO SAY, 'I HAVE NO HUSBAND' (4:17); FOR ALTHOUGH YOU HAVE HAD FIVE, THE ONE YOU HAVE NOW IS NOT YOUR HUSBAND. YOU SPOKE THE TRUTH THERE" (4:18). You know, I can see Jesus with a little smile sometimes, and I think He had one here. I just don't believe that He didn't smile from time to time—there is no way that He could live with Peter and not laugh.

"I SEE YOU ARE A PROPHET, SIR[,]" SAID THE WOMAN (4:19). "OUR FATHERS WORSHIPPED ON THIS MOUNTAIN . . ." (4:20). What has that to do with anything? The God-Man has read her soul, and what has she done? Changed the subject! What happens to you when something comes along that draws out the worst in you? You blame everybody, you blame the economy, circumstances, you just get it away from yourself. Then you don't have to carry the cross—you don't have to imitate the

Passion, you just blame it on everybody else and go your way. So this woman changes the subject. She says, "OUR FATHERS WORSHIPPED ON THIS MOUNTAIN, WHILE YOU SAY THAT JERUSALEM IS THE PLACE WHERE ONE OUGHT TO WORSHIP" (4:20). But He didn't say that. He said, "You have five husbands and one is not your own!" She is the great hedger, but Jesus goes along with her.

JESUS SAID: "BELIEVE ME, WOMAN, THE HOUR IS COMING WHEN YOU WILL WORSHIP THE FATHER NEITHER ON THIS MOUNTAIN NOR IN JERUSALEM (4:21). YOU WORSHIP WHAT YOU DO NOT KNOW; WE WORSHIP WHAT WE DO KNOW; FOR SALVATION COMES FROM THE JEWS (4:22). BUT THE HOUR WILL COME—IN FACT IT IS HERE ALREADY—WHEN TRUE WORSHIPPERS WILL WORSHIP THE FATHER IN SPIRIT AND TRUTH: THAT IS THE KIND OF WORSHIPPER THE FATHER WANTS (4:23). GOD IS SPIRIT, AND THOSE WHO WORSHIP MUST WORSHIP IN SPIRIT AND TRUTH" (4:24). But she still will not admit what she is.

THE WOMAN SAID TO HIM, "I KNOW THAT MESSIAH—THAT IS, CHRIST—IS COMING; AND WHEN HE COMES HE WILL TELL US EVERYTHING" (4:25). Do you see what she is doing? She will not admit what is wrong with her. She is negating the necessity of humility, of pain, of truth. She can't take looking at herself.

Jesus says: "I WHO AM SPEAKING TO YOU . . . I AM HE" (4:26). Imagine the healing that must have gone on in that woman's soul. The one Messiah that the prophets spoke of and promised is speaking to a sinner and asking for love. He still asks us for love; yours and mine. He is trying to shape and mold you through the battles all about us, internal and external. We need Jesus and He says to you and me, "I am He."

AT THIS POINT HIS DISCIPLES RETURNED, AND WERE SURPRISED TO FIND HIM SPEAKING TO A WOMAN, THOUGH NONE OF THEM ASKED, "WHAT DO YOU WANT FROM HER?" OR, "WHY ARE

YOU TALKING TO HER?" (4:27). (They were too chicken to ask about it.)

Look what happens to this woman. THE WOMAN PUT DOWN HER WATER JAR AND HURRIED BACK TO THE TOWN TO TELL THE PEOPLE (4:28), "COME AND SEE A MAN WHO HAS TOLD ME EVERY-THING I EVER DID; I WONDER IF HE IS THE CHRIST?" (4:29). She began to see clearly all the things in her life that were opposed to Christ. She compared herself not to the other women in the village, but to Jesus. The light of Jesus made her understand who and what she was, and there was no fear in admitting it. The people started coming out of the town and started walking toward Him.

Meanwhile, the apostles came back and they WERE URG-ING HIM, "RABBI, DO HAVE SOMETHING TO EAT" (4:32); BUT HE SAID, "I HAVE FOOD TO EAT THAT YOU DO NOT KNOW ABOUT" (4:32). Then He went on to tell them the very thing I want you to remember this week: JESUS SAID: "MY FOOD IS TO DO THE WILL OF THE ONE WHO SENT ME, AND TO COMPLETE HIS WORK" (4:34).

Our food is to do God's will each day, each moment. To look at ourselves with humility and say, "There is nothing in me that is of any value. I am a sinner. I have to struggle and fight to be good, and every morning I begin again and every evening I have to ask forgiveness for all the failings of my day." You never go anywhere without Him. He suffers when you suf-fer. He delights when you delight. I never see a crowd that my heart does not go out to tell them how much He loves us. I never look at an adulterer or a blasphemer when I don't think, "I wish they knew the love of Jesus." Be childlike with God. Have compassion for His pain, for your brother and yourself. Have the love of the Spirit in your heart because God lives in you and loves you, and you must give that love to others.

Walking on Water

❖

Matthew 14:22–33

J esus made the disciples get into the boat and go on
ahead to the other side while he would send the
crowds away (14:22). After sending the crowds away he
went up into the hills by himself to pray. When evening
came, he was there alone (14:23), while the boat, by now
far out on the lake, was battling with a heavy sea, for
there was a head-wind (14:24).

Now, this is the beginning of the night. Jesus prays and
He's watching. He's watching you and me in this age. Nothing
is hidden from Him. Everything is now. He sees us. Even at
that time, He saw us here examining His Word. He also saw
the apostles and they were battling.

He watched them until the fourth watch—anywhere from
three to six a.m. He's just sitting there watching them. With
Jesus there is always a test: there is a pain, an ache, there
is something you don't like to do, or something you find very
hard. And all the while He just watches. It's a great help for
us to understand that we should never deliberately disappoint
Him by doing something goofy or saying no outright, because
He's watching you, all your life.

Now, In the fourth watch of the night he went to-
wards them, walking on the lake (14:25), and when the
disciples saw him walking on the lake they were terrified (14:26). Now you would think they would say, "Wow, look
at that," or, "He must be the Lord, who else could walk on

water?" But they were terrified. His water walk didn't seem to have the result He intended.

Jesus was trying to prove that He was the Son of God. And instead they were frightened out of their minds. What did they say? "Oh, hi-ya, Jesus, thank you for coming. Boy, you're wonderful. We didn't know You could walk on water." Nope. They said: "It is a ghost" (14:26). Ha-ha. Oh, dear Jesus, a ghost! What kind of ghost would walk on water? And why would a ghost be going toward them?

See, they missed the whole point of the miracle. I wonder, very often, how many of those points I've missed in my own life. God loves you to go out on a limb and even though it gets shaky—He loves you to do that so that He can perform a miracle. Would God have walked on the water had there not been a storm? Scripture tells us that the Lord watched their reaction and then when they were scared out of their wits and no longer trusted in themselves and their own capability to steer the ship—He came. Many times that's when He comes to us as well.

At once Jesus called out to them, saying, "Courage! It is I! Do not be afraid" (14:27). You know, if we realized that Our Dear Lord watches us, every one of us individually, as He watched those apostles in that boat, every moment, whether you're awake or asleep, you would love Him and prefer Him to all things. He watches you, not as a Judge, but as One who loves us so much. We don't catch it. We're terrified. We're busy with so many things. And what does He say to us? "Courage! It's I. Don't be afraid." We worry about the past, we worry about the future, and we worry about the present. Instead we should be saying, "He's watching me. He sees me and He loves me."

It was Peter who answered—now here comes the great tester. They're looking at Him, He's walking on the water, and what does Peter say? "Well, if it is You, let me test You." Aren't we strange people? Many of us are so proud we do the same thing. It's a wonder the Lord doesn't just wipe us off the face of the earth. We test God, just as Peter does here. "LORD," HE SAID, "IF IT IS YOU, TELL ME TO COME TO YOU ACROSS THE WATER" (14:28).

And the Lord said, "Come." THEN PETER GOT OUT OF THE BOAT (14:29)—listen to what he's doing: he gets out of the boat and he starts walking across the water. You know, I sometimes wonder how many miracles we begin and then ruin by our own inaction or fear. Do you ever wonder that?

I always pray, "Lord, don't let me chicken out if You have something hard for me to do." The Lord said, "Come," BUT AS SOON AS [PETER] FELT THE FORCE OF THE WIND, HE TOOK FRIGHT AND BEGAN TO SINK (14:30). Peter is on the water and he is walking on it. His feet are wet, but he's walking on the water. And all of a sudden, a big wind comes and he loses his faith. He was distracted from the gaze of Jesus. It was the wind that got him—the world, his knowledge of the world. And so he sank. He started going down.

What does he say now? "LORD! SAVE ME!" (14:30). At least he was smart enough to know he needed the Lord—as we need Him today. We need to say when we're weak, when we're lost, when we're disappointed, when we're just worn out, "Lord, save me." You think, "Well, I'll never walk on water." Oh, I think we do that often, and we sink because we feel the power of the world, the power of people, the power of everybody and everything. . . . That's why nothing is changing in the world, because nobody has the courage of faith. Nobody.

And JESUS PUT OUT HIS HAND AT ONCE AND HELD HIM. "MAN OF LITTLE FAITH," HE SAID[,] "WHY DID YOU DOUBT?" (14:31). Couldn't Our Lord say that now about us? Now you say, "Wait a minute. Peter was told to walk on the water and he did it. He felt the wind, and the wind was pretty hard. It can knock you over. It destroys buildings. Peter was afraid, so he called out." All that is pretty logical, very logical. But what does the Lord answer to something that looks that logical and that reasonable and that right? "MAN OF LITTLE FAITH, . . . WHY DID YOU DOUBT?" (14:31). See, God doesn't think like you. He doesn't want your excuses. He nailed it.

There was absolutely no human excuse for Jesus: you have no faith and why do you doubt? AND AS THEY GOT INTO THE BOAT THE WIND DROPPED (14:32). THE MEN IN THE BOAT BOWED DOWN BEFORE HIM AND SAID—what He wanted to hear— "TRULY, YOU ARE THE SON OF GOD" (14:33). It took failure, fear, and humiliation to give them light. And that's true with us too. Sometimes it takes all of that to give us light.

HALOS

The mistake we make when we read the Scriptures is we put a halo on these men before it was there. We look at every man in the Gospel from afar with great yearning in our heart to be holy and we think, "Oh that's not for me." But God is looking for people willing to accept themselves where they are, and strive for holiness. There is no perfection in this world. But there is holiness.

The Greatest?

❖

Mark 9:33–35

Just imagine twelve unknown, dummy fishermen. The only intellectual was Judas. He was a Judean and the only Judean in the crowd. Shrewd man—that shrewdness did him in. The rest of them weren't too bright. Suffering wasn't even a consideration for them, especially when they were with the Master. When Jesus would speak before the crowds the apostles were strutting around him, looking out at the crowds, thinking: "Don't you wish you were up here?" They acted very smart.

When Our Lord explained the parables they stood there as if they understood. Then at night they would say, "Master, explain the parable to us. What did you mean?" They were too proud to ask in front of the crowd. They lacked simplicity; they were proud, ambitious.

Now, would you have chosen people to be teachers who didn't understand simple things? You wouldn't, but the Lord did, to show His power—the power to overcome their weakness. He does the same with us, if we let Him. The apostles were faulty men.

When the apostles were fussing over which one of them would be the greatest, the Lord very gently looked at them, and He said, "WHAT WERE YOU ARGUING ABOUT ON THE ROAD?"(9:33). They hemmed and hawed as men often do. I can see the gleam in the Lord's eye. I imagine James and John must have been the worst. They were called Sons of Thunder because their father had a hot temper and so did they. I'll bet James and John said, "Jesus prefers us because when He went to Jurius's daughter's house, you know who He took with Him." The other apostles were probably infuriated with these guys. Our Lord looks at them and says, "IF ANYONE WANTS TO BE FIRST, HE MUST MAKE HIMSELF LAST OF ALL AND SERVANT OF ALL" (9:35). This was before Pentecost. After Pentecost there was such a change in these men. They would learn what being a "SERVANT OF ALL" really meant. That's the amazing thing about the Holy Spirit: He transforms—today and always.

THE APOSTLES DIDN'T GET IT EITHER

If you ever feel discouraged that you don't understand the Scriptures and you say, "Oh if I could have just sat there and listened to the Lord and looked at Him, and watched Him . . ." Well, the apostles were there and they apparently never caught on. They were always in another world.

So sometimes you ought to pray to one of the apostles and say, "Look, you know how it is when you don't understand what the Lord is doing or saying in your life, pray for me, so that I will understand."

Calming the Storm

❖

Mark 4:35–41

Mark gives us so many little details. When Jesus was asleep in the boat with the apostles, Mark tells us He had His head on a cushion. Sound asleep. Storms, I understand in that region of the world, come up very quickly. They're rough storms. They're not like little breezes. They're real rough windstorms.

WITH THE COMING OF EVENING THAT SAME DAY, HE SAID TO THEM, "LET US CROSS OVER TO THE OTHER SIDE" (4:35). AND LEAVING THE CROWD BEHIND THEY TOOK HIM, JUST AS HE WAS, IN THE BOAT (4:36). That's an interesting phrase. I wonder what JUST AS HE WAS means? Did they have one of those "come as you are" parties? I never did figure that out.

THEN IT BEGAN TO BLOW A GALE (4:37). This isn't an ordinary windstorm, it's a gale. AND THE WAVES WERE BREAKING INTO THE BOAT SO THAT IT WAS ALMOST SWAMPED (4:37). The waves are now going into the boat, over the boat, and almost sinking the boat. THEY WOKE HIM—but, it says—HE WAS IN THE STERN, HIS HEAD ON A CUSHION, ASLEEP (4:38). THEY WOKE HIM AND SAID TO HIM, "MASTER, DO YOU NOT CARE? WE'RE GOING DOWN!" Boy. AND HE WOKE UP AND REBUKED THE WIND AND SAID TO THE SEA, "QUIET NOW! BE CALM!" AND THE WIND DROPPED (4:39). Boom. No wind.

It's amazing to me how the Lord took care of the storm first—but it always makes me think: God does answer my prayers, but I sometimes wonder if He is disappointed in me

when He answers them. This is a sure case of God answering the apostles' prayers, but He was also rather disappointed in them. Because after He rebuked the wind and said, "QUIET NOW. BE CALM!" and the wind dropped, and all of that, He looked at them and said, "WHY ARE YOU SO FRIGHTENED. HOW IS IT THAT YOU HAVE NO FAITH?" (4:40). He didn't say, "How is it you have little faith?" It's "How is it you have NO faith?"

I want you to really study that for a minute. You're in a boat, the waters are coming over, they're filling the boat. You're getting buckets, and you're trying to get the water out. But as fast as you get one bucket out, twenty-five more come in. The boat is getting heavy, it's beginning to sink, and the One who created the whole thing is lying in the stern of the boat fast asleep. What's your reaction? Had the apostles just kept bucketing it out, I think they would have made it. That's what He was trying to tell them when He said, "Why are you frightened?" In other words, when you're faced with a situation and you're fighting it, keep on fighting! "HOW IS IT THAT YOU HAVE NO FAITH?"

They should have said something else besides, "Master, we're drowning. Don't you care?" To say that God doesn't care is to lack faith—totally—and that's why they were frightened. The apostles lost it when they thought He didn't care about them. They said: "MASTER, DO YOU NOT CARE? WE'RE GOING DOWN!" And the Lord was rebuking this ridiculous idea.

As I said before, I think if they would have just kept bucketing and working hard to get the water out, even though it may have been a couple of coffee cans, they would have been fine. Jesus never sleeps, even when you think otherwise.

And look at what the apostles say afterward. They're all excited over the miracle. THEY WERE FILLED WITH AWE AND SAID TO ONE ANOTHER, "WHO CAN THIS BE? EVEN THE WIND AND THE

SEA OBEY HIM" (4:41). So obviously at this point they were not ready to accept Him as Lord—they were just learning about Him. But learning or not, He upbraided them for not having any faith.

It's an interesting paragraph because it contains so much of our human nature. According to your personalities, you can see what your reaction would be—each one of you. What would you have done in the same situation? What do you do when the storms are sinking your boat? When you get so frightened during life's storms, threatened, and unhappy, do you really believe that Jesus is the Son of God? Is there a purpose in His allowing the storm in your life?

A Sinner Repents (A Meditation)

❖

Luke 7:36–50

These "Journeys into Scripture" are really a chance to practice mental prayer. We use our mind, the faculties of our soul, our memory, our imagination, our will, and our understanding during these "Journeys."

We're going to Jerusalem, and we go to the house of one Simon the Pharisee. We see the Master and His twelve apostles coming into the room. There's a large table there, a very long one, and some semicircular tables. There are couches jutting out and we realize they are reclining at table.

I look at Simon the Pharisee; he's a tall man with a beard. He has a habit of stroking his beard especially when he's in deep thought. His eyes are narrow. He's a nervous man. And as Christ walks in, he scans Him from head to toe. I look at

Christ and I know that He knows He was not invited out of love; He was invited out of hatred. They want to see who this Jesus is, to test Him, to ridicule Him, to make Him look a fool. Christ goes and He takes His place at table. Christ is tall and handsome, and though He looks majestic and kingly, He is so humble and approachable.

I see the apostles and they look a little uneasy. They know why they were invited and they dislike these kinds of dinners. They would much rather be out with the Master under a tree, alone. But the Master is very serene and He looks around, and unlike the apostles, He is in full possession of His peace. I think to myself, "In this circumstance, what would I do? Would I be so conscious of what the men who invited me were thinking and why they invited me?" I look at Christ and He sees this as an opportunity to show love for His Father. His Father permits it, and He accepts it.

Finally the meal begins and the servants are passing the food and all of a sudden there is a silence in the room. A great hush. Through the door comes a woman, a very beautiful woman with long black hair, striking. Simon looks at her and he leans over to his neighbor and he whispers in his ear.

There's Peter and he's looking at her with an odd expression on his face. It seems to say, "Oh no, I hope she's not going to do what I think she's going to do." She makes her way toward the Savior—she seems completely oblivious of everyone in the room, except Jesus. She goes to Him, kneels at the end of the couch where He's reclining, and she begins to cry. Her sobs fill the room. No one moves a muscle. As she cries, her tears fall on Our Lord's feet, so many of them that His feet are soon wet. She takes her long beautiful hair and she begins to dry them and she kisses them with great affection. I feel so sorry for her. I look at Simon the Pharisee. Simon is lost in thought. His eyes

narrow and he strokes his beard and says, "IF THIS MAN WERE A PROPHET HE WOULD KNOW WHO THIS WOMAN IS THAT IS TOUCHING HIM AND WHAT A BAD NAME SHE HAS" (7:39).

Jesus is looking at the woman with great love and compassion. He glances over to the Pharisee and says, "SIMON . . . YOU SEE THIS WOMAN?" (7:44). (And I think to myself, "Who hasn't!") He says, "Have you seen this woman, Simon? When I CAME INTO YOUR HOUSE, YOU POURED NO WATER OVER MY FEET" (7:44). I suddenly realize that Simon skipped the Lord. It was the custom in those days for the host to kneel down and wash the feet of those invited to dinner. They put oil on their beards and gave their guests a kiss. This custom was omitted for Christ deliberately.

Jesus said, "[THIS WOMAN] HAS POURED OUT HER TEARS OVER MY FEET AND WIPED THEM AWAY WITH HER HAIR (7:44). SIMON YOU GAVE ME NO KISS" (7:45). I think to myself, Can it be that God's Son missed the kiss of one like Simon? A proud, arrogant, egotistical man whose one design was to humiliate Him? Could He miss the kiss of one like this? Is that an example of God's infinite love for me? He yearned for the kiss of a traitor, from one who hated Him. But God loved that much.

Jesus said, "This woman, Simon, has not ceased to kiss my feet. And I say to thee, her many sins are forgiven her because she loved much." And I think, Is that all, Lord? Is that all we must do? She didn't even ask forgiveness, she just loved much. As I look at this scene I see the mercy of God making one person bitter and filling another with joy. "My Lord," I say, "I kneel with this sinner at Thy feet. You know what's in my heart. You know Lord that I try and I fail and I try and I fail and I love Thee with all my heart. With all my heart."

The Master looks down at me and He says, "Go in peace, daughter. Thy sins are forgiven thee. Have joy. For I love thee with an everlasting love (Jer 31:3). I have called thee by thy name, thou art mine" (Is 43:1). And so for a few moments, let each one of us kneel at the feet of Christ and tell Him what's on our hearts.

The Truth (And Your Own Business) Shall Set You Free

❖

John 8:31–32

To the Jews who believed in him Jesus said: "If you make my word your home you will indeed be my disciples (8:31), you will learn the truth and the truth will make you free" (8:32).

Be careful of worldly truth! I've told you that a thousand times. The world loves to say that the truth will make you free. The only truth that makes you free is the truth of Jesus. But there are many other truths that can make you proud, make you despair, make you hopeless, make you discouraged, make you morose, make you sad. You need the truth that will make you mind your own business.

Remember that little saying I put up there, Mind your own business. If you all got that one practical thing, setting aside anything spiritual, you would be holy today—by noon. By noon you would be holy if you would just mind your own business. You'd be surprised at how little business you actually have. You'd be shocked to find that your business is so tiny, and that you crowd your mind with everybody else's. It's no good for you spiritually or otherwise. You have very little business, honey.

Trusting Providence

❖

Matthew 6:25–33

There's a beautiful chapter here on trust in Saint Matthew's Gospel, it advises us never to worry about anything. See, this constant worry. Our Lord said one time, "CAN ANY ONE OF YOU, FOR ALL HIS WORRYING, ADD ONE SINGLE CUBIT TO HIS SPAN OF LIFE?" (6:27). See, you can't. Worrying is not an act of trust. Concern, even, is not an act of trust. Thinking you have to do something about this or that is not an act of trust. If we're asked to do anything, just do it! Trust means to trust the world to God, to trust the outcome of our works to God, to trust our day to God, to trust our families to God. It means: Drop it. Drop it. Do you understand? We can't drop things. We've just got to hold on to them. We Americans, for instance, are do-it-yourselfers; and that is an absolute tragedy because you cannot advance in holiness without trust.

Look at what the Lord says in Matthew:

"THAT IS WHY I AM TELLING YOU NOT TO WORRY ABOUT YOUR LIFE AND WHAT YOU ARE TO EAT, NOR ABOUT YOUR BODY AND HOW YOU ARE TO CLOTHE IT. SURELY LIFE MEANS MORE THAN FOOD, AND THE BODY MORE THAN CLOTHING! (6:25) LOOK AT THE BIRDS IN THE SKY. THEY DO NOT SOW OR REAP OR GATHER INTO BARNS; YET YOUR HEAVENLY FATHER FEEDS THEM. ARE WE NOT WORTH MUCH MORE THAN THEY ARE? (6:26) CAN ANY OF YOU, FOR ALL HIS WORRYING, ADD ONE SINGLE CUBIT TO HIS SPAN OF LIFE? (6:27) AND WHY WORRY ABOUT CLOTHING? THINK OF THE FLOWERS GROWING IN THE FIELDS; THEY NEVER HAVE TO WORK

OR SPIN (6:38); YET I ASSURE YOU THAT NOT EVEN SOLOMON IN
ALL HIS REGALIA WAS ROBED LIKE ONE OF THESE (6:29). NOW
IF THAT IS HOW GOD CLOTHES THE GRASS IN THE FIELD WHICH
IS THERE TODAY AND THROWN INTO THE FURNACE TOMORROW,
WILL HE NOT MUCH MORE LOOK AFTER YOU, YOU MEN OF LITTLE
FAITH? (6:30) SO DO NOT WORRY; DO NOT SAY, 'WHAT ARE WE TO
EAT? WHAT ARE WE TO DRINK? HOW ARE WE TO BE CLOTHED?'
(6:31) IT IS THE PAGANS WHO SET THEIR HEARTS ON ALL THESE
THINGS. YOUR HEAVENLY FATHER KNOWS YOU NEED THEM ALL
(6:32). SET YOUR HEARTS ON HIS KINGDOM FIRST, AND ON HIS
RIGHTEOUSNESS, AND ALL THESE OTHER THINGS WILL BE GIVEN
YOU AS WELL" (6:33).

Now it is fine to pray, and after you pray, leave it alone.
That's trust. You trust that whatever you do sincerely in the
eyes of God, whatever the outcome, it will be good for you.
Trusting is to love someone enough that you trust whatever it
is they do. You're willing to stand by them if they fail. God will
stand by me if I fail. But constant worry, depression, anxiety,
frustration, thinking "Nothing's going to change"—that is a total, total lack of trust.

It's so bad because what does it do? It keeps your mind
and heart away from Jesus. And that's the whole thing. It's
one of the cleverest tools of the enemy, because he makes you
think you're doing right. He makes you think that you've got
to solve the problem, so you have no trust that God will solve
the whole thing in His time. That can have a paralyzing effect
on the soul.

If you don't have trust in your life, you have little love,
because trust comes from love. If you love someone deeply,
you trust them. You may not understand God's ways, but you
can trust that everything is going to be okay. That's what the
Blessed Mother did. Just look at what she said yes to. That

takes real trust. Work on trusting God, my friends, in little and big ways throughout the day. There's a beautiful book called *Abandonment to Divine Providence*—that whole book is one total act of trust. You can ask for things, but if you don't get them, keep your peace and drop it. That's trust.

Seeking God

❖

Luke 11:9–10

In the Gospel of Luke Our Lord said: "So I SAY TO YOU: ASK, AND IT WILL BE GIVEN TO YOU; SEARCH, AND YOU WILL FIND; KNOCK, AND THE DOOR WILL BE OPENED TO YOU" (11:9). And I think in here is the secret to all holiness. We need to ask, and we certainly don't have much trouble asking, do we? That is all we do. But knocking, searching, seeking, that's different. To seek someone is to look for them. The Lord promises if we look we will always find. So how do I seek the Lord: His invisible Reality, the very reason for my being, the cause of my existence? How do I reach out and say, "God, where are You and how close are You to me? How do I live with Thee?"

I think the best way to seek the Lord is to search for Him in the mundane duties of the present moment. Don't stare glumly at those egg-stained dishes that you have to scrape in the morning—see the duty of the present moment. Seek God in those dirty dishes, in that rug that you have to vacuum, in that budget that you have to balance. Seek God in the person who bugs you. Why? Because Our Dear Lord, in the Gospel of Saint John, said that if you are bearing fruit, the Father will prune you so that you may bear more fruit (Jn 15:1–8, 16).

Each one of us has a long way to go before we are perfect images of the Father. The Father loves you enough to put you in situations that you can't get away from. Are you supposed to crumble before them? Are you supposed to despair? No, in that very thing your Father, who seeks only your good and loves you with an infinite love, is pruning you. Our Father has sent this thing to make you more patient. He has sent someone to offend you so that in the act of forgiving you will "be merciful as your Father is merciful" (Lk 6:36). In the everyday, mundane things of this life, in the monotony of eating and sleeping and drinking and working—in all of this there is God, there is goodness. But you must *seek* it! If the person who tries your patience is the only thing on your mind, then you're going to be resentful and hateful. You have not sought God and you have not found God. The very thing that God permitted for your good is lost. You have not been pruned. You have become more callous and more impatient and more bitter and more unkind than ever. Seek Him in those moments, and you will find Him.

Receiving an Answer to Prayer
(A Meditation)

❖

Luke 11:9–13

In our "Journey into Scripture" today, we see the Master and the apostles and they are discussing prayer. I go closer to them and listen. The Master says, "ASK, AND IT WILL BE GIVEN TO YOU; SEARCH, AND YOU WILL FIND; KNOCK, AND THE DOOR WILL BE OPENED TO YOU (11:9). FOR THE ONE WHO ASKS ALWAYS

RECEIVES; AND THE ONE WHO SEARCHES ALWAYS FINDS, THE ONE
WHO KNOCKS WILL ALWAYS HAVE THE DOOR OPENED TO HIM"
(11:10).

I look at the Master and say, "I am in doubt. There are
many things that I have asked in your holy Name but not received. Yet You have said, 'He who asks *always* receives.' Will
you explain this to me?" The Master looks up at me and says,
"When you ask the Father in My Name, you must first ask
for everything that is for your good. And sometimes because
your sight is limited you ask for things that seem to receive
no answer, as if all of heaven is closed to your prayer. In your
finite mind you believe if you have this one thing, all else will
be well. But the Father's one desire is to have you as close to
Him in heaven, as possible. Sometimes He says no, but even
in that no you have received an answer to your prayer. Your
prayer should always be for the good of the kingdom and for
your love.

"As a child you must have unbounded confidence in God's
wisdom and know that when you pray for your good and for
the good of the kingdom on earth—you always receive an answer."

I understand that now. I used to think that the answer had
to be the one that I wanted. But perhaps God says no to determine how much I love Him—to bring out from the depths
of my soul a love and a confidence that is so great that it will
increase my glory in heaven and give courage to my neighbor.
In adversity and tribulation we prove that we are disciples by
holding firm.

The Master goes on and says: "When you search you always find." I ask Him, "What does it mean to seek Thee? You
are invisible and I cannot touch You. When I look, I do not
see You." And He says, "To seek Me is to look for Me as you

would look for a friend or a loved one. To seek Me out in the daily duties of your life, to seek Me in joy and sorrow, honor and dishonor, and in everything that life gives you moment to moment—to find good and to find God; to seek Him in everything. For those who love God all things tend to good." I now realize that I have not sought God in this way. In adversity and pain and sorrow it is so hard to find Him, perhaps because I have not sought Him in these things. Then I remember that Jesus sought the Father in every occurrence in His life—in the ingratitude of the healed lepers who never said thank you, in the malice and the jealousy of those who should have loved Him.

Then the Master goes on, "WHAT FATHER AMONG YOU WOULD HAND HIS SON A STONE WHEN HE ASKED FOR BREAD? OR HAND HIM A SNAKE INSTEAD OF A FISH? (11:11). . . . IF YOU WHO ARE EVIL, KNOW HOW TO GIVE YOUR CHILDREN WHAT IS GOOD, HOW MUCH MORE WILL THE HEAVENLY FATHER GIVE THE HOLY SPIRIT TO THOSE WHO ASK HIM!" (11:13).

I suddenly realize that my concept of what is good for me and God's understanding and wisdom of what is good for me are different. I have not been a child who has trusted the Father. I have considered my wisdom superior to His, as if I know what is best for me. But I do not see tomorrow the way He sees tomorrow. I must have confidence in His wisdom and then every time I ask I shall receive, and every time I seek I shall find, and every time I knock He will come and rest in me.

Only the Violent Carry It Away

❖

Matthew 11:12

You will know in greater depth as you see the Lord's Passion and the humiliations He suffered day after day by people who didn't believe, by His own apostles—what violence He did to His purity as God. And yet He did all that violence. "THE KINGDOM OF HEAVEN HAS BEEN SUBJECTED TO VIOLENCE AND THE VIOLENT ARE TAKING IT BY STORM" (11:12). In another translation it reads ". . . only the violent carry it away." What does that mean?

It doesn't mean violence. It means I have to crush my own weaknesses to be like Jesus. I have to die to myself and that sometimes takes violence. Have you ever been on the verge of losing your temper and tried to hold it? It takes violence to do that. It's a violent thing sometimes to be meek when you want to sock somebody in the chops. It's a violent thing I do to my nature when I feel so bad and I don't want anybody around me and I'm sweet and I talk to somebody and I'm loving to them. It takes violence. When I give in to myself, I'm not being violent; I'm being careless with my own soul.

Love and Duty

❖

Luke 17:7–10

WHICH OF YOU, WITH A SERVANT PLOUGHING OR MINDING SHEEP, WOULD SAY TO HIM WHEN HE RETURNED FROM THE FIELDS, 'COME AND HAVE YOUR MEAL IMMEDIATELY'? (18:7) WOULD HE NOT BE MORE LIKELY TO SAY, 'GET MY SUPPER LAID; MAKE YOURSELF TIDY AND WAIT ON ME WHILE I EAT AND DRINK. YOU CAN EAT AND DRINK YOURSELF AFTERWARDS'? (17:8) MUST HE BE GRATEFUL TO THE SERVANT FOR DOING WHAT HE WAS TOLD? (17:9) SO WITH YOU: WHEN YOU HAVE DONE ALL YOU HAVE BEEN TOLD TO DO, SAY, 'WE ARE MERELY SERVANTS: WE HAVE DONE NO MORE THAN OUR DUTY'" (17:10).

The Lord is teaching us a very strong, hard lesson here. A thank-you is a very important thing because it shows people courtesy, that you appreciate what they're doing. But when you're talking about accomplishing a duty for God, He is not obliged to say thank you or to reward you. We can't go to heaven with any concept of an award or reward for all the exterior things we did. Those were inspirations we merely followed because it's our duty to follow the will of God. The only thing I will have when I die is the amount of love I have for God at that moment.

The Woman Caught in Adultery

❖

John 8:2–12

A T DAYBREAK HE APPEARED IN THE TEMPLE AGAIN; AND AS
ALL THE PEOPLE CAME TO HIM, HE SAT DOWN AND BEGAN
TO TEACH THEM (8:2). THE SCRIBES AND PHARISEES BROUGHT A
WOMAN ALONG WHO HAD BEEN CAUGHT COMMITTING ADULTERY
(8:3). I suppose the thing that gripes me the most is that the
guy, who must have also been caught committing adultery, got
off scot-free. But they made the woman stand in full view of
everybody.

THEY SAID TO JESUS, "MASTER, THIS WOMAN WAS CAUGHT
IN THE VERY ACT OF COMMITTING ADULTERY (8:4), AND MOSES
HAS ORDERED US IN THE LAW TO CONDEMN WOMEN LIKE THIS
TO DEATH BY STONING. WHAT HAVE YOU TO SAY?" (8:5). That was
the trick of tricks really. Looks like they were setting the Lord
up. (I know it doesn't say that here.) It says, THEY ASKED HIM
THIS AS A TEST, LOOKING FOR SOMETHING TO USE AGAINST HIM
(8:6).

The Lord was so clever. He bent down and started writing
on the ground with His finger. AS THEY PERSISTED WITH THEIR
QUESTION (8:7)—you get the impression that He may have
been doodling in the sand. Just took His time. He may have
written the accused woman's name in the dirt. And they persisted with the question, probably repeating it again: "Master,
this woman was caught in adultery. The Law says we should
stone her. What do You say?" It's like: "Yoo hoo, are you listening?" Then HE LOOKED UP AND SAID, "IF THERE IS ONE OF YOU

WHO HAS NOT SINNED, LET HIM BE THE FIRST TO THROW A STONE AT HER" (8:7).

Notice that He didn't say the Law should not be observed. He just said, "If all of you have not sinned (and maybe with her), then you can go ahead and punish her." She may have had a few little rendezvous with some of them. Who knows?

THEN HE BENT DOWN AND WROTE ON THE GROUND AGAIN (8:8). I imagine He was writing names, like Joseph, Simon—their names. This next bit makes you think that's exactly what He did: WHEN THEY HEARD THIS THEY WENT AWAY ONE BY ONE, BEGINNING WITH THE ELDEST, UNTIL JESUS WAS LEFT ALONE WITH THE WOMAN, WHO REMAINED STANDING THERE (8:9). She just stood there.

HE LOOKED UP AND SAID, "WOMAN, WHERE ARE THEY? HAS NO ONE CONDEMNED YOU?" (8:10). "NO ONE, SIR[,]" SHE REPLIED. "NEITHER DO I CONDEMN YOU," SAID JESUS[,] "GO AWAY, AND DON'T SIN ANY MORE" (8:11). What a phenomenal gift.

If we ever get discouraged over our faults and weaknesses and imperfections, if we ever even begin to get discombobulated because we have this fault or that fault, we should think on this moment in Jesus's life. Adultery's a pretty bad thing. But the Lord looked up and He said, "Has no one condemned you?" She said no. He said, "Well neither will I. Go and sin no more." He's very merciful and a wonderful teacher.

He forgives her but then adds that little line we often forget: "Don't do it anymore." This is the essence of confession. Any big sin we have made a definite decision to commit, must not be repeated after absolution. Most of the things we're guilty of are little things, spur of the moment things, things that arise from our temperaments. When our temperament riles up very quickly, pride and sensitivity and all of that stuff creep in, and we fall more frequently.

WHEN JESUS SPOKE TO THE PEOPLE AGAIN, HE SAID: "I AM THE LIGHT OF THE WORLD; ANYONE WHO FOLLOWS ME WILL NOT BE WALKING IN THE DARK; HE WILL HAVE THE LIGHT OF LIFE" (8:12). I think we must look upon Jesus as our one love. Look upon Jesus as our only love, and look upon our neighbors as those whom we love because we're so in love with Jesus. When we're with Jesus, when we're in His Presence, when we're in prayer, we are in light. Anything else that occupies our mind is darkness.

He said, "I AM THE LIGHT OF THE WORLD; ANYONE WHO FOLLOWS ME"—that's an important thing: anyone who follows Him—"WILL NOT BE WALKING IN THE DARKNESS; HE WILL HAVE THE LIGHT OF LIFE" (8:12). You see, you can't give people light if you're in darkness. The only way to give light is to be *in* the light. I think it's an important passage for us to understand that if we really love Jesus, we need to live in that light. Live in the light of Jesus and everything else falls away: things, time, people, events, work—it all falls away. What is left is only the light, and that's Jesus.

Do Not Let Your Hearts
Be Troubled

❖

John 14:1–2

DO NOT LET YOUR HEARTS BE TROUBLED. TRUST IN GOD STILL, AND TRUST IN ME (14:1). THERE ARE MANY ROOMS IN MY FATHER'S HOUSE; IF THERE WERE NOT, I SHOULD HAVE TOLD YOU. I AM GOING NOW TO PREPARE A PLACE FOR YOU" (14:2). "DO NOT LET YOUR HEARTS BE TROUBLED." This word is so important. Contrary to all the things that go wrong in our lives, the things that don't come up to par, the things I expected that failed to materialize—in spite of all that, or perhaps because of it, we must trust in the Lord, trust in God. The reason we allow our hearts to be troubled is that we don't trust. Why else would you be troubled? There's no reason to be troubled if you trust the Lord.

Jesus goes on to give us a reason for not allowing our hearts to be troubled. He says, "THERE ARE MANY ROOMS IN MY FATHER'S HOUSE." We must realize that we have something coming that's much greater than what I'm troubled about having or not having, or what I would like or not like, or whether things go my way or not. Our hearts are always troubled, my friends, always troubled when we don't get what we want or expect. Our Lord is saying, "Look to the future."

The Father has many, many rooms in His house, and He's going to prepare a place for me. Think about that. God is preparing that place through all of your joys, sorrows, health, sickness—everything in your life is of value to God, and He uses everything. He never wastes a thing, not even your faults and weaknesses. He makes you want to repent, and even though you rebel against the present moment, He said, "I AM GOING NOW TO PREPARE A PLACE FOR YOU." Shouldn't that take the place of anything you're disappointed in? I have been chosen by God, and He is, at this moment, preparing a place for me. What a reassurance that is.

The Grace of the Word

When we talk about the Word of God, we are talking about Jesus. The Word of the Father is Jesus.

The Word of God is something very awesome and precious. Any book you read can be beautiful and inspiring, it can be searing—meaning it can really convict you—but in no way is it like the Word, because the Word of God pierces the heart, and when it enters the soul it brings with it grace. That is not true of any other book.

If you read this one sentence that I just opened up to— "Do not let your hearts be troubled"—even *reading* the Word brings grace to your heart.

In the Eastern Church they kneel, they genuflect before the Word. And I think we need to renew our love for the Word and recognize that the Word brings grace.

Read your books of the world, but absorb the Word, without which we cannot grow in His image. If I don't know Him, I can't grow in Him. What makes me like Him the most is taking this Word and placing it in my heart and soul, and that is what will make you, and your life, beautiful.

Shake the Dust

❖

Luke 10:5–10, 12

WHATEVER HOUSE YOU GO INTO, LET YOUR FIRST WORDS BE, 'PEACE TO THIS HOUSE!' (10:5). AND IF A MAN OF PEACE LIVES THERE, YOUR PEACE WILL GO AND REST ON HIM; IF NOT, IT WILL COME BACK TO YOU" (10:6). Our problem is we lose our peace if we're not accepted the way we want to be accepted. We're not able to let people go and move on. You know? Our Lord is very clear: You offered peace, they didn't take your peace, let it go.

"STAY IN THE SAME HOUSE, TAKING WHAT FOOD AND DRINK THEY HAVE TO OFFER, FOR THE LABOURER DESERVES HIS WAGES; DO NOT MOVE FROM HOUSE TO HOUSE (10:7). WHENEVER YOU GO INTO A TOWN WHERE THEY MAKE YOU WELCOME, EAT WHAT IS SET BEFORE YOU" (10:8). (So don't be a fussbudget.) "CURE THOSE IN IT WHO ARE SICK, AND SAY, 'THE KINGDOM OF GOD IS VERY NEAR TO YOU' (10:0). BUT WHENEVER YOU ENTER A TOWN AND THEY DO NOT MAKE YOU WELCOME, GO OUT INTO ITS STREETS AND SAY (10:10), 'WE WIPE OFF THE VERY DUST OF YOUR TOWN THAT CLINGS TO OUR FEET, AND LEAVE IT WITH YOU'" (10:11). Our Lord was not interested in the hygiene of your tootsies. He is saying if you're trying to talk to someone and they won't listen to you, don't bring that heartache along with you the rest of the day. Shake it off! If you're not accepted, if what you say is not accepted, whether they like you or they don't—don't permit that dust (He calls it dust), don't permit that incident, that occasion, that person to reside in your house for the rest of the day, the rest of the month, the rest of the year.

If we understood that one principle we'd be saints by tomorrow morning at nine-thirty. Because it isn't the present moment that gripes you, it's what happened two days ago that lingers in your mind and heart. You don't shake it. It goes around like a three-act play, and then it's a four-act play, and then it's a five-act play, and the first thing you know, you've created a drama over nothing. And the Lord said, "Shake it! Wipe off the very dust of it!"

Our Lord is teaching us that if you offer peace and people don't accept it, don't let it bother you. Keep your peace, and shake their dust from your feet.

The Lord pronounces a warning here: "I TELL YOU, ON THAT DAY IT WILL NOT GO AS HARD WITH SODOM AS WITH THAT TOWN" (10:12). That's pretty heavy stuff. The apostle who came there to preach the Gospel wasn't accepted—and there is a price to pay for that rejection.

I think that's a good lesson for us in our daily life when we think we ought to be affecting somebody and we're not. We ought to just shake the dust from our feet! We just have to let it go, and leave it to God. We would like to think we're the ones who are going to convert everybody, but others will follow, other events will follow, other circumstances will follow, and God will take care of them there. That's where prayer is so important. If I pray much, I may not see the fruit of my prayer, I may not see it in this life, but prayer is powerful—and because it's powerful, it never dies.

The Parable of the Two Sons
(A Meditation)
❖

Matthew 21:28–31

During our spiritual journey, we see the Master speaking to a crowd of people. He has been asked by some of the Pharisees by what authority He teaches and acts as He does. He looks out at the crowd and says, "WHAT IS YOUR OPINION? A MAN HAD TWO SONS. HE WENT AND SAID TO THE FIRST, 'MY BOY, YOU GO AND WORK IN THE VINEYARD TODAY' (21:28). HE ANSWERED, 'I WILL NOT GO,' BUT AFTERWARDS THOUGHT BETTER OF IT AND WENT (21:29). THE MAN THEN WENT AND SAID THE SAME THING TO THE SECOND WHO ANSWERED, 'CERTAINLY, SIR,' BUT DID NOT GO" (21:30).

The Lord looks out at the crowd and asks: "WHICH OF THE TWO DID THE FATHER'S WILL?" "THE FIRST," THEY SAID (21:31).

I look at the Master and joy wells up in my heart because I see myself in the first son. How many times has the Lord asked me to do things, some easy and some hard? I have said no, and I have rebelled and then thought it over, and went out and did it. If only I had gone out and done the Lord's will the first time with joy. If only I had not gotten angry and rebelled. And I look at the Master and He looks at me and says, "Fear not. It is the accomplishment of His will that shows love, not how you do it. Sometimes it is difficult and poor human nature rebels, but love conquers all." Then I realize that love demands sacrifice. I went out and did the Father's will even when it was hard.

And He was pleased. If I continue this, I will soon adopt a habit of doing the Father's will and more easily see the Father's love, not just a command. Sometimes that love requires the sacrifice of something in this world, but the Father will make it up to you.

I make a vow never to hesitate before a request of the Lord, but to always say yes and to fulfill it with great haste.

I Am the Vine,
You Are the Branches

❖

John 15:5–6

I AM THE VINE, YOU ARE THE BRANCHES. WHOEVER REMAINS IN ME, WITH ME IN HIM, BEARS FRUIT IN PLENTY; FOR CUT OFF FROM ME YOU CAN DO NOTHING (15:5). ANYONE WHO DOES NOT REMAIN IN ME IS LIKE A BRANCH THAT HAS BEEN THROWN AWAY—HE WITHERS; THESE BRANCHES ARE COLLECTED AND THROWN ON THE FIRE, AND THEY ARE BURNT" (15:6).

What's so marvelous about Jesus is His awesome humility. He calls Himself the vine, which means that unless we're *in* Jesus we become a kind of wild plant. Then the enemy comes and just pushes you back and forth in your heart, your mind, your soul and everything spirals out of control. Without the vine—the root—the branches wither. But the Lord said that His Father is the vinedresser and prunes the branches. Some say, "I don't want to be pruned. I'm strong and I want to go my own way." Well, that "branch" will grow. But the older it gets and the faster it grows, the less value it will have. It is of no use. It begins to wither—it overgrows itself. It self-destructs in time. Unruly vines bear thistles; they don't bear fruit. Sometimes that's the deception in our lives. We think we are growing, we're doing this, we're doing that, but if we don't bear fruit and if we don't allow the Lord to prune us, it may all be for naught.

The fruit of our life is found in a deep union with Jesus. We have to never forget our real vocation. Our real vocation is not the things the Lord asks us to do but to be attentive to the will of God as it manifests itself in the present moment.

God's will is frustrated many, many times, usually when we're not clinging to the Lord. We just don't cling to the Lord in our hearts, minds, and souls. Look at the Gospel: You have Matthew who was not one that Peter wanted around at all. I mean, we're talking about a tax collector who was a thief, a rabble-rouser; he was a traitor who left the synagogue. He left his faith and became a tax collector, and he collected from his own people! Well, here comes Jesus and He says, "Follow me" (Mt 9:9). I bet you some of those apostles, especially Simon the Zealot, must have had a fit. You see, God's ways are not our ways, and He picked a sinner to bear fruit on His vine. But Matthew, and Magdalene, and Thomas (who was a doubter), and Peter (who was a hothead), and John, and all of them, with all their faults and weaknesses, clung to Jesus. And when they clung to Jesus, they bore fruit. So I think in our own lives we need to examine ourselves once in a while and say, "Am I bearing fruit?" If I'm not, it's only because I'm not clinging to Jesus.

Let's ask the Lord, as the Spirit, to make us fruitful branches on His vine, on His Son's vine. Let us ask the Spirit to increase within us a great thirst for God, a great thirst for holiness. Let us ask Him to make us so holy, and so in love with our Bridegroom, that it will be a foretaste of heaven. Whether we have the pains of the martyrs or the dryness of the great mystics; whether we have health, sickness, or death—may we still love Jesus all the days of our lives.

The Kingdom

❖

Matthew 16:28; 3:2

The Lord says, "I TELL YOU SOLEMNLY, THERE ARE SOME OF THESE STANDING HERE WHO WILL NOT TASTE DEATH BEFORE THEY SEE THE SON OF MAN COMING WITH HIS KINGDOM" (16:28). What does that mean?

It refers to the resurrection. That was the Kingdom. Redemption began at the incarnation, but the opening of the Kingdom began at the resurrection and the ascension. Some of those listening to the Lord would see the resurrection. A bit earlier John the Baptist announced, "[T]HE KINGDOM OF HEAVEN IS CLOSE AT HAND" (3:2). What he is saying is: at this point in time there are no more promises. The promise is fulfilled in the Messiah. So the Kingdom of heaven is at hand. Here it is. The Messiah is here, and now there is an opportunity for you to be a son of God by baptism, to be an heir to the Kingdom by baptism. Without this opportunity you and I would be nothing.

Bearing Fruit (A Meditation)

❖

Matthew 7:15–20

I t is the cool of the night, and the Lord is sitting in a semi-circle with the apostles, and one of them asks: "How do you know a real prophet? They all look good and sound so good. How do you know which is from God?" The Lord says to them, "You must beware of false prophets and those who come to you disguised as sheep and underneath are wolves."

Peter looks at the Master and says, "That's the point. How do you know?" And the Master says, "YOU WILL BE ABLE TO TELL THEM BY THEIR FRUITS. CAN PEOPLE PICK GRAPES FROM THORNS, OR FIGS FROM THISTLES? (7:16) IN THE SAME WAY, A SOUND TREE PRODUCES GOOD FRUIT BUT A ROTTEN TREE BAD FRUIT" (7:17).

I catch the Master's eye and I say, "What do you mean by fruit?" He says, "You will know if someone is living the life of a child of God by his conduct." And I say to Him, "You just said false prophets look like sheep but are wolves on the inside." He said, "Yes, their actions are good but their fruit are bad. When a Christian loves his neighbor in the same way God loves him (as he is); when a Christian is patient with the faults of others; when he realizes that sanctity of life takes time and that each fall demands rising to greater heights; when a Christian has joy of heart and can accept anything that life gives him with serenity of soul; when he has unbounded confidence in His Father's love for him—this is bearing fruit. A man and a woman will be known by their fruit. A pagan must see the

Father in you so that he can believe that the Father sent Me and I sent you."

I begin to understand that it means more to *be* a Christian than to be called a Christian. It means that God in me must grow brighter and brighter and as the image of Jesus grows in my soul, I must bear fruit.

The Lord then says something that chills me: "ANY TREE THAT DOES NOT PRODUCE GOOD FRUIT IS CUT DOWN AND THROWN ON THE FIRE (7:19). I REPEAT, YOU WILL BE ABLE TO TELL THEM BY THEIR FRUITS" (7:20).

SAINTLY CONTEMPLATION

Learn to abide with attention in loving, waiting upon God in the state of quiet. Contemplation is nothing else but a secret, peaceful and loving infusion of God, which, if admitted, will set the soul on fire with the Spirit of love.

— SAINT JOHN OF THE CROSS

The Eucharist

❖

John 6:53–69

Whenever Our Dear Lord says, "I TELL YOU SOLEMNLY" (6:53), that means you should listen very closely. So perk up your ears. "[I]F YOU DO NOT EAT THE FLESH OF THE SON OF MAN AND DRINK HIS BLOOD, YOU WILL NOT HAVE LIFE IN YOU (6:53). ANYONE WHO DOES EAT MY FLESH AND DRINK MY BLOOD HAS ETERNAL LIFE, AND I SHALL RAISE HIM UP ON THE LAST DAY" (6:54). This is very, very deep doctrine and Jesus does not dilute it—He doesn't tone it down at all. When He speaks of the vine and branches in John, it is obvious that this is a symbol of our relationship with Him. He didn't say unless you eat my vine you shall not have life in you. Everybody understood that it was a symbol.

But here He is talking about something that if it *were* true would be very, very disconcerting to these people because they had no context to place it in. When He said, "IF YOU DO NOT EAT THE FLESH OF THE SON OF MAN AND DRINK HIS BLOOD, YOU WILL NOT HAVE LIFE IN YOU," the only thing they can think of is the old sacrifices and cannibalism. That's what cannibals do; they eat you up, literally. What a shocking doctrine, and yet He goes on as if it were the most common thing in the world.

"FOR MY FLESH IS REAL FOOD AND MY BLOOD IS REAL DRINK (6:55). HE WHO EATS MY FLESH AND DRINKS MY BLOOD"—again, this is a repetition; He just got through saying it—"LIVES IN ME AND I LIVE IN HIM" (6:56). He is speaking of Holy Communion, the Body and Blood of Christ. It is unbelievable that God would think of such a thing. If we thought of it, it would be blasphemy. The very idea that God would make Himself bread and wine and then be our food—it is unbelievable. But when the Son of God says it, it is *unbelievable* love and *unbelievable* humility. Think about what He has done. He goes wherever you want Him to go. He's there all day long in many churches throughout the world. And too often every door is locked. God is locked away from His people. They say they're afraid of robbers. Well, put an alarm in there or pay a guard, but don't shut the people away from the Lord. What a horrible thing to do.

"As I, WHO AM SENT BY THE LIVING FATHER, MYSELF DRAW LIFE FROM THE FATHER, SO WHOEVER EATS ME WILL DRAW LIFE FROM ME" (6:57). This means that He is the living image of the Father. When Philip said, "LORD, LET US SEE THE FATHER AND THEN WE SHALL BE SATISFIED" (14:8), I would have slapped him down, but the Lord said, "TO HAVE SEEN ME IS TO HAVE SEEN . . ." Who? "THE FATHER" (14:9). Why? Because Jesus is the perfect image of the Father's knowledge of Himself. So he who sees Jesus sees the Father. That's why when you look at the Host you see the Father, Son, and Holy Ghost.

"THIS IS THE BREAD COME DOWN FROM HEAVEN; NOT LIKE THE BREAD OUR ANCESTORS ATE: THEY ARE DEAD, BUT ANYONE WHO EATS THIS BREAD WILL LIVE FOREVER" (6:58). HE TAUGHT THIS DOCTRINE AT CAPERNAUM—very important—IN THE SYNAGOGUE (6:59). This is one of the few times where the word "doctrine" is uttered in Scripture.

AFTER HEARING IT, MANY OF HIS FOLLOWERS—now, you know, it doesn't say just the Pharisees but His *followers*—SAID, "THIS IS INTOLERABLE LANGUAGE. HOW COULD ANYONE ACCEPT IT?" (6:60). They just can't accept it. "This is for the birds," they are saying. It's still that way today: Many consider this intolerable language. Even the Fundamentalists, who take the

Scripture at face value, say, "This is ridiculous." They take this whole chapter and throw it out the window. They never mention it.

This is a point you have to understand: If Jesus did not mean what He said, then He was obliged in justice to explain it.

JESUS WAS AWARE—this is a very important passage, Jesus was *aware*—THAT HIS FOLLOWERS WERE COMPLAINING (6:61). If He was only speaking symbolically, then Jesus, because He was Infinite Justice, was obliged to explain to everybody, "This is a symbol." But instead He says, "DOES THIS UPSET YOU?" (6:61). Oh, Jesus was so strong. He could care less about human respect. "WHAT IF YOU SHOULD SEE THE SON OF MAN ASCEND TO WHERE HE WAS BEFORE?" (6:62).

He's saying: "If this upsets you, how are you going to accept Jesus, Me, as Son of God defying death?" That's what He was saying. "How are you going to accept that I will ascend to the right hand of the Father if you can't accept this?" "IT IS THE SPIRIT THAT GIVES LIFE, THE FLESH HAS NOTHING TO OFFER. THE WORDS I HAVE SPOKEN TO YOU ARE SPIRIT AND THEY ARE LIFE" (6:63). What does the priest say before the consecration? He puts his hand over the host and he says, "By the power of Thy Spirit may this become the Body and Blood, Soul and Divinity of Your Son, Jesus Christ." That's the whole essence of Catholicism.

"BUT THERE ARE SOME OF YOU WHO DO NOT BELIEVE." FOR JESUS KNEW FROM THE OUTSET THOSE WHO DID NOT BELIEVE, AND WHO IT WAS THAT WOULD BETRAY HIM (6:64). Now, most of us would be terribly crushed if some of our faithful friends had turned around and walked away. Crushed to pieces. One of the most crushing blows in life would be to have dear friends walk away. He looks at them walking away and says, "THIS IS WHY I TOLD YOU NO ONE COULD COME TO ME UNLESS THE FATHER

ALLOWS HIM" (6:65). AFTER THIS, MANY OF HIS DISCIPLES—it doesn't say Pharisees; it doesn't say Sadducees; it doesn't say scribes; it says *disciples*—STOPPED GOING WITH HIM (6:66). They went back to the synagogue, back to their old ways. This Man didn't say what they wanted Him to say.

It's an amazing chapter. You ought to read it yourself today and try to mull it over. Find out what the Lord is saying to you there. See, His disciples stopped going with Him—but isn't that true today? How many priests, how many Sisters, how many laity have stopped following the Lord because they no longer believe in the Eucharist? They don't have the guts to stand up and be counted.

The spirit of the Gospel is to love in the same way God loves me, which is most difficult because I cannot love you in the same way God loves me unless I understand the Eucharist. The Eucharist is self-sacrificing, the Eucharist is obedient, the Eucharist is dependent. He's dependent on the priest, dependent on the people for attention and love. You put Him in the tabernacle, He stays there. If someone tramples Him on the ground, He says nothing. When He goes into sacrilegious hearts, He remains silent. He is totally given to His neighbor—totally given. Which means that if I am to love my neighbor as God loves me, I must be totally given. I do not have to feel anything—I must simply give of myself to my neighbor. I must be dependent; I must not be afraid to be dependent on others. Why? Because the love of God is totally dependent. He's humble.

Another way to love my neighbor is to be self-sacrificing like the Eucharist. In other words, I prefer the good of my neighbor to myself. If I can do those things for my neighbor, I can rest assured that I love my neighbor in the same way God loves me.

Now, all of His disciples, many of them, have left. In fact, it looks like they all left Him at this point because it says here that JESUS SAID TO THE TWELVE, "WHAT ABOUT YOU, DO YOU WANT TO GO AWAY TOO?" (6:67). Now, here's Jesus willing to sacrifice even the apostles for the sake of this truth—Jesus, the Eucharist, is the Truth. It is His Body, His Blood, His Soul, His Divinity. He lost most of His disciples. He lost a lot of them there. Now He's looking at the Twelve and He's saying, "You want to go away, too? Are you going?" And Peter said, "LORD, WHO SHALL WE GO TO? YOU HAVE THE MESSAGE OF ETERNAL LIFE (6:68), AND WE BELIEVE; WE KNOW THAT YOU ARE THE HOLY ONE OF GOD" (6:69). So here's Peter saying he doesn't understand it, but he believes. That's what faith is all about.

When you try to understand the Scripture, your faith will be in jeopardy because you cannot understand it. You can get inspiration from it, the Lord will give you some light, but to say you understand—Peter didn't understand any more than did the people who walked away, but he believed, and we must believe as well.

Joy in the Lord

❖

John 16:21–22

Our Lord said: "A WOMAN IN CHILDBIRTH SUFFERS, BECAUSE HER TIME HAS COME; BUT WHEN SHE HAS GIVEN BIRTH TO THE CHILD SHE FORGETS THE SUFFERING IN HER JOY THAT A MAN HAS BEEN BORN INTO THE WORLD (16:21). SO IT IS WITH YOU: YOU ARE SAD NOW, BUT I SHALL SEE YOU AGAIN, AND

YOUR HEARTS WILL BE FULL OF JOY, AND THAT JOY NO ONE SHALL TAKE FROM YOU" (16:22).

The kind of joy that Our Lord is talking about is the serenity of soul that comes from being satisfied with what God is doing in your life, not what YOU are doing in your life.

Look, you can always do better, but to be satisfied with what God is doing in your life, that brings joy. It's a joy that brings a serene acceptance of God's will in the present moment.

Happiness is a spurt of satisfaction, and those feelings come and go very quickly. But joy is different. That's why our Lord said here, "[Y]OUR HEARTS WILL BE FULL OF JOY, AND THAT JOY NO ONE SHALL TAKE FROM YOU."

So the joy we have is in what? The resurrection. The resurrection gives us joy not only because it proves that Jesus is the Lord, but because we too shall be resurrected one day and the difficulties of the moment are all going to pass.

From the Rock to Satan

❖

Matthew 16:16–23

Peter, the great blunderer, the one who always spoke before he thought (you probably know twenty people like that) one day said, "YOU ARE THE CHRIST" (16:16). AND THE LORD SAID TO HIM, "YOU ARE PETER AND ON THIS ROCK I WILL BUILD MY CHURCH (16:18). . . . I WILL GIVE YOU THE KEYS OF THE KINGDOM OF HEAVEN" (16:19). Then what happened?

The Lord starts to tell Peter about His going into Jerusalem to die. Peter takes the Lord aside and says, "[T]HIS MUST NOT HAPPEN TO YOU." LORD, DON'T GO! (16:22). Now if you know the Lord is going to die if He goes to Jerusalem, isn't it logical to ask Him not to go? Wouldn't you say the same thing?

The Lord makes Peter the rock, the foundation of His Church, five minutes before, and now He looks at him and says, "GET BEHIND ME, SATAN" (16:23). Oh what a comedown: the leader one moment and the devil the next. Isn't that your life? Don't you feel so good one moment and like the devil the next? Peter was trying to stop the Lord from completing His mission, and that He could not allow.

But God held onto Peter, kept him as an apostle—and He keeps us too. Because you're human you're going to rise and fall. Scripture says somewhere that "THE VIRTUOUS MAN FALLS SEVEN TIMES" (Prv 24:16). For most of us that would be a good day. So don't lose courage because you fall. You don't need anything else in this life except to become holy and to remain close to God. And don't fail to make the distinction between the rejection of God and imperfections. There's a big difference between the two.

Love Your Enemies

❖

Matthew 5:43–45

In Saint Matthew's Gospel, we find some prerogatives of the Father, given to us so that we might imitate God. Most of the hallmarks of the Father, the attributes of the Father, are beyond us. But here is one we can accomplish: "YOU HAVE LEARNT HOW IT WAS SAID: YOU MUST LOVE YOUR NEIGHBOUR AND HATE

YOUR ENEMY (5:43). BUT I SAY THIS TO YOU: LOVE YOUR ENEMIES AND PRAY FOR THOSE WHO PERSECUTE YOU" (5:44). I must love my enemy as the Father loves His enemies. The Father does good to His enemies and so I must pray for mine, and "IN THIS WAY YOU WILL BE SONS OF YOUR FATHER IN HEAVEN" (5:45).

Then He says: "FOR HE CAUSES HIS SUN TO RISE ON BAD MEN AS WELL AS GOOD, AND HIS RAIN TO FALL ON HONEST AND DISHONEST MEN ALIKE" (5:45). In the Lord's mind there can be no difference between a person who is holy, a person who is faulty, a person who is a big sinner, or a person who is pious. There's no difference. Jesus in His love always said He hated sin—hated sin—but He loved the sinner. We seldom separate the sin from the sinner. So, if I hate your way of life, I hate you. If I despise your faults, I despise you.

Love has a way of minimizing faults. They've got these minimizing bras—what do they do? They're supposed to make something big look like something small. Well, that's what our love should do. Love minimizes the faults of others.

I used to have a superior, and I hated going to spiritual direction with her because when I'd share all my gripes, she'd say, "Well, you have to cover it over with a mantle of charity." I used to just about die. It was the same line every month. I'd never say anything, but I thought, "God, if I hear that one more time . . ." But she was right. See, my solution to every problem was to wipe it out: if you can't change them, get rid of them. My solution seemed a lot simpler than hers; but her solution was right. When I started loving this one particular individual, her faults were still there, but I found it easier to overlook them. It worked for me. The compassion I began to feel for this individual, through loving, overcame my bitterness; it didn't change her in any way, but it overcame my bitterness over what she was or was not doing.

So the first thing we must do is love everybody. In that way we can be perfect as the Father in heaven is perfect. Perfection consists of totally accepting every individual, with all of their weaknesses, their foibles, and loving them exactly as they are.

Advice for Praying

❖

Matthew 6:7–8

The Lord gives you some tips on prayer. He says, "IN YOUR PRAYERS DO NOT BABBLE AS THE PAGANS DO, FOR THEY THINK THAT BY USING MANY WORDS THEY WILL MAKE THEMSELVES HEARD (6:7). DO NOT BE LIKE THEM; YOUR FATHER KNOWS WHAT YOU NEED BEFORE YOU ASK HIM" (6:8). The logical follow-up to this is: Why are you asking at all? If the Father knows what you need, and will provide it, why do you have to ask?

Well, it is God's will that you ask because it gives Him greater joy. Secondly, He wants to build a desire in our hearts to possess what is good and holy. He then wants to fulfill that desire. Making a request of God also gives you a deep awareness of His immediate response to you—His loving concern for you. The Father-daughter/Father-son relationship is built upon asking, that you may receive.

Think about it: Don't you want somebody you love to ask for something? So often surprise gifts are not what the other person really wants. You learn that at Christmas. How many men get umpteen neckties at Christmas because you don't know what else to give them? The immediacy with which something is given (or sometimes refused) is always indicative of the love of the beloved—which means that God Who is

Father wants to act like a father. He just doesn't want to pour stuff into your lap. The asking is so you can appreciate His generosity. What the Lord is saying here is don't *worry* about the things you need. But He still wants you to ask and He wants to fulfill your needs.

The Plank in Your Eye

❖

Luke 6:41–45

Our Lord said, "WHY DO YOU OBSERVE THE SPLINTER IN YOUR BROTHER'S EYE AND NEVER NOTICE THE PLANK IN YOUR OWN? (6:41) HOW CAN YOU SAY TO YOUR BROTHER, 'BROTHER, LET ME TAKE OUT THE SPLINTER THAT IS IN YOUR EYE' WHEN YOU CANNOT SEE THE PLANK IN YOUR OWN?" (6:42).

Our Dear Lord calls all the faults we find in others "a splinter." And knowing us as He does, He says, "You've got an awful lot to account for. Why are you looking at that splinter?" The Lord calls us "hypocrites" (6:42). I think that's funny. That was His favorite word: "hypocrite." He uses it an awful lot.

"TAKE THE PLANK OUT OF YOUR OWN EYE FIRST, AND THEN YOU WILL SEE CLEARLY ENOUGH TO TAKE OUT THE SPLINTER THAT IS IN YOUR BROTHER'S EYE" (6:42).

He's not saying there's not a splinter in your brother's eye. What He's saying is unless you overcome yourself, you can't help somebody else overcome themselves. You haven't gone through the process. Now, just imagine if you took that as a model for your life. Just imagine what would happen to you. You would be so conscious of your own sinner condition that it would never dawn on you that anybody else did anything wrong. Why? Because whatever they do, regardless of what you think, the Lord God calls it a splinter.

Now why does He do that? Because when I offend God, it's a plank, it's a big thing. If my neighbor offends me, it's a very little thing. That's what He's saying. So why can't you forgive little things when God has forgiven some pretty big planks in your life? That's the whole point.

He keeps saying, "If you took that plank out of your own eye, you would see clearly. You would see the difference between your brother's fault and your own. Then you would not be as critical, but more charitable. That would help you love a lot more."

Our Lord always used little things. He transformed bread and wine into His Body and Blood. He said if you give a cup of cold water to one in need you get an eternal reward. If you feed the poor you get a great reward. And so, in our lifetime, in our daily life, you have to look past the big things, to the little things. He even said, "[U]NLESS YOU CHANGE AND BECOME LIKE LITTLE CHILDREN YOU WILL NEVER ENTER THE KINGDOM OF HEAVEN" (Mt 18:3). That's an awesome remark because it says if you're not little in your heart, if you're not humble, trusting, forgiving, and generous with love, you will not see heaven.

Littleness. That's why some people have a hard time being humble, because they can't be little. They cannot be aware of their nothingness without becoming disheartened and discouraged. But littleness of heart is so important.

Let's always remember to take the planks out of our own eyes, and look to little things, understanding that little things make us great, and little things make us extremely imperfect.

Rooted to God's Will
(A Meditation)

❖

Mark 4:3–20

We are in Jerusalem, and the Master is with a great crowd of people, and He tells them: "The kingdom of heaven is like a sower who goes out to sow his seed." I can imagine a farmer going out and sowing seed. Jesus says, "Now it happened that, as he sowed, some of the seed fell on the edge of the path, and the birds came and ate it up (4:4). Some seed fell on rocky ground where it found little soil and sprang up straightaway, because there was no depth of earth (4:5); and when the sun came up it was scorched and, not having any roots, it withered away (4:6). Some seed fell into thorns, and the thorns grew up and choked it, and it produced no crop (4:7). And some seeds fell into rich soil and, growing tall and strong, produced crop; and yielded thirty, sixty, even a hundred-fold" (4:8). And he said, "Listen anyone who has ears to hear!" (4:9).

Later, I listen as Peter asks the Lord to explain the parable of the sower and the seed. The Master gently says to Peter, "What the sower is sowing is the word (4:14). Those on the edge of the path where the word is sown are people who have no sooner heard it than Satan comes and carries away the word that was sown in them (4:15). Similarly, those who receive the seed on patches of rock are people who,

WHEN FIRST THEY HEAR THE WORD, WELCOME IT AT ONCE WITH JOY (4:16). BUT THEY HAVE NO ROOT IN THEM, THEY DO NOT LAST; SHOULD SOME TRIAL COME, OR SOME PERSECUTION ON ACCOUNT OF THE WORD, THEY FALL AWAY AT ONCE (4:17). THEN THERE ARE OTHERS WHO RECEIVE THE SEED IN THORNS. THESE HAVE HEARD THE WORD (4:18), BUT THE WORRIES OF THIS WORLD, THE LURE OF RICHES AND ALL THE OTHER PASSIONS COME IN TO CHOKE THE WORD, AND SO IT PRODUCES NOTHING (4:19). AND THERE ARE THOSE WHO HAVE RECEIVED THE SEED IN RICH SOIL: THEY HEAR THE WORD AND ACCEPT IT AND YIELD A HARVEST, THIRTY AND SIXTY AND A HUNDREDFOLD" (4:20).

It's wonderful to know God's love for me, and that there is a kingdom hereafter, but what kind of root does it have within me?

For some the Word does not last—because the moment some trial comes along, some tragedy, some pain, they lose faith and their joy is gone. They begin to think there is no God. Or perhaps a persecution comes because they did believe, and the faith is completely lost—they fall away. Then there are those who receive the Word, but the lures of the world, the lures of riches, choke the Word—pleasure, the easy way out. These are the people for whom the seed fell on thorny ground. They don't want God; they want only the things of this world. They can't possess anything without being attached to it. And so they lose out, choked by the pleasures and the cares of this world. Then there are those who receive the Word. Their hearts are rich with love, and these, each one, harvests different kinds of fruit. The harvest is different. Some yield a hundredfold and they give and give and give, and when the storm comes their roots go deeper and they withstand the storm and they grow strong like a tree does. It bends with the storm but never cracks.

I look at the Master and say, "How can I bear a hundred-fold?"

He says, "By doing the Father's will with love and with joy."

But I find doing the Father's will so difficult. It isn't as if the Father comes down and tells me what to do. "What is God's will?" I ask.

He says, "In any given situation you do what you think the Father wants you to do. Be guided by the light that you have in the present moment and the Father will stand by you—He understands. Find God and God's will in the duties of the present moment."

"Do you mean every duty?" I ask the Master.

"Yes," He says. "Perform the duty of the present moment with great love and affection and receive whatever the Father sends you moment to moment with great love and you will find God and bear fruit a hundredfold."

NECESSARY READING

It's very necessary, if you want to grow in holiness, to read the Scriptures and other spiritual books. To discover how men and women who had the courage and strength to live the Gospel lived. You need that food, that nourishment, that example. You've got to ask for faith every day and immerse yourself in the experience of those people who exercised their faith. You have to read the Scriptures. You've got to do it, and then act on what you've read.

Up a Tree with Zacchaeus

❖

Luke 19:1–10

Chapter 19 of Luke gives us a glimpse into the virtue of being childlike, the virtue of having no human respect, the virtue of repentance and generosity and great desire. So you have four entirely different virtues that are depicted in this small paragraph of Scripture, and all of these virtues were possessed, quite suddenly, by a sinner. We would all like to possess these virtues—and this man, Zacchaeus seemingly attained them by doing one act. One act. This Gospel proves just how generous the Lord is over one act.

Now, [Jesus] entered Jericho and was going through the town (19:1) when a man whose name was Zacchaeus made his appearance; he was one of the senior tax collectors and a wealthy man (19:2). Here's a man who was a publican, a senior publican, which meant he was head of all the other publicans. They were kind of the first-century Internal Revenue Service, except they were thieves. They were really the Jewish mafia. So the tax was 10 percent for Rome and 15 percent for Zacchaeus. Anyway, that's why they were hated by the Jews. They were in league with Rome, and collected Roman taxes. And if you weren't nice to them, they'd pile another 5 percent on your bill. Needless to say, they were not accepted in the synagogue. But they could care less, they were making a bundle. You've got to keep all of that in mind when we look at this Zacchaeus.

He was anxious to see what kind of man Jesus was

(19:3). He's curious, nosy. The Lord is using even his faults. It's an amazing thing about God: He uses even our faults, our weaknesses, and our imperfections. Zacchaeus probably heard about this man and said, "I wonder what he's like. I'm going to have a peek."

BUT HE WAS TOO SHORT AND COULD NOT SEE HIM FOR THE CROWD (19:3). Zacchaeus was very short—maybe five feet, maybe four foot eleven, who knows—and that would have only made him more hated, because they would have considered him half a man. And you can see the thieving qualities in this guy: he's ingenious, he's undaunted, he's looking for an angle. So he decides to run ahead.

You can just visualize this little guy racing ahead desperate for some way to see over the crowd. In the moment, he decides to climb a sycamore tree. He is determined to catch a glimpse of this Man, that's all he wants. He's just curious, waiting in a tree to see Jesus.

It shows us something, doesn't it? It shows us that sometimes when we're up a tree, it's a pretty good place to be. Many times we're up a tree in our spiritual lives. Maybe we can't see beyond our pettiness and faults. We can't see beyond the pettiness of other people or their cruelty. All of this towers above us and we can feel very short. You ever feel that way? But we've got to rise above all of that spiritually and look beyond people, beyond ourselves, beyond things, to Jesus. That's what Zacchaeus did. He rose above it all to search for the Lord. What he couldn't do by stature he did by climbing a tree.

SO HE RAN AHEAD AND CLIMBED A SYCAMORE TREE TO CATCH A GLIMPSE OF JESUS WHO WAS TO PASS THAT WAY (19:4). WHEN JESUS REACHED THE SPOT HE LOOKED UP (19:5). To me it's a very exciting incident. Here's this guy up in this tree and he's looking around. When he sees the Lord he's probably thinking,

"Boy, He's so tall!" Then the Lord looks right at him, with the most perfect, gentle, beautiful eyes and He calls this man by name. He didn't say, "Hey there, who are you?" He says, "ZAC-CHAEUS, COME DOWN. HURRY" (19:5). Unbelievable. This old sinner. "HURRY, BECAUSE I MUST STAY AT YOUR HOUSE TODAY" (19:5). The Lord didn't just invite Himself over; He is basically saying, "Your house is going to be mine today." And you can almost feel that little heart of Zacchaeus beating like it was coming out of his chest.

AND HE HURRIED DOWN—I imagine him shimmying all the way down to the street—AND WELCOMED HIM JOYFULLY (19:6).

Here's a man who knows he's a sinner: he's ostracized by the people, he's a thief, he's got a lot of money that doesn't do him much good, and along comes the Master: the one they call Messiah. He says, "HURRY. COME DOWN, BECAUSE I MUST STAY AT YOUR HOUSE TODAY." Wouldn't it be great if every sinner knew that all it took was a little desire on their part, and the Lord would come and stay with them? Not only that, but He wants them to "hurry."

You know, the compassion of Jesus at this point is so astro-nomical, but we just can't imagine Jesus desiring us because we think our weaknesses and imperfections stand in the way. The Lord sees beyond all that. When it comes to the heart, Jesus sees all, and He saw the heart of Zacchaeus—that's all He saw. I think what hurts Him the most in us is not our sins or our weaknesses but that we concentrate on them too much. We obsess over them. We're so attuned to our failings and on being perfect that we forget about Jesus.

What happened to Zacchaeus? Well, the people start grumbling. Here's the most hated man in the city and the Lord invites Himself to dinner and for a stay at his house! That means that all the people who wanted to see Jesus had to go to Zacchaeus's house.

When He said He was going to stay at a sinner's house they complained. BUT ZACCHAEUS STOOD HIS GROUND AND SAID TO THE LORD, "LOOK, SIR, I AM GOING TO GIVE HALF MY PROPERTY TO THE POOR, AND IF I HAVE CHEATED ANYBODY I WILL PAY HIM BACK FOUR TIMES THE AMOUNT" (10:8). Whew. If he squeezed a dollar out of you, he's going to give you four.

AND JESUS SAID TO HIM, "TODAY SALVATION HAS COME TO THIS HOUSE, BECAUSE THIS MAN TOO IS A SON OF ABRAHAM (19:9); FOR THE SON OF MAN HAS COME TO SEEK OUT AND SAVE WHAT WAS LOST" (19:10).

This is the beautiful thing about Jesus: When you looked at Him, you either turned to Him or against Him. The Lord never said a word to Zacchaeus except, "HURRY, BECAUSE I MUST STAY AT YOUR HOUSE TODAY." Did you notice that the Lord never convicted him or said, "I want you to make a public apology"? But Zacchaeus was so moved by the mere presence of Jesus that he made a public statement. And it was accepted by Jesus when He said, "SALVATION HAS COME TO THIS HOUSE." So seek Jesus out each day, even if you are up a tree.

Woman with the Hemorrhage

❖

Mark 5:25–34

There was a woman who had suffered from a hemorrhage for twelve years, which meant she couldn't go into the synagogue. She was considered unclean. You can imagine how weak she must have been. They didn't have vitamins and B-12 and iron pills and stuff like that. If you had a hemorrhage for twelve years, you'd be pretty peaked—not to mention the humiliation she suffered from her husband and her neighbors.

[A]FTER LONG AND PAINFUL TREATMENT UNDER VARIOUS DOCTORS, SHE HAD SPENT ALL SHE HAD WITHOUT BEING ANY THE BETTER FOR IT, IN FACT, SHE WAS GETTING WORSE (5:26). SHE HAD HEARD ABOUT JESUS, AND SHE CAME UP BEHIND HIM THROUGH THE CROWD AND TOUCHED HIS CLOAK (5:27). "IF I CAN TOUCH EVEN HIS CLOTHES," SHE HAD TOLD HERSELF[,] "I SHALL BE WELL AGAIN" (5:28). AND THE SOURCE OF THE BLEEDING DRIED UP INSTANTLY, AND SHE FELT IN HERSELF THAT SHE WAS CURED OF HER COMPLAINT (5:29). IMMEDIATELY AWARE THAT POWER HAD GONE OUT FROM HIM, JESUS TURNED ROUND IN THE CROWD AND SAID, "WHO TOUCHED MY CLOTHES?" (5:30).

Now when this woman with the hemorrhage knelt down and said to herself, "If I touch the hem of His garment, I shall be healed," that was a word. That word was a request. She didn't utter it out loud. Nobody knew who she was, or where she came from, or what she wanted. Suddenly Jesus turns around and He says, "WHO TOUCHED MY CLOTHES?" Her word reached THE Word, and immediately something happened—

immediately! I think that would happen to all of us if we had that confidence and knowledge and belief—belief—that the Word in itself is not like any other word in any other book.

Look at this again: JESUS TURNED ROUND IN THE CROWD AND SAID, "WHO TOUCHED MY CLOTHES?" (5:30). Now the apostles get a little bit edgy here: HIS DISCIPLES—probably Peter—SAID TO HIM, "YOU SEE HOW THE CROWD IS PRESSING ROUND YOU AND YET YOU SAY, 'WHO TOUCHED ME?'" (5:31). The apostles were irritable. To them it was a stupid question. With people pushing in on every side of Jesus, how could anyone know who touched Him? The Lord didn't pay any attention to them. HE CONTINUED TO LOOK ALL ROUND TO SEE WHO HAD DONE IT (5:32). THEN THE WOMAN CAME FORWARD, FRIGHTENED AND TREMBLING BECAUSE SHE KNEW WHAT HAD HAPPENED TO HER—see, the reason she came forward in fear was that she was unclean—AND SHE FELL AT HIS FEET AND TOLD HIM THE WHOLE TRUTH (5:33). And He said, "MY DAUGHTER, . . . YOUR FAITH HAS RESTORED YOU TO HEALTH; GO IN PEACE AND BE FREE FROM YOUR COMPLAINT" (5:34). Go in peace. What a sentence.

It's so hard for us to understand the power of the Lord. We do much more than touch the hem of His garment. We receive Him Body, Blood, Soul, and Divinity. So why is it then that we ourselves do not benefit as much as this woman did? There's power coming out of the Eucharist for us. There is the Word made Flesh. Sometimes you look at yourself and you say, "God, I've been in the same rut for how long?" But what we should be asking is "Has power gone out from Jesus? Has my prayer, my faith really released something?" You see, something is released each time you come into the Presence of Jesus. But most people don't believe it.

How little people change. All those people pressing in on Jesus didn't have the faith of that one woman. She alone in that crowd believed she would be healed if she but touched His garment. She was instantly healed.

Go through chapter 5 of Mark, the entire chapter, and read it slowly. Ask the questions: "Jesus, tell me, do You touch me? Do I touch You in return? Am I with You all day? Do I reach out to You in my problems, in my trials, in my aggravations? Do I touch You in my illnesses?" The woman knew. Jesus knew He had been touched. What a beautiful explanation of prayer, the prayer of one who has great faith. Power leaves Jesus by that fact. You don't have to argue with Him, or debate Him—you don't even have to explain. You just have to say, "Lord, I do believe you can do this," and there's a power that leaves Jesus.

He Wants to Love You

❖

John 10:16–18

Jesus says: "AND THERE ARE OTHER SHEEP I HAVE THAT ARE NOT OF THIS FOLD, AND THESE I HAVE TO LEAD AS WELL. THEY TOO WILL LISTEN TO MY VOICE, AND THERE WILL BE ONLY ONE FLOCK, AND ONE SHEPHERD (10:16). THE FATHER LOVES ME, BECAUSE I LAY DOWN MY LIFE IN ORDER TO TAKE IT UP AGAIN (10:17). NO ONE TAKES IT FROM ME; I LAY IT DOWN OF MY OWN FREE WILL, AND AS IT IS IN MY POWER TO LAY IT DOWN, SO IT IS IN MY POWER TO TAKE IT UP AGAIN; AND THIS IS THE COMMAND I HAVE BEEN GIVEN BY MY FATHER" (10:18). So the Father commanded Jesus to come down and save us, and Jesus responded.

It's important that we understand that there was a request made, and acquiescence to that request—meaning Our Dear Lord has free will. He says, "I LAY [MY LIFE] DOWN OF MY OWN

FREE WILL, AND AS IT IS IN MY POWER TO LAY IT DOWN, SO IT IS IN MY POWER TO TAKE IT UP AGAIN" (10:18). There's the mystery of the humanity of Jesus, and the mystery of grace in our hearts too, isn't there? We have so much grace in our hearts and yet we have free will—grace never interferes with our free will. Both the divinity and the humanity of God are present in this statement.

Jesus wanted to lay His life down for us, and the Father had commanded Him to do it. It's very important that we understand that when Jesus manifests His love, He does it on a level we understand: with free will. He *wanted* to do it. So if you have a problem with the love of Jesus, or understanding how much He loves you, just think of this sentence: He *wants* to love you. He has decided to love you.

The Canaanite Woman (A Meditation)

❖

Matthew 15:22–28

As the apostles and Jesus are walking along, a Canaanite woman shouts, "SIR, SON OF DAVID, TAKE PITY ON ME. MY DAUGHTER IS TORMENTED BY A DEVIL" (15:22). The apostles wait for the Master to turn around, but He continues on as if He didn't hear.

BUT HE ANSWERED HER NOT A WORD. AND HIS DISCIPLES WENT AND PLEADED WITH HIM. "GIVE HER WHAT SHE WANTS," THEY SAID[,] "BECAUSE SHE IS SHOUTING AFTER US" (15:23). HE SAID IN REPLY, "I WAS SENT ONLY TO THE LOST SHEEP OF THE

House of Israel" (15:24). But the woman had come up and was kneeling at his feet. "Lord," she said[,] "help me" (15:25). He replied, "It is not fair to take the children's food and throw it to the house-dogs" (15:26).

I think to myself: What strange words. Is He not the Savior of all? Is she not coming to Him in deep faith? She is a Canaanite woman, a pagan who says, "Take pity on me." He looks disturbed almost and says, "It is not right to give bread from the Master's table to dogs." I wonder what this woman will say?

She retorted, "Ah yes, sir; but even house-dogs can eat the scraps that fall from their master's table" (15:27). Then Jesus answered her, "Woman, you have great faith. Let your wish be granted." And from that moment her daughter was well again (15:28).

I have never heard Jesus speak this way. He was so compassionate with Mary Magdalene, with Matthew, with Zacchaeus. This woman seems to be a good woman who is not asking for herself, but interceding for another. I go to the Master and ask, "Is there a lesson for me in this strange conduct of Yours, in this seeming lack of compassion?" He says, "Yes, I knew this woman's heart. Her deep faith and her compassion. But I wanted others to see it. I wanted her to be an example to all mankind of deep humility and perseverance. Even the rebuff she accepted in love. Even when she did not understand she kept asking and loving. Her faith increased each time I said no."

Isn't it the same way with us? I have asked Him for personal things, and for things on behalf of others, and have yet to receive an answer. As this woman was called by God to give an example of perseverance in time of trial, of deep faith when faith can be shaken, so God also permits trials and temptations and tragedies in my life to draw out from my soul those hidden qualities that are unknown, even to me. I know that He looks at me with a deep love, as He looked at this woman, when I persevere under trying circumstances, when I try to see the Father's love in everyone. These are opportunities for greater love, greater patience, greater humility, and a chance to show unselfish love for my neighbor.

As God treated this woman, He often treats me. It seems as if He doesn't care, but I know He does, and He only tries me as much as I can bear. As He told Saint Paul: "MY GRACE IS ENOUGH FOR YOU" (2 Cor 12:8–9). Whatever trial, whatever heartache you have, know that God watches with a deep love and He loves you from all eternity. In this trial, in this pain, in this suffering, when it has made you more like Him, He will tell you, "Go in peace. I have not seen such peace in all of Israel." Have hope.

The Death of Lazarus

❖

John 11:11–15

Jesus told the apostles, "OUR FRIEND LAZARUS IS RESTING, I AM GOING TO WAKE HIM" (11:11). THE DISCIPLES SAID TO HIM, "LORD, IF HE IS ABLE TO REST HE IS SURE TO GET BETTER" (11:12).

THE PHRASE JESUS USED REFERRED TO THE DEATH OF LAZARUS, BUT THEY THOUGHT THAT BY "REST" HE MEANT "SLEEP," SO (11:13) JESUS PUT IT PLAINLY, "LAZARUS IS DEAD (11:14); AND FOR YOUR SAKE I AM GLAD I WAS NOT THERE BECAUSE NOW YOU WILL BELIEVE" (11:15). Now you will believe. . . .

He knew that even among His apostles there was this element of doubt in their hearts and minds. I would suppose the same is true of even the holiest persons walking the earth today. Wherever they are, and whoever they are, they probably share the apostles' frustrations, their doubts, their lack of spirituality, and their inability to place the world and its cares on a spiritual plane. In a word, they are very "human." Like these rugged men, we don't always see the wisdom of God as He allows things in our lives. So often we question Him or we try to evade reality. Jesus comes out at this moment when the apostles are confused and ignoring reality and says, "No, this man is dead and I'm glad for your sake He died, so now you will believe." You can see here one of the hidden sufferings of Jesus.

One of the hidden sufferings of Our Lord was that nobody really understood Him. Very few people understand the visions, concepts, or lights of others; so understanding those of the Lord God is even more difficult. There is a hiddenness, an aloneness in Jesus that shows itself in this moment from Scripture. It's why it was so necessary that Jesus be united to the Father in His Humanity, because He would live a very lonely life. Outside of Our Lady, who wasn't always there with Him, He really didn't have anybody who understood Him.

We should make it our business to spend time with the Lord whenever we can; before His Presence and in His Word. We can never fully understand Him, but we can make the effort to grow closer to Him each day; to put ourselves in a position to be raised by Him and to see life as He sees it.

Will You Be Martha or Mary?

❖

John 11:19–22, 31–35, 39

AND MANY JEWS HAD COME TO MARTHA AND MARY TO SYM-
PATHISE WITH THEM OVER THEIR BROTHER (11:19). WHEN
MARTHA HEARD THAT JESUS HAD COME SHE WENT TO MEET HIM.
MARY REMAINED SITTING IN THE HOUSE (11:20).

I get the impression that Mary was kind of angry, a pouter.
She just sits there in the house as the Lord comes. This is
Mary, the great contemplative.

Now Martha, Mary's sister, is true to her character as she
appears in the Gospel of Luke. She was the one who said,
"Lord, why don't you tell my sister to help me. I've got so much
serving to do and here she is sitting at Your feet" (Lk 10:40).
Well here's that same woman, and she's got that same critical spirit. Instead of saying, "Lord I'm so happy you're here,"
or "My brother passed away," Martha says: "IF YOU HAD BEEN
HERE, MY BROTHER WOULD NOT HAVE DIED" (Jn 11:21). In other
words: "You've got some nerve coming here four days after he
died!" This is her temperament.

Still, there's a little glimmer of hope in Martha, and she
said, "[B]UT I KNOW THAT, EVEN NOW, WHATEVER YOU ASK OF
GOD, HE WILL GRANT YOU" (11:22). So she has faith in Jesus,
but she stops short before she can ask for something so impossible. Jesus says: "YOUR BROTHER . . . WILL RISE AGAIN" (11:23).

This is when Martha "the Enlightener" makes an appearance. Not only does she criticize the Lord; now she's going to
enlighten Him. It's amazing how often we try to teach God

something during our prayers—and that's what old Martha does here. MARTHA SAID, "I KNOW HE WILL RISE AGAIN AT THE RESURRECTION ON THE LAST DAY" (11:24). Which means: "What's that got to do with anything?" She never thought of the Lord raising her brother from the dead right then and there. She didn't say, "I believe that you can raise my brother from the dead." She says only, "I BELIEVE THAT YOU ARE THE CHRIST, THE SON OF GOD, THE ONE WHO WAS TO COME INTO THIS WORLD" (11:27).

Look a little further down. Mary, Martha's sister, comes running out now. WHEN THE JEWS WHO WERE IN THE HOUSE SYMPATHISING WITH MARY SAW HER GET UP SO QUICKLY AND GO OUT, THEY FOLLOWED HER, THINKING THAT SHE WAS GOING TO THE TOMB TO WEEP THERE (11:31).

MARY WENT TO JESUS, AND AS SOON AS SHE SAW HIM SHE THREW HERSELF AT HIS FEET, SAYING, "LORD, IF YOU HAD BEEN HERE, MY BROTHER WOULD NOT HAVE DIED" (11:32). You get the impression that she and Martha talked this whole thing over a few times during the four days that Lazarus was buried. They probably kept saying to each other, "You know, if the Master had been here, Lazarus wouldn't have died." They both say exactly the same thing to the Lord. Sometimes you can tell what people are chitchatting about because they begin to parrot one another in public. That's how you know there's been a little committee meeting.

AT THE SIGHT OF HER TEARS, AND THOSE OF THE JEWS WHO FOLLOWED HER, JESUS SAID IN GREAT DISTRESS, WITH A SIGH THAT CAME STRAIGHT FROM THE HEART (11:33), "WHERE HAVE YOU PUT HIM?" THEY SAID, "LORD, COME AND SEE" (11:34). JESUS WEPT (11:35). That's a magnificent account of the compassion of Jesus, and His emotions living in the present moment. Since He knew what He would do and what was going to happen, there is no reason for these tears, is there? He could have said, "Don't worry, I'm going to raise him up." But He didn't say that. He saw her distress and His heart went out to her: WITH A SIGH THAT CAME STRAIGHT FROM THE HEART (11:33).

And did you notice that Martha for some reason did not elicit this kind of reaction from Jesus even though she said the same thing? I wonder why? She's a little hustle bustle. She's always finding little flaws living on the level of the memory, while Mary lived on a level of the will. The Lord was moved to compassion by Mary's humility, by her faith.

JESUS SAID, "TAKE THE STONE AWAY." MARTHA SAID TO HIM, "LORD, BY NOW HE WILL SMELL; THIS IS THE FOURTH DAY" (11:39). Ah, here's good old Martha again. There she is teaching the Lord. You can plainly see her lack of faith, her lack of belief in a possible resurrection. She has no concept that Jesus is going to raise her brother. She's too busy enlightening the Lord: "Don't move that stone, it'll stink up the whole block." I wonder how many times we do that to the Lord. How many times have we talked the Lord out of what He wanted to do for us? How many times have we tried to bully God into doing our will instead of His? Throwing ourselves at His feet and humbly begging for His mercy is the lesson here.

In your prayer life let someone else play Martha—you play Mary.

The Raising of Lazarus

❖

John 11:44–53

THE DEAD MAN CAME OUT, HIS FEET AND HANDS BOUND WITH BANDS OF STUFF AND A CLOTH ROUND HIS FACE. JESUS SAID TO THEM, "UNBIND HIM, LET HIM GO FREE" (11:44).

MANY OF THE JEWS WHO HAD COME TO VISIT MARY AND HAD SEEN WHAT HE DID BELIEVED IN HIM (11:45), BUT SOME OF THEM WENT TO TELL THE PHARISEES WHAT JESUS HAD DONE (11:46). THEN THE CHIEF PRIESTS AND PHARISEES CALLED A MEETING. "HERE IS THIS MAN WORKING ALL THESE SIGNS[,]" THEY SAID[,] "AND WHAT ACTION ARE WE TAKING? (11:47). IF WE LET HIM GO ON IN THIS WAY EVERYBODY WILL BELIEVE IN HIM, AND THE ROMANS WILL COME AND DESTROY THE HOLY PLACE AND OUR NATION" (11:48). It's unbelievable. It's unbelievable what the enemy does, and that's why sometimes you don't know it's the enemy because it seems so reasonable. Satan makes the unbelievably unreasonable, reasonable. That's what's so bad. For anyone to see these incredible signs—a man walking out of a tomb—and say, "We've gotta stop Him," is just astounding. How many signs did they need to believe? How many signs do you need?

ONE OF THEM, CAIAPHAS, THE HIGH PRIEST THAT YEAR, SAID, "YOU DON'T SEEM TO HAVE GRASPED THE SITUATION AT ALL (11:49); YOU FAIL TO SEE THAT IT IS BETTER FOR ONE MAN TO DIE FOR THE PEOPLE, THAN FOR THE WHOLE NATION TO BE DESTROYED" (11:50). Here a very evil man is prophesying. It says here, HE DID NOT SPEAK IN HIS OWN PERSON, IT WAS AS HIGH

PRIEST THAT HE MADE THIS PROPHECY THAT JESUS WAS TO DIE FOR THE NATION—(11:51) AND NOT FOR THE NATION ONLY, BUT TO GATHER TOGETHER IN UNITY THE SCATTERED CHILDREN OF GOD (11:52). FROM THAT DAY THEY WERE DETERMINED TO KILL HIM (11:53).

This is why I imagine Jesus, knowing all things, sighed so much on the way to perform this great miracle. If you knew you were going to do something so great and that it would turn people totally off—that it would be the cause of your demise—it would certainly cause a heartrending sorrow. So I'm sure He cried, not only for Martha and Mary—I'm thinking He also cried because He knew this was the occasion the Father had set aside, a last sign, the great sign that would force everybody that was against Him to make their last ditch stand. They were determined at this point to kill Him—at that very moment.

It is unfathomable that they would do such a thing after witnessing an amazing sign like this: the raising of the dead! It shows that pride can so harden your heart that you never, never change. And that's what makes hell eternal. If you went to hell at this very moment and asked the people described in this verse what they thought now, it would be exactly the same thought that they had then. That's why it's so important that you give up your will in small things and accept whatever God sends you in the present moment as an act of humility; because if you don't, in time, you can get this hard, this stubborn. And finding God at that point is very difficult.

The Pharisees' Jealousy

❖

John 11:55–57

THE JEWISH PASSOVER DREW NEAR, AND MANY OF THE COUN-
TRY PEOPLE WHO HAD GONE UP TO JERUSALEM TO PURIFY
THEMSELVES (11:55) LOOKED OUT FOR JESUS, SAYING TO ONE AN-
OTHER AS THEY STOOD ABOUT IN THE TEMPLE, "WHAT DO YOU
THINK? WILL HE COME TO THE FESTIVAL OR NOT?" (11:56). THE
CHIEF PRIESTS AND PHARISEES HAD BY NOW GIVEN THEIR OR-
DERS: ANYONE WHO KNEW WHERE HE WAS MUST INFORM THEM
SO THAT THEY COULD ARREST HIM (11:57).

It's an amazing phenomenon how human passions can
overwhelm the intellect, the soul, and the heart. When in the
throes of passion, we are capable of almost operating by instinct instead of reason. If you look at these Pharisees, you'll
notice something: they were living *entirely* on the level of memory, and in their imaginations. They imagine that this Man is
in their way; they imagine that He would disrupt the whole
nation and cause friction with Rome. They imagine that their
positions as high priests are in great jeopardy. So they determine, on a purely emotional basis (there's no reason here), that
the only way to solve the problem is to get rid of the Man.
And so you find in this passage from John what happens to us
when we allow ourselves to live on a memory level. When we
live in memory there is absolutely no way that we can arrive at
anything reasonable.

Why did they want to arrest Him? The motivation of these
Pharisees was jealousy. Hearing that the people were begin-

ning to like Him, they decided they would do away with Him? They were supposed to be the popular ones. When they walked down the streets, people would rush out and always stand so many paces behind them. They began to develop a tremendous amount of pride, and a tremendous amount of hypocrisy because in their human nature they had their faults and their failings. They had a lot of secret sins.

It was the Pharisees who when the adulterous woman came along were going to stone her because that was the Law. Now how did they know she was an adulteress? I'll bet when Our Lord started scrawling in the sand He wrote the days and dates that each one of them had slept with this woman. Who knows? But they did suddenly walk away, and that was not by accident. . . .

But by this time they had begun to concentrate on the popularity of Jesus to the point where they felt that Jesus was taking something that belonged to them legally. Jealousy is a *blinding* vice. It blinds the soul to any reason. It is *unreasonable* and once it begins to blind the soul, people become a threat to you. And the threat is: they are taking away something that's yours. Only what you think is yours is imaginary.

Jealousy is a fire, and it licks up the living water. Remember, the enemy, who is after your soul, plants seeds of jealousy in your memory, and in your imagination. You make them grow. He plants the seed, and then he stands back and laughs at you because you water it, you nourish it, you take care of it, and when it grows into a tree, it will choke you. It will choke you—and that's exactly what happened to these Pharisees. It began to choke them to the point where they couldn't see, they couldn't hear. They benefited absolutely zilcho from the graces and the miracles they were witness to. Every miracle made them want to do away with this Man more. And the last miracle was it! He raised Lazarus from the dead—and that really emptied their cup completely. They had to get rid of Him. There was no choice on their part at that point. This Man was too great and jealousy was consuming them.

The Anointing at Bethany

❖

John 12:1–8

SIX DAYS BEFORE THE PASSOVER, JESUS WENT TO BETHANY, WHERE LAZARUS WAS, WHOM HE HAD RAISED FROM THE DEAD (12:1). THEY GAVE A DINNER FOR HIM THERE; Martha's waiting on table again. MARTHA WAITED ON THEM AND LAZARUS WAS AMONG THOSE AT TABLE (12:2). MARY BROUGHT IN A POUND OF VERY COSTLY OINTMENT, PURE NARD, AND WITH IT ANOINTED THE FEET OF JESUS, WIPING THEM WITH HER HAIR; THE HOUSE WAS FULL OF THE SCENT OF THE OINTMENT (12:3). A pound! Boy, she must have really laid that stuff on thick. I don't know how you would get a whole pound on anybody's feet, but I guess you could. I keep thinking about her hair. Isn't nard kind of oily? If it comes by the pound, it must be pretty thick too. Like a thick lotion. Her hair must have been greasy to say the least.

THEN JUDAS ISCARIOT—ONE OF HIS DISCIPLES, THE MAN WHO WAS TO BETRAY HIM—SAID (12:4), "WHY WASN'T THIS OINTMENT SOLD FOR THREE HUNDRED DENARII, AND THE MONEY GIVEN TO THE POOR?" (12:5). Isn't it strange that the question itself is a very logical one, and one that social people continue to ask today. "Why don't you sell everything and give it to the poor?" A man stopped me one day at the Network and said,

"Why don't you give all that money you're getting to the poor?" And I said, "Do you watch the Network?" He said, "Yes." I said, "Well, if I gave all the funds we get away, you wouldn't be able to see the Network, would you? You would be denied that beauty, that truth in your home, when you need it." He didn't understand; we are giving those funds to the poor: the poor in spirit. I think it was Mother Teresa who said that spiritual poverty was the worst kind of poverty—and in America and the Western world you see it everywhere.

So it says here that Judas SAID THIS, NOT BECAUSE HE CARED ABOUT THE POOR, BUT BECAUSE HE WAS A THIEF; HE WAS IN CHARGE OF THE COMMON FUND AND USED TO HELP HIMSELF TO THE CONTRIBUTIONS (12:6). SO JESUS SAID, "LEAVE HER ALONE; SHE HAD TO KEEP THIS SCENT FOR THE DAY OF MY BURIAL (12:7). YOU HAVE THE POOR WITH YOU ALWAYS, YOU WILL NOT ALWAYS HAVE ME" (12:8).

So you can clearly see God's preference. It doesn't mean we shouldn't do what we can for the poor; it only means that we must understand that the spiritual comes first, that devotion to Jesus comes first. Even our charity to the poor should spring from our desire to reach Jesus through them.

A NITTY-GRITTY GOSPEL

To me if the Gospel is not nitty-gritty and gutsy, forget it. You need to go out there and *live IT*. The Gospel is your marching orders.

The Triumphal Entry
❖
John 12:12–28

THE NEXT DAY THE CROWDS WHO HAD COME UP FOR THE FES-
TIVAL HEARD THAT JESUS WAS ON HIS WAY TO JERUSALEM
(12:12). THEY TOOK BRANCHES OF PALM AND WENT OUT TO MEET
HIM, SHOUTING, "HOSANNA! BLESSINGS ON THE KING OF ISRAEL,
WHO COMES IN THE NAME OF THE LORD" (12:13). JESUS FOUND
A YOUNG DONKEY AND MOUNTED IT (12:14). . . . AT THE TIME HIS
DISCIPLES DID NOT UNDERSTAND THIS, BUT LATER, AFTER JESUS
HAD BEEN GLORIFIED, THEY REMEMBERED THAT THIS HAD BEEN
WRITTEN ABOUT HIM (12:16). . . . ALL WHO HAD BEEN WITH HIM
WHEN HE CALLED LAZARUS OUT OF THE TOMB AND RAISED HIM
FROM THE DEAD WERE TELLING HOW THEY HAD WITNESSED IT
(12:17). It was because of Lazarus, you see, that they came
out to meet Him. That's important to know. This greeting was
very superficial. Very superficial. He had given the sign of rais-
ing Lazarus from the dead and they thought "Now this is the
prophet." And here you have this very sad sentence: THEN THE
PHARISEES SAID TO ONE ANOTHER, "YOU SEE, THERE IS NOTHING
YOU CAN DO; LOOK, THE WHOLE WORLD IS RUNNING AFTER HIM!"
(12:19). They had no desire to know He was Messiah, no desire
to accept Him as Messiah. He was not their kind of Messiah.
They wanted a political leader.

AMONG THOSE WHO WENT UP TO WORSHIP AT THE FESTIVAL
WERE SOME GREEKS (12:20). THESE APPROACHED PHILIP, WHO
CAME FROM BETHSAIDA IN GALILEE, AND PUT THIS REQUEST TO
HIM, "SIR, WE SHOULD LIKE TO SEE JESUS" (12:21). Now that's

a very beautiful sentence that you might use today: "Sir, we would like to see Jesus." Because we don't see Jesus, we manage to get all messed up in our lives. If we could see Jesus in the present moment, in our neighbor, in ourselves, in our actions, even in creation, our whole life would be different because to *see* Jesus is to be united to Jesus, especially in the Eucharist. If you really believe that the same Jesus in heaven is on that altar, then why don't you spend more time with Him when you have free time? It's not a kind of substitute presence; it's the same Presence.

PHILIP WENT TO TELL ANDREW, AND ANDREW AND PHILIP TOGETHER WENT TO TELL JESUS (12:22). That shows zeal. Whenever you're enthused about the Lord, enthused over His desires in your life, you always want to tell somebody. So instead of Philip going directly to Jesus, which he could have certainly done, he goes to Andrew. Some today say, "Go directly to Jesus. You don't have to go to any intercessor." Well, Philip went to Andrew, and I suppose it was for support. After all, if two go, it's better than one going.

JESUS REPLIED TO THEM: "NOW THE HOUR HAS COME FOR THE SON OF MAN TO BE GLORIFIED (12:23). I TELL YOU, MOST SOLEMNLY, UNLESS A WHEAT GRAIN FALLS ON THE GROUND AND DIES, IT REMAINS ONLY A SINGLE GRAIN" (12:24). It takes humility to be like that grain of wheat; to give your opinion, to prefer others to yourself. It takes humility to be guided, it takes humility not to be sensitive, it takes humility to put your pride in your pocket and die to yourself. It takes a lot of humility to have faith. A person who doesn't have humility lacks faith. They don't see God in the present moment. They don't see God anywhere for the simple reason that they're too full of themselves—they refuse to die to self. "I'm going to keep my little grain. I'm gonna keep a cover on it, and I don't want anybody to bother me." Don't worry. The Lord says it's just going to sit on the ground by itself.

Then the Lord doubles back. He knows how stupid we are and so He comes along and says, "ANYONE WHO LOVES HIS LIFE LOSES IT" (12:25). Now, if you didn't get the grain, kiddo, you ought to get this one.

What is it that you do when you're proud or you lack humility? You kind of nourish yourself: "Mmm, I'm wonderful, I'm always right, I'm always good, I'm always persecuted, I'm always this, I'm always that." It's me, myself, and I. You see, you're going to live with a trinity one way or another. The trinity is either me, myself, and I, or it's the Father, Son, and Holy Spirit. The choice is yours. But if you're not with God, you're with yourself.

So the Lord comes back again, hits 'em with the same thing, and says, "ANYONE WHO HATES HIS LIFE IN THIS WORLD WILL KEEP IT FOR THE ETERNAL LIFE" (12:25). Which means you count yourself to be of little concern. The world tells you exactly the opposite.

The world says, "I am getting better and better and I can do it." The world is a positive thinker. So you're never down on yourself, you never lose yourself, you're never one who dies to yourself. You enhance yourself, you make yourself great. What's the difference if you're not great, as long as you think you're great. So the world has totally contradicted the concept of the Gospel, which says, "Die to yourself. Die to this world."

Jesus then tells us: "IF A MAN SERVES ME, HE MUST FOLLOW ME" (12:26). What does Our Lord mean? How am I going to follow somebody who is infinite when I'm finite—Someone who is the strength of the world when I'm total weakness? How can I follow Somebody like that? It's His attitude, His life, His humility—that's what you are to follow. All you can follow is His example. We often say one thing and then we do something else. So the Lord said, 'if you serve me, you must follow me.' To serve is to preach the truth, to embody it, to be an example yourself.

"[W]HEREVER I AM, MY SERVANT WILL BE THERE TOO" (12:26). Wherever you go the Lord is with you. "IF ANYONE SERVES ME, MY FATHER WILL HONOUR HIM" (12:26). He then says, "NOW MY SOUL IS TROUBLED. WHAT SHALL I SAY: FATHER, SAVE ME FROM THIS HOUR?" (12:27).

Most people think when Our Lord had His agony in the garden, He was saying, "Let's forget this Passion stuff. There must be another way to save people." No, He says, "BUT IT WAS FOR THIS VERY REASON THAT I HAVE COME TO THIS HOUR" (12:27). There was no way He was going to change His mind in the garden. So what do you suppose He was agonizing over for three hours? Perhaps those who refuse Him, those who reject Him: the lost.

Our Lord is just talking to people. He's not demonstrating. He's not yelling. He just clearly says, "FATHER, GLORIFY YOUR NAME!" (12:28)—a very simple little prayer while He's talking. And boy, BOOM. A voice comes from heaven and says, "I HAVE GLORIFIED IT, AND I WILL GLORIFY IT AGAIN" (12:28). Which shows what? The Father is ever present. Omnipresent. The Psalmist says, "WHERE COULD I FLEE FROM YOUR PRESENCE? (7) IF I CLIMB THE HEAVENS, YOU ARE THERE, THERE TOO IF I LIE IN SHEOL" (8). (Ps 139:7,8). The Presence of God is everlasting.

The Last Testament of Jesus

❖

John 14:14–21; 17:4–20

I f you want to read the last will and testament of Our Lord
flip to chapters 14 and 17 of Saint John's Gospel. If you were
dying, you would think hard about what you wanted to say and
would certainly remove any frills—leaving just the essential
points for your family to remember. This is also true of Our
Lord in the Gospel of Saint John.

He says here: "IF YOU ASK FOR ANYTHING IN MY NAME, I
WILL DO IT" (14:14). Of course, we know that if you do something in a person's name, like the ambassador of a country, you
fulfill the will of the country or the president regardless of your
personal opinion. You can't speak your mind, or you're not an
ambassador for very long. It is similar here.

Today we've denigrated this aspect of "asking in (His)
name" and we've become name-droppers. So now people say,
"In the name of Jesus," and then everything is supposed to
happen, like some magic formula. What the Lord is saying is
if you're going to speak in the name of Jesus, you've got to be
with Jesus; you've got to think like Him; you've got to be totally
united to the Father's will. You must be united to the Trinity in
your heart and your soul so that you're one with Jesus. Then
when you speak in His Name, you know what He wants. You
have a relationship with Him. That's why it's inevitable that
you will get what you ask when you do so IN HIS NAME, because you're united to the Lord and His will. You request only
what He wants for you. It's not a magic formula for prayer. So

when you speak the name of Jesus, be extremely careful that you are not just dropping His name but asking IN His will.

Jesus then says, "IF YOU LOVE ME YOU WILL KEEP MY COMMANDMENTS" (14:15). You've got to watch these little words in Scripture, these two-letter words. They'll knock you right out of the box. This "if" changes the picture: "IF YOU LOVE ME YOU WILL KEEP MY COMMANDMENTS" (14:15). So all of us have to wonder, "Do I love God?" Am I keeping His commandments? . . . The person who continues to commit adultery and goes to church, whether he's born-again or not, isn't loving God. You can't be a part of Satan's kingdom and God's kingdom at the same time. Light and darkness have nothing in common. So you can't do both.

Now the Lord says, "I SHALL ASK THE FATHER, AND HE WILL GIVE YOU ANOTHER ADVOCATE" (14:16). That means what? It means that Jesus is an advocate—and there is going to be "another" Advocate. So we have an advocate with the Father, and in Jesus and in the Holy Spirit—"THAT SPIRIT OF TRUTH WHOM THE WORLD CAN NEVER RECEIVE SINCE IT NEITHER SEES NOR KNOWS HIM; BUT YOU KNOW HIM, BECAUSE HE IS WITH YOU, HE IS IN YOU" (14:17). This is one of the most gorgeous sentences on this page. How do you know the Spirit? "BECAUSE HE IS WITH YOU, HE IS IN YOU." You feel the Spirit inside, you're aware of His working, you're aware of His inspirations, you're aware of His effect on other people.

To be aware of and attuned to Him is a gift from God. And that's why Our Lord says here: "I WILL NOT LEAVE YOU ORPHANS; I WILL COME BACK TO YOU" (14:18). Once He was gone, had He never sent the Advocate, we would be orphans. With His physical presence, He could only be one place at one time—only a few people could be around Him. But now, through the Spirit, He can be with everyone, at all times.

Then He goes on to say: "IN A SHORT TIME THE WORLD WILL NO LONGER SEE ME; BUT YOU WILL SEE ME, BECAUSE I LIVE AND YOU WILL LIVE" (14:19). So the world has seen the last of Jesus, but we can see Him in His risen life, we see Him in the Eucharist, we see Him in the sacraments, and we see Him in each other. We do all these things through the power of the Spirit. You could not see Jesus in the Eucharist without the Spirit.

"ON THAT DAY YOU WILL UNDERSTAND THAT I AM IN MY FATHER AND YOU IN ME AND I IN YOU" (14:20). Oh, the Trinity. It is the Spirit that makes you understand that the Father is in Jesus, Jesus is in the Father, They are in us and we are in Them. I suppose one of the greatest things we could do is let the Father love Jesus in us. Just allow the Father to love Jesus in us.

In John 14:20 we have the whole beautiful revelation of the Indwelling. There are so few people today who understand the Divine Indwelling, and they would never understand if it wasn't for the Scripture here. The cause of the Divine Indwelling is the Holy Spirit. He comes into our hearts. Now, we've got to know: How do you keep Him?

Jesus says, "ANYBODY WHO RECEIVES MY COMMANDMENTS AND KEEPS THEM WILL BE ONE WHO LOVES ME; AND ANYBODY WHO LOVES ME WILL BE LOVED BY MY FATHER, AND I SHALL LOVE HIM AND SHOW MYSELF TO HIM" (14:21).

So in order to keep the Divine Indwelling, you will have to be one who loves Jesus—and we know if you love Him, you will "keep [His] commandments." Are you keeping them? You've got to constantly ask yourself that question. In your quest for God, self-knowledge is extremely important, because unless you know who you really are and where you really are, improvement is impossible—contrition and true repentence are impossible. Spirituality faces reality. The world doesn't face reality—those living worldly lives can't face it. They have to pretend. So you have guys who tell you, "You're somebody. You can really do it." But the Christian says, "I'm nobody. Without God, I'm nothing," and rejoices in the fact that God is doing so much.

Look up ahead at chapter 17 of John. Jesus says, "I HAVE . . . FINISHED THE WORK THAT YOU GAVE ME TO DO (17:4). NOW, FATHER, IT IS TIME FOR YOU TO GLORIFY ME WITH THAT GLORY I HAD WITH YOU BEFORE EVER THE WORLD WAS (17:5). I HAVE MADE YOUR NAME KNOWN TO THE MEN YOU TOOK FROM THE WORLD TO GIVE ME. THEY WERE YOURS AND YOU GAVE THEM TO ME, AND THEY HAVE KEPT YOUR WORD" (17:6). He is referring to the twelve apostles here. "NOW AT LAST THEY KNOW THAT ALL YOU HAVE GIVEN ME COMES INDEED FROM YOU" (17:7).

There's a beautiful thing in here in verse 8 of chapter 17; it says "FOR I HAVE GIVEN THEM THE TEACHING YOU GAVE TO ME" (17:8). In other words, "the teaching You gave Me, I have given them." It's amazing Our Lord is constantly giving credit to the Father. Isn't it a shame how we constantly give credit to ourselves for everything? I did this, I did that. Psychologists tell us today you've got to have self-confidence. What you need is confidence in God. Whatever you have, you have from God. "[T]HEY HAVE TRULY ACCEPTED THIS, THAT I CAME FROM YOU, AND HAVE BELIEVED THAT IT WAS YOU WHO SENT ME (17:8). I PRAY FOR THEM; I AM NOT PRAYING FOR THE WORLD BUT FOR THOSE YOU HAVE GIVEN ME, BECAUSE THEY BELONG TO YOU (17:9): ALL I HAVE IS YOURS AND ALL YOU HAVE IS MINE, AND IN THEM I AM GLORIFIED" (17:10). He looks at His disciples and continues: "I AM NOT IN THE WORLD ANY LONGER, BUT THEY ARE IN THE WORLD, AND I AM COMING TO YOU. HOLY FATHER, KEEP THOSE YOU HAVE GIVEN ME TRUE TO YOUR NAME, SO THAT THEY MAY BE ONE LIKE US" (17:11).

It's very difficult to imagine the challenge the Lord gives us with that one sentence. You and I are to be one with each other as the three persons of the Trinity are one with each other. Then the Lord says, "As YOU SENT ME INTO THE WORLD, I HAVE SENT THEM INTO THE WORLD (17:18), AND FOR THEIR SAKE I CONSECRATE MYSELF SO THAT THEY TOO MAY BE CONSECRATED IN TRUTH" (17:19). That means that Jesus is going to sacrifice Himself for them and they're going to in turn sacrifice themselves for Him. We also learn that Jesus is praying for us. We rarely think of the Lord praying for us. But He says, "I PRAY NOT ONLY FOR THESE, BUT FOR THOSE ALSO WHO THROUGH THEIR WORDS WILL BELIEVE IN ME" (17:20).

So you have an intercessor, a mediator in heaven, Jesus, continually petitioning the Father and atoning for all your sins.

The best definition of love was given to us by Saint John when he said, "God is love." That's why it's so important for us to live the life of the Trinity, because He bears fruit. This is what He keeps saying here: "I only gave them what You gave Me." So if you're living the life of the Trinity in your heart then you are able to love with detachment and trust.

The Arrest of Jesus
(A Meditation)

❖

John 18:1–11

AFTER HE HAD SAID ALL THIS JESUS LEFT WITH HIS DISCIPLES AND CROSSED THE KEDRON VALLEY. THERE WAS A GARDEN THERE, AND HE WENT INTO IT WITH HIS DISCIPLES (18:1). JUDAS THE TRAITOR KNEW THE PLACE WELL, SINCE JESUS HAD OFTEN MET HIS DISCIPLES THERE (18:2), AND HE BROUGHT THE COHORT TO THIS PLACE TOGETHER WITH A DETACHMENT OF GUARDS SENT BY THE CHIEF PRIESTS AND THE PHARISEES, ALL WITH LANTERNS AND TORCHES AND WEAPONS (18:3).

Now you notice in Saint John's Gospel he does not give us a rendition of the Agony in the Garden. Maybe he was humiliated at having fallen asleep.

Close your eyes and begin to see with your imagination. You see Our Lord; He leaves the Last Supper and He walks to the Garden of Olives. There's no account here of the three apostles who followed Him. At a distance, you see lanterns flickering, you begin to hear a little hum of distant voices; you begin to hear these voices coming closer and closer. You see the apostles finally beginning to wake up and wondering what the din is about.

Now, you see Our Lord standing there looking in the distance, and then you realize that these are not His usual followers. These are soldiers, and they're a different kind of soldier; they're the guards of the Pharisees. As you see these men coming closer, you realize they have weapons, they have spears, and they're very determined and angry.

KNOWING EVERYTHING THAT WAS GOING TO HAPPEN TO HIM, JESUS THEN CAME FORWARD (18:4). There's a good place to stop. Our Lord knew what was going to happen. We would run. He went forward.

Ask yourself a question: Would I have gone forward or would I do what the apostles did and run? It was dark, He certainly could have run and He could have probably hid Himself. He used to hide Himself in the middle of a crowd when they wanted to nab Him or throw Him over the mountainside. You would have probably run like the apostles. But Jesus goes forward; He goes forward to meet them.

JESUS . . . SAID, "WHO ARE YOU LOOKING FOR?" (18:4). THEY ANSWERED, "JESUS THE NAZARENE." HE SAID, "I AM HE" (18:5). Now you see the absolute courage of Jesus. They don't even know who He is at this point, and Jesus asks, "Who are you looking for?" They should have said, "You. We're looking for You." But they didn't know what He looked like. Jesus said, "I am He." He enlightens His enemies. He tells them who He is. Isn't that a strange thing? He *enlightens* His enemies.

Of all the times to be thoughtful of others, you would think this moment would not be one of them. You would think that God would expect us to worry only about ourselves during moments of crisis. But look at the example of Jesus: all He can think of are His poor apostles, scared to death. And He says, "[L]ET THESE OTHERS GO" (18:8). Do you see the awesome compassion of Jesus? THIS WAS TO FULFIL THE WORDS HE HAD SPOKEN, "NOT ONE OF THOSE YOU GAVE ME HAVE I LOST" (18:9).

SIMON PETER—now this is a little touch of humor—WHO CARRIED A SWORD—and you wonder why he carried a sword because he was a fisherman—DREW IT AND WOUNDED THE HIGH PRIEST'S SERVANT, CUTTING OFF HIS RIGHT EAR (18:10). The poor guy couldn't even hit the target, couldn't even reach a head that was right there in front of him. He was not a soldier. THE SERVANT'S NAME WAS MALCHUS (18:10), and JESUS SAID TO PETER, "PUT YOUR SWORD BACK IN ITS SCABBARD; AM I NOT TO DRINK THE CUP THAT THE FATHER HAS GIVEN ME?" (18:11). Right now there are a lot of fervent Christians, true believers who would like to get a sword and just lob off the heads of all these liberals—just do them in. But this is a wonderful part of Scripture that should calm their passions a bit. Peter reacted the way most of us would.

Do you see the difference between Jesus and the apostles? The apostles right away start running and lashing out at others because things did not come up to their expectations—even though Our Lord told them three or four times what was coming, they were caught by surprise. They didn't want to drink that same cup. If you remember, the Lord asked John and James and their mother, "Can you drink the cup that I am going to drink?" They said, "Yeah, sure." He said, "Very well, you shall drink My cup" (Mt 20:20–23; Mk 10:35–40). It is the Father who gives us the cup, but we must have the serenity and the love of Jesus. He knew all that He would endure. He knew everything He had to go through. We have to go through it as well, and we know it. This is not a time for swords or for fleeing. It's a time to accept God's will and pray more, or when the worst comes we'll do what the apostles did.

Judas and Peter

❖

Matthew 27:3–5; 26:75; *Luke* 22:62; *John* 21:7–17

The suffering of Jesus is complex. There is, of course, the physical pain. But imagine the spiritual and emotional pain. I would suppose it would be a very difficult cross to know the will of God and to watch people constantly oppose it.

When someone like Judas, for example, who was with Him for three years, saw His miracles, saw the fruit the Lord bore, and still could not recognize that He was the Messiah— that had to hurt. Judas became possessed by his greed. You see, the Lord was not chasing money. He was after the poor, He was after sinners, He was after the destitute. Judas may have come in with a good intention—I don't think the Lord would have chosen him otherwise—but when he saw the opportunities for gain, for *personal* gain, he bolted. It says in the Scripture, he used to take the money (Jn 12:6), that's stealing. So he began by stealing. Then he continued by satisfying that personal greed for money. When things weren't going as he imagined, he could have very easily said, "Well, this is not the Man I want to follow," and just left. That would have been sensible. Just go. But he decided to do away with Jesus. Not only was he possessed by greed; he was overwhelmed by jealousy and anger. The anger came from the Lord's inability to live up to Judas's image of the Messiah. Jesus was not fulfilling *his* needs. There had to be an anger in Judas beyond greed or disillusionment—an anger that ended with a decision: "I'm going to do away with this Man."

Look at this line from Scripture: WHEN HE FOUND THAT JESUS HAD BEEN CONDEMNED, JUDAS HIS BETRAYER WAS FILLED WITH REMORSE AND TOOK THE THIRTY SILVER PIECES BACK TO THE CHIEF PRIESTS AND ELDERS (Mt 27:3). "I HAVE SINNED"; HE SAID[,] "I HAVE BETRAYED INNOCENT BLOOD." "WHAT IS THAT TO US?" THEY REPLIED[.] "THAT IS YOUR CONCERN" (27:4). AND FLINGING DOWN THE SILVER PIECES IN THE SANCTUARY HE MADE OFF, AND WENT AND HANGED HIMSELF (27:5).

That's just awful. You have to understand why he committed suicide while Peter repented. Judas said, "I have betrayed an innocent man." But his greed and his anger prevented him from repentance. So what did he do? He rebelled against repentance. To the very end he rebelled against God.

Even his suicide was an act of rebellion. Some people say, "He felt sorry." No he didn't feel sorry. He regretted his actions because they weren't going to work. He didn't get what he wanted, so he rebelled against the Lord by taking his own life. He was the only educated apostle. He was from Judea, and the only intellectual among all the apostles—so he knew the Law. He says, "I have sinned." His reason leads him then to say: "I have done such a terrible thing. This is an innocent man. And I have betrayed Him." He must have seen Our Lord suffering in some manner. Still, he admits what he does, but instead of repenting for it, he only has regret—which leads him to suicide, the final act of rebellion against God. That's why he is condemned.

Peter, on the other hand, did not rebel. As soon as he realized what he had done, HE WENT OUTSIDE AND WEPT BITTERLY (Mt 26:75; Lk 22:62). He cried.

Remember that moment in the courtyard, when the Lord looked at Peter and the cock crowed (Lk 22:60–62). It must have been a look of deep sorrow and compassion. Peter couldn't take it. You see Peter's act of denial sprang from his weakness, whereas Judas's was an act of the will.

Look at what Peter does later. After the resurrection, John recognizes Jesus and says, "It is the Lord." But who gets to him first? Peter. The Scripture says he put a cloak on, jumped out of the boat, and went to Jesus. The Lord asks him at that point to feed His sheep and His lambs (Jn 21:7–17).

See Judas, who was full of regret and despair, left the Lord and hung himself. Peter who did about the same thing (not quite as bad, but bad for his office) ran to Jesus. Wherever he saw Jesus he ran to Him. Why? Because he knew that without Jesus he could not be whole. We need to run to Jesus in His resurrected body in the Eucharist. We need to run to Jesus. Think of Him daily. When things get a little hard, a little tough, a little disagreeable, when we fall, think of Him. Think of that agonized Body on the cross. Run to Him and repent.

Jesus on the Cross

❖

John 19:30

God's concept of love is vastly different from our own. Jesus on the cross is the Father's ideal—the essence of love. Imagine the depth of that sacrifice. See the Lord's bloody, mangled body and all the while He is being miraculously sustained by a loving Father until the very end. Think about it: There is no way that a human being could be intellectually alert enough to speak once a certain level of blood has been lost. The circulation to the brain would be nil. But you have to realize that it took the power of the Spirit to maintain Jesus until the very end, until He could say in a loud voice, "IT IS ACCOMPLISHED" (Jn 19:30). No mere human could have done it. And no one else in the history of this world could have redeemed us. So it was a miracle of the Spirit and the Father that kept Jesus alive to suffer to the very last drop of blood for your sins and mine. That is the ultimate in love.

On the cross, the bitter vinegar they gave Jesus was not meant to torment Him—at least they had some sympathy for the Lord. He tasted it, the Scripture says, but not until moments before His death. He wanted to suffer until the end. Now that doesn't mean that we should run around looking for pain. But it means we have to accept what God gives us in the present moment with love. Love through pain is a higher form of love. Anybody can love when everything is fine. What's hard about that? Love is proved by sacrifice.

Jesus demonstrates how we must love God and His will always. Loving God when things are sunny is loving what He gives you; you're loving His goodness to you. The real proof of love is when you feel dry, when you feel terrible, when things are falling apart around you and yet you remain loyal to the Lord and persevere in loving Him. Pain and sacrifice perfect love and transport it to another level far beyond mere feelings.

IN A NUTSHELL

His whole Gospel is daily living in, and total abandonment to God's will. It's very simple. Very simple.

The Thieves

❖

Luke 23:39–42; Mark 15:23

You know, I was reading the Scriptures the other day and it said that both the thieves crucified on either side of the Lord spoke ill of Him (Mt 27:44, Mk 15:32). Both of them. And one of them, after seeing Our Lord suffer so patiently and asking the Father to forgive His enemies, then says, "Jesus . . . remember me when you come into your kingdom" (Lk 23:42). He realized that only God could do that. I was surprised. You know you can read Scripture a thousand times and you always find something new.

Both of the thieves reprimanded the Lord and said, "You're supposed to be the big one, why aren't you taking us all down from these crosses?" (23:39). The other one said at some point, "Look we have what we deserve, but this is an innocent man, he hasn't done anything" (23:40–41). So somewhere along the line Our Lord's beautiful example of love and patience in the midst of great insults and trials touched that thief's heart. He found faith at the very end, and stole heaven.

The wine they gave Our Lord is another interesting detail in the Scripture. It was a bitter wine with a kind of narcotic in it to dull the pain; they gave it to a lot of the people who were crucified. Our Lord wouldn't drink it. He refused it, Saint Mark tells us (Mk 15:23). So there again, He deliberately chose to give His last drop of blood for us—which would have to take a miracle of the Holy Spirit because there's no way a man could endure such pain. You'd go unconscious. When the centurion pierced His heart, blood and water flowed out. When you reach the point that all the blood has been drained, water begins to come out of the body. That's why Saint John mentioned water. Blood and water came out (Jn 19:34). Every drop of His blood was shed, everything given for you.

THE LIGHT OF THE WORD

Nothing is greater than the mind of man, except God. Learn to fix the eye of faith on the divine word of the Holy Scriptures as on a light shining in a dark place until the day dawns and the day star arises in our hearts. For the ineffable source from which this lamp borrows its light is the Light that shines in the darkness, but the darkness does not comprehend it. To see it, our hearts must be purified by faith.

— SAINT AUGUSTINE

Belief in the Resurrection

❖

Luke 24:1–12

ON THE FIRST DAY OF THE WEEK, AT THE FIRST SIGN OF DAWN, THEY WENT TO THE TOMB WITH THE SPICES THEY HAD PREPARED (24:1). THEY FOUND THAT THE STONE HAD BEEN ROLLED AWAY FROM THE TOMB (24:2), BUT ON ENTERING DISCOVERED THAT THE BODY OF THE LORD JESUS WAS NOT THERE (24:3). AS THEY STOOD THERE NOT KNOWING WHAT TO THINK, TWO MEN IN

BRILLIANT CLOTHES SUDDENLY APPEARED AT THEIR SIDE (24:4). TERRIFIED, THE WOMEN LOWERED THEIR EYES (24:5).

Isn't it funny how we're always terrified by the supernatural? The people I meet on the street scare me more. Well, these women who went to Jesus's tomb were terrified. They're standing there looking at this empty tomb, when, all of a sudden TWO MEN IN BRILLIANT CLOTHES are there standing next to them (24:4). [T]HE WOMEN LOWERED THEIR EYES (24:5). I don't know whether the light was too great or they were just awestruck, but they lowered their eyes. Women in those days lowered their eyes, but today we'd probably say: "What do you want?" And reach for some sunglasses.

[T]HE TWO MEN SAID TO THEM, "WHY LOOK AMONG THE DEAD FOR SOMEONE WHO IS ALIVE?" (24:5). Now remember, these women are the ones who were there with Jesus throughout His Passion. They didn't cop out like the men did (except for John). These women were the faithful ones. So why do the angels challenge these faithful women? Well, *they're* the ones who saw Jesus before Pilate, they saw Him before Caiaphas, they saw Him dragged up the street, they saw Him fall, they saw Him crowned with thorns, hang on the cross for many hours, die, His body practically shredded just from the scourging—most men would have died then and there, but He kept Himself alive so that He could suffer more for you and me. They witnessed all of that and still they are looking among the dead for Christ, seeking Him the way the world would seek Him.

"WHY LOOK AMONG THE DEAD FOR SOMEONE WHO IS ALIVE?" "Why are you having these doubts?" they're asking the women. Then the angels say: "HE IS NOT HERE; HE HAS RISEN" (24:6). What a bomb that is. "REMEMBER WHAT HE TOLD YOU WHEN HE WAS STILL IN GALILEE" (24:6). So what does that mean? It means: "Why didn't you believe Him? Why didn't you stay here all night waiting for Him to resurrect? He told you three times. Why didn't you come earlier to watch and wait for Him? Why are you just asking where He is? He told you! If He told you, why don't you believe it? Why are you looking for the living among the dead?" When you look at this Scripture, you should ask yourself: "How much do I really believe?"

"REMEMBER WHAT HE TOLD YOU WHEN HE WAS STILL IN GALILEE?" (These angels know the whole story.) Remember "THAT THE SON OF MAN HAD TO BE HANDED OVER INTO THE POWER OF SINFUL MEN AND BE CRUCIFIED"—they explained the whole thing to the women—"AND RISE AGAIN ON THE THIRD DAY" (24:7). Don't you remember that? There's such a difference between our remembering the Truth and the actions that follow. Our knowledge and our actions—there is a vast difference between them. We know a lot, but we do little about it.

The angels are telling these women that there is no excuse. He told you! If you want to know what faith is, my friend, it's to believe in what He said *totally*. Nothing else holds water. You can think what you want, you can excuse yourself all you want, but when you face Him on that special day, you won't have any excuses. It all falls away like water off a duck's back. No more excuses. We know we should forgive, but we refuse; we know we should be loving and cheerful with one another, but we aren't; we know we are our brother's keeper, but we could care less. We know what the Lord said, but are we doing it? Well, someday you will answer *not* for what you knew, but for what you did!

And that's what the angels are saying here: "Didn't He tell you?" Haven't I told you 1,588 times to get rid of all the junk and rot and fussing and fuming in your heart and mind and soul? Haven't I asked you a thousand times? Haven't I asked you not to gripe, not to be critical, not to gossip, not to go behind somebody's back, not to criticize, not to judge rashly? Haven't I told you a thousand times? But you don't do it. That's what the angels are saying here. Didn't He tell you back in Galilee? What are you doing here, right now?

Well, THE WOMEN RETURNED—all excited, probably shouting, "He's risen! He's risen! He's not there!"—THEY TOLD ALL THIS TO THE ELEVEN AND TO ALL THE OTHERS (24:9). . . . BUT THIS STORY OF THEIRS SEEMED PURE NONSENSE, AND THEY DID NOT BELIEVE THEM (24:11). Isn't that something? THEY DID NOT BELIEVE THEM (24:11). They told them the whole story—the tomb is empty, He's alive, and they were reminded of the prophecies. Our Lord warned them (told them three times) "I will go to Jerusalem" and that's where Peter said, "Well, if you're going to be crucified, don't go." And still they didn't believe the women.

PETER, HOWEVER, WENT RUNNING TO THE TOMB (24:12). This is one of Peter's hidden virtues, because if you or I had denied Jesus so miserably, I wonder if we would have run to the tomb. Most people, because they're so self-centered and scrupulous and self-oriented and guilty, would not have gone, they would have hidden somewhere—"Tell me where He is and maybe I'll go see Him." But Peter ran. He was repentant and he trusted. HE BENT DOWN AND SAW THE BINDING CLOTHES BUT NOTHING ELSE (24:12). No Jesus. Still, Peter doesn't understand that the Master is truly risen. Jesus said He would rise, but they didn't believe it.

How often are we in the same situation? After the cross, after tragedy, after years have passed, I look back and see that that cross was good. I didn't see it at the moment, I didn't understand it at the time, but it was good. I can see how a particular decision would have been the wrong one. If God had granted this to me, it would have been a disaster. Why didn't I see it then? Why didn't I believe Him when He said no? Why didn't I trust Him? But we still have a chance. We can still look at Peter and the others and learn from their example, learn from their mistakes—that we must trust the Master now! We must believe what He says—that as He rose, we shall rise. God Himself will wipe away every tear from our eyes (Rv 21:4), and He will love us and we will know we are loved by God and by every beautiful soul in heaven. We will be needed, we will be cherished, we will be understood. We SHALL KNOW AS FULLY AS [WE ARE] KNOWN" (1 Cor 13:12), and we shall be happy forever because Our Lord is risen.

After he visits the tomb the Scripture tells us Peter WENT BACK HOME, AMAZED AT WHAT HAD HAPPENED (Lk 24:12).

But see, he didn't hear what the Lord told him. He didn't believe. Say what you want about the Pharisees, at least they heard what Jesus said. Remember, they paid three or four soldiers to stand outside the tomb. The Scripture tells us that the Pharisees instructed the soldiers, "Just say His disciples stole Him when you fell asleep. If you have any problems we'll take care of it" (Mt 28:12–14). Isn't it interesting how evil made arrangements to disguise the truth while those who should have known didn't believe at all? The Pharisees believed at least on some level—that's why they could make arrangements to disguise what was coming.

Let us believe as the apostles eventually did. Let us strive to follow the Truth and to believe even when we see nothing.

The Road to Emmaus

❖

Luke 24:13–35

THAT VERY SAME DAY, TWO OF THEM WERE ON THEIR WAY TO A VILLAGE CALLED EMMAUS, SEVEN MILES FROM JERUSALEM (24:13), AND THEY WERE TALKING TOGETHER ABOUT ALL THAT HAD HAPPENED (24:14).

These disciples here, going to Emmaus, are a typical example of the wrong way to act. They had already been told by Mary Magdalene and some of the other disciples—friends, they called them—that the Lord had risen. And what did they do? They walked away from the Lord! They walked away from Jerusalem to go to Emmaus. What they hoped to find in Emmaus I don't know. They just wanted to get away. They're thinking: Let's leave this place. There's a bunch of nuts here, a bunch of hysterical women. And literally, that's what they said. And Our Lord was so kind . . . so gentle.

NOW AS THEY TALKED THIS OVER, JESUS HIMSELF CAME UP AND WALKED BY THEIR SIDE (24:15); BUT SOMETHING PREVENTED THEM FROM RECOGNIZING HIM (24:16). Their lack of faith is what did it. You wonder how many times, in the very trials we suffer, why we don't see Jesus? Because we're so blinded. We're blinded by ourselves, blinded by the flesh, blinded by the world, and sometimes blinded by the enemy—and that's why we don't see. We don't see. And HE SAID TO THEM, "WHAT MATTERS ARE YOU DISCUSSING AS YOU WALK ALONG?" THEY STOPPED SHORT, THEIR FACES DOWNCAST (24:17). And Cleopas says, "YOU MUST BE THE ONLY PERSON STAYING IN JERUSALEM

WHO DOES NOT KNOW THE THINGS THAT HAVE BEEN HAPPENING"
(24:18). He's very irritable. He's in no mood to answer a nice
question.

The Lord asked, "WHAT THINGS?" (24:19). Ha ha, Oh
Lord. And the disciple answered: "ALL ABOUT JESUS OF NAZA-
RETH . . . WHO PROVED HE WAS A GREAT PROPHET BY THE THINGS
HE SAID AND DID IN THE SIGHT OF GOD AND OF THE WHOLE
PEOPLE" (24:19).

See, that was their first mistake: They didn't believe He
was the Son of God. They heard what Peter said but they
thought, oh, Peter, he's always opening his mouth and getting
his foot in it. He always spoke and then thought. They believed
it was part of the same routine when he said, "You are the
Christ, the Son of the Living God." They thought, "Oh, there
he goes again." Many thought Jesus was only a prophet, even
His own disciples. They continue on: "WHO PROVED HE WAS A
GREAT PROPHET BY THE THINGS HE SAID AND DID IN THE SIGHT
OF GOD AND OF THE WHOLE PEOPLE; AND HOW OUR CHIEF
PRIESTS AND OUR LEADERS HANDED HIM OVER TO BE SENTENCED
TO DEATH, AND HAD HIM CRUCIFIED" (24:20). Here comes the
worst sentence of all (and their second mistake): "OUR OWN
HOPE HAD BEEN THAT HE WOULD BE THE ONE TO SET ISRAEL
FREE" (24:21). They didn't want a Savior; they wanted a deliverer. And I wonder sometimes if in our own interior life we
don't want a deliverer instead of a Savior. We want to be delivered from ourselves, from our weaknesses, from our faults,
from our imperfections—we want to be delivered from whatever is difficult for us. We don't want a Savior who makes us
know, in His infinite goodness, that we're rotten and fallen. We
don't want to know ourselves, so we don't look for a Savior; we
look for a deliverer.

Deliver me, Lord, from this temptation. Deliver me from

this fault. Deliver me from this imperfection—which may be the only source of humility you have, to know that you desperately depend upon God's grace to persevere in the least good thing.

Now, their third mistake: Not only did Jesus disappoint them, not only was He crucified by the leaders of the people (which means if He had been a true prophet this may not have had to happen), He was not going to deliver anyone. Now, to add to all these problems: "[S]OME WOMEN FROM OUR GROUP HAVE ASTOUNDED US: THEY WENT TO THE TOMB IN THE EARLY MORNING (24:22), AND WHEN THEY DID NOT FIND THE BODY, THEY CAME BACK TO TELL US THEY HAD SEEN A VISION OF ANGELS" (24:23). These were men who had heard Jesus speak of angels. They saw miracle upon miracle: the two multiplications of loaves, all the healings.

So you have to wonder in your heart: How did these men get so blinded? But we're the same, we're the same—aren't we? We don't see our nose for the rest of us.

Then they said, "SOME OF OUR FRIENDS WENT TO THE TOMB AND FOUND EVERYTHING EXACTLY AS THE WOMEN HAD REPORTED, BUT OF HIM THEY SAW NOTHING" (24:24). What incredulity—but don't criticize. We do the same thing. We read spiritual books that say that dryness is the greatest purification there is. We read with great anticipation that we're going to go through a "Dark Night of the Soul," but man, you haven't even reached the letter *D* let alone the "Dark Night of the Soul." We're astounded that the Lord would dare to purify us.

You know what the Lord said? [H]E SAID TO THEM, "YOU FOOLISH MEN!" (24:25).

You have to realize He didn't say, "Oh, you foolish *man*." There was nothing feminine about Our Lord. He was strong.

He said, "You foolish men!" He never said that to women, by the way. "So slow to believe the full message of the prophets!" (24:25).

Are we also not slow, when we take ourselves so seriously? Whatever I'm thinking, it's gospel truth. If I'm feeling something, it has to be right. We're no different from these disciples going to Emmaus. No different at all. It's the same pride these men had.

The Lord said: "Was it not ordained that the Christ should suffer and so enter into his glory?" (24:26). Oh, now, isn't that kind of interesting? Is it not ordained that we shall suffer? Is it not ordained that as children of a Crucified Lord we shall be crucified in some manner, even if only upon a splinter? A splinter. It's going to be terrible if we meet the Lord and He says, "You couldn't carry my splinter. You couldn't carry my splinter." When pain appears in my life I must understand that if it was necessary in His life, it is more necessary in mine. There is so much within me that must be brought out, and in the crucible of suffering, everything is purified. Then, starting with Moses and going through all the prophets, he explained to them the passages throughout the scriptures that were about himself (24:27).

When they drew near to the village to which they were going, he made as if to go on (24:28); that's the second time He did that. After the multiplication of the loaves He told the apostles to go on and He would dismiss the crowd. They were so irritable by that time that the Lord said, "Look, you go ahead. I'll take care of them." Instead, He went to the top of a hill and watched these men battle a storm. Finally, He comes walking on the water and they're scared to death. He made as if He was going past them because He wanted them to cry out,

"Lord, help us." And so it's the same here, the second time He made as if He was passing them, BUT THEY PRESSED HIM TO STAY WITH THEM (24:29).

They said, "Ah, don't go. You know, we didn't see the light. We enjoy what You say. Come on, stay with us."

He says, "No, I really have to go."

"Aw, come on. Please stay with us."

"No, I really have other things to do."

"Just break bread with us. Just have some supper."

"Well, okay," the Lord says. What a beautiful thing for God to do, to make you want to want Him. See, at the start of this little walk they could have cared less.

The personality of Jesus is so fascinating because as we stray, looking for our own answers to our own problems, trying to discern how to get out of this mess—if we would just press Jesus and say, "Lord, You know I can't do this without You, stay with me"—He will.

SO HE WENT IN TO STAY WITH THEM (24:29). NOW WHILE HE WAS WITH THEM AT TABLE, HE TOOK THE BREAD AND SAID THE BLESSING; THEN HE BROKE IT AND HANDED IT TO THEM (24:30). AND THEIR EYES WERE OPENED AND THEY RECOGNISED HIM; BUT HE HAD VANISHED FROM THEIR SIGHT (24:31).

All of a sudden, they saw Him. What is so fascinating about this is that they did not recognize His human person; they only recognized Him in the Eucharist. How pitiful that after two thousand years we're almost the opposite. We don't recognize Him in the Eucharist. "Oh," we say, "if He would just appear to me once, I would know for sure," or "I would recognize Jesus." Do you recognize Jesus in each other? These men didn't see Jesus. They didn't want Him at that point.

So their eyes were finally opened, they recognized Him and off He went. Why? It's faith He wanted. He didn't want them hanging on to Him because He appeared to them. He wanted faith, and their faith was enkindled when He broke the bread. They recognized Jesus and all of a sudden they saw He was Lord. I've got to recognize Him in you. THEN THEY SAID TO EACH OTHER, "DID NOT OUR HEARTS BURN WITHIN US AS HE TALKED TO US ON THE ROAD AND EXPLAINED THE SCRIPTURES TO US?" (24:32).

THEY SET OUT THAT INSTANT (24:33)—they forgot their dinner, they forgot they had already walked a long way—AND RETURNED TO JERUSALEM. THERE THEY FOUND THE ELEVEN ASSEMBLED (24:33), who said to the two, "YES, IT IS TRUE. THE LORD . . . HAS APPEARED TO SIMON" (24:34).

What a wonderful thing. He appeared to the very man who betrayed Him. Poor Simon. We only say "poor Simon" because of our own weaknesses and imperfections. You know what's so amazing to me: with all our problems and trials, we don't look to Jesus. When the disciples of Emmaus recognized Jesus, all of their problems were gone. Isn't that funny? When Peter recognized Jesus, all of his problems were gone. Why is it that ours don't go? Why is it that we wallow in the same darn things over and over and over: the same imperfections, the same weaknesses, the same idiosyncrasies—why is it we don't see Jesus?

"THE LORD HAS RISEN AND HAS APPEARED TO SIMON" (24:34). THEN THEY TOLD THEIR STORY OF WHAT HAD HAPPENED ON THE ROAD AND HOW THEY HAD RECOGNISED HIM AT THE BREAKING OF BREAD (24:35)—in the Eucharist.

So here are two kinds of recognition. The recognition of Jesus in your neighbor: Jesus has appeared to Simon—He hadn't appeared to them yet as a group. He has appeared to Simon, appeared to the women, appeared to Mary Magdalene, appeared to these men going to Emmaus—but they didn't recognize Him in His resurrected body. I would think that was because they were so obstinate. Isn't it strange that Magdalene recognized Him pretty quickly? She thought the fellow moving around the tomb was the gardener. She said (and it really is ridiculous), "Tell me where you laid Him, and I'll get Him." She's going to pick up a man nearly six feet tall—deadweight—and take Him away. Now, if that isn't the extravagance of love. That's Mary Magdalene. The women ran, they got so scared. Mary Magdalene was beyond scared. He said, "Mary." And she said, "Rabboni! Master!" Wow. And these men were walking with Him and talking with Him—He's explaining the Scriptures for Pete's sake—and nothing! Closed minds. Then Jesus broke the bread and there He was. He had to disappear at that point because the Eucharist would not be the Eucharist if He hadn't.

Man had fallen through a tree, and by a tree man would be redeemed. Oh why didn't they see it? And why don't I see it? Why is it so hard for me to understand that there are times in my life when pain is necessary if I am going to enter into my glory? If I am going to be like my Lord I must be like the whole Christ, not only the glorified Christ. I too will have my passion, and the glory to come. We must keep our eyes on the Risen Lord and our hearts will burn within us no matter what happens—for our God is risen. He is truly risen!

Jesus Returns to the Apostles and Thomas (A Meditation)

❖

John 20:19–29

IN THE EVENING OF THAT SAME DAY, THE FIRST DAY OF THE
WEEK, THE DOORS WERE CLOSED IN THE ROOM WHERE THE
DISCIPLES WERE, FOR FEAR OF THE JEWS (20:19). Suddenly
there is a silence in the room. Everyone feels a presence. They
recognize it. It is the Lord, but they are afraid. Right in the
midst of them is the Risen Lord. They look at Him and their
hearts pound within them. They are so afraid they dare not say
a word. And they are ashamed. The Lord looks at them and He
says, "PEACE BE WITH YOU" (20:19). If I could only remember
that one word when I am distraught as these apostles were distraught; when it is hard to have faith; when doubts assail me
and hope seems so far away; when I am discouraged, if only I
would look at the Master and hear Him say to me as He said
to them, "Peace be with you."

Then the Lord SHOWED THEM HIS HANDS AND HIS SIDE
(20:20). Each apostle and disciple looks at the glorified wounds.
They're closed and yet you know that there was once a nail
through those hands and those feet. Jesus kept His wounds
to show us how much He loves us. He will always keep those
wounds for they are the sign, a greater sign than the miracles
He performed, a greater sign of how much He loves us. From
those wounds rays of light and grace flow to you and to me.
Will it not be the same with our pains? Will not the suffer-

ings of this life glow? Will they not have their own beauty in heaven, and will not all men see what we have suffered for the Lord—what we have suffered with patience, with love, and with hope in deep faith? It will all be plain there.

THE DISCIPLES WERE FILLED WITH JOY WHEN THEY SAW THE LORD (20:20), AND HE SAID TO THEM AGAIN, "PEACE BE WITH YOU. AS THE FATHER SENT ME, SO AM I SENDING YOU" (20:21). AFTER SAYING THIS HE BREATHED ON THEM AND SAID: "RECEIVE THE HOLY SPIRIT (20:22). FOR THOSE WHOSE SINS YOU FORGIVE, THEY ARE FORGIVEN; FOR THOSE WHOSE SINS YOU RETAIN, THEY ARE RETAINED" (20:23).

THOMAS, CALLED THE TWIN, WHO WAS ONE OF THE TWELVE, WAS NOT WITH THEM WHEN JESUS CAME (20:24). WHEN THE DISCIPLES SAID, "WE HAVE SEEN THE LORD," HE ANSWERED, "UNLESS I SEE THE HOLES THAT THE NAILS MADE IN HIS HANDS AND CAN PUT MY FINGER INTO THE HOLES THEY MADE, AND UN- LESS I CAN PUT MY HAND INTO HIS SIDE, I REFUSE TO BELIEVE" (20:25).

Thomas is sure that these men are so distraught that they only imagine they saw Him. Their love for the Master was so great; they just think they saw Him. It couldn't be. That Man was so mangled. . . . He bled to death. He cannot, cannot, be alive. Thomas looks at the apostles and the disciples with dis- gust and he says, "UNLESS I SEE THE HOLES THAT THE NAILS MADE IN HIS HANDS AND CAN PUT MY FINGER INTO THE HOLES THEY MADE, AND UNLESS I CAN PUT MY HAND INTO HIS SIDE, I REFUSE TO BELIEVE." I look at Thomas and I think to myself, "I know. I have been incredulous so often, and I wish I hadn't been."

EIGHT DAYS LATER THE DISCIPLES WERE IN THE HOUSE AGAIN AND THOMAS WAS WITH THEM. THE DOORS WERE CLOSED, BUT JESUS CAME IN AND STOOD AMONG THEM. "PEACE BE WITH

YOU[,]" HE SAID (20:26). THEN HE SPOKE TO THOMAS, "PUT YOUR FINGER HERE; LOOK, HERE ARE MY HANDS. GIVE ME YOUR HAND; PUT IT INTO MY SIDE. DOUBT NO LONGER BUT BELIEVE" (20:27). Thomas falls to his knees. He will not feel those wounds. He knows indeed it is the Master.

THOMAS REPLIED, "MY LORD AND MY GOD!" (20:28). JESUS SAID TO HIM: "YOU BELIEVE BECAUSE YOU CAN SEE ME. HAPPY ARE THOSE WHO HAVE NOT SEEN AND YET BELIEVE" (20:29). I realize what a tremendous gift faith is. I have not seen Him, but I believe that He is risen, that He died for me, that He rose for me and that He lives within me.

CONTEMPLATION AND BEARING FRUIT

Contemplation is to be lost in the awesome wonder of God. I think that's one of the best definitions of contemplation. The whole reality, and necessity, of pondering the Word of God is so that Jesus might "live in me and I in Him." It implies that some live "in" Him and others do not. . . . He just didn't say, "Whoever remains *with* me, bears fruit in plenty." No. He says, "Whoever remains *in* me" (Jn 15:5). That's sanctifying grace, but I must remain *in* Him by the perfect accomplishment of His will.

If I do that, I have all the freedom and clarity of mind to ponder the truths of God. Otherwise your mind is cluttered with somebody or something else. Most of the time we run around with cluttered minds, and even when we come to prayer we complain that we can't pray. We're distracted.

(Sometimes we try so hard that we don't live in God; we

---

live in ourselves. We're so easily tempted to think of ourselves, or our comfort, that God becomes an afterthought. The worst thing during temptation is to think about it; because the more you think about it, the worse it gets.)

Prayer is important, because the fruit of prayer is love. The fruit that God bears in us is always the fruit of love. I can have all kinds of motivations for doing things or not doing things, but if the fruit is love, I can be sure that God bore it in me. Evil is also fruit; it's just bad fruit. Everything we do will bear fruit. The only way we can bear good fruit—because the Lord said, "without Me you do nothing"—is to remain in Jesus. Prayer, the sacraments, and contemplation of His Word are the only ways to remain *in* Him throughout the day.

The Mirror

When it comes time to live the Scripture you are looking at the *mirror of Jesus.* When you put yourself in front of that mirror, you know how you should be acting at every moment of your life.

Throwing Your Net Out

❖

John 21:4–7

Did you ever read chapter 21 of Saint John's Gospel? Do you realize that there is not one place in Scripture where the apostles caught fish without the Lord doing it for them? Look at this Scripture and you will know why God chose them and what He is looking for today.

Now, imagine you are one of the apostles: you've fished all night, you're soaking wet, and you've caught nothing. As you come to shore there is a stranger there, and He says, "HAVE YOU CAUGHT ANYTHING, FRIENDS?" (21:5). Can you imagine what you would say to that? My Italian temper would have gone right off the charts. I would have said, "I didn't go fishing," or "It's none of your business." I'm talking to a stranger after all; I don't know it's Jesus. Anything but the truth, never admit failure—that's the world today. But you know what Peter did? He said, "No, we didn't catch a thing." Very simple. He had something we don't have today. He had honesty and integrity.

The stranger says to them, "THROW THE NET OUT TO STAR-BOARD AND YOU'LL FIND SOMETHING" (21:6). This is totally unreasonable. God was asking them to do three ridiculous things: throw their net on the starboard side, in shallow water, at the wrong time of day. And they did it! They were simple men who were not afraid to do the ridiculous—they were dodos! What did they have to lose? They admitted their failure.

You see God is not looking for the successful and the competent who can do it on their own. He is looking for people like you and me.

If God were to say to you right now: "Throw your net on the starboard side of the boat," would you cling to it saying, "Oh Lord, the timing is not right"? Or would you say, "Lord, I just couldn't do that, people will think I'm nuts"? You have to be willing, in your interior life, to throw your net on the starboard side every day of your life. There's going to be a lot of shallow water and wrong timing. But you'll have the thrill of knowing that He does it all.

There were so many fish in the apostles' net that they could not pull them all in. At that point, John said, "IT IS THE LORD" (21:7). And here is a strange phenomenon: As soon as the net was full, as soon as they realized they had nothing to do with the catch except to be obedient—suddenly the fish were no longer important. It says that Peter (how I love Peter; I think he had to be an Italian Jew), Peter throws a cloak around himself, because he had practically nothing on, and leapt into the water to see Jesus. He didn't care how he looked. He didn't care what people would say. He wanted to get to Jesus and would use any means to get there.

Do you understand what God tries to do in your life sometimes? He is telling you to "Let go. Don't hang on. I'll take care of your future and your past. You let go." Throw your net and let Him fill it. Feel the thrill that must have been in the apostles' hearts on that magnificent day. They had an empty net and they kept doing the ridiculous and God kept filling it. It's only when we refuse to throw the net over that we catch nothing.

A Breakfast of Effort and Desire

❖

John 21:10–12

It says when they came to shore there was some bread there and a charcoal fire and fish cooking. JESUS SAID TO THEM, "COME AND HAVE BREAKFAST" (21:12). Isn't that tremendous? Jesus cooked breakfast for His apostles. Doesn't that tell you something? You see how human Jesus is, even after the resurrection? With His glorified body He's making breakfast. Isn't that fantastic? Tomorrow morning think about that and really savor your bacon and eggs. Jesus is totally unselfish. He looks at the apostles and says, "BRING SOME OF THE FISH YOU HAVE JUST CAUGHT" (21:10). Who caught what? He told them how, when, and where, then He put the fish in the net. But the apostles caught the fish. Jesus did it all, and the apostles did it all. They both had a part. In our lives it's very important for us to admit that all of the successes, all of the good in our lives, was put there by God. Sure you play a part, but so does He.

It seems to me that in our spiritual lives we don't have that deep reality of the invisible. Saint Paul says in Second Corinthians: "WE HAVE NO EYES FOR THINGS THAT ARE VISIBLE, BUT ONLY FOR THINGS THAT ARE INVISIBLE; FOR VISIBLE THINGS LAST ONLY FOR A TIME, AND THE INVISIBLE THINGS ARE ETERNAL" (2 Cor 4:18).

Now I want to go back again to that Sea of Tiberias scene after the resurrection. We know that those fishermen didn't catch one of the fish they ate for breakfast on their own. It was a miraculous catch. The Lord put the fish there. But the apostles had to do two things: They had to have a tremendous *desire* for a catch. They also had to exert *effort* to pull it in. So He could truly say to them, "Bring some of the fish you have caught."

It seems to me we lack something between the visible and the invisible in our lives. What is it that keeps us always in the same spot? What am I failing to do that keeps the Spirit from permeating my whole being? The Sea of Tiberias scene has the secret: We lack desire and we lack effort. We are either all effort and no desire or vice versa. We must right this imbalance and apply both effort and desire to do God's will.

The Ascension and the Descent of the Holy Spirit

❖

Acts 1:3–14; 2:1–3

Lets look at the Acts of the Apostles. Tradition tells us that Acts was written by Saint Luke. This book really gives us a sense of what the early Church was truly like.

HE HAD SHOWN HIMSELF ALIVE TO THEM AFTER HIS PASSION BY MANY DEMONSTRATIONS: FOR FORTY DAYS HE HAD CONTINUED TO APPEAR TO THEM AND TELL THEM ABOUT THE KINGDOM OF GOD (1:3). You know we just can't imagine being with the Lord in His Risen Body, and having Him give us instructions in the faith. Of course, at Mass you're at Calvary, and at communion, you're at the resurrection. Throughout your day, He's teaching you all day long. We don't always like the lessons He teaches. We don't always like what He's saying, but, nonetheless, He does speak to us through the events and the situations and the people we encounter.

WHEN HE HAD BEEN AT TABLE WITH THEM, HE HAD TOLD THEM NOT TO LEAVE JERUSALEM, BUT TO WAIT THERE FOR WHAT THE FATHER HAD PROMISED. "IT IS[,]" HE HAD SAID[,] "WHAT YOU HAVE HEARD ME SPEAK ABOUT (1:4): JOHN BAPTISED WITH WATER BUT YOU . . . WILL BE BAPTISED WITH THE HOLY SPIRIT" (1:5).

After forty days with Our Lord, they ask Him an amazing question. They said, "LORD, HAS THE TIME COME? ARE YOU GOING TO RESTORE THE KINGDOM TO ISRAEL?" (1:6). Now, we know we should never be discouraged about our ignoramus condition after hearing these apostles speak. They are as unenlightened as we are—maybe worse. That is kind of an encouragement. The Lord said, "IT IS NOT FOR YOU TO KNOW TIMES OR DATES THAT THE FATHER HAS DECIDED BY HIS OWN AUTHORITY (1:7), BUT YOU WILL RECEIVE POWER WHEN THE HOLY SPIRIT COMES ON YOU, AND THEN YOU WILL BE MY WITNESSES . . . TO THE ENDS OF THE EARTH" (1:8).

Then along comes another shock to these poor men. You know, you just have to feel sorry for them. I don't know what they thought was going to happen, but they could never have thought THIS would happen. All of a sudden the Lord starts rising up. HE WAS LIFTED UP WHILE THEY LOOKED ON, AND A CLOUD TOOK HIM FROM THEIR SIGHT (1:9). What is this cloud? Spirit. The Spirit always comes in a cloud. The Holy Spirit is a favorite theme of Saint Luke.

SO FROM THE MOUNT OF OLIVES, AS IT IS CALLED, THEY WENT BACK TO JERUSALEM (1:12), . . . AND WHEN THEY REACHED THE CITY THEY WENT TO THE UPPER ROOM WHERE THEY WERE STAYING (1:13); AND THEY JOINED IN CONTINUOUS PRAYER, TOGETHER WITH SEVERAL WOMEN, INCLUDING MARY THE MOTHER OF JESUS, AND WITH HIS BROTHERS (1:14)—which means Jesus's cousins. Joseph had brothers and sisters; Mary must have had aunts, who had, in turn, cousins.

WHEN PENTECOST DAY CAME ROUND, THEY HAD ALL MET IN ONE ROOM (2:1), WHEN SUDDENLY THEY HEARD WHAT SOUNDED LIKE A POWERFUL WIND FROM HEAVEN, THE NOISE OF WHICH FILLED THE ENTIRE HOUSE IN WHICH THEY WERE SITTING (2:2). They weren't praying on their knees. They were probably sitting around chitchatting, wondering what was going to happen. Somebody probably said, "Well, we've been here nine days. How long are we gonna stay in this place?" One of the others may have said, "What's the difference? You got someplace to go?" This is the first novena. [A]ND SOMETHING APPEARED TO THEM THAT SEEMED LIKE TONGUES OF FIRE; THESE SEPARATED AND CAME TO REST ON THE HEAD OF EACH OF THEM (2:3).

When Jesus sent His Spirit, He really sent His love upon the apostles. The Holy Spirit is the love the Father has for the Son, and the love the Son has for the Father. That is what Jesus left: He left His love for us. And that Spirit, that love that loves in me, is fruitful when I begin to imitate it. If my actions are loving, my words are loving, my thoughts are loving—then the Spirit reigns in my life.

His body went up to heaven but the Spirit became a fire. That's what love is; love is a fire; it gives people the grace to be martyrs, the grace to do great things, the grace to be heroic in virtue. Love is a force.

Love was the most important thing in the lives of the saints. They judged everything in their lives by love. They didn't judge by justice or truth or weakness or strength—they asked one question: Was I loving? Everybody is a lover, if you get out of the way. Because you're made by Love to love—so don't ever say "I can't love." You may love differently than others, but God made you and created you to be a lover.

The Spirit, I believe, came as a fire because nothing survives in a fire. Nothing brash, nothing rough—nothing survives a fire. When this fire came upon the apostles, weak men were made strong, frightened people were made courageous, timid people were made bold, the fearful were made so brave. Remember, all of these people were hiding for nine days in a locked room. Just imagine yourselves now, all of us locked in two rooms for nine solid days. You'd be chewing each other up.

So why did the Lord come as a fire? What does a fire do? It did exactly what it was sent to do: it consumed all of the dross, all the dust, all the sins, all the weaknesses of these apostles, and turned them around—because love consumes, and that's what fire does. Fire like love knows no bounds. You can see this at Pentecost when you read the Acts of the Apostles. The fire that came upon their heads consumed their hard-heartedness, their weaknesses, their fear, and their lukewarmness. Pentecost is an influx of Someone Who is Love.

The Father is God, and the Son is God, and the Spirit is God. So there's only one God, and only one Spirit, and there's only one Love expressed in different ways—expressed by the Father, expressed by the Son, expressed by the Spirit—but it never ceases being one Love. So when we take our love and we allow the Spirit to burn up our frailties, we live in Love, and we live by Love, and we live through Love. The Spirit and I become one, because I disappear and He takes over—and that's what happened at Pentecost.

The Invisible Reality of the
Holy Spirit

❖

Acts 2:13, 15

Here are men and women in the upper room, scared to death. The doors are bolted out of fear! In comes the Holy Spirit who permeates each one of them and leaves a visible sign of an invisible reality: a tongue of fire over each apostle.

They unbolt the door, go out, and they were so filled with God that they appeared to be drunk. Some of the people seeing them after this little experience said, "THEY HAVE BEEN DRINKING TOO MUCH NEW WINE" (2:13). You know how drunks look? They're silly, they can't walk straight, they might be dancing. The apostles were so filled with God and joy that they appeared drunk. They had to be doing something for the people in town to think they were loaded. The Spirit took such hold of them that they were completely changed into new people, like a new birth. They were born again in the Spirit.

Saint Peter then stands up with the eleven and announces in a loud voice: "THESE MEN ARE NOT DRUNK, AS YOU IMAGINE. . . . ON THE CONTRARY, THIS IS WHAT THE PROPHET SPOKE OF: IN THE DAYS TO COME — IT IS THE LORD WHO SPEAKS — I WILL POUR OUT MY SPIRIT ON ALL MANKIND" (2:15).

The Lord after His resurrection breathed upon the apostles and told them to receive the Holy Spirit. They had the Holy Spirit before Pentecost. What happened at Pentecost?

They received the seven gifts of the Holy Spirit. I think that on that day the invisible became visible. They had been with the Lord, but on this day the Holy Spirit touched their minds and reminded them of all the words and actions of Christ's life. They came out of that upper room infused with habits of virtue and the ability to constantly see the invisible. How conscious are you of the invisible?

An atom is invisible. Yet science tells us within an atom there are so many neutrons and electrons and protons, and so forth. Look at the power when you split an atom: a natural, invisible reality. The power can destroy a city. The Holy Spirit has a power as well—not a destructive power—but a supernatural, invisible power that is just as real as that of an atom. Call upon Him and ask Him to fill your life.

The Epistles

Mother Angelica's Notes on the Epistles of Saint Paul

❖

*S aint Paul is among Mother Angelica's favorite biblical figures,
and certainly one that she repeatedly turned to in her public
and private teachings. In the following excerpts she explains her
affection for Saint Paul and puts his writings in context.*

God uses crosses—hatred, misunderstandings, pain, and
suffering—for the good of His saints. Saint Paul wrote all of
his epistles under great pressure. Every epistle was inspired
because a particular community was in trouble. At times they
were misinterpreting him, or criticizing him, or in error. Saint
Paul had to write to these people, and from the tone of the writing you can tell that the apostle was having a difficult time.

Everything that he had worked for seemed to be falling
apart. When he went to Galicia and converted them and moved
on, they began to fall apart. When he went to Corinth and converted them, and left, that community began to fall apart. New
doctrines sprang up and new controversies. Saint Paul was in
a constant state of confusion. So to read Saint Paul's epistles
and grow from them you must know that they were written
under pressure, often in a state of heartache. Saint Paul could
be very angry. He had a caustic sense of humor and a deep,
real-world faith.

The True Saint Paul, the True You

❖

2 Corinthians 5:11–17; 6:3–10; Assorted

I thought perhaps we would look at Paul in the Second Epistle to the Corinthians. Here we see a man who was not always appreciated by the Christians. He was not considered an apostle by many. They thought him a usurper who had no right to be called an apostle, and so he constantly had to defend his right to preach God's word. I would like to explore with you today Paul, the man: the egotist, the arrogant intellectual, the humble Christian. He was a man who began his ministry in a very odd way, by hating. God chose Paul WHILE . . . STILL IN [HIS] MOTHER'S WOMB, he says in one of his epistles (Gal 1:15). And in another place the Lord says, "THIS MAN IS MY CHOSEN INSTRUMENT TO BRING MY NAME BEFORE PAGANS . . . AND BEFORE THE PEOPLE OF ISRAEL" (Acts 9:15).

But what kind of man did God choose in Paul? You know, I think there's a secret here. I'm always looking for secrets. I think all women love secrets; that's why we can't keep any. . . . But when we look at this man all we can think about is "Saint Paul the great orator." And he really wasn't that, you know.

During one of his great orations some poor fellow fell asleep, slipped off a windowsill, and killed himself (Acts 20:9). So Paul was the type of speaker who didn't always hold his audience's attention. He was a little bit of a bore. One day somebody complained to him and Paul got very angry. They said he was "NO PREACHER AT ALL" (2 Cor 10:10). They called him a half-pint (2 Cor 10:10). He was short, kind of stocky. Yet this is the man whom God chose. He had great zeal for the honor and glory of God and a love of souls.

In his earlier life when he saw that some of the Jewish people were going over to the other side (converting to Christianity), his zeal consumed him. He runs over to the Sanhedrin at one point and gets papers authorizing him to arrest the followers of Jesus (Acts 9:1–2). He's going to do this right. If he's going to drag you away in chains, he's going to do it legally. And he does. We don't know how long he did this, but one day riding his horse on the way to Damascus, with only one thing in mind, "crush these Christians," a bolt of light comes along. God says, "SAUL, SAUL, WHY ARE YOU PERSECUTING ME" (Acts 9:4). It was such a powerful moment he fell off his horse, and he goes into Damascus blind. It takes Ananias to come and cure him of his blindness and baptize him.

Now we have this concept of Paul at that moment: rising up, getting back on his horse, going to Jerusalem, and beginning to preach. Well, he didn't. He went into the desert for three years to pray (Gal 1:17). It's about ten years before he begins a missionary journey to preach the word of God. Just imagine, it took time even after he was knocked off his horse; it took time for this egotistical intellectual to become a humble servant of the servants of God. In our lives we have the impression that after I have said, "Jesus is Lord," I've got it made. I just walk off and shine my halo every morning before breakfast—off I go being the most patient, kind, loving person this world has ever known. Boy, are we kidding ourselves? You know the world is full of potential saints. We're all potential saints. If we just understood that we're *potential* saints and will be until we die, we'd never say (as some do), "I've made it." Until you reach heaven you haven't made anything.

Now I want to explore a little bit from the Second Epistle

to the Corinthians and show you the man Paul, and try to show you how you are not only going to be saints, but how you're already on your way. No matter how miserable you are, or how miserable you feel, you're on the way.

There are some clues right here in the Scripture that show you how defensive Paul was, and I think they reveal the man. He says: AND SO IT IS WITH THE FEAR OF THE LORD IN MIND THAT WE TRY TO WIN PEOPLE OVER. GOD KNOWS US FOR WHAT WE REALLY ARE (5:11). You see, somebody probably didn't think Paul was too hot. THIS IS NOT ANOTHER ATTEMPT TO COMMEND OURSELVES TO YOU (5:12). Somebody must have also told him, "All you do, brother, is boast, boast, boast." They were tired of it. But he can't help it—this is the man. In fact, in one of his epistles he writes, I WOULD RATHER DIE THAN LET ANYONE TAKE AWAY SOMETHING THAT I CAN BOAST OF (1 Cor 9:15). Isn't that beautiful? WE ARE SIMPLY GIVING YOU REASONS TO BE PROUD OF US (2 Cor 5:12), . . . IF WE SEEMED OUT OF OUR SENSES—somebody must have called him a nut—IT WAS FOR GOD; BUT IF WE ARE BEING REASONABLE NOW, IT IS FOR YOUR SAKE (5:13). . . . BECAUSE THE LOVE OF CHRIST OVERWHELMS US (5:14).

FROM NOW ONWARDS; THEREFORE, WE DO NOT JUDGE ANYONE BY THE STANDARDS OF THE FLESH. EVEN IF WE DID ONCE KNOW CHRIST IN THE FLESH, THAT IS NOT HOW WE KNOW HIM NOW (5:16). AND FOR ANYONE WHO IS IN CHRIST, THERE IS A NEW CREATION (5:17). That's what you are, a new creation. Like Paul, you're a Christian, and God lives in your soul. You have a dignity above all dignities. There is no dignity in this world that can compare with the dignity of having God within you and being called to, and being in, Truth. As Saint John says, we are CHILDREN OF GOD (1 Jn 3:2). Just imagine that: children of God.

Paul goes on and tells them that WE ARE AMBASSADORS FOR

CHRIST (5:20). WE DO NOTHING THAT PEOPLE MIGHT OBJECT TO, SO AS NOT TO BRING DISCREDIT ON OUR FUNCTION (6:3). This is one of the obligations you have: to be a good witness to the faith; to do nothing in your life that might *discredit* the faith. If you yield to any passion habitually, you discredit the faith.

Then he says, WE PROVE WE ARE SERVANTS OF GOD BY GREAT FORTITUDE IN TIMES OF SUFFERING (6:4). Uh-huh. These are the little things in Scripture that we would very much like to skip over. Yet we're constantly griping about our problems, our tension, our pain, the disappointments in life, and all the people who are hard to get along with. And what are you to do? Buckle under? Look what Paul did. He said, FORTITUDE IN TIMES OF SUFFERING—you prove you are a servant of God by fortitude in suffering. You don't pretend it isn't there; you face it head-on and stand tall.

WE PROVE WE ARE SERVANTS OF GOD BY GREAT FORTI-TUDE . . . IN TIMES OF HARDSHIP AND DISTRESS (6:4); WHEN WE ARE FLOGGED, OR SENT TO PRISON, OR MOBBED (6:5). Can you imagine being mobbed? Being flogged, being hated? Just walk-ing down the street and having somebody spit on you? If any-body did that to us that would probably be the end of our faith, our life, our hope, our love—we would flatten out in the gutter. But Paul went through all of it because THE LOVE OF CHRIST OVERWHELMS US (2 Cor 5:14).

Look at what Paul says: WE PROVE WE ARE GOD'S SER-VANTS BY OUR PURITY, KNOWLEDGE, PATIENCE AND KINDNESS; BY A SPIRIT OF HOLINESS, BY A LOVE FREE FROM AFFECTATION (6:6). You know we have a tremendous amount of affectation in our lives. I asked a woman one time, "How's so-and-so?" And she said, "Oh, I don't know, I never ask her. I'm afraid she'll tell me." That's affectation. Some people come up to you and they say, "Oh you look just beautiful." It nauseates you. Because you just got through looking in the mirror and you looked horrible. You've got bags under your eyes and you're tired. But they have this affected way of talking and you know it isn't from the heart. So Paul says we must practice A LOVE FREE FROM AFFECTATION (6:6), a love that comes from down deep and accepts a person as he is.

Do you really want to love God or do you want people to *think* you love God? Paul said we are OBSCURE YET FAMOUS; SAID TO BE DYING AND HERE ARE WE ALIVE; RUMOURED TO BE EXECUTED BEFORE WE ARE SENTENCED (6:9); THOUGHT MOST MISERABLE AND YET WE ARE ALWAYS REJOICING; TAKEN FOR PAUPERS THOUGH WE MAKE OTHERS RICH, FOR PEOPLE HAVING NOTHING THOUGH WE HAVE EVERYTHING (6:10). Now how do I get to that state, huh? It's beautiful to read. Beautiful. But now we come to the nitty-gritty living.

You have husbands and wives that bug you—well, you bug them too, so let's make it even steven. Don't forget, you are not only the bugged, you are also the bugger! Somewhere, somehow, somebody is under the impression that you are NOT God's gift to humanity either. This is life. I had a woman tell me the other day she's very unhappy because her husband's a salesman and he's constantly coming home with glowing tales about the cuisine he eats in all these restaurants while she's eating hot dogs at home. I said, "I wouldn't worry about that. Does he tell you the times he goes into an office and he's rebuffed by the executive who doesn't want his line of stuff or thinks it's inferior to what he's already using? Does he tell you about the nights he doesn't sleep wondering where he's going to go next?" Oh let's be real. Instead of thinking about how much you're suffering and how much so-and-so is bugging you, why don't you start to think: This is life. How am I going to become a saint with all of this? Because these things are

never going to leave you, and you will battle your faults until you die. You can go to Timbuktu or Bangladesh and you'd still be there with yourself. You are your biggest problem.

In the Scripture you'll find hope to transform your life. Don't despair and don't think holiness is not for you or that God doesn't love you. Though you fall a million times a day, our Father will reach down and lift you up and teach you humility. . . . That's what holiness is. It's about falling and rising with God. If you reject God, it is you who reject Him. He never rejects you. God's hand is the last one to let go. That's the message of Paul and that's the message of Christ.

You see, I find the apostles' faults very encouraging. I like to go through Scripture looking for all the human things that nobody ever mentions—the disgusting disease that Saint Paul mentions in Second Corinthians (12:7). We don't like to think that Paul had a disgusting disease. He is supposed to be this towering figure, this great holy man, like that statue in Rome. Well, he might have had epilepsy. Can you imagine Saint Paul an epileptic? He might have had dysentery. "Oh, no saint would have dysentery!" some will say. The saints had dysentery and they had a lot of other things. This is life! They lived it with God, and so must we.

The Marks of a Christian

❖

Titus 1:5–15

Today we're going to look at the letter of Saint Paul to Titus, because it is seldom read. There must be something in Titus that keeps everyone away. It says, THE REASON I LEFT YOU BEHIND IN CRETE WAS FOR YOU TO GET EVERYTHING ORGANISED . . . AND APPOINT ELDERS IN EVERY TOWN, IN THE WAY THAT I TOLD YOU (1:5): THAT IS, EACH OF THEM MUST BE A MAN OF IRREPROACHABLE CHARACTER; HE MUST NOT HAVE BEEN MARRIED MORE THAN ONCE, AND HIS CHILDREN MUST BE BELIEVERS AND NOT UNCONTROLLABLE OR LIABLE TO BE CHARGED WITH DISORDERLY CONDUCT (1:6). Paul was very strict with the ministers. Not only did the ministers have to be holy, but their families had to be holy as well. SINCE, AS PRESIDENT, HE WILL BE GOD'S REPRESENTATIVE, HE MUST BE IRREPROACHABLE: NEVER AN ARROGANT OR HOT-TEMPERED MAN (1:7). This applies to all Christians because we all share the priesthood, though we don't all perform the function in the same manner. So he is telling us never to be hot-tempered, NOR A HEAVY DRINKER OR VIOLENT, NOR OUT TO MAKE MONEY (1:7). Today this is accepted and no longer considered wrong.

Paul says that the ideal candidate must be A MAN WHO IS HOSPITABLE (1:8). It is something that is indicative of a Christian. Now, sometimes we get the wrong idea of hospitality. We think this means that grandma, Uncle George, and your mother-in-law are going to come for Christmas and you have to kind of brace yourself for this awful trial. It makes for

one miserable holiday. Hospitality is not only inviting some-one into your home, but it is inviting someone into your heart. The essence of hospitality is to make someone feel that they are important to you. It means showing a willingness to help others no matter the cost. A Christian must be HOSPITABLE AND A FRIEND OF ALL THAT IS GOOD; SENSIBLE, MORAL, DEVOUT AND SELF-CONTROLLED (1:8). Most people have no sense of these anymore. Self-control means that you have mental and physical discipline. If more people practiced self-control there would be true peace and less evil.

He goes on to say HE MUST HAVE A FIRM GRASP OF THE UNCHANGING MESSAGE OF THE TRADITION (1:9). Don't forget, he said "tradition" because when Paul was writing to Titus there were no epistles. None of the people reading these letters had any concept that we would later consider them Scripture. At the time they were considered by some to be the letters of a madman, a former persecutor of the Church. Everything that Jesus did was passed on to them by word of mouth, gesture, and practice.

He goes on to say there are A GREAT MANY PEOPLE WHO NEED TO BE DISCIPLINED, WHO TALK NONSENSE AND TRY TO MAKE OTHERS BELIEVE IT (1:10). What do you do with these people? How far do you go with someone who is in error? You never stop loving him, but at what point do you no longer condone what he does or thinks? Saint Paul is quite clear: THEY HAVE GOT TO BE SILENCED: MEN OF THIS KIND RUIN WHOLE FAMILIES, BY TEACHING THINGS THAT THEY OUGHT NOT TO (1:11). . . . YOU WILL HAVE TO BE SEVERE IN CORRECTING THEM, AND MAKE THEM SOUND IN THE FAITH (1:13). So we must not let corrupt teach-ers slide, but be clear and bold in correcting their errors. But at the same time we must be charitable enough so that they continue to listen and return to a sound faith.

Paul says, To ALL WHO ARE PURE THEMSELVES, EVERYTHING IS PURE; BUT TO THOSE WHO HAVE BEEN CORRUPTED AND LACK FAITH, NOTHING CAN BE PURE—THE CORRUPTION IS BOTH IN THEIR MINDS AND IN THEIR CONSCIENCES (1:15). THEY CLAIM TO HAVE KNOWLEDGE OF GOD BUT THE THINGS THEY DO ARE NOTHING BUT A DENIAL OF HIM; THEY ARE OUTRAGEOUSLY RE-BELLIOUS AND QUITE INCAPABLE OF DOING GOOD (1:16). It's an awful indictment.

There are people, even in the world today, who are delib-erately trying to confuse you, to ruin the Christianity that you have learned your whole life through. When they aggravate you to the point where you're ready to pop them they say, "Hey, a Christian wouldn't do that." Don't strike them, reach out and give them the truth. We must be kind to all, but know that there are some whom you must stay away from, who will never listen to you. Leave them to the Lord and walk away.

Picking Up the Pieces

❖

Acts 20:9–12

I love Saint Paul, but I'm going to deck him when I get to the Kingdom. Because I have often used him as an example of how human and faulty you can be while still achieving holi-ness. This little man was a terrible preacher and he knew it.

One day he talked all night and this kid up in a windowsill fell asleep—flopped right out the window to his death. Paul didn't strike his breast and say, "Oh I spoke too long." He ran out to this poor body splattered all over the ground and he said,

"Son, get up." Then he went back upstairs, continued eating, and preached the rest of the night.

He was human and he let God's grace build on that human nature. He knew what it meant to be holy: being faithful to the state of life where God has placed you, accepting everything as coming from the Lord, living in the present moment, and being enthused. We lack this in the Church today. Loving God is not a joyless thing, and it shouldn't be a passionless thing either.

Reaching the Promised Land

❖

Hebrews 4:1–3, 6–7

In chapter 4 of Hebrews it speaks of the forty years that the Israelites wandered through the desert. They were unfaithful to God. Yet it is amazing to me how faithful God is to us. No matter how unfaithful people are, God constantly pursues them as a shepherd pursues a lost sheep. He is always faithful.

Saint Paul says: BE CAREFUL, THEN: THE PROMISE OF REACHING THE PLACE OF REST HE HAD FOR THEM STILL HOLDS GOOD, AND NONE OF YOU MUST THINK THAT HE HAS COME TOO LATE FOR IT (4:1). The "place of rest" Paul speaks of is the Messiah, the new covenant, the new kingdom. They had gone through the desert to arrive at the Promised Land—the promised Messiah. Paul also says, WE RECEIVED THE GOOD NEWS EXACTLY AS THEY DID; BUT HEARING THE MESSAGE DID THEM NO GOOD BECAUSE THEY DID NOT SHARE THE FAITH OF THOSE WHO LISTENED

(4:2). This is one of the greatest phenomena I would say. You can go to any church and you will find that people week after week are being told the same thing. They are all listening, but they do not all *hear*. They never reach the Promised Land.

Every sermon you hear, everything you read should help you arrive at that Promised Land. Your heaven, or hell, or purgatory begins here. You don't just die and go to heaven. I see people in hell here; they do the same evil thing over and over and over. They are miserable. They spend forty years in the desert of misery, suffering, and spiritual hunger. They never arrive at that place of rest, that tranquility of spirit. Human passions and human greed keep them away. Saint Paul says we indulge ourselves. We think of our pleasure and our pet hatreds—everybody has one. And these things bar us from freedom of the soul. WE, HOWEVER, WHO HAVE FAITH, SHALL REACH A PLACE OF REST (4:3), Paul says. Is he only talking about the final rest? No, your eternity begins here. You are right now in heaven or hell. Most people hop back and forth.

IT IS ESTABLISHED, THEN, THAT THERE WOULD BE SOME PEOPLE WHO REACH IT, AND SINCE THOSE WHO FIRST HEARD THE GOOD NEWS FAILED TO REACH IT THROUGH THEIR DISOBE-DIENCE (4:6), GOD FIXED ANOTHER DAY (4:7). Now, some would look upon this as predestination and claim that God looked upon everything and said, "You people on the left go to hell. You people on the right go to heaven." No. It's only that God, to whom all things are present, knows what I will do. Do you think it was a surprise that He chose Judas? Because God follows the pattern that He has set before all men. You as an individual must choose. And to choose well, Saint Paul offers this nugget of advice: "If only you would listen to Him today; do not harden your hearts" (Heb 3:15). Listen to what the Lord is telling you in each moment, watch what He is sending you in each moment. He wants you to follow Him, but He won't force you—and He won't impose a final destination on you. You do.

When you hear people say that there is no hell because God is loving, and being a loving God He would never condemn anyone to hell, that's a truth, but only half a truth. God does not put anyone in hell, God does not want anyone in hell, but they themselves will it. God loving lets you go where you want to go. The individual puts himself in hell. You see God didn't do His people some great injustice by allowing them to wander through the desert for forty years. If God gave you everything you wanted, He would not be treating you like a father. A father chastises. When God says no to you, it is a blessing, because He is acting toward you as a Father who knows best. When He lets you go, when His infinite justice allows you to go your own way, then you are in trouble. So long as God gives you some things and denies you others, rest secure.

We shall all travel toward heaven, but we shall not all arrive. Some of our pagan brothers will get there and we will not. Each shall be judged by the light we have been given. Remember, we are intended to arrive, so let's not linger in the desert. Don't hug your little passions: the bottles, the sex, the meanness, the greed. Stop hugging misery as if it were livable, leave the desert once and for all, and journey on toward the Promised Land.

Patient Perseverance

❖

Romans 5:3–4

Saint Paul says here, THESE SUFFERINGS BRING PATIENCE, AS WE KNOW (5:3), AND PATIENCE BRINGS PERSEVERANCE, AND PERSEVERANCE BRINGS HOPE (5:4). One would imagine that suffering could be of no use to our poor human nature. We don't want to suffer. We don't. We like to persevere, but we don't understand that suffering makes us persevere.

Perseverance in itself is a virtue, a moving virtue—it pushes you to keep going in the face of all obstacles. It's a very active virtue, and that's why when I read this I never cease to wonder how sufferings bring patience. We think sufferings make us impatient, but Paul says that "sufferings bring patience." During suffering we must accept what God has sent us. In that acceptance we find patience. And if we can be patient long enough, we are persevering. The constant giving of oneself to God's will, persevering through pain and suffering, is itself an act of hope, isn't it? Patient perseverance—what a beautiful definition of hope. No matter your condition, be hopeful each day, each moment, and remember that God perseveres in His love for you.

The Light

❖

2 Corinthians 4:6

In Second Corinthians Saint Paul says Jesus is the "LIGHT SHINING OUT OF DARKNESS," WHO HAS SHONE IN OUR MINDS TO RADIATE THE LIGHT OF THE KNOWLEDGE OF GOD'S GLORY, THE GLORY ON THE FACE OF CHRIST (4:6). We learn a few things here.

We learn, first, that there must be light shining out of darkness. This part is amazing to me: WHO HAS SHONE IN OUR MINDS (4:6). That's where the light is. We're always looking for somebody radiating light by their holy life, by what they accomplish, by what they do, by their virtue—aren't we? And all of that is fine. But what Saint Paul is saying here is when we talk about Jesus, it is THE LIGHT OF THE KNOWLEDGE OF GOD'S GLORY (4:6) that gives us light. So we take light from light.

God's Choice

❖

Galatians 1:15

Let's go to Galatians: GOD, WHO HAD SPECIALLY CHOSEN ME WHILE I WAS STILL IN MY MOTHER'S WOMB, CALLED ME THROUGH HIS GRACE AND CHOSE (1:15) TO REVEAL HIS SON IN ME (1:16).

You have to grasp the reality that through God you were

present from all eternity. He had you in His mind from the beginning. If you want to ponder something sometime, that would be a wonderful thing to ponder because it is beyond our realization.

It says here WHILE I WAS STILL IN MY MOTHER'S WOMB (1:15), He called me and chose me. Paul was specially chosen, as you and I are chosen. We cannot even comprehend "before time began." But to be specially chosen *then,* I had to be in the mind of God *before* time began. God doesn't do anything haphazardly. He's not impetuous. He doesn't say, "Oh I think I'll create this one." Before the angels fell, before time began, you were in the mind of God. Stop to think for a moment that God really designed you—decided that you would be, then waited for how long? Only Someone who truly loves you would wait that long for your appearance.

Spiritual Warfare

❖

Ephesians 6:10–18

Saint Paul says here, GROW STRONG IN THE LORD, WITH THE STRENGTH OF HIS POWER (6:10)—not my power, His power. PUT GOD'S ARMOUR ON (6:11).

Why are you supposed to grow strong in the Lord and why are you supposed to put on His power and His armor? SO AS TO BE ABLE TO RESIST THE DEVIL'S TACTICS (6:11). FOR IT IS NOT AGAINST HUMAN ENEMIES THAT WE HAVE TO STRUGGLE, BUT AGAINST THE SOVEREIGNTIES AND THE POWERS WHO ORIGINATE THE DARKNESS IN THIS WORLD, THE SPIRITUAL ARMY OF EVIL IN THE HEAVENS (6:12).

SO STAND YOUR GROUND, WITH TRUTH BUCKLED ROUND YOUR WAIST (6:14). Do you understand? You cannot resist the enemy without the Lord. You cannot be strong without the Lord. You cannot do anything without the Lord. We're all different—kind of like a sassafras tree. Sassafras trees have different leaves. One looks like a glove, one looks like a clenched fist, and one has a little thumb protruding from the side. They're all of the same tree, but have different forms. This to me is one of the best things to analyze: to look at the diversity in God's Kingdom. Even though we are all pummeled by the enemy, the flesh, and the world (mostly the flesh), the solution for each of us is the same: God. In other words, we all come from the same tree, and the tree is God.

As we strive for holiness, all we have to say is yes to God, and He does it all. He does it all. We MUST RELY, he said, ON GOD'S ARMOUR (6:13). See, that's the freedom He wants for all of us. As I enjoy poor health—and I do enjoy it—it's a marvel to me that since I laid down and said, "Lord, if this is all You want for me to do at this point, it's all I need to do"—I've never seen so many wonderful fruits and so many wonderful things happen.

Saint Paul tells us to put on INTEGRITY FOR A BREASTPLATE (6:14), WEARING FOR SHOES ON YOUR FEET THE EAGERNESS TO SPREAD THE GOSPEL OF PEACE (6:15)—Zeal, Zeal—AND ALWAYS CARRYING THE SHIELD OF FAITH SO THAT YOU CAN USE IT TO PUT OUT THE BURNING ARROWS OF THE EVIL ONE (6:16). Faith actually counters the temptations and lures of the devil. Pretty good.

We've got to keep fighting. The only people who don't get anything accomplished or don't feel anything are mummies, but as long as you're breathing there is something happening in your soul. You're either going up or down. There's no way you can remain in the same place. In this struggle, you have to fight to keep moving upward. That's what we have to re-member. As we struggle for holiness, without any consolations, we often don't have the slightest idea that we're being trans-formed by God. But that is what's happening. You don't get a report card in the spiritual life, you get pain and sufferings and temptations. That's the report card. And it says: "You're making progress."

AND THEN YOU MUST ACCEPT SALVATION FROM GOD TO BE YOUR HELMET AND RECEIVE THE WORD OF GOD FROM THE SPIRIT TO USE AS A SWORD (6:17)—to fight back. And then here's the clincher: PRAY ALL THE TIME (6:18). All the time. How do you pray all the time?

Saint Paul says to PRAY ALL THE TIME, ASKING FOR WHAT YOU NEED (6:18). How do you like those apples? ASKING FOR WHAT YOU NEED (6:18). Sometimes we think of that as a kind of infe-rior prayer, like vocal prayer—petition prayer. In a petition we say, "Lord, please give me what I need." So let's try to put that into practice here and see what the Lord is saying. How many times do we say, "Lord, help me do something I do every day?"

What a prayer, to say, "Lord, at this meal let me not sin with my tongue." "Help me to have patience with my children at this event." "Lord, keep me from slugging this man." See, I can go from exercise to exercise, from event to event and never talk to the Lord in the course of the day. Saint Paul instructs us to keep PRAYING IN THE SPIRIT ON EVERY POSSIBLE OCCASION (6:18). Saint Paul is telling us how to pray without ceasing, how the Lord wants us to pray. To pray in the Spirit is to pray as the apostles prayed.

Praying in the spirit is to pray with the mind of Jesus. Saint Paul's talking about spiritual warfare. He wants our hearts and minds to be aligned with God's will. It means that I am open on every possible occasion, open to the power of God. That's the most important interpretation. To pray in the Spirit is to pray with the mind of God, to pray in love, out of love, to pray with the same will as the Father, and to pray with the same mind as the Father. On every possible occasion, pray that way.

NEVER GET TIRED OF STAYING AWAKE TO PRAY FOR ALL THE SAINTS (6:18). Pray for each other. Pray for the world. Pray for the Church. Pray for priests. Pray for religious. Pray for all those in cults, and all those Christians who have lost their faith. We've got so much to pray for. Ask the Lord for His help throughout your daily activities. When you do that you are saying, "Lord, I need You. I can't do anything without You. I can't make a recipe. I can't get to work. I can't answer the door or the phone. I can't do anything unless I get Your help." I assure you the Holy Spirit will rush to your aid. As the Lord said to Nicodemus of the Spirit, THE WIND BLOWS WHEREVER IT PLEASES. . . . YOU CANNOT TELL WHERE IT COMES FROM OR WHERE IT IS GOING (Jn 3:8).

The Behavior of a Christian and Discovering God's Will

❖

Romans 12:1–20

The following excerpt is fascinating. In addition to sharing her great insights on Saint Paul's letter to the Romans, Mother reveals a biographical detail that I had never seen before. She has often told this story from her childhood, but the detail here is arresting in its own right. As with Saint Paul, Mother's personal reference only sweetens the teaching.

Saint Paul writes in Romans: THINK OF GOD'S MERCY, MY BROTHERS, AND WORSHIP HIM, I BEG YOU, IN A WAY THAT IS WORTHY OF THINKING BEINGS, BY OFFERING YOUR LIVING BODIES AS A HOLY SACRIFICE, TRULY PLEASING TO GOD (12:1). Which means that we should give God whatever comes our way whether it's dry hair, or pimply skin, or a headache, a toothache, or just the weather—little things, not big things, but give Him a lot of little things.

DO NOT MODEL YOURSELVES ON THE BEHAVIOUR OF THE WORLD AROUND YOU, BUT LET YOUR BEHAVIOUR CHANGE, MODELLED BY YOUR NEW MIND (12:2). So Saint Paul was telling the Christians that they couldn't even think the way they used to think. They had to think differently. We have to examine ourselves once in a while, take an inventory of where we are and adjust the way we think. I don't know if you examine your conscience before your night prayers, but you should.

THIS IS THE ONLY WAY TO DISCOVER THE WILL OF GOD (12:2). Now isn't that kind of a switch. You'd think you'd discover the will of God first and then practice virtue. Well, here he's saying you practice virtue and THEN you'll discover the will of God. That's a real switch. That's something entirely different. We often pray that we may know the will of God. But it is only in accepting the opportunity of the present moment (whether it be one of joy or sorrow) that we begin to know the will of God for us. By looking for Jesus in the present moment, searching for Him in the occassions of our lives, we can begin to understand the will of God.

Let me read that again. LET YOUR BEHAVIOUR CHANGE, MODELLED ON YOUR NEW MIND. THIS IS THE ONLY WAY TO DISCOVER THE WILL OF GOD AND KNOW WHAT IS GOOD, WHAT IT IS THAT GOD WANTS, WHAT IS THE PERFECT THING TO DO (12:2). It's an amazing paragraph. The Scripture is filled, filled with short paragraphs that boggle your mind, and this is one of them. By not modeling myself on the behavior of the world, not thinking as the world thinks, but by changing my behavior, modeled by my new mind, I can discover the will of God. I can know what is good, I can know what God wants, and I can know the perfect thing to do. My Lord, that's a revelation.

See, we've got it twisted around. We think, "I must first know what God wants, know the perfect thing to do, then I can practice this virtue." Saint Paul is saying just the opposite. He says, "When my behavior's like Jesus's, then I know the will of God and what He wants and what the perfect thing to do is." So many people seek the will of God. What God has permitted in this present moment is His will. You only discover it after you have done it.

IN THE LIGHT OF THE GRACE I HAVE RECEIVED I WANT TO URGE EACH ONE AMONG YOU NOT TO EXAGGERATE HIS REAL IMPORTANCE (12:3). Somebody somewhere was kind of strutting his Christianity around and Saint Paul was saying, "Lay off it. You're not that important."

I remember once I was given this award, the Mercy Award in Toledo, Ohio. There were about two thousand people at this luncheon. For some reason or other, it took four people to introduce me. The man introduced me and then the head of the organization introduced me, then some Sister came up and introduced me, and as I was listening to all these introductions and all these compliments and so forth, I looked out among the tables and all the people, and suddenly the whole thing disappeared right in front of my eyes. It was as if the whole room was suddenly emptied. And I saw an incident in my mind's eye. I must have been eleven years old. I saw myself in bed with my mother. She was sound asleep. I saw the one-room apartment we were in. The whole thing became very real again. I was on my right side facing the wall. We used to hear rats gnawing at the floorboards at night. This one little guy had been gnawing for days and finally he got through—and I saw this rat. You know, rats are like little raccoons—they're big with long tails. And this guy came up and was scurrying on the floor. Well, I looked at him, and my heart stopped beating. I was petrified. I was cold all of a sudden. What was scary was he stopped in the middle of the floor, turned, and looked right at me. I thought for sure he'd jump because those rats will eat anything and he was obviously hungry. I was petrified. But he just looked at me and turned around and went his way. There was a door in our apartment that led to a room where the apartment owners used to keep garbage. The door didn't fit, and the rat squeezed himself under that door and left. This whole scene appeared to me while these people were giving me all these accolades and compliments.

I knew what the Lord was doing. I don't know whether I had begun to believe what they were saying, or whether the Lord wanted to remind me that whatever had been accomplished was from Him—but I got the point anyway. That little moment brought to mind what Saint Paul said, "Don't exaggerate your real importance because you have to judge yourself soberly by the standard of faith." I have to judge myself and examine my conscience by the standard of faith. How do I measure up to the standard of faith? How does my conduct measure up to the standard of faith?

JUST AS EACH OF OUR BODIES HAS SEVERAL PARTS AND EACH PART HAS A SEPARATE FUNCTION (12:4), SO ALL OF US, IN UNION WITH CHRIST, FORM ONE BODY, AND AS PARTS OF IT WE BELONG TO EACH OTHER (12:5). We are truly one body. We all have different functions, and we all represent different parts of this one body, but we're one body. We belong to each other. Our gifts differ according to the grace given us, but we are a crucial part of the whole.

DO NOT LET YOUR LOVE BE A PRETENCE, BUT SINCERELY PREFER GOOD TO EVIL (12:9). LOVE EACH OTHER AS MUCH AS BROTHERS SHOULD, AND HAVE A PROFOUND RESPECT FOR EACH OTHER (12:10). We have to learn to respect each other's very different personalities, different gifts, different ideals and ideas. We have to respect those differences as something beautiful, and God given.

IF YOU HAVE HOPE, THIS WILL MAKE YOU CHEERFUL. DO NOT GIVE UP IF TRIALS COME; AND KEEP ON PRAYING (12:12). Sometimes we forget that. We don't keep on praying. And IF ANY OF THE SAINTS ARE IN NEED YOU MUST SHARE WITH THEM; AND YOU SHOULD MAKE HOSPITALITY YOUR SPECIAL CARE (12:13). That's why when people come to visit, we must be hospitable. They must always feel that they're not only welcome, but we're happy to see them. I think that's such a great thing because people see and feel our joy. Elsewhere in the Scripture it says: we must be hospitable because some people entertain angels as Abraham did (Heb 13:2).

I would advise you to read Romans chapter 12 because it has an awful lot of goodies in it. BLESS THOSE WHO PERSECUTE YOU: NEVER CURSE THEM, BLESS THEM (12:14). REJOICE WITH THOSE WHO REJOICE AND BE SAD WITH THOSE IN SORROW (12:15). TREAT EVERYONE WITH EQUAL KINDNESS; NEVER BE CONDESCENDING BUT MAKE REAL FRIENDS WITH THE POOR. DO NOT ALLOW YOURSELF TO BECOME SELF-SATISFIED (12:16). Never think that you've done enough, or you've worked hard enough, or you've been kind enough. NEVER REPAY EVIL WITH EVIL BUT LET EVERYONE SEE THAT YOU ARE INTERESTED ONLY IN

THE HIGHEST IDEALS (12:17). DO ALL YOU CAN TO LIVE AT PEACE WITH EVERYONE (12:18). NEVER TRY TO GET REVENGE; LEAVE THAT, MY FRIENDS, TO GOD'S ANGER (12:19).

Paul is kind of funny, he doesn't believe in exacting revenge on your enemies, but he has a quotation here that is classic. He says, Vengeance is mine—I WILL PAY THEM BACK, THE LORD PROMISES (12:19). . . . IF YOUR ENEMY IS HUNGRY, YOU SHOULD GIVE HIM FOOD, AND IF HE IS THIRSTY, LET HIM DRINK. THUS YOU HEAP RED-HOT COALS ON HIS HEAD (12:20). I think that's the funniest line in Scirpture. So being nice to your enemy, you heap red-hot coals on his head. We can try to make something nice out of it, but somehow I think he meant red-hot coals! Oh well.

Mother's Favorite Line in Scripture

❖

2 Corinthians 3:18; Assorted

Saint Paul's epistles are a theology of the spiritual life, a theology of Christianity. You can't read Saint Paul's epistles for even a moment without realizing that he is talking about living in holiness and charity (to the Thessalonians), explaining Christian behavior, and warning against errors (in Colossians).

In Second Corinthians, Saint Paul speaks a lot about our human nature. He says, TO STOP ME FROM GETTING TOO PROUD I WAS GIVEN A THORN IN THE FLESH (2 Cor 12:7). There's no human being in the whole wide world who does not have a thorn in their flesh. There's one weak spot in your spiritual life, in your nature, in your soul that is like an internal Achilles' heel. We all have one. Paul says, I HAVE PLEADED WITH THE LORD THREE TIMES FOR IT TO LEAVE ME (12:8), BUT HE HAS SAID, "MY

GRACE IS ENOUGH FOR YOU: MY POWER IS AT ITS BEST IN WEAK-NESS" (2 Cor 12:9). This is a concept lost on the world. That's why I encourage you to read the epistles so often. God says, "MY POWER IS AT ITS BEST IN WEAKNESS." And a typical Saint Paul remark is I AM QUITE CONTENT WITH MY WEAKNESSES (2 Cor 12:10). We must embrace that weakness, embrace that cross and let God transform it.

Paul speaks in Second Corinthians about the ultimate in transforming union. The ultimate. AND WE, WITH OUR UNVEILED FACES REFLECTING LIKE MIRRORS THE BRIGHTNESS OF THE LORD, ALL GROW BRIGHTER AND BRIGHTER AS WE ARE TURNED INTO THE IMAGE THAT WE REFLECT; THIS IS THE WORK OF THE LORD WHO IS SPIRIT (2 Cor 3:18). That's my favorite line in Scripture.

In another translation it reads: BUT WE ALL BEHOLDING THE GLORY OF THE LORD WITH OPEN FACE, ARE TRANSFORMED INTO THE SAME IMAGE FROM GLORY TO GLORY AS BY THE SPIRIT OF THE LORD (3:18).

Our lives have to reflect something of Jesus. You know, each of us is attracted to a different aspect of Our Lord's life. Some are attracted to His ministry, some are attracted to His Sacred Heart, the gentleness of Jesus, His compassion, His strength, His mercy, His patience. We all have something or some aspect of Our Lord's life that we're attracted to. And if we're attracted to it, we try to reflect it. We have to know that even the holiest of us is a mere reflection.

Now, is that all we are, reflections? Are we just here to REFLECT LIKE MIRRORS THE BRIGHTNESS OF THE LORD? No. We ALL GROW BRIGHTER AND BRIGHTER. And that's what the con-templative life is supposed to accomplish. We not only grow bright but we grow brighter and brighter. For what reason? To be TURNED INTO THE IMAGE THAT WE REFLECT (3:18). So it is not just an image we reveal to others; we're supposed to be turned *into* that image.

The other day I was reading about a favorite saint of mine. During the canonization process, people were asked to come and share their recollections of him. A peasant came forward and said, "I went to see a man, but I saw God." This is exactly what Saint Paul is talking about. We should reflect like a mirror the brightness of the Lord. But you can't do that if you're not totally obsessed with accomplishing the will of God and practicing love and charity. Charity is different from love. Ordinary love is my love for you. Charity is my love for God.

Remember, what we do is of no consequence, what we accomplish is of no consequence if our hearts, our souls, our bodies, our minds, our spirits are not being transformed. And the only way to transformation, the only way to reflect the "brightness of the Lord" is to hug the cross. In the spiritual life sometimes you're searching and searching for something you already possess. We look for holiness, but we rebel against the cross. We don't want dryness of spirit, soul, and mind. We don't want to go through that desolation or crisis or loss. We want holiness, but we don't want to spend time in prayer, and we don't want to keep our minds straight and clear and occupied with the Lord alone. See, I think that somewhere along the line we feel that holiness is a gift from God that requires nothing of us—that you wake up one morning and presto! You're suddenly holy. Sorry. It takes a lot of guts, guts right down here in your stomach, and it takes a lot of effort, and a tremendous amount of grace and emptying of self to achieve holiness. What must we rid ourselves of to permit God entry into our lives? Identify those thorns in your flesh and let God help you overcome them. In the doing, you'll find holiness.

A Life of Love

❖

2 John 1:4–6

In the Second Epistle of Saint John, the very short one, he says, IT HAS GIVEN ME GREAT JOY TO FIND THAT YOUR CHILDREN HAVE BEEN LIVING THE LIFE OF TRUTH AS WE WERE COMMANDED BY THE FATHER (1:4). AND I AM WRITING NOW . . . NOT TO GIVE YOU ANY NEW COMMANDMENT, BUT THE ONE WHICH WE WERE GIVEN AT THE BEGINNING, AND TO PLEAD: LET US LOVE ONE ANOTHER (1:5). It would be wonderful if we would remember this commandment of the Lord. If we did, the Lord would be so much within us, and we so united to Him. We would be able to live this commandment, and live it in such a way that everyone would know that we are Christians.

I read a line the other day and it said, "If you were jailed because you were a Christian, would they have enough evidence to convict you?" And I wonder how many of us would display enough evidence that we are Christians to be convicted in a court. Do our daily actions and our way of life demonstrate to people that we are Christians?

Then Saint John says, TO LOVE IS TO LIVE ACCORDING TO HIS COMMANDMENT: THIS IS THE COMMANDMENT WHICH YOU HAVE HEARD SINCE THE BEGINNING, TO LIVE A LIFE OF LOVE (1:6). To live a life of love. Perhaps the reason the world has grown cold is that Christianity has become just a code of ethics and not a way of life. Our lives are no longer a way of love. We are kind to people because it seems to be the thing to do. But we do not love them as the Master loves us, and we should—no—we must.

A Last Warning

❖

Jude 1:3–23

Saint Jude only has one epistle, but he had the same problem that Paul and Timothy and Peter had. No matter where the apostles went it seems someone came behind them and sowed bad seed. Jude says that he had been wanting to write for a long time and that we must FIGHT HARD FOR THE FAITH WHICH HAS BEEN ONCE AND FOR ALL ENTRUSTED TO THE SAINTS (1:3). A real Christian is a saint—the two words should be synonymous. We shouldn't think of saints as just wonder-workers. Those are charisms, but it has nothing to do with faith or sanctity.

Jude says, CERTAIN PEOPLE HAVE INFILTRATED AMONG YOU, AND THEY ARE THE ONES YOU HAD A WARNING ABOUT, IN WRITING, LONG AGO, WHEN THEY WERE CONDEMNED FOR DENYING ALL RELIGION, TURNING THE GRACE OF OUR GOD INTO IMMORALITY (1:4). They had the same problem we have today: the love bit. Everything is love, love, love. As long as it is "love," there is no sin. You just need to love, that's all. They turned the grace of God into immorality and used love as an excuse to do what they pleased, when they pleased.

Saint Jude reminds his readers of THE ANGELS WHO HAD SUPREME AUTHORITY BUT DID NOT KEEP IT AND LEFT THEIR APPOINTED SPHERE; HE HAS KEPT THEM DOWN IN THE DARK, IN SPIRITUAL CHAINS, TO BE JUDGED ON THE GREAT DAY (1:6). He brings up the fall of the angels: creatures who had fantastic light and pure intelligence—and they fell. We too can fall. This is a warning so that we do not become self-sufficient and arrogant. He continues: THE FORNICATION OF SODOM AND GOMORRAH AND THE OTHER NEARBY TOWNS WAS EQUALLY UN-NATURAL, AND IT IS A WARNING TO US THAT THEY ARE PAYING FOR THEIR CRIMES IN ETERNAL FIRE (1:7). We are not dealing with a vengeful God who condemns people to hell. Everyone who goes to hell wants to go. Hell is a choice you make. It is a total rejection of God and His love—and once you reject God's love there is only hate.

He says later: THESE PEOPLE ARE (1:8) . . . LIKE UNREA-SONING ANIMALS (1:10) . . . THEY ARE LIKE CLOUDS BLOWN ABOUT BY THE WINDS AND BRINGING NO RAIN, OR LIKE BARREN TREES WHICH ARE UPROOTED IN THE WINTER . . . TWICE DEAD (1:12); . . . LIKE SHOOTING STARS BOUND FOR ETERNITY OF BLACK DARKNESS (1:13). It is strange that men who were with the gentle Christ for three years, men who preached love, who performed beautiful miracles, had to be hard at times. And Saint Jude is being hard here. He is trying to awaken us to the reality of evil in the world, warning us that there are people who will destroy your faith if you allow them to. We too must discern when it is time to be hard, to be tough with ourselves and others.

Then Jude goes on: REMEMBER, MY DEAR FRIENDS, WHAT THE APOSTLES OF OUR LORD JESUS CHRIST TOLD YOU TO EXPECT (1:17). "AT THE END OF TIME," THEY TOLD YOU[,] "THERE ARE GO-ING TO BE PEOPLE WHO SNEER AT RELIGION AND FOLLOW NOTH-ING BUT THEIR OWN DESIRES FOR WICKEDNESS" (1:18). THESE UNSPIRITUAL AND SELFISH PEOPLE ARE NOTHING BUT MISCHIEF-MAKERS (1:19). Now the apostles thought they were at the end of time, as every generation since them has believed. Since Christ, every generation has looked for His Second Coming. There will be a generation that will see it. Take a look around:

never have so many people sneered at religion as they do today. The mischief makers are everywhere.

Jude then says: BUT YOU, MY DEAR FRIENDS, MUST USE YOUR MOST HOLY FAITH AS YOUR FOUNDATION AND BUILD ON THAT, PRAYING TO THE HOLY SPIRIT (1:20); KEEP YOURSELVES WITHIN THE LOVE OF GOD AND WAIT FOR THE MERCY OF OUR LORD JESUS CHRIST TO GIVE YOU ETERNAL LIFE (1:21). WHEN THERE ARE SOME WHO HAVE DOUBTS, REASSURE THEM (1:22); WHEN THERE ARE SOME TO BE SAVED FROM THE FIRE, PULL THEM OUT; BUT THERE ARE OTHERS TO WHOM YOU MUST BE KIND WITH GREAT CAUTION, KEEPING YOUR DISTANCE EVEN FROM OUTSIDE CLOTHING WHICH IS CONTAMINATED BY VICE (1:23). I marvel sometimes at the wholesale evil in the world today. Today we like to test ourselves by putting ourselves in the middle of the fire, in the presence of sin. The evil one uses scandal in other people's lives to ruin your faith and you cannot let that happen. You cannot let your faith rely on people, or churches, or ministers, but on God. People will disappoint you, but His Word and His Church will not.

Mother Angelica's Advice for Examining Your Conscience

❖

Before we go, let's talk a little bit about examination of conscience. I think it's necessary every night, or every afternoon if you wish, to examine your conscience. Examination of conscience should not be something picky; it is not to encourage scrupulosity. This examination is simply an exercise to clean this dish, this earthenware jar, our souls, inside and out—just as you would clean anything else. I don't think too many of you go without taking a bath every day; at least I hope you don't. But we allow our souls to get full of dust, full of cobwebs, full of all kinds of dirt.

The examination of conscience should be very calm, and conducted at a time of day when you have a moment to reflect—and be extremely honest. Do it in your room at night. You can't do it in the morning because you're just getting started, and in the afternoon you've got a long way to go. It's a time when you should look at yourself objectively, almost as a third person. That's the best way to do it, without providing any reasons and excuses. Simply say: *I did this.* It doesn't matter who enticed you to do it; it doesn't matter whether the occasion was just or unjust—none of that matters. *I did this thing: "I was unloving, I was unkind, I was impatient, I was angry, I was lustful, I showed disgust, or I showed annoyance. I committed these things, and I missed these opportunities."*

We should just sit before the Lord and say interiorly, *"Lord, what did I do today that was not pleasing to You?"* Leave everybody out of your examination of conscience. Forget saying: *"I don't like Mike, or I'm jealous of Sally"*—that is of no concern, because at death the Lord isn't going to ask you one thing about Mike, about your family, about your relatives, or Sally. He'll want to know what *you* did.

It's extremely important that you make an examination of conscience every day, no matter how brief, and keep your neighbor out of it. If you're honest with Him, you'll find yourself less and less disturbed with everybody else. It should sound something like this:

Lord, I was rotten today. I was arrogant, I was proud, I was impatient, I was unloving, I was unkind. I was not obedient in my mind; I was obedient in action but I missed being obedient in my reason. I missed so many opportunities today, Lord. I missed occasions of grace, Lord. I did not forgive readily. I was not thoughtful today. I was not able to overcome myself. I was cruel to a coworker. I was disinterested in what my wife said this morning at breakfast. I lied to get out of the dinner early so I wouldn't have to see that woman. I am constantly making excuses, Lord. Forgive me. Help me.

You see, with an examination like that, you give it all to the Lord. And after you say it, you forget it, like you do in confession. Say, *"Lord, I'm sorry for all of this, and I do most of this out of pride, and I'm going to try harder tomorrow."* You put it to rest. You bury it; it's gone now. You've had the courage to admit *you* are the one at fault. There's nobody else but you. It's very important that you do this every day. It's a cleansing of the soul. It's not a replacement for confession, because your sins are not forgiven, but it makes you more sensitive to the root causes of sin. It's kind of like a daily spiritual checkup.

Without an examination of conscience every day, I don't know how you can sincerely progress in the spiritual life, because if you don't know what's wrong with you, how are you going to improve? If you just eat, sleep, drink, pray, and thoughtlessly go to bed at night, how are you ever going to know yourself? How will you know what part of you is not like the Lord? Be very honest, my friends.

You know what's so strange? I find that some Sisters who very rarely make an examination of conscience refuse to be honest even when they're alone. Some laypeople probably have the same problem. Do they think they're kidding God? You were a louse all day long. You may as well admit it. When we're dealing with the Lord, we need to be totally transparent. And although we think everybody and his uncle are the cause of our transgressions, it is not true. They are merely occasions.

You can't go to heaven disliking even one person. Oh, dear Lord. Now, unless we overcome that totally and really love everybody, we're going to spend some time in purgatory.

Saint Paul brings out this point beautifully: YOU ARE GOD'S CHOSEN RACE, HIS SAINTS; HE LOVES YOU, AND YOU SHOULD BE CLOTHED IN SINCERE COMPASSION, IN KINDNESS AND HUMILITY, GENTLENESS AND PATIENCE (Col 3:12).

You ought to type this out and keep it in your pocket: Colossians 3:12–17. It's a wonderful examination of conscience. Paul goes on: BEAR WITH ONE ANOTHER; FORGIVE EACH OTHER AS SOON AS A QUARREL BEGINS—because, he says, THE LORD HAS FORGIVEN YOU, NOW YOU MUST DO THE SAME (3:13). OVER ALL THESE CLOTHES, TO KEEP THEM TOGETHER AND COMPLETE THEM, PUT ON LOVE (3:14). It's an awesome little paragraph. First of all it tells you who you are, what you are, and then it tells you how to change it. AND MAY THE PEACE OF CHRIST REIGN IN YOUR HEARTS . . . That's another little examination of conscience: Does the peace of Jesus reign in your heart? In heaven it has to, all the time. You must have the kind of humility to know you're not God's gift to humanity, never were and never will be—unless you become a great saint. That's your only value: You've got to be what God wants you to be.

Now go down to the next verse: LET THE MESSAGE OF CHRIST, IN ALL ITS RICHNESS, FIND A HOME IN YOU. TEACH EACH OTHER, AND ADVISE EACH OTHER, IN ALL WISDOM. Most of the time we only chitchat about incidentals, our faults and weaknesses. But we should be teaching each other, advising each other. WITH GRATITUDE IN YOUR HEARTS SING PSALMS AND HYMNS AND INSPIRED SONGS TO GOD (3:16). That doesn't mean you've got to sing out loud, God help us all . . . AND NEVER SAY OR DO ANYTHING EXCEPT IN THE NAME OF THE LORD JESUS. So, can you say all the things you say in front of Him? In His name? And finally, give THANKS TO GOD THE FATHER THROUGH HIM (3:17).

Here you've got an entire examination of conscience, the solution, and you have the reason—peace of heart.

You could concentrate on these few lines for the rest of your life. This examination of conscience could be the very best. It gives you light, it gives you hope, and you see the end of the tunnel, but it's realistic and it doesn't pat you on the back. And don't forget: if you have to forgive your neighbor, you also have to forgive yourself.

Use this time of examination to thank God for the occasions when you did come up to par. *"Lord, I thank You that I didn't sock Frank right in the kisser. I felt like it, but I didn't do it, and I thank You for that grace. I thank You for the chance to go on for another hour and maintain my composure, because I was so tired today. I thank You for that."* See, that's honesty. It's so critical that you perform a daily, honest to goodness evaluation of your miserable day. If you do that, tomorrow will be a lot less miserable, and so will you.

FINAL PRAYER

Lord God, I ask pardon for all our sins.

Lord, for all the times we've offended You in thought,

word, or deed;

for the selfishness in our lives and the ego that blocks

You out of our minds and hearts.

I ask pardon for the distractions that keep

leading us away from You.

I ask for Your mercy upon us, and on the whole world.

Prepare our hearts and minds, Lord, for what is to come.

Prepare our souls, our thoughts, our will, and give us strength

to fight the good fight. Give us communal love, Lord,

the kind that will bind us together as one in the heart of Jesus.

We ask, Lord, small and insignificant as we are,

that we may give You comfort and love.

We ask for pardon, Lord, for those who crown You with thorns by

their pride and arrogance. We ask pardon for those who scourge

You at the pillar by their immorality.

Lord, we ask pardon for those who strip You of your garments

by their greed and ambition for worldly things.

We ask pardon for all mankind. We ask pardon,

Lord, for the whole world, for all of our sins.

Be merciful to us, Lord. We praise and glorify Your name,

for You are holy, You alone.

We glorify Your justice, Lord, and Your mercy.

We praise and bless You.

Amen.

Acknowledgments

❖

I must first thank the woman who spent much of her life speaking the truths assembled on these pages. Today, even hidden in the silence of her monastery in Hanceville, Alabama, Mother Mary Angelica continues to spend long hours with her spouse, interceding for her spiritual children around the world. And though she is no doubt still seeing "invisible things" and hearing "unutterable words," she can no longer share them with us as she once did. Today she reflects what she has beheld. I am thankful to her for her prayers, her example, and for her continuing affection. This and the two books that preceded it are small tokens of my gratitude.

There is no way I could have assembled this book without the martyrlike labors of Sister Maria Consolata PCPA of Our Lady of the Angels Monastery. Sister spent many weeks transferring Mother's lessons from disintegrating audiotapes. She not only saved these priceless teachings; she then carefully transcribed them along with Sister Mary Paschal PCPA. The good cheer and humor of Sister Consolata never flagged, nor did her ability to locate just the right lesson for me. Sister Grace Marie PCPA has my appreciation for the splendid shot she snapped of Mother, which truly *made* the cover of this book. I am also thankful to the vicar of Our Lady of the Angels Monastery, Sister Mary Catherine PCPA who has been a constant encouragement and a wonderful collaborator. For their continuing prayers, I thank all of Mother's Sisters, some of whom are now relocated to foundations in France, Arizona, Ohio, and elsewhere.

There are so many people I have to thank for sustaining me through yet another book. First, there is my wife, Rebecca, and our children: Alexander, Lorenzo, and Mariella. They sacrificed so many nights and weekends for this work, allowing me to hide out in my office, litter the kitchen table, or run to the coffee shop to complete it. The process of assembling a collection like this is long and arduous, but my family was always there to bolster the editor. Any success this work enjoys is the direct result of their love and support. They are the animating spirit that gives me meaning, and my greatest hope for the future. I love you all so very much.

There are also many dear friends to whom I am indebted for their persistent devotion and encouragement: Christopher Edwards, my steadfast producer and wing man, who is always there; Doug Keck, my long-suffering executive producer; Laura Ingraham, one of the few people who never fails to send me into hysterics, even when her dog is devouring my chair; Michael Paternostro; Jim Caviezel; Umberto and Maryellen Fedeli; Andrew T. Miller; Ron Hansen; Kate O'Beirne; Carl Amari; and Joseph Looney. Your friendship means more to me than you know.

At EWTN I am grateful to James Faulkner, Lee South, Peter Gagnon, Michael Warsaw, and Bill Steltemeier for keeping Mother and her editor on the air.

At Doubleday my editor Trace Murphy has done it again. He has been there for all three of the Mother Angelica books, displaying his usual great taste and kindness throughout. Thank you, Trace. For his steady support of my efforts, the president of Doubleday, Steve Rubin, has my gratitude and esteem. For bringing me to Doubleday, I need to thank Michelle Rapkin, my first publisher—and for making me feel at home, I thank her successor, the brass-tacks visionary Bill Barry. Bill made sure that my work was everywhere, and beat the drum until the audience took notice. He is the best there is.

Then there are special people who have assisted me in ways I could never thank them enough for: my fearless agent Loretta Barrett is always in my corner, and her crew Nick Mullendore and Gabriel Davis are simply incredible; Greg Mueller and Peter Robbio of Creative Response Concepts, as well as Cari Beckman publicized my work like no one could. They are miracle workers all.

And finally there is you. But for your attention and commitment, Mother's full story would still be untold and her best lessons would be confined to her monastery archive. I am so thankful for you, my literary and broadcast family, who continue to support my work. Thank you for being there, and I promise to keep bringing you work that inspires and challenges . . . so stay tuned.

Doubleday kindly allowed me to quote from the 1966 edition of their *Jerusalem Bible*. It is Mother Angelica's favorite Bible, and the one she used for all her scriptural teachings, both on air and off.